Pillad felt something tugging at his mind. It took him only a moment to understand that it was the Weaver reaching for his magic and that of the others. He abruptly felt power flowing through his body like sunlight through glass.

A flame appeared in front of the Qirsi army, brilliant blue at its center, bright yellow above that, and orange at its top. For a single heartbeat it was suspended in midair. Then it moved toward the Eandi soldiers, slowly at first, but building speed quickly. As it rushed forward, it grew larger, until it towered over the battle plain like a huge fiery cloud. It lit the faces of Galdasten's warriors, so that all the Qirsi could see their fear and despair.

Pillad saw Duke Renald then. The man's mouth was open as if he were wailing, the killing blaze shining in his eyes. The minister almost hoped that Renald would look at him, so that he might know that Pillad had killed him, that he had contributed his magic to this spiraling storm of flame. But the duke seemed incapable of looking away from the fire. He was still staring up at it when the full force of the magic crashed down upon his army, swallowing him and the soldiers around him, blackening the ground, lighting the Moorlands as if a piece of Morna's sun had fallen to the earth. Renald hadn't even drawn his sword.

"Fans of Terry Goodkind's brand of fantasy intrigue will be pleased." —*Publishers Weekly* on *Shapers of Darkness*

Weavers
of
War

✦

DAVID B. COE

BOOK FIVE

OF

Winds of the Forelands

TOR®

A TOM DOHERTY ASSOCIATES BOOK
NEW YORK

WEAVERS OF WAR: BOOK FIVE OF WINDS OF THE FORELANDS

Copyright © 2007 by David B. Coe

Edited by James Frenkel
Maps by Ellisa Mitchell

A Tor Book
Published by Tom Doherty Associates, LLC
175 Fifth Avenue
New York, NY 10010

www.tor.com

Tor® is a registered trademark of Tom Doherty Associates, LLC.

ISBN-13: 978-0-7653-5106-7
ISBN-10: 0-7653-5106-4

First Edition: February 2007
First Mass Market Edition: January 2008

Printed in the United States of America

0   9   8   7   6   5   4   3   2   1

Once again, for Alex and Erin,
who teach me so much about the world around us
as they discover its wonders for themselves

Acknowledgments

Again, many thanks to my terrific agent, Lucienne Diver; my publisher, Tom Doherty; the great people at Tor Books, in particular David Moench and Fiona Lee; Carol Russo and her staff; Terry McGarry for her friendship and unbelievably thorough copyediting; my fine editor and good friend, Jim Frenkel; his editorial assistants, Liz Gorinsky and Stosh Jonjak; and his interns, in particular David Polsky and John Payne.

Once more, my deepest thanks go to Nancy, Alex, and Erin, whom I love more than words can say.

—D. B. C.

The Forelands

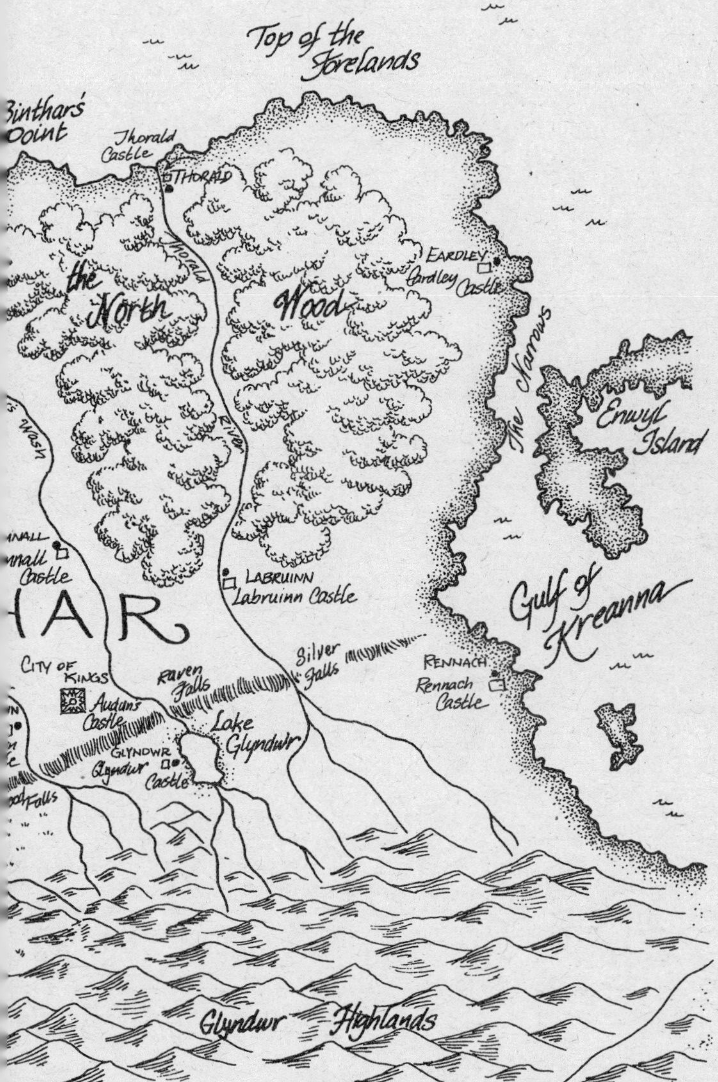
Top of the Forelands
Binthar's Point
Thorald Castle
THORALD
the North Wood
Thorald River
EARDLEY
Eardley Castle
The Narrows
Enwyl Island
Wash
LABRUINN
Labruinn Castle
Gulf of Kreanna
HAR
City of Kings
Audun's Castle
Raven Falls
Silver Falls
RENNACH
Rennach Castle
Lake Glyndwr
GLYNDWR
Glyndwr Castle
Glyndwr Highlands

Characters

KINGDOM OF EIBITHAR

City of Kings

KEARNEY THE FIRST, king of Eibithar, formerly duke of Glyndwr

LEILIA, queen of Eibithar, formerly duchess of Glyndwr, wife of Kearney

KEZIAH JA DAFYDD, archminister of Eibithar, formerly first minister of Glyndwr

GERSHON TRASKER, swordmaster of Eibithar, formerly swordmaster of Glyndwr

AYLYN THE SECOND, king of Eibithar, formerly duke of Thorald (deceased)

WENDA JA BAUL, high minister of Eibithar

PAEGAR JAL BERGET, high minister of Eibithar (deceased)

DYRE JAL FRINVAL, minister of Eibithar

House of Curgh

JAVAN, duke of Curgh

SHONAH, duchess of Curgh, wife of Javan

LORD TAVIS OF CURGH, son of Javan and Shonah

GRINSA JAL ARRIET, formerly a gleaner in Bohdan's Revel

FOTIR JAL SALENE, first minister of Curgh

HAGAN MARCULLET, swordmaster of Curgh

DARIA MARCULLET, wife of Hagan (deceased)

XAVER MARCULLET, pledged liege man to Tavis of Curgh, son of Hagan and Daria

House of Kentigern

AINDREAS, duke of Kentigern

IOANNA, duchess of Kentigern, wife of Aindreas

LADY BRIENNE OF KENTIGERN, daughter of Aindreas and Ioanna (deceased)

LADY AFFERY OF KENTIGERN, daughter of Aindreas and Ioanna

LORD ENNIS OF KENTIGERN, son of Aindreas and Ioanna

SHURIK JAL MARCINE, formerly first minister of Kentigern (deceased)

VILLYD TEMSTEN, swordmaster of Kentigern

House of Galdasten

RENALD, duke of Galdasten

ELSPETH, duchess of Galdasten, wife of Renald

LORD RENALD THE YOUNGER OF GALDASTEN, son of Renald and Elspeth

LORD ADLER OF GALDASTEN, son of Renald and Elspeth

LORD RORY OF GALDASTEN, son of Renald and Elspeth

PILLAD JAL KRENAAR, first minister of Galdasten

EWAN TRAYLEE, swordmaster of Galdasten

House of Thorald

FILIB THE ELDER, duke of Thorald (deceased)

NERINE, duchess of Thorald, wife of Filib the Elder

LORD FILIB THE YOUNGER OF THORALD, son of Filib the Elder and Nerine (deceased)

TOBBAR, duke of Thorald, Filib the Elder's brother

MARSTON, thane of Shanstead, Tobbar's son

ENID JA KOVAR, first minister of Thorald (deceased)

XIVLED JAL VISTE (XIV), minister of Shanstead

House of Glyndwr

KEARNEY THE YOUNGER, duke of Glyndwr, son of King
   Kearney the First and Queen Leilia

House of Heneagh

WELFYL, duke of Heneagh
DUNFYL, thane of Cransher, Welfyl's son
RAB AVKAR, swordmaster of Heneagh

House of Tremain

LATHROP, duke of Tremain
EVETTA JA RUDEK, first minister of Tremain

House of Labruinn

CAIUS, duke of Labruinn
OTTAH JAL BITHLAN, first minister of Labruinn

House of Domnall

SEAMUS, duke of Domnall

House of Eardley

ELAM, duke of Eardley
CERRI JA RONTAF, first minister of Eardley

KINGDOM OF ANEIRA

House Solkara (formerly Aneira's royal house)

TOMAZ THE NINTH, king of Aneira, duke of Solkara (deceased)
CARDEN THE THIRD, king of Aneira, duke of Solkara, Tomaz
   the Ninth's son, Kalyi's father (deceased)

CHOFYA, formerly queen of Aneira, formerly duchess of Solkara, Carden the Third's wife, Kalyi's mother

KALYI, duchess of Solkara, formerly queen of Aneira, daughter of Carden and Chofya

GRIGOR, marquess of Renbrere, Carden's younger brother, known as one of the Jackals (deceased)

HENTHAS, duke of Solkara, Carden and Grigor's younger brother, known as one of the Jackals (deceased)

NUMAR, formerly marquess of Renbrere, formerly regent to Queen Kalyi, Carden, Grigor, and Henthas's younger brother, known as the Fool

PRONJED JAL DRENTHE, formerly archminister of Aneira

TRADDEN GRONTALLE, master of arms of Aneira

House Dantrielle

TEBEO, duke of Dantrielle

PELGIA, duchess of Dantrielle, wife of Tebeo

LORD TAS OF DANTRIELLE, son of Tebeo and Pelgia

LADY LAYTSA OF DANTRIELLE, daughter of Tebeo and Pelgia

LORD SENAON OF DANTRIELLE, son of Tebeo and Pelgia

EVANTHYA JA YISPAR, first minister of Dantrielle

BAUSEF DARLESTA, master of arms of Dantrielle (deceased)

GABRYS DINTAVO, master of arms of Dantrielle

House Orvinti

BRALL, duke of Orvinti (deceased)

PAZICE, duchess of Orvinti, Brall's wife

FETNALLA JA PRANDT, formerly first minister of Orvinti

TRAEFAN SOGRANO, master of arms of Orvinti

House Bistari (now Aneira's royal house)

CHAGO, duke of Bistari (deceased)

RIA, duchess of Bistari, wife of Chago

SILBRON, king of Aneira, duke of Bistari, son of Chago and Ria

House Mertesse

ROUEL, duke of Mertesse (deceased)
ROWAN, duke of Mertesse, son of Rouel
YAELLA JA BANVEL, first minister of Mertesse

House Noltierre

BERTIN THE ELDER, duke of Noltierre (deceased)
BERTIN THE YOUNGER, duke of Noltierre, son of Bertin the Elder
MEQIV JAL WANAERE, first minister of Noltierre

House Kett

ANSIS, duke of Kett

House Rassor

GRESTOS, duke of Rassor

House Tounstrel

VIDOR, duke of Tounstrel (deceased)
VISTAAN, duke of Tounstrel, son of Vidor

MATRIARCHY OF SANBIRA

House Yserne

OLESYA, queen of Sanbira, duchess of Yserne
ABENI JA KRENTA, archminister of Sanbira
OHAN DELRASTO, master of arms of Sanbira

House Curlinte

DALVIA, duchess of Curlinte (deceased)
SERTIO, duke of Curlinte, husband of Dalvia, master of arms of Curlinte

DIANI, duchess of Curlinte, daughter of Dalvia and Sertio
LORD CYRO OF CURLINTE, son of Dalvia and Sertio, brother of Diani (deceased)
KREAZUR JAL SYLBE, first minister of Curlinte (deceased)

House Brugaosa

EDAMO, duke of Brugaosa
VANJAD JAL QIEN, first minister of Brugaosa

House Norinde

ALAO, duke of Norinde
FILTEM JAL TORQATTE, first minister of Norinde

House Macharzo

NADITIA, duchess of Macharzo
CRAEFFE JA TREF, first minister of Macharzo

Other Sanbiri nobles

VASYONNE, duchess of Listaal
AJY, duchess of Kinsarta
RASHEL, duchess of Trescarri
TAMYRA, duchess of Prentarlo

EMPIRE OF BRAEDON

HAREL THE FOURTH, emperor of Braedon, Lord of Curtell
DUSAAN JAL KANIA, high chancellor of Braedon
URIAD GANJER, master of arms of Braedon
KAYIV JAL YIVANNE, minister of Braedon (deceased)
NITARA JA PLIN, minister of Braedon
STAVEL JAL MIRAAD, chancellor of Braedon
B'SERRE JA DOSH, minister of Braedon
GORLAN JAL AVIARRE, minister of Braedon

ROV JA TELSA, minister of Braedon
BARDYN JAL FENNE, chancellor of Braedon

THE QIRSI CONSPIRACY

CRESENNE JA TERBA, formerly a chancellor in the Qirsi movement, formerly a gleaner in Bohdan's Revel

BRYNTELLE JA GRINSA, daughter of Cresenne and Grinsa jal Arriet

JASTANNE JA TRILN, a chancellor in the Qirsi movement, a merchant in Kentigern and captain of the *White Erne*

TIHOD JAL BROSSA, a merchant and captain of the *Silver Flame,* the man who pays gold to members of the movement (deceased)

UESTEM JAL SAFHIR, a chancellor in the Qirsi movement, a merchant in Galdasten

MITTIFAR JAL STEK, member of the Qirsi movement, owner of the White Wave tavern in Galdasten (deceased)

CADEL NISTAAD, also called Corbin, an assassin (deceased)

Chapter
One

T he touch of his mind on hers was as gentle as the Weaver's had been brutal, as tender and loving as the Weaver's had been vengeful and cruel. She sensed in that touch his passion, his longing to be with her, his hope that he could shield her from the pain that seemed to have enveloped all the land. And she wanted nothing more than to hold him in her arms—really to hold him, beyond this haven he had created so that he might speak with her as she slept—to show him that she yearned for him, too.

Theirs was the most unlikely of loves, having overcome deception, betrayal, and her devotion to the Weaver's conspiracy. But feeling the caress of his thoughts, Cresenne could not question the power of what they shared.

"Tell me about Bryntelle," Grinsa whispered, still holding her close amid the sun-warmed grasses of the plain he had conjured for this dream.

How could she not smile at the mention of their daughter? The girl had been the lone spark of light in a darkness that had consumed her days and nights over the past several turns.

"Bryntelle's fine. She's been up much of the day, crying, but I think that's because she's getting her first tooth."

He pulled away slightly, looking down at her, his face lit by a dazzling smile. "A tooth? Really?"

Cresenne nodded. "It's not much right now—just a little bump on her gums. But one of the healers tells me that once it appears it'll grow in very quickly."

Grinsa was still smiling, but there was a pained look in his eyes. "I wish I could be there to see it."

"Soon," she said, looking down, her chest tight. She sensed that he wanted to kiss her, and she kept her face turned away from his. "Has the fighting begun?"

"Yes, we fought our first skirmish this morning."

At that she did look up. "Are you all right?"

"Yes, fine."

"And Keziah?"

"She is, too. As are Kearney and Tavis."

"Good." She nodded again, shivering as if the warm breeze had grown icy and harsh. "That's good." She hesitated. Then, "Have you seen the Weaver yet?" Her stomach turned to stone as she spoke the words, but she tried to keep her voice even.

Grinsa shook his head. "Not yet. I expect he wants the war to begin in earnest before he reaches the Moorlands. The more damage the Eandi do to each other, the easier his task when the time comes."

She felt certain that he was right. While Grinsa and the Weaver had little in common beyond their powers and their formidable appearance, Grinsa had come to understand the conspiracy's leader quite well. Only a year before, Grinsa had been but a gleaner in Eibithar's Revel, concealing the true extent of his powers and spending his days and his magic showing others glimpses of their futures. Now he was an advisor to kings and nobles, though still they called him gleaner. Cresenne of all people, having been one of the Weaver's most trusted servants—a chancellor in his movement—knew how strong the enemy was, and so how great the land's need. If anyone could destroy the Weaver and his movement, her beloved could. So why did she find it so difficult to take comfort in Grinsa's arms, to believe that he could prevail in this war that loomed before them, as black and menacing as some seaborne storm summoned by Amon himself?

For a long time, neither of them spoke. Cresenne sensed that Grinsa was gathering himself to end the dream. She could feel his despair at the distance between them, how he begrudged every day they spent apart. No, there could be no doubting the power of their love.

All of which made what the Weaver had done to her that much more galling.

"I should return to the front lines," he said, grimacing. "Who knows when the empire's men will attack again?"

"I understand."

"You'll kiss Bryntelle for me?"

Again she smiled. "Of course."

Grinsa pulled her close again, kissing her deeply. Cresenne returned the kiss with as much passion as she could muster, not wanting him to sense how she suffered for it.

At last he released her, a frown on his handsome face.

"What's the matter?" he asked.

"It's nothing."

"Cresenne—"

"Please, Grinsa," she said, closing her eyes, wishing she could just sleep. "I just . . . It's going to take some time for me to . . . to heal."

"I want to help."

"You can't. No one can," she added, seeing how this hurt him. "Just make certain that you win. Killing the Weaver will do more to help me than you can know. Destroy him for me, and I'll see to the rest."

He just gazed at her, looking so sad. "I'll do what I can."

That's not enough! she wanted to say. *You can't fail at this! He'll kill me! He'll kill Bryntelle!* But he knew all of this. As much as she wanted Dusaan jal Kania dead, Grinsa wanted it more.

"I know you will."

He brushed a strand of hair from her brow with the back of his hand. And even this gesture, done with such care and tenderness, was nearly enough to make her shudder with the memory of the Weaver's brutality.

"I love you, Grinsa."

"And I love you, more than you know."

She awoke to the sound of swifts chattering as they soared past the narrow window of her chamber. Bryntelle still slept in her cradle, her arms stretched over her head, her mouth making suckling movements. Cresenne sat up, taking a long breath and running both hands through her hair. Grinsa deserved better from her. He carried the burdens of every man and woman of the Forelands on his shoulders, and all she could think to do was tell him what he already knew: that in order to be whole again she needed for him to destroy the Weaver.

Her wounds had healed, and in recent days she had finally begun to eat again, slowly regaining her strength after the poisoning that almost killed her. But the Weaver had left her with other scars that remained beyond a healer's touch. True, she had managed to fight Dusaan off and then to end that horrific dream before he could take her life, but the memory of rape clung to her bed, her hair, her body—the stench of his breath, hot and damp against her neck. She could still feel him driving himself into her again and again, tearing her flesh, his weight bearing down on her until she wondered if she could even draw breath. She could hear him calling her "whore." It had only been a dream, she tried to tell herself, an illusion he had conjured by using her own magic against her. But did that lessen the humiliation or deepen it? It had been a violation in so many ways and on so many levels. Did his invasion of her mind make what he seemed to have done to her body any less real?

She feared that she might never again be able to bear Grinsa's touch. The Weaver had poisoned all of her dreams, even those in which her love spoke to her. Grinsa's merest kiss when he walked in her sleep, his most gentle caress, made her feel once more the savagery of Dusaan's assault. Cresenne wanted desperately to believe that it was the dreams that did this, that once she and Grinsa were together again, and he could hold her in his arms without touching her mind, everything would be all right. But she had no way of knowing this for certain, and doubt lay heavy on her heart.

Grinsa would have told her to sleep more. The sun would be up for several hours yet, and since she still didn't dare sleep at night, for fear of another attack from the Weaver, she wouldn't have another opportunity to rest for quite some time. But she was awake now, and she knew herself well enough to know that she could lie on her bed from now until dusk, and she wouldn't get back to sleep. Instead, she stared out the window and waited for Bryntelle to wake, knowing that the baby would be hungry when she did.

She didn't have long to wait. After nursing Bryntelle and changing her wet swaddling, Cresenne took her daughter in her arms and left their small chamber to wander the grounds of Audun's Castle. It was a rare treat for them to be out of doors during the daylight hours; Cresenne savored the warm touch of the sun on her skin, and the mild breeze that stirred her hair. Bryntelle seemed to enjoy the day as well. She squinted up at the sun repeatedly and squealed happily at the sight of clove-pink and irises blooming brightly in the gardens.

One of the advantages of wandering the castle at night was that Cresenne rarely found herself in the company of others. She had no desire to make conversation with ladies in the queen's court, and she dreaded being recognized as the "Qirsi traitor." Nurle, the young healer who saw her through the poisoning, occasionally joined her after tending to patients during the course of the night, but mostly she and Bryntelle kept to themselves. On this day, however, there were several people walking the castle grounds, and though Cresenne was loath to return to her chamber, she dreaded the thought of being among other people, particularly since everyone she saw was Eandi.

Hesitating, yet eager to find some way to enjoy this day without having to endure the stares of all these people, Cresenne ducked into a small courtyard off one of the main paths that meandered through the garden.

She knew immediately that she had erred. Cresenne had seen Leilia of Glyndwr, Eibithar's queen, only once before, but she recognized the woman immediately. The queen was seated on a small marble bench in the middle of the courtyard. Sunlight angled across her face, making her skin look pale and thick. Her black hair was tied up in a tight bun, and the dress she wore appeared so tight around the bust that Cresenne found it hard to imagine that she could be comfortable.

Several of the queen's ladies stood around her, chatting amiably, and four guards stood at attention nearby.

Cresennne had every intention of leaving the courtyard, but at that moment Bryntelle let out a small cry, drawing the stares of every person there. The guards turned toward her, glowering, and the ladies regarded her with frowns and pursed lips.

"Forgive me," she muttered, not entirely certain that they could even hear her. "I didn't know there was anyone here." She curtsied quickly and started to leave.

"You there! Wait a moment!"

Cresenne turned back to them. Leilia was eyeing her with obvious interest, though there was no warmth in her expression.

"Yes, Your Highness," Cresenne said, curtsying again.

For a moment she wondered if the queen expected her to approach, but then Leilia stood, and as the guards rushed to her side the queen began to walk toward her. Leilia paused, regarded them with obvious disdain, and waved a hand, seeming to dismiss them. One of the men said something to her in a low voice, but she merely glared at him until he bowed and backed away. Then she started toward Cresenne again.

Bryntelle had begun to make a good deal of noise—she wasn't crying, fortunately, nor did she seem particularly unhappy. But she certainly was being loud. Leilia glanced at the babe as she drew near, but only for a moment. Mostly, she kept her dark eyes fixed on Cresenne.

"They tell me that you're the renegade," the queen said, stopping just in front of Cresenne, and gesturing vaguely at the soldiers behind her. "The one who had Brienne killed. Is this true?"

Cresenne stared at the ground before her, her cheeks burning. A thousand replies sprang to her lips, any one of which would have earned her a summary hanging. In the end, she merely muttered, "Yes, Your Highness."

"They also warn me that you might make an attempt on my life. Is that your intent?"

"No, Your Highness."

"Good. Walk with me."

Leilia stepped out of the courtyard, and turned toward the north corner of the gardens, leaving Cresenne little choice but to follow. Emerging from the courtyard, she found Leilia waiting for her a few strides away, an arch look on her face.

"Well?" the queen said. "Aren't you coming?"

"Yes, of course, Your Highness. Forgive me."

But even after Cresenne reached her, the queen didn't resume her walking, at least not immediately. Instead, she regarded Cresenne's face critically, as if examining a new piece of art. It took Cresenne but a second to realize that Leilia was staring at her scars. She had to resist an urge to stomp off.

"You've healed well."

"Thank you, Your Highness."

"I can see why some think you pretty."

"Do they, Your Highness?"

Leilia began to walk again, sniffing loudly. "Come now, my dear. Let's not be coy. I'm certain that you've had no shortage of men in your life. Certainly, Eandi men seem fascinated by your kind."

Something in the way the queen said this caught her ear. As she hurried to keep up with the woman, Cresenne remembered that during her many conversations with Keziah ja Dafydd, Eibithar's archminister, she had found herself speculating about Keziah's relationships with both Grinsa and Kearney, the king. On several occasions she had wondered if one of the men might once have been Keziah's lover. The same thought came to her now. Leilia sounded very much the wounded wife, though clearly she had no cause to be jealous of Cresenne.

"Silenced you, have I?" the queen said, glancing at her sidelong.

"Have I given offense in some way, Your Highness? Is that why you wished to speak with me?"

That, of all things, brought a smile to Leilia's lips, though it was fleeting. "No. You haven't given offense. I've been . . . curious about you."

"I see."

"Do you?"

"I've been a curiosity since I arrived here, Your Highness."

"Yes, I'm sure you have. Is that why you spend your days in your chamber and your nights wandering the castle corridors?"

She thought the queen a strange woman. Her directness was both disconcerting and refreshing, and while Cresenne thought it best to keep her replies circumspect, she sensed that Leilia would not have taken offense had she chosen to be more candid.

"Actually, Your Highness, I sleep during the day to avoid the Weaver who attacks me in my dreams."

"I'd heard that, but I wondered if there were other reasons as well."

Cresenne said nothing.

"The child doesn't seem to mind?"

"She's hardly known any other way to live."

Leilia nodded, and they walked in silence for several moments, Cresenne gazing at a bed of brilliant ruby peonies.

"Tell me of the child's father," the queen said abruptly.

Cresenne made herself smile, sensing that their conversation had taken a perilous turn. "Her father, Your Highness?"

"Yes. This tall Qirsi who's been the subject of so much talk throughout the castle."

"I didn't know that people were speaking of him."

"Shouldn't they? He's little more than a Revel gleaner, yet he was Tavis of Curgh's lone confidant over the last year, and my husband thinks highly enough of him to include him in councils of war. Doesn't that strike you as odd?"

"Grinsa is a wise man, Your Highness, as I'm sure Lord Tavis will attest. I've no doubt that he'll serve the king well."

"I'm not questioning his worth, my dear. I'm merely asking you to tell me more about him. And I sense your reluctance."

"I'm not—"

"Don't dissemble with me." Leilia glanced at her again, as if gauging Cresennne's reaction. "Is he a traitor? Is that it? Have you both contrived this elaborate farce to gain Kearney's trust?"

"No, Your Highness! I swear it! Grinsa's no traitor!"

Again, the queen smiled. "I believe you. You love him very much."

Cresenne nodded, afraid to speak. She had come close to losing him so many times, all of them her own fault. She had

betrayed him, sent assassins for him, and nearly driven him
away with her stubborn, foolish devotion to the Weaver and
his movement. And she knew that she might lose him still. Or
he her. Who could say whether he would survive the fighting
between the Eandi armies, much less his inevitable encounter
with Dusaan? Who knew how many more of the Weaver's
servants had been sent to kill her?

"You fear for him."

"I fear for all of us, Your Highness. I've seen how wicked
this Weaver is, though I was blind to it for too long."

"Kearney will find a way to prevail." The corners of her
mouth twitched. "He always does." When Cresenne didn't respond, the queen looked at her again. "War is hardest on the
women, you know. It's always been so, though men will deny
it. Remaining behind, awaiting the outcome, fearing that the
next messenger will bear word that your husband or lover or
brother has fallen." She gazed up at the sky, as if to judge the
time. "I envy the women of Sanbira, who fight their own battles alongside the men. Their way strikes me as being far
more just."

"Yes, Your Highness."

"You're humoring me." She wore a smirk on her fleshy face.

"No, Your Highness! I was just—"

"It's all right, my dear. I suppose I deserve it. I find it easy
to complain here, safe behind Audun's walls. But given the
opportunity to ride to war, I'm not at all certain that I would."
She frowned. "Does that make me a coward?"

"I believe it makes you honest, Your Highness."

Leilia laughed. "Well said, my dear! I'll take that as a compliment!"

Bryntelle started at the sound of the queen's laughter, but
then let out a squeal and offered a grin of her own.

"What's the child's name?"

"Her name is Bryntelle, Your Highness."

"Bryntelle. That's lovely." She regarded the baby for a
time, looking as if she wished to hold her. But the queen
never asked, and Cresenne thought it presumptuous to offer.

"Is she the reason you did it?" the queen finally asked,
meeting Cresenne's gaze.

"Your Highness?"

"Is she the reason you turned away from the conspiracy?"

Cresenne didn't want to talk about this, not with Grinsa, or Keziah, or the king, and certainly not with this odd woman standing before her. But how did one refuse a queen?

The truth was, everything she had done, both on behalf of the Weaver and to thwart him, she had believed she was doing for this child, or at the very least, for the promise of her. She joined the movement to create a better world, not only for herself, but also for the child she knew she would someday bear. After Bryntelle's birth, Grinsa threatened to take the child from her in order to compel Cresenne to confess her crimes to Kearney. He knew as well as did Cresenne that she would do anything to keep her child. And in the days since, she had come to see that the future once promised to her by the Weaver—a future in which Qirsi ruled the Forelands through torture and murder and deception—was not the one she wanted for her daughter. More than anything, she wished to see Dusaan's movement defeated, and she had resolved long ago that she would not allow herself to be killed, not merely because she wished to live, not merely because by surviving she defied the Weaver, but because she would not allow her child to grow up without a mother's love. Bryntelle had been the most powerful force in her life for as long as she could remember, going back far beyond the consummation of her love affair with Grinsa.

"Yes, Your Highness, I did it for Bryntelle, at first because I feared having her taken from me, and more recently because I've come to realize that I don't want the Weaver's tyranny to be my legacy to her and her children."

"That's more of an answer than I expected."

Cresenne looked down at Bryntelle, whose pale yellow eyes shone in the lateday sun like torch fire. "It's merely the truth."

"I've never had much use for your kind, and I never thought I'd go looking to a Qirsi for any kind of truth. But you impress me."

Cresenne couldn't help the small noise that escaped her.

"You find that amusing?"

She knew that she should just deny it and end their conversation, but she had been honest up to this point, and pride would not allow her to be anything less now.

"Not amusing, Your Highness. But I have to wonder if you truly think I should be flattered by what you just said."

Leilia's face shaded to scarlet and Cresenne felt certain that she had pushed the queen too far. The woman surprised her, though.

"No," the queen said, the smirk returning. "I don't suppose I do. You'll have to forgive me. My past . . . encounters with Qirsi women have been rather unpleasant."

Now she was certain about Keziah and the king, although she knew better than to reveal as much to the queen.

"There's nothing to forgive, Your Highness. Our peoples have struggled with such misunderstandings for centuries. Perhaps if more of us simply spoke our minds, we'd find a way past these conflicts."

"Perhaps." A faint smile touched her lips and was gone. "I should return to my ladies before they send the guards out to search for us."

"Yes, Your Highness. Shall I accompany you back to them?"

Leilia waved the suggestion away. "No need, my dear. I daresay I know the way." She started to turn, then paused, eyeing Cresenne once more. "Is there anything you need?"

"Anything I need?" she repeated, knowing how foolish she sounded.

"Yes. Are you comfortable? Are you and your child getting enough food, enough blankets? Would you feel better with more guards outside your door?"

On more than one occasion in the past several turns, Cresenne had been surprised by the kindnesses shown to her by Eandi men and women, be they wandering merchants in the Glyndwr Highlands or lords and sovereigns in the noble courts. But nothing that any of them had done surprised her more than this question from Eibithar's peculiar queen.

"Thank you, Your Highness. We're just fine."

"Very well. If you think of anything, you only need ask."

"Again, Your Highness, my thanks."

Cresenne curtsied once more, then straightened and

watched the queen walk away. Only when Leilia had disappeared into the small courtyard did Cresenne leave the gardens and make her way to the castle kitchen. It would soon be dark, and the kitchenmaster had made it clear to her long ago that she was to be out of his way before it came time to feed the queen and the ladies of her court.

Besides, after dusk the courtyards and corridors emptied, leaving Cresenne and her daughter free to wander in solitude. It was her favorite part of the day.

Chapter

Two

✦

Dantrielle, Aneira

Not long ago—only a few days by his reckoning, though it was hard to keep track in this prison cell—Pronjed jal Drenthe had been archminister of Aneira, the most powerful Qirsi in all the realm. Now, with the failure of Numar of Renbrere's siege at Castle Dantrielle and the collapse of the Solkaran Supremacy, which Pronjed had served, he was but a prisoner of Dantrielle's duke, his ministerial robes tattered and soiled, his hair matted, his skin itching with vermin and sweat. For another man, this might have been a humiliation, cause to despair in his dark, lonely chamber. But not for Pronjed. He was a powerful sorcerer, a man with resources beyond the imaginings of the foolish Eandi who guarded him day and night. He possessed shaping power with which to shatter the iron door to his cell. He wielded mind-bending magic with which he could turn Dantrielle's guards to his purposes. He could raise mists and winds, which would allow him to elude his captors once he was free of the tower. Even the silk bonds holding his wrists and ankles wouldn't be enough to stop him, though they presented something of a challenge. He had been planning his escape almost since the moment of his capture. He knew just how he would win his freedom. Despite what the Eandi might have thought, this prison of theirs couldn't hold him.

And yet here he remained. Pronjed had thought to escape several nights before, in the tumult just after the breaking of Numar's siege, when Tebeo, duke of Dantrielle, was still occupied with removing dead soldiers from the wards of his castle and determining, with the aid of his allies, how best to proceed now that the Supremacy had been toppled.

But somehow one of his own people, Evanthya ja Yispar, Dantrielle's first minister, had divined his mind. Not only did she know of his intent to escape; she had guessed as well that he planned to head north from Dantrielle to meet the Weaver in Eibithar, on the battle plain near Galdasten. She claimed that she would do nothing to hinder him, that all she wanted was to follow, so that she might find her lover, Fetnalla ja Prandt, Orvinti's first minister, who had betrayed and killed her duke. But Pronjed had been so badly shaken by their conversation that he now found himself afraid to make the attempt. He had sensed no deception on Evanthya's part—it truly seemed she wished only to find her love. But what if he was mistaken? What if he allowed himself to be followed, only to find that the minister had found some way to thwart the Weaver's plans? He thought this unlikely, but he would have been a fool to dismiss the idea entirely.

The Weaver expected him to join the Qirsi army; Pronjed desired this, as well. He expected his service to the movement to be rewarded with power and wealth. The Weaver had often spoken to him of creating a new class of Qirsi nobility, and the archminister had every intention of claiming his place among them. The previous night he had resolved at last to escape his chamber, notwithstanding the risk of being followed by the first minister. Although still unwilling to trust that she meant no harm to the movement, he was confident he could kill her should the need arise.

And yet, even after the midnight bells tolled in the city he couldn't bring himself to try. Fear held him in the chamber; fear as unyielding as that iron door, as immune to his power as the silk bonds. How had Evanthya known so much about him and his intentions? She was but one woman—what danger could she pose to a movement as vast as theirs? Though blessed with a keen mind and more courage than he would have expected from one with such a slight frame and reserved manner, she would have been no match for Pronjed in a battle of magic. Yet, several hours later, when the dawn bells rang and the sky began to brighten, the dark of night giving way to the soft grey light of early morning, Pronjed still sat in his prison.

He had made the mistake of angering the Weaver once—when he killed Carden the Third, Aneira's king, assuming incorrectly that the Weaver would be pleased. He could still feel the way the bone in his hand had shattered, the pain so severe he could barely remain conscious. The Weaver, who could be so generous with his gold, was no less stingy with his punishment when the occasion demanded. That memory, as much as anything, kept Pronjed in his chamber, grappling with his uncertainty.

Nothing in his past, however, could have prepared him for the conversation he had later that same morning. The last peals of the midmorning bells were still echoing through the castle when he heard a light footfall in the corridor outside his chamber and then a woman's voice he recognized immediately.

"Open the door and then leave us," Evanthya told the two guards.

"We're to remain in the corridor at all times, First Minister," one of the men answered. "Duke's orders."

Silence. After several moments, she said, "Fine then. Let me into the chamber."

"Yes, First Minister."

It took the man but a moment to find the correct key. After he opened the door, Evanthya stepped past him into the chamber, then pulled the door shut behind her.

"One of us should be in there with you, First Minister."

"It's all right. I've a dagger with me. I'll call for you when I'm ready to leave."

She faced Pronjed, her cheeks flushed, her expression grim. Her yellow eyes were as bright as blooms in the castle gardens, and her fine white hair hung loose to her shoulders. Pronjed knew that she loved another, a woman at that, but he couldn't help noting how attractive she was.

"You realize, of course, that your dagger will do you no good against me," he said quietly, not bothering to stand. He held up his wrists so that she could see the silk ties. "There's a reason I'm bound with these."

"Yes, Archminister. You may remember, they were my idea in the first place. We both know that I won't need the weapon at all. You have no intention of harming me."

"How can you be so sure?"

She had stepped closer to him and now she cast a quick glance at the door. "Because," she whispered, "if you try to hurt me you'll either be executed or thrown in the castle dungeon. You aren't ready to die, and if you're placed in the dungeon, you'll have a much harder time escaping."

Pronjed's eyes flicked toward the door. Neither of the guards appeared to be listening. "I don't know what you're talking about."

"Stop it. Of course you do. And I want to know why you've yet to make the attempt."

"What?"

"Why haven't you tried to escape?"

Perhaps there was an opportunity here. "Because I have no intention of escaping. I never have."

"You're lying."

"You seem terribly sure of yourself, First Minister, and yet, as you yourself point out, I've made no attempt to win my freedom. Isn't it possible that you've been wrong about me, that in your haste to pursue Fetnalla, you've imagined a traitor where there is none?"

"No, it's not," she said. But Pronjed heard doubt in her words and pressed his advantage.

"I can imagine how hard it must have been for you, hearing of Lord Orvinti's death, knowing that there could be little doubt but that Fetnalla was responsible."

"Be quiet!"

"Still, just because the first minister proved false, doesn't mean that I will as well. I'm sure that would be of great comfort to you, but it's just not—"

"I told you to be quiet!" In a swirl of her ministerial robes and a blur of white and steel, she was on him, her forearm pressed against his chest so that he was forced back against the stone wall, her blade at his throat.

It was all Pronjed could do not to shatter the dagger instantly. He tried to reassure himself that she needed him too much to kill him, and that she couldn't risk harming him in any way and thus raising the suspicions of her duke. But he was trembling, and the edge of her blade felt cold and dangerous against his neck.

"First Minister?" one of the guards called from the grated window in the iron door, sounding alarmed.

"Leave us alone!" she said.

The man looked at Pronjed briefly, a smirk on his lips. Then he turned away.

"Why don't you shatter my blade, Archminister?" she said, her voice dropping once more. "Or do you intend to tell me now that you're not really a shaper?"

"This is foolishness, Evanthya. As you've already made clear to me, I can't afford to harm you. Nor are you going to hurt me. You still believe that I can lead you to Fetnalla. So put your dagger away, and let's speak of this civilly."

Evanthya glared at him another moment, her weapon still held to his throat. Finally, slowly, she released him and sheathed the blade. "All right," she said. "Tell me why you're still here, or I'll go to the duke and convince him to put you in the dungeon."

"Another empty threat. As I say, you need me, or at least you think you do."

"I need you as an excuse to go after Fetnalla, Archminister. Nothing more. Tebeo won't let me pursue her—he sees no sense in it so long after Brall's murder. But if you escape, I can prevail upon him to let me follow you. He hasn't enough men left to send soldiers after you, so he'll send me."

"As I said—"

"But if you don't tell me what I want to know, I'll send you to the dungeon and then leave Dantrielle without his permission. I'll forfeit my title and place in his court if I have to. As I've told you once before, all I want is to get Fetnalla back. I don't care about anything else. I certainly don't give a damn about you."

A braver man might have been willing to test her resolve, to force her either to give up her position in Tebeo's court or prove that her threats amounted to nothing. But Pronjed felt his nerve failing him at the mere suggestion of being sent to the castle dungeon.

"I haven't made the attempt," he said at last, "because I've been unable to decide whether you truly wish to find her, or have been hoping to lure me into a trap."

That, of all things, seemed to leave her speechless. She opened her mouth to respond, then closed it again. The archminister would have laughed had he not been trembling at the realization of what he had done. With that small admission he had, in effect, confirmed for her all that she had been assuming about him.

"Is that true?" she finally asked him, her voice so soft that he could barely hear her.

"It is."

"Damn." She raked a hand through her hair, closing her eyes briefly. "We've lost a good deal of time. There's no telling where she is by now."

"Perhaps then, it no longer makes sense for you to follow me."

"I didn't say that I was ready to give up."

"And I didn't say that I was ready to let you follow me." She started to respond and Pronjed raised a hand, stopping her. "I know: you don't need my permission, and I might not be able to prevent it. But I'm obligated to try. I'd be a fool not to."

After a moment, she nodded. "So, when?"

Pronjed shook his head. He must have been an idiot. "Tonight," he whispered. Seeing the doubtful look on her face, he added, "I swear it. I can't afford to wait any longer either."

She glanced toward the door. "Don't hurt the men. You have delusion magic. Use it."

He should have denied this, too. But like before he found

himself helpless in the face of her certainty. He could argue the point for the rest of the day without convincing her. Instead, he shook his head. "I make you no promises in that regard. I'll do whatever I have to. If you really want to ensure their safety, you'll have these silk bonds removed. I can shatter manacles, but with these . . ." He shrugged.

"But your powers—"

"I can't control two men at one time, which means that the second guard will have to be incapacitated somehow. It's up to you, First Minister. If you truly care about these men, you'll help me."

Evanthya offered no reply, save to hold his gaze for a few moments more before straightening and crossing to the door.

"Guards!" she called.

One of the men was there immediately, unlocking the door and letting her out. An instant later he clanged the door shut again and threw the lock, the sound echoing in the chamber.

"Watch him closely," he heard Evanthya say to Tebeo's men. "It wouldn't surprise me if he tried to escape."

Pronjed just gaped at the door. The silk at his wrists and ankles felt tighter than ever.

Evanthya was trembling as she descended the stairway of the prison tower. Tonight.

She had never known that she could be afraid of so many things at one time. The archminister, the Weaver, the castle guards, her duke and his reaction if he learned what she intended. And behind it all, the fear of her next encounter with Fetnalla. She no longer doubted that her beloved had betrayed the realm or that she had killed her duke, Brall of Orvinti. Nor did she have any illusions as to her own power to turn Fetnalla from the dark path she had chosen. Yet she had to try. She owed that much to herself, to both of them.

The two soldiers outside Pronjed's chamber had regarded her strangely when she stepped back into the corridor, a testament to how deep suspicions of the Qirsi still ran in Aneira. All the men in Castle Dantrielle knew how she had fought against the soldiers of Solkara and Rassor during the recent siege. They had seen her doing battle, back to back with the duke, risking her life on Tebeo's behalf. They had seen as well the mist and wind she raised to protect Dantrielle's men from enemy archers when Numar's invaders briefly took control of the castle ramparts. After all that, none could question her loyalty to Tebeo and his house.

Or so she had thought. For some still did, and these few would see a dark purpose in her whispered conversation with the archminister. And would they be wrong? Hadn't she been plotting the traitor's escape, ignoring the fact that he may well have been responsible for the death of Aneira's king? She had used her own gold to buy the murder of a Qirsi traitor in Mertesse. Wasn't she then an enemy of the conspiracy? Did sharing a bed with a traitor and wishing desperately to lie with her again negate all that she had done before?

These questions plagued her as she made her way across the castle's upper ward. Evanthya didn't even notice the two soldiers standing in her path until she had nearly walked into them.

"Pardon me," she said, flustered and feeling slightly dazed. "I didn't see you."

"Actually, First Minister, we was waitin' for you."

"For me?"

"Yes. The duke wants a word right away."

The minister looked up at the window of Tebeo's ducal chamber and saw that he was watching her, his round face lit by the morning sun.

She nodded, swallowing. "Of course."

The two men fell in step on either side of her and in silence the three of them entered the nearest of the castle towers, climbed the stairway, and walked to Tebeo's chamber. One of the guards knocked, and at the duke's summons, he pushed open the door and motioned for Evanthya to enter. She nodded at the two men, trying with little success to smile, and stepped into the chamber. Neither man entered with her and an instant later she heard the door close.

Tebeo was still at the window, his back to her. "Please sit, First Minister."

Evanthya took her usual seat near the duke's writing table. Her heart was pounding so hard it was a wonder Tebeo didn't notice.

"Would you like some tea?"

"No, thank you, my lord."

"Wine perhaps?"

She smiled, despite her fright. "I'm fine, my lord."

He turned at that. "Are you?"

Evanthya shivered. "What do you mean?"

"I've been impressed with your strength this past half turn since the breaking of the siege. You've done all that I've asked of you; as always your service to House Dantrielle has been exemplary."

"Thank you, my lord."

"I can only imagine how difficult it's been for you."

She felt the blood rush to her face and looked away. There would have been no sense in denying it. "Yes, my lord."

"To be honest, I'm a bit surprised that you're still here."

Evanthya could only stare at him.

"I have some idea of how much you love her, and I know as well that you hate the conspiracy, that you've risked a great deal to strike at its leaders."

Not long ago, Evanthya had told him of hiring the assassin to kill Shurik jal Marcine, and though he hadn't approved, neither had he punished her, which would have been well within his prerogative as her sovereign.

"Had it been me," he went on, "I would have gone after her already. That you haven't speaks well of your devotion to me and this house."

"You honor me, my lord," she managed to say.

"I'm merely being honest. And I'd ask the same of you."

"My lord?"

He came and sat beside her, a kindly look on his face. "What were you doing in the prison tower just now?" he asked, his voice so gentle it made her chest ache.

She tried to answer, to say anything at all, but instead she began to cry.

"There are only two men in the tower right now," he said.

"Numar and the archminister. And I doubt that you have much to say to the regent. That leaves Pronjed."

When she didn't answer, he took a long breath.

"After all we've been through these past few turns, I'll never again question your loyalty. I think you know that."

Evanthya nodded, tears coursing down her face.

"Still, I need to know what you and he discussed. As much as I trust you, I fear the archminister. You've told me yourself how dangerous he is. If my castle is in peril—"

"It's not, my lord."

In the next moment she thought of the last words Pronjed had spoken to her and the danger his escape might pose to Tebeo's guards, and she regretted offering even this meager assurance.

"You're certain of this?"

She lowered her gaze again. "Not for certain, no."

"You must tell me, Evanthya. You know you must."

A thousand denials leaped to mind, all of them lies. How different would she be from Fetnalla if she resorted to any of them?

"He means to escape, my lord."

"Escape? How?"

"He has mind-bending magic, mists and winds, and shaping power. It should be a fairly simple matter."

"Then why hasn't he done so already?"

"Because several days ago I informed him of my intention to follow him, and he fears a trap."

The duke expressed no surprise. His expression didn't even change, save for a momentary closing of the eyes.

"In other words, you meant to let him go, though surely his escape would strengthen the conspiracy."

"He can lead me to her, my lord."

"That hardly justifies it."

"We'd merely be exchanging one traitor for another. Pronjed might join them, but Fetnalla won't."

His eyebrows went up. "You believe you can turn her from the renegades?"

"I have to try. If that doesn't work, I'll find some other way to keep her from joining them. In any case, she won't be fighting alongside her Weaver."

Tebeo frowned. "I hate to have to say this, Evanthya, but Fetnalla is dangerous, too. She used magic to kill Brall, and as you've often told me, yours are not the powers of a warrior. You're still thinking of her as your love, but she's your enemy now. You may not be strong enough to defeat her."

"I'm not without advantages of my own, my lord," Evanthya said. "She may be formidable, but so am I, in my own way." The minister was surprised at herself. Pride had always been Fetnalla's failing.

Tebeo smiled, as might an indulgent parent. "You needn't try to convince me of your worth, First Minister. I saw you fight for this castle. I stood and did battle with my back to yours, and never did I fear that a killing blow would come from behind."

"Thank you, my lord."

"I fear losing you, not only because I value your counsel, but also because I count you as a friend."

"Then think for a moment as my friend, rather than as my duke. Do you honestly believe that I can simply remain here while Fetnalla fights beside the Weaver? After what she's done, how can I not go after her?"

He shook his head. "This wasn't your fault, Evanthya. You couldn't have known—"

"But I should have! There's no one in the world who knows her as I do. She was acting so strangely the last time we were together." She brushed a tear from her cheek. "It should have been obvious."

"You ask too much of yourself."

"The person I love most in this world has revealed herself as a traitor and murderer. How can I not blame myself?"

The duke winced, seeming to cast about for something to say.

"You want to tell me that you can't answer, that the duchess would never do anything of the sort. And of course you're right. But until just a short time ago, I had no reason to think otherwise about Fetnalla."

The duke stood and walked back to his open window. "I can't even begin to imagine what that must be like," he said, gazing out at the castle ward. He said nothing for a long time, until Evanthya began to wonder if he was waiting for her to say more. At last, however, he faced her again. "If it were simply a matter of giving you leave to go, I'd do so in an instant, despite my fears for your safety. But you're asking me to allow Pronjed to escape, and that I can't do. We suspect him of the foulest crimes against the realm, and I fear he remains a threat to all of us."

"I can't find her alone, my lord."

"I'm sorry."

"He's going to escape whether I follow him or not! It's simply a matter of how much damage he does to your castle and how many men he manages to maim and kill in the process!"

"Don't you believe I can stop him?"

"Not if he's determined to win his freedom, no."

Tebeo let out a short harsh laugh. "Evanthya, I command an entire army. He may be powerful, but he's only one man."

"Then why is it so important that you keep him here?"

The duke hesitated, then smiled wryly and shook his head. "You're playing games with me, now."

"I assure you, my lord, this is no game. He can lead me to Fetnalla, and she, in turn, can lead me to the conspiracy. There's far more to be gained by letting him go. If I can find Fetnalla, if I can turn her from this dark path she's on, perhaps she and I together can strike a blow against the renegades. Wouldn't that be worth something?"

"It would, were it possible. But I don't believe it is. I'm sorry, Evanthya, but I believe that Fetnalla has gone too far to turn back. And as you've told me yourself, the archminister is a threat to us all. I can't let him escape, and I'll look upon any attempt on your part to help him do so . . . as a most serious offense."

He had been going to say, "as an act of treason." She was certain of it. It was a measure of how much he cared for her that he didn't.

The duke crossed to his door, pulled it open, and beckoned to one of the guards. "Have the master of arms sent to me immediately," he said.

"What are you going to do, my lord?" Evanthya asked, as Tebeo closed the door again.

"I'm going to double the guard in the corridor outside his chamber, and place extra guards in every corridor that offers access to the prison tower."

The minister shook her head. "All you're doing is placing more men in danger, my lord. A shaper can shatter bone with a thought. A Qirsi with delusion magic can make a man do nearly anything—it's quite possible that Pronjed made the king kill himself."

"So what can I do?"

"That's my point. I'm not certain you can do anything without putting more lives at risk. This is one instance in which your army can't help you. If he was in a courtyard surrounded by one hundred archers, you might be able to stop him, though his power of mists and winds would make it difficult. But he's in a prison tower, where the corridors are narrow, and only a few men can stand against him at any given time."

"Surely four men outside his door will make his escape more difficult than would two."

"A bit. But in the end you'd merely have to build four pyres rather than two."

Tebeo rubbed a hand over his face, looking forlorn. "How does one fight such an enemy?"

No doubt this was a question Eandi lords were asking themselves throughout the Forelands.

"You fight them just as you would any cunning, powerful foe: by forging alliances, by using tactics that you've never thought to employ before, and by choosing your battles carefully."

He eyed her for several moments. "What do you suggest?"

"You know what I want you to do, my lord. Let him go. Remove one of the guards from the corridor outside his chamber."

"What?"

"If only one man is there, Pronjed can use his mind-bending magic on the man. He can free himself from the chamber without harming anyone. Indeed, if we plan this well, he can escape without hurting a single man."

"Did you speak to him of this as well?"

Evanthya felt her face coloring once again. "Yes, my lord. Forgive me. I was—"

"No. It's all right. We're living in extraordinary times. My loyal minister is conspiring with a Qirsi renegade to effect his escape in a way that saves Eandi lives. I suppose it's funny, in a way."

"It's a bitter jest, my lord. You should know that I hate this man. I do this for Fetnalla, and because I believe that I can help those who are fighting the conspiracy."

A lengthy pause, and then, "You'd be the only one of us."

Evanthya frowned. "My lord?"

"Men from Mertesse and Solkara marched north to fight the Eibitharians, but I doubt that they'll join forces with the enemy to fight this Weaver and his renegades. And even if we had a king to lead us, I'm not certain that we could provision an army and send it north in time to take part in a war against the conspiracy. Be it through our own foolishness or the machinations of the traitors, Aneira has been effectively removed from this battle. You'd be the only one of us who could strike a blow."

She couldn't quite believe what she was hearing. "Does that mean you'll let me go, my lord?"

He exhaled heavily, his whole frame seeming to sag with his surrender. "I must be mad," he muttered.

"My lord?"

"I won't try to stop you."

Her heart was pounding once more, with excitement, with fear, with the anticipation of war. "And the archminister?"

"You say that if there's only one guard up there, he won't harm the man?"

"He'd have no reason to."

"Save for his hatred of the Eandi."

She shrugged, then nodded, conceding the point.

Before she could answer, there came a knock at the door. Tebeo stared at her a moment, before calling for whoever had come to enter. The door opened and Gabrys DinTavo, Tebeo's master of arms, entered the chamber.

Seeing Evanthya, the man hesitated and gave a small nod. Then he faced the duke and bowed.

"You sent for me, my lord?"

"Yes, armsmaster." The duke returned to his writing table and sat, his face pale. "How many men do we currently have standing guard in the prison tower?"

Gabrys cast a quick glance at Evanthya. "There are four, my lord, two each outside the chambers of the regent and archminister. Plus we have men in the ward outside the tower, and along the corridors that lead to it. That would be sixteen men in all, my lord."

"That strikes me as being quite a few."

"Yes, my lord. It would be for ordinary prisoners. But these men are far from ordinary. We've felt all along that one or both of them may try to escape."

"But wouldn't we be well served to have some of these men working on the ramparts and battlements? The repairs are going slowly."

The master of arms looked at Evanthya once more, suspicion in his dark eyes.

"Perhaps he should know, my lord," she said, thinking again of the soldiers outside Pronjed's chamber.

Tebeo nodded. "Very well."

"Know what, my lord?"

"We intend to allow the archminister to escape. I want only one guard positioned by his door, and I want the south corridor on the ground level cleared of men entirely."

To Gabrys's credit, he offered no reaction, other than to say, "May I ask why, my lord?"

"This was my idea, armsmaster," Evanthya said. "I'm going to follow him when he leaves the castle. I believe Pronjed can lead me to . . . to the leaders of the Qirsi conspiracy."

Before becoming master of arms, Gabrys had seemed wary of her, as so many Eandi warriors are distrustful of all Qirsi. But after Tebeo named him as successor to Bausef Dar-Lesta, who was killed during the recent siege, the new master of arms put aside his suspicions, appearing to recognize that

Evanthya had the duke's trust. And Gabrys, of all people, understood how desperately she fought to save Castle Dantrielle. She sensed that he no longer doubted her loyalty.

Still, she was not yet ready to reveal to him that she sought her beloved. And he was not ready to trust her on this matter.

"With all respect, First Minister, this is madness. What's to stop him from killing you once he's free? For that matter, what's to stop him from helping the regent escape and allowing the Solkarans to menace us once more?"

She shook her head. "He has no interest in helping the regent, armsmaster. All he wants to do is go north to join his fellow renegades. As for killing me . . ." She looked away. "That's my concern, not yours."

"My lord—"

"I know what you're going to say, Gabrys. I've already argued as you would. But Evanthya has convinced me that we risk more by trying to keep the archminister here. He means to escape, and given the powers he wields, we'll have a difficult time stopping him."

"We can put him in the dungeon."

To her horror, Tebeo appeared to consider this.

"Please don't," Evanthya said, crying again, cursing herself for her weakness. "You have to understand, armsmaster. I need this man. No one else can help me find her." She regretted the words as soon as they crossed her lips.

"Her?" the master of arms repeated, his eyes narrowing.

"It's all right, Gabrys," the duke said quietly. "She refers to Lord Orvinti's first minister. She believes the archminister can lead us to her as well."

The man frowned. "Again, my lord, I must advise you not to do this."

"I know. I share your concern, Gabrys, but against my better judgment I'm going to do as Evanthya requests."

Gabrys was a soldier, and Evanthya had to give him credit for his discipline. Clearly he wished to argue the matter further, but he nodded once, not even glancing in the first minister's direction, and said, "Is there anything else, my lord?"

"No, armsmaster, thank you. See to the removal of the guards."

"Yes, my lord."

He let himself out of the chamber, closing the door quietly, and leaving Evanthya alone with her duke. Perhaps for the last time.

"You're certain about this?" Tebeo asked.

Abruptly she was trembling. "I am, my lord."

Tebeo stood and walked to where she was sitting. Taking her hands in his, he made her stand as well, and then he gathered her in his arms.

"You have served me as faithfully as any minister has ever served a noble," he whispered. "And you've defended this house as bravely as any soldier who's ever worn its colors. Whenever you return, you'll still be first minister of Dantrielle, and so long as I live, no other person will ever bear that title."

Evanthya knew she should say something, but she couldn't speak for her weeping and the aching in her throat. After several moments Tebeo released her, though he took hold of her hands again.

"Do you have everything you need?"

Evanthya nodded.

"Do you need gold?"

"I have some, my lord."

"You should have more." He let go of her hands and returned to his writing table. Opening a small drawer, he produced a leather pouch that rang with the jingle of coins. Crossing back to her, he opened the purse and began to count out gold rounds. After a few seconds he put them back and handed her the entire pouch.

"Just take them all. It's not much, really. Fifty qinde perhaps. But it should help."

"Thank you, my lord."

"You should get food from the kitchens as well."

But Evanthya shook her head. "No one else should know that I'm leaving."

"Oh . . . of course."

They stood in silence, their eyes locked. Evanthya's tears still flowed, and Tebeo seemed to be searching for something more to say. In the end, the first minister merely stepped forward, kissed his cheek, and fled the chamber.

Just a short while after the ringing of the midday bells, the archminister heard men speaking in the corridor outside his chamber. The soldiers there and whoever else had come kept their voices low, and though Pronjed strained to hear them, he could not. He hoped, though, that men had come with orders to replace the silk ties that still held him with iron shackles.

After some time, however, the conversation in the corridor ceased and still no one entered his chamber.

Had the first minister betrayed him? Had she tricked him into confessing his intentions only to turn to her duke and warn him of the danger? He didn't think so—he wasn't even certain that Evanthya was capable of such duplicity—but in truth, he couldn't really be sure of anything anymore.

Actually that wasn't quite true. He knew, with the assurance of a condemned man, that if he didn't join the Weaver in this war he would be killed, either in the dungeons of Dantrielle, or in his dreams by the Weaver himself. And so he resolved, despite his doubts, to carry through on his promise to escape this night.

His decision did little to calm him. In fact, as the day wore on, marked by the tolling of first the prior's bells and then the twilight bells, his apprehension only grew. Yes, he wielded deep magics. But if Evanthya had deceived him, even they might not be enough.

As night settled over the city of Dantrielle, darkening the narrow window of his chamber, he again heard footsteps in the hallway outside his door. A few moments later, one of the guards unlocked his door and stepped into the cell, bearing Pronjed's evening meal. The man placed it on the floor near the archminister, and straightened, clearly intending to leave again.

Before he could, Pronjed reached out with his power and touched the man's mind. Immediately the soldier's face went slack.

"Where is the other soldier?" Pronjed whispered.

"There is no other," the man said, his voice flat. "I'm here alone."

Pronjed gaped at him. "What?"

"I'm here alone."

"Since when?"

"Earlier today. The duke says you're not a threat anymore and we need only one man to guard you."

He eyed the man closely, searching for some sign that he was lying, that he had found some way to resist Pronjed's mind-bending magic. During the last days in Solkara, as Numar planned for his siege, Pronjed had found himself unable to turn the regent or Numar's brother, Henthas, to his purposes. He had assumed at the time that the two men had learned of his abilities and were warding themselves. But what if his power was simply failing?

"Hit your head against the wall," Pronjed said, pushing with his magic again.

The man stepped to the wall, and pounded his forehead against the stone. His powers were working just fine.

"What else has the duke done?"

"He's moved men out of some of the corridors leading to the tower."

"Which corridors?"

"I don't know."

He pushed harder with his magic until the man winced and held a hand to his temple. "I don't know," he said again, whining slightly, like a hurt child.

It would have been useful information, but Pronjed could hardly complain. Evanthya had done more for him than he had dared hope. It was time for him to do his part.

"Come here and untie my wrists."

The man complied instantly. In just a few moments his hands were free, and he had removed the bonds from his ankles.

"Now, tell me where I can find the nearest sally port."

The man's directions were a bit muddled, and Pronjed had to tell him to repeat several parts, but Castle Dantrielle was somewhat similar in design to Castle Solkara, where he had served for so many years. He'd have little trouble finding the hidden doorway.

"Give me your sword and dagger."

The soldier appeared so docile as he handed Pronjed the weapons that the archminister nearly laughed aloud. "The mighty warriors of the Eandi," he said, regarding the man with contempt. "Our Weaver has nothing to fear from any of you."

The man simply stood there, slack-jawed and helpless. Pronjed would have liked to strike at him with the blade. Let Tebeo and his noble friends think on that. But he had struck a bargain of sorts with Evanthya, and she had kept up her end of it.

"Lie down and go to sleep," he said.

And as the man stretched out on the stone floor, Pronjed slipped from the chamber to begin his long journey toward freedom and the triumph of his people.

Chapter

Three

Curtell, Braedon

Somehow his life had become a waking vision of terror. Somehow he had allowed himself to be drawn into matters that were far weightier, far more dangerous, than any with which he had the capacity or desire to cope. Once, as a much younger man, he had hoped to wield influence within the emperor's court, to make himself high chancellor and act as the leader of the imperial Qirsi. Not anymore, not since Dusaan jal Kania's arrival in the court nine years ago. Stavel was too old now. He had none of the high chancellor's ambition. His powers had faded, like muscle that is allowed to grow flaccid with years of neglect, and though he was loath to admit it, he lacked Dusaan's intelligence as well. He always had. He had been clever enough to get by in the Imperial Palace, and even as old age had robbed him of his magic and his physical strength, his mind had remained nimble. But he had never been as brilliant as the high chancellor. Fortunately, he had never been fool enough to make an enemy of the man.

Until now.

It was all the fault of Kayiv jal Yivanne. If the young minister hadn't come to him a turn or so before, accusing the high chancellor of lying to the emperor, and trying to foment rebellion among the chancellors and underministers, perhaps none of this would have happened. If Kayiv hadn't tried to force himself on Nitara ja Plin, who, it seemed, had once been his lover, and who was forced to kill the man to protect herself, the emperor wouldn't have grown so suspicious of all his Qirsi.

Stavel still couldn't say for certain why Harel the Fourth had singled him out in this way. In all the years Stavel had served the imperial court, he and the emperor had barely even spoken, except—and here was an irony—on the day Dusaan told Harel the very lie over which Kayiv eventually became so agitated. Stavel had suggested a possible solution to a dispute in the south, and Harel, happening upon him in the gardens, had complimented him on his inspiration.

He had come to believe that this was why the emperor had approached him, of all people. Still, he thought it strange. Was it possible that Harel had so little contact with his advisors that this one encounter had made Stavel his most trusted Qirsi? It seemed impossible, yet the chancellor could think of no other explanation for what had happened that night near the end of Elined's waxing.

Kayiv had been dead but two days, and for the first time in memory, the emperor's court no longer felt like a haven from the violence that seemed to have gripped every other court in the Forelands. Stavel had just retired for the night, when there came a knock at his door. Surprised—he so rarely had visitors at any time of day—and just a bit frightened, he lit the candle by his bed with a thought, crossed to the door, and opened it cautiously.

Two of Harel's guards stood in the corridor, resplendent in their uniforms of gold and red.

"Th' emperor wants a word with ye, Chanc'lor," one of them said, with the icy courtesy that such men always seemed to reserve for the palace's higher-ranking Qirsi.

His apprehension growing by the moment, Stavel quickly changed back into his ministerial robes and followed the men through the palace corridors to the imperial chamber.

He found Harel there, pacing the stone floors, gripping his jeweled scepter with both hands. He halted when the guard announced Stavel, and regarded the chancellor for just a moment before dismissing the guards. One of his wives reclined in a nest of lush pillows near the hearth, and he ordered her from the chamber as well.

"Sit down, Stavel," he said, stepping to his marble throne.

The chancellor did as he was told, but the emperor remained standing. After a moment he resumed his pacing.

"Terrible," he said, "this business with Kayiv." He shook his head, a frown on his fleshy face.

"Yes, Your Eminence."

"Did you know him well?"

The chancellor's heart was pounding. Did the emperor know of Dusaan's lie, of the discussions Stavel had with Kayiv as they tried to decide whether to bring it to Harel's attention? Or worse, having heard that Kayiv was a traitor, that he tried to turn Nitara to his cause before forcing himself on her, did the emperor suspect that Stavel was a traitor as well? "Not very well, Your Eminence," he said at last, his voice unsteady.

"Do you believe he was a traitor?"

"I believe what Nitara has told us of their encounter, so, yes, I suppose I do."

The emperor stopped by one of his windows, turning to face Stavel. "Do you believe the woman might be a traitor, too?"

"I don't think so, Your Eminence."

"Are you a traitor, Stavel?"

His eyes widened. "No, Your Eminence! I swear I'm not!"

Harel nodded. "I believe you. Indeed, that's why I've summoned you here."

"I'm afraid I don't understand."

"I'm convinced that there are other traitors in my palace. I've heard a great deal about this conspiracy—how it works, how its leaders entice others to join—and I find it very hard to believe that Kayiv was alone. I think this woman might have been a part of it. She shared his bed for a long time before all this ugliness. Perhaps there was more to their relations than mere lust." He began to wander the room again. "And I suspect others may be involved as well. I want you to find out."

"Me, Your Eminence?"

"Does that surprise you, Stavel?"

"Actually, it does, Your Eminence. I would have thought that you would entrust the high chancellor with such a task."

The emperor gave a small smile. "Who's to say how many people I intend to enlist in this effort? Given the nature of this conspiracy, wouldn't I be foolish to place my faith in only one person?"

Stavel hadn't thought of this, and he found himself impressed with the workings of the emperor's mind. "I see. Your Eminence is most wise."

"I want you to learn what you can about your fellow Qirsi, the high chancellor included."

Stavel felt himself blanch. "The high chancellor, Your Eminence?"

"That frightens you, doesn't it?" the emperor asked, narrowing his eyes. "Why?"

"The high chancellor is a . . . a formidable man, Your Eminence. He's the most powerful Qirsi in your palace. Should he decide that one of us is no longer fit to serve you, he can have us banished from your court."

"Only with my consent, Stavel. Never forget that. Dusaan serves in this court at my pleasure, and should he try to have you banished, as you say, I won't allow it to happen."

Even then, sitting in the emperor's chamber, surrounded by the trappings of imperial power, Stavel could not help but wonder if this man, or anyone else for that matter, could protect him from the high chancellor.

Their discussion ended a few moments later and Stavel returned to his chamber, accompanied once more by the two guards. He hadn't spoken with the emperor since, though he had tried to find out what he could about his fellow Qirsi. He began to take his meals in the kitchens and halls rather than in his private chambers, allowing himself to overhear conversations to which, only a short time before, he would have been too well mannered to listen. He spoke with guards—casually, he hoped—about the comings and goings of the palace Qirsi, not only the ministers and chancellors, but also the healers and fire conjurers. He even dared ask about Dusaan, though to a man they denied having seen him leave the palace even once during the past several turns. This struck Stavel as odd, indeed nearly as much so as if they had told him that the high chancellor left the palace frequently, but he had no idea what to make of it.

There were other peculiarities as well. Several turns before, it seemed, Nitara and Kayiv had left the palace together with some frequency, often returning later bearing some new trinket for the woman. And two other Qirsi, healers both, spent a good deal of time down at the wharves along the riverbank. Again, however, Stavel didn't know what any of this meant. His was not the mind of a conspirator; he had no talent for connivance. He learned what he could, having no sense of what to do with the knowledge he gathered. Knowing nothing for certain, he couldn't very well take any of this to the emperor. Nor could he ask anyone else what they thought of all he had learned, not without revealing himself as Harel's spy.

For the first time in all his years in Curtell, Stavel had truly been taken into the emperor's confidence. And he had never felt so isolated.

Attending the daily discussions with Dusaan and the emperor's other advisors proved to be both the easiest and most difficult part of his work on Harel's behalf. Whenever he spoke with the guards, the chancellor spent every moment terrified that he would be discovered by another of the em-

peror's advisors. He had no such fears during the gatherings
of chancellors and ministers. Even if Dusaan learned later
that someone had reported to the emperor on the substance
of their discussion, the high chancellor would have no way of
knowing which of them was the informer. On the other hand,
Stavel could not help feeling that he had betrayed all of his
fellow Qirsi, and at no time was his guilt more pronounced
than during these deliberations. As far as Stavel was concerned, they couldn't end quickly enough.

Midway through Elined's waning, just over half a turn after the tragedy in Nitara's chamber, Stavel began to hear rumors of a contentious exchange between Dusaan and the
emperor. According to some, guards mostly, the emperor had
the high chancellor disarmed and hooded before allowing
Dusaan into the imperial chamber. Others said that it had
gone far beyond that. The high chancellor, it was whispered,
had been bound hand and foot before being granted entry.
Once inside, it seemed that Dusaan had argued with the emperor, complaining about the treatment of palace Qirsi since
Kayiv's death. Exactly what the two men said remained
vague in these tales, and Stavel might have been skeptical
about the whole affair had it not been for a notable change in
Dusaan's demeanor soon after the day in question.

Thinking about it later, Stavel realized that the first signs of
change in Dusaan's behavior began to manifest themselves
the morning after this alleged argument. The high chancellor
appeared distracted during the ministerial discussion, which
itself was unusual. But more to the point, Dusaan didn't seem
bored, as he often did. Rather, he was seething, as if whatever
occupied his mind so infuriated him that it was all the high
chancellor could do simply to sit still. He ended their discussion abruptly, long before a debate over how best to respond
to an outbreak of pestilence near Pinthrel had run its course.

The following morning was no better, and as the days went
by, Dusaan's mood grew ever darker, until Stavel began to
wonder if he might harm himself or someone else.

Only on this very morning, however, the sixth of the new
waxing, did he understand just how gravely matters stood,
and just how badly he had miscalculated.

He was on his way to Dusaan's chambers when a guard stopped him. It was one of the men who, on several occasions, had given him information about other Qirsi. A young man, no more than a year or two past his Fating, he was, nevertheless, uncommonly tall and broad in the shoulders. When he was fully grown, he would be massive. All of which made the wide-eyed, somewhat frightened expression on his face that much more comical.

"Pardon me, Chancellor," the man said, seeming unsure of himself, "but I know tha' ye've been askin' 'bout th' high chanc'lor."

Stavel looked back over his shoulder, as if expecting to see Dusaan himself enter the corridor at any moment. Suddenly his hands were sweating.

"Yes," he said in a hushed voice, wishing he were elsewhere. "What about him?"

"Well, 'e left th' palace las' night. First time any o' us ca' remember. 'E weren't gone long. Less than 'n hour, I'd say. Bu' when 'e come back, 'e had a large bundle under 'is arm."

"How large?"

"Long like, no' too fat mind ye. Put me 'n mind o' a sword, wrapped in cloth."

Stavel could think of no explanation for this. He couldn't imagine that a man in Dusaan's position would need to purchase a weapon in the city marketplace. Most Qirsi serving in the court of a noble, particularly that of a sovereign, already had a sword. Stavel did. It was old, and for all he knew rusted at this point. He hadn't so much as looked at in several years. But it was there in the back of his wardrobe, sheathed and ready should ever he need it. No doubt Dusaan had one as well. So what could he have been carrying?

"Is there anything else you can tell me?"

The man shook his head. "No, Chanc'lor. I think 'e wen' right t' 'is chamber. None o' us saw 'im th' res' o' th' night."

Stavel fumbled in the pocket of his robe, pulling free a five-qinde piece and offering it to the man.

"No, Chanc'lor," he said, shaking his head a second time. "I's jes' doin' my job."

"Well, thank you," Stavel said. "I'm grateful."

The man nodded and left him, the click of his boots echoing loudly off the vaulted ceiling of the corridor. The chancellor stood there for several moments considering why Dusaan might need a sword. Could it be that he'd never had one? He came to the court of the emperor as a young man, and he'd never actually needed one during his tenure as high chancellor. It was possible, no matter how unlikely. At last, Stavel shook his head, as if rousing himself from a dream, and hurried on to Dusaan's chamber.

He was the last to arrive, which was unusual, and his tardiness did not go unnoticed. Dusaan arched an eyebrow at him, and several of the older chancellors regarded him with open curiosity as he took a seat near the window.

The discussion began unremarkably and soon the older chancellors were immersed in yet another argument over how best to keep the pestilence from spreading beyond Pinthrel. Stavel, who usually would have been debating the matter with the rest of them, found it difficult to keep his mind fixed on what they were saying. Instead, his gaze wandered the chamber, and within moments he had spotted a sword—the sword?—sheathed on a belt that hung over a chair in the far corner. The hilt was gold, but rather plain, as was the leather scabbard. Still, once Stavel saw the weapon, his eyes kept returning to it, as if of their own volition. It might very well have been a new blade, though the sheath seemed worn and scuffed along its edges. But if it wasn't a new sword, why would the high chancellor have gone to the city to get it?

"Chancellor?"

Dusaan's voice cut through his thoughts, forcing him to look away from the weapon. The high chancellor was staring at him, frowning slightly, though there was amusement in his golden eyes, and something else as well, though Stavel couldn't say for certain what it was. He seemed in a lighter mood this day, but that only served to give Stavel a somewhat queasy feeling.

"Yes, High Chancellor?"

"Are you all right?"

"Yes, I'm fine."

"It seems your mind is elsewhere." Dusaan turned, glancing in the direction of the sword before looking Stavel in the eye once more. "Is something troubling you?"

"No, High Chancellor. Forgive me. I was . . . merely thinking of something else. I'll do my best to keep my mind on the matters at hand."

"Of course, Chancellor. We were just saying that with Braedon at war, and so many of the emperor's men committed elsewhere, we would be better off leaving it to the army of Pinthrel to cope with the situation there. Wouldn't you agree?"

"Indeed, I would."

"Good." Dusaan turned his attention back to the others, a brittle smile on his lips. "The emperor has also asked me to discuss with the rest of you his plans for the Emperor's Day celebration, which, as you all know, comes at the beginning of the next turn." Stavel and the others knew that Dusaan was putting a good face on bad circumstance. He hadn't spoken with the emperor since their last confrontation. Harel sent messages to the high chancellor instructing him to raise certain matters with the other Qirsi, and Dusaan sent back reports of their discussions in written form. No one dared correct Dusaan on this point.

The Emperor's Day festivities tended to be much the same from year to year. Planning for the affair usually fell to Harel's wives and their courtiers, but the emperor always made a show of involving his Qirsi and Eandi advisors in the preparations. Clearly Dusaan had little patience for the task this year, but he dutifully led the discussion. For his part, Stavel forced himself to attend to the conversation, though he continually fought an urge to gaze once more at the sword.

When at last Dusaan ended their discussion, the midday bells were tolling in the city. The ministers and chancellors began to leave, Stavel with them.

"Wait a moment, won't you, Chancellor?" Dusaan called.

Stavel turned, hoping that he would find the high chancellor looking at one of the others. Would that it had been so.

"Of course, High Chancellor," he said, his hands starting to shake.

When the other Qirsi had all gone, Dusaan gestured at the chair next to his. "Please sit."

Stavel lowered himself into the chair, feeling as though the tip of that damned sword were pressed against his back.

"I wanted to make certain that you were all right, Stavel. I've never seen you so distracted."

"I assure you, High Chancellor, I'm fine."

"So you said before. Yet I find myself wondering what it is about my sword that would interest you so."

Stavel felt as though there were a hand at his throat. The high chancellor hadn't moved.

"Your sword, High Chancellor?" he asked, trying with little success to sound puzzled, or unconcerned, or anything else other than panicked.

"You've spent the better part of the morning staring at it."

"Have I?"

Dusaan eyed him briefly, then rose, crossed the chamber, and retrieved the weapon from the chair on which it sat. Walking back toward Stavel, he pulled it from its sheath, appearing to examine the blade. The chancellor half expected Dusaan to run him through right there, but the man merely held out the sword to him, hilt first.

"There's really nothing extraordinary about it," the high chancellor said, as Stavel took it from him. "It's a simple weapon. I've had it for years."

Stavel looked up. "For years, you say?"

A strange smile alighted on the high chancellor's lips and was gone. "Does that surprise you?"

"No, of course not. Why should it?"

"A good question, Stavel. Why?"

"As I said, it didn't surprise me at all."

"I'm not certain that I believe you. This is hardly the time for a Qirsi to tell lies, Stavel, particularly to another Qirsi." Dusaan's tone was light, but there could be no mistaking the warning in his words.

Stavel gave a small shrug, sensing that he was far out of his depth. "I heard that you had a new sword, that's all."

The smile returned. "Really? Where did you hear that?"

Too late, the chancellor realized that Dusaan had taken him

just where he didn't wish to go. His mouth had gone dry and that hand at his throat seemed to be tightening slowly. "I . . . I don't recall. I must have heard the guards speaking of it."

"How strange. The weapon's been with a swordmaker in Curtell City for nearly four turns now. I only just retrieved it last night."

"But how could—?" Stavel stopped himself, the blood draining from his cheeks. "How could the guards have known then?"

This time Dusaan grinned broadly. It almost seemed that he knew what Stavel had intended to say. *But how could you have taken it to the city when no one saw you leave the palace?* "I don't know. I suppose the emperor's men have ways of learning such things."

"Yes," Stavel said, the word coming out as barely more than a whisper. "That must be it."

They sat in silence for a moment, their eyes locked. Dusaan appeared amused again, though there was a predatory look in those bright yellow eyes.

"Well, Chancellor," he said, "I'm glad to know that you're well. You can go."

Stavel nearly jumped out of his chair, so eager was he to be away from the man. "Yes, High Chancellor. Thank you." He hurried to the door, then forced himself to stop and bow to Dusaan. "Until tomorrow, then."

Dusaan gave a small nod. "Until tomorrow."

A moment later he was in the corridor. The air felt cooler, tasted sweeter. He felt as though he had escaped a dungeon. Except that he knew better. Through circumstance, or ill fortune, or just plain carelessness, he now found himself caught between the emperor and Dusaan. If he didn't extricate himself quickly, he would be crushed, like an innocent trapped between advancing armies.

It had been the last remaining obstacle. After his humiliating encounter with the emperor—he could still smell the muslin hood, dampened by his breath and his sweat—he had determined that there was nothing more to be gained by waiting.

Tihod jal Brossa, the Qirsi merchant who had arranged payments of gold to the Weaver's servants, was dead. Even if Tihod still lived and his network of couriers remained at the movement's disposal, Harel had taken the fee accountings from Dusaan, placing them under the authority of his master of arms. The high chancellor no longer had access to the emperor's gold, which meant that he no longer had any reason to debase himself before the fat fool.

All that kept Dusaan from beginning immediately to set in motion the next part of his plan was his suspicion that Harel had one or more of his Qirsi working as spies within the palace. Until Dusaan had identified the emperor's agent, or agents, he couldn't risk revealing himself.

He had suspected Stavel jal Miraad from the start. From what Nitara told him just after Kayiv's death, he knew that Stavel had worked with the young minister in his efforts to turn the other Qirsi against Dusaan. At first the high chancellor had been skeptical of this, not because he thought Stavel was loyal to him, but because he didn't think the old man courageous enough to involve himself in matters of this sort. But when Gorlan jal Aviarre, who had wisely chosen to ally himself with Dusaan's movement, confirmed all that Nitara had told him, the Weaver had no choice but to believe it.

Still, the emperor could not have known any of this, and while Dusaan saw the old chancellor as the natural choice to act as Harel's spy, the emperor might have had someone else in mind. Though certain that he was being watched, that one of his fellow Qirsi had been asking questions about him, he couldn't be sure which of them had betrayed him. Hence the sword.

It hadn't really been with the cutler for four turns. Dusaan had taken his blade to the city only a few days before, departing the palace and returning through a sally port on the western side, taking great care not to be seen by any of the guards. It was a simple ruse, one that might not have ensnared someone more adept at court intrigue. That Dusaan's trap worked so well was less a reflection of his own cunning than a testament to Stavel's shortcomings as a spy.

What mattered was that Stavel was the emperor's man.

Dusaan was certain of that now. Which meant that the time to reveal himself was finally at hand. Through years of careful planning, of meticulously laying the foundation for his coming war, he had remained patient, knowing that eventually he would be rewarded. He would wait no longer. A new day was dawning, and with it a new age for the Forelands. The anticipation of his victory, after so very long, nearly overwhelmed him. He would have liked to go to Harel that very moment and show the fat fool just how powerful he was. But though everything was in place, he still needed to proceed with some caution. Harel might be a fool, easily turned to Dusaan's purposes and far weaker than he thought himself, but he was not without his resources.

Only a few moments after Stavel left him, looking like a frightened rabbit, there came a knock at his door. Gorlan and Nitara.

"Enter," he called.

They came in together, but quickly separated, Gorlan taking a seat near the window, Nitara sitting beside the high chancellor. It seemed that his hope of fostering a love affair between them, one that would make her forget her desire for him, had been in vain. A pity: her expressions of affection were becoming more and more distracting.

"What have you learned?" he asked, looking from one of them to the other.

"I believe all of the ministers will join with you," Nitara answered, eyeing Gorlan as she spoke. "And perhaps one or two of the chancellors."

"And the rest?"

"I'm not certain what they'll do. They've served the emperor for so long they've forgotten what it is to be Qirsi."

She said it to please him, he knew, because she thought it sounded like something he might say.

"What do you think?" Dusaan asked, looking past Nitara to Gorlan.

He had chosen to join the movement, just as the Weaver had known he would. The alternative had been death, or a desperate attempt to flee Curtell. Gorlan wasn't the type to choose martyrdom, and he was too wise to think that he might actually escape. What impressed Dusaan, however, was the fervor with which he had embraced the Qirsi cause as his own. It was hard to tell if the minister had considered the possibility of joining the movement prior to that day when Dusaan offered him the opportunity to do so. But once presented with the choice, he committed himself fully to its success. Dusaan would have known if the man was feigning his enthusiasm—such was the power of a Weaver. It almost seemed that having opened his eyes at last to the suffering his people endured under Eandi rule of the Forelands, Gorlan could hardly stand to look upon what he saw. He was everything Dusaan had once hoped Kayiv would be, and more. Intelligent, passionate, but controlled, and above all, honest with his opinions and insights, even when he knew that they were at odds with what Dusaan wanted to hear.

"I'm a bit less certain about the ministers than is Nitara. B'Serre and Rov will probably pledge themselves to the movement. I don't know about the others. And I have little sense of what the chancellors will do."

"What do you think it would take to convince those who are less willing to join us?"

Gorlan shook his head. "I really don't know."

"Do you think telling them of the Weaver would help?"

"It might."

"What if they were to learn that I was that Weaver?"

Dusaan heard Nitara give a small gasp, but he kept his eyes fixed on the other minister. Gorlan was staring at him, looking awed and just a bit frightened.

"You're the Weaver?"

"I am."

"I'm not certain that I believe you." There was no disrespect in his tone. Just disbelief.

Dusaan smiled. He had concealed his powers for so long. He would enjoy proving to this man what he was. "Raise a wind," he said.

"What?"

"I want you to summon a wind, right here in this chamber."

Gorlan regarded him briefly, then gave a small shrug and closed his eyes. A moment later the air in the chamber began to stir. In a few seconds a gale was howling, blowing scrolls onto the floor and making Dusaan's hair dance.

"Good," the Weaver said. "Don't stop."

He reached for his own power, and joining it to Gorlan's strengthened the wind as only a Weaver could. Two of the empty chairs toppled. His sword, still sheathed, fell to the floor. The shutters on his window clattered loudly, until it seemed that they would splinter.

Gorlan's eyes flew open. "Demons and fire!"

"You believe me now?"

The wind died down, and a broad smile broke over the man's face. "Forgive me for doubting you, Weaver."

"You needn't apologize."

"The others will join you," he said, still grinning. "I'm certain of it. How could they not?"

"I hope you're right. If I reveal to them the true extent of my powers, and they still refuse to pledge themselves to our movement, I'll have no choice but to kill them."

"If you tell them that you're a Weaver," Nitara said, "and they still refuse you, they deserve to die."

Gorlan nodded. "I have to agree."

"You both have served me well, and I know that you'll continue to do so. For now, though, speak to no one of this. I've one more thing to do before I can tell the others who and what I am. Do you understand?"

They both stood and bowed to him.

"Yes, Weaver," Nitara said.

Once they had left his chamber, Dusaan stood and began to pace. Now that his time had come, he was eager to act, to put an end to the Eandi courts and begin his reign as ruler of the Forelands. But once more, he had to wait until nightfall so that he might speak with those throughout the land who served him. One last time, the sun would set over the Western Sea with the Curtell Dynasty ruling Braedon. When morning came Dusaan would begin to reap the rewards for which he had waited so long. There was no one in all the Forelands who could stop him.

Chapter
Four

How could a single night take so long to pass? Even with all Dusaan had to do before dawn, it seemed to him that the moons took days to turn their broad arcs across the darkened sky. He had waited years to begin his war in earnest, he had dreamed of doing so since before his Fating. Patience had long been his greatest weapon. But on this final night, his anticipation got the better of him.

He barely touched his evening meal, which a servant brought to his chamber at twilight and removed several hours later. He paced, he sat by his window staring up at the stars, and he waited for the tolling of the midnight bells, his mind churning, his heart pounding so loudly that he thought everyone in the palace must hear it.

When at last he heard the bells, he wasted no time. Closing his eyes, he began to reach across the Scabbard and the Strait of Wantrae for his chancellors, his most trusted and most powerful servants. He found Jastanne ja Triln aboard her ship, the *White Erne,* just off the Galdasten shore, within sight of the warships of Braedon, Eibithar, and Wethyrn. As always, she was naked, her body offered to him as a gift. And, again as always, he sensed her ambition, her daring, and her keen intelligence.

Abeni ja Krenta, archminister in the court of Sanbira's queen, proved more difficult to locate. He had expected to find her in Yserne, but she was riding with the queen and a force of nearly eight hundred men. They were two days out from Brugaosa, just across the border into Caerisse, and pushing hard toward northern Eibithar. Dusaan was pleased;

he had feared that she might not reach the northern kingdom in time. Of all his servants, she might have been the most valuable. As brilliant as Jastanne and as passionate in her commitment to the movement, Abeni was somewhat older, and with that age came a wisdom and calm that the young merchant lacked.

Uestem jal Safhir, solid like the great boulders on Ayven-calde Moor, had proved himself intelligent as well, if some-what unimaginative. He was already in Galdasten. And Pronjed jal Drenthe had managed to escape the prison tower of Dantrielle and was already making his way northward. As always, the archminister was eager to please and, after his questionable decision to kill Carden the Third, king of Aneira, frightened of incurring Dusaan's wrath again.

There were others—men and women who served in courts or sailed ships or journeyed the realms with festivals. And on this night, Dusaan spoke with all of them, telling each the same thing.

The time has come. I will reveal myself within the day and will begin to fight the Eandi courts in earnest. Prepare your-selves and make your way to Galdasten as quickly as possi-ble. I intend to form an army the likes of which has not been seen in the Forelands for nearly nine centuries.

The sky had already begun to brighten when he ended the last of these conversations. He hadn't slept at all. He should have been too weary to stand. Instead, he felt invigorated. The sky over the Imperial Palace glowed indigo and the moons hung low to the west. What a glorious day to begin his reign.

He had a servant bring him his morning meal, and this time he ate, like a newly robed cleric breaking his fast. When he had finished, he sat by the window and dozed until the first of the ministers arrived for the day's discussion. He watched them file into the chamber, singly and in pairs, their hair as white as bone, their eyes a dozen different shades of gold and yellow. He had heard it said among the Eandi that all Qirsi looked the same. Dusaan couldn't have disagreed more. There was as much variety in the Qirsi face as in the Eandi, and far more beauty. Their skin was as pure as new snow, their features as fine as Sanbiri metalwork. He would challenge any man in the Forelands to show him an Eandi woman as beautiful as Jastanne, or Cresenne for that matter.

His mood darkened at the thought of Cresenne. Had she not betrayed him for Grinsa, she would have been one of those whose dreams he entered this past night. She could have had a hand in this momentous day, she could have been his queen and shared with him the glorious future he had conceived and would soon create. Instead, she would die an enemy of the new Qirsi court. A pity. But she had brought this fate upon herself.

"We're all here, High Chancellor."

He looked up to find Nitara standing before him, lovely in her own way, her face flushed with desire for him, and, just perhaps, her anticipation of what was about to happen in this chamber.

Dusaan gazed past her to find that all of them were watching him: Gorlan looking younger than the Weaver had ever seen him, a smile on his lips; Stavel looking old and scared, as well he should. The others appeared oblivious, some even bored. That wouldn't last long.

He smiled at Nitara and gestured for her to sit. "Thank you, Minister."

How many times had he envisioned the scene unfolding before him? For how long had he been composing what he was about to say? It seemed to Dusaan that his entire life had been leading to this very moment.

"Have you any further word from Pinthrel, High Chancellor?"

The Weaver glared at Stavel, causing the old man to shrink back into his chair.

"All of you have heard rumors of the Qirsi movement, the so-called conspiracy that threatens the Eandi courts, that strikes fear into the hearts of nobles throughout the Forelands, that unmans Braedon's emperor. For many turns now, we've denounced this movement, just as the emperor would expect. We've done so to keep ourselves from being branded as traitors, we've done so because as servants of an Eandi lord we could do no less."

"High Chancellor," Stavel said meekly, "what does this have to do with the pestilence and Pinth—?"

Dusaan pounded his fist on the writing table. *"Will you be silent?"* He closed his eyes briefly, trying to compose himself, trying to remember exactly where he'd been in his oration. "As I say, we've denounced this so-called conspiracy because that's what was expected of us. But how many of us have wished for the freedom promised by this movement? How many of us have dreamed of a day when Qirsi ruled in the great cities of the Forelands? I know that I have."

"What are you saying?"

It wasn't Stavel this time, but rather one of the young ministers. He looked nearly as frightened as Stavel. Indeed, with the exception of Nitara and Gorlan, all of them appeared scared, like children caught in a sudden storm.

"I'm saying just what you think I am. I believe the time has come to put an end to Eandi rule in the Forelands. Our people have served inferior men for too long. We possess great powers. Qirsar has given us the gift of his magic. He has allowed us to glimpse the future, to heal flesh and shape matter, to turn the elements to our will. And yet we are expected to humble ourselves before Eandi nobles who possess neither our powers nor our wisdom. Why should this be?"

"Because they defeated us." Stavel again, bolder this time. He was trembling—Dusaan could see his hands shaking—but he held his chin high, defiant and proud. The Weaver hadn't known that he possessed such nerve. "We fought this war nine centuries ago, High Chancellor, and we were beaten back. The Eandi rule the Forelands because we weren't strong enough to take it from them. We failed then, and this conspiracy will fail now."

Not long ago, he would have responded to such words with rage. But he was too close now to care what this one man said, weak and inconsequential as he was. He merely shook his head, grinning fiercely. "No, Stavel, you're wrong. We failed then because we defeated ourselves, through the treachery of a single man." Even now, on the verge of undoing all that this traitor had wrought, Dusaan found it difficult to speak his name. "Carthach ruined us, he doomed our peo-

ple to nine centuries of servitude and humiliation. But all that
is about to end."

"You can't really think to defeat them. Their armies—"

"Their armies are already destroying one another. By the
time we strike at them they will have so weakened themselves that our victory will be assured."

"How long have you been with the conspiracy, High Chancellor?" Rov asked, her tone betraying little.

"I prefer to call it a movement, Minister. And I've been
with it from the beginning. The movement is me, and I am
the movement."

She frowned. "I don't understand."

"It's very simple. I lead the movement."

The woman blinked, wide-eyed.

"I don't believe you." Stavel, of course.

"Don't you, Chancellor? Look into your heart. You know
that it's true." He smiled again. "But there's more." He
looked around the chamber. "Who here knows what powers I
possess?"

No one spoke.

With only the merest effort, he called forth a wind, allowing it to sweep through the chamber, then die away. He held
forth his hand and conjured a flame. Then he held his other
hand over the fire, wincing at the pain. Several of the Qirsi
gasped, including Nitara. He let the fire go out and held up
his burned hand so that all could see the wound. And then he
healed it. He picked up a wine goblet from his writing table,
balanced it in his palm, and shattered it with a thought.

"Mists and winds," he said. "Fire, healing, shaping. Let me
assure you that I have gleaning, language of beasts, and delusion as well."

Stavel looked like he might be ill. "You're a Weaver," he
whispered.

"Yes. Drawing on my own powers and melding them with
the magic of those in this chamber, I could tear this palace to
the ground, killing every Eandi within it. With the force that I
have assembled throughout the Forelands, I can overcome the
combined might of the seven realms."

Gorlan stood and faced the others. "What he's telling you

is true. I've felt his power. It's greater than I ever thought possible."

"You're involved in this, too?"

"We're part of a great movement," Dusaan said, ignoring Stavel. "We're on the verge of changing the course of history. I would gladly welcome all of you to our cause, if you so choose. But you must decide now. You have spent your lives in the service of Eandi lords, men who did not deserve your devotion. Now I offer you the opportunity to join me in building a Qirsi empire. You need only swear your fealty to the movement."

"And if we refuse?" asked one of the chancellors.

"I have revealed to you that I'm a Weaver, and I've declared myself at war with the Eandi courts, including that of the emperor. If you refuse, you declare yourself his ally. You'll have until nightfall to leave the palace without fear of reprisal. After that, if you remain and you still refuse to pledge yourself to our cause, I'll have no choice but to kill you."

"Do you honestly believe that you can win our allegiance with threats?"

Again, the Weaver ignored the question, eyeing the others. Nitara had been right: all of the ministers were with him, and at least one of the older Qirsi.

"All of you who intend to join me, please stand."

All six ministers and two of the chancellors stood, leaving only Stavel and two others sitting.

"You're mad!" Stavel said. "All of you." He pushed himself out of his chair and started for the door.

"Hold, Stavel."

The old chancellor halted, his back to Dusaan. After a moment, he turned. His face was deathly pale, and there could be no mistaking the terror in his eyes. Yet, once more, he surprised the high chancellor with his bravery. "What are you going to do to me?"

"That depends. Where are you going?"

"To the emperor, of course. I must tell him of this."

Brave indeed. "You know I can't let you do that."

"So it's to be murder then."

"I'd rather it not be." Dusaan wouldn't have thought it pos-sible, but he actually meant what he said. Just the day before he wouldn't have thought twice about killing this man. But Stavel had earned his respect this day. Dusaan was forced to admit that there was more to the man than he had ever imag-ined. "I know that we've had our differences over the years. I know that you were jealous of me when I first came to Curtell. I'll even grant that you had reason to be. I was new to the palace, and I was very young to be made high chancellor. It couldn't have been easy for you, being passed over when you had waited so long. But I'd be willing to put all of that aside if you'll pledge your fealty to me now."

"Never."

"Surely you can't think that the emperor deserves such loyalty. The man's a fool. He cares nothing for the Qirsi who serve him. He can barely even remember our names."

"None of that matters, Dusaan, and you know it. I swore an oath to serve the empire, and I will not go back on my word."

"Even if it means turning against your own people?"

"You may be a Weaver, and you may lead a movement that stretches across all the Forelands, but that doesn't mean that you speak for our people." The old man took a long breath, drawing himself up so that he stood straighter than Dusaan had seen in many years. "So if you wish to stop me, you'll have to kill me."

Their eyes were locked, and the Weaver refused to look away, but he sensed that the others were watching him, won-dering what he would do.

"Go ahead, Dusaan. Kill me. Show them what kind of leader you intend to be."

It would have been easiest to break his neck. One simple push with his shaping power would do it, and it would be a relatively painless death for Stavel. But he needed to decide what point he wished to convey to the others—did he want them to think him merciful, or would it be more useful to make them fear his power?—and he had only an instant to make his choice.

Stavel turned again, reaching for the door handle.

"Stop, Stavel." He pushed as he said the words, touching

the old man's mind with his magic. The chancellor hesitated, his hand resting on the door handle for an instant before dropping to his side. The others were watching in grave silence, but Dusaan didn't think they understood quite what was happening.

The Weaver glanced about the chamber, trying to decide what to do with Stavel now that he controlled him. It took him but a moment to decide. "Retrieve my sword, Chancellor, and bring it to me."

Stavel looked at him, despair in his yellow eyes, but he could only obey. He crossed the chamber, pulled the sword from its scabbard, and walked back to where the Weaver stood.

"Lay the point against my chest."

Stavel lifted the blade so that its point rested on the high chancellor's breastbone.

"No doubt he'd like to kill me," Dusaan said so that the others could hear, all the while keeping a tight hold on Stavel's mind. "But I control him. He's helpless to do anything other than what I command."

"Why are you doing this to me?" Stavel whispered, a tear winding a crooked course down his face.

"Because you turned against me. Because you chose service to the Eandi over loyalty to your own people."

"What are you going to do to him?" asked Bardyn, another of the old ones who had refused to join him.

"What would you suggest I do with him, Chancellor? He's been spying on all of us for the emperor. He's guilty of the worst kind of betrayal."

"He was only doing what his sovereign asked him to do. Harel feared for his life and his court—with good reason it now seems—and he ordered Stavel to do this. Surely you can't fault the chancellor for that."

"So you would have done the same thing?" Gorlan demanded.

Bardyn glared at him briefly before looking away. "I wouldn't expect you to understand."

Stavel's hand was trembling. Dusaan could feel him fighting to win back control of his mind and body.

"Turn the sword on yourself," he said.

Another tear slid from Stavel's eye as he turned the blade and held the tip against his own chest.

The Weaver almost told the man to kill himself then. He intended to. He considered Stavel's betrayal a crime against the Qirsi people, one for which the old man deserved to die. But looking at the others once more, he saw apprehension on their faces. Even Nitara seemed to be pleading silently for Stavel's life, her pale eyes wide and brimming with tears. If this woman, who had willingly taken the life of her former lover, couldn't bear to see the chancellor killed, how would the rest respond?

"You understand that it would be nothing for me to take your life, that you've earned such a death with all you've done?"

Stavel nodded.

"And you understand as well, that if you dare go to the emperor with any of this, I will kill you, and Bardyn, too."

His eyes flicked toward his friend, then back to Dusaan's face, the sword still pressed to his heart. "I understand."

"Good." Dusaan took the blade from him and released his hold on the man's mind. Stavel blinked once, his entire body appearing to sag. "You're to leave the palace at once, Chancellor. I don't ever want to see your face again. If I do, your life is forfeit."

Stavel started to say something, then seemed to think better of it. With one last glance at the others, he left the chamber.

"If any of you still intend to oppose me, you should leave now as well. My patience for traitors runs thin."

There was a brief silence. Then Bardyn stood, crossed to the door, and pulled it open. Pausing on the threshold, he turned to stare back at Dusaan. "Stavel is right, you know. You're all quite mad."

Dusaan raised the sword, so that it pointed directly at Bardyn's chest. "Not a word to anyone, Chancellor. You'll find that a Weaver's reach is not limited by walls, or mountains, or even oceans. Defy me now, and I'll find you, no matter how far you run."

The man blanched and pulled the door shut, his footsteps retreating quickly down the corridor.

"Anyone else?" Dusaan asked.

No one moved.

"I'm pleased," he said. "And I welcome you to the Qirsi movement. Before this day is done the Imperial Palace will be ours, and soon after, all of Braedon. From there, it won't be long until we've conquered all the Eandi courts and created a new land ruled by the Qirsi people and defended by Qirsi magic."

"How will we take the palace, Weaver?" Nitara asked.

The high chancellor allowed himself a smile. "Leave that to me."

Dusaan left his chamber a short time later, instructing the other Qirsi to remain there and await his return. He wouldn't need them for what he intended to do next, nor did he wish for any aid. Harel was his. He had been anticipating this day for too long to share its pleasures with anyone else.

The guards at Harel's door stopped him, of course.

"The emperor isn't expecting you," one of them said.

"I know that, but it's rather urgent that I see him."

The one who had spoken stepped into the imperial chamber, closing the door quietly behind him. After some time he reemerged, eyeing Dusaan with manifest distrust.

"What is it you want?"

"It's a rather delicate matter, involving the fee accountings. I'd prefer not to say more than that."

The man frowned, but went back into the chamber. When he returned to the corridor once more, he nodded to the other guard then faced the high chancellor. "You'll have to remove your weapons."

"Yes, I know. And I suppose I'll have to wear that hood again as well."

"I'm afraid so," the man said, sounding more insolent than apologetic.

They took his dagger, tied the hood in place, and led him into the chamber. Dusaan sensed four guards in the chamber,

two by the throne and two more by the door. Two of Harel's
wives sat in a far corner whispering to one another as a
harpist played nearby. Harel was sitting on his throne as
Dusaan entered, but he stood immediately and began to pace.
The two guards who had accompanied the Weaver into the
chamber withdrew, closing the door behind them.

"Well, High Chancellor?" Harel said, his voice tight.
"What is it you want?"

"I thought your man explained that, Your Eminence."

"Yes, yes, the fee accountings. What about them?"

The guards seemed content to remain where they were, no
doubt believing that the hood rendered Dusaan powerless to
harm the emperor. Within the muslin the Weaver smiled.

"I fear that some of your gold has been misused, Your Eminence."

Harel stopped pacing. "What? How much?"

"Quite a lot actually. Several thousand qinde, at least."

"Several thousand! How is this possible?"

"It's difficult to say, Your Eminence. I found some notes
that I had written down some time ago and I realized that the
numbers on those notes were not consistent with what I remember being requested by the fleet commanders in the
strait."

"I don't understand."

"It would be easier to explain if we had the accountings
here with us. Perhaps you can have the master of arms summoned."

"Yes. Yes, I'll do that." Harel approached the guards at the
door. "Have the master of arms brought here at once, and
make certain that he brings the fee accountings." Harel hesitated, then turned to Dusaan. "All of them?"

"No, Your Eminence. Only the current one."

"The current fee accountings," Harel repeated to the guard,
as if the man couldn't hear.

The soldier left them, and Harel resumed his pacing.

For a long time the emperor merely walked, saying nothing, though Dusaan sensed his impatience mounting. The
high chancellor would have liked for Harel's wives to leave.

The harpist, too. He had no desire to harm them, but neither could he have them running through the palace raising the alarm.

"How could this have happened?" Harel finally demanded, sounding like a petulant boy. "Where could the gold have gone if not to the fleet?"

"Your Eminence, it might be best if we discuss this matter in private."

"What? Oh, yes, of course." Dusaan heard him snap his fingers. An instant later the music stopped, as did the whispers and soft laughter. "Leave us. I'll call for you again later."

The two wives rose and walked quickly from the chamber, followed closely by the harpist.

"Now, Dusaan, can you tell me where this gold might have gone?"

"Actually, Your Eminence, I believe so."

He sensed the emperor's surprise. "You can? Where?"

"I think it will be easier to explain when the master of arms arrives with the fee accountings."

"Damn you, Dusaan! Stop weaving mists and tell me what's happened to my gold!"

Before the Weaver could respond, there came a knock at the door.

"Enter!" Harel shouted.

A guard stepped into the chamber to announce the master of arms, but the emperor cut him off and called for Uriad, who stepped past the man and knelt. The guard remained by the door, which Dusaan had expected. Four guards in all, the emperor, and Uriad.

"You asked for this, Your Eminence?" said the master of arms, apparently referring to the fee accountings.

"Yes. According to the high chancellor, some of my gold has been lost."

He sensed Uriad turning to face him. "Before or after I took control of the accounts?"

"Before. The fault is mine, armsmaster, not yours."

"I've been trying to get him to tell me where the gold has gone, but he won't answer me."

"It's not that I won't answer, but rather that I wanted Uriad to hear what I had to say." He reached up and began to untie the cords that held his hood in place.

"What are you doing?" Harel demanded.

"I'm removing this damned hood."

"Don't you dare!"

Dusaan continued to work the knot loose.

"Stop him!" the emperor said, his voice rising.

The guards converged on him. The two who had been nearest the throne were closer, and so he struck at them first, hammering at them with his shaping power. He heard the muffled snapping of bone and the clattering of swords and mail as they fell to the floor. He didn't even turn to kill the other two. His magic was as precise and lethal as a war hammer; it was as effortless to wield as an Uulranni blade.

The two guards from the corridor burst into the chamber. Dusaan whirled and conjured a great killing flame that enveloped them like a mist. Within seconds he heard their blades fall to the floor.

He sensed that Uriad was gathering himself for an assault.

"Don't do it, armsmaster," Dusaan warned, turning once more toward Harel and his master of arms. "The emperor would be dead before you took your first step. And neither of you had better call for help. I'll kill you for that as well." Without even looking back he summoned a wind that blew the doors closed.

"But you can't see!" the emperor whispered.

The Weaver laughed. "You're a fool, Harel. You collect Qirsi the way other men collect fine blades or Sanbiri mounts, but you've never bothered to learn anything about us or our magic. I don't need to see you to use my power against you. I can sense your every movement." He pulled off the hood to find Harel staring at him as if the high chancellor had grown into some beast from a child's darkest dream. Uriad stood near the emperor, his sword drawn, as if that might protect them. Just for amusement, Dusaan shattered the blade.

"What is it you want?" Harel asked, his voice quavering.

"It's not a matter of what I want, Your Eminence. You're the one who asked me what happened to your gold. I can tell you exactly what happened to every qinde, every silver that was diverted from your treasury. It has been given to the Qirsi movement."

It took Harel a moment. "The Qirsi movement? You mean the conspiracy?"

"No, you fat fool, I mean the Qirsi movement. That's what we call it. What I call it."

"So you're a traitor." Uriad sounded calm, as a warrior should. Perhaps Kayiv had prepared him for this before his death.

"I'm more than that, armsmaster. I'm *the* traitor. I created what you call the conspiracy, and I'm its leader. And still, I'm even more than that. I'm the most powerful Qirsi either of you has ever known." He smiled. "I'm a Weaver."

That morning, when he revealed his powers to the emperor's other Qirsi, he had reveled in their awe. *This,* he had thought at the time, *is how Qirsi across the Forelands will receive me. With wonder and reverence.* But that was nothing compared with the fear he now sensed from both the emperor and his master of arms. While his own people would exalt him, the Eandi would tremble before him. His people would see in him the embodiment of a glorious future; the Eandi would see in his powers the promise of their own doom. Harel's terror strengthened Dusaan, until he felt that he was invincible, that entire armies were not enough to quell his power.

"A Weaver," the emperor repeated, as if he had never heard the word before.

"By law, Weavers are to be executed."

Dusaan regarded the master of arms, noting the fighter's stance, the way his hand wandered toward the hilt of his dagger. "I respect you, Uriad. I want you to know that. I have nothing but contempt for our emperor here, for most Eandi really, particularly those one finds in the courts. But I've always thought that you were an uncommonly thoughtful man for one of your race."

The man raised an eyebrow. "Really? I've always thought you an arrogant bastard, who was more smug than he was intelligent."

Dusaan blinked. After a moment, he tried to laugh away the remark, but he felt as though he'd been slapped. And perhaps sensing that he had caught the Weaver off guard, Uriad chose that moment to launch himself forward, his dagger in hand, his arm cocked to strike at Dusaan's heart. Recovering quickly, the Weaver battered the man with his shaping power, fracturing not only the blade, but also Uriad's wrist and forearm.

The master of arms staggered back, clutching his arm to his belly and gritting his teeth against the pain.

"You're a fool, Uriad. You could have escaped with a quick, painless death."

The man glared at him. Then he opened his mouth, taking a breath as if he intended to shout for help. Dusaan never gave him the chance. He lashed out with his foot, catching Uriad full in the face. The master of arms sprawled backward onto the floor, bleeding from his nose and mouth. And as he lay there, Dusaan reached once more for his shaping power, applying pressure slowly to the man's head. Uriad clawed at his temple with his good hand, a moan escaping him. Still pushing with his magic, Dusaan stepped forward and put his foot on the armsmaster's throat to keep him from screaming. Uriad's mouth was stretched open in a silent wail, his eyes were squeezed shut, his fist was closed tight around a handful of hair. After a time Uriad began to flail with his feet.

"Stop it!" the emperor cried. "Let him go."

Dusaan eyed him briefly. "No. But I will end his pain." With a final push, he crushed the man's skull. Uriad's struggles ceased abruptly, a thin trickle of blood seeping from his ear and staining the floor.

The Weaver removed his foot from Uriad's neck and strode toward the emperor. "Now it's your turn, Your Eminence."

Harel dropped to his knees, tears streaking his face. "No, please! I beg you!"

Dusaan grabbed him by the hair and hauled him to his feet. "Do you know how long I've dreamed of killing you?"

"Why? Haven't I always treated you well? Haven't I paid you more than any noble in the Forelands pays his Qirsi?"

The Weaver slapped him, leaving a bright imprint of his hand on Harel's corpulent face. "You don't understand, do you? I don't aspire to being the wealthiest minister in the land, nor am I willing to have myself hooded, like some sort of common brigand, so that I can continue to earn your gold. I intend to rule the Forelands myself."

"You what?"

"Before the snows return to Braedon, every Eandi noble in the land will bow before me, or they'll suffer the same fate as poor Uriad."

"You can't be serious!"

He slapped Harel a second time. "Do you think I jest?"

"What is it you want from me?"

"Your empire, Harel. Isn't that clear? You've given me everything else I could want. A position of authority from which to make my preparations, gold for my movement, an invasion that is destined to weaken the fleets and armies of Braedon, Eibithar, Aneira, Wethyrn, and Sanbira. You've been most helpful, Your Eminence, but I'm afraid you've outlived your usefulness."

"No, I haven't! I can give you more! I can keep my soldiers from harming you."

Dusaan laughed, and Harel's face fell. "Do you have any idea what a Weaver does, Harel? I can bind together the power of other Qirsi. I'm but one man, and I've killed seven of your warriors. Think what I can do with the other ministers and chancellors by my side. I have nothing to fear from your army."

"The others?"

"Yes. They've all joined with me. Well, not all. Stavel and Bardyn have fled the palace, but the rest have pledged themselves to my cause. I suppose that's one more thing you've given me, Your Eminence. Before you began to treat all of us like we were traitors, a good number of them might have refused to join me. In essence, you've made my movement stronger."

"I'll abdicate to you! I'll sign whatever you want me to sign! I'll tell my men to fight on your behalf! You'd command an army of both Eandi and Qirsi!"

He had been ready to kill the emperor. Indeed, he had been eager for Harel's blood. But for the second time that day he was forced to wonder if he might be better served by showing mercy. He doubted that the emperor's men would willingly fight on behalf of the Qirsi movement. On the other hand, he was certain that they would lay down their arms if they thought that it would save the emperor's life. Wouldn't it be better to win the surrender of the emperor's men peacefully, than to risk a battle that might cost the lives of his new adherents?

"All right, Harel. I accept your offer. I'll spare your life, and in return you'll surrender the empire to me. If you renege on this arrangement, or if you try to turn even one of your men against me, you'll suffer a fate far worse than that of your master of arms. Do I make myself clear?"

The emperor nodded, dread filling his small green eyes.

Dusaan smiled. "I'm glad to hear it." He crossed to the emperor's writing table and quickly drafted a statement of surrender. "Come here, Harel," he said when he had finished. "I want you to sign and seal this."

The emperor joined him at the table and read the statement, tight-lipped and pale. His hand trembled as he penned his name, dripped a small puddle of red wax below, and pressed his seal into it.

Dusaan started toward the door. "Now follow me."

"Why? You said you'd spare me! You gave me your word!"

"Calm yourself, Harel. I'm not going to kill you. But I am going to place you in the prison tower."

"No! I want to stay here!"

"I'm afraid that's impossible. You're not a brave man, but you just might be fool enough to try to escape through those glazed windows of which you're so proud."

"I swear, I wouldn't."

"I don't believe you. Now come along."

Harel crossed his arms over his chest, managing to look Dusaan in the eye. "No."

He didn't have time for this. With a quick thought, he snapped the bone in Harel's little finger. The emperor cried out, cradling his maimed hand with his whole one.

"Defy me again and the next thing I break will be your arm."

Harel nodded, and when Dusaan opened the door and entered the corridor, the emperor followed closely.

They went first to Dusaan's chamber, where the other Qirsi were waiting for him. They passed two guards, but at Dusaan's instruction, the emperor said nothing to them. When they entered the chamber the other Qirsi stood, looking first at Harel and then at the Weaver, as if uncertain of what they should do.

"The emperor has surrendered Braedon to me." He held up the rolled parchment. "I have his written word right here." He paused, regarding the others. He could sense what powers they possessed simply by looking at them. He would need to face the soldiers next, and so he sought out those with shaping and fire magic. "I'll take B'Serre, Gorlan, and Rov with me. Nitara, I want you and the rest to gather the emperor's wives and servants and take them, along with Harel here, and put them in separate chambers in the prison tower. If they give you any trouble at all, kill them."

"Yes, Weaver."

"I want the emperor in the highest chamber. When he's there, place a flame in the window that faces into the courtyard. That will be our signal to begin. At some point I'll also want you to put Harel in front of the window so his men can see him. Can you do all that?"

She nodded and smiled, her cheeks flushed with excitement.

"Good. Now go."

"Yes, Weaver."

Harel stared back at him as he was led away, but he said nothing. Dusaan worried that they might encounter guards along the way, but there were several in Nitara's group who had fire magic, and one other who was a shaper. They would be able to meet any challenge that presented itself.

"The three of you come with me," he said, returning to the corridor and going in the direction opposite that taken by the others. They walked to the nearest of the tower stairways and descended to the courtyard, remaining in the archway. There they could conceal themselves, while watching the windows of the prison tower.

They waited a long time, and still the narrow windows remained dark. Dusaan began to fear that something might have gone wrong. Perhaps Nitara and the others had encountered more guards than they could handle. Perhaps Harel had managed somehow to win his freedom. Still they waited, and still they saw no sign of Nitara and her company.

"Weaver," Gorlan began.

Dusaan shook his head. "Not yet. Give her a few moments more."

The minister nodded and fell silent.

They had to wait a bit longer, but at last their patience was rewarded. A bright flame appeared in the highest window of the prison tower, and a moment later windows in the other chambers began to glow softly as well.

At the same time, however, shouts went up from the guard house in the upper courtyard. Soldiers began gathering in a tight knot near the building, many of them bearing torches.

"Let's go," Dusaan said. He and his three companions left the tower and strode to where the men stood.

"Where's your captain?" Dusaan demanded as they drew near the soldiers.

A man stepped forward, his sword drawn. "I'm the day captain, High Chancellor." He raised his weapon. "I'd suggest you stop right there."

"Gorlan?"

The minister grinned. An instant later there was a sound like the chiming of a bell and the soldier's blade splintered like glass.

Other men came forward, weapons readied.

"Call them back, Captain, or the same magic that shattered your blade will break their necks."

"Stand your ground, men."

The soldiers halted, though they kept their swords up.

"What is this, High Chancellor?"

Dusaan held up the parchment. "The emperor has surrendered this palace and this realm to me. From now on, I am your sovereign."

"I don't believe you."

"Look for yourself." He handed the parchment to the captain and waited while he read it.

"You made him sign this. That's the only explanation that makes sense."

"Such documents are often coerced. That doesn't make it any less valid." He held out his hand for the parchment, ready to use mind-bending power if the man refused to return it to him. But the captain handed it back without a fight.

"It means nothing to me, or to my men. You'll have to defeat the emperor's army to take Braedon."

"I'm prepared to do just that. I assure you, Captain, my powers, and those of my friends here, are more than enough to destroy your army. And if you're not convinced, I suggest that you look up at the prison tower."

The captain turned toward the tower, as did Dusaan. Clearly Nitara had anticipated this, for Harel was already standing there, peering out through the narrow window.

"Demons and fire," the captain muttered.

"I'll kill him if I have to, though I'd rather not."

"What do you want us to do?" he asked, still gazing up at the emperor.

"Surrender your weapons and leave the palace. If you and your men do that, all of you will be spared. The emperor, too. If you choose to fight, you'll die."

"There's only four of 'em, Captain," said one of the men. "How much can four Qirsi do?"

"I need to talk to my men," the captain said.

Dusaan nodded. "Of course."

The captain led his men a short distance off, and began talking to them in low tones.

"What do you think they'll do?" Rov asked.

"They'll attack. Rov, Gorlan, we'll strike first with shaping power. Just reach for your magic and let me do the rest. After that we'll try fire. Rov, you'll be doing both, so you're likely to tire first. Give me what you can, and I'll draw the rest from B'Serre."

"Yes, Weaver."

Dusaan saw two men slip away from the captain's group and run back toward the guard house. There would be more men coming.

"Be watchful," he said. "They'll try to flank us."

"Are you certain that we can do this?" Gorlan asked.

"You've never fought beside a Weaver before. Savor this moment. We're about to win the first battle in a glorious war."

The assault began abruptly. The captain shouted something—Dusaan couldn't make out the words—and perhaps two hundred men charged toward them, battle cries echoing off the palace walls, swords and battle hammers glittering in the sun.

Dusaan reached for his magic and then for that of Gorlan and Rov. Both were young and powerful, just the sort of warriors who would help him to destroy all the armies of the Eandi courts. He didn't bother to aim the blow; he didn't care whether he cleaved steel or bone. He merely struck at the soldiers, his power slicing through the cluster of Eandi like an invisible scythe. Steel shattered in sweet ringing tones, bones fractured in rapid succession so that the sound resembled the snapping of a great fire. Men screamed in pain, dropping to the ground, writhing pathetically.

A second wave of attackers, at least a hundred strong, rushed from the towers to their left and right.

"B'Serre! Rov!" Dusaan called, his voice carrying over the war cries.

Again they offered their power to him, willingly, even eagerly. No doubt they had never felt so strong, had never realized that they could be such fearsome warriors. Rov, who had already given her shaping power, showed no sign of weariness. She would serve the movement well.

The fire Dusaan conjured radiated out in all directions, a glowing yellow ring of power, rampant, indiscriminate, deadly. It hit the soldiers like an ocean wave, knocking them backward, hammering some of them to the ground. And every man it touched was consumed by the flames—clothing, skin, hair. The shrieks of Eandi warriors filled the courtyard; the stench of their charred flesh made the Weaver's eyes water.

There would be archers on the ramparts soon. Dusaan was certain of it. And they would be harder to kill.

"Hear me!" he called over the death cries and the groans of the wounded. "I can kill all of you if I have to. And your emperor, too. Or you can surrender to me as he has and spare yourselves. This is your last chance to live. Lay down your weapons before me and you may leave the palace today as free men. Continue to resist, and you'll die as these men have."

For a long time nothing happened. Dusaan eyed the ramparts watching for the archers. He could shatter the arrows if he had to, but that demanded a more precise use of shaping power, and he wasn't certain how much more his companions could give him.

After several moments, however, soldiers began to emerge from the towers and guard house. They held their weapons low, swords pointing toward the ground, bows hanging from their hands. And one by one, they laid the weapons at Dusaan's feet, eyeing him with unconcealed hatred, but with fear as well. Swords, hammers, bows and arrows, daggers, and pikes lay in a pile before him. And a column of men filed toward the palace gate and the freedom he had promised them.

The first battle was his, and with it the Imperial Palace.

He looked up at the tower. Harel was no longer by the window, but Nitara was there, gazing down at him. He could imagine her expression, the look of adoration in her eyes. Just this once, he didn't mind.

Chapter

Five

The Moorlands, Eibithar

The skirmish had begun without warning, just like the others. One moment all had been quiet; the next the silence was riven by war cries and the clash of steel on steel, the rhythmic shouts of army commanders and the whistle of arrows soaring high into the hazy sky before beginning their deadly descent. Once again, the encounter was initiated by the Braedon army, which seemed capable of striking at any given moment, anywhere on the battle plain.

Eibithar's king had arrayed the three armies—his own guard, as well as the soldiers of Curgh and Heneagh—as best he could. But they were outnumbered, and would be until the soldiers of Thorald, Labruinn, and Tremain arrived. Add to that the fact that Heneagh's men lacked the discipline and skill of the other two armies, and it was something of a miracle that they hadn't been overrun already. Had Galdasten sent soldiers, or Sussyn, or Domnall, or any of the other houses that stood with Kentigern in defiance of the king, matters would have been different. As it was, it seemed to Tavis that the survival of the kingdom was in doubt.

The previous night, Braedon's warriors had struck at Kearney's lines, on the eastern front, nearest to the river. The battle had been short-lived—a few volleys of arrows exchanged and a brief, fierce engagement between swordsmen which left several men dead and many more injured—and had ended as abruptly as it began, with the soldiers of Braedon breaking away and retreating. The morning before that, the enemy had staged a similar attack on the Curgh lines, striking and withdrawing with astonishing swiftness.

This time, the empire's men were attacking the western end of the Eibitharian lines, which were defended by the army of Heneagh.

"They're testing us," said Tavis's father, the duke of Curgh, his face grim and etched with concern as he watched this latest skirmish unfold. "They're looking for weaknesses in our lines, trying to decide where to concentrate their assault when it begins in earnest."

"Can Heneagh hold them?" Xaver MarCullet asked, standing beside his father, Hagan, Curgh's swordmaster.

Hagan shrugged. "I don't know. But if the duke's right, I think they've probably found what they were looking for."

Within just a few minutes, the Braedon raiding party had withdrawn. They were pursued briefly by a large group of Heneagh's men, but Welfyl's swordmaster quickly called them back. It had seemed to Tavis that this skirmish was even briefer than the previous night's, but he couldn't say if he thought this boded well or ill for Eibithar's forces.

"We should check on them," the duke said, swinging himself onto his mount. "They may need healers." Javan glanced down at Tavis. "Come with me?"

The young lord nodded, a smile springing to his lips. Then he climbed onto his horse. Grinsa followed, as did Xaver and Hagan.

Tavis and Grinsa had finally caught up with Kearney's army four days before, finding the king some ten leagues north of Domnall, where he waited for the armies of Curgh and Heneagh to join his own. From there they had ridden northward with the king and dukes for two days until finally encountering the empire's invading force on this plain in the northeastern corner of the Moorlands, within sight of Binthar's Wash and only seven leagues or so from Galdasten Castle. The skirmishes had begun almost immediately, and though Tavis's father had brought most of the Curgh army and also commanded five hundred men of the King's Guard, the duke had been alarmed by his army's showing during their brief encounter with the enemy. A number of his men had been wounded. Qirsi healers had little trouble mending most of their injuries, but Curgh's soldiers should have fared better.

Still, even under these extraordinary circumstances, Javan had clearly been pleased to see his son; Tavis, in turn, had been surprised by how happy he was to be with his father again. Theirs had never been an easy relationship, even before the brutal murder of Tavis's promised bride, Lady Brienne of Kentigern, and the young lord's imprisonment in Kentigern. Tavis hadn't been certain how the duke would receive him. But Javan had openly welcomed both Grinsa and the boy, and Kearney had done much the same.

The soldiers of the King's Guard, however, had made it clear from the moment Tavis and Grinsa joined them that they still considered the young lord a murderer who had lost all claim to nobility. Since his arrival, they had offered naught but glares and vile comments uttered just loud enough for Tavis to hear. The boy had thought, or at least hoped, that once he proved his innocence their hostility toward him would abate. But though Cresenne ja Terba had confessed to hiring an assassin to kill Brienne, and Tavis had managed to kill that assassin on the shores of Wethyrn's Crown, little had changed.

"It's going to take them some time," Grinsa had whispered that first day, as they rode past the soldiers, Tavis's face burning as if it had been branded. "Not all of them will have heard yet that you killed the assassin, and even after they do, some of them will never accept your innocence."

Tavis had simply nodded, unable to bring himself to speak.

Curgh's men had been far more welcoming. As word of his encounter with the assassin, Cadel, spread through his father's army, men began to treat him like a hero, a conquering lord returning to his homeland. This made Tavis nearly as uncomfortable as the rage he saw on the faces of Kearney's men. He had been fortunate to survive his battle with Cadel, and the man had been defenseless when Tavis killed him. *I'm no hero,* he wanted to yell at them. *And I'm not a butcher, either. I'm just a man. Let me be.* But that, he was beginning to understand, would never be his fate.

Still, despite all of this, he was glad to be with his father again, and also with Hagan and Xaver MarCullet, and Fotir jal Salene, his father's first minister. For a year he had been an exile, denied the comfort of his friends and family, denied the right to claim his place as a noble in the House of Curgh. Now his life as a fugitive was over. He had told Javan all that he could remember of his final encounter with the assassin, and though he knew that many in the realm might be slow to believe him when finally his story was told to all, he had no doubt that his father did. He longed to see his mother, to set foot once more in the castle of his forebears, but already he felt that this was a homecoming of sorts.

Just as Tavis's father had expected, the Braedon attack, brief as it was, had taken a heavy toll on Heneagh's army. At least two dozen men lay dead in the long grass; most of them bore ugly, bloody wounds. Nearly three times that number had been injured. Already healers were tending to them, but Tavis could see immediately that they had need for more.

"Go to the Curgh camp," Javan told the nearest of Heneagh's uninjured men. "Tell them to send all our healers."

"What of the king's healers?" the man asked.

"Curgh's should be enough. Go. Quickly." As the man ran back toward the Curgh lines, Javan surveyed the Heneagh army, shielding his eyes with an open hand. "Where is Welfyl?" he muttered.

"You don't suppose he fell in the battle."

The duke glanced at his son. "He shouldn't have been anywhere near the battle." He made a sour face. "He shouldn't be here at all."

Welfyl was by far the oldest of Eibithar's dukes. Indeed, he came to power the same year Aylyn the Second, Kearney's predecessor, began his reign as king of the realm. Javan, Tavis knew, had always liked Heneagh's duke, but there could be no denying the fact that the man was simply too old to be riding to war. He was frail and bent—Tavis wondered if he could even raise a sword, much less fight with one. But he had led his army to the Moorlands, and unless the king said otherwise, he would lead them into battle.

"My lord, look." Fotir was pointing farther west, his white hair gleaming in the sun, his bright yellow eyes seeming to glow like coals in a fire.

Following the direction of his gaze, Tavis saw the old duke kneeling in the grass, cradling a man in his arms, a stricken expression on his bony face.

Kicking at his mount, Javan rode toward the man, Tavis and the others following close behind.

"Get a healer!" the old duke cried as they drew nearer. "He's dying!"

It was true. Even Tavis, who knew little of such things, could see that the man in Welfyl's arms had lost too much blood. He had a deep gash on the side of his neck, and another that had nearly severed his leg just above the knee. Blood pulsed weakly from both wounds and already the man's uniform was soaked crimson, as was the duke's.

"More healers are on the way," Javan said, dismounting and crouching beside Welfyl. "I've sent for all the Qirsi who accompanied my army."

"Can you help him?" the duke asked Fotir, seeming to ignore Javan. "Please."

Fotir looked pained as he shook his head. "I haven't that power, Lord Heneagh. I'm sorry."

It had to be Welfyl's son. Looking at the face of the wounded man, Tavis saw that he had the duke's nose and chin. The man's hair was yellow, rather than white, and his face was fuller than Welfyl's, but the resemblance was strong. He glanced back at Grinsa and read desperate frustration in his friend's eyes. No doubt he wanted to try to heal the man, but couldn't without giving away who and what he was.

A moment later, one of Heneagh's Qirsi arrived, breathless, her cheeks flushed.

"Ean be praised," the duke said, looking up at her. "Save him! I beg you!"

She frowned. "I'll do what I can, my lord."

Javan placed a hand on Welfyl's shoulder. "Perhaps we should leave them—"

"No!" The duke seemed to tighten his hold on the man.

"Your healer will do all she can for him."

"I'm not leaving him!"

Javan gave a low sigh and nodded. "Very well." Straightening, he stepped away a short distance, gesturing for his company to follow.

"He won't make it," Hagan said, his voice low.

"Probably not." Javan closed his eyes and ran a hand over his face. "Damn."

"That's his son, isn't it?" Tavis said, careful to keep his voice down as well.

Javan eyed him briefly, then nodded. "Dunfyl, thane of Cransher. He's a good man, and a fine warrior."

"Why isn't he duke?"

Tavis's father looked over his shoulder, as if to make certain that Welfyl couldn't hear, then he walked a bit farther from where the thane lay dying. "That's a good question. The two of them had a falling-out many years back—I never learned what caused it. But Welfyl is given to pride, and the son doesn't step far from his father's shadow. For years they didn't even speak to each other. To be honest, I never thought I'd see the day when they rode together to battle. It seems they reconciled none too soon."

They heard horses approaching and turned, seeing Kearney and his archminister riding toward where they stood. Behind them, on foot, came several more Qirsi and a small contingent of soldiers.

"What's happened?" the king asked, as he climbed off his mount. His eyes fell on Welfyl then quickly darted away. "Is that the thane?"

"It is, my liege."

"Will he live?"

There was an uncomfortable silence.

Kearney shook his head slowly, his lips pressed thin. "Demons and fire. How many others were lost?"

"Twenty-five. Maybe more. I expect many of the wounded won't make it."

"Were your losses this high, Lord Curgh?"

"No, my liege. About half, though even that was too many."

"Yes. Ours were similar."

"If I may, Your Majesty," Hagan said, "Heneagh has never been known for her might. And I've never seen an army that could strike as quickly as that of the empire."

"I agree with you, Sir MarCullet. I've been thinking that perhaps we'd be better served by giving Lord Heneagh command of the five hundred men I originally gave to you, Javan."

Curgh's duke gave a single nod. "Of course, my liege." But he wasn't pleased by this. Kearney didn't notice, but Tavis did. He had spent all his childhood gauging his father's mood changes by inflections far more subtle than this one.

"You can't do that, Your Majesty!"

"Hagan!"

"It's all right, Lord Curgh. Let him speak." The king faced Javan's swordmaster, a slight smile on his youthful face. "Why can't I do this?"

Hagan had colored to the tips of his ears, and he was staring at the ground, looking for all his height and brawn like an abashed child. "Forgive me, Your Majesty. I shouldn't have spoken."

"It's all right, Hagan. Clearly you feel that I'm making a mistake. Why?"

"Th-the Curgh army holds the center, Your Majesty. Braedon's soldiers have been testing us, looking for where we're weakest. If they see that we've shifted so many men, they'll strike at where they had been. And if our center fails, we're lost."

"Thorald's army should reach us by tomorrow, Hagan. They can reinforce the center. But right now our weakest point lies here. If Braedon's army strikes at the western lines, the entire Heneagh army could be lost. Surely you see that I can't allow that."

"Yes, Your Majesty."

Kearney grinned, though the look in his eyes remained bleak. "Don't humor me, swordmaster. Gershon Trasker has served me for quite a few years now, and whenever he agrees with me in the manner you just did, I know that I've done something wrong."

Kearney's archminister cleared her throat. "If I may offer a suggestion, Your Majesty: you've also given five hundred men to Lord Shanstead. If we wait until nightfall to move the men from Curgh's army to Heneagh's, the enemy might not notice. And tomorrow, when the Thorald army arrives, Lord Shanstead can send half of those five hundred men to Lord Curgh."

The king smiled again, more convincingly this time. "A fine idea, Archminister."

"It is, Your Majesty," Fotir said. "But I don't think we should wait until dark. As the archminister just said, Lord Shanstead should reach here tomorrow. If Braedon's scouts learn of his approach, the empire will attack today. Certainly that's what I'd advise them to do. We should move half the men immediately."

"You make a good point, First Minister."

"Thank you, Your Majesty."

"What do you think, Hagan?"

The swordmaster smiled as well, though clearly it was forced. "Very well, Your Majesty. We'll send two hundred and fifty men to the Heneagh lines. I'll see to it right away."

The king nodded. "Good." He glanced at Welfyl, his smile fading. The old duke was weeping, and though his son's chest still rose and fell, the healer had stopped working on him. It was but a matter of time.

"Excuse me," Kearney said, his voice hardly more than a whisper. He stepped to where Lord Heneagh still knelt and placed a hand on the man's shoulder. Welfyl seemed to collapse at the king's touch, falling against Kearney's leg and sobbing.

"Two hundred and fifty men is nothing," Hagan said, pitching his voice so that Javan could hear but Kearney could not.

"I know. But it's all we have. Half of the King's Guard is in Kentigern, and half of Eibithar's houses have chosen not to fight at all. We're fortunate to have as many men as we do."

"Yes, my lord."

"There's nothing for us to do here," the duke said, looking once more at Welfyl and wincing, as if the man's grief pained him. Tavis couldn't help but wonder if Javan was thinking about how close he had come to losing his own son the previous year. "We should return to the Curgh lines."

Tavis saw Grinsa and Keziah exchange a look.

"I'll be along shortly, Tavis," the gleaner said. Then, facing Fotir, he raised an eyebrow. "Will you join us for a moment, First Minister?"

"My lord?" the minister said, seeking Javan's permission.

"Yes, of course."

The duke had climbed onto his mount again, as had Hagan. They started away to the east, and Tavis and Xaver followed, scrambling onto their horses and following some distance behind the duke and his swordmaster.

For a time the two young men rode in silence, Tavis enduring the stares of his father's soldiers as best he could.

"I wonder if they'll even let us fight now," Xaver finally

said, his voice so low that Tavis wasn't certain he had heard correctly.

"Let us fight?"

His liege man nodded, then glanced toward their fathers so that Tavis would know who he meant.

"Why wouldn't they let us fight?"

"Dunfyl, of course. My father didn't even want to bring me along from Curgh; he made up some nonsense about how he needed me to take command of the castle guard while he was gone. After seeing Dunfyl killed he'll have me standing watch over the provisions or some such thing. You watch, your father will be the same way."

"I doubt that."

"Tavis, you and your father might not always see eye-to-eye—"

"No, it's nothing to do with all that. I've been gone for a year now, evading Aindreas's guards, journeying through Aneira, tracking down Cadel. He doesn't get to choose anymore whether or not I fight. I know he's my father, but the fact is that I've been taking care of myself for some time now. I don't need his permission to pick up a sword." He looked over at Xaver, who was regarding him as if they'd never met before. "I guess to you I sound pretty full of myself, eh?"

"Not really. Somebody else saying all that, maybe. But not you. Not after what you've been through."

He continued to stare at Tavis, until the young lord began to feel awkward, the way he did when the soldiers cheered for him.

"Stop looking at me like that."

Xaver dropped his gaze, a smile tugging at the corners of his mouth, his light curls stirring in the wind. "Sorry."

"What are you staring at, anyway?"

"You look different."

"Yes, well, Aindreas saw to that with his blade, didn't he?"

"That's not what I mean. I'm used to the scars now. In a way, I find it hard to imagine you without them."

Tavis looked away. Grinsa had said much the same thing to him not long ago. For his part, Tavis still imagined himself without them all the time. Indeed, even now, whenever he saw his reflection, he found the lattice of scars on his face jarring. He wondered if he'd ever get used to them.

"You look older, Tavis," Xaver said, drawing the boy's gaze once more. "Older even than you did when I saw you in the City of Kings."

"A lot's happened since then."

Xaver hesistated. "You still haven't told me about . . . about the assassin."

He shook his head, staring straight ahead. "I'm not sure I can. I killed him. That's really all that matters."

"I don't believe that."

He could see it all again. The storm that had battered the Wethy Crown that day, the serene expression on the assassin's face just before he died, the way his own sword cleaved the man's neck. And he could remember as well being held under water, with Cadel kneeling on his back, the man's hands clamped on his neck and head. He could feel his lungs burning for air, the frigid waters of the gulf making his head ache.

"I almost died, Xaver. He had me, and he let me go. When I killed him, he wasn't even trying to protect himself anymore."

His friend was watching him, seemingly at a loss for words.

"I thought that I'd find peace once I'd killed Cadel, that avenging Brienne would make up for everything that's happened since she died. But I was wrong."

"It's too soon to know that. You may find peace yet, but it can't be easy when everyone around you is preparing for war."

A smile touched his lips and was gone. "I suppose."

"Maybe once this war with the empire is over, and you've—"

"You know what, Stinger," he broke in, "I understand that you're trying to help, but I just don't want to talk about any of this."

Xaver's jaw tightened and he lowered his gaze. "Fine."

"Why don't we talk about you for a while?"

The boy looked up again, a slight frown on his lean face. "About me?"

"Yes. You haven't told me anything about home."

"There's nothing to tell."

"There has to be something. Tell me about your studies, or your training. I don't even know if you have a girl."

That, of all things, made Xaver's face shade to scarlet.

"You do! I knew it!"

The boy shrugged, grinning sheepishly. "She's not really . . ."

"What? She's not really a girl?"

Xaver laughed. "Oh, she is that."

"Well, now I really want to hear."

His friend was a bit sparing with details—her name was Jolyn, and she was the daughter of one of the ladies who served Tavis's mother. Other than that, Xaver offered precious little information. But Tavis hardly cared. Long after he and Xaver had returned to the Curgh camp, they continued to talk, laughing and teasing one another as they had long ago, before their Fatings and all that followed. And for a brief time, as the day grew warm and the sun turned its slow arc over the Moorlands, Tavis gave little thought to Cadel or the conspiracy or the war that loomed over them like a dark cloud.

Later in the day, however, after they had talked themselves into a lengthy silence, Xaver eyed the young lord, suddenly appearing uneasy.

"I have a favor to ask of you," he said, meeting Tavis's gaze for but a moment before looking away.

"Of course. Anything."

"Don't say that until you've heard what it is."

Tavis felt his stomach tighten.

"I'm not certain that my father's going to let me fight," said the liege man. "And if he asks your father to keep me out of the battle, your father will do just that."

"I really don't think—"

"Please, let me finish. You're my lord—I swore an oath to serve you. And since we're both past our Fatings, you have the authority to overrule my father."

"Xaver, the last thing I want to do is get between you and Hagan. Besides, if my father decides to keep you out of combat, there's nothing I can do."

His friend scowled at him.

"Why are you so eager to fight, anyway?"

"You have to ask? You're just as avid for it as I am."

Tavis shook his head. "That's different. I have reasons that have nothing to do with this war and everything to do with Cadel and Brienne and all the rest."

"Well, I have reasons, too, Tavis! You're not the only one who wants to strike back at the Aneirans and the Qirsi and the empire, and everyone else who's been attacking us for the past year. You're not the only one whose father . . ." He shook his head. "I know it's hard between you and your father, but it's not easy being the son of Hagan MarCullet either. He's been the best swordsman in the land for just about all my life. And everyone expects me to be just like him." *Including me.*

Xaver didn't have to say this last aloud. As his friend spoke Tavis found himself remembering what Xaver had told him of the siege at Kentigern, which was the first and only time the young man had fought in a battle of any sort. He said at the time that he had acquitted himself poorly, that he had embarrassed himself in front of Javan. For his part, the duke never had anything but praise for Xaver's courage as a warrior, but that wouldn't have kept Xaver from feeling that he had something to prove to himself, to his duke, and to his father in this newest war.

"I'm sorry, Stinger. You're right, I'm not the only one. As I said before, I have no desire to put myself between you and Hagan, but I'll do what I can."

Xaver nodded, still looking displeased.

"Personally, I'd be honored to march into battle beside you."

He smiled at that. "We've been talking about it since we were five."

"Longer than that, if my mother is to be believed."

"Thanks, Tavis."

"I'm not promising anything. You understand that."

"I know. But I'm grateful anyway."

"Just promise me that you'll watch my back, and I'll do the same for you."

Xaver grinned. "Done."

After Javan and Tavis rode away, Keziah turned her attention back to Kearney, who was still giving comfort to the duke of Heneagh. There was a pained expression in her pale eyes. She held a hand to her mouth, as if afraid that she might weep at any moment.

"Perhaps we should find someplace where we can speak," Fotir suggested.

She nodded, but her gaze never left the king.

"Keziah."

She looked at Grinsa, seeming to rouse herself from a dream. "Yes, of course."

It looked to the gleaner that she hadn't slept in days. There were circles under her eyes, and her skin was so wan that she almost looked gray. He wondered how many times in the past few nights she had dreamed of the Weaver.

The three Qirsi walked away from the king toward the rear of the Curgh camp where there were fewer soldiers. After a few moments, Grinsa realized that one of Kearney's men was following a short distance behind them.

"My shadow," Keziah said, seeing him glance back.

"Kearney's having you watched?"

"It's necessary. We still need for everyone to believe that he doesn't trust me."

Fotir looked from one of them to the other. "Am I to understand that the king knows of your attempt to join the conspiracy?"

Keziah gave a rueful smile. "That was necessary as well. He was preparing to send me away from his court."

"This seems to be growing more perilous by the moment."

Grinsa said nothing, though it occurred to him that it had all been far too dangerous from the very beginning. Keziah had contrived to join the Qirsi conspiracy, making it seem to the Weaver that she served his cause, and convincing all those around her that she had betrayed her king and her land. Kearney knew the truth now, but that seemed small consolation to Grinsa. If the Weaver learned that Keziah had been deceiving him, he would make her suffer terribly before killing her.

"Can we speak frankly with that soldier hovering at our shoulders?" Fotir asked.

"We haven't much choice, First Minister," Keziah said, impatience creeping into her voice. "Believe me when I tell you that these inconveniences mean little to me at this point. I have far greater matters weighing on my mind."

The gleaner thought that Fotir might respond in anger—the minister was no more accustomed than was Keziah to having people speak to him so. To his credit, however, the man gave a small smile and inclined his head. "You're right, of course. Forgive me, Archminister."

Keziah frowned, as if she had expected more of a fight.

"Have you heard from the Weaver again?" Grinsa asked in a whisper.

"I last heard from him about a half turn ago," she answered, whispering as well, "just after we marched from Audun's Castle. He was angry with me for failing to kill Cresenne."

"Did he hurt you?"

His sister tried to smile, failed. After a moment she looked away. "It wasn't too bad."

Grinsa didn't believe her, but he let it pass, his heart aching for her.

"He told me that he would find another way to kill her. Don't worry," she said, seeming to believe that she was anticipating Grinsa's next question. "I sent word back to the castle. She knows to expect an attack."

The gleaner looked away. "The attack's already come."

She gaped at him.

"Is she—?"

"She's all right." Actually, the gleaner couldn't say with any certainty that she would ever truly recover from all her encounters with the man. The Weaver had tortured her, leaving scars on her face that might have looked like those Tavis bore had Grinsa not been able to heal her so soon after the assault. One of the Weaver's servants had poisoned her, very nearly taking her life. And the last time he entered her dreams, the Weaver had raped her, or come as close to rape as a man could without actually touching her physically.

"What did he do to her?"

"It's not important. What matters is that Cresenne drove him from her dreams. She won." *Though at what cost?*

Keziah still stared at him, but the horror on her face had given way to a look of wonder.

"Did she really?"

"Yes. And as I've been telling you all along, you have the power to do the same."

After his own unsuccessful encounter with the Weaver half a turn before, as he and Tavis were riding across the southern Moorlands, Grinsa had come to doubt that anyone could prevail against the man. But despite all that she had endured during her dreams of the Weaver, Cresenne had given him hope, not only for himself, but for Keziah as well. He still feared for his sister—for all of them, really—but he had to believe that Dusaan could be beaten.

"She did it," Keziah whispered, sounding awed and shaking her head slowly.

"You were telling us of your own encounter with the Weaver," Fotir prompted gently.

She ran a hand through her hair, smiling self-consciously. An instant later, though, she had grown deadly serious. "Yes, of course. He gave me a new task to complete. He wants me to kill Kearney."

"What?" Fotir said, far too loudly, his eyes widening. He glanced back at the soldier. "How?" he asked a moment later, his voice lowered once more.

"He left that to me. He wants it to happen in battle, so that no one suspects the Qirsi."

"Does Kearney know?"

She looked at Grinsa. "I've warned him, yes."

"Why bother?" Fotir asked. "It's not as though you intend to go through with it, right?"

"Of course she doesn't. But if the Weaver really wants Kearney dead, and if her failure to kill Cresenne has made him question Keziah's commitment to the conspiracy, then he'll have given the same order to others who serve him."

Fotir shook his head slowly. "You both seem to understand him so well. I'm out of my depth."

"We have an advantage, First Minister," Grinsa told him. "If you care to call it that. We've both spoken with the man. He's walked in our dreams."

Keziah gaped at him. "You dreamed of him, too?"

"Yes, not long after you did, it seems. He tried to attack me, and he threatened Cresenne."

"But he couldn't hurt you, right? You're too strong for him."

Grinsa's stomach turned at the memory of what the Weaver had done to him, of the pain in his temple as the man tried to crush his skull. Seeing how Keziah looked at him, begging him with her eyes to say that his magic had been a match for that of the Weaver, he almost lied. Qirsar knew that he wanted to.

Instead he shook his head. "I wasn't strong enough."

"He did hurt you." Her voice shook and terror was written plainly on her face.

"I was able to wake myself before he could do any real harm. And I managed to summon a flame that lit his face and the plain on which we stood. I know for certain who he is."

"Were we right about him?" Fotir asked. "Is it the emperor's high chancellor?"

"Yes. Dusaan jal Kania. He was on Ayvencalde Moor. He tried to keep me from using my fire magic, but I have to say that once I'd seen him, he didn't seem overly concerned."

"Still," the first minister said, "we know who he is. That has to count for something."

"Does this mean that he's more powerful than you are?" Keziah asked, sounding so young, so scared.

"I don't know, Keziah. Truly I don't. As Tavis pointed out to me, we were hardly on equal footing. He was in my dream, so he could hurt me, but I couldn't hurt him. The most I could do was illuminate his face and the moor, and I managed that."

She nodded, but he read the despair in her expression, and

he knew its source. If he, a Weaver, couldn't keep this man from hurting him, how was she to protect herself? Any hope she had drawn from Cresenne's success was already gone.

For a long time, Keziah didn't speak. She just stood there, staring off in the distance, until Grinsa began to wonder if he and the first minister should leave her. But after several moments, she seemed to gather herself. Looking first at Grinsa and then at Fotir, she said, "There's another matter we need to discuss, before the empire strikes at us again." She cast a quick look at Kearney's soldier, as if to assure herself that he wasn't close enough to hear. "When the fighting begins, how far will we go with our magic to aid Kearney and the dukes?"

"Do you mean will I weave your powers with mine?"

She nodded.

"I think the risk is too great," Fotir said. "The emperor sent Qirsi with his army—quite a few really. And they'll be watching us closely. I don't know what powers you possess, archminister, but I'm a shaper and I have mists and winds. If the gleaner and I raise a mist together, Harel's Qirsi are likely to know it. Word of a Weaver would spread across this battlefield in no time."

"But what if it's the only way to keep them from breaking through our lines?" Keziah demanded. "Kearney already knows that Grinsa's a Weaver, and if Eibithar's other nobles find out because he used his powers to save the realm, they can hardly turn around and have him executed."

"It would be foolish of them, I agree. But that doesn't mean they won't do it."

"Careful, First Minister," Grinsa said with a smile. "That's something one of the renegades might say."

Fotir's expression didn't change. "Well, in this case they may be right. This is no time for us to underestimate Eandi fear of Qirsi magic. With all that the conspiracy has wrought in the last few years, I'm afraid our nobles will be more inclined than ever to put a Weaver to death, even one who uses his magic to protect their realm."

"Is that what you think?" Keziah asked.

Grinsa shrugged. "I suppose it is."

She nodded, though clearly unhappy with his answer.

"But I can't see allowing the empire to prevail in this fight, no matter the danger to me."

"The danger isn't yours alone," Fotir said. "They'll kill Cresenne and your child as well."

"They may try, First Minister, just as they may try to execute me. I assure you that they'll fail. But we're getting ahead of ourselves. We have a number of Qirsi on our side; I may not need to weave at all. And if it does come to that, I believe I can join our powers without anyone realizing it." He looked at Keziah again, wanting to brush a strand of hair away from his sister's face. But he didn't dare, not with the soldier so close. Even Fotir, who knew so much about him, didn't know that Keziah was his sister. The danger was still too great to reveal that to anyone. Fear of Weavers ran deep among the Eandi, and for centuries, when Weavers were executed, so were all those in their families. Add to that the fact that Dusaan might have spies on the battle plain ready to report back to him any strange behavior on Keziah's part, and they were risking her life merely by standing and talking to one another. "I won't let them get past us. You have my word on that."

"Shouldn't the three of us be together then, fighting in the same place?"

"The first minister and I will be together on the Curgh lines, and if I need your power too, I can find you."

She nodded again, but appeared tense and uncertain.

"I should return to my duke," Fotir said, his gaze wandering northward, to the Braedon army. "And I'd suggest, Archminister, that you find Kearney. I expect that we'll be raising mists and summoning winds before long."

Chapter
Six

That Fotir was right shouldn't have surprised Keziah at all. She had spent enough time with Curgh's first minister to realize that he was every bit as brilliant as he was reputed to be. When he warned that Braedon's attack would come before the day was out, she should have believed him.

Nor should she have been taken aback by the ferocity of the empire's assault. She had seen combat before, only a year earlier. The fight to end the siege at Kentigern had not lacked for violence or blood, and though she had been horrified by what she witnessed, she had also believed that the experience had hardened her, preparing her for the day when once again she would have to follow her king into battle. Nothing, though, could have readied her for the storm of steel and flesh and blood that raged before her now.

It seemed as well that she was not the only one. Even with scouts from Heneagh, Curgh, and the King's Guard keeping watch on the Braedon army, the enemy's attack caught the Eibitharians off guard. The empire's army gave no warning at all. Among the houses of Eibithar it was tradition to loose a single arrow into the sky over the battle plain before commencing an attack. Braedon offered no such gesture. Nor did their Qirsi raise a mist to conceal their numbers. Keziah did not even hear an order shouted to the empire's archers before their first volley. One moment all seemed as it had for the past several days, the next a thousand arrows were carving across the sky and pelting down on Eibithar's warriors.

Even before the first of the darts struck, Braedon's soldiers had begun their charge across the moor, sunlight glinting off their blades and helms, the earth seeming to tremble with the roar of their war cries. Kearney and his dukes barely had time to call their men to arms, much less marshal an ordered defense. They had thought that the attack would be concentrated on Heneagh's lines—clearly Welfyl's army was no match for Javan's or Kearney's.

But Braedon's commanders, rather than striking at the weakest point in Eibithar's defenses, aimed their assault on the King's Guard itself, the strongest of the three armies. Curgh and Heneagh weren't spared. Far from it. Within moments of that first volley of arrows, all three armies were under attack, but Kearney's guard bore the brunt of the onslaught. Poorly prepared for the intensity of Braedon's attack, Eibithar's men were forced to fall back. Kearney and Javan had managed to get their archers in place soon enough to loose one barrage of arrows at the charging Braedony soldiers, but after that, their bowmen had little choice but to draw swords and fight with the rest. Heneagh's archers didn't loose a single arrow before the empire's men crashed into their lines.

"Why would they attack this way?" Keziah called over the din of battle, as she rode beside Kearney, who was rallying his men as best he could.

"Because it's working!" he shouted back, green eyes blazing, his face damp with sweat.

She nodded, wishing she hadn't asked.

"I'm not sure," he said a moment later. "None of us expected this. But I think they wanted to keep our armies from working together. Had they focused their attack on Welfyl, Javan and I would have banded together to try to flank them. This way we have no chance to combine our forces."

Keziah nodded a second time, eyeing the battle with apprehension. The king's men were still giving ground, more grudgingly now, but there could be no mistaking the trend. It wouldn't be long before Kearney rode forward to join the fighting. He had deployed his men as best he could under the circumstances, and already he was glancing toward the lines, his hand wandering to the hilt of his sword. And as much as Keziah feared for him, she envied him more. She felt useless.

She had no place in this battle. Though competent with a blade, she was neither skilled enough, nor strong enough, to fight beside these men. None of Braedon's soldiers were on horseback, so having the magic her people called language of beasts did her no good, and with the men already fighting at close quarters, it did no good to raise a mist or wind.

Looking toward the middle of the fighting, Keziah tried to catch sight of Grinsa or Fotir. The fighting there appeared every bit as vicious as it did along Kearney's lines, and like the King's Guard, Curgh's army looked to have slowed Braedon's advance somewhat. Gazing beyond Javan's army, however, she could see that the men of Heneagh were still being driven back with alarming speed. She didn't need Kearney's knowledge of military matters to understand how vital it was that Welfyl's men keep the Braedony force from breaching their lines.

"Keziah."

She forced herself to meet his gaze, knowing what he would say.

"I have to join my men. I can't just—"

"I know," she said. "Go. Orlagh guide your blade and keep you safe."

"And you."

They stared at one another for just a moment more, Keziah doing her best to commit his features to memory, every line on the youthful face, every strand of silken hair, silvered before its time and gleaming in the bright sun.

I love you, she mouthed.

And I love you.

An instant later, so suddenly that she actually started, Kearney pulled his sword free and swung his mount around, plunging into the bloody tumult. Even as the tide of the fighting drew him away from her, she could still see him, towering and fell atop his mount, his sword rising and falling, its blade stained crimson. It didn't take long for the battle to close in around him, as if cutting him off from her, from any path to safety.

Such confusion, such frenzy, such carnage. As Keziah watched the battle unfold, one thought kept echoing in her mind, and it scared her more than all that she saw. *Anything could happen in conditions like these; what a perfect place to kill a king.*

She could even imagine different ways it might be done, ways she might do it herself. "You possess both language of beasts and mists and winds," the Weaver told her the last time he walked in her dreams, just after he punished her for failing to kill Cresenne. "They should serve you quite well in this regard."

He was right, of course. She could see it now, how easy it would be. A sudden gust of wind might alter the path of an arrow aimed at another. Or even better, a single word whispered to Kearney's mount might make the beast throw the king into the fury around him. No one, no matter his skill as a warrior, would survive long on his back amid the steel and the blood.

Keziah was horrified at herself for thinking any of this, but once she began, she couldn't stop. As more died, falling at the feet of Kearney's mount, it would be more and more difficult for the horse to step true. A shaper might break one of the beast's legs and drive the king to the ground that way. Or he might shatter Kearney's blade as the king struck at another, leaving the king defenseless. Working with a second person, an assassin perhaps, a Qirsi might raise a mist to conceal the other's approach. With so many sorcerers on the battle plain, with so many dying in this fight, almost anything was possible.

How many of the Qirsi around her served the conspiracy? To how many of them had the Weaver given the order to kill her king? Surely she wasn't the only one. As the Weaver himself had reminded her, she had already failed him once. Knowing that she had loved Kearney, that she might love him still, he would not trust her with this unless he had others poised to act should she falter.

Frightened now, convinced that one of the Weaver's servants would make an attempt on Kearney's life at the first opportunity, Keziah very nearly spurred her mount forward into the fray. She had no idea what she would do when she reached the king, she only knew that she wanted to be there, to guard him, to watch for the Weaver's killers. The archminister had gone so far as to adjust her sword in preparation for entering the battle, when she felt something brush her mind as a stranger might brush one's arm in a crowded marketplace.

For a single, horrifying instant, she thought it was the Weaver, reaching for her, attempting to read her thoughts or compel her to kill Kearney. In the next moment, however, she realized that there was something familiar in the touch, and something gentle as well. Turning to gaze toward the Curgh lines, she saw Grinsa atop a mount, looking back at her. She couldn't understand why he would have reached for her now. Fotir, perhaps, but not her. She hadn't any magic that would be of use to them. Certainly he couldn't think that raising a mist would do any good. But after catching her eye ever so briefly, no longer than the span of a single heartbeat, he looked away, his touch gone from her mind. It almost seemed that he had only wished to reassure himself that she was all right. Or maybe he had sensed what she was about to do, and had wanted to stop her, if only for a moment, so that she might reconsider. Whatever the reason, she realized that she could do Kearney no good by rushing to his side. Her presence would only distract him, making it easier for agents of the conspiracy to strike at him.

Unable to do anything more than watch the battle, Keziah began what could only be called a vigil. She kept her gaze riveted on Kearney, straining to see him through the sun's glare and the haze of dust and dirt kicked up by the warriors. So long as she could see his bright silver hair, and the gleaming blur of his sword slicing through the air, she knew that he was safe, or at least alive.

As the seething shadows of men and beasts and weapons lengthened across the bloodstained grass, the tide of the battle began to turn. Eibithar's forces were not able to gain back much of the ground they had lost initially, but they managed to halt Braedon's push forward. Even in the west, where it had seemed that Heneagh's lines must surely be broken, Welfyl's men rallied, aided by reinforcements from the Curgh army. When at last the sun dipped below the western horizon, leaving a fiery sky of yellow and orange and scarlet, the empire's men broke off their attack and pulled back.

Raising a ragged cheer, some of Kearney's soldiers began to give chase, only to be called back by their king. Kicking her mount to a gallop, Keziah rushed to Kearney's side, resisting an urge to throw her arms around his neck. He had several gashes on his legs and a deep wound on his side, where blood oozed through his chain mail.

"You need a healer," she said.

Kearney flashed a smile. One might have thought that he'd come through nothing more dangerous than a battle tournament. "I'm all right. I need to speak with my dukes."

"Your Majesty—"

"Find them for me, Archminister. Bring them here as quickly as possible. Their ministers as well."

Keziah frowned, but nodded. "Yes, Your Majesty."

She wheeled her horse and started toward the Curgh lines, only to halt after a few paces, her stomach heaving. The grass, once lush and green, had been trampled and soaked in blood, so that the earth itself seemed to be bleeding from some gaping wound. Scattered among the corpses of more soldiers than she could count were severed limbs, disembodied hands that still clung to swords and battle-axes, and heads that stared up at the darkening sky through sightless eyes, some of them with their mouths open in silent wails, as if with death cries still on their lips, waiting to be given voice. She should have been looking at their surcoats, trying to determine which side had gotten the better of the day's fighting, but she couldn't look away from those faces, those hands, that blood.

"Keziah."

She flinched, looked toward the voice. Kearney gazed back at her, the smile gone, his brow furrowed with concern.

"Are you all right?"

"I . . ." She swallowed, fighting another wave of nausea. "I will be."

"Don't look. Just find Javan and Welfyl. Send them to me, and then ride away from the lines, away from all this. Do you understand?"

She nodded, but even as she did, her eyes dropped again. One of the dead seemed to be staring at her, a look of surprise on the young face that might have been amusing had it not been—

"Keziah."

Her eyes snapped up again.

"Find the dukes."

"Yes, Your Majesty."

She started forward again, allowing her mount to navigate among the corpses as best he could, forcing herself to keep her eyes on the men ahead of her, the ones who lived still and who wore the brown and gold of Curgh. She spotted Grinsa and Fotir, and hurried toward them, knowing that the duke would be nearby. A moment later she saw Javan, standing with Tavis, Curgh's swordmaster, and another young man who she had gathered from previous conversations was Tavis's liege man and the swordmaster's son. Like Kearney, Javan bore a number of wounds, but none of them appeared grave. Grinsa, too, was bleeding. Indeed, all of them were. Aside from the healers, she was probably the only person on the Moorlands who hadn't been injured.

At her approach, the duke raised a hand in greeting. "Archminister. What news of the king?"

"He's well, my lord. He wishes to speak with you and your minister."

"Of course. We'll go to him immediately. How fared the King's Guard?"

"I'm not certain, my lord. I wasn't in the fighting. I don't . . . I don't have the magics of a warrior."

"Of course, Archminister. Forgive me."

"Not at all, my lord. I'll see you shortly. I must find the duke of Heneagh as well."

Javan glanced quickly at Fotir before facing her again, and she knew from his expression what he would say. "The duke is dead, Archminister. He fell in battle."

Her first thought was of Heneagh's duchess, who had no idea that she had lost a husband and a son on this day. Keziah didn't even know the woman's name. As archminister to the king, she should have, but they had never met, and because

Welfyl was duke of a minor house, he and the king had little contact before these last few turns.

"Archminister."

She shook herself, as if waking from a bad dream. She was not cut out for war. "Yes, my lord. Who commands Heneagh's army now?"

"Welfyl's swordmaster, a man named Rab Avkar."

Keziah looked westward to the Heneagh army. She didn't relish the idea of entering the camp and searching for a warrior she'd never met before.

"I know him," Hagan MarCullet said, sensing her unease. "With my lord's permission, I'll go and find him."

"Of course, Hagan."

"Thank you, swordmaster," Keziah said.

He nodded to her and walked away, reminding her so much of Gershon Trasker, Kearney's swordmaster, who was marching south to fight the Aneirans, that she had to smile.

Javan climbed onto his mount, moving stiffly, a rueful grin on his lips. "What I wouldn't give to be ten years younger."

"Only ten?" Tavis said, drawing laughs from all of them.

Within moments Keziah, the duke, Tavis, Grinsa, and Fotir were on their way back toward Kearney. The MarCullet boy followed as well; Keziah couldn't remember the last time she had seen Tavis without the other young man nearby. Almost immediately, Grinsa steered his horse to Keziah's side—the side nearest the battle plain, she noticed, as if he wished to shield her from the horrors there.

"Are you all right?" he asked softly.

"No."

He turned and stared at her.

"Don't look so surprised. After all that you've seen today, can you honestly tell me that you are?"

"It's only going to get worse, Kezi."

"I know." She glanced at his wounds, deep cuts on his arms and hands, and a nasty bruise just below his right temple. "Do they hurt much?"

"No. If they did, I'd have healed them by now."

"Why haven't you?"

He shrugged. "I'm too weary."

"There are other healers, Grinsa. One of them . . ."

"I'm fine, Keziah. I'll heal myself later. I promise."

She nodded, pressing her lips in a tight line.

They soon reached Kearney, who was walking among the injured men of his guard, offering what comfort he could as the soldiers waited for healers to tend their wounds. Two of his captains stood nearby. Seeing Javan approach, the king came forward. He, too, had not yet had his own injuries healed.

"Well met, Lord Curgh. I'm glad to see you're well."

"Thank you, my liege. I could easily say the same, except it seems you're hurt."

Kearney glanced down at the bloody gash on his side. "It's nothing of concern. We have more pressing matters to discuss."

"Forgive me for saying so, my liege. But we can speak of these things while the Qirsi minister to you." Javan caught the eye of one of the healers and beckoned him over.

A healer could do much damage under the guise of trying to help him. An herbmaster could easily exchange poison for a tonic. . . .

"No!" Keziah said, a bit too quickly. The healer hesitated. "The . . . the matters we need to discuss are of a sensitive nature."

Grinsa was eyeing her strangely. But after a moment he appeared to catch on. "She's right, Your Majesty. I'm not a healer by trade, but perhaps I can help in this instance."

Kearney seemed to understand as well. He even paled a bit. "Very well, gleaner." He faced the healer and forced a smile. "Thank you anyway."

The healer stood there a few seconds longer, then returned to the soldiers, appearing nonplussed by the exchange and leaving Keziah to wonder if she should have kept silent.

"What was that about?" Fotir asked.

"We have cause to think that the conspiracy will make an attempt on the king's life," Grinsa said. "We should be wary of allowing any Qirsi we don't know to get near him."

Javan narrowed his eyes. "What makes you think they want

to kill the king? Did that woman you imprisoned tell you this as well?"

"I can't say," Grinsa told him.

"But surely—"

"Leave it, Father." Tavis placed a hand on the duke's shoulder. "Grinsa wouldn't have said anything if he didn't have good reason to believe it was true. Trust him as I do and let it be."

Javan regarded his son briefly, as if seeing him anew. Then he nodded. "Very well."

They found a pallet on which Kearney could sit, and Grinsa knelt before him, laying his hands over the wound on the king's side.

"Tell me of your battles," the king said, clearly uncomfortable with having Grinsa tending his wounds with the others nearby. His expression changed. "Where's Welfyl?"

Javan took a long breath. "He's dead, my liege."

Kearney closed his eyes briefly. "Demons and fire. This is a black day for the House of the River."

"Yes, Your Majesty."

"How severe were Heneagh's losses?"

Curgh's duke shook his head. "We don't know for certain yet, my liege, but it appeared that they had lost nearly a third of their men. Perhaps more."

"Damn. And yours, Lord Curgh?"

"Not quite as bad as that, though close."

"Same for my guard. We've yet to make a count of the enemy dead and wounded, but I'm sure they fared better than we did."

"I'm afraid so, my liege."

Hagan MarCullet returned, accompanied by a lanky man with a shaved head and trim beard who Keziah assumed to be Rab Avkar.

"Swordmaster," the king said, looking up at the man. "All of us are deeply saddened by the loss of your duke, none more so than I."

"Thank you, Your Majesty," the swordmaster said, his voice thick, his eyes reddened. "I tried to reason with him, to

keep him from joining the battle—a man his age . . ." He
shook his head. "He insisted. He said he wanted to strike a
blow for his son. And for some time he fought as a man possessed. But he wasn't strong enough. I saw him go down—"
His voice broke and he turned his head, swallowing hard.

"Songs will be written of his bravery, and of Dunfyl's as
well. The Underrealm will shine like Morna's sky with their
light."

"Yes, Your Majesty," the man whispered. "Thank you."

Grinsa removed his hands from Kearney's side and sat
back on his knees, his face shining with sweat.

"Thank you, gleaner," the king said, twisting his body ten-
tatively and then lifting his arm. "That's much better. You
have a deft touch."

"You have other wounds, Your Majesty. I can heal them as
well."

Kearney stood. "Thank you. Perhaps later." He stepped to
where Welfyl's swordmaster stood. Immediately the man
dropped to one knee, bowing his head. "Rise, Sir Avkar." The
man did as he was told. "I know that you grieve for Lord Heneagh," the king went on, "but this is not the time for mourning. Braedon's army will attack again, perhaps as soon as
dawn. I need for you to command your duke's army. Can you
do that for me?"

"Yes, Your Majesty."

"You've suffered terrible losses. I can offer you a few hundred men, but it won't be enough to take the place of all those
who have fallen."

Rab straightened. "With all respect, Your Majesty. We
don't need any more men. We may not be as well trained as
the soldiers of Curgh or the King's Guard, but we fight now
for the memories of our duke and lord. The empire's army
won't get past us."

For a moment it seemed that the king might insist, but then
he appeared to think better of it. "Your duke would be proud,
swordmaster. Very well. We'll leave the armies as they are for
now."

It had grown dark. Throughout the camp, soldiers were
lighting small fires. A few could be heard singing softly, their

voices mingling with the low moan of the wind and the cries of the wounded. A short distance to the south a great fire burned, the pyre for Eibithar's dead. Gazing up at the sky, Keziah saw stars beginning to emerge in the blackness, bright and clear. The moons weren't up yet, but already she could see that it was going to be a glorious night.

"We need to be ready when they attack again," Kearney was saying. "I want archers posted at the front of our lines at all times. Have them stand in three shifts."

Javan, the swordmaster, and Kearney's captains murmured their agreement.

Fotir glanced at Grinsa, who nodded. "Pardon me, Your Majesty," the minister said. "But Grinsa, the archminister, and I all have magic of mists and winds. On your authority, we can summon a wind to aid our archers and hinder Braedon's."

"Yes, First Minister, that would be fine. But remember that the empire has Qirsi as well. Any wind you raise may well be countered before it can do much good."

"Wait," Javan broke in, staring at Grinsa. "You have mists and winds? I thought you were just a gleaner."

Keziah felt her entire body growing tense, but her brother merely smiled.

"I'm somewhat more than I seem, my lord," he said, "as your son will attest." He gave the king a meaningful look. "And I assure you, Your Majesty, the wind we raise will be more than a match for that of Braedon's Qirsi."

Again the king blanched, appearing to remember in that moment that Grinsa was a Weaver. "Yes, of course, gleaner. Thank you." He took a breath, as if to gather himself. Then he turned to the older of his captains. "What news of Shanstead?" he asked. "Do you still expect him to reach here tomorrow?"

"Last we heard, Your Majesty, he was approaching the far banks of Binthar's Wash. But that was a day ago, and still we haven't seen them on the moors."

Kearney's mouth twitched. "We may have to fight without them again."

"They won't catch us unaware again, my liege." Javan gave

a thin smile. "The first battle went their way. But the dawn brings a new day, and it will be ours."

The king's smile was brittle and pained. "Of course, Lord Curgh. My thanks."

They continued to speak of the day's battle for some time, eating cold provisions just as did the men around them. Some of what they discussed would serve them in devising tactics for their next encounter with the empire's forces, but much of it, Keziah could tell, was simply warriors exchanging tales of combat. She had little to add of course, but she remained with them, watching with pleasure how Kearney came alive when he spoke of wielding his blade and dancing his mount amidst a sea of enemy soldiers. Even Tavis, who usually seemed so withdrawn around anyone other than Grinsa and the MarCullet boy, offered a tale or two of his own and laughed with the others.

Grinsa said very little, though, like Keziah, he made no effort to excuse himself. After a time he moved so that he was beside her. Kearney eyed him as he did, but said nothing.

"Feeling left out?" Grinsa asked, his voice low, a small smile on his lips.

"A bit. I was wondering if I should ride to the North Wood, find something to kill, and then come back and tell all of you about it."

He laughed. "You don't have to go to such lengths. These are warrior tales. They don't have to be accurate."

"I heard that, gleaner," Hagan MarCullet growled from nearby.

Her brother grinned at the man, then faced her again. "Earlier, when I asked if you were all right, you made it sound like you weren't. I was wondering if there's anything I can do."

"I shouldn't have said that. I had just seen some things, and then hearing that Welfyl was dead . . ." She shrugged. "I'm better now."

"But this day took its toll on you, didn't it?"

"No more than it did on others."

"Kezi—"

"I'm fine, Grinsa."

"I don't believe you."

Keziah almost got up and walked away. She was tired, and though Kearney's soldier—her shadow—would follow her wherever she went, at that moment she would have preferred his silent stares to Grinsa's questions.

During the lengthy silence that ensued, Grinsa seemed to sense how angry she was. "I'm sorry, Kezi," he said, his voice dropping to a whisper.

Forgiveness came grudgingly. "It's all right."

"No, it's not. You don't need me taking care of you anymore. I shouldn't even try."

She couldn't help herself. For years he had treated her as though they were still children, as though she still needed the protection of an older brother. "No, you shouldn't. You may be the older one, the more powerful one, but that doesn't mean that I'm helpless."

"I know that. Truly I do. But the ones who really need my protection are beyond my reach. And so I try to protect you instead."

The ones who really need . . . Cresenne and Bryntelle. Sometimes her own capacity for selfishness and stupidity took her breath away. He had meant well. His questions had done no harm, except perhaps to her pride. But she was so absorbed with her own concerns that all she could see was the meddling of an older brother. She gazed at him now, marveling at how little he had changed over the years. He seemed ageless, save for his eyes. They were medium yellow, like the sun early on a harvest morning, and they appeared to carry within them the cares of all the land. For all the youth she still saw in Kearney's face, her king had aged considerably in the last year. Tavis of Curgh had grown to manhood, it seemed, almost before her eyes. And when she looked in a mirror, she saw time marking its progress with small lines around her own mouth and eyes. But Grinsa remained as she remembered, the man who had loved and protected her all her life, who had always borne burdens the likes of which she could scarcely comprehend.

"I'm sorry," she whispered, her eyes stinging. "I didn't think . . ." She trailed off, not knowing what to say, realizing that what she had said, though incomplete, was as true as anything else she might have offered. "You told me that she won," she said a few moments later. "She shouldn't have anything to fear from him anymore."

Grinsa just nodded. They both knew all too well that the Weaver wouldn't give up so easily.

"I'll trust you to watch out for yourself," he said, staring at the fires burning throughout the camp. "But let me give one last caution. If he has eyes watching this war, keeping him apprised of its ebbs and flows—and I'm certain he does—he'll know that the fighting began in earnest today. If I were you, I'd be prepared to dream of him tonight, and tell him why your king still lives."

Keziah didn't need to feel the familiar dread washing over her, like the waters of Amon's Ocean during the snows, to tell her that he was right. She knew the Weaver better than he did. She should have thought of this hours ago. Despite all her claims that she didn't need her brother caring for her anymore, she found herself struggling to keep up with the speed and clarity of his thinking. Yet, once she looked past her chagrin, she realized as well that she was ready for the Weaver, that she knew just what she would tell him. The time was fast approaching when her lies wouldn't serve her anymore, when she'd either take control of her own magic and banish the Weaver from her mind, or she'd die, a victim of her dreams. But this was not that night.

"I'll be ready for him," she said.

Grinsa actually smiled. "I believe you will."

Pride demanded that she not let him see just how much this pleased her, but she couldn't keep the grin from springing to her lips, or the blood from rushing to her cheeks.

A short time later, Kearney stood, announcing that he intended to retire for the night. Though he said no more than this, all understood that he expected them to do the same. None among them doubted that the fighting would resume with first light. Grinsa smiled at her one last time before walking off toward the Curgh camp, and Keziah turned to follow her king.

"He loves you, you know," she heard behind her before she could take a step.

Looking back, she saw Tavis standing nearby, his face in shadows. He looked taller than she remembered, and broader as well.

"Aside from the woman and his daughter, there's no one who matters more to him than you do."

It seemed a strange comment coming from this young noble whom she had long considered a spoiled court boy. She sensed though that he was trying to help, that he had taken note of the anger she directed at Grinsa.

"I know that," she said. "But I'm grateful to you just the same."

"Well, if you know it, you should show some gratitude. He's sacrificed more than any of us and he deserves better than your anger and your jealousy."

She felt her anger flare, and opened her mouth to lash out at the boy. But as she did, the breeze shifted slightly and a torch sputtered nearby. The light didn't change much, but it was enough to illuminate the scars on his cheek and jaw. If this boy, who had suffered so much, could speak of Grinsa's sacrifice, how could she not? Which of them was the spoiled child?

"You're right," she said at last, and walked away, gratified by the look of surprise on the young lord's face.

It didn't take her long to find her sleeping roll, or for her shadow to find her, lowering himself to the ground only a few strides from where she lay. She worried that he might hear her if she cried out in her sleep, but there was nothing to be done. If she tried to move away from him, he would only follow, positioning himself even closer to her than he was now.

Instead, she closed her eyes and tried to sleep, bracing herself for the coming encounter with the Weaver.

But sleep did not come easily this night. She found herself haunted by images of the battle and its aftermath, and troubled by her conversation with Grinsa and her brief exchange with the Curgh boy. Horror and fear, anger and remorse warred within her, making her toss and turn, keeping her mind racing until she wondered if she'd ever sleep again.

So it was that despite Grinsa's warning and her meager preparations, she was unprepared for the dream when finally it began. One moment she was staring up at the stars over the battle plain, watching as Panya and Ilias climbed into the night, and the next, the sky had turned purest black and the familiar grasses and boulders of the Weaver's plain surrounded her.

Before she understood entirely what she was doing, she had begun to walk, trudging up the hill toward the spot where the Weaver awaited her. By the time she reached the top, and the Weaver's brilliant white sun stabbed into her eyes, she had gathered herself, remembering all that she had intended to tell him.

"You expected to dream of me."

"Yes, Weaver."

"Is that why you took so long to fall asleep? Did you fear this encounter?"

"No more than usual, Weaver," she said, and sensed his amusement. "I tried to make myself sleep, but I couldn't."

"Because of the battle?"

She nodded, summoning the images that had troubled her so.

"I see. You understand that there will be more of this. Eventually, it will be my army—including you—that does the killing but the results will be much the same."

"Yes, Weaver."

"I take it Kearney still lives."

"Yes, Weaver. He was hurt, but his wounds were easily healed."

"I didn't expect you to kill him today, knowing that the first battle might be difficult for you, but my expectations haven't changed."

She had been waiting for this, planning what she would say. And so she nodded her understanding, and began to tell him all the ways she had thought of to kill her king, the sudden gust of wind that changes the flight of an arrow, the dark words whispered to Kearney's mount, the shattering of his horse's leg, the harm that could be done by a healer, the poison that could be slipped into an herbmaster's tonic.

"Just when I had been ready to give up on you, you exceed all of my expectations." She could tell from his voice that he was beaming at her. "All the methods of which you speak will work, though some will require that you find another Qirsi to help you, unless you've added shaping and healing to your magics since last we spoke."

"No, Weaver," she said.

"I'd suggest you use language of beasts. That's least likely to draw anyone's attention."

"Yes, Weaver."

"You hesitate. Why?"

"That man is here. The gleaner. He might know that it was me." The Weaver would know already that Grinsa had joined the Eibitharian army. But having spoken to her of the gleaner in the past, he might find it suspicious if she didn't mention his presence on the battle plain.

"What makes you say that?"

"He speaks of you, Weaver. He warns the king about you. And I just wonder if he knows you're a Weaver, mightn't he be one as well?"

"Does he fight beside Kearney?"

"No, Weaver. He stays with the Curgh boy and fights with Javan's army."

"Good. That should make this easier. Make certain that the gleaner is far away when you do this and you should be fine."

"I will, Weaver. Thank you."

"I want this done soon. When next we speak, Kearney should be dead."

Before she could answer, the Weaver was gone, and she was blinking her eyes open. The sun had yet to rise, but a faint silvery light had already begun to light the Moorlands, shimmering on the dancing grasses and great stones. Keziah could smell the rank smoke from Eibithar's pyre, and, after a moment, she realized that she could hear singing.

She knew immediately that these were not the soft notes sung by Kearney's men the night before. This was a battle hymn, and the voices were those of Braedon's men, loud and boisterous and too damned confident.

Keziah sat up, pushing the tangle of hair back from her face.

"The king is asking for you, Archminister."

She looked up to see her shadow standing over her. She hadn't noticed before how young he was, but it was said that fear did that to a soldier, robbed him of his years as well as his nerve, making him a babe once more.

"All right," she said, stiffly getting to her feet. "Tell him I'll be along in a moment."

He nodded and started to walk away.

"Are the empire's men moving yet?" she asked.

"No, not yet. But soon. Captain says they want to wear us down before Shanstead arrives."

It was more than he had said to her since they marched from Audun's Castle.

It's only going to get worse, Grinsa had told her the day before. And the Weaver had echoed that in her dream. *You understand that there will be more of this.* Imagining the unimaginable, a war between Weavers, Keziah knew that they were right. The soldier was watching her, not with suspicion, as he usually did, but with need, his eyes begging her to reassure him, to tell him that Marston and the Thorald army would arrive in time.

All she could do was turn her back on him and reach for her belt and blade.

Chapter

Seven

Galdasten, Eibithar

t was a siege without blood, a war without swords, at least for the people of Galdasten. Bodies still washed ashore occasionally, bloated and foul, still held together by the purple and gold uniforms that bound them. Braedon's men had recovered their own from the waters after the naval battle ended and Eibithar's fleet, or what little was left of it, fled Falcon Bay. But they had left Eibithar's dead to the surf.

It was but one indignity among many. The emperor's men had set fire to much of the city before marching past the castle and on toward the Moorlands. Those soldiers who remained—perhaps six hundred—had garrisoned themselves in the few homes and buildings they left standing. They patrolled the city as if they owned it, enforcing a strict curfew, closing the taverns, taking the ale and food for themselves, and confiscating the wares of those peddlers foolish enough to enter Galdasten. They maintained a presence outside the walls of Galdasten Castle, but they needn't have bothered. Renald, Galdasten's duke, had no intention of challenging their supremacy within his city, nor had he shown any willingness to pursue the bulk of Braedon's army, which had long since marched southward.

Pillad jal Krenaar, Galdasten's first minister, felt certain that even as the men and women of the city took refuge in the wards of the duke's castle, they cursed Renald's name, seeing him as a traitor to his realm and his people. Had the minister been in their position, he would have done the same. He was just as certain that Renald suffered for his own compliance with the enemy. He seldom left his chambers, speaking only with the duchess, his swordmaster, and Pillad, who had managed at last to regain the trust of Galdasten's Eandi leaders.

Pillad's betrayal of the Qirsi barkeep in Galdasten City had been but the beginning of an ordeal he thought might end with his own execution. Indeed, had he known what his accusations against Mittifar jal Stek would do to his own life, he might never have made them in the first place. But on that day in Elined's turn he hadn't been thinking at all. He had been angry, still smarting from the humiliation of the tavern keeper's refusal to serve him Thorald ale. He had also grown weary of being ignored, of being viewed by Qirsi and Eandi alike as useless. He was eager to reclaim his influence within Renald's court, and he had known that by sacrificing Mittifar, like Pillad, a member of the Weaver's conspiracy, he would enhance his own influence.

He had been pleased with himself when the duke's men left the castle to arrest the man. When they returned empty-handed and reported to Renald that the tavern keeper was dead, Pillad felt his entire world shudder, as if Elined had pounded at Galdasten Tor with her mighty fist. The duchess accused him of being a liar and traitor, of arranging the tavern keeper's murder in order to gain the duke's trust while at the same time masking his own treachery. She even speculated that he had broken Mittifar's neck himself, though this much Renald and his swordsmaster told her was impossible. Ewan Traylee pointed out that the tavern keeper had been too large and powerful for a man of Pillad's stature to best in a physical fight, and the duke made it clear that Pillad didn't possess shaping power. Still, the accuracy of her accusation left the first minister so badly shaken that he barely managed to speak in his own defense.

Yet what disturbed him even more than Elspeth's allegations was the fact that Mittifar had been murdered. He never had any doubt that the conspiracy was responsible, which meant that they knew what Pillad had done before Renald's soldiers reached the tavern, quite possibly before they even left the castle. There were other traitors in Galdasten, at least one of them in Renald's court.

Having no proof that Pillad was a traitor, they could not imprison him. So it was that he was in his chamber two nights later when the Weaver came to him in a dream, incensed and bent on vengeance. Never before had the minister endured such torment, and he hoped that he would die rather than suffer it again. The man burned him with white-hot flames, blackening the flesh on Pillad's chest and back. He broke the minister's ribs one by one, healed them, then broke them again. And all the while he raged at him for his betrayal. Pillad couldn't remember any of what the Weaver said, having heard the words through a blinding haze of agony, but he did recall that the Weaver understood why he had done it, and that he expected Pillad to regain Renald's confidence eventually.

Pillad remembered something else from that night as well, a detail that reached him through the pain and terror and stuck in his mind long after he had awakened. All of the injuries dealt him by the Weaver were to his torso, where they would remain hidden from Galdasten's Eandi. Even as he seethed, the Weaver recognized that Pillad had made himself valuable to the movement once more. Renald would turn to him again, would heed his advice and share with the minister his plans for answering the Braedony invasion. That must have been why the Weaver didn't kill him, why, in fact, he mended all the wounds he inflicted on him. In the midst of his torture, this realization sustained Pillad, gave him strength he hadn't known he possessed, served as a balm for his injuries. He mattered again. He had wondered for so long if he would.

The duke's suspicions lingered for some time. Elspeth's had yet to fade entirely. But finally, in only the last few days, the minister had been welcomed back into the court. There was never any formal acknowledgment of this; he received no apology from Renald for his lack of faith, nor did the duke even ask him to join his daily discussions with the swordmaster. Just the other morning, nearly a full turn after the tavern keeper's death, Pillad was in Renald's chambers answering yet another round of questions about Mittifar and what Pillad had seen in his visits to the White Wave. After perhaps an hour Ewan arrived to discuss military matters with the duke, as he did every day. On this morning, however, Renald did not ask the minister to leave. Instead he launched directly into his conversation with the swordmaster. Pillad's exile was over.

That very night the Weaver came to him once again, and though Pillad's climb to the plain where the man awaited him might have been somewhat more arduous than he recalled from previous dreams, nothing else about the encounter struck him as unusual. The Weaver asked him if Renald had come to trust him again, but clearly he knew the answer already. He asked about Renald's plans, and he told the minister that the time was fast approaching when he would reveal himself to all the Forelands.

"I want Galdasten to be at war when I do," he went on. "I want Renald and his army on the Moorlands, fighting the empire's invaders. Can you convince your duke to ride to war?"

"I can, Weaver," he said, knowing it was true. "Renald wants to fight. Every day that goes by with Braedon's men in his city and the realm at risk, pains him. His swordmaster is much the same and will support me."

"Good. Then I expect this will prove quite easy for you."

"Not entirely. The duchess will oppose me."

"The duchess?" He sounded genuinely surprised.

"Yes, Weaver. She holds sway in Renald's court. If she can't be convinced, Renald may resist."

"See that he doesn't."

He knew better than to argue. If he failed the Weaver in this, his punishment would make their last encounter seem pleasant by comparison. "Of course, Weaver."

"You possess healing and fire magics."

"Yes, Weaver."

"They'll prove useful when our war begins. I'll weave your fire with that of a hundred other Qirsi. Entire armies of Eandi soldiers will fall before you."

Pillad had never considered himself a warrior, but he couldn't deny that the idea of this thrilled him. "My magic is yours, Weaver."

The following morning, the eighth of Adriel's waxing, the minister made his way to the duke's presence chamber intending to raise the matter immediately. When he arrived there, however, he found the duchess with Renald and Ewan.

"What is he doing here?" Elspeth asked, eyeing the minister warily as he stepped into the chamber.

Renald winced, but quickly gathered himself, saying, in a reasonably steady voice, "I asked him here."

The duchess started to say something, then stopped herself, a thin smile flitting across her exquisite face. "I'm not certain that was wise, my lord. We don't know yet that we can trust him."

"I believe we can."

Pillad could not remember ever hearing the duke speak so to his wife, and it made him all the more certain that he could be persuaded to march to war. By the same token, though, the minister decided then that he would not broach the matter that day, in Elspeth's presence. Renald could only be expected to stand up to her so often before falling back into his usual submissiveness. In some respects Pillad and his duke were quite similar.

The minister sat near the chamber door, far from the duchess and from the duke as well. He merely listened as their discussion began slowly and soon foundered. Ewan spoke of his own frustration and that of his men, their eagerness to fight, and the suffering of Galdasten's people under the authority of the empire.

Renald wore a pained expression and nodded his agreement several times, but he said little more than did Pillad. It fell to the duchess to answer the swordmaster's plea for action, and she did so with no apology.

"There's more at stake here than a warrior's pride, swordmaster," she said, sounding like a parent scolding a thoughtless child. "I'd have thought that you understood that by now. How long has it been since a man from Galdasten sat on the throne, Renald?"

She didn't even look at him, and still the duke quailed, his normally ruddy face turning pale. "Nearly a century."

"Nearly a century," she repeated. "And it's been more than three hundred and fifty years since anyone challenged Thorald's supremacy under the Rules of Ascension. We seek to change the course of history. We cannot rush this."

"And what of the people, my lady?"

There could be no denying Ewan's nerve.

"That they suffer is regrettable," she said, without any trace of regret. "But always there is a price for such momentous change."

That ended their discussion. The duke asked his swordmaster a few questions about the castle's stores and readiness of the army should the time to march come soon, but within a few moments Ewan had stood and crossed to the door, clearly troubled by what the duchess had said.

Pillad stood as well, intending to leave with him. Perhaps if they worked together, they might more easily convince the duke to oppose his wife.

"Stay a moment, won't you, First Minister?"

He turned. Elspeth was eyeing him as a spider might regard a newly caught fly. "Of course, my lady."

She stood and began to pace as Ewan left the chamber. "You disagree with me," she said.

"I do, my lady."

"Why?"

"Because I believe that the conspiracy was responsible for Lady Brienne's death, and I fear that the duke is mistaken in opposing the king. I fear for the realm, indeed for all the Forelands."

She raised an eyebrow. Apparently she hadn't expected him to speak against the conspiracy so forcefully. "So you believe that the Qirsi plot is connected in some way to the empire's invasion?"

"I believe it's possible. The barkeep in Galdasten City saw me in his establishment every day for more than a turn, but he didn't offer me gold or speak to me of the conspiracy until after Braedon's ships had appeared in Falcon Bay." He shrugged, pleased with himself. "That isn't proof, of course, but it does make me wonder."

"I see." She continued to circle the chamber, as if lost in thought. After a time, she glanced at Pillad again. "That's all, First Minister. You may go."

He cast a look at the duke, who gave a small nod and, Pillad thought, the barest hint of a smile. Offering a quick bow, he left them.

Over the course of the next few days, Pillad met with the duke several times, but always with Elspeth present. It almost seemed that she was afraid to allow them to speak in private. Their discussions covered little that was new, while avoiding any mention of the war being fought on the Moorlands. For all Pillad knew, the duke was receiving daily reports on the fighting to the south, but Renald didn't speak of them.

Finally, on this, the thirteenth day of the waxing, Pillad arrived at Renald's chamber to find that the duchess was not yet there. While still in the corridor he had heard Ewan's voice, though he had been unable to make out any of what the swordmaster said, and with two guards standing by the door, he didn't dare try to listen. Once he saw that the two men were alone, he had a good idea of what the swordmaster had been saying.

"Come in, First Minister," Renald said, waving him into the chamber and then pointing to an empty chair.

"Are you certain I'm not interrupting, my lord?"

"Not at all. The swordmaster has been telling me once more that it's time we joined the fighting."

He didn't even have to raise the subject himself. The gods were with him.

"You know where I stand on the matter, my lord."

"Yes, I believe I do. You weren't swayed by what the duchess said the other day?"

"I'm certain you would make a fine king, my lord," he said, speaking carefully. "And I think it possible that the situation on the Moorlands is already desperate enough that your arrival there will save the realm, placing you in a position to demand the crown. But I fear that if you wait too long in the hope of positioning yourself to be king, there will be no realm left for you to rule."

"Exactly!" Ewan said, sitting forward so suddenly that he nearly propelled himself out of his chair.

"We always knew that I would have to strike a fine balance," the duke said. "Els— The duchess merely wishes to make certain that we succeed."

"If I may, my lord," Pillad said. "Such considerations ought to be secondary. Your people are suffering. The city of your forebears is overrun with the emperor's soldiers. You should strike at them, drive them back to their ships. If you take the crown, so be it. But the time has come to act like a king."

As soon as he spoke the words, Pillad feared that he had gone too far. But Renald merely sighed, running a hand through his fiery hair.

"You're right, of course. But the duchess—"

The door opened.

"What about me?" She stood in the doorway, wearing a gown of red that nearly matched the duke's hair, her dark eyes flitting from Renald to Ewan to Pillad, and then back to the duke. She stepped into the chamber and closed the door. "Well? What were you saying about me, Renald?"

The duke stood. Pillad could see his hands trembling, but the duke still held himself straight. "I was saying that you still wish to wait before sending the army south. And I was going to add that I think you're mistaken, and that I intend to strike at the emperor's men come morning."

"I knew it," she said, her voice heavy with contempt. She turned to glare at Pillad. "I knew that you'd turn him against me at the first opportunity."

Ewan stood as well. "Actually, my lady, I was the one who began this discussion. The first minister came in later and only added to what I had been saying all along."

"Then you're all fools. And my husband is the biggest fool of all, for listening to you."

"Oh, Elspeth, be quiet."

Her cheeks colored as if he had slapped her, but after only a moment, she smiled. Clearly it was forced, a mask for her rage and humiliation, but it seemed as natural on her features as any smile Pillad had ever seen there. "Fine, Renald. If you wish to strengthen Glyndwr's hold on the throne, and destroy any hope we might have had of ending the Rules of Ascension, so be it. I'll not have any more to do with you."

The duke gave a curt nod. "Very well. As you pass the guards on your way out, please tell them that we're not to be disturbed. We have preparations to make."

She glowered at them all, the muscles in her jaw clenched. Then she whirled away from them, flung the door open, and stormed from the chamber, saying nothing to the soldiers as she strode past them.

For several seconds, none of the men spoke. They didn't even move. Pillad and Ewan were both watching the duke, wondering whether he would go after her. But at last, he merely stepped to the door, closed it quietly, and turned to face them. He still appeared to be shaking, but he looked pleased with himself, as if he had just come through a sword fight unscathed.

"We have a great deal to discuss," he said. "I want Braedon's men out of my city, but I don't wish to spend too much time driving them off, and we can't afford to lose many men. Suggestions?"

Ewan was grinning now—it almost seemed that he, too, had won a battle of sorts. "Yes, my lord," he said. "I've given this a good deal of thought."

Pillad had no doubt that this was so.

Renald knew that he would pay a price for what he had done this day. One did not spurn Elspeth, lady of Prindyr, duchess of Galdasten, as he had done, without inviting her wrath. For a time, she would refuse to speak to him at all, and after that she would take to insults, small barbs cast at him in front of his soldiers, his advisors, noble guests of the castle. The affections she had shown him in recent days were now forfeit. She would not share his bed again for some time, if ever. She might even seek to turn their sons against him, telling the boys that his cowardice and folly had cost them their chance to sit on the Oaken Throne. Elspeth had always been a proud woman, and today Renald had dealt her pride a blow. She would be slow to forgive; she would never forget.

The duke, however, didn't care. He would not go so far as to blame his wife for the humiliation of Galdasten's people or the damage to the realm done by his own timidity. She had urged this course of action, but he was duke, and he had made the decision not to oppose Braedon's invasion. She had preyed on his ambition, as well as on his fear of her, and he had allowed her to have her way. Ashamed as he was of what he had become, Renald would accept responsibility for it, not only in his own mind, but also when it came time to face Kearney. The hour was late, but at last he was ready to comport himself as befitted a duke.

And it pleased him to do so. Merely sitting in his presence chamber, speaking with Ewan and Pillad of military tactics, he felt more like the leader of a great house than he had in many turns. Yes, he feared death. He would be as scared riding to this war as any boy newly enlisted in the Galdasten army. But there was some satisfaction to be found in that fear.

Even the most frightened soldier marching to war was less a coward than the man who did nothing while his realm burned. Renald would endure Elspeth's contempt, he would explain to his sons that ambition and duty to one's realm were not always compatible, that honor should mean more to a man than should power. He didn't want the crown—not this way. As to the rest, he thought with some chagrin, he would have to get used once more to bedding serving girls and ladies of the court.

It became clear from the very start of their discussion that the swordmaster had spent days thinking of how they might break Braedon's hold on Galdasten City. Ewan believed that under cover of a fierce assault from Galdasten's archers, several large raiding parties could leave the castle by way of the sally ports and strike at the Braedony soldiers who were camped outside its gates. Once they were defeated—and the swordmaster didn't believe that would take long—Renald could send the full force of his army into the city to drive the invaders back to their ships.

Ewan actually believed that the duke's reluctance to act before now would work to their advantage.

"They've grown lax, my lord. They don't expect you to do anything."

The irony wasn't lost on any of them.

"No doubt generations from now, my descendants will celebrate the brilliance of our strategy."

Pillad grinned. "No doubt, my lord."

"Prepare your soldiers, swordmaster."

"My lord, I would suggest that we wait until dawn. If we do it in the middle of the day, Braedon's men will have little trouble spotting the soldiers leaving the castle by way of the sally ports."

"What about dusk? The light will be more favorable then."

"Aye, my lord, dusk might be better for the initial assault. But if we wait until dawn—"

"I don't want to wait another night. We'll strike at dusk. Ready your men, swordmaster."

Ewan frowned, but stood. "Yes, my lord. I'll begin preparations immediately."

"Very good. Keep me informed of your progress."

Ewan bowed and hurried from the chamber, leaving Renald alone with his first minister. Renald had convinced himself that Pillad served him loyally, seeing Elspeth's suspicions of the man as another of her ploys. The minister advocated going to war, and so she accused him of treason hoping that this would keep Renald from heeding his counsel. Yet, though certain of this, he couldn't help but feel discomfited being alone with the Qirsi. He tried to tell himself that it had always been this way, that the white-hairs were strange, their powers unfathomable. Who among the Eandi enjoyed being around them? But he knew that there was more to his uneasiness. Try as he might to put the doubts out of his mind, he could not help but wonder if the man had betrayed him.

"Perhaps I should leave you, my lord."

Could he read Renald's mind? Did Qirsi magic run that deep?

"As you wish, First Minister," he said, struggling to keep his voice steady. "We have much to do in the next few hours."

"Yes, my lord." He pushed himself out of his chair.

"Do any of the other Qirsi in the castle have mists and winds?"

"I'm not sure, my lord. I would doubt it. It's one of the deeper magics and not terribly common."

"Ah, well. I was merely curious. I take it you'll be helping the healers."

"As you wish, my lord. Though I had thought that I would stay with you. You may wish for my counsel when the fighting begins."

"Yes, of course. I haven't decided yet if I'll be joining the fighting when it comes time to take back the city."

"Even then, my lord, I'm willing to go into battle with you." He smiled. "I'm not much of a swordsman, but I ride well, and I might be of some use in a fight."

Renald forced a smile in return. "I'm sure you'll do just fine, First Minister. I'll let you know what I decide to do myself, and what I expect of you."

The Qirsi's pale eyes narrowed for just a moment, his

smile fading. Then he nodded. "Of course, my lord. I think I understand." He started toward the door.

The duke knew that he should let the man go, that he should end this awkwardness before one of them said something foolish. But he couldn't stop himself. "What is it you think you understand, Pillad?"

The minister halted just a step or two from the door. He kept his back to the duke, taking a long breath. "Forgive me, my lord. I shouldn't have said anything."

"But you did."

Pillad turned at that. "Yes, I did. I sense that you still don't trust me entirely. I wonder if you don't want me riding to battle with you because you fear I might make an attempt on your life."

"The conspiracy has disturbed us all a great deal, First Minister. The death of the tavern keeper only served to heighten our fears. I find it hard to believe that he was the only traitor in Galdasten, which would mean that there are still Qirsi in this city, perhaps in this castle, who wish to do me harm."

"I'm certain that you're right, my lord. But to my mind that makes those of us you know you can trust all the more valuable."

"That may be so, but it also makes the task of distinguishing loyal Qirsi from traitorous ones that much more daunting. Surely you can appreciate that."

"Yes, my lord. As always I'll serve as you see fit. If that means remaining with the healers, so be it. I'll await word of your decision." With that, he bowed and let himself out of the chamber.

Renald didn't know what to think. For just an instant he considered going after the minister, and saying that he wanted to ride with him into battle. But he couldn't help wondering if that was just what Pillad wanted him to do, if the Qirsi's words and bearing had been intended to produce just such a response. What scared the duke most was that in the past he had relied on Elspeth to help him make such judgments.

Unable to find any humor at all in this irony, the duke left his chamber and went in search of Ewan. Better to help the swordmaster with his preparations than sit alone in his chamber with his doubts and fears.

By the time the prior's bells began to toll in the city, Renald's archers were ready. They remained in the castle wards, where the enemy soldiers couldn't see them. Only when the sunlight began to fail would they climb the towers to the ramparts. Standing together in the courtyards, their quivers full, many of them testing the tension of the bows for the tenth time, they reminded the duke of boys awaiting the start of their first battle tournament. Clearly they had been hoping for this moment, eager for a chance to strike at the invaders who had taken their city. Renald heard more laughter in those hours before dusk than he had in the last turn and a half. It lightened his spirit, gave him hope that they might really succeed in breaking the empire's hold on Galdasten.

At one point, gazing up at the windows overlooking the upper ward, he thought he saw Elspeth. But when he looked again, no one was there, and he was left to wonder if he had only imagined her face in the late-day sun.

When at last the sky began to darken, Ewan ordered the archers onto the walls, imploring them to take their positions with as little noise as possible. He also sent his raiding parties to the castle's sally ports, instructing them to wait just inside the hidden gates until they heard the bells ringing in the cloister tower. That would be their signal to attack.

Convinced that all was ready, Renald and the swordmaster climbed the nearest of the stairways to the turret atop one of the towers, where they could watch the battle unfold without getting in the way of Ewan's bowmen.

The sky above the tower had deepened to a dark velvet blue, and the western horizon glowed brightly, the thin clouds over the North Wood touched with yellow and orange and pink. There was still enough light to see—Renald could make out the soldiers standing at the base of the castle, leaning against siege engines that had seen little use in the past half turn. From the beginning, it had seemed that Braedon's men had known Galdasten wouldn't oppose them. They had prepared for an assault on the gates, but had done nothing more, as if believing that the mere threat of attack would be enough to keep Renald from fighting back.

And for too long it had worked.

"Give the order, swordmaster. I grow tired of seeing the emperor's men on my soil."

Ewan grinned. "With pleasure, my lord."

He took a torch from a bracket on the stone wall beside them, raised it over his head, then brought it down in a chopping motion. Immediately, two hundred archers stepped forward to the outer wall, arrows already nocked in their bows, and let their darts fly, the thrum of their bowstrings echoing off the castle walls like the roar of some great strange beast from the Underrealm. Screams rose from below, cries of alarm and rage filled the lanes surrounding the castle. Ewan raised and lowered his torch again, and the archers loosed a second volley.

More shouts reached them from the streets, repeated now farther off, as word of what was happening spread toward the piers. Ewan turned toward the cloister tower and swept his torch back and forth. A moment later the bells began to toll, and an instant after that, a different kind of cry arose from the soldiers around the castle. In just a few seconds Renald heard the clash of steel on steel, the urgent calls of men doing battle.

His eyes were adjusting to the evening light, but the shadows at the base of the castle walls were deepening. He couldn't tell who had the upper hand. In just a few moments, however, he saw men retreating down the lanes that led to the port, and he knew that the invaders had been driven off. The men below gave a ragged cheer that was repeated by Ewan's archers.

"Well done, swordmaster!" Renald said over the din, clapping the man on the shoulder.

It was not something the duke would normally have done, and Ewan gave him a strange look. "This is only a small victory, my lord. Braedon's men gave up too quickly. No doubt they've simply gone to join their comrades in the city. They haven't been beaten yet. Far from it."

"I know that," the duke said, forcing a smile so the sword-master wouldn't see how much the words had sobered him. "Still, I'm pleased. Surely this is a good beginning."

"Yes, my lord, I believe it is." He looked down at the city again, seeming to mark the progress of the retreating soldiers. "We have to choose now, my lord. Do we wait until morning to attack their strongholds in the city, or do we pursue them immediately?"

Renald stared at him a moment, suddenly out of his depth. "I'm . . . I'm not certain. What would you do?"

"Well, on the one hand, we would do well to attack before they have a chance to marshal their defenses. On the other hand, they're already entrenched in the city, and with night falling, they have the advantage of being able to conceal themselves more easily. If we attack, our men may be rushing headlong into a trap."

The duke felt his face coloring. He had pushed to begin all this sooner. Had he been willing to wait for daybreak, there would be no question as to what they should do.

"Our men know the city, swordmaster," he said, trying to sound confident. "Braedon's soldiers may be established there now, but the city has been home to many of our warriors since they were children. I believe we can pursue them now without placing the men in too much danger."

"Very well, my lord." He nodded once—it took Renald a moment to recognize it as a bow—and started to walk away.

Is that what you would have done? he wanted to ask. *Am I doing the right thing?* But he didn't dare show the man how uncertain he was, how ill-equipped to be leading this army to war. And then a thought came to him, one that turned his innards to water and nearly made his knees buckle. He would be leading this charge into the city. How could he not? He almost ran after the swordmaster to tell him that he had changed his mind, that they would wait for daybreak. But did he really want to lead a charge into an ordered defense, one that the emperor's captains had all night to plan?

Ean have pity, what have I done?

"Are you well, my lord?"

Renald turned so quickly that he nearly lost his balance.

Pillad was standing just beside him, having snuck up on him like a cat stalking prey.

"Yes, I'm fine," the duke said, a bit too quickly.

"You look pale, my lord."

"A trick of the light, no doubt. As I said, I'm fine." He had no desire to be anywhere near this man just now. "We ride into battle within the hour. We'll be attacking the Braedony strongholds in the city. I want you with the healers. I'm sure they're already tending to the men who were wounded in our first assault. You should find them now."

"But, my lord—"

"You'll have an opportunity to ride with me when we go south to the Moorlands. Right now I want you with the healers. Do I make myself clear?"

"Of course, my lord." The Qirsi bowed, his expression revealing little. He looked like he might say more, but instead he withdrew, descending the tower stairs.

Renald intended to go that same way, but he waited until he was certain that Pillad had reached the bottom of the winding stairway. He could feel some of the archers watching him, but he kept his eyes fixed on the city. When he finally left the ramparts, he welcomed the solitude of the tower stairs as he would rain on a sweltering day. He had to resist an urge to leave the stairs at the castle's second level and take to his quarters until the fighting was over. Reaching the bottom of the stairs, he stepped into the ward and was greeted by a sight that did little to calm his nerves.

The wounded had been brought back into the castle and placed on pallets in the ward, where the Qirsi healers were now ministering to their wounds. Pillad was among the healers, looking slightly lost, and flinching at much of what he saw.

The duke hurried past, keeping his eyes trained on the ground. Still, he could hear the moans and cries of the injured men, and he nearly gagged on the smell of the herbmaster's tonics and poultices. When at last he entered the lower ward, he rested, leaning against the stone wall and trying to slow his pulse. Nearby, the people of his city, who had been driven from their homes, eyed him with curiosity, and, he thought, some contempt. He tried to ignore them, and when he couldn't, he started across the ward. At the far end of the courtyard, near the main gate, Ewan was mustering his soldiers, barking commands and sending his captains scurrying in all directions. He didn't stop when he saw the duke, but he did stride in Renald's direction, even as he continued to yell at his men.

Stopping beside the duke, he asked in a low voice, "Is everything all right, my lord?"

For a moment, Renald considered telling the swordmaster that he had decided to put off the assault until dawn, but he wasn't any more certain about the wisdom of that course of action than he was about the one they were on already.

"I was going to ask you the same," he said at last.

"My lord?"

"I sensed before, on the ramparts, that you preferred to wait for dawn. If you feel strongly that we should, I'll heed your counsel."

Ewan turned his back on the soldiers. "Please turn as well, my lord. I don't want the men to know what we're saying."

Renald turned, feeling somewhat foolish standing shoulder to shoulder with the swordmaster, facing the castle wall.

"If you're at all uncertain, my lord, we shouldn't attack. The men will sense it, and their confidence will suffer."

Of course I'm uncertain! I don't know what I'm doing! "I merely meant to ask if you disagree with my decision."

"It's not my place to disagree."

"Well, damn it, I'm making it your place!" The duke winced at what he heard in his voice. "Forgive me, Ewan. I don't . . . I don't have a great deal of experience with such matters."

"None of us do, my lord. But we've begun to ready the men. To change our tactics now would be to put doubts in their minds. I'd rather not do that."

"So we march tonight."

"I believe we should."

"Very well."

"Is there anything else, my lord?"

"The archers are still atop the walls. Shouldn't they be marching with us?"

"I thought to leave them on the battlements, my lord. I'm having oil and tar brought to them now. In case the empire's men circle behind us and try to take the castle, I want the archers ready. I've instructed them to fire flaming arrows in case of attack. That will alert us to the danger, and we can return here and see to the defense of the fortress."

Renald regarded the man, not bothering to mask his admiration. "Very impressive, swordmaster. Very impressive indeed."

"Thank you, my lord. Now if I may return to the men, I'll have them ready to march within the hour."

True to his word, Ewan and his soldiers were ready to march from the castle just as the bells rang in the city's Sanctuary of Amon, marking what would have been the gate close had the Braedony army not held all the city gates. Renald and the swordmaster sat atop mounts at the head of the column, and now the duke raised his sword, silencing his men.

"I know that you've waited a long time for this night," he said, his voice echoing off the stone walls. "Believe it or not, so have I. We fight for our people, for our city, for our realm. Let the men of Braedon learn the peril of awakening the Galdasten eagle! Let them feel the bite of our steel and rue the day they set foot on our hallowed land! Let them scurry to their ships like vermin and leave these shores forever!" He reared his mount, holding his sword high again. "For Galdasten!" he cried.

And his men called out as one, "For Galdasten!" the might of their voices threatening to topple the castle. Even the city folk cheered.

Renald felt a chill go down his spine, and he wished that Elspeth could have seen him, armed, astride his horse, leading these fine men to war. The thought was fleeting, however, replaced as they rode through the castle gate and into the lane leading down to the city, by the same debilitating fear he had felt earlier, atop the walls.

"Well done, my lord," Ewan said, his voice low.

Renald merely nodded, unable to speak.

"Stay close to me, my lord, and together we'll see this enemy defeated. I'll do all I can to keep you safe."

At that, he glanced at the man, a grateful smile on his lips. "Thank you, Ewan."

They rode slowly, keeping pace with the soldiers, who were on foot. Still, it wasn't long—not nearly long enough, as far as the duke was concerned—before they were in the heart of the city, making their way past a burned-out smithy and a tavern that seemed eerily quiet. The marketplace was completely empty, save for a stray dog that sniffed about for scraps of food. They saw no signs at all of the enemy.

Ewan had appeared composed as they approached the city, but once on its lanes, he had grown increasingly tense. He was frowning now, shaking his head.

"I don't like this at all," he said under his breath. Renald wondered if he was keeping his voice down for the sake of his men, or to keep the empire's soldiers from overhearing. "We should have seen them by now."

"You've said all along that you were surprised they left so few men in the city. Perhaps they saw how large a force we brought, and retreated to their ships."

"I suppose it's possible," the swordmaster said, but Renald could tell that he didn't really believe this, that he was merely humoring the duke. He continued to glance about anxiously, as if expecting an attack at any moment.

In the next instant it came. An arrow buried itself in Ewan's shoulder, tearing a gasp from the man. Before the duke had time to act a second barb hit Renald in the thigh, the pain stealing his breath. An instant later, arrows were whistling all around them. It was as if they had disturbed a nest of hornets.

"Shields!" the swordmaster roared through clenched teeth. "Take cover!"

The men broke formation, scattering in all directions. And even as the arrows continued to fly, Renald heard the ring of steel and saw that the enemy had been waiting for his army to do just this. Abruptly he was surrounded by a melee. Everywhere he looked, men were fighting and falling. Soldiers in

Braedon's gold and red pressed toward him, and he hacked at them with his blade, making his horse rear again and again so as to keep them at a distance. Ewan battled as best he could, though he had taken the arrow in the right shoulder and so was forced to fight with his weaker hand.

Another arrow struck the duke's shield and others streaked past him, making him cringe repeatedly. He would have liked to jump off his horse—as it was he presented Braedon's bowmen with an inviting target—but he didn't dare descend into the maelstrom of steel and flesh that swirled all around him. All he could do was fight, clinging desperately to his mount with his legs, the wound in his thigh screaming agony, his back and buttocks aching, his sword arm flailing at the enemy time and again until the muscles in his shoulder seemed to be aflame. Time came to be measured by the rise and fall of his blade. He thought nothing of the realm or the throne or the renegade Qirsi. He cared only for his own survival, not for years to come, nor even for this night, but for each moment as it passed. Would he live long enough to kill this man in gold and red who sought to pull him off his mount? Would he survive the next volley of Braedony arrows? Would the next pulse of anguish from his leg make him fall to the street?

He had thought to lead Galdasten's army into battle, but there was nothing for him to do other than live and fight; there was no command he could give, no plan he could follow. All around him, men fought and died. They would decide the outcome of this conflict; in pairs and skirmishes they would write the history of Galdasten's war. Even in pain, in battle fury, in this madness that passed for war, Renald had the sense to see that it had always been thus, that his forebears who claimed war's glory as their own had done little more than live to declare victory. The realization sobered and humbled him, made his struggle more bearable even as it forced him to admit that its outcome mattered little. And still he fought on.

After a time that shaded toward eternity, it occurred to the duke that there were fewer men around him, that he had more room in which to turn his mount, and that the clashing of swords and cries of dying soldiers had somewhat abated.

Ewan was still beside him, his face damp with sweat, his skin ashen and his lips shading to blue. The arrow was still in his shoulder and a second jutted from his right side, blood staining his shirt of mail. His grey eyes had a glazed look to them, and yet he continued to fight, turning his horse in circles, looking for more of the enemy to strike.

"Swordmaster!" Renald called. And when the man stared back at him, seeming not to recognize his face, he said, "Ewan."

The man blinked and looked at him again, tottering in his saddle. "My lord," he said, his voice weary and hoarse.

"You need a healer."

"No, my lord. I'm all right."

"I think it's ending. I can't tell who's won, but the fighting appears to have ebbed."

Ewan glanced up and down the street, nodding. He sat a bit straighter in his saddle, the color returning to his cheeks. It almost seemed that he drew strength from the mere suggestion that the fighting might be over. "We've won."

"You know this?"

The swordmaster faced him again. "You and I are alive. We wouldn't be if your army had been defeated."

Indeed, the arrows had stopped flying, and now soldiers began to wander back into the lane, all of them wearing the bronze and black of Galdasten. One of the captains approached Renald and the swordmaster, a deep gash on his upper arm, and several smaller ones on his face, hands, and neck.

Ewan sheathed his sword, grimacing at even this small movement. "Report," he said.

"Most of the enemy are dead, sir. Those who still live have fled to their ships. Some of our men pursued them—there's still fighting at the piers."

"And our losses?"

"I don't know for certain yet. If I had to guess, I'd say several hundred, but fewer than half."

"All right, Captain. Go back to the piers. Tell the men there to let the rest go. We've won already; I don't want to lose any more men. Then get yourself to a healer."

"Yes, sir." He looked at the duke and bowed. "For Galdasten, my lord."

Renald nodded. "Thank you, Captain."

"You need a healer, too, my lord," Ewan said, as the man walked back toward the quays.

"No more than you do."

"Shall we go together, then?"

"That would be fine. Pillad can minister to us both."

Ewan grimaced again. It took Renald a moment to realize that he was grinning. "Yes, my lord."

They found a soldier who had come through the fighting relatively unscathed and sent him back to the castle to fetch the healers.

"Assuming that your captain was right," the duke said after the man had gone, "and that we lost several hundred men, how long will it be before we can march to the Moorlands?"

"It depends upon how many men you wish to take, my lord. If you'll be satisfied to take seven or eight hundred, we can leave in three days. Perhaps two, if the quartermaster works quickly."

"Then let's plan on that." Renald glanced down at the arrow protruding from his thigh. His leggings were soaked with blood, and the wound throbbed mercilessly. He could hardly believe that he was already contemplating his next battle, but what choice did he have? For better or worse, at long last, he had become a warrior.

Chapter
Eight

Curtell, Braedon

On the morning following their capture of the emperor's palace, Dusaan sent Nitara and several of the other ministers to Curtell City with instructions to scour the inns and taverns and marketplace for all the Qirsi they could find.

"For now, you're simply to tell them that the emperor's high chancellor wishes to speak with them," he said, sitting in the middle of what had been Harel's imperial chamber.

Nitara had stared back at him, her pale eyes wide, still so afraid of giving offense. "But Weaver, they know that you've taken the palace. Everyone does. Many will have heard that you're . . . that you lead our movement."

"They still know me as the high chancellor," he told her, keeping his voice low so that she would know that he wasn't angry. "And I'm not ready to announce myself as Weaver to all in Curtell."

"What if the Qirsi refuse to come with us?" another asked.

The Weaver considered this briefly. "For now, that's their right, though if they've heard of our victory over Harel's guards, I don't think they'll refuse you. Now go."

Nitara had bowed then, lovely and eager to please, despite her fear of him, and she had led her small band of Qirsi out into the lanes of the imperial city.

A short time later, Gorlan came to him, a grin on his lean face. "The emperor is demanding to speak with you."

Dusaan barely looked up from the treasury accountings— not much had changed in the short time they had been out of his control, but he wanted to make certain he knew just how much gold was at his disposal.

"Is that so?" he said evenly. "About what?"

"I believe he's dissatisfied with his quarters."

At that Dusaan did look up, nearly laughing aloud. "You're not serious."

"Yes, Weaver, I am. He's also demanding a healer. It seems you wounded him last night."

He shook his head and turned his attention back to the accountings. "I'll deal with it later. In the meantime, take some of the others and gather whatever weapons are left in the guard house and armory."

"Weapons, Weaver? Do you mean to destroy them?"

"No. I plan to use them."

"But our magic—"

"I mean to lead a conquering army, Minister." He had decided that he would allow the Qirsi to keep their titles for now. For many of the older ones, the changes of the past few days had been difficult; best to let them hold on to a few harmless remnants of the old ways. "While you and I know that our magic is the only weapon we need, the Eandi do not. I want them to see us as warriors. Besides, it never hurts to be too careful. I happen to be quite skilled with a blade, and I expect the same of those who serve me."

"Yes, Weaver. I'll do it right away."

Dusaan had much to occupy his day, and even had he not, he would have gone out of his way to make Harel wait. He wasn't even certain he ought to go to the man at all, but in the end curiosity got the better of him. Late in the day, some time after the ringing of the prior's bells, the Weaver made his way to the prison tower.

There were no Eandi guards in the corridor of course—all who had survived the previous day's battle were gone—and Dusaan hadn't enough Qirsi to leave even one to watch over the emperor. In all likelihood, Harel had been alone in his chamber since Gorlan's visit several hours before. Even before he opened the door to the sparse, round chamber, Dusaan knew that the emperor would be in a foul temper. He would enjoy this.

"It's about time!" Harel said, as soon as the Weaver turned the lock. "I called for you hours ago!"

Dusaan stepped inside, saying nothing, but walking a slow circle around the perimeter of the emperor's prison. A platter of half-eaten food sat on the floor near the door—a rind of hard cheese, a few scraps of stale bread, and a small, empty cup that might once have held water. Closer to the lone window, a chamber pot sat unattended, foul-smelling and buzzing with flies. Dusaan wrinkled his nose as he walked past.

"You see what I've had to put up with?"

The Weaver said nothing. Pausing by the window, he gazed down on the palace courtyard where the battle had taken place the day before. His Qirsi had used fire magic to dispose of the bodies, but the soldiers' weaponry still lay in an enormous pile on the bright grass.

"They've brought me only the one meal."

Dusaan turned to face the man. Harel looked a mess, his round face flushed, his brown curls sticking out at odd angles, his imperial robes disheveled.

"There's little I can do about your food," the Weaver said. "It seems your kitchenmaster and all your cooks have fled the palace."

Harel held up his hand, which was swollen and purple around the little finger, the bone of which Dusaan had snapped the previous night. "And what of the healers? Surely your own people didn't flee."

"No, they didn't. But they've been busy attending to other matters."

"Other matters?" the emperor repeated, his voice rising.

"Yes. But allow me."

Dusaan crossed to where Harel stood, and gently taking hold of his maimed hand, closed his eyes and began to mend the bone with his healing magic. It was a clean break and a small bone—it healed quickly. After just a few moments he looked at Harel again and released his hand. "Is that better?"

The emperor gazed at his hand with unconcealed wonder. "Yes, it is. Thank y—"

The dry sound of cracking bone echoed in the chamber.

Harel dropped to his knees with a shriek, clutching his arm to his chest and whimpering like a beaten dog.

Dusaan stood over him, fighting an urge to kick him in the gut. "I told you last night that if you defied me again I'd break your arm. Next time it will be your neck."

"But all I did—"

"Don't ever summon me again. It's not your place to make demands of me or my Qirsi. You're no longer emperor, Harel, and I'm no longer your chancellor. You ceded the realm to me, in writing. I am your sovereign, and I will be treated as such. Do you understand?"

Harel nodded.

"Good." Dusaan started for the door.

"But what about my food? And my arm? What about . . . ?" He glanced at the chamber pot. "What about that?"

"If I think of it, I'll send a healer for your arm. As for the rest, so long as you don't eat, the pot shouldn't be a problem."

He let himself out of the chamber to the sound of the emperor's sobbing, and descended the stairs. When he reached the courtyard, Nitara was there with the five Qirsi who had accompanied her, and well over a hundred more. Dusaan strode to where she stood smiling at him, her pride evident in her stance, the squared shoulders and straight back. He had never seen her look more beautiful.

"Report," the Weaver said.

"We've brought one hundred and fifty-four Qirsi to serve you, Weaver. There were even more who were willing, but many were the husbands and wives of those you see before you, and they had children who couldn't be left alone."

"Of course. Did you have any trouble?"

"Just a bit at first. We encountered a group of soldiers, the emperor's men. They attacked us, but B'Serre used fire magic on their leader, and the rest ran off. We saw them again later, but by then we were a far larger group—they didn't dare come near us."

"Very good, Minister. Very good indeed."

She fairly beamed as he stepped past her to address the newcomers.

"Welcome," he said, opening his arms wide, "to what is now my palace, the seat of power for what will soon be a Qirsi empire extending the length and breadth of the Forelands. I know that a great deal has happened here in the past day, and no doubt you've heard much from the former emperor's soldiers. You have questions, I'm sure. I'll be happy to tell you what I can."

For several moments no one said anything. Most of the Qirsi before him simply stared at the ground, fidgeting like embarrassed children. After a time, however, one man stepped out from the middle of the group, glancing about nervously, but eventually meeting Dusaan's gaze. He looked old, particularly for a Qirsi. He was bald save for a few wisps of white hair that clung to the back of his head, and his face was bony and thin. Yet his eyes were bright, the color of elm leaves during the harvest, and he narrowed them now as he regarded the high chancellor.

"Are you really a Weaver, like they say?"

"Yes, I am."

"How can we know that for sure?"

"What's your name, friend?"

He hesitated, but only for an instant. "Creved jal Winza."

"And you're a healer, aren't you, Creved?"

"You've heard of me?"

"No. I sense that you have healing magic, and so I assumed."

"You sensed—?"

"A Weaver can do that. You also have language of beasts. Those are two of the deeper magics. How is it that you never ended up in an Eandi court?"

At first the man gave no response. He merely stared back at Dusaan, without a trace of the skepticism he had exuded just moments before. "I . . . I never wished to serve, my . . . your . . ."

"Call me Weaver."

"Yes, Weaver, thank you. And besides, Eandi nobles seek out gleaners. They want their ministers to be able to see the future."

"Quite right, Creved. Isn't it fascinating," he went on,

speaking to all of them now, "that the Eandi value us precisely for the magic we know to be the least potent. Don't get me wrong. Gleaning is a talent, and gleaners will be as welcome as all other Qirsi in the new world we're building. But the Eandi want gleaners for their courts and for their festival tents. Yet gleaning is not one of the deep magics—all of us know this. Perhaps they do as well. They fear our powers. They use what they can, but they fear the rest, which is why for nearly nine hundred years, they have made us their servants, their entertainers, objects of curiosity and contempt." He smiled. "Well, those days are over." He looked at the healer again. "You said something else that interested me, Creved. You said that you never wished to serve in their courts. Why not?"

The man shrugged, looking afraid, as if he thought that he had said something wrong. "I don't know, Weaver. I just . . . I don't know."

"It's all right, Creved. For too long, our people have willingly given ourselves over to the Eandi. We need more men and women like this fine healer, who can see the virtue of using magic simply because it is our gift, the source of our distinctiveness and our strength."

Was it just his imagination, or were the others staring at this old healer with admiration and envy, wishing that they, too, might earn the Weaver's praise? He eyed the men and women Nitara had brought him, divining their powers, searching for any who looked like they might betray him. Like Creved, most of them appeared so awed by the notion of serving a Weaver that Dusaan knew he had nothing to fear from them. One or two remained wary, but this was to be expected.

Nearly all of those standing before him possessed only one or two powers; a few wielded three. Many of the men and women were healers, and a good number of the others possessed fire magic. There were, of course, quite a few gleaners. And a small number wielded the greater magics. Several had mists and winds, a few, like Creved, had language of beasts, and seven were shapers.

"All of you will serve our cause in some capacity. For

many of you that will mean helping to protect and maintain this palace. Others among you will accompany me across the Strait of Wantrae to Eibithar, where we will wield our powers as one and destroy the armies of the Eandi courts. Whatever your role in this struggle, I promise you that you will be paid in gold, that your lives will be better than you ever imagined possible under the emperor's rule, and that someday your children will thank you for what you do now." He smiled again. "Are you with me?"

"Yes, Weaver!" they answered as one, their voices resounding off the courtyard walls.

He turned to Nitara, B'Serre, and the other ministers. "Find quarters for these people and then assign them tasks. We need some in the kitchens," he said, lowering his voice. "And others, those with fire power, should be stationed as guards at the gates and in the prison tower."

Nitara nodded. "Yes, Weaver." She often spoke for the others, almost as if he had made her one of his chancellors. He didn't mind, but he found it somewhat curious, and he wondered if her fellow ministers and chancellors thought that she and Dusaan were lovers.

He pointed out the seven shapers. "Bring them to me. They'll be sailing with us to Eibithar. Oh, and send a healer to Harel. He's hurt himself again."

Dusaan returned to the imperial chamber a short time later, and was joined soon after by Nitara and the seven shapers. Five of them were old for his people—thirty years old at least, as far as he could tell, and of the two who were younger, one struck him as being somewhat less than eager to pledge himself to the Weaver's cause. This man was watching him now, a slight smirk on his oval face. He wore his white hair long and pulled back from his face, and his eyes were so pale as to be ghostlike.

"You," Dusaan said, nodding toward him. "What's your name?"

"B'Naer, High Chancellor."

Nitara cast a quick look Dusaan's way, seeming to gauge his response. The Weaver hadn't explicitly instructed the other Qirsi not to use his old title, but he felt that they should

have known. Normally he wouldn't have tolerated such an in-
discretion but in this case he decided to give the man a bit of
latitude. A very little bit.

"That's all? Just B'Naer?"

The man shifted his weight from one foot to the other, an
amused look on his face. "B'Naer jal Shenvesse."

"And from the looks of you I'd say you're a peddler."

"Close enough."

The Weaver raised an eyebrow. "A brigand then."

The smile vanished from his face.

"It's all right, B'Naer. Whatever laws you've broken were
Eandi laws. That's not to say that I won't deal harshly with
your kind now that I lead the realm, but consider this your
one opportunity to change the course of your life, to choose a
brighter path, if you will." Dusaan crossed to the emperor's
throne and sat. "Tell me, B'Naer, why do you think you're
here? What do you think you have in common with these
other six people?"

"I don't know? Are they brigands, too?"

One of them, an older woman, actually laughed out loud.

"No," the Weaver said with a smile. "They're not brigands." He eyed the man for a moment longer, and when he
shook his head, Dusaan looked at the others. "Do any of you
know?"

"You know what powers we possess," the woman answered
at last. "Are we all shapers?"

The Weaver smiled. "And your name?"

"Qidanne ja Qed, Weaver. I'm a healer in the city."

This name he did know. She wasn't just a healer—she was
the most renowned healer in all of Curtell. On several occasions the emperor had asked her to serve in the palace. Each
time she had refused him, claiming that her duties as a healer
called her into the countryside too often, and that some of
those to whom she ministered would not trust another healer.
Dusaan had long wondered if these excuses had served to
mask her dislike of the emperor. Now he felt certain that they
had.

"We're all honored to have you with us, Qidanne. Your reputation precedes you."

"Thank you, Weaver."

"You're right, of course. All of you are shapers, and as such, will prove invaluable to our movement in battle."

"In battle?" she said, frowning. "I'm no warrior, Weaver. Surely you understand that all to which I've devoted my life is at odds with the very notion of armed conflict."

"I do understand that, healer. But I know as well that the fate of our people rests with our ability to defeat the combined might of the Eandi armies. I'll need shapers to do that. The sooner I can destroy the enemy, the fewer of our people will need your talents."

"I minister to Eandi as well as Qirsi, Weaver, and though I sympathize with your movement, I can't bring myself to kill anyone, no matter the color of their eyes."

Dusaan detested cowardice, and had he sensed in her words even a hint of pretense, he would have killed her where she stood. He could tell, however, that she spoke not out of fear of being killed herself, but rather out of a true aversion to killing others, and he knew that to force this woman to fight against her will would diminish him, not only in her eyes, but in those of the men and women around her.

"Will you accompany me to the battle plain as a healer, then?"

"I will, if you will allow me to tend to all who are wounded, no matter the color of their eyes."

Dusaan gave a small laugh. "You're a difficult woman."

"Why is it, Weaver, that I'm called 'difficult,' while men who behave as I do are called 'determined' and 'strong'?"

"A fair point, healer." He nodded. "You can tend to all who are wounded, and I'll enjoy having you with me, to keep my wit honed." He eyed the others. "And what of the rest of you? Will you wield your shaping power on behalf of the Qirsi cause?"

"You mentioned gold before," the brigand said, a sly look on his handsome face. "Just how much will our role in this battle—?"

Before he could finish, Dusaan had taken hold of his shaping power and used it to press on the man's temples. B'Naer gasped at the pain, both hands gripping his head. The Weaver was willing to tolerate a good deal from a woman like Qi-danne. But this man was another matter entirely.

"This is not a negotiation, cousin. The healer has earned some consideration, even from me. You haven't. Push me too far, and you'll learn what it is to face the wrath of a Weaver."

He maintained his grip on the brigand's magic for a moment longer, then released him. B'Naer toppled to the floor, his chest heaving, his eyes squeezed shut. The other Qirsi were gaping at Dusaan, all of them looking awed and terrified. In a way, the brigand had done him a service. Qidanne had given him the opportunity to show his compassion, his willingness to accommodate those who served him well. B'-Naer had allowed him to demonstrate what happened to those who defied him. He knew that it wouldn't take long before all the Qirsi who had come to the palace that day heard of both the depth of his kindness and the power of his rage.

"Now, I'll ask all of you again," he said. "Will you join me in this fight against the Eandi?"

"Yes, Weaver." They spoke as one, without the enthusiasm that all the Qirsi had shown in the courtyard, but with a tone of reverence that Dusaan found quite satisfying.

"Good. We leave for Ayvencalde in two or three days. Until then, you're to do as Nitara commands. In my absence, in all matters of importance, she speaks with my authority." He glanced at Nitara, who nodded in return. "You may go." They began to file out of the chamber. "A word please, B'Naer."

The brigand halted, glancing toward the door as if considering whether he might be better off fleeing. The others looked back at him, and judging from their expressions, they could well have been thinking the same thing.

B'Naer walked slowly back to the center of the chamber, stopping at last just before the Weaver's throne and flinching slightly when the door clicked shut behind him.

"I hurt you," Dusaan said.

"Yes, Weaver."

"And now you think I'm going to kill you."

"Aren't you?"

"That depends in large part on you. Even as high chancellor to the fat oaf who used to sit in this chair, I grew accustomed to people heeding my commands and speaking to me with deference. If you can do so from this day forward, you'll live. If not, your death will serve as a lesson to others foolish enough to defy me."

"Of course, Weaver. I'll do as you say."

Dusaan reached for him so swiftly, wrapping a powerful hand around the man's throat, that the brigand had no time to react. He grabbed for the Weaver's hand, no doubt to try and break Dusaan's grip. After a moment, however, he appeared to think better of this.

"You'll find, B'Naer, that I don't take kindly to being humored. I'm not some merchant ripe for being cheated, nor am I a simpleminded Eandi soldier to be mollified with a smile and a kind word. I'm the most powerful man you've ever met, and the most intelligent as well. Anger me again, and I will kill you. You have my word on that. Do I make myself clear?"

B'Naer nodded, his pale eyes wide.

Dusaan let go of the man's neck, sitting back in his throne. "What did you do as a brigand?"

"What do you mean?"

"Well, you must have had a specialty. Men of your sort usually do. Isn't that so?"

"Yes, Weaver." His face colored. "I . . . I began as a road thief. Later I turned to city thieving, first in Refte, then in Ayvencalde, and finally here."

"I see. How does a man choose such a profession, B'Naer? Surely your Determining didn't show you as a brigand."

The man smiled—it almost seemed he couldn't help himself. "No, Weaver, but my Fating did. I'm good with a blade, and I'm strong for a Qirsi. And having shaping power made it that much easier to take care of myself."

"Yes, I'm sure it did," the Weaver said, narrowing his eyes, staring intently at this man before him. He couldn't deny that there was need in his army for men like this one. He had more than enough ministers and healers; shouldn't he have a brigand or two as well, men who could be ruthless, perhaps even cruel? After all, soon they would be marching to war. "I think I'm glad you're here, B'Naer. I sense that you may prove useful to me yet."

The brigand grinned.

They rode from the palace three days later, seventy strong— a laughably small army by Eandi standards, but powerful enough to topple every fortress in the Forelands if victory demanded it. To her delight, Nitara rode with the Weaver at the head of their column. The other chancellors and ministers— Gorlan, Rov, B'Serre, and the rest—followed just behind them, and they, in turn, were trailed by those newly enlisted in the Weaver's cause. All told, there were ten shapers in their ranks, as well as twenty who had language of beasts, nearly thirty who could summon mists and winds, dozens of others who could call forth a killing fire, and a good number of healers who would prove of great value when the fighting began.

And, of course, they had the Weaver, who could wield their power as a single weapon more fearsome than any that had been seen in the Forelands for nine centuries. The armies of Eibithar and Aneira and Sanbira had their kings and queens, but what were these sovereigns other than mere men and women? Perhaps they inspired their soldiers to fight and die with a bit more courage than the pathetic souls would muster otherwise. But beyond that, they were nothing; their crowns and thrones signified nothing. To Nitara and the other Qirsi, Dusaan jal Kania was their strength and their hope, their power and intelligence, the link to their past and the path to their future. He was everything—king, commander, god. Nitara would have followed him into Bian's Underrealm to face hordes of demons and wraiths if only he asked it of her, and though others might not have loved him as she did, the minister sensed that many in their army had already devoted themselves wholly to him and his cause.

They thundered across the moor toward the city of Ayvencalde, knowing that they might meet resistance there from the Eandi lord, who had been a close ally of the emperor. They needed only to reach the pier and seize a ship, but the

Weaver made it clear that they would not shy away from a battle if the lord decided to challenge them.

"No doubt he's heard of what happened in Curtell," Dusaan told them before they left the palace. "He'll think this no more than a rebellion, easily beaten back by a show of force. I intend to prove him wrong and then add the willing among Ayvencalde's Qirsi to our army."

Pushing their mounts to the limits of the beasts' endurance, the Weaver and his army were able to cross the moor in only two days, coming within sight of Ayvencalde Castle's great towers a short time before dusk on the second day. There, on the plain, positioned just before the city walls, the lord was waiting for them, an army of more than a thousand men behind him, their weapons gleaming gold in the dying sunlight.

The Weaver led his Qirsi directly toward the lord and his men, only halting when he was well within range of Ayvencalde's archers.

"Your advance ends here, High Chancellor," the lord said, his square face ruddy, as if he had been sitting in the sun and wind for much of the day. "I will not allow you to set foot in my city, nor will I let you take your evil magic to any other lordship in the realm. You may have caught the emperor unawares, but that's not likely to happen again."

Dusaan glanced back at the sun, as if judging the hours left until nightfall. "I haven't time for this, Lord Ayvencalde. Surrender now and let us pass, or you and your men will be destroyed."

The lord actually laughed. "You don't suffer for a lack of confidence, do you, High Chancellor?" His smile vanished and he raised a hand. "Bowmen!"

Several hundred archers stepped forward, readying their bows.

"You were warned," the Weaver said, his voice even and devoid of regret. "We'll use fire," he said more quietly, glancing back at the other Qirsi.

For Nitara, who didn't have fire magic, there was nothing to do but watch. The Weaver closed his eyes and stretched forth a rigid hand. The plain was eerily silent—even the

Eandi seemed to be waiting, as if frightened of what would come next, but too fascinated to prevent it. Slowly, as if emerging from the sunlight, a gleaming sphere began to take shape just in front of the Weaver. It appeared to Nitara that he had summoned a bright yellow star from beyond the sky. As she watched, the ball gathered strength, brightening, growing larger, until it seethed and churned like a mighty river in flood.

Ayvencalde shouted to his archers again, and the minister saw them draw back the cords of their bows. Before they could loose their arrows, though, the ball of flame surged forward, flattening as it went, so that it struck the lord and his soldiers as might a great fiery sword. They didn't even scream. Every man in the army was cut down and consumed in the storm of flame. Only the lord, who had been sitting atop his mount, was spared, and he lay sprawled on the ground, dazed, his leg bent beneath his body at an impossible angle. The horse was dead, its carcass blackened and smoking a short distance from the lord.

Slowly, the Weaver dismounted and walked to where the noble lay, drawing his sword as he went.

"You should have listened," Dusaan said, resting the point of his sword on Ayvencalde's chest.

"You'll never prevail," the lord said, glaring up at him. "You may have won today, but someone will stop you."

Dusaan smiled. "You're wrong." And he thrust the blade into the noble's heart. Pulling the sword free, he stooped to wipe the blood from the shining steel, then he sheathed his weapon and walked back to his horse. "Victory is ours again," he said. "Do you see now that we can't be beaten, that the might of Eandi armies is nothing against our power?"

"Yes, Weaver."

"We'll ride into the city and find as many Qirsi as we can. But we won't tarry here long. I want to be sailing by morning."

He swung himself into the saddle once more and they rode toward the city gates. As they drew near, a swarm of arrows rose into the sky and began to fall toward them. Instantly, Nitara felt something tugging at her mind and a moment later, she sensed the Weaver drawing upon her magic. A great wind stirred from the grasses, building rapidly until it howled in the stones of the city wall, though Nitara's hair barely stirred. The arrows were beaten back, dropping harmlessly to the ground in front of them.

Nitara nearly laughed aloud. It seemed that their power knew no bounds. Never had she felt so close to her people, and glancing back at her companions she saw mirrored in their faces the same joy and wonder at what they had become. They continued to advance on the gate, and as they did, she heard a great rumbling, as from an approaching thunderstorm, and in a billowing cloud of dust, the city wall collapsed on either side of the gate, sending the Eandi archers stationed there tumbling to the ground.

Moments later the Qirsi army entered the city unopposed. They divided into smaller groups and navigated Ayvencalde's narrow stone lanes in search of others to join their cause. Nitara remained with the Weaver, who sat straight-backed atop his horse like a conqueror. His face, though, was covered with a fine sheen of sweat, and she could see that he had tired himself.

"Shall we rest, Weaver?" she asked, her voice barely more than a whisper.

His eyes snapped toward her, blazing angrily. Then his gaze softened and he shook his head. "I'm fine. And in the next several days I'll be taxed far beyond this. I need to be ready."

More than anything she wanted to reach out and touch his face, to run her hands through his wild hair and feel the strength of his shoulders and chest. But she merely nodded. "Yes, Weaver."

Word of what the Weaver's army had done to Lord Ayvencalde and his men spread swiftly through the city. A few of the soldiers who remained chose to fight the Qirsi invaders, and all of them perished. Most fled, however, and with them many of Ayvencalde's Eandi inhabitants. The city's Qirsi—who numbered slightly over one hundred—greeted the Weaver and the others warily, but quickly pledged themselves to Dusaan's cause. As with the Qirsi in the imperial city, most of them were healers and gleaners. A good number had fire magic and a few possessed one or more of the deeper magics.

After addressing them briefly, telling them of his coming battle with the armies of the Forelands and the fine future his victory would bring, he instructed almost all of them to remain in Ayvencalde and protect it from any attack that might come from other Eandi courts in Braedon. Four of the city's Qirsi were shapers, and fourteen had mists and winds. These he added to his army.

He led his force to the Ayvencalde piers and quickly took control of one of the lord's great war ships. A group of Qirsi went below into the hold and rowed the ship free of the docks, while others held flames aloft to light their way through Ayvencalde's shallow harbor. Once free of the quays, they raised the vessel's sails.

A breeze freshened from the west, and the ship started across the Scabbard toward the coast of Eibithar.

"Forgive me, Weaver," Nitara said, approaching him, and lowering her gaze, "but I can summon a wind to take us across the Scabbard. So can any other Qirsi who has mists and winds. You should rest."

He regarded her briefly, his expression mild. "You serve me well."

"Yes, Weaver."

The wind died away. "All right then. Share the burden with others. I don't want any of you growing too weary. Steer us east of Cormorant Island, and then follow the Eibithar shore toward Falcon Bay. Wake me when we're close enough to see . Braedon's war ships."

"Yes, Weaver."

He started to walk away, then paused, touching her cheek with a gentle hand. It seemed to Nitara that he summoned a soft flame, so great was the warmth that traveled through her body during that brief caress. A moment later he moved on, leaving her shivering in the cool night air as she gazed after him.

The ship sailed the glasslike waters of the Scabbard throughout what remained of the night, no doubt presenting a strange sight to those who saw her from the shores of Braedon and Eibithar. It was a windless night, still as death, and yet the vessel skimmed across the brine like a shearwater, her sails full, her bow carving the surface of the inlet. Nitara summoned the wind herself for some time, before giving over to Gorlan. He, in turn, passed the task to one of the men recruited in Curtell City, who then gave way to a woman from Ayvencalde. All told, seven summoned winds to propel the ship toward Falcon Bay. By the time morning broke and the Weaver returned to the deck, they were well past Cormorant Island. Wantrae Island loomed before them, pale blue in the early morning light. The waters remained calm, the sky clear. They would have no trouble with the weather.

"You've done well," the Weaver said after looking about for some time, as if to determine their position. "But we have need of haste." All of them were watching him. It seemed to Nitara that the others couldn't help themselves. Certainly she couldn't. He turned to her now, beckoning to her with a gesture. Crossing to where he stood, she bowed, then waited.

"Open yourself to me," he commanded, his voice low.

A moment later, she felt him touch her mind, and there arose around her a gale the likes of which none of the Qirsi, herself included, had been able to raise alone. The ship leaped forward, leaning heavily alee, and the others scrambled to grab hold of something.

"I want others with winds to join us here," Dusaan called over the rush of the wind he had summoned. Several stepped forward, and the gale began to strengthen, until it seemed that the ship would tear itself apart. The hull held, however, as did the sail, and the Weaver's windstorm propelled them past Eibithar's coastline and the islands of the upper Scabbard as if the ship were being pulled by a team of Sanbiri stallions.

Nitara knew that she should be tiring—a Qirsi's powers were finite. To tax oneself beyond endurance was to risk utter exhaustion, even illness or death. Yet with the Weaver wielding her magic for her, blending it with his own and that of the other Qirsi, she hardly grew weary. She might have been doing gleanings in a festival tent for all the effort the Weaver required of her. Glancing at the others, she saw them smiling with wonder at the wind they had called forth. At midday they rested, taking a meal and speaking of how easy it had been to drive the ship toward Galdasten. Clearly the Weaver had been taxed far more than had they. As soon as they stopped, he went below deck, his face wan and damp. Nitara wanted to follow, but she knew that he didn't want her with him. Instead she waited with the others, and before long Dusaan returned, looking refreshed.

"Shall we continue?" was all he said. Soon they were cutting through the tide once more, gliding beneath Curgh Castle, perched atop the rocky cliffs above them, and past the sheer cliffs of Eibithar's northwest coast.

Late in the day, as they approached the mouth of Falcon Bay, Nitara saw the Braedony war ships, sails lowered and sweeps extended for combat, the red and gold painted on their bows glowing in the light of the setting sun. Beyond them, arrayed as if for battle, a second set of ships advanced, their sails lowered as well.

She glanced at the Weaver, wondering if he had expected this, afraid that perhaps he hadn't.

"The Wethy fleet," he said. "No doubt the men and women of Galdasten believe their salvation is at hand. If any ships can best those of the empire, Wethyrn's can." He smiled. "It doesn't matter."

They sailed on, steering toward the heart of the emperor's navy, and as they drew close, the Weaver strengthened his gale still more, sending it beyond the sails of the Qirsi vessel so that it battered the ships of Braedon. At first the men of the emperor's fleet ignored the Qirsi vessel. It was but one boat and the soldiers were far more concerned with the strange, powerful wind that had struck at them so suddenly. But as the Weaver's ship bore down on them, the soldiers finally noticed. Rowing furiously, the oarsmen on several of the vessels managed to turn their boats toward the Qirsi ship, increasing their speed as if to ram. As the distance between the ships closed, one of the men on the lead vessel recognized Dusaan.

"High Chancellor!" he called, raising a hand in greeting, his face a mask of puzzlement.

"Shapers," the Weaver said without raising his voice. Immediately the shapers stepped forward, and an instant later, the advancing ships crumpled, as if some unseen fist had hammered down upon them. Men tumbled into the cold waters of the bay, some of them screaming, others too shocked to make any sound at all.

Too late, the fleet captains tried to turn their vessels to meet this new challenge. The Weaver and his shapers destroyed these ships as easily as they had the others, spilling more bodies into the sea, turning Braedon's vaunted navy into little more than jagged scraps of wood and shattered oars. Still the Qirsi ship sailed on, barely slowing as it passed by the ruins of the fleet.

"Fire," Dusaan said, and more Qirsi moved to stand near him.

The men on the Wethy vessels, who had cheered upon seeing the Braedony ships smashed, now began to shout warnings to one another. A thin line of golden flame appeared on the surface of the water and began to roll toward Wethyrn's navy, building like a wave as it went, until it towered above the vessels, menacing them like some demon sent by the fire goddess. The Wethy oarsmen tried to reverse course and outrun the wall of fire, but to no avail. The blaze crashed down upon them, blackening wood and flesh alike, making the water hiss and seethe, sending great clouds of steam into the sky.

The ship slowed and the wind around them diminished until it was but a faint breeze. The Weaver looked weary again, but he wore a grim smile as he surveyed the waters around them.

Eandi soldiers would have cheered after such a victory, but the Qirsi standing near the Weaver made not a sound. They seemed awed by what they had done, perhaps even a bit frightened, though Nitara felt certain that this would pass.

"What now, Weaver?" B'Serre asked, her voice barely carrying over the sound of water lapping at the sides of the ship.

"Now, I rest, and those of you with mists and winds steer us into the port of Galdasten. If you meet resistance, call for me. Otherwise, come for me when we've tied on to the pier.

We'll take Galdasten tonight. Two of my chancellors await us in the city, to join our assault on the castle and add their number to my army. Tomorrow we ride to the Moorlands. And there, we'll destroy what's left of the Eandi armies."

Chapter
Nine

Galdasten, Eibithar

t had been two days since Renald led his soldiers out of the castle in pursuit of Braedon's army, four since he defied her, choosing to follow the counsel of his fool of a swordmaster and the first minister who, Elspeth was certain, had betrayed them all to the conspiracy. The duchess tried to tell herself that it didn't matter, that Renald would have made a poor king whose reign would do more to sully the Galdasten name than glorify it. But it wasn't her husband for whom she had harbored ambitions; the fact that none of her sons would ever wear the crown made her seethe like Amon's Ocean on a stormy day. If only she had been born into the Matriarchy of Sanbira where her keen mind would have allowed her to do more than merely recognize her duke's many flaws, and her path to power wouldn't have been blocked by the man's weakness and timidity.

Even if he returned from this battle to which he had ridden, she would never again allow him into her bed. Let him fill his court with bastards, he'd take no more pleasure in her flesh. She would gladly take a lover herself and bear him a child, announcing to all that the babe wasn't Renald's, if the punishment for such a thing were not so severe. A part of her wanted just to kill Renald and be done with it, and not for the first time she found herself hoping that he wouldn't survive the war. She knew, however, that the man's death would do little to enhance the station of her sons. Renald the Younger would become duke a bit sooner, but he'd never have more. And Adler and Rory would both still be tied to their paltry thaneships. They deserved better fates.

More to the point, Galdasten deserved to be led by a great man. Elspeth had lived in the dukedom all her life and was as devoted to the house as any soldier or noble could be. Her father, the thane of Prindyr, whose title Rory would one day inherit, had been a great friend of Kell, the duke before Renald. Indeed, her father had planned to attend the feast that Kell hosted in Galdasten Castle during Morna's turn in 872. At the last moment, however, amid fears that Elspeth, at the time a young lady just past her Fating, had come down with the pestilence, he remained in Prindyr. Hers turned out to be an ordinary fever, one that saved her father's life. For that was the feast to which a madman brought vermin infected with the pestilence, killing the duke and his family, and dooming Galdasten to four generations of inconsequence. The House of Eagles should have been leading this realm, its banner flying above Audun's Castle along with the purple and gold of Eibithar. Instead, its people bowed to a false king from Glyndwr, the weakest of the five major houses, and its foolish duke rode to fight on behalf of that king, thus preserving the very laws that barred his sons from the throne.

It all made Elspeth want to scream. Of course the duchess of a great house didn't resort to such displays, so she spent her days on the castle walls, staring out at Falcon Bay and the Braedony war ships that controlled its waters. The guards stationed atop the battlements usually ignored her, having learned that they invited a sharp rebuke if they chose to offer her even the mildest greeting. She had to admit that Galdasten's soldiers seemed in far better spirits since retaking the city. They gave little indication that they minded the presence of the emperor's ships off their shores, as if they expected that once the war on the moors had been won, driving off the Braedony navy would be but a small matter. Elspeth doubted it would be so simple, but she kept this to herself.

It was late in the day; sunlight slanted sharply across the castle walls, casting long shadows and making the stone glow like gold. Liked winged wraiths, gulls circled lazily over Galdasten's port, their cries plaintive and haunting. The air was still and the surface of the bay looked as smooth as polished steel.

Which made the sudden appearance of the lone ship that much stranger.

It sailed into the mouth of the bay as if pushed by Morna's hand, skimming lightly across the surface, its sails full, its hull leaning so steeply that the straining cloth nearly touched the water. The ship flew no colors, but it sailed directly at the Braedony ships, leading Elspeth to believe that it had been sent by the emperor. Perhaps it carried a message to his commanders, or provisions of some sort, or additional men for combat.

But how could it be moving so quickly? Then it turned slightly, adjusting its course for just an instant, allowing the sun to hit its decks. And Elspeth gasped. Every person she saw aboard the vessel had white hair. Sorcerers, of course.

She should have run for help. She should at least have pointed out the ship to the soldiers standing nearby. But all the duchess could do was watch.

A sudden wind swept toward the first of the empire's ships—she could actually see the gale move across the water. It seemed that the vessels were attempting to turn so that they might ram the Qirsi ship, but the wind hindered their movements. An instant later the ships were crushed, as if the same goddess that had guided this strange vessel into the harbor now smote the others. In mere moments the entire imperial navy had been destroyed; what Eibithar's fleet had fought for days to do, to no avail, these Qirsi accomplished in the span of a few heartbeats.

Yet that was nothing compared with what they did next. It started as a faint golden glimmering along the surface of the bay, but it quickly built into a curling wall of flame that rose from the brine like Eilidh herself, indomitable, insatiable, merciless. Higher and higher it grew, racing toward the Wethy fleet. Elspeth heard herself cry out, was aware of the guards turning to look at her. But she couldn't bring herself to look away as that wall of flame fell upon the vessels, in an eruption of fire and steam and charred fragments of wood.

"Demons and fire!" one of the man muttered. "What in Ean's name was that?"

"It's a Qirsi army," Elspeth said, knowing as she spoke that it was true, that for all the dire warnings she had heard of a coming war with the renegades, she had not believed it until now. She faced the man. "Go find your captain! Have him place all his archers on the battlements and all his swordsmen at the north gate!" She glanced out at the bay again. The ship was already turning southward, toward the port. "Quickly! They'll make land soon!"

Never before had she given a command to one of Renald's men, but this soldier responded as if the order had come from the duke himself. He and his comrade bowed to her and strode, swords jangling, toward the arched entrance to the nearest tower.

Elspeth turned back to the bay, and saw that the Qirsi ship was speeding toward the city piers, driven once more by its phantom wind. She shook her head, terror gripping her heart. There wasn't nearly enough time. They would be at the docks in mere moments. She crossed to the inner side of the wall and looked down on the ward in time to see the two soldiers emerge from the tower and run toward the armory.

"Hurry!" she shouted. The men didn't even look up at her. *They're doing the best they can,* a voice told her. Renald's, naturally. *Besides, what good will swords and arrows do against such magic?* That question, for which she had no answer at all, forced her into motion.

The boys would be in the cloister for their devotions. All three of them had swords, and wore them proudly on their belts, but she didn't want them fighting. Once more she saw in her mind that hideous wall of flame and she shuddered. She had ordered Galdasten's warriors to their deaths, but she wouldn't have her sons fighting a hopeless battle, not if there might still be some way to save them.

Men in the courtyard were shouting to one another and to the soldiers on the ramparts even before she entered the winding stairway, and before she reached the second level of the castle, where the cloister was, she heard soldiers entering the tower from the ward to make their way up to the top of the wall. Elspeth managed to leave the stairway before any of the men saw her. She ran through the corridor to the cloister.

The prelate had his back to the entrance as she entered the shrine, but he whirled on her, drawing a blade. Elspeth had to smile, despite her fear. The man was new to Galdasten—the old prelate had died during the previous harvest and this young man, Coulson Fendsar, who had once been an adherent in this very cloister, was elevated to the prelacy. He still seemed a bit unsure of himself at times, but the boys liked him a good deal and Elspeth thought his approach to the devotions refreshing if a bit unconventional. More to the point, she could hardly imagine the old prelate raising a weapon at all, much less putting himself between her children and armed invaders.

Seeing her, the prelate let out a long breath and lowered his sword. "My lady. I heard voices in the ward and feared the worst."

"And with good reason, Father Prelate."

"Have the empire's men returned?"

She looked past him, saw her sons watching, the youngest, Rory, looking pale and frightened, as if he had just awakened from a terrible dream.

"No," she said, lowering her voice. "A ship bearing a Qirsi army has just destroyed the fleets of Braedon and Wethyrn. They sail toward our piers even as we speak."

"Ean save us all!"

"I don't know that he can, Father."

"Do you wish to take shelter here, my lady?" He straightened. "I'm not much with a blade, but I'd give my life in your defense."

Again Elspeth smiled. "Thank you. I've come for my boys. I'm going to take them from the castle while there's still time."

Coulson nodded. "I understand, my lady. The duke would want no less. If I may be so bold, I'd suggest that you make your way to the Sanctuary of Amon. Most Qirsi still adhere to the Old Faith. Even these renegades may respect its walls."

"Thank you, Father Prelate," she said with surprise. "I hadn't expected such . . . sound counsel to come from the cloister."

A grin flashed across his youthful face and was gone. An instant later, he turned and beckoned to her sons. "Come, my lords," he called. "Quickly now. You need to follow your mother."

"What is it, Mother?" Renald the Younger asked. He was the image of his father, straight and thin as a blade, with unruly red hair and bright blue eyes. But he had Elspeth's strength and nerve, and he looked eager for battle. "Braedon's men again?"

"Not this time," she said, ushering them all toward the doorway.

"Then who?"

"I bet it's the Qirsi."

She stopped for just an instant, staring at Adler, who had spoken. He was still a year shy of his Determining, but already he showed signs of being the cleverest of them all.

"What makes you say that?" she asked.

He shrugged. "Who else would it be, if it's not the empire?"

"I'm scared, Mother," Rory said.

She put an arm around him and kissed the top of his head. "Hush, child. Everything will be all right. Just come with me and do as I say. Can you do that?"

He nodded solemnly.

She urged them forward once more, stopping on the threshold to look back at the prelate.

"Thank you, Father Prelate. Ean keep you safe."

"And you, my lady."

She tried to smile, but failed, certain in that moment that she would never again see the man alive.

A moment later, fear for her sons overmastered all other concerns, and she was again in the corridors, hurrying the boys along toward the nearest of the sally ports. Everywhere she looked soldiers ran toward gates or towers, many with bows and quivers filled with arrows, others with swords and gleaming shields.

"Where are you taking us?" Renald asked, a frown creasing his smooth brow.

"Away from here."

He stopped. "No! In Father's absence I lead our house! I can't flee, like a child or a woman!"

Elspeth gritted her teeth. She hadn't time for this.

"Your father would be very proud," she said thickly. "But he'd also tell you that you can't fight this enemy."

"Why not?" the boy demanded, proud, stubborn, defiant. Hadn't she nurtured these very qualities, trying to make him more like his grandfather, more like her?

"Because this army is Qirsi. They'll destroy this castle, and they'll kill all who defend it."

"I'm not afraid of dying."

But I'm afraid of losing you! She remembered what it was to be this young, though the memory seemed to grow dimmer with each passing day.

"I know how brave you are," she said, forcing a smile. "How brave all three of you are. It makes me very proud. But the fact is that all of you are still boys. Even you, Renald," she said, raising a hand to keep him silent. "You've another year until your Fating, which means that you can't yet lead this house, not even in your father's absence. That responsibility falls to me, and I'm commanding you to follow me." The smile returned for just an instant. "I need you to protect me, as well as your brothers. Father would tell you that your first duty is to our family."

He stared at her a moment longer, his mouth twisting as it always had when he was deep in thought. Surely the Qirsi ship had reached the port by now. She wanted to grab the boy's arm and pull him along behind her as she might a child half his age, but she knew how important it was that Renald accept this for himself.

"All right," he said at last, reluctantly sheathing his sword.

"Come on then. We haven't much time."

They continued on to the sally port at the southern end of the fortress. The south gate road wasn't the quickest way to the sanctuary, but it kept them a good distance from the pier and, Elspeth hoped, offered them their best chance of eluding the Qirsi.

By the time they were outside, however, the duchess could hear screams coming from the city, and before they were off Galdasten Tor, she could see the first of the white-hairs advancing on the castle. It occurred to her that she should have had them all change into plainer clothes, but by then it was too late.

"Hold, Duchess!" came a man's voice.

The distance was great, but Elspeth didn't know how far Qirsi magic could reach. She resisted an urge to look back at the white-hairs.

"Just keep moving," she told the boys, her voice low and taut.

"Not another step, my lady!" the man called again, closer this time, the tone harder.

Still she didn't slow.

Suddenly, a stone just beside the road exploded in a cloud of white dust, the report making her jump.

"Another step, and I do the same to one of you."

Elspeth stopped, holding out a hand so that her sons would do the same. Turning slowly, she saw a tall Qirsi approaching her, followed by a company of perhaps two dozen sorcerers. But it was the leader who drew her eye. She had never seen a Qirsi like this one—comparing him in her mind with Pillad, her husband's unremarkable first minister, she found it hard to believe that they were of the same race. This man was powerfully built and had an elegant bearing. He was even handsome in a chilling way, with his unruly white hair, brilliant golden eyes, and square face. He had the look of a noble—she could see why these others followed him.

Before she could stop the boy, Renald pulled his sword free and stepped in front of her.

"Get back, white-hair," he said. Elspeth could see his hand trembling.

A sharp, ringing note echoed off the tor, and shards of steel fell to the ground, clattering off the stone road.

"I could do the same to your skull, whelp," the man said.

He gestured at the Qirsi standing with him. "So could any of my warriors. You may think yourself brave, but in this case you'd be wise to let fear stay your hand."

Her son's face shaded to crimson and Elspeth worried that he might say something rash. But he merely stared at the useless hilt of his sword.

"Your husband rode south with his army?" the man asked.

Elspeth regarded him for several moments. She wasn't about to do anything foolish, but neither was she ready to just give him whatever information he wanted. "Who are you?"

The man grinned, though the look in his eyes remained deadly serious. "Very well. My name is Dusaan jal Kania."

She narrowed her eyes. The name sounded familiar.

"Until recently, I was high chancellor to the emperor of Braedon." His smile broadened at what he saw on her face. "This surprises you. Perhaps you think that a man in my position would have too little to gain and too much to lose from a movement such as ours."

Elspeth opened her mouth, closed it again, shook her head. "I don't know what I thought," she admitted.

"It may also surprise you to learn that I'm a Weaver."

"Gods save us all!"

"Indeed. Now I'm going to ask you again, and I won't be so patient this time if you refuse to answer. Has the duke ridden south with his army?"

She hesitated, pressing her lips together. Then she nodded, feeling as she did that she was betraying her husband, wondering that she should care.

"And the first minister with him?"

"Yes, he—" She stared at him. "Pillad's a traitor, isn't he? He's part of your conspiracy."

The predatory smile returned. "As you might imagine, we don't think of ourselves as traitors. But yes, he serves our movement."

"I warned him," she said, her voice low. "But the fool just wouldn't listen." The duchess nearly asked the man what orders he had given Pillad, but she wasn't certain that she wanted to hear his answer, at least not in front of her children. Just a short time ago she had wished for Renald's death.

Faced now with the realization that he most likely would be killed, she found herself grieving for him, her eyes stinging with tears she had never believed she would shed.

"I see you understand," he said.

"Understand what?" Renald the Younger demanded. He glared at her. "Mother?"

She ignored him, keeping her eyes on the Weaver. "What is it you want of us?"

"You're to accompany us back to the castle and convince your soldiers to surrender the castle."

Renald shook his head fiercely. "Never!"

"And if I don't?"

"We'll take it anyway, hundreds of men will die, and the fortress of your forebears will be destroyed."

"You could do that?" But already she knew the answer. She had seen what this man and his army had done to the fleets in Falcon Bay.

"Weaving the magic of these other shapers, I can lay waste to the entire city."

How could Kearney possibly prevail against this man? How could any sovereign? In that moment, Elspeth understood that she was looking upon the future of the Forelands.

"Very well. I'll do as you command. In return, I ask that you spare my life and those of my sons."

"Mother! You can't do this!"

She looked at the boy. "Be quiet, Renald. Only a fool would doom so many men to their deaths simply out of pride and obstinacy. It's time you learned what it means to lead a great house."

The irony hit her as soon as she spoke the words. If this Qirsi standing before them truly intended to rule the seven realms, all Eandi nobility would be overthrown. Her sons would never rule in any court. Not even in Prindyr or Lynde, much less in Galdasten or the City of Kings. If the Weaver was thinking the same thing, he had the good grace to keep it to himself.

"Well?" she asked, eyeing the Qirsi once more.

"I make no promises, my lady, except to say that so long as you cooperate with us, you'll not be harmed."

She couldn't be certain whether he meant only her or the boys as well, and she had the sense that his ambiguity was intentional. Fear for her sons seized her, and for a moment she couldn't even bring herself to draw breath.

"Lead the way, my lady," the Weaver said, his square face as placid as a morning tide. With a slender hand, he indicated the road back to the castle.

Run! she wanted to yell to her children. *Make your way to the sanctuary and don't look back!* But she had little hope that they could escape the Qirsi, and every expectation that the Weaver would punish them all for making the attempt. So she turned, defeated and helpless, and meekly led them back toward the castle gate. The duke wouldn't have recognized her; her sons wouldn't so much as glance at her.

She kept her eyes fixed on the ramparts as she walked up the road, half hoping that Galdasten's archers would loose their arrows despite her presence at the head of the Weaver's army. Instead, they lowered their bows and called for the gate guards to open the portcullises. Just as the Weaver had known they would.

For all her talk of Renald's cowardice, his weakness and poor leadership, Elspeth couldn't imagine him giving up his castle without a single weapon being drawn. *What have I become?*

Within moments, they stood in the center of the lower ward, surrounded by men who even now looked to her for leadership. The archers still carried their bows, and the swordsmen held their blades ready. Elspeth could see murder in their eyes. She could still save Galdasten, if she were willing to sacrifice herself and her boys.

Perhaps the Qirsi read these thoughts in her eyes, for abruptly he grabbed Renald the Younger by the arm, pulling the boy away from her and in the same motion drawing his sword. For one terrifying instant, Elspeth thought the Weaver would kill the boy right there, but he didn't. He merely laid the edge of his sword against Renald's neck and looked at her, his expression unchanged.

"Tell them to lay down their weapons."

"No, Mother, don't!" the boy said gamely. "He's not—"

"Quiet!" the Qirsi said. He pressed harder with his blade, so that a thin line of blood appeared at the boy's throat and trickled over the steel.

Elspeth had to bite her tongue to keep from crying out.

"Now, my lady. Do it, or he dies."

"Surrender your weapons," she called to the soldiers, her eyes never straying from the steel and the blood. When several of the men hesitated, looking at one another, she said, "Please. I've seen what these Qirsi can do with their magic. They destroyed the entire Braedony fleet, and Wethyrn's as well. We cannot defeat them; if we try, they'll kill us all."

The men stared at her for what seemed an eternity, until finally one of them stepped forward and dropped his sword and dagger only a few paces from where she stood. Then he bowed to her and took a step back. Slowly, others did the same, all of them offering obeisance to her as they added their weapons to the growing mound of steel.

Adler and Rory stood on either side of her, clinging to her hands, but though the Weaver had released Renald, the boy still would not look at her, nor did he bother to wipe the blood from his neck. He stood perfectly still, staring straight ahead, like a soldier bravely awaiting execution.

Soon archers were filing out of the towers to place their bows and quivers with the other arms. As the surrender continued, the Weaver whispered something to two of the other Qirsi, one of them a waif-like woman with eyes as bright as his own, and the other a man with pale yellow eyes in a lean face. A moment later these two started off in different directions, the woman with a half smile on her face.

"You two," the Weaver said, pointing to the captains Renald had left behind to protect the castle. "Come here."

The soldiers approached him, as a low murmur swept through the courtyard. They stopped just before him, both of them pale and tight-lipped.

"Your duke left the two of you in command of the army?"

Neither man spoke.

"Answer me."

The Weaver didn't move at all, but it seemed that both men suddenly sagged, as if they had abruptly taken ill.

"Yes," one of them said. "We're in command."

He's using magic on them, she had time to think.

"Get on your knees."

The men dropped to their knees, their heads bowed.

The Weaver still held his sword, and now he stepped forward, raising the weapon as to strike them.

"No!" Elspeth cried.

The Qirsi glanced at her. "They're soldiers, my lady. They understand that I can't allow them to live. So long as these captains live, your husband's soldiers remain an army. Without them, they become nothing more than a collection of defeated men."

He faced them again, and with swift, powerful strokes hewed off the head of one man and then the other. Their bodies toppled sideways to the earth, blood darkening the grass. The other men said nothing nor did they make any move to retrieve their weapons.

Rory, on the other hand, was sobbing, his face pressed against her dress. Elspeth stroked his head, fearing that she'd be ill.

"See what you've done?" Renald said, glowering at her. "You made those men surrender and now they're dead!"

She should have said something. She should have had some answer for the hatred she saw in her son's eyes. But she couldn't think of anything adequate. And in the next moment matters grew far worse.

"What are they doing with Father Coulson?" Adler asked.

The duchess's head snapped up in time to see the man the Weaver had sent away moments before leading the prelate down the broad stone stairway that linked the castle's upper and lower wards. Even from this distance, she could see that Coulson was trembling, and that his legs seemed barely to support him.

"What are they going to do to him, Mother?" Adler asked again.

She glanced at Renald, whose face had gone white and whose eyes still held such contempt.

"I don't know, child," she said. A lie, for who in that ward didn't know, save for the young ones? The cloisters had long been tied to the courts and were known to be hostile to the Qirsi and their adherence to the Old Faith. Was it so surprising that these renegade white-hairs should strike at the prelacy?

"They're going to kill him," Renald said bitterly.

"They are not!" Adler shot back. "Are they, Mother?"

"Hush, child."

The Qirsi man pulled the prelate with him until they stood before the Weaver. Then he threw Coulson to the ground and handed the Weaver the hilt of a shattered sword.

"This is his?" the Weaver asked.

"Yes, Weaver."

The Qirsi nodded. "Thank you, Uestem." He looked down at Coulson, a smile playing at the corners of his broad mouth. "So you fancy yourself a warrior, do you, Father Prelate?"

"I'm a man of the cloister," he answered in a quaking voice. "But I'll gladly take up arms to defend my house and my realm."

"Bravely said. Of course, your house is defeated, and your realm will soon be mine. So it seems your courage has been wasted."

Without another word, the Weaver raised his weapon once more and hacked off the prelate's head.

Adler screamed, Rory's sobbing grew louder.

Several of Galdasten's soldiers looked away. Others shouted angrily, a few of them taking a step toward their weapons.

There was a strange, dry cracking sound, and the nearest of these men collapsed to the ground clutching his leg and howling with pain.

"That was his leg," the Weaver said, his voice carrying across the ward. "It could just as easily have been his neck. And it will be for the next man who takes even a single step toward those weapons. Do I make myself clear?"

The others who had started toward the weapons stood utterly still, but several of them continued to eye the swords.

Apparently the Weaver noticed this as well, for a moment later there was a second snapping noise and another soldier fell to the ground. This one, however, didn't cry out, nor did he writhe in pain. He simply lay still, his head tipped at a wrong angle, his eyes gazing sightless at the sky. The other men stepped back.

"You're going to kill us, too, aren't you?" Renald said, drawing the Weaver's gaze.

"I have no intention of killing you today, Lord Galdasten."

"What about tomorrow, or the day after that?"

The man smiled thinly. "Gleaning has always been my least favorite of the Qirsi magics."

Renald said nothing.

"For now, you'll be placed in the prison tower with your mother and your brothers. Beyond that, I can't say."

"You intend to rule the Forelands, and to be served by Qirsi lords, just as our king is served now by Eandi nobles. You can't have men like me about, reminding your subjects of the day when the great houses ruled the seven realms."

For some time the Qirsi just stared at him. Then he smiled faintly and said, "No, I don't suppose we can." With that, he turned away and beckoned to another of his Qirsi soldiers. "Take them to the prison tower," he said, his voice so low that Elspeth had to strain to hear any of it. "Put the mother in one chamber, the boys in another. Make them comfortable, be certain that they're fed, but don't allow any of the Eandi to see them."

"Yes, Weaver."

"Can't we be in the same chamber?" the duchess asked. "The younger ones are frightened."

The Weaver frowned at her, as if annoyed that she had overheard. "I don't think that would be wise."

Rory still clung to her and now she indicated the boy with an open hand.

"But look at him. He's only a boy. Surely there would be no harm—"

"I said no!" He spun toward the Qirsi soldier. "Take them away from here now!"

There could no longer be any doubt. Renald was right. The Qirsi intended to kill all three boys. Perhaps her as well, though she cared far less about that. They wouldn't do it here. The executions of the captains and prelate had been intended to dishearten Galdasten's soldiers, to sap them of their will to fight. But the killing of the duchess and her sons would enrage them. No, they would have to wait, though not long, for there was also danger in keeping them imprisoned for too long. It would be this night, perhaps the morning. No later. Elspeth felt her legs give way and suddenly found herself sitting on the grass only a short distance from the headless body of Father Coulson. Rory stared at her, a puzzled look on his puffy, tear-streaked face.

"Mother?"

"Get up," the Qirsi soldier said, his voice flat.

"Please," she sobbed, hot tears coursing down her cheeks. "Don't do this."

The Weaver kept his back to her, speaking in low tones with another of his soldiers.

"For pity's sake, they're just children!"

At that, he glanced back. "Yes. But one day they'd be men."

Chapter

Ten

T he Weaver had told Nitara that they would be there, much the way a parent might tell a child that she was to have a younger sibling.

Two of my chancellors await us in the city, to join our assault on the castle and add their number to my army.

They had been at Galdasten's pier waiting to greet the ship. When Dusaan stepped off the vessel, they knelt before him, compelling the rest in the army, those who had already ridden with him and killed with him, to do the same. A man and a woman. The man was a merchant, with an air of success and wealth about him. He was lean of face, but his body was thick and his belly round. He had lived well.

The woman was said to be a merchant as well, but Nitara found that difficult to believe. She was as young as Nitara, perhaps younger, with thick white hair that she wore loose to her shoulders, and brilliant yellow eyes that were almost a match for Dusaan's. She was as lean as the other merchant was broad, as beautiful as he was plain. It took Nitara but a moment to understand that they weren't a couple, that this woman had her sights set higher. One need only see how she looked at Dusaan to know just how high. Nitara hated her before they left the pier. By the time they reached the walls of Galdasten Castle, she was ready to plunge her blade into the woman's back.

Jastanne ja Triln. The man's name she already had forgotten, but the woman's name stuck in her mind like a child's rhyme, repeating itself again and again. Both merchants had shaping power and mists and winds—it was small wonder they had become chancellors in the Weaver's movement, or that Dusaan welcomed them into his army with such enthusiasm.

Perhaps he didn't notice how this woman eyed him, how her cheeks reddened every time their eyes met. Surely he would have been as discomfited by her affections as he had been by Nitara's. This was no time for such thoughts. They were at war, fighting for the freedom of all Qirsi in the Forelands, fulfilling the dream that had brought them all to the Weaver's cause in the first place. That was what the Weaver had told her, and that was what he would have told this woman, this Jastanne ja Triln, had he only noticed.

Except that as the Weaver strode toward the great fortress, flanked by his two chancellors, and followed by the rest, including Nitara, Dusaan did appear to notice. When had she ever known him to miss anything? In Jastanne's case, it seemed he simply didn't mind.

The ease with which they took the castle should have been cause for rejoicing. Even the unfortunate but necessary execution of Galdasten's three young lords the following morning would not have been enough to dampen such a victory. But Nitara could think only of how the Weaver had trusted Jastanne and the other chancellor with tasks that would have fallen to her just a day before. He sent Jastanne into the city to find other Qirsi to join their cause; he had the man lead a group of several shapers to imprison Galdasten's soldiers. In the span of a single day, she had become merely another servant of the Weaver, but a single soldier in a growing army.

The morning after their victory, with the grievous cries of the duchess still echoing through the castle and many of the newly recruited Qirsi guarding the fortress walls, they took nearly every horse in the city and castle, and started southward in pursuit of Galdasten's army. Again, the chancellors rode with the Weaver; the rest trailed behind. Dusaan had barely said a word to Nitara since they docked in Galdasten; she had little choice but to ride with B'Serre, Rov, and the others from the court of Curtell. If the other ministers had noted her fall from the Weaver's favor, they had the good sense not to mention it. They made room for her, so that she could ride beside them, and they continued their conversation. Nitara said nothing—she couldn't take her eyes off the woman riding with her Weaver—but at least she didn't have to ride alone, looking foolish and pitiable.

Late in the day, as they rested along the banks of a small rill, Jastanne approached them, leading her mount on foot, the wind making her hair dance, the setting sun gleaming like gold in her eyes. In spite of herself, Nitara could see what the Weaver might find attractive in this woman.

"Hello," she called to them as she approached, a hand raised in greeting.

B'Serre and the others nodded, and Rov called out a tentative "Hello" in return.

"I hope I'm not interrupting."

"Not at all, Chancellor."

She smiled, though it never reached her eyes. "Good. The Weaver asked me to speak with you. He intends to divide the army into smaller forces, and he's placed Uestem and me in charge of doing so."

"Has he really," Nitara said, her voice flat.

Gorlan shot her a look, and gave a small shake of his head, but Nitara ignored him.

"You've been with us for less than a day, and already we're to take orders from you?"

The smile lingered on Jastanne's face as she eyed Nitara. Then she turned to the rest of them. "Shapers are to go with Uestem, as are those with fire magic. If you have mists and winds or language of beasts, you're to stay with me. And if your powers place you with both of us, follow the deeper magic—if you have mists but also fire, stay with me, language of beasts and shaping, go with Uestem."

"Yes, Chancellor," Gorlan said. "Thank you."

"We'll ride a bit further today. We'll divide into units tonight when we stop. Uestem will be on the west end of camp, and I'll be to the east."

The others nodded, and the woman's smile broadened.

"I don't know how all this will separate out, but I look forward to working with as many of you as possible." She started to walk away, then halted, glancing back over her shoulder at Nitara. "Minister, would you walk with me for a moment?"

Nitara almost refused. She would have given anything for the courage to tell this woman exactly how much she hated her. But Jastanne was the Weaver's chancellor, and Nitara knew that he would be furious with her. Besides, having both mists and winds and language of beasts, Nitara would be under the woman's command. What could she do but follow? She knew the others were watching her, wondering if she had already pushed the chancellor too far, but Nitara didn't look back at them.

"The Weaver has told me a good deal about you," Jastanne said, when they were alone.

"Has he?"

"Yes. He tells me that you've served him quite well since joining the movement. He said you even killed an old lover who betrayed us."

Quite unexpectedly, she found herself angry with the

Weaver. She had never thought she could feel such a thing, but it was not his place to tell this woman what had happened with Kayiv. "What of it?" she demanded.

Jastanne stopped and stared at her, that smile on her lips once more. "You don't care much for me, do you?"

Nitara looked away. "I hardly know you."

"I could make the same point."

"Was there something you wanted, Chancellor? A reason why you pulled me away from my friends?"

"I sense your hostility, Minister. I did before as well. And I want to know if I need to speak with the Weaver about this, if it compromises your ability to serve his movement."

Nitara felt the color drain from her cheeks. "No, Chancellor."

The woman regarded her for several moments. "What is it about me, Minister? Why do you hate me so?"

She shook her head. "It's not . . . I don't hate you."

"Now you're lying."

"You wouldn't understand."

"Wouldn't I? Or are you afraid that I would, all too well?" The smile again, kinder this time. "You love him very much, don't you?"

"I don't want to talk about this."

"There are others, you know. There are women in every realm who serve this movement. Do you really believe that you're the only one who feels this way about him?"

"No," she said, her voice barely more than a whisper.

"Look at him," the woman went on. "Do you really think that a man like that—a Qirsi king—will take but one wife? How many women did your emperor have?"

Nitara shrugged. "I don't know. Several."

"Yes. And so will the Weaver. You may well be one of them. And I might as well. We're going to have to get along, you and I, not only during this war, but after it. So I'd suggest you put your hatred aside. The Weaver feels that you could be of value as a noble once we control the Forelands. You'd be a fool to do anything to change his mind."

"I understand, Chancellor."

"I have others to inform of our plans. We should be riding again shortly."

Before Nitara could even nod to her, Jastanne turned and walked away, lithe and confident. Nitara watched her go, then started toward her mount, having no desire to face her companions again. Before she reached her horse, however, she heard Gorlan calling to her. She stopped, closing her eyes for just a moment.

"What?" she said, looking at the other Qirsi.

"Are you mad?" Gorlan asked, stopping just in front of her. "You can't afford to anger that woman, no matter what you might think of her."

"I know that, Gorlan," she said crossly. "Thank you."

"What did she say to you?"

"Basically the same thing you just did."

"Well, you'd better listen. I don't even understand why you're so angry with her. What could she have possibly done to you?"

"Nothing, Gorlan. Nothing at all. Just leave me alone."

He frowned, shaking his head. After a moment he left her, as did several of the others. Only B'Serre remained with Nitara.

"I think I understand," the minister said softly. "And I don't really blame you."

Nitara raked a hand through her hair. "I'm a fool. I don't know what I was thinking."

"Sure you do. It seems pretty normal to me. Clearly the Weaver thinks highly of you. You were the one riding beside him before the chancellors arrived." She gave a conspiratorial smile. "If I were you, I'd hate her, too."

Nitara had to grin. "Watch what you say. You'll get yourself in trouble."

They stood in silence for some time, the smiles lingering on their faces. Nitara stared at the ground, uncertain of what to say next. She had few friends to speak of. Kayiv had been a friend once, before he began to share her bed. Before she killed him. She would never have been so bold as to call the Weaver a friend, but other than Dusaan, she had spoken to few people in the past several turns. She wasn't quite certain how to behave around this woman who had gone out of her way to declare her friendship. She knew only that she didn't want to do anything to drive B'Serre away.

"Gorlan's probably right, you know," the minister said at length, drawing Nitara's gaze. "You shouldn't anger her again. I don't think you want her as an enemy."

Nitara gave a small laugh. "It might be too late for that." When B'Serre didn't respond, she grew serious again. "I know. I'll be careful."

A short time later, the chancellors called for the army to ride on, and soon they were thundering across the moor again, their shadows stretching eastward in the dying light of the sun. When they stopped for the night, Nitara followed Jastanne to the eastern side of the camp. Most of the others who had ridden with her from Curtell, including B'Serre, Gorlan, and Rov, went to the other side, further darkening her mood.

Once the army had been divided, the chancellors began to divide it a second time between those who possessed the two magics each would command. A few on Jastanne's side had both language of beasts and mists and winds. As before, she instructed them to follow the deeper magic. When Nitara started toward the group with mists, however, the chancellor stopped her.

"You have both?" she asked.

"Yes, Chancellor."

Jastanne considered this. "Stay with those who have language of beasts."

Nitara felt her face color. She knew that this was Jastanne's revenge, that the chancellor was looking for some way to humiliate her for what Nitara had done earlier. But the minister refused to let herself grow angry. She merely bowed and murmured, "Yes, Chancellor."

"You think I'm punishing you."

"If you are, I'm sure you feel you have reason."

Jastanne grinned—it seemed she responded to everything with a smile. "You're controlling your temper, I'll give you that much. But you have much to learn about me. I want you to remain with the other group because I need to choose a commander from among those with language of beasts. And I choose you."

Nitara opened her mouth. Closed it again. "Why?"

"Because I trust you. I know that you'll give your life for the Weaver's cause. And I sense that you're clever enough to lead them."

"But I've never—"

"None of us has, Minister. You'll be fine."

"Thank you, Chancellor." She had no idea what else to say.

"Your task, and that of your unit, will be to get as close to the mounted soldiers and nobles as possible. It promises to be dangerous work. The Weaver has also told me that he's least likely to weave those with language of beasts. In most cases, it'll be easier to unnerve their mounts one by one."

"Of course."

"That said, if you face a larger force on horseback, the Weaver may have to weave your powers with his own. You'll need to be prepared for that."

"I'll make certain that we are, Chancellor."

"I don't doubt that you will."

Nitara had never before thought of herself as a commander, and after the chancellor walked away, she knew a moment of panic. What if the others wouldn't follow her? What if she made some terrible blunder and all of them were killed? She nearly ran after Jastanne to ask her what to do next, but she immediately thought better of it. The chancellor had given her a gift, in spite of how Nitara had treated her earlier in the day. No doubt it wouldn't take much to make the woman reconsider her decision.

Taking a breath, Nitara turned to face the Qirsi standing near her. They were already watching her. A few she recognized, but most were strangers.

"My name is Nitara ja Plin," she said. "I was a minister in the court of the emperor of Braedon until the Weaver revealed himself." She hesitated. Their expressions hadn't changed, and she wondered if she were going about this the wrong way. "The chancellor has asked me to command this unit of the army." Still no response. She repeated for them what Jastanne had just told her, about how they would need to get close to the mounted Eandi, and how the Weaver would likely leave them to use their powers individually.

"Do you have questions?" she asked after another silence. Nothing.

"Perhaps I'll take some time to speak to each of you, learn your names and where you're from."

Were they simple? Had they understood any of what she told them? Or did they merely resent taking orders from a young minister?

"In the meantime, make camp. Start finding wood for fires and preparing your suppers."

That set them in motion. Given something to do, they seemed to rouse themselves from a stupor. Perhaps there was a lesson there—to succeed as a commander, one first had to give commands.

Once the fires were burning, the smell of roasting fowl and boar hanging in the still air, Nitara began to make her way through the camp. Her conversations with the Qirsi in her unit quickly convinced her that they did not in fact resent her authority. None of them had ever been warriors before, and none aspired to command. Many of them had long sympathized with the Weaver's cause, but didn't know how to go about joining the movement until Dusaan captured their cities. Others had joined when they did because they feared what might happen to them if they didn't. All of them, it seemed, merely wanted someone to tell them what to do.

By the time she had spoken with all the soldiers under her command and returned to where her horse stood, chewing noisily on the moorland grasses, Nitara was exhausted. She wanted nothing more than to eat something and sleep. Before she could even take a bite of the cold fowl left for her by one of the soldiers, however, she heard someone calling for her. It wasn't until she turned and realized the man approaching her was a stranger that it occurred to her that he had been addressing her as "Commander."

"Yes," she said, with as much brightness in her voice as she could muster.

"The chancellors wish a word with us."

Of course they did. She nodded. "Lead the way."

She fell in step beside him, eyeing him briefly.

"Forgive me," she said. "I don't recognize you."

"There's no reason you should. I was an underminister in the court of Ayvencalde and was never fortunate enough to travel to the imperial city. The chancellor chose me to lead those with mists and winds. I'm Yedeg jal Senkava."

"Nitara ja Plin."

"Yes, I know," he said, surprising her.

"You do?"

"You're obviously quite important to the Weaver. He trusted you with a great deal in Ayvencalde."

"Yes," she said, facing forward again, her jealousy returning in a rush. "He did there."

"I also heard that you challenged one of the chancellors today."

She felt her face grow hot. "People are speaking of that?"

"Oh, yes. It seems you were fortunate to end up on Jastanne's side of the army."

"Actually," she said, somewhat sheepishly, "it was Jastanne I challenged."

His eyebrows went up. "Really? Can I ask what your . . . dispute was about?"

She closed her eyes briefly. What a fool she had been. "I'd rather not say."

"Of course. Forgive me."

They walked the rest of the way in silence, soon coming to a small fire on the southern edge of the Qirsi camp. Jastanne and Uestem were already there, along with Uestem's two commanders, who turned out to be Gorlan and Rov. Both of the ministers nodded to Nitara as they made room for her and Yedeg around the fire, but neither of them spoke.

"This won't take long," Uestem said, regarding each of them in turn. "It's been a long day and all of us need to rest. But the Weaver wanted us to speak with you briefly, to make certain that all went smoothly with your units."

Nitara's eyes flicked toward Jastanne. The chancellor was already watching her, wearing that same inscrutable smile on her lips.

"Well?" Uestem asked, after a lengthy silence.

"Commander," Jastanne said, still watching Nitara. "Why don't you begin? Tell us about your first night of command."

"It was fine," she said, meeting the chancellor's gaze. "I was a bit hesitant at first. I've never commanded warriors before, and I wasn't certain that I was going about it in the right way."

"What do you think is the right way?"

She shrugged. "I'm still not sure. Maybe there is no right way. When I finally gave them an order, they couldn't carry it out fast enough. I think they were just waiting for someone to tell them what to do."

"Very good," Jastanne said, nodding. "What about the rest of you?"

Gorlan cleared his throat. "Actually, my experience was much the same as Nitara's."

The others turned toward him, including Jastanne, and Nitara exhaled, relieved just to have the chancellor looking elsewhere. She gathered from what the others said that they all had been somewhat unsure of themselves at first, a point that was not lost on the chancellors.

"Let this be a lesson to all of you," Uestem said, when Yedeg, the last of them, had finished speaking. "Command is, above all else, a matter of confidence, of believing in your ability to lead others. If you trust in yourself, those you command will trust you as well."

"Surely there's more to it than that," Nitara said without thinking. In the next moment she winced. How often did she think she could contradict the chancellors before they turned on her?

But Uestem just grinned. "Yes, there is. But it's a good place to begin."

The others laughed.

"Get some sleep," the chancellor said. "We ride at dawn. The Weaver wants to strike at Galdasten's army before they can join with the rest of the Eandi forces. They're two days ahead of us, perhaps more, although they are on foot. Still, we'll probably have to ride through much of the night tomorrow, and perhaps the next as well. Whatever it takes, we'll ride them down before they reach the others. We have enough horses to keep the animals fresh, and we've ample provisions from Galdasten. Make certain your units are prepared to push themselves and their mounts."

"Yes, Chancellor," the four of them said as one.

The others started away, but Jastanne called to Nitara, stopping her. Though the minister had been expecting this she felt herself growing tense once more. She still didn't quite trust the woman.

"You did well," Jastanne said.

"Thank you, Chancellor."

"You don't hesitate to speak your mind. I like that about you. It speaks well of your courage."

"Some would say it casts doubt on my judgment."

"There are times when you'd do best to keep your thoughts to yourself. But I'd rather a commander who thinks and questions, than one who just blindly follows my orders."

Nitara narrowed her eyes. "Why are you being so nice to me? After our first conversation, I expected you to do everything you could to make my life miserable."

The chancellor grinned. "Maybe I should have. But I see much of myself in you—the good and the bad. Given the chance, I think we could be friends." She turned to walk away. "Sleep, Commander. This war begins in earnest tomorrow."

The army of Galdasten was up and moving before dawn, their swords and shields and shirts of mail catching the silver-grey light of early morning so that the entire column of soldiers seemed to gleam faintly, like stars partially obscured by a high haze. Renald had hoped that three days of marching would have taken them farther than it had, but his swordmaster assured him that they were making good progress. Still, he found their pace maddeningly slow, and he longed to kick at the flanks of his mount and thunder southward across the Moorlands until he found the king.

We're coming! he would say. *Keep the empire at bay for another few days and the men of Galdasten will join your battle!*

And Kearney, in his desperate gratitude for this last spar of hope where none had been expected, would praise the duke as a hero and his house as the greatest in all the realm.

Instead, Renald rode at the head of his company, flanked by Ewan Traylee and Pillad jal Krenaar, his first minister, forced to discuss the weather and fighting to keep thoughts of his wife from darkening his mood. *Their minds are no more nimble than yours,* she had once said of his swordmaster and minister. And once more, having suffered their companionship for these last several days, he could only marvel at her acumen.

With every hour that Galdasten's army squandered on this toilsome march, with every battle the king waged in Renald's absence, the duke knew that Kearney and his allies would grow more convinced that Renald wasn't coming and that his house was in rebellion. If they were defeated by Braedon's army, Galdasten, no doubt along with Aindreas's house, would bear much of the blame. History would remember Renald as the leader of a house of traitors. Nearly as troubling was the thought that Kearney might succeed in defeating the invaders without Galdasten's help. Renald would still be labeled a traitor, but as one whose betrayal had little significance.

Clearly they had need of haste. Yet his swordmaster did nothing to increase their pace, and the first minister seemed content to stroll along beside them, chatting amiably about anything other than the war.

"It's a cooler day by far than I would have expected so late in Adriel's waxing," he was saying now. "We've been fortunate."

"Yes, and what of it?" the duke demanded irritably. "Perhaps you care to comment on the health of the farmers' crops as we amble past the fields."

Pillad and Ewan exchanged a look.

"My lord, I believe the first minister's point was that, because of the cooler weather, we can probably keep the men marching without a rest clear through to sundown, allowing us to cover more distance today."

Renald looked at the Qirsi, who nodded. "That would be . . . helpful," he said, trying not to sound too contrite.

"Yes, my lord."

"Do you have any idea how far we are from the battle plain?"

"No, my lord," Ewan answered. "But it can't be too far now. The king marched from Audun's Castle some time ago. I expect his army met the enemy well north of Domnall, in which case it should only be another day or two."

"Two days," the duke said, exhaling. "I begrudge the time, swordmaster."

Ewan lowered his gaze. "Yes, my lord."

Renald knew what the man was thinking. If he was in such a hurry to fight, why had he waited so long before leaving Galdasten? Why had he suffered the presence of the empire's soldiers in his city for so many days? In truth, the duke had no answer for him other than the obvious. It had been a grave mistake, born of his ambition, and Elspeth's uncanny ability to gauge his darkest desires. He should have been able to admit this to them. Whatever their limitations, both Ewan and Pillad had ridden with him to war, risking their lives. They deserved far more from him than he seemed capable of offering, and so too did his men.

"Tomorrow is the Night of Two Moons, my lord," the first minister said. "There'll be ample light to march even past dusk. We can rest at twilight before continuing on for a few more hours."

Ewan frowned. "Certainly we can take advantage of the moons' light to march the men another league or so. But I don't want to push them too hard. They need some rest along the way, or they won't be fit to fight."

Renald almost told the swordmaster that he coddled the men too much. But it occurred to him that he couldn't remember the last time he had marched any distance at all. Since he was a boy accompanying his father on hunts or visits to another of Eibithar's great houses, he had ridden while common soldiers remained on foot. Perhaps in this instance Ewan knew better than he did what was best for Galdasten's army.

"I agree," he said. "We'll rest at sundown, continue southward for another league, then stop for the night."

Ewan nodded. "Very good, my lord. I'll inform the captains."

Before Renald could object, the swordmaster was riding back along the edge of the column leaving the duke with Pillad.

He had tried to spend as little time as possible alone with the Qirsi. In spite of his decision to let the minister ride with him to this war, he still had doubts about the man's loyalty. And even before he began to suspect that Pillad was a traitor, even before he had heard of the conspiracy, Renald had never felt entirely comfortable around white-hairs. He found them strange in both appearance and manner. Pillad was no exception to this.

"Shall I leave you, my lord?"

Whatever his faults, Pillad was observant.

"Perhaps so, First Minister. We'll speak again later."

The Qirsi smiled thinly. "Of course."

He slowed his mount, allowing the duke to pull ahead of him a short distance. They rode this way for several moments, and though Renald was relieved to be rid of the man, he could feel the minister watching him from behind, as if Pillad's eyes could cast heat upon his back. If the Qirsi did wish him ill, wasn't it safer to ride alongside the man, instead of in front of him, vulnerable and unguarded? After considering this briefly, he slowed his mount in turn, so that the minister pulled abreast of him.

"My lord?" Pillad asked mildly.

Faced now with having to make conversation with the man, Renald wasn't certain what to say. If only he'd just remained in front of him.

"I was wondering, First Minister, if you feel the swordmaster is too easy on the men."

It was the first thing that came to mind, and immediately he regretted saying it.

Pillad's brow creased, and he tipped his head to the side, as if pondering the question. "I'm not certain I know what you mean, my lord."

"Well, no matter."

"If you refer to his concerns about tiring them, I suppose I do think it odd. He certainly trains them hard enough. Yet he seems reluctant to put that training to the test when it comes time for war." His yellow eyes were so wide that he looked like some great pale owl. "Please don't misunderstand, my lord. I have great respect for the swordmaster. But other armies have had to march longer distances over shorter spans of time, and they've fought effectively."

Despite himself, Renald was swayed by this. "I've thought much the same thing," he said, feeling that by admitting even this much, he was betraying Ewan's trust. "I would like to cover more ground before we stop for the night."

"Of course, my lord. I know how eager you are to join the king. Still, it's probably best to be prudent under these circumstances."

"Perhaps so."

Pillad looked back over his shoulder, no doubt to see if Ewan was returning. "It might also behoove you to give some consideration to the swordmaster's command, my lord."

"His command?"

"Yes. If he's told the men that they'll only cover a certain distance in a given day, then any deviation from that plan could undermine his authority. It may even convince the men that you've lost faith in him."

"So now you believe that we should keep to the swordmaster's pace?" Renald shook his head. "I'm afraid you have me a bit confused, First Minister. One moment you seem to agree with me that Ewan is being too easy on the men, and the next you tell me that we'd be best off doing as he counsels. It almost seems that you're trying to confuse me."

The duke said this without giving it much thought, but almost as soon as the words crossed his lips, he found himself wondering if this was precisely what the first minister had meant to do. Mightn't a traitor to the court have reason to do so?

Pillad replied with an easy laugh, though Renald thought he saw something else flash in those ghostly eyes. "Forgive me, my lord," he said. "That wasn't my intent. The fact is, I know little of military tactics and even less about leading an army. Sir Traylee is the expert on such matters, not I."

"Well, thank you, First Minister," the duke said, eager now just to be away from the man. "I'll give some thought to what you've said."

"Very good, my lord."

Before Pillad had finished saying this, Renald was already kicking at his horse's flanks, putting as much distance as he dared between the Qirsi and himself. Yes, the man was behind him again, but Renald no longer cared. Just as long as he didn't have to speak with him, or see the minister's strange features. Or so he told himself. For some time after he pulled ahead of Pillad he found himself anticipating a sword thrust between the shoulder blades, flinching at every unexpected noise, and turning his head ever so slightly to try to see where the Qirsi was and what he was doing.

When Ewan finally rejoined him, the duke nearly wept with relief.

"I've spoken with the captains, my lord. They're in agreement that we can try to march two more leagues after dusk. I knew that you would prefer this, so I told them that we would. I hope that was all right."

This was how a man serving in a noble court should speak to his duke, with the clarity and purpose of a soldier. Whitehairs seemed always to be weaving mists with their words.

"Yes, swordmaster. I'm pleased to hear that. Well done."

"Thank you, my lord. Shall I leave you?"

"No!" Renald said, a bit too quickly. "I'd be grateful if you rode with me for a time."

"You honor me, my lord."

Over the next several hours, riding side by side, the two men said little. But Renald felt far safer with Ewan nearby. Let the minister make an attempt on his life. He'd die before he could raise a weapon or draw upon one of his powers. Thinking this, the duke tried to recall what magics Pillad possessed, but he could only remember healing and gleaning. There was a third, he knew. What was it?

They stopped just as the sun disappeared below the western horizon, the sky above it aflame with orange and red. Most of the men sat beside a narrow stream that wound past the grasses and stones of the northern Moorlands on its way to Binthar's Wash. The duke and swordmaster left their horses grazing on the moist grass, and walked among the men, offering words of encouragement. It had been Ewan's idea—a way to raise the men's spirits, he said—and it did seem to do his warriors some good.

At one point, Renald looked up to see Pillad, still atop his mount, gazing northward, as if he could see the towers of Galdasten Castle from this distance. A moment later one of the soldiers said something to him, drawing his attention once more. And when he finally had the opportunity to look for Pillad again, he spotted the minister standing near the soldiers, watching the duke. When their eyes met, the Qirsi nodded and smiled, as if nothing were amiss. But once more Renald had the sense that the man was deceiving him.

"I want you to send out scouts," Renald told Ewan, as they returned to their horses.

"We already have scouts ahead of us, my lord, watching for imperial soldiers or any sign of the King's Guard."

"Fine. But I also want you to send men back to the north. I want to make certain that we're not followed."

The swordmaster looked puzzled. "We left few of Braedon's men alive in Galdasten, my lord, and fewer still alive and at large. Surely there weren't enough of them to muster a force of any consequence."

"It's not the empire I fear."

"My lord?"

"Humor me, swordmaster. Send back two men. Tell them to watch the northern horizon."

"We have only a few spare mounts left, my lord."

"I don't care."

Ewan shrugged, then nodded. "Yes, my lord."

They set out again a short time later, the column of men stretching behind Renald in the gathering gloom, so that the duke could barely see the last of his men. Panya, the white moon, appeared in the east soon after nightfall, huge and pale and just a night shy of full. Even low in the sky, her glow was enough to cast long faint shadows across the moors. As she rose, her light strengthened until the grasses and stones themselves seemed luminous. Some time later, red Ilias rose below her, adding his radiance to hers: the lovers, one night before the Night of Two Moons in the turn of Adriel, Goddess of Love. Once more Renald's thoughts returned to Galdasten and Elspeth. Tomorrow would mark seventeen years since their joining, and tomorrow night seventeen years since the consummation of the their love. According to lore, lying together for the first time on Lovers' Night ensured a lifetime of love and passion. So much for the moon legends.

"My lord, listen!" Ewan said, abruptly reining his mount to a halt.

Renald did the same, and heard it as well. Two faint voices calling, "My lord! My lord!"

"What could it be?" the duke asked.

"Scouts," Ewan said, and kicked his horse to a gallop back toward the end of the column.

Renald followed, cold panic sweeping over him like an ocean wave in the snows.

The two men Ewan had sent to scout the north rode into view as the duke and his swordmaster neared the rear of Galdasten's army. Both men looked terribly young, their faces ashen in the moonlight.

"Report," Ewan commanded.

"We watched th' northern horizon as ye ordered, swordmaster. An' at first we saw nothin'. But a few times we heard horses, or thought we did. And so we slows down and waits a bit. And then we sees 'em. A large army of riders followin' behind us."

"Riders?"

"Not just riders," the other one said. "White-hairs. Must be two hundred of 'em."

"Qirsi?" Ewan said, breathless, fear in his eyes.

"Where's Pillad?" the duke asked, looking around for the man.

The swordmaster stared at him. "I don't remember seeing him when we stopped."

Renald closed his eyes and ran a hand over his face, fearing that he might vomit. "He wasn't there," he said, as certain of this as he was of his own name. "He's already gone to join them."

"You said there's two hundred of them?" Ewan asked, turning to the men once more.

"Yes, swordmaster."

"We've five times that many, my lord. Magic or no, we should be able to defeat them. We'll marshal the men, make our stand right here. Archers on the flanks, swordsmen in the center."

Renald nodded, but said nothing. Let the swordmaster and his men believe this. He knew better. These Qirsi had gotten past the force he left in Galdasten, and perhaps the Braedony fleet, as well. It would be a slaughter.

"Do you know what powers Pillad possesses?" he asked at last, gazing northward, waiting for a glimpse of the Qirsi army.

"Not all of them, my lord. I know he can heal, and I once saw him start a fire in his hearth with only a thought."

Fire, yes. That was it. They'd all be killed by Qirsi fire.

Slipping away from Renald's army was laughably easy, though it soured his mood for a time. That none of them should notice or care struck him as insulting, one final indignity among too many to count. Still, had a soldier spotted him, forcing him to fight or flee, it would have made matters considerably more difficult. It might have cost him his life. Better to be ignored than pursued.

Once he was clear of the Eandi army and the two scouts sent back by the swordmaster, he rode northward at a full gallop. And when at last he spotted the Qirsi army, he raised a hand, summoned a flame and his healing magic, and bore a bright beacon on his palm, announcing himself to his fellow warriors. Abruptly his heart was pounding, not with remorse at what he had done, nor with fear of the battle to come, but rather with anticipation. At long last, he was to meet the Weaver, to bow before the man who would lead the Forelands and guide his people to their rightful destiny. He wondered briefly if he'd recognize this man who he had only encountered previously in dreams.

He needn't have worried.

The Weaver rode at the head of the army, his mane of white hair flying behind him like a battle pennon, his face chiseled as from alabaster. Uestem jal Safhir, the merchant who first recruited Pillad into the movement, rode on one side of him. On the other rode a slight, pretty woman who looked to be no more than a year or two past Fating age. And behind the three of them came an army of his people, mounted as he was, armed as well. The force was a mere fraction of the size of Renald's, yet they had the look of conquerors from some tale of old.

Seeing Pillad, the Weaver raised a hand and his army came to a halt. The minister slowed his mount, but didn't stop until he was only a few paces from the Weaver. Then he dismounted and dropped to one knee.

"Weaver. I am Pillad jal Krenaar, first minister of Galdasten. I offer myself to your service."

"Rise, Pillad."

He straightened.

"Your duke's army is near?"

"Yes, Weaver. Perhaps half a league ahead. No more."

"Good. You've done well. You'll ride with Uestem, who commands those with shaping and fire."

The minister bowed again. "Yes, Weaver. Thank you." He started to remount, but then hesitated. "My pardon, Weaver. I know that it's not my place, but I'd ask that you use fire magic against my duke."

"Why?"

"It's the one magic I wield that can be used as a weapon. I want Renald to know that I was part of the army that destroyed him."

The Weaver regarded him briefly, then nodded. "So be it."

Pillad climbed onto his horse and fell in behind Uestem. The merchant nodded to him as he rode past, but kept silent. Once the minister would have been desperate for any word of greeting from the man, having harbored affection for him. But he cared now only for war and flame. There would be time for other considerations after their victory. For now, Pillad was just as glad to have the merchant treat him as merely another warrior.

They started southward and soon encountered the scouts. The woman riding beside the Weaver said something, but he shook his head.

"Let them go. They're nothing."

Not long after, they saw the army of Galdasten arrayed before them on the Moorlands in a great crescent.

"There will be archers on the flanks, Weaver!" Pillad cried out.

The Weaver looked back at him, and for a moment the minister worried that he had angered the man. But the Weaver simply nodded. "I know." He swept the others with his gaze. "Mists and winds!" he called.

Immediately a wind started to blow, building swiftly to a gale that howled in the stones and flattened the moorland grasses. Pillad grinned. Let Renald's archers contend with that!

The Weaver turned to Uestem and his warriors. "Fire!"

An instant later, Pillad felt something tugging at his mind. It took him only a moment to understand that it was the Weaver reaching for his magic and that of the others. He made no attempt to resist and abruptly felt power flowing through his body like sunlight through glass.

At the same time, a flame appeared just in front of the Qirsi army, brilliant blue at its center, bright yellow above that, and orange at its top. For a single heartbeat it remained where it was, seemingly suspended in midair. Then it began to move toward the Eandi soldiers, slowly at first, but building speed quickly. As it rushed forward, it grew larger as well, until it towered over the battle plain like a huge fiery cloud. It lit the faces of Galdasten's warriors, so that all the Qirsi could see their fear and despair.

Pillad saw his duke then. The man's mouth was open as if he were wailing, the killing blaze shining in his eyes. The minister almost hoped that Renald would look at him, so that he might know that Pillad had killed him, that he had contributed his magic to this spiraling storm of flame. But the duke seemed incapable of looking away from the fire. He was still staring up at it when the full force of the magic crashed down upon his army, swallowing him and the soldiers around him, blackening the ground, lighting the Moorlands as if a piece of Morna's sun had fallen to the earth. Renald hadn't even drawn his sword.

Pillad wanted to laugh aloud. Never before had he felt so strong, so alive. Never before had he been so free.

Chapter

Eleven

Glyndwr Highlands, Eibithar, Adriel's Moon waning

beni ja Krenta, archminister of Sanbira, lay on the damp ground, staring up at the few pale stars that still lingered in the brightening blue sky. Around her, the camp was coming to life slowly, warriors awakening, horses nickering in anticipation of another day's ride.

The archminister had been awake for some time. Her encounters with the Weaver always left her too unsettled to sleep, and on this past night he had come to her when the sky was still black, speaking to her only briefly before leaving her, no doubt to walk in the dreams of another of his servants. She had not entertained any hope of falling asleep again, but neither did she think it prudent to leave her sleeping roll and walk, as she often did back in Yserne after the Weaver came to her. So she lay where she was, trying to still her racing heart and slow her breathing, and turning over in her mind all that the man had told her.

Any doubts that might have lingered in her mind as to the purpose of this war in the north to which she and Sanbira's army were riding had been dispelled tonight. Braedon's invasion of Eibithar had been contrived by the Weaver's movement—he had all but said so. The armies of the Eandi were destroying one another, so that when the Weaver and his army struck at them, they would be too weakened to defend themselves. That Sanbira's queen had elected to join this war pleased him greatly.

"Your army should arrive at nearly the same time as the Solkarans," he had said. "With so many of the Foreland's powers there, making war on one another, our task grows simpler by the day. By convincing the queen to fight you've made our victory that much more certain. You're to be commended."

Abeni explained that she had little to do with the queen's decision, but he continued to praise her, particularly after learning that the first ministers of Macharzo and Norinde, both of whom served his movement as well, rode with her.

"Three of you together," he said. "Truly the gods must be with us."

There was little she could say, except, "Yes, Weaver."

"Don't reveal yourselves yet. Do nothing to delay your queen's arrival at the battle." She could hear the excitement in his voice, and she found that she felt it, too. They were approaching the culmination of their efforts, the final battle for which they had been preparing these long years. Yet, even recognizing this, she hadn't been prepared for what he said next.

"Look for me when you reach the battlefield."

"What?"

"I'll be there. I'm not going to reveal myself to you now, but you'll know me, you'll feel me as I reach for your power. Be prepared to give your magic to me so that I can wield it as my own against the enemy. Tell the other two to do the same. Our time is at hand. The Forelands will soon be ours."

The archminister had nodded, too overwhelmed to speak.

"One more thing. There's a man with Eibithar's army, a Qirsi named Grinsa jal Arriet. He claims to be a mere gleaner, but he's far more. This man is dangerous. Keep away from him. When the time comes, I'll deal with him myself. Do you understand?"

"Yes, Weaver," she whispered. "Do we also have allies among the Eibitharians?"

For a moment the Weaver said nothing, and Abeni wondered if she had angered him. When he did answer, however, his tone was mild. "Actually, yes. Usually, I don't reveal such things, but it may be time that I started to bring together those who serve me in different realms. There is a woman—your counterpart actually."

"The archminister?"

"Yes. But don't approach her unless you absolutely must. The risks are far too great."

"Yes, Weaver."

"The hour of our victory approaches. Until then." An instant later, she was awake, shivering in the darkness, though with excitement or fear or simply the cold, she couldn't say. She tried to imagine what it would be like to have another take hold of her magic, to give herself over to a man so completely. Though she had never taken a husband, she had shared her bed with many, both men and women. She wondered if it would be anything like the act of love.

Since learning that the queen intended to ride to war, and listening as Olesya speculated as to whether this conflict was connected in some way with the conspiracy, Abeni had feared that the Eandi might yet find a way to thwart the Weaver's plans. In the wake of her dream, however, she was reassured. The Weaver had spoken of the coming war with such confidence that she couldn't help but take heart. There was a portent in this dawn she was witnessing, the promise of a new era in the singing of the larks and the earliest golden rays of sunlight. For the first time since leaving Yserne with the Sanbiri army, she was anxious to be riding. When at last the soldiers and nobles and other ministers began to stir, she rose, bundled her sleeping roll, and saddled her mount with the exuberance of a young warrior riding to her first battle.

Olesya, the queen, expected Abeni to ride with her, just as the dukes of Brugaosa and Norinde, and the duchess of Macharzo assumed that their ministers would ride with them and their armies. The nobles of Sanbira had long since lost faith in their Qirsi, their trust shaken by the attempts on the life of duchess Diani of Curlinte and the death of Kreazur jal Sylbe, her first minister—or, more precisely, his murder, for

which Abeni was responsible. Eager as the archminister was
to tell Craeffe and Filtem of her dream, she would have to
await an opportunity, or create one. Diani herself had ridden
with the queen as well, and seemed to have taken it upon herself to keep watch on the archminister. Whether she expected
Abeni to make an attempt on Olesya's life or to flee the war
party at her first chance, the minister couldn't say, but as their
journey into Eibithar continued, she had found the woman's
constant presence increasingly bothersome. On this day, she
no longer cared. Let Diani of Curlinte indulge her suspicions
and her lust for vengeance. Abeni had nothing to fear from
her, nor did the movement. The woman would be crushed
with the rest of them, destroyed by the combined might of the
Weaver and those who served him.

Abeni actually smiled at the duchess as they began to ride.

"Good day, my lady. I trust you slept well?"

Diani frowned, as if confused by Abeni's courtesy. "Yes,
thank you. And you?"

"Very well, thank you." The lie came to her with such ease
that she nearly laughed aloud.

Even the prospect of another lengthy ride was not enough
to dampen her spirits. They had come a great distance
already—the ride from Yserne to Brugaosa alone had been
over forty leagues—and Abeni, who had spent little time riding before then, was in agony day and night, her muscles
aching.

Once the duke of Norinde and the duchess of Macharzo
reached Edamo's castle with their warriors, the journey began in earnest. After fording Orlagh's River into Caerisse,
the Sanbiri army rode northwest, between the duchies of
Aratamme and Valde. They then forded the headwaters of the
Kett River and began the arduous climb into the Glyndwr
Highlands, crossing into Eibithar in the midst of a violent
storm. Throughout their travels, Olesya had assured the minister that she would grow accustomed to riding, that her body
would soon learn to move with her mount, but Abeni's discomfort only grew worse, until she wondered how she would
ever make it all the way to Eibithar's Moorlands.

Over the past few days, however, as they made their way

through the highlands passing close to Glyndwr Castle and its sparkling jewel of a lake, her pain had finally begun to subside.

Hearing the cheer with which Abeni greeted Curlinte's duchess, the queen slowed her mount, allowing the two of them to catch up with her. Her master of arms, Ohan Delrasto, slowed as well, though he didn't look pleased. Abeni had noticed that he often seemed to resent those who intruded upon his time with the queen, and she wondered if the old warrior fancied himself a suitor for Olesya's affections.

"You're in a fine mood today, Archminister," the queen said. "I take it you and your mount have reached an understanding."

Abeni grinned. There were times when she did like Olesya. "I suppose you could say that, Your Highness. It may be more accurate to say that my horse has finally succeeded in training me."

The queen laughed. "Well said! I've long believed that the first step in becoming a true rider is giving up the illusion of control. As my mother used to say, we may hold the reins, but the horse holds us."

Diani frowned again. "I've been riding since I was a child, and I always have control over my mount."

"My mother also used to speak of the arrogance of youth," Olesya said, a conspiratorial tone in her voice.

"Yes, Your Highness."

"It seems I'm outnumbered," the duchess said, raising an eyebrow.

They crested a small rise, and beheld a sight that took Abeni's breath away. Ahead, less than half a league off, the earth seemed to fall away, as if Elined had carved a great hole in the surface of her world. They had reached the edge of the Caerissan Steppe. To the east, the waters of Binthar's Wash churned and rumbled, glimmering like a river of sapphires, toward a great waterfall from which rose a fine white mist. Beyond the rim of the steppe and a thousand fourspans below them, the Moorlands stretched toward the horizon. Brilliant green, they were bounded on the east by the wash, which looked like little more than a thin blue ribbon, and on the west by the great Sussyn River. Farther to the east, so dark that it looked almost black, stood Eibithar's North Wood, nearly as vast as the Moorlands and divided by yet another river, the Thorald, if she remembered correctly.

"What are these falls?" Diani asked in a hushed voice.

"Raven Falls, I believe," the queen said. "I'd never go so far as to say that any realm was as beautiful as our own, but surely Eibithar comes closest." She inhaled deeply, as if trying to breathe in the splendor. "We'll rest here briefly before beginning the descent." She cast a sympathetic glance at Abeni. "I'm afraid going down from the highlands will be no easier than the climb into them."

A moment later they were joined by the dukes of Brugaosa and Norinde, the duchess of Macharzo, and their Qirsi.

Craeffe and Filtem still looked ill at ease atop their mounts, and Abeni took some solace in knowing that however much she would suffer on the way down from the highlands, they would suffer more. She shared their cause, but she had never liked either of the Qirsi, particularly Craeffe, who had long envied Abeni's status as a chancellor in the Weaver's movement. Fortunately, their mutual dislike made it far easier for them to spend time in each other's company without drawing the attention of Olesya and her nobles. The real danger was not Diani or the queen—Abeni and her allies knew better than to say anything revealing in front of them. But the fourth Qirsi in their midst, Vanjad jal Qien, Brugaosa's first minister, remained loyal to his lord and to the realm. As far as Abeni could tell, the man had never even considered whether his duke deserved such devotion. He was, in her mind, the worst kind of Qirsi traitor.

But he stood with them now, as the Eandi spoke among themselves, keeping Abeni from relating to Craeffe and Filtem what the Weaver had told her.

"I trust you slept well, cousin?" Abeni said, eyeing Craeffe.

The woman seemed as unprepared for her graciousness as Diani had been. "I suppose," she said. And then as an afterthought, "You?"

"Actually, no. I had a dream that kept me awake for much of the night."

Craeffe's eyes widened, and she looked sharply at Filtem. After a moment, he gave a nod that was almost imperceptible.

"Minister," he said, placing a hand lightly on Vanjad's shoulder, "I wonder if I might have a word with you, in private."

"Of course, cousin."

The two men walked off a short distance, leaving Abeni alone with Craeffe, who would tell Filtem later all he needed to know.

Abeni and Macharzo's minister gazed out at the distant Moorlands, the wind stirring their white hair. To anyone watching, they would have seemed to be discussing the terrain.

"The Weaver came to you?"

"Yes. Our conversation was brief, but quite illuminating."

"Strange that he didn't contact Filtem or me as well."

Abeni smiled, as if the minister had said something amusing. "Actually, cousin, it's not strange at all. This is precisely why he has chancellors in his movement. He told me knowing that I would, in turn, tell you." She extended an arm, as if pointing at some feature of Eibithar's landscape, and Craeffe nodded, though Abeni could see that the muscles in her jaw were bunched. "I'm surprised that after all this time, you still haven't gotten used to this."

"Just tell me what he said, and be done with it."

Craeffe pointed at something else, and Abeni looked off in that direction, passing a hand casually through her hair.

"Very well." The archminister related her conversation, repeating as best she could exactly what the Weaver had said about how they would know him on the battlefield, and how he would reach for their power. Speaking the words, she felt her excitement return in a rush; by the time she had finished, her hands were trembling, and her cheeks burned as if she were a love-struck girl.

For all her carefully rehearsed indifference, Craeffe could not entirely conceal her own astonishment at what she heard.

"How long did he say it would be?" she asked, breathless and grinning.

"He didn't. He just said to look for him when we reached the Moorlands. For all we know, he's already there."

"I've been with the movement for some time now," she whispered. "I've dreamed of this for even longer. But until now, I don't think I ever really believed it would happen." She looked at Abeni with a diffidence the archminister had never seen in her before. "Forgive me, Chancellor. I hope you understand."

Abeni wasn't certain what to say. It occurred to her that if the promise of seeing the Weaver could humble Craeffe ja Tref in this way, his powers must truly be great. But this she kept to herself. "I think I do understand, First Minister," she said at last. "We've all been waiting so long. But we can't allow our anticipation of what awaits us on the Moorlands to make us careless, not when we're so close."

Craeffe nodded. Were those tears glistening in her pale eyes?

"You'll speak with Filtem?"

"Of course, Archminister."

"What powers does he possess?"

"Gleaning, fire, and mists and winds," she said. "And I have gleaning, fire, and shaping."

Abeni nodded. "I have gleaning, shaping, and mists and winds. No wonder he's so pleased that we're together. Our powers blend quite well."

Filtem and Vanjad were walking back in their direction, chatting amiably, though Filtem had an eye on Craeffe.

"Sorry to abandon you, cousins," the minister said, grinning at them. "But occasionally the common interests of our dukes make it necessary for us to speak beyond the hearing of those who serve Sanbira's matriarchs."

It was a fine cover for what he had done. Norinde and Brugaosa were closely allied, in large part because the two dukes did not trust Olesya or her duchesses.

"You're forgiven, cousin. At least this time."

Vanjad gave an earnest look. "I assure you, Archminister, we spoke only of matters pertaining to our houses. We did not speak ill of the queen or those who serve her."

"The thought never entered my mind, First Minister."

A few moments later, the queen, her master of arms, and the nobles returned as well. Behind them, soldiers were climbing onto their mounts once more. Diani was regarding the ministers warily, as if she regretted going off with the queen and leaving the Qirsi to themselves.

Olesya swung herself onto her horse and glanced back at the ministers. "Are you ready to ride on, Archminister?"

"I am, Your Highness."

The queen nodded and kicked at her mount.

Abeni gave a quick smile to Craeffe and the others. "See you at the bottom," she said. She remounted and soon had pulled abreast of the queen and the duchess of Curlinte.

Diani refused to look at her, but Olesya glanced over, her dark eyes dancing.

"Judging from the way your fellow ministers looked, I gather that Qirsi don't ride much."

"Some do, Your Highness, but not many. Still you needn't worry; I have no doubt that we'll all manage the descent."

"I should hope so. We'll have need of you once we reach the Moorlands."

Abeni had to smile. "We'll be ready, Your Highness. You have my word on that."

She knew the Qirsi was lying, that in fact everything the archminister said and did was a pretense intended to disguise her treachery. Diani was galled by every kind word that came from the woman's mouth, every courtesy she extended to the queen or Sanbira's other nobles. The duchess could almost see the blood staining her hands, the wraiths hovering at her shoulder, reminders of every murder committed in the name of the conspiracy. She looked at the woman, and she felt anew her grief over the garroting of her brother. She heard Abeni's voice, obsequious and smooth, and she winced at the remembered pain of the arrows that had pierced her own flesh on the Curlinte headlands.

Abeni ja Krenta, archminister to the queen of Sanbira, was a traitor. Diani wanted to shout this at the top of her voice, she wanted to brand the woman as such with hot irons. But she hadn't the proof.

Ean knew that it wasn't for lack of trying—she and her father had searched Castle Yserne time and again for any sign that the archminister had joined cause with the renegades, and Diani had hardly allowed the woman out of her sight since they left the royal city. Thus far, she had found nothing. She would have liked to listen to Abeni's conversation with Macharzo's first minister that morning, as they stood at the edge of the steppe. For that matter, she would also have been interested to know what the first ministers of Norinde and Brugaosa discussed as they walked off on their own. As far as the duchess was concerned, they were all traitors until they proved their fealty. Her father would have scoffed at her suspicions, seeing in them the rash prejudice of a child. Olesya would have felt the same way. So, Diani didn't speak to anyone of her suspicions. She needed evidence, and though Abeni had been uncommonly clever thus far, Diani remained convinced that she could not conceal her treachery much longer.

The ride down the face of the Caerissan Steppe consumed much of the day. The distance wasn't great, but the steepness of the path at times forced the riders to dismount and lead their horses on foot. With Raven Falls thundering nearby, filling the air with a fine, cool mist and the soft, sweet scent of lush ferns and mosses, the day never grew too hot. But even for an experienced rider like Diani, the descent was exhausting.

When at last they reached the base of the slope, her back and legs were aching, and her riding clothes were soaked with sweat. At the bottom of the steppe they turned eastward, riding to the banks of Binthar's Wash. There they made camp, though nightfall was still some time off. This close to the bottom of Raven Falls, the river churned and frothed like some great beast, its wild waters reflecting the brilliant golden light of the late-day sun. Diani could see the famed walls of Eibithar's City of Kings in the distance, also bathed in the sun's glow, and she wondered briefly if they would stop there before continuing on to the Moorlands. It made no sense to do so, she knew, but she had always dreamed of seeing Audun's Castle.

After unsaddling her horse, she returned to where the queen was speaking with her master of arms. Diani had long since decided that even if she couldn't convince Olesya that her archminister was a traitor, she could do everything in her power to make certain that the queen came to no harm. She rarely let Olesya out of her sight and had privately vowed that she would give her own life before she allowed the conspiracy to strike at Sanbira's queen.

Diani nodded once to Ohan before facing the queen. "The soldiers are making camp, Your Highness. The captains tell me that we have ample stores to see us through the rest of the journey, but a few of the archers have gone back up the slope to hunt for supper. I didn't see anything wrong with this, so I told them to carry on."

Olesya gave an indulgent smile, reminding Diani of her own mother. "That's fine, Lady Curlinte. Thank you."

"Is there anything I can do for you, Your Highness?"

"No, thank you. The master of arms and I are going to walk back to the base of the falls. I've never been so close to them, and have heard about them all my life."

"Of course, Your Highness. That sounds very nice." Diani continued to stand there, waiting for the queen to lead the way.

"Actually, we intended to go alone."

The duchess blinked, then glanced at the master of arms. Ohan was blushing to the tips of his ears, his dark eyes fixed on the ground. He was tall and lean, with the shoulders and chest of a warrior, but at that moment he resembled nothing so much as a shy boy. Quite suddenly Diani understood that Ohan and the queen were in love, or close to it. The young duchess, her own cheeks growing hot, stared at the queen, who gazed back at her placidly.

"But, Your Highness, it could be dangerous." She wasn't quite sure what she was warning Olesya against, but still she forged on. "I believe it would be best if I accompanied you—"

"Diani, think for a moment. Don't you think that Ohan is

capable of protecting me? He is, after all, the finest swordsman in the land."

"With the possible exception of your father," the master of arms added hastily.

"Of course, but—"

"Rest, Diani. Go find Naditia. She's been riding with Edamo and Alao all day. I'm sure she'd be grateful for your company."

The duchess looked away, feeling foolish. "Yes, Your Highness. Enjoy your walk."

"Thank you. We will."

The two of them strolled off, leaving Diani alone with her embarrassment. After standing there for several moments, she decided that she would seek out the duchess of Macharzo as Olesya had suggested. She and Naditia had never been close, but if Diani had been forced to spend the entire day with the dukes of Norinde and Brugaosa, she would have been grateful for any companionship at all. She had just started walking in Naditia's direction, however, when she saw Abeni speaking with one of the other Qirsi. As she drew nearer to them, she realized that it was Macharzo's first minister. It was perfect—just the excuse she needed to intrude.

She walked to where they stood, noting that they fell silent at her approach.

"Forgive the interruption, Archminister, but I was wondering if the first minister could tell me where I might find her duchess."

"You're not interrupting at all, my lady," Abeni said pleasantly.

But the other woman regarded her cautiously, overlarge yellow eyes staring out from a small, thin face, so that she looked more like a waif than a minister.

"I believe she's down beside the river, my lady," the first minister said at last. "That's where I saw her last."

"Thank you." Diani faced Abeni again, scouring her mind for anything that she might say to prolong their conversation and learn what the two women had been discussing.

"Is there anything else, my lady?" the archminister asked, eyeing Diani as if she thought the duchess simple.

"Actually," she said, "I've been wondering if you've given any more thought to the questions my father and I asked you while we were still in Yserne."

She sensed the woman's annoyance. "You mean about traitors in the queen's court?"

"Yes."

"I'm afraid, my lady, that I have little more to tell you than I did the last time we spoke of this. After Kreazur's death, I tried to think of who in Yserne might have been working with him, but I hadn't cause to suspect any of the Qirsi in our court. That hasn't changed."

"A pity." She glanced at the other woman. "And you, First Minister?"

"My lady?"

"Well, surely you've heard of the attacks on me, and the death of my first minister."

The minister nodded, her expression revealing little. "Yes, I did, my lady. I was horrified, as was all of Macharzo."

"I'm sure. And since then, has anything happened to make you question the loyalty of the Qirsi in your duchess's castle?"

"No, my lady. But then, that's not my way."

Diani narrowed her eyes. "What do you mean?"

The woman faltered. "Nothing, my lady," she said, shaking her head. "Forgive me. I should have simply answered your question and left it at that."

"But you didn't. And I want to know what you meant."

The minister glanced at Abeni, but the archminister was staring at the ground, her lips pursed. "It just seems to me that you've allowed the treachery of one minister to color your perceptions of all Qirsi. I wouldn't do that."

Diani knew that she should have been enraged. This might not have been her own Qirsi speaking to her so, but the woman was just a minister and Diani was a duchess. Instead she felt like crying. The criticism stung too much for her to respond at all. Hadn't her father said the same thing to her before she left Yserne with Olesya's army? Hadn't the queen herself done so as well? Here she had thought to trick these women into revealing something of themselves, and all she had done was give them cause to hate her and question her motives.

"Yes, well, you shouldn't presume to judge me, First Minister. If the attempt had been made on your life, you might feel differently."

She knew that this made little sense, but she didn't care. She only wished to be away from them, and without another word, she stalked off toward the river, her face flushed with shame. Diani no longer felt much like speaking with Naditia, but she had asked the minister where to look for the duchess, and she couldn't very well walk in the opposite direction.

She found Naditia sitting on a large stone by the water's edge, staring up at the rim of the steppe, a large hand raised to her brow to shield her eyes from the sun. Seeing Diani approach, she stood, looking uncomfortable, as though she wished to be alone.

"Forgive the intrusion, Lady Macharzo."

"Not at all. Has something happened?"

"No. The queen told me you might like some company after spending the day with the dukes."

Naditia smiled at that. She was a large woman, built more like a man, and a powerful one at that. Her features were blunt, her yellow hair cropped short. It was said that she favored her father, and that this was unfortunate, for her mother, the old duchess of Macharzo, had been quite beautiful. But her smile softened her face, even made her pretty, in a coarse way.

"If I'm disturbing you, I'll go."

Naditia sat again, shaking her head. "It's all right."

Diani found a stone on which to sit, and gazed up at the steppe. Much of the cliff face was shrouded in shadow, but she could make out the rocky crags and gnarled old trees that lined the top. Swifts darted along the edge of the bluff, chasing one another in tight circles and veering so suddenly that it took her breath away just to watch them.

"The dukes weren't that bad," the duchess said after a long

silence, her eyes still fixed on the ridge. "They mostly just talked to each other and ignored me."

Others might have been offended by this, but Naditia, Diani knew, was so painfully shy that she probably was grateful.

"Well, I'm glad to hear that. But I'm certain that if you wanted to ride with the queen tomorrow, she'd be pleased to have you join us. I know I would."

The woman smiled again, glancing at Diani just for an instant, then shaking her head. "Thanks, but I should ride with my warriors."

It was custom for the army of a lesser house to ride or march behind that of the queen. Because Macharzo was considered a weaker house than either Brugaosa or Norinde, Naditia's warriors rode last in the column.

"I understand," Diani said. "But I couldn't do it. I'd rather ride alone than with Edamo and Alao."

"If I was in your position I'd feel the same."

"I'm not certain I know what you mean."

Naditia looked panicked, as if she wished she hadn't spoken. Why did everyone around her seem so afraid of making her angry?

"I shouldn't have said that. I just was . . . I meant that with your brother . . . and then the attempt on your life. It's no secret that Curlinte and Brugaosa have been enemies for a long time."

"It's all right. My father hates Edamo a lot more than I do. I actually believe that the conspiracy was behind both the attack on me and the murder of my brother." She gave a small smile. "Still, I know what you mean. Edamo and I will never be friends."

Naditia nodded, her relief palpable.

"Have you seen any evidence of the conspiracy in Macharzo?" Diani asked, thinking once more of her strange conversation with Naditia's first minister.

"None at all. That doesn't mean it's not there, of course. Only that its members have been careful."

"Do you trust your minister?"

"Craeffe?" She shrugged, a frown creasing her forehead. "I used to. I'm not certain anymore."

"Why not?"

"She's changed in recent turns, grown quieter, more sullen. But I'm sure I've changed, too. She may sense that I have doubts about her, and probably she resents it."

"I often see her speaking with the archminister."

Naditia stared at her, nodding. "I've noticed that, too. And she spends a good deal of time with Alao's first minister. I believe they're lovers." She blushed and looked away. "Though that doesn't mean anything."

"Maybe it does." Diani paused. "Some time ago, not long after my first minister was killed, the queen asked me to keep watch on the archminister. I haven't been able to prove anything yet, but I don't trust her. If you'd be willing to keep an eye on her as well, along with your own minister and Alao's, I'd be grateful."

"Of course."

Diani smiled. "Thank you."

They spoke for a while longer. It turned out that Naditia remembered Diani's mother quite vividly. Once, while visiting Yserne with her own mother, she had entered a chamber uninvited only to find Dalvia and the queen having a private conversation. The queen had said little, but Diani's mother spoke to her quite sternly before sending the girl on her way. The incident had left enough of an impression that even after becoming Macharzo's duchess, Naditia had still been intimidated by Dalvia.

"That sounds like mother," Diani said, laughing at the story. "She was very kind, really, but she could seem terribly cross when she wanted to."

"That's a fine skill for a noble to have. I know, because I don't."

Diani grinned, realizing that she liked this woman far more than she had imagined she would.

A moment later, they heard voices calling out from west of the river. Scrambling up the riverbank with Naditia at her side, Diani saw that the archers had returned, carrying four stags, several does, and a good number of partridges.

"It seems we're going to eat well tonight."

Naditia nodded, and together they walked back to the camp.

"You're a fool!" Abeni said under her breath, as she watched the duchess walk away. "You couldn't just leave it, could you? You should have just answered her question and let it be. But no. You had to say more. 'That's not my way.' Demons and fire, Craeffe! What were you thinking?"

"Calm yourself, cousin," the minister said, though without her usual composure. "She's just a dull-witted girl, barely old enough to rule her house."

"And you're an idiot. That dull-witted girl has managed to convince the queen that Kreazur's death was more than it seemed."

"That would seem to be your fault, wouldn't it?"

"She has Olesya's ear, and she's just gone to speak with your duchess. If we give her cause to question our loyalty— as you just did—she'll destroy us."

Craeffe gave a small breathless laugh. "Now I know that you're fretting for no reason. My duchess is no more a threat to this movement than my horse. Even if she learned something of our movement, she'd be too afraid to voice her suspicions. If her mother was still alive, perhaps I'd share your fears. But the daughter is nothing."

"I hope you're right. As it is, the Weaver won't be pleased to hear about this."

Craeffe blanched. "There really isn't any need to mention it to him, is there, Chancellor?"

"That depends on you, Minister."

Craeffe lowered her eyes. "Yes, of course. I didn't mean to imply that you had made a mistake with Kreazur."

"Yes, you did. But I'll take that as an apology and assume that you won't speak of it again."

"I won't, Chancellor," the woman said through clenched teeth. "You have my word."

Abeni grinned, knowing that she was enjoying herself far too much.

A short time later, the soldiers returned with food for the evening meal. Gradually the nobles returned as well. Diani and Naditia gave no indication that they had gleaned anything from Craeffe's insolence, but they did seem to have forged a bond at the river, and once more Abeni found herself cursing the minister's recklessness.

The balance of the evening passed without incident, as did the next several days. Now that the army had reached the moors of Eibithar, Olesya pushed them harder than ever. They covered nearly ten leagues each day, riding due north toward Galdasten, where the empire's army was said to have made land. On the third day after their descent from the steppe, as they drew nearer to the central moorlands, they began to see columns of smoke rising into the sky far off toward the horizon. Sensing that they were near the warring armies, Olesya began to send out scouting parties, several at a time ranging to the east and west as well as to the north.

Early the following morning, just after they had set out from camp, the western party returned, bearing news of a great army marching from the southwest.

"Is it Kentigern?" Olesya asked the lead rider as he steered his mount next to hers.

"No, Your Highness. They're burning crops and homes as they go. This is an invading army."

"What colors do they fly?"

"Gold and red, Your Highness."

The queen cast a dark look at Ohan and Diani.

"What would the empire be doing down here?" the duchess asked.

"It's not the empire. Think, Diani. Braedon isn't the only realm that flies banners of gold and red."

Diani's eyes widened. "Solkara! It's the Aneirans."

Olesya nodded. "Yes." She faced the rider again. "How many are they?"

"More than a thousand, Your Highness. But they're on foot."

"We can stop them," Ohan said. "Keeping to our mounts and using our bowmen wisely, we can defeat an army that size."

"No!" Abeni bit her tongue, furious with herself for speaking so rashly. Both Olesya and Diani were staring at her as if she had just told them of the Weaver.

"You have something to say, Archminister?" the queen demanded. Abeni could hear the distrust in her voice.

"Forgive me, Your Highness. I was merely going to suggest that we might be better off joining with Kearney's army first. We're on horseback. Aneira's men aren't. We'll reach Eibithar's army well before they do, and we can warn the king of Aneira's approach. That way, Kearney won't be caught unawares, and we won't have to risk fighting a larger army."

The master of arms appeared to weigh this. "Actually, she makes a good point."

The duchess continued to glare at her as if she hadn't heard.

"Did they see you?" the queen asked her scout.

"I don't believe so, Your Highness, but I can't be certain."

"All right. Go tell the dukes and Lady Macharzo what you've seen. Tell them we'll continue to ride through the day and well into the night. By the time the sun sets we'll be far enough from the Aneirans to light torches. Except for brief rests, we won't stop again until we find Kearney and his army."

"Yes, Your Highness."

"Once you've delivered that message, I want you and your party to ride west again. Keep pace with us, and watch the Aneirans for as long as you can. If they change direction or do anything unexpected, return here immediately and inform me. Do you understand?"

"Yes, Your Highness." He bowed to her as best he could atop his mount before riding off toward the other nobles.

Abeni gazed straight ahead, revealing nothing with her expression, but inside she was smiling with relief. The Weaver wanted both armies at the battle on the Moorlands. And he would have them.

The queen, with Ohan at her side, had pulled ahead of the archminister again. It took Abeni a moment to realize that the duchess wasn't with them.

"You're one of them."

The archminister started at the sound of Diani's voice. Somehow the woman was right beside her, hatred in her black eyes.

"That's why you didn't want us to attack. I'm sure of it now."

"I don't know what you mean." But Abeni could hear the flutter in her own voice.

"Yes, you do. You got your way this time. I commend you for that. Somehow you convinced the master of arms that you had the army's interests at heart. But I'll be watching you as never before. And at the first move you make against the queen, I'll kill you."

She kicked at her mount and rode ahead of Abeni, her back straight, her dark hair dancing in the wind.

Despite the pounding of her heart, Abeni nearly laughed aloud. At the first move . . . By then it would be too late.

Chapter

Twelve

The Moors of Durril, Aneira

ou know that she pursues you, even as we speak."

"Yes, Weaver."

"And you know what you must do?"

Terror and grief warred within Fetnalla's heart, threatening to rend it in two. She wanted to hide her feelings from the Weaver, but despair overwhelmed her; even if she had the wherewithal to try, he would have seen through her deception.

She hadn't needed the Weaver to tell her that Evanthya was following her; she'd known for days. She hadn't yet seen any sign of her beloved, but Fetnalla felt her presence in other ways: the tingling of her skin as she slept at night, dreaming of the unmistakably tender touch of Evanthya's lips and slender hands on her back and her breasts; the hint of the woman's voice in the cry of a falcon circling overhead; the elusive scent of her hair and skin riding the warm wind. Illusions, of course, brought on by her longing for Evanthya, and by her loneliness. When these sensations persisted, Fetnalla tried to tell herself that her fear of being caught and her guilt at all she had done were getting the best of her. But the feeling that she was being trailed remained with her, growing stronger with each passing day. And the more she considered the matter, the more certain she became that in fact Evanthya was following her. It made sense. Evanthya would never just let her go, particularly after Fetnalla killed Brall, duke of Orvinti, and revealed herself as a traitor to the realm.

The truth was, Fetnalla would have been devastated if Evanthya had not come after her. For her part, had their roles been reversed, Fetnalla would have followed her love to the farthest reaches of northern Eibithar and across Amon's Ocean. She had fled not only to save her own life and find the conspiracy, but also to shield Dantrielle's minister from harm. All of which made answering the Weaver's question all the more difficult. Fetnalla knew what he expected of her, but the very idea of it made her tremble like a palsied child. She couldn't even bring herself to speak of it.

"Do you still think she can be turned?" he asked her, his voice as close to gentle as she had ever heard it.

"No, Weaver."

"A brave answer. I sense what it cost you to admit that." He paused, seeming to search for the right words. "I need to ask you if you can do this—and I must have the truth."

"You want me to kill her." She sounded dull, but she couldn't help herself, and for once the Weaver didn't lose patience with her.

"She has to die," he said. "She is a threat to you and to this movement."

"She's not interested in the movement. She only cares for me, and she's no threat."

"You know this?"

"I know her."

Fetnalla saw him shake his head, the wild mane of hair, made black by his brilliant white sun, moving back and forth slowly, even sadly. "That's not enough. A year ago, perhaps, but not now, when we're so close. I can't risk allowing her to live. And since you know her so well and you're so near to her, you're the one to kill her."

She felt tears coursing down her face, but she didn't bother to wipe them. "Isn't there anyone else?"

"Actually, there are others who are near, who are making their way northward as you are, but I want you to do this. You and I have spoken of this before, and I've long believed that this would be the greatest test of your loyalty to our movement. If you can take the life of this woman you love, then you will have earned a place at my side. You will become part of the new nobility, the Qirsi nobility, that is to rule the Forelands."

"And what if I can't?"

"As I said, there are others. You won't be saving her life, you'll only be imperiling your own. You've done so much more than I ever expected you would. I had questioned whether you could kill your duke, or any of his men, for that matter. Don't disappoint me now."

He had been kind to her thus far, but Fetnalla knew that his generosity only went so far.

"Yes, Weaver."

"You're on the Moors of Durril."

"Yes, in the northeast corner."

"How far from the Tarbin?"

"Not very. A day's ride at the most."

"Very well. Remain there. Allow her to find you; build a fire if you must. I don't want her to cross into Eibithar."

Fetnalla wanted to plead for Evanthya's life, or, failing that, to beg him to find another to kill her love. It was all she could do not to fall to the ground sobbing, berating him for his cruelty, cursing his tests and his promises and his threats. But somehow she managed it. She stood utterly still, afraid even to draw breath. She knew that he could read her thoughts, but there was little she could do about that.

"You're brave," he said at length. "And I sense your strength."

"Thank you, Weaver," she whispered.

In the next instant she opened her eyes, blinking several times to clear her sight. White Panya and red Ilias were climbing to the east, though they were still low enough in the sky so that their light did not obscure the brilliant stars overhead. The night was warm, but Fetnalla found that she was shivering. Her clothes and hair were soaked with sweat, as they always were after these encounters with the Weaver, and her face was damp with tears. Alone save for her mount, she removed her wet clothes and sat naked, allowing the mild breeze to dry her skin and soothe her heart.

Eventually she lay back down, pulling her blanket up to her chin and staring at the moons until she fell back asleep.

When next she woke, the sun was high in the eastern sky, warming the moor. She sat up quickly, cursing herself for sleeping so late into the morning. Then it all came back to her, crashing down like a wave, stealing her breath. *Remain there,* the Weaver had said. *Allow her to find you.*

But what if she didn't? What if Fetnalla explained to him that in spite of her best efforts, Evanthya had passed her by? No sooner had she formed the thought, however, than she realized that such a transparent lie would never work. The Weaver would find Evanthya eventually and he'd kill Fetnalla, too.

What did it say about the love Fetnalla shared with Evanthya that she should choose to kill the woman herself rather than allow another to do it? She tried to tell herself that she feared another Qirsi might be too cruel in carrying out the Weaver's command. She desperately wanted to believe that.

Not wishing to ponder the matter further, she rose, dressed, and gathered what wood she could find for a fire. No trees grew in this part of the moor, but there were enough low shrubs to feed a small blaze. The branches were fresh and gave off far more smoke than heat, but under these circumstances, that was just what Fetnalla wanted.

She spent much of the day sitting beside the fire, feeding more branches into its low flames, and foraging for additional fuel. All the time, she kept an eye on the southern horizon, searching for some sign of her love. As the hours stretched on, she began to wonder how long the Weaver would expect her to wait. Wasn't it possible that Evanthya had taken another route northward? Even as she formed the question, however, Fetnalla knew that she hadn't. Any farther east, and she would have had to climb onto the steppe; any farther west and she would have had to cross Harrier Fen, or worse, brave the waters near Kentigern, where there was war. Fetnalla had chosen to come this way because it was the quickest and safest path to Galdasten, and Evanthya would do the same.

Late in the day, at long last, a figure appeared in the distance, riding a horse, white hair flying in the wind. At first Fetnalla was certain that this was Evanthya, and her heart began to race, not with dread at having to kill her, but with the familiar thrill of knowing they would soon be together.

As the rider drew closer, however, she realized that this wasn't Evanthya at all. It was a man, tall, with narrow shoulders and a thin face. Pronjed jal Drenthe, archminister of Aneira. Fetnalla stood. For just an instant she even considered drawing her sword.

"I saw your fire," he said, as he approached. He reined his horse to a halt a few fourspans from where she stood, but he made no move to dismount. "You want her to find you?"

Fetnalla and Pronjed had never spoken of the conspiracy. After Carden's death, she and her duke had speculated that the archminister might be a traitor, but they had never confronted him. Since joining the movement herself, Fetnalla had spent almost no time in the man's company. Yet it seemed now that each knew where the other's loyalty lay. Why else would Pronjed be riding northward? Why else would she?

"I've been instructed to wait for her."

He nodded, showing no surprise. "She's about a day's ride behind me—she's been following me almost since the moment I escaped from Dantrielle."

There are others. "The Weaver sent you this way."

"He didn't have to. When I left Dantrielle, my only aim

was to reach the Moorlands as quickly as possible. But when he learned that I could lead the first minister to you, he told me to go slowly enough to keep her close." He hesitated. "Are you going to . . . ? What is it he expects of you?"

"I think you know."

His eyes widened slightly, but otherwise his expression didn't change. "Can you do it?"

Fetnalla found herself wondering if Pronjed was asking for himself or on behalf of the Weaver, and she answered cautiously. "The Weaver has told me what needs to be done. What else matters?"

"I could do it for you. The Weaver need never know."

She eyed him doubtfully. "Why would you take such a risk?"

"It's the least I can do. You once healed me when I came to you in need, and you guarded my secret. I haven't forgotten that."

Fetnalla had, though hearing him speak of it, she remembered it all quite clearly. They had been in Castle Solkara for Carden's funeral, not long before the poisoning that nearly killed her. The archminister came to her quarters early in the morning with a shattered bone in his hand, which, he said, had come from a fall he had taken the night before. And with the memory, came a sudden insight.

"The Weaver did that to you!" she whispered. "He broke your hand—it didn't happen in some fall."

He smiled weakly. "Very good, cousin."

"But why did he hurt you?"

"It was punishment for something I did, something that angered him greatly."

"What?"

The smile lingered, but there was a haunted look in Pronjed's pale yellow eyes as he shook his head. "It's not a matter I wish to discuss."

"Yet you offer to risk angering him again by helping me."

"As I say, I feel that I owe you this much. And if neither of us tells the Weaver, there is no risk."

"I think we both know better. Keeping secrets from him is

no small task." She looked away from him, gazing southward once more, as if expecting to see Evanthya at any moment. "Besides, I think it's best that I do this."

"I believe I understand. Perhaps I should be on my way then."

A part of her would have liked for him to stay. She had been alone for so many days that it felt good to talk to someone, even about this. But she couldn't bring herself to ask him to remain with her, so she merely nodded. "May the gods treat you kindly, Archminister. I'm grateful to you for offering to help me."

"Gods keep you safe, Fetnalla. I'll look for you on the Moorlands."

He clicked his tongue at his mount and the beast turned, resuming the journey toward Eibithar. Fetnalla watched him ride off for a time, until he was little more than a speck in the distance. Then she threw another branch on the fire and sat facing south, scanning the moors for her love.

Nightfall brought a sense of relief. Even early in the waning, the moons didn't rise until several hours after dusk—they didn't climb high enough to light the moors until well past midnight—and Evanthya wouldn't ride far in the darkness. Fetnalla tried to eat, but she had no appetite. She unrolled her sleeping roll and lay down, staring at the low flames. Her clothes stank of smoke and horse and sweat. She could only imagine how she must look. How strange it was to worry about her appearance now, when she was waiting to kill her lover. Eventually, she fell into a deep, dreamless slumber, waking only when she felt the sun warming her face. Again, she had slept far into the morning.

Sitting up, she noticed that her fire had burned out. Zetya nickered and bobbed her head.

"Good morning to you, too."

The horse whinnied again and stomped a hoof.

"What is it you—?"

She froze, her heart suddenly pounding. Not a hundred fourspans from where she lay, Evanthya sat on her horse, her sword in hand, her fine white hair stirred gently by the breeze. Their eyes met and locked, and for what seemed an eternity Fetnalla could do nothing but gaze back at her love, struggling to remember how to breathe.

Finally, she forced herself to her feet, running a hand through her ragged hair. She glanced at Evanthya's sword and made herself grin. "Are you planning to use that on me?"

Evanthya looked down at it for a moment, then shrugged. "I don't know." Her voice sounded small and thin, as if the distance between them were much greater than it appeared.

"You know that I can shatter it if I must."

"Is that what it's come to, then? Are we to fight?"

"I'd rather we didn't."

Evanthya whispered something to her mount, and the beast began to step closer. She kept her sword out, and her eyes, bright as gold and as lovely as ever, never left Fetnalla's face.

"You broke the siege," Fetnalla said, watching her love approach.

"Yes, with help from the other dukes, and from Orvinti's army." Evanthya halted just in front of her and dismounted, her blade still in hand.

"Your duke survived?"

"Yes."

"Good. I always liked Tebeo. Put your sword away, Evanthya."

Her love had started to walk toward her, but now she faltered, appearing uncertain as to what she should do.

"I said, put it away."

"And if I won't?"

It was as easy as drawing breath, as immediate as thought. There was a sound like the chiming of a small bell, and in the next instant the blade of Evanthya's sword lay shattered on the ground. Once more, as she had the night she killed Brall and his men, Fetnalla marveled at her own power, at the mastery with which she wielded her magic. The Weaver had given her this, simply by speaking to her of the wonders their people could accomplish working together, by forcing her to become more than she had been.

And gazing at her love as she stared at the broken weapon in her hand, Fetnalla realized that Evanthya could never truly understand. She still equated loyalty with fealty to the Eandi courts. She still measured strength by counting Eandi warriors and gauging the quality of their weapons. She could no more contemplate joining the movement than she could hacking off her own arm. Yet, standing on the plain, feeling the sun and wind on her face, feeling more alive than she ever had, Fetnalla also understood that the only way to save Evanthya's life was to force the woman to become more than she was, just as the Weaver had done for her. Probably it wouldn't work. Probably Fetnalla would have to kill her. But she owed it to herself and to Evanthya to try.

"You knew that I was a shaper," she said, speaking softly, as to a frightened child.

Evanthya nodded, still looking at the hilt of her sword. A single tear rolled down her cheek, but she made no effort to wipe it away. "That's how you killed Brall."

"Evanthya—"

Her eyes snapped up, meeting Fetnalla's once more, silencing her. "When did you join them?" she demanded. "How long have you been a traitor?"

Fetnalla's anger flared, and she struggled to control it. She had to make Evanthya see the world as she saw it, which meant, at least for the moment, accepting what a limited notion she had of the Weaver's cause.

"I'm not a traitor," she said, pleased by how calm she sounded.

"Don't lie to me!"

"I'm not lying. I'm with the movement. I killed Brall and his men. But that doesn't make me a traitor."

"What kind of madness is that? The movement?"

"Yes. That's what we call it. We're led by a Weaver, Evanthya. He wants to unite all the realms of the Forelands and rule them as king. Think about that. A Qirsi king. Qirsi nobles. How long have our people been forced to serve the Eandi, to put up with their foolish wars and their limited minds? Isn't it time we claimed the land as our own?"

"Would you listen to yourself? Less than a year ago you gave me all the gold you possessed in this world so that I could hire an assassin and strike at the conspiracy. You

knew—both of us knew—that this movement, or whatever
you want to call it, was a threat to all that we cared about."

"We were wrong. I was wrong."

"No, you weren't! These renegades have been responsible
for murders in every realm. They killed Chago and the
king—"

"The king was a brute and a despot, and Chago was no better."

"So they deserved to die? Did Brall?"

"Yes. You know how he treated me for the past half year."

Evanthya gave a high, desperate laugh and threw her arms
wide. "He treated you that way because he thought you had
betrayed him. And I hated him, too, because I thought that he
was mistaken, that he was treating you unfairly. But now . . ."
She shook her head.

"Now you think he was justified."

"You betrayed me, as well. You lied to me, and you nearly
killed me."

"I did not!"

"You murdered Brall to keep Orvinti's army from reaching
Dantrielle. You wanted the castle to fall—or rather, your
Weaver wanted it. And if it had, I would have been executed,
along with my duke and his family. You know that's true."

Fetnalla did know it, and she had known it at the time. "I
assumed you'd get away," she muttered, but she had little
hope that her love would believe her.

"You never answered me. How long?"

She didn't have to answer, of course, and yet she felt compelled to do so. "Not long," she said, her voice low. "Four or
five turns. The Weaver first came to me shortly before you
and Tebeo arrived in Orvinti to speak of opposing the regent."

"That makes sense. You acted so strangely when we were
together. Just as you did later, when you and Brall came to
Dantrielle." She looked at her sharply. "You had that dream.
You were dreaming of him, weren't you?"

"That's how he communicates with us. He walks in our
dreams."

"I remember that you were terrified of him. You cried out in your sleep. This is the man you want to lead the Forelands?"

"It's not terror; it's awe. Do you know what it's like to be in the presence of one who is so powerful, to feel that power touching your own mind? All my life I've thought that I was fortunate to be the servant of an Eandi lord. But he's shown me that I can be so much more than that. He's promised me that I will be."

"And he's already making good on the promise. Only a short time ago you were just first minister of a great house. Now you're a murderer and a fugitive. He must be very great indeed."

"Stop it!"

"Do you love him?"

"What?"

"You heard me."

"I love him as I would a king, Evanthya. A true king. Or maybe even a god."

Evanthya's mouth twisted in disgust. "Please!"

"I still love you. That's why I want you to join me and be part of this new kingdom the Weaver is making."

"I can't believe what you're saying! Think of what this man has done, of what others have done in his name! Look what he's made you do! This kingdom you're helping him make will be built on a foundation of lies and betrayals and murders!"

"I told you to stop!" She leveled a finger at Evanthya's heart, her hands trembling with rage. "I will not allow you to speak that way of the Weaver and his movement!"

"You won't allow me?"

Once more Fetnalla fought to control her ire. She had known that Evanthya would say such things. It had to be difficult for those Qirsi who had spent their lives in the service of the Eandi, and who had yet to learn of the Weaver's cause. He called into question all in which they believed and on which they had based their lives.

"You make him sound evil," she said. "And he's not. We're living in a land ruled by despots. You can't think that it would be easy to win our freedom."

"Our freedom? We're not slaves, Fetnalla!"

"We might as well be. But," she went on, cutting off Evanthya before she could reply, "it's not too late to change all that. He wants you to join us. He wants you to be part of his movement and the new world he's creating."

The color drained from her love's face. "He knows of me?"

"Of course."

"You told him about us?"

"He walks in my dreams, Evanthya. He can read my thoughts." She smiled. "And many of my thoughts are of you."

"Does he know that we hired the assassin to kill Shurik?"

"Well, yes." She lied. She had yet to muster the courage to tell him this, and somehow he had yet to read it in her thoughts. "But he's forgiven us for that."

"He's forgiven you."

"He wants to forgive you, too. He wants you to join him."

"I don't believe you. He has no reason to forgive me, or to care for me at all. He only has reason to want me dead—indeed, he has several."

"That's not true!" Fetnalla spoke the words forcefully, but she couldn't look her love in the eye as she did.

"You're lying. I can always tell." Evanthya looked about, as if noting their surroundings for the first time. "That's why you're waiting for me here, isn't it? He's ordered you to kill me, just as you did Brall."

"If only you'd join us, everything would be all right."

"Knowing me as you do, do you really think I could ever join you in serving this Weaver?" Her love actually managed a smile as she said this, though she still looked sad, and heartrendingly beautiful.

"You have to," Fetnalla whispered. "It's the only way."

"No, it's not. You and I have fought the conspiracy before and we can still fight it now. Renounce your Weaver and come back to me."

"I can't do that. He'll kill me. And if he doesn't, the Eandi will. I murdered Brall, Evanthya. I couldn't leave the movement even if I wanted to. So long as the Eandi rule the Forelands, I have no future. Only the Weaver can save me now. But there's room in his world for both of us, if only you'll come with me."

Evanthya shook her head. "No."

"Don't make me do this."

"If you love your Weaver this much, you'll have to prove it by killing me. Because I have no intention of letting you go any farther."

Fetnalla felt panic well in her chest. In spite of all she knew of her beloved, she had continued to hope that Evanthya's love for her would prove stronger than her loyalty to Aneira and her duke. "You know you can't stop me," she said. "Your magic runs deep, Evanthya, but I'm a shaper. If you force me to do this, you'll die right here."

That sad smile returned. "You won't hurt me."

"I will. The Weaver will kill me if I don't. There's no escaping him. I told you, he walks in my dreams. He can find me anywhere in the land, and he knows how to hurt me, how to punish me if I fail him."

"He sounds like a fine man," Evanthya said, her voice dripping with sarcasm, "a worthy leader for this new world of which you dream."

"I told you not to speak of him that way!"

"Yes, you did. But I don't give a damn. You say that you won't allow me to mock him. Well, I won't allow you to join him."

"And how do you intend to stop me? Will you raise a mist or summon a gale? Do you really believe that you can keep me from going north?"

"No. But I can slow you down." She turned to Fetnalla's horse and stared at her. An instant later Zetya reared, then bolted southward.

Language of beasts.

"Damn you!" Fetnalla said, running after her mount briefly. Realizing that she couldn't catch the animal, she faced Evanthya again. "Call her back!"

"I won't. And if you refuse to come back to Dantrielle with me, I'll send her off to where you'll never find her. You can walk to Galdasten."

"Zetya!" Fetnalla called. The horse didn't move. She whistled sharply, which nearly always brought the beast back to her. Still Zetya stood there, nibbling on grass and ignoring her.

"Call her back, Evanthya!"

"She'll return eventually. The commands don't work forever. But if you don't want to lose her for good, you're going to have to do as I say."

"I don't want to have to hurt you."

"You're supposed to kill me. If you really want to join the Weaver, you'll do so now. As I say, your horse will come back to you after a time, and you can be on your way."

"This isn't a joke!" Fetnalla said, growing more desperate by the moment. "I will kill you if you force me. I have to. That's what he wants."

"Then do it."

She felt tears on her face, and she wiped them away quickly. "Please, Evanthya. Just . . ." She took a breath, knowing how she would suffer for this when next she stood before the Weaver. "Just go. Leave me now and I won't have to hurt you."

"I thought he expected you to kill me."

"He does."

"But you can't."

"No. Now leave me."

Evanthya smiled. "I knew it. You're no traitor. I know how much Brall hurt you, with his mistrust and his accusations. But you're still one of us. This Weaver can't change that."

"You're wrong. I'm glad Brall is dead. I've pledged myself to the Weaver and to his movement. No matter what you say, or what you think you know about me, I'm not going back with you. Now leave—please—before it's too late."

"You have to come back with me."

"I won't."

"Then you leave me no choice." Evanthya turned toward Zetya, who was watching them now, still standing off amid the grasses.

"No!" Fetnalla shouted. And before she knew what she had done, the magic flew from her, hot and angry and wild. She heard the muffled crack of bone, saw Evanthya fall, crying out in pain, clutching at her shoulder.

"Demons and fire!" Fetnalla sobbed, rushing to Evanthya's side. Her love writhed on the ground, gritting her teeth, her eyes squeezed shut. "Do you see what you made me do? I warned you!"

"Just finish it, damn you! He wants me dead, so go ahead and kill me."

Fetnalla glared at her. So stubborn, even now. So be it. "No, I won't kill you. I've done enough. Stay away from me, Evanthya. The next time I see you, I'll have no choice."

"Then you might as well do it now," Evanthya said, her jaw clenched against the pain. "Because as soon as you ride, I'll follow. You can no more escape me than you can your Weaver."

Fetnalla stood, still staring down at her, still crying. "You're a fool." Reaching for her magic a second time, she shattered the bone in her love's leg, wincing at the sound of cracking bone and at the scream she tore from Evanthya's lips. "Try following me now."

She whistled for Zetya again, and this time the horse trotted to her.

"You're just going to leave me?" Evanthya asked in a ragged whisper.

"You've given me no choice."

She started to swing herself onto her mount, but the horse reared again and danced away from her.

"Stop it, Evanthya!"

She reached for the reins, but Zetya evaded her again.

"Stop it!" she cried, whirling toward her love, tears flying from her cheeks. "Can't you just let me go? Do you want me to have to kill you?"

"I won't let you go to him. You've done enough damage."

"Then I'll have to end this now."

"You have already. How long do you think I can survive out here with a shattered shoulder and leg?"

Fetnalla considered this. She wasn't certain that it was true, but it did give her a way out, something she could tell the Weaver when he asked how she had dealt with Evanthya.

"Fine then." She grabbed Zetya's reins before her love could touch the beast again with her magic. Climbing into the saddle, she glanced back at Evanthya once more, cringing at what she saw.

Perhaps she should have ridden away then. She would never be able to explain to the Weaver why she hadn't, though probably she wouldn't have to. Already, he knew her quite well.

Dismounting again, she walked back to Evanthya and knelt beside her. Her love tried to flinch away, but Fetnalla placed her hands on the broken shoulder.

"It's all right," she whispered, probing the mangled bone with her mind. "This will hurt for just a moment." With a quick jerk she set the bone back in place. Evanthya howled, but she managed to lie still. A moment later, Fetnalla began to pour her magic into the woman's shoulder, mending the splintered bone. After a time, she moved to Evanthya's leg and did the same. This was a cleaner break and setting the bone proved much easier.

She didn't do much more than knit the bones together and start the healing process. If she healed Evanthya too thoroughly, the two of them would be right back where they began. This way, the leg and shoulder remained weak and tender. Perhaps that would be enough to keep Evanthya from following her, at least for a while.

"Why did you do that?" Evanthya asked, when she had finished.

Fetnalla stood. "I'll leave that for you to figure out."

"I'll come after you."

"I know. Don't put too much weight on the leg or strain the shoulder. The bones need time to heal or they'll just snap again."

She walked back to Zetya, who stood perfectly still while she climbed onto her back.

Evanthya sat up, wincing.

"Don't come to the Moorlands. The Weaver will kill both of us if you do."

Her love said nothing.

"I know you won't believe this, but I love you. I've never stopped loving you."

Expecting no response, unable to bear the silence, Fetnalla turned her mount immediately and kicked her to a gallop. The sun was high over the Moors of Durril by now, warming the air. But the wind felt cold against her tears, and for a long time she couldn't swallow past the aching in her throat.

She rode Zetya hard for the rest of the day, resting only when she had to, eating nothing, drinking little. She kept her eyes fixed on the northern horizon, and her thoughts fixed on the Weaver and the war he had promised her. The past was lost to her; all that mattered now was the future—hers, that of the Qirsi, that of the Forelands. Not once did Fetnalla look back, not even when she thought she heard the pounding of hooves pursuing her.

Chapter
Thirteen

The Moorlands, Eibithar

Slash. Parry. Duck. Parry again. Lash out with the right foot and chop downward with the blade arm. Wipe blood from the blade if time allows, and then start again. It seemed to Tavis that Hagan MarCullet was beside him, shouting instructions as he fought, exhorting the young lord to draw on all the lessons he had learned in the sunlit wards of Curgh Castle.

Hagan was fighting his own battles, of course—he had no time to offer instruction to a young noble far out of his depth. Somewhere to the west his son, Tavis's liege man and closest friend, fought as well, summoning memories of the same training. Nor could there be any mistaking his own weapon or those around him for the wooden practice swords with which he and Xaver had exercised not so very long ago. Wooden swords didn't gleam so in the sun, they didn't ring like a smith's hammer when they met. They didn't even sound quite the same as they whistled past his head. And of course, wooden swords didn't draw blood; they didn't sever a man's arm from his shoulder, or cleave his head in two. Since killing the assassin Cadel on the shores of the Wethy Crown, Tavis had prayed for the opportunity to fight in this war, to prove himself in battle. "Beware the boons you ask of the gods," it was said in the streets of Curgh, "for the great ones might just be listening." Indeed.

He battled to survive, to kill the man in front of him before he himself was killed, and to do the same to every Braedony warrior who took the place of those he slew. Though Grinsa fought only a few fourspans from where he stood, the boy was but dimly aware of him. He would have liked to believe that if the gleaner was in trouble, or if, gods save them all, he fell, Tavis would sense it, and would be able to leap to his aid. But in truth, the young noble wasn't even certain of this much. He had no idea how the rest of Eibithar's army was faring.

The empire's assault on the second day of fighting had been even more ferocious than its initial attack. Braedon's archers had loosed volley after volley into the morning sky, until it seemed that a constant storm of arrows rained down on Kearney's army forcing the men to huddle beneath their shields. Eibithar's bowmen could not return fire without imperiling themselves, and her swordsmen could only watch, helpless, fearing for their lives, as Braedon's warriors marched toward them, under cover of the archers' barrage. Grinsa, Fotir, and Keziah raised a powerful wind to knock the arrows back, but the empire's Qirsi raised a countering gale. Tavis knew Grinsa could have done more, but he also knew the gleaner didn't dare, for fear of revealing himself too soon.

Braedon's men halted just short of where the arrows were falling and let out an earsplitting cry. A moment later, the last of the darts rose into the pale blue and fell. And when it hit, embedding itself in a soldier's shield, the empire's army surged forward, swords raised, helms glinting in the sunlight.

Once again, as they had the previous morning, Eibithar's soldiers gave ground, fighting desperately to keep from being overrun. For a time it seemed to Tavis that they could do nothing against such an onslaught. He fought desperately, as did those around him, but he felt that he was taking a step back with every parry. The young lord was sure that had it not been for the timely arrival of Thorald's army under the command of Marston of Shanstead, Kearney's army would have been defeated before midday. As it was, the addition of Marston's men only served to stop Braedon's advance. When Heneagh's remaining soldiers were overrun late in the day, the Thorald army rushed to take their place on the western lines and succeeded in keeping the enemy from flanking the king. Under the circumstances, that was all anyone could have asked.

Sundown brought an end to the fighting, mercifully. Tavis wasn't certain how much longer Eibithar's men could have gone on. For a second consecutive day, the two armies had fought viciously with neither side making significant gains.

The following morning, Kearney's captains, and those of his dukes, roused the soldiers before dawn and made preparations for the coming day's battle. But the warriors of Braedon did not attack, and given the opportunity to allow his men to rest and heal, the king did not take the fight to the invaders. The armies rested a second day as well, forcing Tavis and the others to wonder what new horror the empire had in store for them.

Late that day, a mounted army came into view from the south. Fearing that Kearney and his men faced some new threat, Tavis and Xaver called out in alarm, causing several hundred men to scramble into formation. Only when the king joined them, chuckling in amusement, did the young lord and his friend see that this army was accompanied by two of Kearney's scouts.

"I believe that's the queen of Sanbira," the king told them. "I'm sure she'll be grateful for the welcome you've arranged."

Many of the men laughed at them. Others, who already hated Tavis and thought him a butcher, merely glared at them. Tavis felt a fool, as did Xaver. But the liege man's father offered them some comfort.

"Don't worry about them," Hagan said, waving a dismissive hand at the warriors. "Better you should be shouting warnings that amount to nothing, than ignoring threats that get men killed."

The queen's force was small—eight hundred warriors, more or less. But riding on Sanbiri horses, and wielding Sanbiri steel, they were a formidable sight. The armies of Eibithar made the soldiers welcome, particularly when they realized that there were women warriors in the Sanbiri ranks. Kearney greeted the queen and her nobles, inviting them to share a meal with his dukes and launching almost immediately into a long description of all that had happened so far on the battle plain.

"We've seen no sign of reinforcements," Kearney said, when the queen asked him about Braedon's decision not to attack in the past two days. "I suppose it's possible that they arrived under cover of darkness, or will do so tonight, but I think it more likely that the emperor's captains are doing as we are: healing the wounded, giving their men time to rest, preparing for the next battle."

Olesya nodded thoughtfully, staring into a bright fire. "That may be," she said. "But they might also be awaiting support from the south. My scouts have seen an army marching north from Kentigern, a thousand men strong. They burn crops and villages as they go, and march under banners of red and gold."

"Numar's men."

"I'm afraid so. We thought to fight them south of here, but decided to ride on instead. That way we could warn you of their approach and fight them off as part of a larger force. We should be a full day ahead of them. Perhaps a bit more."

Kearney nodded. "I would have done the same."

No one else spoke, and Tavis felt much of his relief at the queen's arrival giving way to a renewed sense of dread. He had wanted to believe that the Aneirans would never be able to fight their way past Kentigern, but he should have known better than to place such faith in the fealty of Aindreas and his men.

After a time, the king sent most of the Qirsi and lesser nobles away, staying up late into the night to discuss tactics with Hagan and his dukes, and the queen and her nobles. Tavis wished that he could have been party to the discussion, and he tried to remain awake so that he might ask his father what was said. But before long this day's fighting caught up with him and he fell asleep. He slept fitfully, as he always seemed to these days, his slumber disrupted by every unexpected noise and troubled by strange dreams.

On this, the fifth day of the war, Braedon's archers renewed their assault, allowing the empire's swordsmen to advance on Eibithar's lines. Once again, however, Kearney and Queen Olesya had readied their armies before sunrise. The soldiers of Eibithar and Sanbira were prepared for the attack. Kearney's bowmen matched those of Braedon volley for volley, and when Braedon's soldiers finally began their charge, the warriors of Eibithar and Sanbira rushed forward to meet them. Battle cries from both armies pierced the stillness of morning, and the first crash of steel upon steel, flesh upon flesh, seemed to cause the ground beneath their feet to buck and roll.

That had been hours ago. At least Tavis thought it had been. The sun had turned a slow arc overhead and now was beating down on the armies and the dead, harsh and relentless. But time had lost meaning for him. His life at this moment was measured in sword strokes and blood, the sweat soaking his face and hair and clothes, the screaming muscles in his back, shoulders, and arms.

He knew that he was fighting well, that his father would be proud of him. During his first battle, at the siege of Kentigern, he had acquitted himself poorly, allowing cowardice to get the better of him. There was none of that now. He had killed and had nearly been killed himself. Bian's realm didn't frighten him anymore, at least not as it once had. He wouldn't call it courage—that was a word reserved in his mind for men like Grinsa and Kearney, for Keziah, who dared offer herself to the Weaver so that she might defeat him, and oddly, for Cresenne, whose treachery had cost Tavis so much and whose redemption had come at a far higher price to herself. In the absence of true bravery, though, it was all he could ask of himself. Anyway, it kept him fighting.

The soldier before him now was a large man, more powerful than he, just as all the others had been. And like the others, his strength could not hide his lack of skill with a blade and shield. Hagan had always told Tavis and Xaver that brawn was not always an asset, that in fact it could be a hindrance at times.

"If your opponent is stronger than you are, but unskilled with a sword, he'll rely on his power to beat you. His attacks will be slower, more obvious. In a contest between two men, one quick and clever, the other big and strong, I'll take the former every time."

Once Tavis had asked, "What if we find ourselves fighting someone who's both stronger and quicker?"

To which the swordmaster replied, "Run."

That wasn't the case here. After eyeing Tavis for just a moment, the Braedony swordsman lunged forward swinging his weapon with all his might and leaving himself open to the young lord's counter. Tavis didn't hesitate. Dodging the man's sword, he leveled a blow of his own at the man's side. The soldier's mail coat kept Tavis's weapon from cutting into his flesh, but he doubled over with a grunt, and Tavis hacked at his neck, knocking him to the ground and loosing a torrent of blood that stained the grass and soil.

The boy spun, dropping into his crouch in anticipation of the next assault, but no one stepped forward to take the soldier's place. After a moment he straightened and turned toward the gleaner. Grinsa was standing in a circle of dead warriors and shattered blades, leaning heavily on his sword, his face damp, his breathing labored. There was a gash on his cheek, but otherwise he appeared unhurt.

"You're bleeding," Tavis said.

"So are you."

Tavis frowned, having no memory of being wounded.

"On your brow," Grinsa said. "And on your left shoulder."

He glanced at his shoulder, then lifted a hand to his forehead and dabbed at it gingerly with his fingers. They came away sticky and crimson.

"It seems our army is making progress."

Tavis looked at the gleaner again before following the line of his gaze. Perhaps twenty paces to the north, soldiers of Eibithar were still fighting a pitched battle.

He started in that direction. "We should help them."

"Tavis, wait. Rest a moment."

"They're not resting," he said over his shoulder, not bothering to stop.

"Some are. All of them should, as should you."

"We'll rest when the fighting's over." But even as he spoke, he felt fatigue crash down upon him like a wave. When was the last time he had eaten or taken a sip of water? When had he last slept a full night without awakening to strains of Braedony war songs? He slowed, then stopped, facing the gleaner again.

"Just for a moment," Grinsa said. "You don't look well."

"I feel fine." Yet he made no move to rejoin the battle. How had has throat gotten so dry so quickly?

Grinsa walked to where Tavis stood, eyeing him closely. "You're pale as a Qirsi."

"I've been spending too much time with you."

"You'll get no argument from me."

Tavis had to grin, though he quickly turned serious again. "Truly, gleaner, I'm fine. Now let me go and fight for my realm."

He shrugged. "Go, then."

Before the young lord could start forward again, however, shouts went up from the south. Both of them turned, and what Tavis saw nearly made his stomach heave.

An army was approaching, marching under a red, black, and gold banner bearing the panther of Solkara. The queen had said that Aneira's army consisted of a thousand men, but the column Tavis saw seemed to stretch for miles. How could there be so many, and how could they have arrived so soon?

"Demons and fire!" the gleaner murmured.

Tavis scanned the lines, looking for anyone who might hold off this new force. But the Sanbiri warriors were fighting alongside the King's Guard, and all of Eibithar's men were engaged as well. "They'll carve right through us," he said, looking at the Solkarans once more.

"Perhaps not. Go find Fotir and bring him to me. Quickly, Tavis."

"Where are you going?"

"To get Keziah."

Comprehension hit him like a fist. "You're going to weave their magic with yours."

"We haven't a choice. Now go, before their archers are close enough to attack!"

Tavis had never run so fast. He could see his father atop his mount leading the Curgh army, and sprinted toward him, knowing that Fotir would be nearby. Already the soldiers battling at the front had noticed the Solkarans' approach. Tavis could hear cries going up from both sides and the fighting seemed to have taken on new urgency, particularly among the empire's men. Heartened by the appearance of their allies, the Braedony swordsmen pushed forward, shouting wildly, like demons from the Underrealm. Within moments, the small gains made in the past few hours by the armies of Eibithar and Sanbira were almost completely erased.

Reaching his father, he found Fotir and Xaver doing battle side by side. Both of them were bleeding, but at least they were alive.

Xaver was fending off two men, giving ground quickly, and Tavis rushed to his aid, his sword held high. One of the men broke off his attack on the liege man aiming a swift, chopping blow at Tavis's head. Tavis blocked the sword with his shield, his knees nearly buckling. Still, he managed to strike back at the man, hitting only his shield.

The soldier came at him a second time, weapon raised, shield held ready. A simple attack—no feint. As if sparring with probationers in the Curgh wards, Tavis stepped around the assault, allowing the man's blade to glance off his shield, and slashed at the man's gut. As with the last Braedony soldier, this man's mail coat saved his life, but only for the moment. The blow staggered him, and before he could recover Tavis thrust his sword through the soldier's throat.

Without hesitating, the young lord sprang toward Xaver's other attacker. But seeing how his friend died, this soldier retreated.

"Thanks," Xaver said, sounding winded and slightly awed. "What are you doing here, I mean other than saving my life?"

"I need Fotir."

There was a chiming sound, which Tavis recognized as the splintering of a blade, and then the harsh cry of a dying man.

"Did I hear you say that you needed me, my lord?"

"Yes. You've seen the Solkarans?"

The first minister nodded, glancing southward. "The duke ordered his archers to the rear to hold them off."

"That might help, but Grinsa was hoping you and he might join that fight as well."

The man's bright eyes widened, owllike and eager. "Are you certain?"

"What can they do?" Xaver asked, brow creasing.

"Right away, First Minister. There isn't much time. He's at the rear of the king's line."

"Yes, my lord. The duke—"

"I'll explain it to him as best I can."

"I think you'd be better off telling him nothing, my lord. I'll think of something later."

Tavis nodded and watched as the minister ran off toward where Grinsa and Keziah awaited him.

"What's going on, Tavis?"

"It's best you don't know, Stinger."

"Why? Because I haven't been through all that you have? Because I've just been in Curgh all this time, while you've been traveling the length and breadth of the Forelands?"

He faced his friend, who, despite his cuts and bruises, looked terribly young. "Grinsa is a Weaver, Xaver," he said wearily. What did it matter anymore? With that army approaching, all was lost. "Do you know what that means?"

Xaver's face paled, his green eyes widening much as had Fotir's a few moments before. "A Weaver?"

"Yes."

"The conspiracy . . ." He stopped, shaking his head.

"Grinsa has saved my life more times than I care to count. He's no traitor. In fact, I believe he's the only person in the Forelands who can defeat the Weaver who leads the renegades."

"Then why not tell your father?"

"Because he's not ready to understand all of this. He'll hear the word 'Weaver' and nothing else." He looked southward again, marking the progress of Solkara's army. "Until the nobles in this land see for themselves what this other Weaver can do, they won't be willing to put their trust in Grinsa."

"Does Kearney know?"

"Yes. As I understand it, he'd pretty much figured it out for himself. Grinsa had no choice but to admit it."

"A Weaver," Xaver said again, as if the word were new to him. "I suppose I should be pleased. Having one on our side evens matters a bit, doesn't it?"

Tavis looked to the south again. "It might. He's still our only chance of defeating the Weaver. I hope he doesn't get himself killed."

"Should we go after him now?"

Tavis shook his head. "Fotir and the archminister are with him. They won't let anything happen to him."

"Wait a moment. How does Fotir know? Surely if your father—"

"You remember how I escaped from Kentigern?"

"The hole in the castle wall!" the liege man said, breathless, a look of wonder on his face. "Grinsa did that?"

"Grinsa and Fotir did it together."

"Demons and fire!"

"He risked a great deal saving me from Aindreas."

"How does the archminister know?"

Tavis hesitated, then shook his head. "Some secrets aren't mine to tell. I'm sorry."

Xaver dismissed the apology with a wave of his hand. The resentment he had expressed just a short time before seemed to have vanished. "Thanks for telling me as much as you did."

The young lord grimaced. "I suppose you feel that I've been keeping a lot from you."

"I understand," his friend said, shrugging.

"I've wanted to tell you more, Stinger. Really. But I couldn't. I probably shouldn't have even told you this, but you were bound to find out eventually, I expect sooner rather than later."

"I won't tell anyone."

"I know. It's never been a matter of my not trusting you. As I said before, they're just not my secrets to tell." He gazed southward once more. He couldn't be certain, but it appeared that the Solkarans had halted their advance. "I never knew that so many people in this realm had so much to hide."

"What's going on back there?" Xaver asked, shielding his eyes from the sun as he gazed toward the Aneirans.

"I'm not sure. It looks like they're fighting."

"You're right, but against who? Surely not Grinsa and the others."

"No, there's another army behind them." They shared a look, the realization hitting both of them at once. "Come on!" Tavis said, breaking into a run. "We need to tell my father!"

It galled him to ride under Kearney's banner and Gershon's command. Aindreas knew that he deserved far worse, having defied the king at every opportunity, having betrayed the realm, though none of his companions knew this. Still, he led one of the realm's leading houses. Surely he deserved to ride under his own colors, as did Tremain and Labruinn. But with all that he had done, with the prospect of admitting his treachery hanging over him like the black smoke of siege fires, he couldn't bring himself to protest. Gershon, Lathrop, and Caius had saved his castle from Aneira's siege before setting out after the Solkaran army, which had marched northward to join forces with Braedon's warriors. And Aindreas, faced with the prospect of remaining behind with his wine and the ghost of his daughter, or riding to war with these men, had chosen the latter. He had sensed Gershon's reluctance to let him join the king's army, and truly, he could hardly blame the man. What choice did he have but to submit to the swordmaster's authority? He ordered his men to march at the rear of the King's Guard, and he rode beside Gershon and the other dukes, saying little, enduring their sidelong glances and strained courtesy as best he could. In the rush to leave Kentigern Tor, he hadn't thought to bring any wine. A pity. Not a night went by when he wouldn't have sold his dukedom for a cup of Sanbiri red.

He had no cause to resent Gershon. The swordmaster had treated him civilly since their departure from Kentigern, though clearly it pained him to do so. Nor did he have any right to hate the king. Hadn't Kearney's decision to grant asylum to the Curgh boy been vindicated long ago? Hadn't the man given Aindreas every opportunity to redeem himself and his house? Hadn't he saved Kentigern from the Aneirans twice now, despite Aindreas's continued defiance? Kearney's grace, his willingness to forgive, left Aindreas humbled and ashamed, which might well have been why he did it. No doubt it was the source of the duke's bitterness. For when he asked himself if he would have been so generous being in the king's place, he was forced to admit that he would not.

Despite his hostility toward the swordmaster, Aindreas could not help but admire the man's qualities as a leader. He pushed the armies hard as they pursued the Aneirans northward, resting only when absolutely necessary, and marching well into the night. It was hard to say whether the enemy knew they were being followed—they set a punishing pace for themselves as well. Still Gershon and the dukes gained on them, slowly but steadily.

As demanding as Gershon was of the men under his command, his orders never provoked a single complaint, at least none that the duke heard. Perhaps it was because Caius and Lathrop and Aindreas himself deferred to the man. Perhaps the soldiers understood that the very survival of the realm was at stake. Or perhaps it was just that Gershon looked so formidable on his mount, with his clean-shaven head, blunt features, and icy blue eyes. Whatever the reason, Aindreas had seen few swordmasters who were as revered by their men as Gershon Trasker was by his.

By the end of the seventh day of their march, the Aneirans certainly knew that they were being followed. Gershon had brought his vast army within sight of the invaders, and though the enemy didn't flag or turn to face the Eibitharians, neither could they increase the distance between the two forces. Like wild dogs snapping at the heels of a stag, the armies of the realm drove the enemy across the Moorlands. The Aneirans might reach the rest of the Eibitharian army first, but they would barely have time to raise their swords before Gershon's force struck at them.

Eibithar's army continued to close the distance throughout the following day. By the approach of dusk, as the sun was balanced huge and orange on the western horizon, they were close enough to the Aneirans for Aindreas to make out the red Solkaran panther on the army's banner. With luck, they would catch the enemy the next day.

"Still no sign of the empire's army," he heard Gershon say, as they continued to ride.

For a moment he thought to answer himself, but Lathrop responded before he could say anything. They hadn't gone out of their way to speak with him thus far. Why should they start now?

"I'd been thinking the same thing," Tremain said. "Perhaps it means that the king withstood the first assault."

"And more, I'd guess. If the empire's army had overrun the king and his allies, they'd be farther south by now."

"I hope you're right, swordmaster."

"In either case, we have no choice but to keep moving until we catch the Solkarans. We must be getting near to the king's army and we can't allow the enemy to reach them first. With the empire attacking from the north, they'll cut through his lines like a sword through parchment. And if by some chance Braedon's forces have already defeated him, we'd do well to defeat the Aneirans before they can join with a larger force. Tell your men that we march through the night. We're not going to stop until we catch the enemy."

Lathrop nodded, as did the duke of Labruinn. A moment later, they both turned their mounts and headed back to speak with their men. Gershon glanced over his shoulder at Aindreas, as if expecting him to comply with the order as well.

"Do you disagree, my lord?"

"Not at all."

"You just don't like the idea of taking commands from a man who's common-born."

Aindreas opened his mouth, then closed it again.

"I thought so," Gershon said, a thin smile springing to his lips and vanishing as quickly.

"Actually that's not it either."

"Then what? You feel you've been treated unfairly? To be honest, my lord, I believe you're fortunate to be a free man. I don't mind telling you that if I'd had my way, you would have been thrown in your own dungeon and left there to rot. But I had orders from His Majesty, and unlike you, I do as my liege tells me."

He should have been outraged. Had his soldiers been nearby, they would have had to be restrained from killing the man. At least, the duke wanted to believe that this was so. The truth was that he deserved to be spoken to in this way. He hadn't seen Brienne's ghost—or whatever it was that haunted his days and nights—since leaving Kentigern, but he didn't need her to tell him that he had placed the realm at risk with all he had done since her murder, and for no good reason at all.

"You think me impudent for speaking to you so."

"Please stop putting words in my mouth, swordmaster. The truth is, I wish that I hadn't done so much to deserve your contempt. I'll see to my men right away."

He wheeled his mount, intending to do just as he had said.

"My lord, wait."

Aindreas would have liked to ride away and leave this insolent swordmaster to chew on whatever it was he wished to say. But something stopped him—the man's tone, his own surety that he had already done too much to drive a wedge between his house and the Crown. Reluctantly, he faced the swordmaster again, saying nothing.

"I'm—" Trasker looked away briefly. "I shouldn't have spoken to you so. It was . . . inappropriate."

The duke could think of no reply. After several moments, he simply nodded and rode back to his men.

Aindreas had left his swordmaster, Villyd Temsten, in Kentigern, refusing to trust anyone else with the protection of his castle and family. The captains he had brought with him were good men—brave, loyal—but they were not deep thinkers, and they had even less sense of what the duke had done to earn the king's enmity than did Villyd. Clearly they did not feel that soldiers of Kentigern should be marching under the king's banner. They accepted their duke's orders, and began immediately to convey them to the rest of the Kentigern army, but they made it clear to the duke, with their expressions and their flat voices, that they disapproved of his willingness to yield to Gershon's authority. Returning to the head of the great column, Aindreas was forced to wonder anew if he had been wrong to make this journey.

An image of Jastanne ja Triln entered his mind, pale and lithe and lovely. He saw her as she had appeared that night he forged his alliance with the conspiracy, looking young and unassuming, an illusion she shattered, along with a wine goblet, using her shaping power. What would she do when she learned that he had marched with Kearney's army? Would she and her Qirsi allies reveal his treachery immediately? Would they seek vengeance against Ioanna or his children, or would they content themselves with destroying his name? Perhaps these fears should have given him pause, made him wonder how he might aid the conspiracy here on the Moorlands. Instead they emboldened him.

For so long he had allowed his shame and fright to render him helpless. Not anymore. Casting his lot with the Qirsi had been the greatest mistake of his life, a desperate gambit born of grief and rage and drunken foolishness. He would pay for that error until his death, and long after he was gone his family would continue to pay. But maybe he could mitigate some of the harm he had done by making a hero of himself in the coming war. Not this one with Aneira and Braedon, but the real war against the Qirsi renegades, the one that would decide the fate of all the Forelands. That was the hope that drove him onward, that left him unmoved by the dismay of his captains. They couldn't possibly understand. Up until a few days ago, he hadn't either, though he should have. It remained to be seen if the realization had come to him too late.

True to his word, Gershon kept the army moving well past sundown, stopping only long enough to feed and water the horses, allow the soldiers to eat, and light their torches. The Solkarans didn't stop for long either, but they could not increase their lead on the Eibitharians. When the two moons finally rose high enough into the star-filled sky to illuminate the grasses and boulders of the moor, Eibithar's men doused their torches and quickened their pace, but it seemed the Solkarans did the same, for the enemy's torch fire had vanished.

Their first indication that the Aneirans had halted was the barrage of arrows that pelted down just in front of the column. Aindreas's horse reared, more because of the duke's startled response than because of the arrows themselves, but Aindreas managed to keep himself from falling.

"Damn!" Gershon spat, fighting to control his mount as well. More arrows struck the ground before them, but all of them fell short.

"We were fortunate," Lathrop said.

"We were careless. *I* was careless," Gershon corrected. He peered ahead, eyes narrowed, trying to see the enemy in the dim glow of Ilias and Panya. Then he beckoned to one of his captains, who was marching a short distance behind the dukes and swordmaster. Immediately the man hurried forward. "Call our archers forward," he said quietly.

The man nodded and ran back toward the king's soldiers.

Lathrop frowned. "Do you think they mean to fight us here?"

"I'm not certain what they have in mind. But they've loosed two volleys now to no avail. I expect they'll move their bowmen closer and try again. I want to be ready when they do."

It didn't take long for Kearney's archers, three hundred strong, to reach the front of the column.

"I'd suggest you move back, my lords," Gershon said. "I don't want a chance dart to strike one of you."

Caius shook his head. "I have a better idea." He waved Gershon's captain to his side. "Please, Captain, have my bowmen brought forward as well."

The captain glanced at Trasker, who, after a moment's pause, nodded.

"Mine as well, Captain," Lathrop said.

Aindreas twisted his mouth for just an instant. "Better call for mine as well." The others regarded him silently. "Well, I can't let it be said that Kentigern shied from a fight, can I?"

"Thank you, my lords," Gershon said, the ghost of a smile on his lips. "Though I'd still feel better if the three of you moved back a bit."

Lathrop glanced briefly at Aindreas and the duke of Labruinn before looking at Gershon again. "It would seem, swordmaster, that your authority over us only goes so far."

Gershon's smile broadened. "Yes, my lord. May I at least ask that you dismount and ready your shields?"

This the dukes did.

Soon the king's archers were joined by six hundred more from the dukes' armies. Moments later, another swarm of arrows descended upon them, and this time many of them struck true. Eibithar's bowmen had brought shields as well as their bows and quivers, but still a number of them fell, their screams making Aindreas flinch beneath his shield.

"Loose your arrows at will!" Gershon called.

And a moment later the moor seemed to sing with the thrumming of so many bows. Cries of pain rose from the Aneiran army, like a distant echo of those that had come from Eibithar's sons a few seconds before.

More darts fell around Aindreas, and more were sent hurtling toward the enemy.

"This is madness," the duke muttered.

"I quite agree."

Gershon was closer than Aindreas had known.

"I didn't mean—"

"It's all right, my lord. I believe I understand. But I'm at a loss as to what to do. It's too dark and too dangerous to send the swordsmen forward, particularly with both armies loosing arrows blindly at one another."

"What if we set one volley aflame?"

"My lord?"

"We wouldn't even have to light all of them. We wouldn't want to, because it would make them too easy to avoid. But if we light some of them, we might be able to see where the enemy is."

"A fine idea, my lord," Gershon said, sounding as if he thought Aindreas a genius. "I'll speak with the captains right away."

It took some time to get the arrows wrapped in oilcloth and lit, and in the meantime the armies traded volley after volley. Finally Eibithar's archers loosed the flaming arrows and the duke followed their arcing flight wondering what their fires would reveal.

Only when they struck, though, did he understand how badly he and the others had miscalculated. Several of Aneira's bowmen lay dead on the ground and perhaps two hundred others could be seen dodging the arrows that continued to fall. But the rest of the army was gone.

"Demons and fire!" Gershon rasped. "They've gone on. It was all a ruse."

The Aneiran archers turned and ran, and after a moment's hesitation, the swordmaster called for his men to attack. Instantly the king's army surged forward, followed closely by the soldiers of Labruinn, Tremain, and Kentigern.

"How far ahead do you think they are?" Caius asked, as the soldiers overran Aneira's men.

Gershon had already remounted. "They could have gained an hour on us. Maybe more." He spat a curse. "I'm a fool!" He rubbed a hand over his face. "We'll have to drive the men even harder now, keep them at a trot for as long as we can."

The dukes climbed onto their horses, and Eibithar's army resumed its pursuit of the Solkarans. There were fewer of the enemy ahead of them now, but still enough to make a difference in Kearney's battle with the empire. The soldiers, heartened by their easy victory over the archers, maintained a remarkably brisk pace for some time before finally flagging as the night wore on. As dawn approached, Gershon was forced to call a respite. The soldiers seemed utterly spent, and Aindreas felt what little hope he had left wither and die.

But when the sky began to brighten at last, revealing the Solkaran army, the duke's spirits lifted. It seemed that the Aneiran swordsmen had not left their bowmen as early as Aindreas had feared. Or perhaps they too had taken some time to rest during the night. The Aneirans had increased their advantage, but not so much that they could not still be caught. He sensed that the soldiers behind him realized this as well and he felt the lethargy of a long night being lifted from Eibithar's army.

Looking past the enemy, the duke saw far in the distance several thin plumes of pale smoke rising into the morning sky. He thought he could see tents as well, and a great host of men. The battle plain. It would still be several hours before the Aneirans reached the other armies gathered there—he could only assume that Kearney's forces held the southern ground—but that made the morning's pursuit even more urgent.

"It seems the king has held them," Lathrop said, already mounted and ready to ride on.

Gershon gave a curt nod, his expression grim. "All the more reason to keep moving."

Lathrop eyed him in the dim grey light. "I quite agree, swordmaster," he said pointedly. "I was merely observing what I suppose was already obvious to you."

The swordmaster's mouth twitched. "Forgive me, my lord."

"I already have. I believe it's time you forgave yourself. We all shared equally in what happened during the night. And to be honest, I'm not certain there was anything else we could have done. The Solkaran's deception didn't make their arrows any less deadly. Until we defeated the archers, we couldn't resume our pursuit. I thought you dealt with them as well as anyone could have. And your decision to light our arrows aflame was quite brilliant."

"That was Lord Kentigern's idea, my lord."

Lathrop looked at Aindreas, raising an eyebrow. "Really."

"Don't look so surprised, Tremain. I still have occasional lucid moments."

"So it would seem."

Aindreas had to grin. Truth was, he had always liked Lathrop.

Gershon rode back to address the men, and though Aindreas couldn't hear all that the swordsmaster said, he could imagine well enough. He had rallied armies himself, and the words never changed much. Judging from the earsplitting roar that greeted Trasker's words, it seemed to work on this morning.

They started forward again moments later, and almost immediately began to gain on the enemy. It seemed that the Aneirans were slowing their pace deliberately, as if they suddenly understood that they were to be crushed between the two armies of Eibithar. Throughout the morning Gershon's forces drew nearer to them, his soldiers singing so loudly that the Solkarans could not help but hear.

Aindreas kept an eye on the distant armies as well. They were fighting again, and though the distance was too great to make out much of what was happening, it didn't seem that the battle lines moved at all. He could only imagine the carnage.

"Our soldiers may well tip the balance."

He turned to find Lathrop riding beside him.

"They may indeed, if there's anyone left alive when we get there."

"I'm sorry to have to ask this, Lord Kentigern, but I feel that it is my duty as a loyal subject of the king. Can you be trusted not to betray us at the end?"

He should have expected this. It shouldn't have stung at all. Just because he had chosen to turn from the path he had been on did not mean that the arrogance and self-righteousness of Glyndwr and his allies would magically disappear. Yet the question cut his heart like a blade, perhaps because he had always thought that Tremain was different from the rest, that he might have understood, even as he continued to stand with the king.

"Yes, Lord Tremain. I can be trusted. Before leaving Kentigern, I swore to you on Brienne's memory that I would keep faith with you and your king. Do you honestly think that I would dishonor her in that way?"

"Aindreas, I'm sorry. But I had to—"

"No," the duke said. "You didn't." He kicked at his horse's flanks and rode ahead of the man. And for the rest of the morning he kept to himself.

By midday, they were once again as close to the Aneirans as they had been the previous evening. They were also near enough to the battle to make out the colors of the pennons fluttering in the wind above the armies of the realm. The purple and gold of Eibithar flew over the King's Guard, and Aindreas also saw the colors of Thorald, Heneagh, and, of course, Curgh.

Seeing the brown and gold of Javan's house, the duke felt his chest tighten with old, familiar pains—grief, fury, bloodlust. Maybe Lathrop had been justified in asking about his intentions after all. Could he really fight beside Curgh's duke, beside his son?

His son didn't kill your daughter. The Qirsi did.

He knew this to be so, but his hatred for the men of Curgh ran deep.

As the Solkarans drew ever nearer to Kearney's army, they began to slow, then halted altogether. Aindreas saw a small group of Aneiran archers—perhaps a hundred—position themselves between their army and Gershon's force. He could only assume that the enemy's other bowmen had gone to the far side of their army to loose their arrows at the king's men.

"Archers!" Gershon cried, and the word was echoed by the captains marching behind them. Within moments, several hundred of Eibithar's bowmen had come to the front of the column, arrows already nocked.

At Gershon's command the army resumed its advance until it seemed that the bowmen were within range of the enemy. Then the swordmaster called a halt and ordered the archers to begin their assault. The Solkarans tried to answer, but there were few of their bowmen left to face those of Eibithar.

"They'll attack His Majesty first," Gershon said, his voice taut. And it did seem that they would. Though their archers sent volleys of arrows at Gershon's force, the swordsmen behind them appeared to be massing for an attack northward. "If they can fight through to the empire's army all is lost."

Before the Aneirans could strike, however, a great gale began to rise from the north, abrupt and unnatural.

Many of Gershon's archers, who had been about to fire again, paused, glancing at one other with puzzled expressions. The swordmaster stared up at the sky, as if expecting to see some great beast swoop down upon them from the clouds. The squall continued to gain power, until Aindreas felt that he would be swept off of his mount.

"This is no natural wind," the duke said, shouting to be heard. "It's sorcery. I'm certain of it."

The swordmaster nodded, staring up at the sky. "Aye, but who among the Qirsi is powerful enough to summon such a gale?"

Chapter
Fourteen

 rinsa could see now that this was in fact two armies—the Aneirans had another force following on their heels—and even without seeing the banners of this second army, the gleaner had an idea of who they were.

"They're trapped now," Keziah said over the roar of their gale, reasoning it out for herself. Fotir gave a puzzled look and she added, "That's Gershon behind them."

"You're certain?"

"I'd know the swordmaster from any distance. They must have followed the Solkarans from Kentigern."

"Then we've hope after all."

Grinsa nodded, his eyes fixed on the Aneiran captains riding at the head of the column. "There's hope for the king and

his men, yes, but our situation hasn't improved much at all."
He glanced about quickly before staring at the captains
again. The three of them had ridden a fair distance from
Kearney's lines to meet the Aneiran threat, thinking to protect the king from an attack on the rear of his lines. They
were quite alone on this side of the Solkaran army.

Keziah frowned. "Of course it has. They'll have to fight off
Gershon's assault as well as ours. How can that not help us?"

"We're still three against hundreds."

"When we first rode to meet them we thought we were
three against thousands. Or had you forgotten that?"

"That was when I thought we had no choice!"

She glared at him. "So now you've changed your mind?"

"Can you do this?" Fotir asked. "Or are they too many?"

"We can do it."

Keziah was still eyeing him, the wind howling all around
them, though her hair remained still. "Then why does it
sound like you've lost your nerve?"

He rounded on her. "Have you ever used your powers to
kill a thousand men, Keziah? Or a hundred? Or even one?"
She appeared to waver. "I thought not! Until you have, do not
presume to judge me or my nerve!" Grinsa had never spoken
to her so and he could see the hurt in her eyes, but at that moment he couldn't have cared less. "If we choose to fight now,
it will be my weaving that kills, and Fotir's shaping! Even
now, down to the three of us, you won't bear the cost of this
battle! So I'll thank you to keep silent and do as I say!"

A tear rolled down her smooth cheek and she looked away,
back toward the army of Solkara.

"Grinsa, she didn't mean—"

"It's all right, First Minister," she said, her voice steady. "I
shouldn't have said what I did." She swiped at the tear and
faced the gleaner again. "Should we retreat then?"

Before he could answer, a swarm of arrows rose from the
Aneiran army, arcing toward them. The wind they had summoned ensured that the darts would fall well short of them,
but Grinsa sensed that Solkara's bowmen were merely testing
the gale.

"We need to decide now, Grinsa!"

She was right, of course. Not only about needing to make his choice immediately, but also about the rest of it. They had ridden forth to oppose an army of thousands, and though the Aneirans presented less of a threat than they first thought, he and the others still needed to protect the king's army from any assault. More to the point, it was time to stop this killing, to make the Eandi see that they were wasting lives and strength warring with each other while the true enemy bided his time, waiting until they were too weak to resist his magic.

"We'll stay."

The Solkarans loosed their arrows again and instantly Grinsa could tell that this second volley would reach them. Still drawing on Fotir and Keziah's power, he shifted the wind a quarter turn, so that it blew the arrows to the side.

Before the archers could fire a third time, cries rose from the far side of the Aneiran force. Gershon's men had attacked.

"Damn!" If he could have shattered every weapon held by the two armies, he would have, but even a Weaver's power was not so precise. A burst of magic that strong would splinter bone as well.

"No, it's all right," his sister said. "The king's men can defeat them, even without our help."

"Don't you understand, Keziah? That's not what I want! We have to stop thinking like Eibitharians! These men aren't the enemy! Neither are the Braedony soldiers fighting your king to the north! We have to find a way to end the fighting, before Gershon's force kills them all."

"How?" Fotir asked.

Grinsa shook his head, his desperation growing with every scream that came from the warring armies. "I don't know."

A large contingent of Eibitharian soldiers had moved up from the rear of Gershon's company and flanked the Aneirans to the east. They fought under a green and white banner and appeared to be led by Lathrop of Tremain. No doubt the swordmaster had sent Labruinn's men to the west—few understood military tactics better than did Gershon Trasker. It would be a slaughter.

Keziah gazed toward the fighting with a crease in her brow.

"What about a mist? Perhaps if they can't see, they'll break off their assault."

"I don't want the Aneirans fleeing so that they can join with the empire's men and attack again. A mist might allow them to escape. I just want to stop them from killing each other."

"A wind then," she said, turning to face him. "Like at the Heneagh."

A year before, when they had sought to keep the armies of Curgh and Kentigern from destroying one another on a battle plain near the Heneagh River, the two of them had summoned a powerful wind. It hadn't been so strong as to keep the men from fighting, but it had gotten their attention long enough for Kearney to place himself between the two armies. Perhaps it would work again. First though, Grinsa had to be close enough to make himself seen and heard.

"Follow me," he called, kicking his mount to a gallop and steering the beast around those fighting on the west and then toward the center of the battle.

Keziah and Fotir rode after him, and together the three Qirsi plunged into the fighting, Grinsa drawing on their magic once more to summon a staggering wind. He made it build swiftly, so that to the soldiers it would seem that it had risen without warning. As he and Kezi had hoped, it did force many of the men to break off their combat, including Gershon Trasker, who sat on his horse, his sword still poised to strike, his hot glare directed at Grinsa and the others. Already many warriors had fallen, most of them Solkaran. Only a few hundred Aneirans remained alive, and the gleaner guessed that they would not survive long if the fighting resumed.

"Break off your attack, swordmaster!" Grinsa called as he drew nearer.

"I will not! These men are invaders. Their lives were forfeit as soon as they crossed the Tarbin."

The soldiers around them were eyeing each other warily, their weapons ready. The merest twitch by one of them would launch all into combat once more, no matter the wind that raged about them.

"We've a more dangerous foe, swordmaster," Keziah said, drawing the man's eye. "You know that as well as anyone. We'll need these men before all is done."

Gershon said nothing, the expression on his blunt features and in his hard blue eyes offering little promise that he would relent.

"Men of Aneira!" Grinsa called. "Lower your weapons! Surrender now, or all of you will die!"

"Never!" came a reply. Others echoed the sentiment, and Eibithar's men began shouting for their deaths. They were a heartbeat away from bedlam.

"Fotir, their swords. Quickly."

The minister nodded. A moment later an Aneiran blade shattered, and then another. Grinsa broke several as well.

"We'll break them all if we have to! Now put them down, and perhaps you'll survive this day!"

Reluctantly, the nearest of the Aneiran captains dropped his blade to the ground. Slowly, other men began to follow his example.

After several moments, Gershon nodded to his captains, who began ordering their men to lower their weapons.

"I do this against my better judgment, Archminister."

From what Keziah had told him, Grinsa gathered that she and the swordmaster had feigned many conflicts recently in order to maintain the illusion that her fealty to the king had wavered. Now, however, he sensed no trickery in the man's tone. He was deadly serious.

"I understand," Keziah said. "I had to be convinced as well."

Gershon's eyes flicked toward the gleaner, then back to her.

"You spoke a moment ago of another foe, Archminister. Of whom do you speak?"

Grinsa turned toward the voice. A stout man with yellow hair and a trim beard was leaning forward in his saddle, regarding the gleaner with obvious distrust. It took Grinsa a moment to recognize him as the duke of Labruinn. But his eye was drawn beyond this young duke to the towering figure who sat just behind him on the largest stallion Grinsa had ever seen. Aindreas of Kentigern, his ruddy face flushed to crimson, and his jaw clenched tight.

"You need to ask, my lord?" Fotir answered.

"The conspiracy."

"Yes, my lord. Many of us believe that this war—"

"Yes, I know. You think the Qirsi have, through treachery and deception, led us to this conflict so that we'll weaken ourselves." Labruinn looked at Grinsa again. "I just wonder if keeping the Aneirans alive is intended to strengthen us, or weaken us."

"Why would I want to weaken us, my lord?"

"He's not questioning your motives, First Minister," Grinsa said. "He's questioning mine."

"I don't know you, sir," the duke said. "I have no reason to question the first minister's loyalty, but in these times all strange Qirsi are suspect. And for many turns I've been hearing of odd behavior on the part of the archminister."

Gershon started to say something, but a glance from Keziah silenced him.

"I know this man," Aindreas said, murder in his voice. "I know all three of them."

"This is Grinsa jal Arriet, Lord Labruinn," Fotir said, with the merest of glances toward Aindreas. "And I assure you, he's no stranger to me. If it wasn't for Grinsa, Lord Tavis might still be a prisoner in Kentigern's dungeon. He has as much reason to hate the conspiracy as any man in the Forelands. For that matter, so does the archminister, and I have every reason to believe that she serves our king loyally and always has."

"I'd like to believe you," Caius said. "But I'm afraid even your word on the matter isn't enough."

"Nor should it be," Aindreas said. "The Qirsi can't be trusted."

Grinsa met the duke's glare, their eyes locking. "Last I heard, my lord, you were saying much the same thing about all men of Curgh and Glyndwr. Yet here you are fighting in the service of the king. Isn't it possible that you're as wrong about me as you were about them?"

Aindreas pulled his sword free. "You white-hair bastard!"

"That's enough from both of you," Gershon said, eyeing one of them and then the other. "It doesn't matter now. The Aneirans have surrendered." He faced his captain again. "Collect their weapons, see to their wounds, and prepare them for review by the king. I don't want them mistreated, but neither will I tolerate any resistance on their part." He cast a look at Keziah as he said this last, but she offered no response. As the king's men began to herd the Solkarans into a tight cluster, Gershon regarded Caius and Lathrop. "Take your armies forward to the king," he said. "I don't know how his soldiers are faring, but I'm certain he'll welcome your aid."

"There's no need," Fotir said. "The empire's men have broken off their attack. At least for the moment."

They all turned to look northward. Indeed, it did seem that Braedon's warriors were in retreat.

"Then perhaps we should find His Majesty, and ask him how he wants us to proceed."

The others agreed and after leaving their captains with instructions to make camp and watch over the prisoners, Gershon, the dukes, and the three Qirsi rode to the front lines. They found Kearney with Javan of Curgh, Marston of Shanstead, and Rab Avkar, Heneagh's swordmaster. The queen of Sanbira was there as well, with four of her nobles, including a dark-haired young woman who the night before had eyed Grinsa and the other Qirsi with manifest distrust.

Reaching the king, Gershon dismounted and dropped to one knee, as did all the others, including Aindreas.

Kearney, limping slightly, strode to his swordmaster, ordered Gershon to rise, and gathered him in a fierce embrace. "Well met, Gershon! Well met!" he said. "All this time I've felt like I've been fighting with one hand." He released the man and looked him up and down. "I take it you're well."

Trasker was grinning. "I am, Your Majesty. Thank you. And you?"

"Well enough." He looked past Gershon to the dukes. "Lord Tremain, Lord Labruinn, I'm deeply grateful to both of you. I've no doubt that your counsel and your men were of tremendous value to the swordmaster. I believe it's time the people of this realm stopped referring to the 'minor houses.' As far as I can tell, there's no such thing."

Lathrop and Caius bowed.

"Thank you, my liege," Tremain said. "We did only what any man of the realm would have done for his king." As soon as he spoke the words, Lathrop paled, casting a furtive look at Aindreas.

"What do you think of that, Lord Kentigern?" Kearney asked.

Aindreas glowered at the king, but after a moment he nodded, as if compelled to do so by some unseen hand. "I'm sure my lord duke is correct, my liege."

"Is that why you're here?"

Neither man had moved, though it seemed that both had weapons drawn.

"I'm here to defend Eibithar, and to strike back at the men who attacked Kentigern."

"No other reason?"

"None that I can think of, my liege."

"I see." The king held Aindreas's gaze for another moment, then turned to Keziah, as if dismissing the duke. "How did you end up with Gershon and the others, Archminister? I thought you were behind our lines. When you weren't there, I . . ." His face colored briefly. "I grew concerned."

"Forgive me, Your Majesty. Grinsa suggested that the three of us ride back to stop the Aneirans' advance. We didn't know at the time that the swordmaster was pursuing them."

"What?" Javan asked. He had been watching Aindreas all this time, as a seaman might watch an approaching storm. But now he stared at Keziah, a slight frown on his lean face. "The three of you thought you could stand against a thousand Solkaran soldiers? Are you truly that powerful, or just that foolish?"

"All three of us have mists and winds, my lord," she said, giving no indication that his question discomfited her. "We were afraid that Aneira's archers would attack the king's army from behind. We merely wished to protect His Majesty."

"Every time I turn around you seem to grow more powerful," Javan said, looking directly at Grinsa. "I find myself wondering if your magic knows any bounds at all."

Aindreas was staring at Grinsa as well. "I thought you were just a gleaner."

"Grinsa's a bit more than he seems, my lord," Fotir said. "But there can be no question of his loyalty to the realm."

"More than you seem, eh?" Aindreas asked, his eyes narrowing. "Is that how you got the boy out?"

"What boy?" Javan demanded, though clearly he knew.

"Yours, of course. This man put a hole in the wall of my castle that I could have walked through."

Grinsa opened his mouth to deny it, but before he could Fotir said, "No, Lord Kentigern, that was me."

"But you said that you couldn't have done such a thing. Shurik told me much the same."

"Normally I couldn't have. But that night called for extraordinary measures, and somehow Qirsar gave me the power to win Lord Tavis's freedom."

In strictest terms it wasn't a lie. Fotir had used his power on the wall, though without Grinsa weaving the minister's magic with his own, augmenting and controlling it, he never would have succeeded. As for Grinsa's presence there being an act of the god, the gleaner couldn't say that he believed this, but neither could he say with complete certainty that it wasn't so. In any case, Fotir's confession appeared to satisfy the duke and lay the matter to rest. Or so he thought.

"It seems that our Qirsi friends are full of surprises," said Marston of Shanstead, whose distrust of all Qirsi had nearly led the king to banish Cresenne and Keziah from Audun's Castle.

Grinsa saw the dark-haired duchess nod slightly, her eyes fixed on Marston.

"You wish to say something more, Lord Shanstead?" Kearney asked, his voice hardening.

"Nothing I haven't said to you before, my liege."

"Fine then. I've heard it once, I needn't hear it again."

The thane lowered his eyes. "Yes, my liege."

The queen of Sanbira cleared her throat. "Perhaps, Your

Majesty, we should continue this conversation later. Braedon's men have retreated for now, but I daresay they could renew their assault at any moment."

Kearney nodded. "You're right, of course, Your Highness." He looked at Gershon. "I want the soldiers who've just arrived added to our lines as quickly as possible. Swordmaster, you're to assume command of the King's Guard—take the men who have been under your authority and combine them with those I took north from the City of Kings."

"Yes, Your Majesty."

"Lord Tremain, I'd like your men to join with the Curgh army. Lord Curgh, with Gershon's men joining my own, the King's Guard will take the center. I want you and Lathrop on the eastern flank."

"Of course, my liege."

"Lord Labruinn, I want your force in the west, along with Thorald's army and what's left of the army from Heneagh." He paused, looking at Aindreas. "Lord Kentigern, you and your men will go with Caius. For now you'll be under his command."

"Very well."

"You and I have a good deal more to discuss. But I'm afraid that'll have to wait."

Aindreas's face reddened, but he merely nodded. "As you wish, my liege."

"Your Highness, I would ask you to keep your army where it's been today, unless of course you have another idea."

"We are here at your request, Your Majesty," Olesya said. "Use us as you will."

The king smiled and bowed. "My thanks. That's all," he said, looking at the others. "I hope the empire's men will think twice before attacking again. They've seen how easily their Aneiran allies were defeated, and they know that we've added several thousand men to our defenses. Still, I agree with the queen that we must remain watchful. I want your armies positioned quickly. They've surprised us before and may well do so again."

Eibithar's dukes and their ministers bowed to the king and

began to move off, Grinsa following Fotir so that he might thank the first minister for helping him keep his secret a bit longer. Before he had gone far, however, Kearney called to him.

"A word please, gleaner."

Keziah was beside the king, her face colorless, her lips pressed together in a taut line. Grinsa returned to where they stood.

"Yes, Your Majesty?"

Kearney hesitated. "Walk with me."

They started away from the armies, skirting the portion of the moors where the battle with the Solkarans had been fought, and where bodies were now being piled. Glancing back, Grinsa noticed that Marston and the dark-haired duchess were watching them. They were too far away for the gleaner to see their expressions, but he could guess.

"The first minister didn't make that hole in Aindreas's castle, did he?" the king asked, drawing Grinsa's gaze.

"Not alone, no. He couldn't have without my help."

"So he's the other."

"Your Majesty?"

"The day you told me you were a Weaver, you listed those who knew—Keziah, Tavis, Cresenne, and another you wouldn't name. It was Fotir, wasn't it?"

"Yes."

"And how much longer can our circle remain so small?"

Grinsa shook his head. "Not much, I fear."

"Aindreas will call for your head. So will Shanstead. I don't know about the others, but I can't imagine they'll be willing to embrace you as an ally."

"They have to!" Keziah said. "Who else among us can fight the Weaver?"

"I don't disagree with you, Kez. I'm just telling you what I know to be true."

"The question is, Your Majesty, what will you do? If you support me, the others may follow. Perhaps not Kentigern, nor even Shanstead, but the rest. Certainly Javan will. He knows what I've done for Tavis, and the boy will speak to him on my behalf. I sense that the queen might support me as well, though some of her nobles might speak against it. Ultimately, though, this is up to you."

Kearney looked back across the battle plain, then stared up at the crows and vultures circling overhead. "My father used to say that we don't choose our allies so much as find them. The hardest part, he said, was recognizing them in time." He met Grinsa's gaze. "I'll support you, gleaner. I haven't much choice in the matter, and even if I did, you've proved your good faith time and again. I'd be a fool not to stand with you."

Grinsa bowed. "Thank you, Your Majesty."

"Shall we speak to them now?"

"Not yet. There's something I want to do first. With your permission, I'd wait until morning."

"All right. May I ask what it is you intend to do?"

"I'm going to try to enter the Weaver's dreams."

"What?" Keziah whispered.

"We need to know where he is, and, if possible, what he's planning. This is the only way I can think of to learn both."

"Is there any danger to you?" the king asked.

"No. I'll be in his mind. The worst he can do is drive me out. But it may be that I can hurt him."

"Very well." The king halted, as did Keziah and Grinsa. "I'll be eager to hear how you fare."

"Thank you, Your Majesty."

"I should return to the armies."

"May I have a moment with Grinsa, Your Majesty?"

"Of course." He nodded to the gleaner, who bowed once more in return. Then he turned and started back toward the soldiers.

"You think I'm wrong to try," Grinsa said.

"I think the risks are greater than you made them sound just now."

"He can't hurt me, Kezi."

"Maybe not. But he can sense your thoughts, your fears. I know, because I've sensed his. Not enough to learn much, but I'm not a Weaver. You may give away as much as you learn. You could even reveal that I'm your sister."

"I won't."

"But you could."

"At the first sign of danger, I'll break contact with him. You have my word."

She looked like she might say more, but in the end she merely nodded and walked away, leaving Grinsa alone amid the grasses and stones.

The truth was, Grinsa didn't have to enter the Weaver's dreams at all. He had only to reach for him. He could search the land for the man without actually entering his mind. That would tell him where Dusaan jal Kania and his army could be found. But Grinsa wanted this confrontation. Twice before they had met, once when he pulled Cresenne out of her dream of the man, thus saving her life, and again when the Weaver came to him, and nearly managed to turn Grinsa's own magic against him. Eventually they would face each other in battle, probably on this very moor. It seemed as inevitable as the new day. They were tied to one another, their strange bond forged of hatred and the powers they shared; of the Weaver's ambition and Grinsa's need to avenge all that Dusaan had done to Cresenne and Keziah. But during their previous encounter, when Braedon's high chancellor entered his dreams, Grinsa had found himself overmatched. Before their final battle, he needed to prove to himself that he could defeat this man, that his powers ran as deep as those of the renegade Weaver.

After some time, as the sun finally began to dip toward the western horizon, Grinsa returned to the Curgh camp to look for Tavis. Before he reached the boy, though, he was accosted by Marston of Shanstead. The thane had two soldiers with him, as if he feared approaching a Qirsi unguarded. His grey eyes were watchful, scanning from side to side as he walked, and he rested a hand on the hilt of his sheathed sword.

"I know what you have in mind to do," Shanstead said without preamble, his voice low and tense. "And I'd advise you against it."

For just an instant, Grinsa wondered if the man really did know, if he had discovered Grinsa's secret and learned of his intention to speak with the Weaver. In the next moment, he dismissed the idea. This man hated all Qirsi, save his own minister. No doubt he meant to accuse Grinsa of some foul crime against the king.

"What is it you think you know, my lord?"

"I know that the archminister is a traitor, and I see the two of you plotting together. I know as well that you've lied about your powers in the past. Aindreas and Javan, who can barely agree on the time of day, concur on that much." He took a step closer, tightening his grip on his weapon. "I'm watching you, gleaner. And your friend as well. If one of you should so much as look askance at the king, I'll crush you both. Do you understand?"

Shanstead, he realized in that moment, was precisely the sort of Eandi that drove Qirsi to the Weaver and his movement. This type of blind distrust and blustering animosity had done more to weaken the Forelands than had any white-haired traitor. Grinsa would have liked to shatter the man's blade, or set his hair ablaze. Instead, he offered a thin smile. "I assure you, Lord Shanstead, the king has nothing to fear from his archminister or from me. What's more, he knows this. It's a pity you're too much a fool to see it for yourself."

"How dare you speak to me so!"

"I could say much the same thing, my lord." And stepping around the man, Grinsa continued on toward the Curgh lines. He half expected Shanstead to follow, and a part of him wished the man would, so that he'd have an excuse to use his magic. But the thane merely stared after him as Grinsa wove his way through a maze of soldiers and past the wounded. When he found Tavis, his hands were still trembling with rage.

"There you are," the young lord said as Grinsa approached him. "I've been hearing all sorts of stories about you." He had been smiling, but seeing the gleaner's expression he grew serious. "What's happened?"

Grinsa shook his head. "Nothing."

"Don't lie to me. I know you too well, Grinsa."

"Nothing of importance. Really." Knowing the boy wouldn't be satisfied by this, he gestured vaguely at the battle plain. "Shanstead just accused Keziah and me of plotting against the king."

"Shanstead's an idiot."

"I'm inclined to agree with you."

"Do you want me to speak with the king?"

The gleaner had to smile. Tavis had grown a good deal in the past year. "No, thank you," he said, dropping his voice to a whisper. "Shanstead's suspicions will prove useful as long as Keziah is still maintaining her deception."

"I suppose."

"Tell me about these stories you're hearing."

"Actually most of them are coming from my father. He's saying that along with Fotir and the archminister, you held off the entire Aneiran army."

Grinsa laughed. "That's not quite true."

"Still, that's what he's saying. He also told me that Aindreas accused you of putting a hole in his castle so that I could escape. Now, he said as well that Fotir claimed to have shaped the hole himself, but my father doesn't believe that for a moment." He paused, eyeing the gleaner. "You do see where I'm going with all this."

"I do," the gleaner said, rubbing a hand over his face. It wasn't as funny anymore.

"He wasn't just telling stories, Grinsa. He took me aside and started asking questions about you, about your powers, about what I've seen you do during our journeys together. My father's no fool. He may not know as much about Qirsi magic as I do at this point, but he's going to figure this out. He might have already."

"What will he do when he does?"

"I don't know."

"I need his support, Tavis. With Shanstead telling everyone who'll listen that I'm a traitor, and Aindreas still bitter over your escape, I'll need all the friends—"

"You're going to tell them?"

"I haven't much choice. Even now, the king is preparing for a final battle with the empire. I can't allow that to happen. If these armies destroy one another, we've no hope of defeating the Weaver. As it is, we might have lost too many men already. I intend to reveal to the nobles that I'm a Weaver, to try to make them see what it is we face. I'm hoping that I can convince them to sue for peace with the Braedony army."

"They won't do it."

"They have to."

Tavis shrugged. "They won't. You've taught me a good deal about your people and your magic during this past year. Now, let me tell you something about the Eandi courts of Eibithar. They don't tolerate invasions. It amazes me that you convinced them to spare the lives of those Solkarans. You might get them to do the same with what's left of the empire's force, but you'll never convince them to sue for peace, much less fight beside them. I do know what's at stake, and I've half a mind to destroy their army anyway."

"I understand what you're telling me. But still, I have to try."

"I know you do," Tavis said, sighing. "I'll do all I can to convince my father. He can be stubborn, although no more so than I." A smile touched his lips and was gone. "After all you've done for me, he won't be one of those calling for your execution. I can promise you that."

"Thank you, Tavis."

"Have you told Keziah what you intend to do?"

"Yes." Grinsa faltered, but only briefly. Tavis should know all of it. He had earned that much. "You should also know that I intend to enter the Weaver's dreams tonight."

He expected the young lord to express amazement, or perhaps to tell him that he was a fool. Instead Tavis just nodded, and said, "Be careful."

"I will."

They stood in awkward silence for several moments. It seemed to Grinsa that they had reached some sort of ending, as if all that they had shared since Tavis's escape from Kentigern was drawing to a close. And strangely, the gleaner found himself saddened by this.

"I suppose everything is going to be different once others know," the boy said. The smile sprang to his lips again, looking forced and bitter among the scars Aindreas had left on his face. Once Grinsa had thought that the scars fit the boy, giving him a hardened look that was a match for his difficult manner. That was when they first began to journey together. Over the course of the past year, however, as they searched for Brienne's assassin and prepared for this war, their relationship changed. Tavis changed. Where once he had been a selfish, undisciplined child, he now stood before Grinsa a man, still with his faults to be sure, but more mature than the gleaner would have thought possible. With time, perhaps, as Tavis's face aged, adding other lines, and softening the effect of the old wounds, he'd look wise and strong. That struck Grinsa as more apt now.

"I won't be the notorious one anymore," Tavis said after a moment. "They'll all be looking at you."

"I'd think that you'd welcome that."

"I guess I should."

"But?"

Tavis shrugged, then shook his head. "But nothing." The smile lingered, grew warmer. "What a pair we make."

Before Grinsa could answer, Tavis stepped forward and gathered him in a rough embrace.

"Thank you, Grinsa," he whispered. Then he pulled back, turned away, and hurried off.

The gleaner wandered off in a different direction, eventually taking a seat on a large grey stone and watching the sun set. As darkness gathered around the armies, the soldiers lit fires and the faint smell of roasting fowl reached him. He hadn't eaten since morning, but he wasn't hungry. He remained where he was, watching as stars began to spread across the night sky. Fragments of conversations reached him, occasionally he heard a burst of laughter, or the sound of rough voices singing some Eibitharian or Sanbiri folk song. After some time, Keziah came to him and sat as well. He thought that she would resume her argument against what he was planning, but she said nothing, just rested her head on his shoulder, and stared up at the stars. Eventually she began to nod off, jerking herself awake more than once. At last she stood, yawning deeply. Gazing at him in the darkness, she smiled sadly. Then she kissed his cheek, gave his hand a gentle squeeze, and moved off, leaving him alone with the soft wind and the distant, mournful cry of an owl.

Still he waited, watching for the moons. Only when both were up, did he finally close his eyes and stretch his mind forth, searching for the Weaver. He had known to look north- ward, expecting that Dusaan would be on the waters beyond Galdasten. Instead, he found the Weaver in the company of nearly two hundred Qirsi on the moors south of the castle, only a few days' ride from the battle plain. Fear gripped him and he nearly opened his eyes once more and went immedi- ately to Kearney. But such a warning could wait a short while—Dusaan and his army weren't on the move just now. And the truth was, Grinsa wanted to face this man again. He wanted to prove to himself, and to the Weaver, that he could stand against the high chancellor's power. He wasn't proud of this—it was something he would have expected of Tavis, not himself—but there could be no denying the strength of the impulse. It was more than he could resist.

Taking one long, final breath, he entered Dusaan's mind.

He had chosen the moors near Eardley for their encounter—the same place he usually spoke to Keziah when he entered her dreams. It was where he felt most comfort- able; he wanted to keep all his attention on the Weaver and what he said, without having to give a thought to their sur- roundings. Still, he made certain that the sun was high over- head. Dusaan liked to hide his face during such encounters. Grinsa wouldn't allow him that luxury.

An instant later, Dusaan stood before him, dressed in war- rior's garb, an amused grin on his square face.

"I've been expecting you," he said.

Without bothering to respond, Grinsa reached for the man's power—shaping first, then fire, then healing. Dusaan blocked his efforts with ease.

"You disappoint me, gleaner. You didn't really think that you'd best me with such a predictable attack."

"It was worth trying."

Dusaan shrugged indifferently. "I suppose, though it seems to me that you do our relationship a disservice."

"We have no relationship."

"No? I walk in your dreams, you walk in mine." He smiled. "People will talk."

Again Grinsa tried to take hold of the Weaver's healing power, but Dusaan had an iron grip on all his magic. The gleaner sensed no fear in the man. Only confidence, an unshakable faith in his own strength and the inevitability of his victory.

"Be honest with me, Grinsa. You've never known another Weaver, have you?"

"No," he admitted.

"Nor have I. We share something unique. Before this moment, no one had ever entered my dreams as you've done. Just as I was the first to walk in your dreams. You can protest all you like, but we share a kinship, even if it is based solely on our desire to kill one another."

"We're both Weavers, but beyond that we have nothing at all in common. I've seen the things you do—you're cruel, arbitrary, ambitious beyond reason."

The Weaver shook his head, making a clicking noise with his tongue. "All this because I hurt your love? You judge me too harshly."

Grinsa didn't answer immediately. He needed to be more careful. As Keziah had told him, the Weaver could sense his emotions, and the last thing Grinsa wanted was to betray his sister's secret.

"I know what I've seen," he said at last.

"Cresenne betrayed me. Can you honestly say that an Eandi lord wouldn't do the same to a traitor?"

"That's a strange defense of your actions. You speak of a new future for the Qirsi people, and yet you look to the Eandi courts to justify torture."

"Don't try to goad me, Grinsa. It won't work, nor is it necessary. No doubt you wish to know my plans, to divine the ploys I intend to use against your Eandi friends. The truth is, there are no ploys. I plan to lead my army onto the Moorlands and defeat the armies of the Forelands in battle. You found me, so you know where we are and how many I command. I don't care. I'm sure you count it a victory that you can see my face, but at this point that doesn't concern me, either. I've nothing to fear from Kearney and his allies, or from you for that matter. I defeated the emperor's army with but a handful of Qirsi. I took Ayvencalde with less than half the number of Qirsi I have now. My army is the most powerful force to travel the Forelands in nine hundred years. There isn't an army you could assemble that would stand against us."

"That army of nine centuries ago was defeated, and yours will be as well."

A bright angry grin lit the Weaver's face. "No, Grinsa. You're wrong. The Qirsi army of old was betrayed. But I know these Qirsi—my Qirsi. There's no Carthach here."

"How can you be so certain?"

Dusaan's grin deepened. "Because you're the only Carthach in the Forelands. You've already betrayed your people, and we're going to prevail in spite of you."

Now who was doing the goading? Grinsa shouldn't have been bothered, but this talk of Carthach—why had he even mentioned the ancient traitor in the first place?—hewed too closely to his own deepest fears to be ignored. He knew that this man before him was not fit to lead his people, much less all the realms of the Forelands. But he knew as well that his people deserved to be treated better than they were by Eandi nobility, and he couldn't help but wonder if he would be remembered as the Weaver who betrayed his people by fighting to save their oppressors.

"I've silenced you," the Weaver said. "How glorious."

There was nothing for him to say. All that was left, in his desperation and his fear, was to make one last attempt at killing the man. He grappled for the Weaver's power once more, lunging for it with his mind, battering at Dusaan's defenses. Fire, shaping, healing—any magic that might allow him to exact revenge for what the Weaver had done to Cresenne, what his schemes had done to Tavis, what the need to defeat him had done to Keziah. And again, he failed. Dusaan actually laughed at him, as if Grinsa were a child leaping to catch hold of wonders that hung beyond his reach.

Then, without warning, the Weaver did something Grinsa hadn't anticipated, hadn't even thought possible. With one quick stride forward, he stretched out a hand, taking hold of the gleaner's throat. Abruptly Grinsa couldn't breathe. It shouldn't have been possible. There was nothing in Grinsa's knowledge of Qirsi magic to explain it. Yet there could be no denying the pressure on his neck, the sudden burning of his lungs.

"You thought to enter my dreams?" the Weaver demanded, his hot breath on Grinsa's face. "You believed yourself powerful enough to use my magic against me? You're nothing, *gleaner*." He said the word with contempt, as if he were calling Grinsa a whoreson. *Or a traitor.*

He struggled to free himself, then stopped, realizing that this was just what the Weaver wanted him to do, just what he had warned Cresenne and Keziah not to do. Instead, he took hold of his own magic again, breaking free of Dusaan's control. An instant later, he drew breath again. Dusaan still stood just before him, his hand at Grinsa's throat. But the gleaner no longer felt the man's touch.

Dusaan gave a wry smile. "Very good, gleaner. You did that quite well. Of course a man of your power shouldn't have allowed me access to your magic in the first place, but I'm sure that when you tell your king of this encounter, you'll leave out that small detail."

An instant later, everything went dark. Grinsa warded himself, grasping at his magic as if it were a battle shield. Only after a few moments did he understand that the Weaver had ended their conversation, waking himself with ease. The gleaner couldn't help but remember how he had struggled to thrust the Weaver from his mind when Dusaan invaded his dreams.

He opened his eyes, bracing himself with his hand to keep from toppling over. The stars above him seemed to pitch and spin, as if he were a feather blown about by a harvest wind. He squeezed his eyes closed, opened them again. After some time, the stars began to slow.

When he could walk again, he made his way to Kearney's tent. Most in the camp were asleep, but a candle still burned within the king's shelter and after a word with Kearney, a guard allowed Grinsa to enter.

The king sat at a small table, a modest, half-eaten meal before him. He looked weary. Even in the candlelight, Grinsa could see the dark lines under his pale eyes. "Yes, gleaner. What is it?"

"I went to the Weaver, Your Majesty, as I told you I would."

Kearney stood, nearly upsetting the table. "I had forgotten. Did you . . . ? Were you able to hurt him?"

"No, Your Majesty. But I did learn something of his plans. He's closer than we thought—no more than two or three days' ride from here. He leads an army of some two hundred Qirsi."

"Two hundred?" the king repeated, frowning.

"It's more than it sounds, Your Majesty. With two hundred Qirsi he can destroy all of the armies on this plain."

"But you're a Weaver as well, with Qirsi on your side. Surely you can help us defeat him."

"I'll do my best, Your Majesty. He's . . . he's very powerful."

"As are you."

"Yes, but he has more Qirsi with him than I do. And he's been using his power as a weapon far longer than I have."

"Still, your presence here must mean something."

"I hope it will, Your Majesty, but I'm not strong enough to do this on my own. You need to end this war with Braedon."

"I intend to try. I've been trying."

"No, Your Majesty, you don't understand. I don't mean defeat them. I'm asking you to sue for peace and end this conflict before others die."

"You can't be serious."

"It's the only way. We can't afford to lose any more men."

"The empire invaded this land! Harel seeks the conquest of Eibithar! And you want me to make peace with him?"

"Harel no longer rules Braedon, Your Majesty! Dusaan has defeated the part of his army that remained in Curtell. For all we know, the emperor is dead. The conspiracy is your enemy, just as it's the enemy of every sovereign in the Forelands. Even if you defeat Braedon's men, this war you're fighting now will destroy you. I beg of you: end it while you can, and prepare for the true battle."

Kearney sat again, looking confused and more than a bit frightened. "He defeated Harel? You're certain?"

"Yes. He also took Ayvencalde, and though he didn't say so, his presence on the Moorlands tells me that he defeated Galdasten as well."

The king stared at the candle flame. "Demons and fire."

"Please, Your Majesty. Make peace with the empire's men. It may be our only hope."

"I'll think on it." He looked up, meeting the gleaner's gaze. "Truly, I will."

"Thank you, Your Majesty."

Grinsa bowed, then left the tent, wondering if even an alliance between Eibithar and her enemies would be enough to withstand the Weaver's onslaught. The king, he realized, was depending upon him to win this war. So were Keziah and Fotir and Tavis. The others might revile him when first he revealed himself as a Weaver, but with time they would see him much the same way. He was their hope, and yet he had no hope himself. This, as much as anything, explained why Dusaan had been right, why Grinsa hadn't mentioned to Kearney the ease with which the Weaver took hold of his magic.

Chapter

Fifteen

iani awoke before dawn, roused from her slumber by the voices of soldiers around her, the ring of steel as swords were drawn, checked for notches, and resheathed, the impatient snorting and stomping of the horses, and the jangling of saddles being fastened. She sat up, winced at the pain. Every muscle in her body was screaming. Her back and legs were so stiff that she wondered how she would ever manage to stand, much less fight. The previous day's battle had been her first, and though she had come through it unscathed save for a few small cuts and bruises, she knew already that she was no warrior. Her ability to avoid injury was due far more to her skill as a rider than to any prowess with the blade. She had inflicted no more wounds than she had sustained. Mostly she had sought to stay alive and to keep out of the way of Sanbira's real soldiers.

Much to Diani's surprise, Naditia was one of them. The duchess of Macharzo, so painfully shy during audiences with the queen and in private conversations alike, was a skilled and powerful fighter. She wielded her blade aggressively and with uncommon agility, and she was as fearless in battle as she was shy at court. It seemed to Diani that the woman had been born for combat. More than once during the course of the previous day, Naditia had saved Diani's life. Yet after the fighting ended, she instantly became again an awkward, tongue-tied young duchess.

Sweating and out of breath, too relieved by the end of combat to care how her army had fared, Diani thanked the woman for protecting her.

"You fight magnificently," she said. "I wish I wielded a blade as you do."

Naditia had given an embarrassed smile and ducked her head, swiping at the hair that clung to her damp brow. "My father taught me."

"You almost seem to enjoy it."

The tall woman shrugged. "I do. As long as I'm fighting, I don't have to say anything."

Struggling to get to her feet on this cool, dark morning, gasping at the pain of every movement, Diani wondered if Macharzo's duchess was actually looking forward to another day of battle. Ean knew that Diani was not. She stood for a moment, stretching her back, then walked stiffly to where the queen and her master of arms were eating a small breakfast. Both were already dressed for battle. Abeni, the queen's archminister, lurked nearby, ghostly pale in the dim light.

"Good morning, Lady Curlinte," Olesya called as she approached. "Are you hungry?"

"No, thank you, Your Highness."

"You should have something, Diani. If the fighting begins again, there's no telling when you'll have a chance to eat."

Reluctantly, Diani took some bread and a piece of hard cheese, thanking the queen and, as an afterthought, Ohan as well. "Do you expect the fighting to begin soon?" she asked between bites.

"I don't know. We're awaiting word from Eibithar's king."

"If the Braedony army chooses not to attack," the swordmaster added, "I expect that Kearney won't force the matter." From his tone, it seemed that Ohan thought this a mistake on the king's part.

Diani felt differently. "Then let's hope the enemy thinks better of it," she said.

Olesya nodded. "Indeed."

They continued to eat, saying little, as the sky slowly brightened. Gazing northward, Diani saw no sign that the empire's men were readying themselves for battle. There was some movement in the Braedony camp, but nothing threatening. One by one, the other nobles joined them, Naditia first, the dukes of Norinde and Brugaosa soon after. Their Qirsi came with them, joining the archminister a short distance off and speaking in hushed tones among themselves.

"I still think we should take the battle to them," Ohan said at last, his eyes fixed on the enemy lines.

Alao glanced at the master of arms. "I tend to agree. With the men who joined Kearney's force yesterday, we have enough to overwhelm Braedon's force. Let's attack and be done with it."

"It's not our decision to make, Lord Norinde," the queen said.

"I mean no disrespect, Your Highness, but I must say I find that troubling as well. It's bad enough that we've allowed ourselves to be entangled in Eibithar's conflict with the empire. But for us to submit to the king's authority seems to me foolhardy and dangerous."

"Yes, Lord Norinde," Olesya said, sounding weary. "I'm quite aware that were you sovereign, matters would be very different. But you're not, and I have made my decision. Kearney appealed to us for aid and we chose to grant it. You disagreed at the time, and you've made it clear that you still think our course an unwise one. Repeating your opinion will accomplish nothing, save to annoy me further."

Alao's face turned crimson, and there was rage in his eyes. But he nodded once, and said simply, "Yes, Your Highness."

"I'll raise the matter of the battle with Kearney when I can. In truth, I don't relish the idea of waiting for another assault either."

A few moments later an Eibitharian soldier approached, resplendent in purple and gold. He bowed to the queen and told her that his king requested a word with her at her convenience.

"Did he want me alone?" Olesya asked.

"No, Your Highness. He asks that you bring your nobles and ministers."

"My ministers?"

"Yes, Your Highness. He made a point of that."

"Very well," the queen said, frowning slightly. "Tell him we'll be along shortly."

The man bowed a second time and left them.

"Now he's summoning us, as if we served in his court."

"Oh, Alao, do be quiet! He did nothing of the sort." She looked at Diani. "It is strange, though, that he's asked us to bring the Qirsi."

It was more than strange; it was disturbing. In this instance, Diani agreed with the duke of Norinde. By asking the queen to bring her Qirsi, Kearney had overstepped propriety and whatever authority he held on this battle plain. More to the point, from what Diani had observed in her short time with the king of Eibithar, the man placed far too much faith in the white-hairs. It almost seemed that he had never heard of the conspiracy, that nothing had happened in the past year to shake his faith in the loyalty of his ministers. She wanted to speak against honoring Kearney's request, but after hearing Olesya reprimand the duke, she didn't dare.

"Yes, Your Highness, it is strange," was all she said.

"Still, I'm sure he has his reasons."

The queen beckoned to Abeni, who led the other Qirsi to where Olesya and her nobles stood.

"The king wishes to speak with us, Archminister. We're to join him at his camp presently."

"Very good, Your Highness," the archminister said, with a smile that was clearly forced. "We'll wait for you here."

"Actually, Archminister, Kearney has asked that you and the ministers come with us."

Abeni made no effort to conceal her surprise. "Did he say why?"

"No. Nor did I ask. I take it you have no objection."

"None, Your Highness." She glanced uncomfortably at the other ministers. "We're ready when you are."

Olesya nodded and led them all to the Eibitharian camp. Kearney was waiting for them outside his small tent. His nobles were already there, as were several Qirsi, including the tall, broad-shouldered man Diani had noticed two nights before. He was unlike any Qirsi she had ever seen. He had the body of an Eandi warrior, and though his skin and eyes were pale like those of other white-hairs, they did not make him appear frail or sickly. On the contrary. He was, perhaps, the most formidable man of either race she had ever seen. A young Eandi man stood near him, his dark blue eyes watchful. He might once have been handsome, but his face now was lined with scars that made him appear both sad and menacing.

Diani recognized some of the other Eibitharian nobles and was able to assign names to a few of the faces. When Marston of Shanstead caught her eye, she nodded to him and smiled. He nodded in return, but his expression remained grim.

"Your Highness," Kearney said, bowing to her. "Thank you for honoring my invitation so quickly. It seems for now that the empire's army is content to rest this day, but we must remain wary. I won't keep you long."

"Actually, Your Majesty, if I may interrupt, a few in my company have suggested that we take the battle to Braedon. They point out that we now outnumber the enemy by a sizable margin. Wouldn't we be wise to end this threat as quickly as possible?"

The king's eyes flicked toward the tall Qirsi. "Indeed we might, Your Highness. I've considered this as well, and have heard much the same thing from several of my dukes. But I'd ask your indulgence before we make this decision. There are . . . other factors at work here that bear consideration."

"What other factors?" Alao demanded, drawing a scowl from the queen.

"I have good reason to believe that there's more to this invasion than Harel's lust for power and land. I fear that much of what's happened in the Forelands in the past year, particularly here in Eibithar, has been contrived by others."

Alao made a sour face. "You speak of the conspiracy."

"Yes."

"All the more reason to end this conflict quickly and decisively."

"Not necessarily," said the broad-shouldered Qirsi.

They all looked at him.

"And who are you, sir?" the queen asked. "I saw you with the king yesterday, but I didn't hear your name or title."

The man bowed. "My name is Grinsa jal Arriet, Your Highness. I'm a gleaner in Eibithar's Revel."

"A gleaner? Hearing these dukes speak of you, I had the impression that you're somewhat more than that."

"I'm a gleaner by profession."

"So am I to gather that you've had a vision of what's to come, and this has convinced you that we shouldn't attack?"

"It's more than that. As we speak, a Qirsi army approaches from the north. They're led by a man named Dusaan jal Kania—"

"Harel's high chancellor?"

"Yes. But he's far more than that. He's a Weaver."

Olesya raised a hand to her mouth. "A Weaver?"

"Yes, Your Highness. A powerful one. He and his warriors have the power to destroy all the armies on this battle plain. If we continue this war—even if we prevail—we only assure Dusaan's victory. We have to end this conflict now. The

Weaver is our true enemy and we can only defeat him by joining forces with Braedon's men and fighting as one."

"This is too much!" said one of Kearney's dukes, a stout man with yellow hair and dark eyes. "It was bad enough when you made us spare Numar's men. But now you want us to make peace with Harel's invaders? I won't do it!" He turned to the king. "I beg you, Your Majesty! Don't listen to this man!"

Diani had to agree, and she was pleased when others spoke against the Qirsi.

"Lord Labruinn is right, Your Majesty," said Marston of Shanstead. "This is not some border skirmish we're fighting. This conflict wasn't caused by some minor land dispute. The empire invaded our realm and until its soldiers are driven from Eibithar, there can be no talk of peace." He pointed a finger at the tall Qirsi. "This man speaks of the conspiracy as if he's the first to bring its perils to our attention. He's not, of course. All of us have suffered for its treachery, including our friends from Sanbira. And in Eibithar, no one has spoken against the Qirsi renegades more strongly than I. There has been no greater threat to our land in my lifetime. But to weaken ourselves in the cause of fighting the Qirsi threat makes no sense at all." He faced the Qirsi. "I find myself questioning this man's motives. If he truly cares about this realm, why does he speak only of accommodating our enemies?"

The young man with the scarred face stared at the thane, shaking his head. "Are you really that stupid?" he asked at last.

"Tavis!"

"I'm sorry, Father, but this has to stop!" He faced the thane again. "Grinsa is no traitor, Lord Shanstead. The king can tell you so, my father and his first minister can tell you so, I can tell you so. If it wasn't for him, I'd be dead by now, or at best, still a prisoner in Kentigern. He's saved my life time and again, and he has spent the last year fighting the conspiracy at every turn."

"I've heard all of this before, Lord Curgh. And I've always

wondered how he knew to find you in Kentigern in the first place. As I understand it, he was a mere Revel gleaner before he 'saved' you."

"He knew because he gleaned for me."

"How convenient. It seems to me that this man contrived your rescue, just as the Qirsi have been contriving wars and murders for the past several years."

"You're wrong, Marston."

This man Diani knew, not only because she had overheard his conversation with the king the day before, but also by reputation. Aindreas of Kentigern was the largest man she had ever seen. Tall, broad—some might have called him fat, as well. But she thought the name by which he was known in Sanbira—the Tor atop the Tor—fit him best. He was a mountain; solid, immovable, enormous.

All were looking at him now, and from the reddening of his face, it seemed that he regretted speaking at all.

"You agree with the Qirsi, Lord Kentigern?" Marston asked, as if unable to believe what he was hearing.

"I'm not saying that. I don't know what we should do about the invaders. But I do know that Tavis's escape was not contrived by the conspiracy. If they were responsible for my daughter's . . . for what happened to her, then the last thing they wanted was for Tavis to be free, trying to prove his innocence."

"This is quite a change for you, Lord Kentigern."

"Yes, Your Majesty."

"Would you care to explain how you've come to feel this way?"

The duke faltered, his gaze darting from face to face. "No, Your Majesty. I wouldn't. At least not just now."

Kearney narrowed his eyes. "Very well."

"Forgive me, Your Majesty," the queen said, "but I'm interested in hearing more of what this gleaner has to say. You tell us, sir, that an army of Qirsi approaches, led by a Weaver. Yet you tell me that you haven't gleaned this. How then do you know?"

The gleaner took a long breath, then glanced at the king,

who nodded, as if to encourage him. "I know, Your Highness, because I spoke with him last night."

"What? He's that close?"

"No, Your Highness. He and his army are still two days away on horseback."

"Then how—?"

A gasp stopped her. Turning toward the sound, Diani saw that Abeni was gaping at the man, her mouth open, her cheeks as pale as Panya, the Qirsi moon. "You . . . ," she whispered. "You're one, too!"

"What is this nonsense, Archminister?" Olesya asked, sounding petulant as a child. "He is what?"

"A Weaver, Your Highness. I'm a Weaver."

Silence.

Soldiers laughed in the distance. Horses whinnied, and a soft wind rustled the grasses of the moor. But no one in their circle spoke. They stared at him, some with open curiosity, others with distaste, all with some measure of fear.

"You realize," Marston finally said, "that by admitting as much, you give us little choice but to execute you."

"I'll grant, Lord Shanstead, that were you to follow the ancient laws, putting me to death would be your only course. But to say that you have no choice simply isn't true."

"The law is clear."

"The law is asinine," Tavis said, "as are those who would follow it blindly! Don't you understand the gift we've been given? We're about to go to war with a Weaver, and we have among us the one man in all the Forelands who can defeat him." He gave the thane a look of utter contempt. "And all you can think to do is call for his head."

"A Weaver," Aindreas muttered, eyeing the Qirsi. "I suppose I shouldn't be surprised."

"You spoke to this other Weaver last night," Marston said, defiant as ever. "Why? And for that matter, how?"

"I entered his dreams. A Weaver can do that with other Qirsi. I tried to kill him by using his own magic against him, but I failed." He looked at the rest of them. "This other Weaver is coming, and he has far more Qirsi on his side than

I do. That's why it's so important that we have as large an Eandi army as possible. Now I'm asking all of you to put your hatred aside and make peace with the empire's men before it's too late."

"You've known of this Weaver for some time, haven't you? How else would you have known to seek him out this way?"

"You're right, Lord Shanstead. I've known about him for several turns."

"And why haven't you told anyone?"

The gleaner gave a thin smile. "I have, my lord. I just haven't told you."

"I've known for some time now, Lord Shanstead," the king said. "I've also known that Grinsa is a Weaver. He kept these matters from the rest of you with my consent. If you wish to take issue with that, address your concerns to me, not the gleaner."

"Am I then to understand, Your Majesty, that you intend to follow this man's counsel?"

"He's placed his life in our hands, Marston. He's offered to wage war against the Weaver on our behalf. And if you had seen what the Weaver did to the woman this man loves, then you'd know, as I do, that he has as much reason as anyone to hate the conspiracy." Again, he glanced at the others. "As much as I would like to see the empire's army crushed, I'm inclined to do as the gleaner suggests. But I won't impose my authority on the rest of you. I'll leave it to my dukes to vote on the matter, and of course, Your Highness, you and your nobles must do as you see fit."

"How many Qirsi does this man command?" Olesya asked.

"Two hundred, Your Highness. Perhaps a few more."

"Two hundred?" Aindreas said, incredulous.

"Do you recall the wind we raised yesterday, Lord Kentigern?" the gleaner asked. "I wove that gale with the power of only two other Qirsi. Imagine what I could do with the shaping power of ten, or the fire magic of fifty. They may be few, but their power is greater than this army alone can withstand."

"That raises another matter," Shanstead said. "If Weavers are so powerful, why haven't you used your magic to help

His Majesty win this war? Our realm has been in peril, yet you've done little to protect it. You could have ended this threat a long time ago."

Tavis shook his head again. "Not without revealing to all that he's a Weaver. And not without destroying the Braedony army, which is just what he seeks to avoid."

"That's Qirsi logic, Lord Curgh. I believe this man has you ensorcelled, and he wishes to do the same to the rest of us."

Before Tavis could answer, Kearney turned to the boy's father. "Lord Curgh, what say you about all this? Surely you've formed an opinion of this man who's been traveling the Forelands with your son."

"I have, Your Majesty. I trust him with Tavis's life, and I trust him in this as well. We should make peace with the enemy and enlist their help against the Qirsi."

Shanstead shook his head violently. "This is madness!"

"I'll take that as a vote against suing for peace, Lord Shanstead."

"I must agree with the thane, my liege," said the duke of Labruinn. "I'm not questioning the gleaner's loyalty, but I can't abide making peace with the invaders."

"I understand, Caius. Lord Tremain, what about you?"

"The Qirsi are the real threat, my liege. We should end this war."

"Lord Kentigern?"

Aindreas pressed his lips in a thin line, looking first at the Qirsi, and then at Tavis and his father. Emotions chased one another across his broad face—rage, hatred, deepest sorrow, and something else Diani couldn't quite name. At last he closed his eyes. "Join with the empire's men. Defeating the Qirsi is everything."

The king eyed him for some time, nodding slowly. "That can't have been easy, Lord Kentigern. You have my thanks."

Aindreas looked away without a response.

"Swordmaster," the king said to a tall, bald man, "your lord is dead, and his son as well. You speak for the House of Heneagh now. What say you?"

The man shuffled his feet, clearly discomfited by the question.

"It's all right, Rab. Your duke would want you to speak your mind."

"They invaded our land, Your Majesty. How could they ever be our allies?"

The king frowned. "Of course, swordmaster. I understand."

"Thank you, Your Majesty."

Kearney sighed, rubbing a hand across his brow. "Damn."

Caius gave a small shrug. "Your vote tips the balance, Your Majesty."

"I was hoping it wouldn't come to that."

"But it has," the queen said. "I feel quite certain that my nobles would also be divided, but I believe we must make peace with the empire's men, and so that's what we'll do. I admire you for asking your nobles, Your Majesty, but this is a king's decision, and I suggest you treat it as such."

Kearney straightened, and for just a moment, Diani thought he would grow angry. Instead he grinned. "I've long heard it said that Sanbiri steel was the strongest in the Forelands. It seems Sanbiri queens and Sanbiri swords are forged in the same fires."

Diani had to smile, though she wasn't certain how she felt about all this. Her land hadn't been invaded, and so her hatred of the empire didn't match that of Marston and the others. Still, she had little desire to ally herself with the emperor, and she couldn't quite bring herself to trust this Qirsi, even though he had taken a great risk by revealing himself as a Weaver.

"Gershon," the king said, turning to his master of arms, "prepare a flag of truce. I'll ride forward with Her Majesty, if she'll be so kind as to join me." He paused, looking to Olesya, who nodded her assent. "Grinsa, I'd like you with me as well."

"Of course, Your Majesty."

"Is there anyone else you care to bring, Your Highness?" Gershon asked.

"No. I daresay the three of us can handle this."

"You'll need guards, Your Majesty."

"We'll have a Weaver with us, Gershon. I'm sure we'll be safe."

The swordmaster didn't look pleased, but neither did he argue the point.

"It's decided then," Kearney said. "The rest of you ready your armies, just in case this doesn't work."

Diani looked to the queen, who gave a small reassuring smile before walking off with Kearney and the gleaner. The duchess had no army here, and was at a loss as to what to do next. Turning, she saw Abeni and the other Sanbiri ministers hurrying off by themselves. She would have liked to follow, but before she could, she heard someone calling to her.

Marston of Shanstead was walking toward her, his expression grim. "May I have a word please, my lady?"

Masking her impatience, she made herself smile. "Of course, Lord Shanstead. How may I help you?"

He looked around quickly, as if to be certain that no one else could hear. "I sense, my lady, that you and I are of one mind when it comes to trusting these Qirsi. Am I right?"

Diani hesitated. "I'll grant that I have cause to hate the conspiracy—more than most. And I'll grant as well, that I trust few of them anymore."

"Do you trust this Weaver in whom my king places so much faith?"

"He risked a great deal by revealing himself, my lord. You must admit that."

"Perhaps. If his powers are as great as he claims, he might have risked less than you think. Even if we wished to put him to death, who among us could carry out the sentence?"

"A fair question. But Weavers have been executed in the past, as have their families, as I understand it."

He frowned, looking toward his army. "So you do trust him."

"Even if I didn't, my lord, what could we do about it? I won't defy my queen, and I'd advise you not to defy Kearney. Under Sanbira's laws, doing so during war is tantamount to treason. I'd guess that the laws of your land are similar."

The thane nodded. "They are. Don't worry, my lady, I have

no intention of holding back my soldiers or any such thing. But if I can prove this Qirsi a traitor, I will."

"And if you can, my lord, you'll have my support."

He smiled at that. "Thank you, my lady. Now, if you'll pardon me, I must see to my army."

"Of course."

Marston bowed to her and strode back to his men. Watching him go, Diani was surprised to find herself hoping that he'd fail. As much as she distrusted the white-hairs, she wanted this gleaner to prove himself an ally. She sensed that without him, they had little hope of defeating the renegades. Thinking this, she went in search of Abeni and the other Qirsi.

"He's a Weaver!"

"Could he be our Weaver?"

"No. Our Weaver warned me about this man. He named him to me and told me that he was more than he claimed to be."

"You never mentioned this to me!"

"No, Craeffe, I didn't. There's much I don't tell you. You seem to forget with some frequency that I'm the Weaver's chancellor, and you're but one of his servants."

"How dare—!"

Filtem laid a hand on Craeffe's arm, silencing her. "What did the Weaver say we should do about this man, Archminister?"

She continued to glare at Craeffe a moment before responding. "He said we should do nothing. He'll deal with the gleaner himself."

"We may not have that luxury anymore," Filtem said.

"What do you mean?"

"I've no doubt our Weaver knew of this man's powers when he gave you that warning. But I'm equally sure our Weaver assumed the gleaner would keep his secret, and that this man's fear of being discovered would keep him from harming our cause before the Weaver's arrival. Clearly that's no longer the case."

"An interesting point. What do you suggest we do?"

"I wish I knew, Archminister."

"You're the chancellor," Craeffe said, all bitterness and wounded pride. "Why don't you think of something?"

"Craeffe—"

"It's all right, Minister. She's right. I will think of something." Abeni glanced toward Brugaosa's army. Vanjad, Edamo's loyal minister, was returning. "We'll talk more later."

"Forgive me, Archminister," Vanjad said, rejoining them. "My duke wished to know what I think of this Weaver in our midst."

"Of course, Minister. What did you tell him?"

"Well, I don't really know the man, but if he truly is a Weaver, and, if the threat we face is as grave as he says, we're quite fortunate to have him on our side." He glanced at the others, looking nervous and old. "Wouldn't you agree? No doubt you've been speaking of him, as well."

"Of course we agree, cousin," Craeffe said. Her eyes flicked toward Abeni. "A Weaver. Who would have thought it possible?"

The archminister frowned. "Indeed." She needed to end this conversation now, before Craeffe said something foolish. "You should return to your dukes. I intend to seek out the master of arms. With the queen occupied, he may need my help."

"Yes, of course," Vanjad said, always so eager to serve. "Thank you, Archminister."

Craeffe eyed her briefly, as if she wanted to say more. In the end, though, she and Filtem walked off together without a word.

Intending to return to the queen's army, the archminister turned, then froze. The duchess of Curlinte stood nearby, staring at her. How long had she been watching? And how had Abeni been so careless as to not notice her sooner? After a moment she nodded to the woman and continued as if nothing unusual had happened. But she still felt the duchess's eyes upon her, and she cursed her own stupidity.

Diani of Curlinte, though, was the least of her concerns. Filtem was right. Her Weaver might have known of Grinsa jal

Arriet's powers, but he couldn't have anticipated that he would reveal himself so soon, or that the sovereigns of both Eibithar and Sanbira would be so willing to embrace him as an ally.

Don't approach her unless you absolutely must, the Weaver had told her. *The risks are far too great.*

What choice did Abeni have now? The time had come to forge an alliance of her own, with Kearney's archminister.

"It's about time," Kearney mumbled, when at last they saw the four Braedony captains riding out to join them.

By the gleaner's reckoning they had been waiting on horseback for the better part of an hour, watching for some sign that the empire's army would respond to their flag of truce. They heard a few jeers as they sat, and they noticed the Braedony archers positioning themselves to the west, where the slow winds blowing that morning would be of most aid should it come to an attack.

"You can protect us, can't you, gleaner?" Kearney asked at the time, eyeing the bowmen.

"I certainly hope so, Your Majesty," Grinsa said drily.

Kearney had given him a sharp look. Olesya laughed aloud.

Now, watching the captains approach, the king shook his head. "This isn't going to work," he muttered.

"We don't know that yet, Your Majesty."

"Actually, gleaner, we do. These men are soldiers—battle commanders. There's no one here from the court. Either they're dead, or Harel never sent anyone. These captains haven't the authority to do what we ask."

Grinsa glanced at the king. "So, what do we do?"

"We talk. We try anyway. We've offered the flag. There's no sense in turning back now. But stay alert. This could end badly."

The captains reined to a halt a short distance away. It took Grinsa but a moment to understand that the gap they had left would be enough to ensure their safety should the archers loose their arrows.

One of the captains, a bald man, clearly several years older than the other three, raised a hand in greeting. "Your Majesty, Your Highness. What is it you want?"

"To discuss terms of peace, Captain. Isn't that clear?"

"So you're ready to surrender?"

Kearney laughed, though his eyes were hard as emeralds. "With the men who arrived yesterday, we have the larger force by far. Why would we surrender to you?"

"I don't know, Your Majesty. But you fly the truce flag, you call us out here to discuss peace. Surely you don't expect us to surrender."

"I don't seek surrender on either side, Captain. I wish for a truce. Indeed, I wish to forge an alliance."

The man's eyebrows went up. "An alliance?" He cast a quick look at the other men, a smile playing at the corners of his mouth. "An alliance against whom, Your Majesty?"

"Has word of the Qirsi conspiracy reached Braedon?"

"Of course it has. You're not speaking of Uulrann, Your Majesty. We are the Braedon empire."

"Then you understand the danger posed by these renegades."

"Yes. But I don't see what any of this has to do with the war we're fighting."

"Even as we speak, Captain, a Qirsi army rides toward us, led by a Weaver and composed of enough sorcerers to destroy either of our armies. But if we unite, if we fight the traitors together, we may yet prevail."

The captain's eyes had narrowed, and he stared warily at the king and then at Grinsa. "Trickery. I don't believe any of this."

"It's true, Captain," the gleaner said. "I've seen it. And the Weaver is none other than your high chancellor."

"What?"

"Dusaan jal Kania leads the conspiracy and rides at the head of this army of which His Majesty speaks."

"I don't know you, white-hair. Why should I trust you? Why should I trust any of you?"

"Because," the king answered, "we have nothing to gain from ending this war. As I said: we outnumber you. We can drive you from our shores, or we can simply crush you. But we share a common enemy, you and I. And I need your help defeating him."

Grinsa winced at what he heard in Kearney's voice. He would have handled this more delicately, but he didn't dare try to soften what the king had said.

"You and I both know it wouldn't be as easy as all that to drive us off, Eibithar. But I want to hear more from the white-hair. You say you've seen the high chancellor leading this Qirsi army. How could you see any of that? It's just sorcery, right?"

"I suppose you could say that. But it is true."

"What's your name? Are you a minister?"

"I'm no minister. My name is Grinsa jal Arriet." He glanced at Kearney, who gave a small nod. "I'm a Weaver as well," the gleaner said, facing the man again. "That's how I saw your high chancellor."

"You're a Weaver."

"Yes."

"Well, now I know this is trickery. How many Weavers do you want me to believe there are in the Forelands?"

Grinsa had done this once before, at a small inn on the Moors of Durril, when he tried to impress upon Tavis what it meant to face a Weaver. He drew upon his power of mists and winds, summoning a gale that made the truce flag snap like a harvest blaze, and raising a mist that hung heavy all around them, as if in defiance of his wind. He then raised a hand and called forth a brilliant golden flame. With a whisper to the horses of the four captains, he made the beasts rear and whinny. As an afterthought, he drew upon his shaping power as well. When the older captain heard the faint chiming of steel, his eyes grew wide. He grabbed for the hilt of his blade and pulled the weapon free of its sheath. Only half the sword emerged, the break clean and almost perfectly straight.

The man glared at him, rage and fear in his eyes. "Damn you!"

"Believe what you will, Captain," Grinsa said, as he allowed his gale to die away. "You've just seen me use shaping magic, mists and winds, fire, language of beasts. In order to hold this flame in my palm, I have to use healing magic. I spent my years in Eibithar's Revel as a gleaner. Who but a Weaver could wield all those magics? I swear that all the rest of what I've told you is also true. A Weaver is coming, and I intend to destroy him. But I need as many warriors with me as possible."

"I won't ally myself with any of you! If the emperor commands me to fight by your side, I will. Until then, you are the enemy."

"Your emperor is dead, or imprisoned in his own palace. His was the first army the high chancellor destroyed. Don't you understand? Your empire is at war, but not with us, not anymore."

"Lies! The Qirsi can't be trusted! That much you have right! Your Majesty, Your Highness, I know that we're enemies, but if you have any sense at all, you'll rid yourself of this white-hair and fight as Eandi are meant to fight."

"We don't wish to fight you at all, Captain," the queen said. "I believe that Grinsa is telling the truth. We have to end this war and join forces."

"The king can have his peace. If he surrenders the land we've won thus far, the fighting will end."

Kearney bristled. "This isn't a negotiation, Captain! I'm offering a truce that will save both of our armies, and quite possibly all of the Forelands!"

"And I'm telling you that there will be no truce!" The captain stared darkly at Grinsa. "You've allied yourself with a demon. I won't make the same mistake."

"Captain—"

"Enough! If this is all you have to offer, then this parley is done. Ride back to your army, Eibithar." He glanced at his archers. "I can't guarantee your safety much longer."

Kearney started to say something, then clamped his jaw shut, wheeled his mount, and began to ride toward his army. After a moment, Olesya started back as well, leaving Grinsa alone with the four soldiers.

"When the Qirsi attack—and they will attack, I promise

you that—have your archers aim their volleys at the high chancellor. If you can kill him, you have a chance against the others."

The captain just stared at him. After a few moments, Grinsa turned his mount and followed the king and queen. Pulling abreast of them, he chanced a look at Kearney.

"Forgive me, Your Majesty. I thought they'd listen. I was wrong."

"It's not your fault, gleaner. Nor is it the captain's. He's just a soldier feeling his way through a war beyond his depth."

"Yes, Your Majesty."

"We need another plan, Your Majesty," said the queen. "Despite our best efforts, it seems we'll be facing the Weaver and his army without any aid from the empire. We'd best make our preparations accordingly."

Kearney nodded, looking at Grinsa. "Gleaner?"

"Yes, Your Majesty. I'll begin right away. And I'll need permission from both of you to form an army of my own, using your Qirsi."

Chapter

Sixteen

It was strange for Keziah, watching Grinsa assume so much responsibility for the coming war. He had always been the strong one, the older brother who protected her and guided her through difficult times—the deaths of their mother and father, the end of her first love affair so many years ago. And of course, he was the Weaver, bearing burdens she could never fully understand.

Through all these long years, however, he had kept his strength and his hardships hidden, out of necessity to be sure, but also, she had always believed, by choice. His was a private life. The role of Revel gleaner suited him. He could travel the land, seeing all, prowling the edges of spectacle, his duties with the gleaning stone demanding an endless stream of intimate conversations. Keziah, on the other hand, had long enjoyed the company of many and her life's path reflected that. She was the minister, the one who felt at ease attending court functions, speaking pleasantly of the weather or the harvest with Eibithar's most powerful dukes and nobles from other realms.

Only now, having revealed to all that he was a Weaver, did Grinsa find himself at the center of weighty discussions among sovereigns, parleys of war, and today, a gathering of Qirsi. Keziah shouldn't have been surprised to find that he appeared comfortable in his new role, or that he could match wits with any noble and any minister in the Forelands. Still, it was hard for her to accept the changes she saw in her brother. They seemed to her undeniable proof of how swiftly and profoundly the world itself was being transformed.

Soon after returning with Kearney and Sanbira's queen from the parley with Braedon's captains, Grinsa sent word to Keziah that she was to join him south of the soldiers' camps. She thought that he wished to discuss something with her alone. Only when she found him speaking with several other ministers and a number of Kearney's battlefield healers did she realize that her brother had summoned all the Qirsi in the Eibitharian and Sanbiri armies.

"Archminister," he said crisply as she approached. "Thank you for coming." Some secrets it seemed were not to be revealed, even under these extraordinary circumstances.

"Of course . . ." She frowned. "Forgive me, but I'm not certain what we should call you now."

He smiled at that. "Gleaner is fine. It's what I'm used to. Or you can call me by my name."

"Thank you, gleaner."

Fotir joined them, accompanied by Xivled jal Viste, Marston of Shanstead's young minister, who had accused Keziah of being a traitor the first time they met. Several moments later the Sanbiri ministers arrived as well.

"I believe that's everyone," Grinsa said, as the rest of them fell silent. There were seventeen Qirsi in their small circle, and it seemed to Keziah that one or two of Kearney's healers hadn't joined them yet, or had chosen not to come at all. "I thank you for coming. I know how unusual this must seem to you. All your lives you've been told that Weavers were little more than legend, or else that we're demons, the worst kind of Qirsi, men and women to be feared and shunned. Yet now you find that there are two Weavers in your world, that one of them intends to lead you to war against the other. In your position, I'd be a bit bewildered."

It struck Keziah as an odd way to begin their discussion until she saw how his eyes moved from face to face. He wasn't saying this for them. He was saying it for himself, gauging their responses, trying to determine which of the Qirsi before him were loyal, and which had pledged themselves to the Weaver's movement. Abruptly, Keziah found herself glancing about as well, as if she could divine the thoughts of her companions.

"As most of you have heard by now, a Qirsi army rides this way, led by a Weaver. This Weaver commands two hundred men and women. It's not a large force—it hasn't been enough to impress our Eandi friends—but you and I know how powerful two hundred of our people can be, particularly when their powers are woven as one. I've convinced the king and queen that we'd be wise to create a Qirsi army of our own. Obviously we won't be a match for the Weaver's army, but perhaps with the Eandi warriors fighting beside us, we'll be enough."

"I take it," Fotir said, "that the parley with Braedon's men went poorly."

"Yes. They weren't ready to ally themselves with Eibithar or Sanbira, much less with a Weaver."

"So am I to understand," said Sanbira's archminister, "that the Eandi have given you permission to form a separate army of Qirsi that will fight alongside the Eandi warriors?"

"Essentially, yes." Grinsa continued to watch her, his eyes narrowing. "You don't approve?"

"I neither approve nor disapprove. I'm just surprised. I didn't think they trusted us enough to allow such a thing."

Labruinn's first minister gave her a quick glance. "They're scared. Trust has nothing to do with it."

Several others nodded their agreement.

"How can seventeen Qirsi hope to stand against an army of two hundred?" asked one of the healers, an older woman. "I mean no disrespect, gleaner, but even the most powerful Weaver can't overcome those numbers."

"It won't be easy. As I said already, I'm hoping that the armies of Sanbira and Eibithar will give us an advantage, or at least lessen the Weaver's advantages. The renegades fight alone, without archers or swordsmen. These thousands of warriors fighting beside us must count for something. And we may be a small force, but we have with us some of the most powerful Qirsi in the seven realms. Five of you are shapers, eight of you have mists and winds, and nine of you have fire magic. All are valuable powers in—"

"How can you know that?" Xivled asked.

Grinsa gave a small shrug. "A Weaver can sense the magics wielded by other Qirsi."

"I'd never heard that," the young man said, shaking his head, and sounding awed.

."There are a few of you who also have language of beasts, and since the Weaver's army is mounted, that could be of great help to us."

"They'll have these powers as well," the healer said. "And in far greater numbers."

"Probably. But this is what we have. Let's keep our attention fixed on that."

The woman nodded, though her mouth twisted sourly.

"So do we answer to you now?"

The woman who asked this, another of the Sanbiri ministers, was slight, with a lean face and overlarge yellow eyes. There was a note of challenge in her voice, as if she were more interested in starting a fight with Grinsa than she was in hearing the answer to her question. Sanbira's archminister gave her a dark look, but kept silent.

"You answer to your duke, as always, First Minister."

"Actually I answer to a duchess, but I take your point."

"When the fighting begins, however, you'll report to me immediately. The king and queen have both instructed me to say that any order I give is to be considered a royal command."

The minister raised an eyebrow. "They must be quite impressed with you."

Grinsa smiled thinly. "They merely understand, Minister, that I represent their best hope of defeating the conspiracy. Now it may be that you see that as a reason to despise me. They don't."

What little color that woman had in her cheeks drained away, leaving her pale as a wraith. "I didn't mean to imply—"

"You'll have to forgive Craeffe, Weaver," the archminister said, an easy smile on her lips. "She often speaks without thinking. I assure you, though. When the time comes to fight this war, she'll be ready."

"Thank you, Archminister. I've no doubt that this is true." Grinsa smiled again; this time it appeared genuine. "And you weren't here when I told the others to call me 'gleaner' or 'Grinsa.'"

It was the archminister's turn to blanch. "Of course," she said, recovering quickly. "Thank you, gleaner."

Grinsa's eyes flicked toward Keziah for just an instant. She had noticed as well. Calling him "Weaver" had come to the woman quite naturally.

"There's not much more for us to discuss just now. The last thing I'd like to do is draw upon your powers as I will when we go to battle."

"Why?" Craeffe asked.

"It can be a bit disorienting the first time a Weaver takes hold of your magic. I want to make certain that all of you are ready when the time comes to battle the Weaver, and I don't want my use of your power to come as a shock." He regarded the woman briefly. "Of course, if you object I can draw upon the magic of the others, without troubling you."

She shook her head. "I just wanted to understand."

"Very well. Between fire and mists, I can try this with all

of you. Why don't we begin with a wind? If you have mists and winds, open your mind to me. Allow me to take hold of your magic."

Keziah did as she was told, feeling Grinsa's familiar touch on her mind. Within moments a great gale was whipping across the moor, flattening the grasses and keening like a great demon as it passed over the stones. After a time, Grinsa allowed the wind to subside, leaving the other Qirsi speechless and wide-eyed.

"Very good," he said. "Shall we try it with fire now?"

Soon he had conjured a ball of flame that rose into the sky like a great yellow sun, then streaked downward to the grasses, crashing into the ground with a mighty roar and scorching black an enormous circle of earth.

By this time all of the healers and many of the ministers were gaping at Grinsa as if he were Qirsar himself, a god standing among mortals. Glancing back toward the armies, Keziah saw that the Eandi were watching them, no doubt impressed by what they had seen, and fearful as well.

"I expect the Weaver and his army will reach here in the next day or two," Grinsa said. "Do what you can to ready yourself for battle. I'll try not to tax any of you for too long, but we are outnumbered. All of us will be pushed beyond what we believe we can endure." He bowed to them and started to walk off, sixteen pairs of eyes fixed on him as he went. Keziah thought to go after him. She was anxious to know what he had learned from their discussion and from touching their minds briefly to draw upon their power.

Before she could call to him, however, she heard a soft footfall just behind her.

"Excuse me, Archminister."

Keziah turned to find herself face-to-face with Sanbira's archminister. "Archminister. What can I do for you?"

"I thought we might speak privately for a moment. It occurs to me that we have a good deal in common, more even than is immediately apparent. I believe we have much to discuss."

Puzzled, Keziah made herself smile. "Of course. Shall we walk?"

"That would be fine."

They started southward, separating themselves from the other Qirsi and increasing their distance from the Eandi camps. For a time neither of them spoke, and Keziah found herself stealing quick glances at the woman. She was uncommonly pretty, with a lean, oval face, medium yellow eyes, and long silken white hair which she wore pulled back from her face. Like Keziah, she was petite, even for a Qirsi woman, though there was a strength to her that seemed to belie her size.

"Would it be all right if I called you Keziah?" the woman asked at last, a disarming smile on her lips.

"Yes, of course."

"Thank you. My name is Abeni."

Keziah nodded, uncertain of what the woman expected her to say.

"You seem to know this gleaner rather well."

She felt her stomach tightening. "What makes you say that?"

"You and he raised that wind yesterday to fight off the Aneirans. It seems you knew already that he was a Weaver."

Again, she wasn't certain how to respond. Her first impulse was to deny that she knew anything about Grinsa, but something stopped her. Instinct, perhaps, or her suspicions about the archminister. Somehow she knew that it would be dangerous to lie to the woman. "The gleaner and I met in the City of Kings and rode to war together. I don't know him well, but he knew that I had mists and winds, and that the first minister of Curgh did also. I assume that's why he chose us when he decided to oppose the Solkarans."

"I see," the woman said, a note of skepticism in her voice. "I fear I've gone about this the wrong way. I've put you on the defensive. Forgive me." She halted, holding out a hand so that Keziah would stop as well. "I know that you're with the conspiracy."

"Don't be—"

Abeni raised a finger, silencing her. "I know it because the Weaver told me. Our Weaver." A smile spread across her face. "Don't you see? We're allies in this war. And there are others who are also with us. Three of the four ministers who rode from Sanbira with the queen are loyal to the movement."

Keziah's mind was racing, trying to keep up with all of this. True, she had been suspicious of the woman. But she had never expected Abeni to approach her this way. Nor had she thought it possible that so many in Grinsa's army could be traitors. Three of the four. . . . Had her brother sensed this? "Did the Weaver instruct you to approach me?" she asked at last, stalling, though for what purpose she couldn't say.

"No. He told me you served his cause, but he said that I wasn't to approach you unless it was absolutely necessary. When the gleaner revealed himself as a Weaver, I decided that I had no other choice."

"Yes, of course."

"You don't believe me."

Keziah licked her lips, which had gone dry. "I'm not sure what to believe."

"I understand. I assure you, this is no trick. I'm one of his chancellors. The others who serve him are the first ministers of Norinde and Macharzo."

Keziah nodded. "All right."

"Now I need to ask you again: how well do you know this gleaner? Does he trust you?"

What had she told the Weaver the last time he entered her dreams? "He's starting to trust me. There's a woman in Audun's Castle. She was the gleaner's lover, and she was once a chancellor like you. But she betrayed the movement. I befriended her, and so won a modicum of the gleaner's trust. But he's wary of everyone."

Abeni's eyes had grown wide. "I knew nothing of this," she whispered. "But I've no doubt that you're right. A man like the gleaner, who had hidden his true powers for so long, would have to be distrustful." She paused, gazing off into the distance, as if lost in thought. Finally looking at Keziah again, she asked, "What is it the Weaver has asked you to do?"

She hesitated, afraid to answer. It was bad enough knowing that the Weaver might come to her any night, demanding to know why Kearney still lived. "I'm not certain the Weaver would want me to tell you."

She feared that she had made the woman angry. If Abeni truly was a chancellor in the movement, she was not one with whom to trifle. But after a moment, the archminister began to nod.

"You're probably right. Can you at least tell me if it has anything to do with the gleaner?"

"It doesn't."

"I thought not. He told me that he would deal with the gleaner himself, though he never told me exactly why. I don't think he expected this man to reveal himself so soon, nor would he have guessed that your king and my queen would be so willing to embrace a Weaver as an ally." She took a breath. "I think we may have to take matters into our own hands."

"But . . . but he's a Weaver. What can we do?"

"There are four of us. Together we may be able to over-power him."

"Wouldn't we be better off making him believe that he commands a loyal army of sixteen? Let him ride into battle thinking that he's surrounded by allies. By the time he real-izes his error, the Weaver will be attacking him, and it will be too late."

Abeni's eyebrows went up. "I'm impressed. That's a fine idea, Keziah."

"Thank you, Chancellor."

"It's a shame we come from different realms. I have a feel-ing you and I could be wonderful friends."

Her stomach felt hollow and sour. "I'm sure that's true. Shall I keep away from the gleaner then?"

"Whatever for?"

"He scares me. I'm afraid he might manage to read my thoughts."

"I understand, but if he hasn't yet, he won't now. Just act normally. Continue to win his trust. I'd do so myself, but were I to try, he might grow suspicious."

"All right."

"We should return to the camps, lest we draw any more attention to ourselves." She gave a rueful grin. "Diani of Curlinte has been trying to prove me a traitor for several turns now. And I've seen her speaking with that thane of yours."

"You mean Shanstead?"

"Yes. He seems to have little more affection for our people than does Lady Curlinte."

Keziah nodded as they began to walk back toward the armies. "You're right. He thinks me a traitor, and he's accused Grinsa, too."

"Grinsa?"

"The gleaner." She felt her cheeks burning.

"Careful, Keziah. If I didn't know better I might think you were taken with the man. Not that I'd blame you, but I don't think our Weaver would be so understanding."

"Of course, Chancellor. I'm sorry."

"Think nothing of it." They were near the Sanbiri camp now, and she slowed. "We'll speak again later."

Keziah nodded and continued on toward Kearney and the others. Her hands were trembling so badly that she had to cross her arms over her chest. At least the archminister had encouraged her to cultivate a friendship with Grinsa. She had a good deal to tell him.

"Look at them," Marston of Shanstead said, glaring at the Qirsi who had gathered in a small cluster south of the camps. "Any of them could be traitors. And our sovereigns allow them to meet without any Eandi present. They even encourage them to form their own army! It's madness!"

"Surely they're not all traitors," Diani said, surprising herself. "And it seems to me that those who are will have to conceal their betrayal from those who remain loyal."

"But what if this gleaner is one of them? We could be giving him the means to destroy us all."

The duchess shook her head. "Honestly, Lord Shanstead, I don't believe he'd betray us."

He said nothing, just stared at the white-hairs, dismay furrowing his brow.

Marston appeared to be about her age, perhaps a year or

two older, though he seemed younger at times like these. Diani thought him handsome, in a somewhat plain way. He looked like so many of the nobles of the northern realms—straight brown hair, grey eyes, square chin. But she admired his passion, the ferocity with which he fought for all that he believed, even as she occasionally found herself disagreeing with him.

He glanced at her, and a smile broke across his ruddy face. "What are you staring at?"

She looked away, feeling her cheeks color. "Nothing."

"A fine thing to say of a man."

Diani laughed. "My apologies, my lord." She looked at him again. "How is it that you're still only a thane, and yet you command the army of Thorald?"

"My father is duke of Thorald. But he's too ill to leave Thorald Castle, much less lead an army to war."

"I'm sorry."

He shrugged, facing southward again.

"I recently lost my mother," Diani said. "She had been sick for a very long time."

"You have my sincere condolences."

This time Diani turned her face away, her eyes suddenly stinging.

"I'm curious about something, Lady Curlinte. You said yesterday that you had more reason than most to hate the Qirsi. Can you explain?"

"I believe the conspiracy killed my brother. And I'm certain that it was responsible for an attack on me that nearly proved fatal."

"Demons and fire! I had no idea!"

"As you can see, I've recovered." Yet even as she spoke the words she felt a dull throbbing in the scars she bore from that terrible day on the promontory, as if the assassins' arrows had hit true once again.

"Still, I hate the Qirsi for one woman's betrayal of my father's trust. You've endured far more at the hands of these demons, yet you find it in your heart to give them your trust."

"I didn't always," she said, remembering the rage and fear

that drove her to imprison briefly every white-hair in Castle Curlinte. She almost told him all that she had done in those dark days following the attempts on her life. But shame stopped her.

They stood in silence for some time watching as the gleaner and his small army continued to speak among themselves. Eventually, they summoned a mighty wind and then a tremendous ball of flame.

"What have we done?" the thane muttered, shaking his head at the sight of the blackened ground.

"The gleaner will be a powerful ally."

"If he's true."

Soon after this display of their might, the Qirsi began to disperse, returning to their lords. Diani turned to the thane, strangely reluctant to end their time together.

"I suppose I should rejoin the queen," she said.

He nodded, his gaze still fixed on the white-hairs. "And I should return to my men."

"I've enjoyed this time with you."

Marston looked at her. "As have I, my lady." His eyes flicked back toward the Qirsi. "I hope that we can . . ." The man's expression hardened. "Now what are those two doing?"

"My lord."

He pointed. "The two archministers. They're going off on their own." He faced her again, his grey eyes boring into hers. "Didn't you tell me that you've been suspicious of your queen's archminister for some time now?"

"Yes, though I haven't been able to prove anything."

He gave a harsh grin. "And I've had just the same problem with Kearney's archminister. I've no doubt that she's betrayed the king, but I haven't yet found proof, and Kearney refuses to send her away." He stared at the two women again. "It has to be more than a coincidence, the two of them being together like this." Abruptly he took her hand. "Come with me. We must speak with the king."

He very nearly yanked her off her feet compelling her to follow.

"I want you to tell Kearney of your suspicions. Make him

see that his archminister is speaking with a woman you feel certain is a traitor."

"We should find my queen as well. She's been reluctant to believe that Abeni could betray her."

"Look," he said. "They're together."

They walked directly to the two sovereigns, heedless of interrupting their conversation.

"Your Majesty," Marston said, as he and the duchess stopped in front of them. "We must have a word with you."

"I was having a word with the queen, Lord Shanstead."

"Yes, Your Majesty. Forgive me, but this can't wait."

"Diani?" Olesya said. "Is everything all right?"

"We're really not certain, Your Highness. After the gleaner met with all the Qirsi, Abeni and the king's archminister went off together for a private conversation."

"And?" the king demanded, glaring at the thane.

"Your Majesty," Marston said, "the duchess has long suspected that Sanbira's archminister is with the conspiracy."

Olesya nodded. "I'm afraid that's true. And while we know nothing for certain, I've grown wary of her, too."

"And what does this have to do with my archminister?"

"Your Majesty, please. We both know that you've had your doubts about her. You came very close to banishing her from Audun's Castle."

"That was a long time ago, Lord Shanstead. I've since come to realize how foolish I would have been to act on my suspicions."

"But don't you see, Your Majesty? You weren't being foolish at all. Even now, she consorts with a woman who might very well be a traitor to her realm."

Kearney looked like he might argue the point further. Then he stopped himself, though it appeared to take some effort. "What is it you'd have me do?"

"She should be placed with the Solkaran prisoners, Your Majesty."

"*What?*"

"Don't you think that's somewhat extreme, Lord Shanstead?" the queen asked.

Marston turned to her. "Forgive me for saying so, Your

Highness, but the same should be done with your archminister."

"For having a conversation?"

"For plotting against their realms!"

"Lady Curlinte," Kearney said, his bright green eyes meeting hers. "Surely you don't agree with what the thane proposes."

Her eyes slid toward the queen, who was watching her keenly. No doubt the memory of what Diani had done in Curlinte was as fresh in Olesya's mind as it was in her own.

"Let me ask you this," the king went on, his voice dropping to a whisper, so that all of them had to lean closer to him. "Do you trust the gleaner?"

Marston shook his head. "Not especially."

"I do, Your Majesty," Diani said. "He risked a great deal revealing to all that he's a Weaver. A man who would do that must be trustworthy."

Kearney gave a small smile. "I agree. What I'm about to say must not leave this circle, for it's not really my secret to tell. But under the circumstances it's the best way I can think of to put your fears to rest." He paused, eyeing Marston and then the duchess. "Do I have your word that you'll keep this to yourselves?"

"Yes, Your Majesty."

The thane nodded. "Of course."

"Perhaps you've heard that in the past, when Weavers were discovered, they were not the only ones who were executed."

"Their families were as well," Diani said.

"Yes. Which is why the gleaner and my archminister have long kept it secret that they're brother and sister."

"Impossible!"

"Why, Marston?" the king asked. "Because it proves her fealty?"

"But she and the archminister—"

"Whatever Keziah is doing, I assure you, she has the best interests of the realm at heart. You have to trust me, Marston, as your father does. Keziah has risked more in this fight against the conspiracy than anyone I know, except perhaps her brother and Lord Curgh."

"Risked in what way, Your Majesty?"

"I can't tell you that. Again, you have to trust me."

Marston nodded. "Yes, Your Majesty." He didn't look pleased, but it did appear to Diani that he had been swayed by what the king had told him. Certainly she had been.

"Does this change your opinion of Abeni, Lady Curlinte?"

"No, Your Highness, it doesn't."

Olesya shook her head. "I didn't think so. Continue to watch her, and the others as well."

She heard a dismissal in the words. "Yes, Your Highness." She bowed, as did Marston. "Thank you."

They walked away together, the thane staring at the ground, muttering to himself.

"I was so certain," he said at last.

"I know." Diani made the decision abruptly. She was still ashamed of what she had done, but perhaps there was a lesson here for both of them. And if anyone could understand, this man would. "After the attempts on my life, I had every Qirsi in my castle imprisoned. I didn't know which of them to trust, so I refused to trust any of them. Olesya the queen made me release them, but to this day, my first instinct when I encounter a strange Qirsi is to look for signs of treachery."

"Is that what you think I do?"

Diani shrugged. "Isn't it?"

He looked away. "Perhaps."

"I'm not saying that there aren't traitors among the Qirsi—there may be several here with us. But they can't all be with the conspiracy."

"I suppose not. I just hope you're right about this gleaner."

"If I'm not, and it turns out that there are two Weavers arrayed against us, it won't matter who else is a traitor."

"That's true." Marston paused, and after a moment he shook his head again. "Something still bothers me about all this. If the king's archminister—"

She held a finger to her lips. There were too many people around them, and Kearney had made it clear that this was not to be shared with anyone. "Not here." Taking him by the hand, she led him away from the armies again, until they were alone on the moor with the swaying grasses and the hulking grey stones.

"Now, you were saying?"

"It's probably nothing," he said. "You're right about me. I'm looking for reasons to doubt them, seeking out enemies when that's the one thing we have in abundance."

The sun shone in his eyes and the breeze stirred his hair. He really was quite attractive, and charming as well, despite his youth.

"Then let's not talk about this anymore," she said, stepping closer to him. "I'm tired of worrying about the gleaner and his sister and whose side they're on and all the rest of it."

He reached up and brushed a strand of dark hair from her brow. "I take it," he said, his voice suddenly rough, "that there is no duke of Curlinte."

She smiled, putting her arms around his neck. "Actually, there is."

He looked so surprised that she actually laughed aloud.

"It's true," she said. "His name is Sertio."

"Sertio," the thane repeated dully.

"Yes. He's my father."

Marston closed his eyes briefly, and gave a small shake of his head. "You enjoyed that, didn't you."

Diani giggled. "Yes."

A moment later their eyes met, and for just an instant she found that she couldn't move at all, that she could hardly breathe for the pounding of her heart. Then he encircled her waist with his arms, pulling her to him, and the world and the war fell away, leaving only the sun and the wind and the kiss they shared amid the grasses.

Filtem found the place, a small bed of grass in a cluster of great grey boulders, sheltered from the wind and blissfully private. Actually, others had found it before him—he had seen a couple emerge from the stones the night before, two Sanbiri warriors. Though the queen allowed women and men to fight side by side, she prohibited them from having romances. Those who defied her had to be discreet. And so did two ministers serving in different courts.

After their conversation with the gleaner, Craeffe had thought that Abeni would want to speak with them. But she went off with Eibithar's archminister, affording Craeffe and Filtem an opportunity to steal away.

There was no one in the circle of stones when they reached it, and they quickly slipped out of their robes, before falling into each other's arms and stretching out on the lush grasses. The sun was high enough to warm their skin and soon both of their bodies were flushed and covered with a fine sheen of sweat, the rhythm they shaped together growing more urgent by the moment. At last Craeffe climaxed biting back a cry, her back arching, her breasts bared to the sky. Then she lay forward, kissing Filtem deeply.

He bit gently on her lip, and she started to laugh.

But just then the sound of voices reached them, and they both froze. At first, Craeffe couldn't make out any of what was being said. She sat up again, holding a finger to her lips to keep Filtem from speaking and closing her eyes in concentration.

". . . I'm looking for reasons to doubt them," a man said, "seeking out enemies when that's the one thing we have in abundance."

"Then let's not talk about this anymore." That voice Craeffe recognized. Lady Curlinte.

"I'm tired of worrying about the gleaner and his sister and whose side they're on and all the rest of it."

Craeffe's eyes flew open and she stared down at Filtem. Clearly he had heard it as well, for he was gaping back at her.

The conversation continued for another few moments—nothing else that caught her attention. But they didn't need to say anything more. The gleaner had a sister! And since the man was a Weaver, it was likely that few others knew of her.

She hadn't heard Lady Curlinte and this man she was with leave, and she wondered idly if the duchess had found love out here on the moor.

Craeffe rolled off of Filtem and both of them began to dress as quickly and silently as possible. Still they waited—

something told the minister that Diani was still there, and she half-wondered if they too might seek refuge within the circle of stones. Eventually, however, she heard them speaking again, their voices so low that Craeffe couldn't hear any of it. Soon there was nothing but silence. Stepping lightly out of the circle, Craeffe saw that the duchess and her consort had gone.

"Come on," she called softly to Filtem. "We have to find Abeni."

As it turned out, the archminister was looking for them as well.

"Where have you two been?" she demanded upon seeing them.

"That doesn't matter. We overheard something."

"Overheard what?"

Craeffe smiled. She couldn't help it. She knew that Abeni disliked her, that the woman hated depending on her for anything. She would have enjoyed stretching this out a bit, making the archminister wait. But in this case, her tidings were too important.

"The gleaner has a sister, and I believe she's here."

"What?"

"We heard Diani speaking of it—it was just in passing, but there could be no mistaking what she said."

"Which was?"

" 'I'm tired of worrying about the gleaner and his sister and whose side they're on,' or something to that effect."

"And how does that prove that his sister is here?"

"Why else would Diani be concerning herself with it at all? If the man had a sister elsewhere, it wouldn't be of concern to the Eandi. But if she's here, and they're still trying to figure out if they can trust him, or both of them, then it would be of great concern."

Abeni appeared to consider this. Finally, she looked at Filtem. "Is that what you think?"

"Yes."

"I suppose it does make sense."

"Do you know who it could be?"

Abeni shook her head. "No, I wouldn't know where to—"

She stopped, her mouth falling open. "Demons and fire!" she whispered.

"You do know."

"I might." She looked at them both. "Don't speak of this to anyone, not even to each other. I'll take care of it."

She started to walk away.

"But—"

Abeni spun to face her, a finger leveled at her heart. "Not a word!"

Craeffe glared after her. "Who does she think she is?"

But Filtem didn't have to reply. Craeffe knew the answer. Abeni was the Weaver's chancellor.

Chapter

Seventeen

hey were walking around the camp—it seemed to Keziah that she had spent much of this day circling the Eandi soldiers, first with Sanbira's archminister and now with her brother. Usually Grinsa was quite skilled at concealing his emotions. He had spent his life hiding not only the true extent of his powers, but also his fear of being discovered, and his concern for Keziah's safety. But at this moment, turning over in his mind what she had told him, he had the look of a man confronting his own doom. Passing a hand over his haggard face, he shook his head.

"You're certain of this?" he finally asked.

As if she could be wrong about such a thing.

"Yes. She left little doubt about any of it."

"Three of them."

"She told me who they are, Grinsa. The first ministers of Macharzo and Norinde, and of course Abeni herself."

"Knowing who they are isn't enough."

"But surely you can defeat three Qirsi."

"Yes, but that's not the point either. I knew that one of them was a traitor, maybe even two. But three? That leaves me with an army of thirteen." He shook his head again. "Even if the imperial army was with us, that wouldn't be enough."

She sensed his fear, his desperation. But someone had to say it. "That's all you've got. It has to be enough."

He cast a look her way, but he didn't grow angry. He merely nodded.

"Abeni wanted to make an attempt on your life immediately, but I convinced her to wait, saying it would be better to make you think that you commanded a loyal army. I hope that was the right thing to do."

"Actually, I'm not certain it was. I'd rather face the Weaver with a small army than have to fight traitors and his force at the same time."

Keziah had thought of this as well, though only after her conversation with the archminister ended. "I'm sorry. She spoke of killing you and I panicked."

"It's all right."

"Do you want me to go back to her and convince her to strike at you sooner?"

He shook his head. "You risk raising her doubts."

"Then maybe we should go to the nobles and tell them that we've learned of traitors in their courts."

"That's also too dangerous. Abeni will know that the information came from you."

"Couldn't you say that you sensed their treachery?"

But even before he answered, Keziah knew that this wouldn't work either. If Abeni and her fellow renegades were executed as traitors, leaving Keziah as the only survivor among those who claimed to support the movement, the Weaver would know that she had betrayed them.

"There's nothing to be done about it now, Kezi. She'll make her plans, and you'll have no choice but to follow along."

"What will you do?"

He smiled, looking so weary that it made her chest ache. "Whatever I have to."

"We should turn back," she said, glancing over her shoulder, trying to catch a glimpse of Kearney.

"You need to be careful, Keziah."

She faced him again, putting on her bravest smile in turn. "I always am."

"I'm serious. Norinde's first minister isn't much of a threat, but both women are shapers. Either of them can kill you with a single thought, and I won't be able to do anything about it."

"Why would they kill me? Abeni is ready to declare herself my closest friend, and I get the sense that she keeps a tight rein on the others."

He looked away, the muscles in his jaw bunching as they often did when he wanted to say something but feared her reaction.

"Hasn't this gone on long enough?" he finally asked. "You've learned the names of the other traitors in this army, you've learned that the Weaver intends to have Kearney killed on the battlefield. We know as much about Dusaan's plans as we need to, in large part thanks to you. But this war—the real war—will begin in the next day or two." He winced, as if suddenly in pain. "Actually, I suppose it's already begun. Dusaan is done making plans. It seems to me that the time has come to end this deceit, before you get yourself killed."

"How do I end it, Grinsa? Do you see a way out of this? Because I certainly don't. Until the Weaver is killed, I won't be safe, no matter how much you try to protect me. You saw what he did to Cresenne when she betrayed him. He'll be no less brutal with me."

"So what are you going to do? Kill Kearney? Fight me? Do all the things Dusaan and his servants expect of you?"

"Of course not!"

"Then what choice do you have, Kezi? You're fast reaching a point where you can't risk staying with them anymore."

"That may be so, but I'm not there yet!"

Keziah started to walk away, not quite understanding why

she was so angry with him. She knew that he was right. She had barely slept the past several nights, fearing that the Weaver would come to her demanding to know why Kearney still lived, and she was still shaken from her conversation with Sanbira's archminister. How much longer could she continue to deceive Abeni and the others? How many more times could she allow the Weaver to enter her mind without revealing her true feelings for Kearney or her love for her brother?

But even knowing all this, she couldn't bring herself to admit that it was time now to end the lies. She tried to tell herself that there was still more that she could learn, that her access to the conspiracy could still help Grinsa and the king. But in truth she wasn't even certain that this was true anymore. A part of her wondered if this were a matter of pride. When she succeeded in joining the conspiracy she assumed a unique role in this war. Never before had she felt so important, and it occurred to her that she might have been allowing vanity to cloud her judgment. But after considering this possibility for but a moment she dismissed it. In the end it came down to fright. Keziah was just scared. She had survived for this long through cunning and lies; she could survive that way a bit longer. But if she revealed to the Weaver that she had deceived him . . .

Keziah shuddered. Yes, that was the reason.

"Keziah," Grinsa called, after she had taken only a step or two.

She halted, but didn't turn.

"I'll do everything I can to keep you safe. You know that."

Probably she should have said something. She could have thanked him in some way, or at least told him that she wasn't really angry with him. Instead, she just nodded and left him there.

She walked northward toward the battle front, her pace quickening as she went. Abruptly she needed to be near Kearney. Grinsa's warnings had taken her thoughts in a new direction. War with the Qirsi army was almost upon them, and the Weaver had made it clear to her that he wanted the king dead before that final conflict began. Clearly she couldn't kill him, but it seemed to her equally clear that in a matter of such importance, the Weaver would not depend solely on her.

When at last she found the king, he was checking the blade of the broadsword he usually carried in the silver, red, and black baldric of his forebears. Another sword hung on his belt, and his horse stood nearby, saddled and bearing battle armor.

"What's happened?" she asked, her apprehension mounting.

He looked up, his eyes meeting hers for just an instant. Then he sheathed his blade and nodded toward the north. "Braedon's men are on the move. I expect them to attack any time now. You shouldn't be here. It's not safe." He stepped to his mount and began to tighten the saddle.

Keziah gazed at the enemy lines. There did appear to be a good deal of activity there, though she couldn't make any sense of it.

"I'll ride with you," she said.

He stopped what he was doing and stared at her. "What?"

"I can wield a blade. And I have language of beasts and mists and winds. I can help you."

"You could be killed."

She raked a hand through her hair. Why were the men in her life constantly reminding her of that?

"He wants you dead!" she said, her voice dropping to a whisper. "I've told you that. I know that you have to fight, but someone has to be near you, to protect you."

"The Weaver isn't even here yet."

"No, but he's near, and he wanted me to do this before he arrived. If there are others who have been told to kill you, they'll make the attempt today."

She had no proof of this, of course, but as she spoke the words she knew in her heart that it was true.

"We're at war, Kez. Anyone who isn't an ally will be trying to kill me. Do you really think that one more Qirsi assassin will make that much difference?"

"*I* can make a difference."

"And who will keep you alive?"

Keziah started to answer, then closed her mouth, unsure of what she had intended to say.

Kearney smiled with such tenderness that it was all she could do to keep from crying. "You see? You're asking me to exchange my life for yours, and that's not a trade I'm willing to make."

Men called out from both ends of the Eibitharian camp, and Kearney's eyes snapped back to the front.

"They must be bringing their archers forward." He looked at her again. "I have to go."

She said nothing.

The king swung himself onto his horse, gazed at her once more.

"They'll try for your mount first," she said. "The Weaver wants you dead, but he wants it to appear to be the empire's fault, so the attempt will be subtle. They'll try to make him rear suddenly, or they'll break his leg."

Kearney nodded. "I'll do my best to be ready."

Their eyes remained locked for another moment before he wheeled his mount away and started toward the front.

She could hear singing coming from the soldiers of Braedon, and though Grinsa had counseled peace time and again, trying to make all who would listen understand that they would need every soldier on both sides of the battle plain to defeat the Weaver, she couldn't help hating them.

Soldiers ran in all directions, archers taking position on the flanks, preparing to answer the Braedony volleys that were already pelting down on the Eibitharian army, and swordsmen taking positions in the center, where they would meet the inevitable charge from the army of the empire. As always, Hagan MarCullet was beside the duke of Curgh, giving voice to Javan's commands, and offering advice when the duke asked for it. And as always, Xaver stood a few paces from his father, waiting to learn if he would be allowed to fight. He had fought in the previous battle, but only because Hagan had been distracted as the fighting began and hadn't noticed his son charging forward with the other soldiers. Afterward, when Hagan was certain that Xaver was all right, he gave the boy a tongue-lashing that Xaver would not soon forget.

Tavis was nearby, his face pale, so that his dark scars stood out even more starkly than usual. Though Xaver and the young lord were the same age, Tavis was strapping on a sword, preparing for combat, while Xaver, his liege man, could only watch.

The injustice of it made Xaver want to scream out loud.

He didn't blame his friend. With all that he had endured the past year, Tavis had earned the right to fight for his realm. But hadn't Xaver as well? Hadn't he fought bravely, albeit clumsily, during the siege of Kentigern a year before? Hadn't he borne the hardships of the march from Curgh along with the other men in Javan's army? Hadn't he acquitted himself well in the recent battle? Didn't he wield a blade as skillfully as any soldier on that battle plain?

Of course he did. For he was Hagan MarCullet's son, trained to fight by the Sword himself. And there lay the problem. As long as his father remained in command of Curgh's army, Xaver might never be allowed to fight again. In a way, Xaver understood. Ever since the death of Xaver's mother, Daria, Hagan had done all he could to protect his son. Matters had only gotten worse since Kentigern, when Xaver accompanied the duke and Tavis to the tor only to find himself imprisoned and then caught in the midst of a siege. The recent deaths of the duke of Heneagh and his son had made Hagan even more cautious. Still, understanding was one thing; tolerating this treatment was quite another. Xaver was a year past his Fating now. Younger men had marched to the Moorlands with Javan's army. Yes, some of them had died, but others had fought bravely, even gallantly. Xaver could well be one of those young heroes, if his father would only give him the opportunity. He could almost see himself ten years from now, a father in his own right, still standing behind Hagan as others marched to battle. It would be funny, if it didn't gall him so.

He had asked Tavis to speak with the duke on his behalf, but he knew that there was little his friend could do for him.

The young lord might have been his liege, but he had no real authority on this battle plain. Javan was duke, Hagan his swordmaster. On matters pertaining to the army, a duke almost always deferred to his swordmaster's judgment.

Tavis glanced at him now, even as he checked his weapon one last time, and there was an apology in his dark blue eyes. "It won't be much of a battle," he said. "We have twice as many men as they do."

"All the more reason for my father to let me fight."

Tavis shrugged, seeming to concede the point. Then he started toward his horse.

"Tavis, wait!"

His friend turned.

Xaver looked toward his father, who was intent on his conversation with the duke and the battle unfolding before them. "I'm coming with you."

Tavis shook his head. "Stinger—"

"Don't call me that."

Even the old nickname rankled. A stinger was what soldiers called a child's training weapon, and since Hagan had long been called the Sword, it had always seemed fitting that they call him Stinger. But didn't it imply that he was still but a boy, not yet as tempered as his father's steel, not yet ready to fight alongside men?

"I'm sorry," Tavis said, frowning. "But I don't think this is a good idea."

"I'm your liege man. If you tell me to stay behind, I have no choice but to obey. But you know that I don't deserve to be left here. I'm as good with a sword as any of these men."

His friend looked truly pained, and Xaver knew that he was being unfair to him, placing him in an impossible position. "The last thing I want to do is get between you and Hagan," Tavis had said the last time they discussed this. Yet that was precisely where Xaver had just put him.

"I'll tell my father that it was my idea," he said. "And your father, too. I'll take all the blame."

"I'm not worried about getting in trouble, Xaver."

He felt his face growing hot. "You think I'm going to get myself killed. You don't think I can fight either."

"That's not true. But this is a war. Anything can happen. Any of us can be killed. I don't know that I'll survive."

"But you choose to fight anyway." Seeing Tavis hesitate, Xaver pressed his advantage. "Shouldn't I be allowed to make that same choice?"

Tavis stood there chewing his lip, looking for just that moment like the boy Xaver used to play with in the gardens of Curgh Castle. At last he exhaled through his teeth, shaking his head. "Your father is going to thrash us," he said. "And if he doesn't, mine will."

Xaver grinned. "They'll never know," he said, and ran to get his mount.

Lenvyd jal Qosten had ridden north, just as the Weaver commanded, leaving Audun's Castle and the City of Kings even before he knew whether the poison he gave to the woman there had killed her. The Weaver had long told him that his time would come, that someday his service to the movement would prove invaluable. Now, it seemed that the time was at hand. First he had been called upon to kill the traitor, Cresenne ja Terba, to punish her for turning against the Weaver and his great cause. Today he would strike a second blow, using his other magic, the one nobody knew he possessed. Nobody, that is, except the Weaver.

The Eandi thought him harmless, an old healer whose talents were limited to mending insignificant wounds and mixing tonics for the foolish ladies of the king's court. But he had always been clever—how else could he have concealed his fealty to the Weaver's cause for so long? The Weaver had recognized this, of course. He had rewarded Lenvyd handsomely for his role in the killing of old King Aylyn, and had promised to do the same if he managed to kill Cresenne.

"But even that payment will be nothing next to what I'll give you if you succeed in this last endeavor," the Weaver had told him one night just before Lenvyd left the castle. "You'll have riches beyond your wildest imaginings, and you'll spend your last days serving in my court."

He was only too happy to comply.

None of the Eandi knew which of the castle healers Minqar, the master healer, had ordered to the Moorlands and which had been instructed to remain behind. Even the king did not trouble himself with such matters. Some of the Qirsi knew—Minqar would have had to speak of this with the archminister, and of course the other healers would know who among their brethren had gone north. But if necessary Lenvyd could always claim that the master healer had sent him to join the others, fearing that the king didn't have enough healers with him. No one would question him. And even if Minqar thought to send a messenger north to warn Kearney of Lenvyd's betrayal, Lenvyd would reach the army first. By the time the missive arrived, it would be too late.

He expected, though, that lies wouldn't be necessary, and that no message would come. He was right.

Lenvyd had come within sight of the Eibitharian camp several days before. He sent his horse away, waited until nightfall, then covered the remaining distance on foot, slipping into the camp unnoticed and lying down to sleep near the other healers. When morning broke and they woke to find him there, no one said a word. One or two looked at him strangely, as if wondering how he had gotten there, but most seemed to take for granted that he had been with them all along. Old Lenvyd, whom no one ever noticed.

For a few days he tended to the wounded, saying little, trying only not to be noticed. But finally last night, the Weaver entered his dreams again.

"You're with Kearney's army," the man said to him, as Lenvyd shielded his eyes from the brilliant light that shone behind him.

"Yes, Weaver."

"And the king still lives?"

"He does, Weaver."

For several moments the Weaver didn't speak. Lenvyd sensed his fury and lowered his gaze, afraid that he might be punished, though he knew he'd done nothing wrong.

"I would have preferred that another see to this task, but she has failed me, so it falls to you. You know what it is I want?"

"Yes, Weaver."

"Good. My army and I are but a day's ride away from your battle plain. I want this done tomorrow, so that when we arrive the soldiers of Eibithar will be grieving for their king and blaming the empire for his death."

"Kearney doesn't allow his healers to venture so close to the fighting. It will be difficult for me to do this in the midst of a battle. Were I a younger man, my magic still strong and new, I could do it from some distance. But now . . ." He shrugged, again fearing the Weaver's wrath.

But the man merely said, "I understand. Still, there is no one else. You must not fail me. Get as close to him as you dare, but not so close that you arouse the suspicions of those around you. I want this to seem an accident or an act of the Eandi warriors. There are times when we must become more than we are, perhaps more than we ever were. For you, that time has come."

"Yes, Weaver."

"If you do this, you will never again want for anything. Your last days on Elined's earth will be glorious, and when you die, Bian will offer you a special place in his realm."

"Thank you, Weaver."

Lenvyd had awakened to a starry sky, exhausted and awed. He had never thought to see a day when a Weaver walked the Forelands. Certainly he had never dared hope to draw the attention of one so powerful. Truly he had been blessed to live in such times.

As the day progressed however, Lenvyd began to wonder if there would even be a battle. When he heard that Kearney had ridden forward to sue for peace, his hands began to tremble so badly that he had to leave the other healers for a time in order to compose himself. But at last, late in the day, after the king's attempt to forge a truce failed, the armies finally began to ready themselves for combat.

The sun had already started its slow descent toward the western horizon when the first arrows flew. Screams went up from both sides, the Braedony swordsmen commenced their charge and were met by Kearney's warriors before they had covered half the distance between the two armies. In moments, the battle plain was in tumult and Eibithar's healers were called upon to mend shattered bone and repair mangled flesh. As always, their work took them dangerously close to the front, and just this once Lenvyd didn't mind at all.

He could see the king from where he tended to the first of the fallen, but the distance was still too great. Others were struck down closer to the fighting, and Lenvyd hurried toward them, continually marking the king's position, doing all he could to narrow the gap between them.

"Lenvyd!" one of the other healers called to him. "You're too close! It's not safe there!"

"What choice do I have?" he called back. "This is where the injured are!" He turned his back on the man.

"You'll get yourself killed!"

He ignored the healer, kneeling down beside a wounded soldier and placing his hands over a deep, bloody gash high on the man's chest.

"Thank ye, healer," the soldier whispered.

Lenvyd nodded, but he was watching Kearney, who steered his mount skillfully, first to one side, then to the other, his blade rising and falling with terrible grace, the steel stained crimson.

He was almost close enough.

Another man dropped to the ground several fourspans ahead. Lenvyd glanced down at the soldier he was healing. The wound had nearly closed.

"That should hold for a time," he said quickly. "Make your way back to the other healers. They'll do the rest."

"Yes, healer. Again, my thanks."

Lenvyd was already scurrying forward, his head held low. Yes, this one would get him close enough. His heart pounded in his chest, fear and elation warring within him. Old Lenvyd. He'd be so much more than that after this day.

He had hoped that this next soldier would already be dead, but he wasn't. The soldier bled from a cut on his temple, and his leg was broken, but he was alive, and, worse, awake.

"Ean be praised!" the warrior said, as Lenvyd knelt beside him. "I though' I was goin' t' die here."

Lenvyd didn't answer. He was watching the king, waiting

for the right moment, gathering his power. Not healing, of course, but his other magic. Language of beasts.

Keziah strained to keep Kearney in view. As long as she could see him, she told herself, he was alive. So she watched, her fists clenched so tightly that they ached, her throat dry, her stomach feeling hollow and sour. Yet even now, struggling with her fear, she couldn't help but take pride in what she saw.

She had never been a woman to be impressed with a man's brawn or prowess with a blade. She had been drawn to Kearney by his wit and his intelligence; she had fallen in love with his tenderness and compassion. But seeing him now, his sword a gleaming blur in the golden sunlight, his mount whirling under his command like the Sanbiri horses that danced in Bohdan's Revel, Keziah felt as though she were watching Binthar himself. This was the stuff of myth and song. She knew that she and the king would never again be together, but she knew as well that she would always love him, that his death would kill her as well.

A moment later she saw the healers making their way toward the front, and she wondered where her brother was, and who had fallen. Where were Tavis and his father, Fotir and Evetta and the other ministers? Where was Sanbira's queen? With the Weaver and his army bearing down on them, they could ill afford to lose anyone.

Once again, she had to fight her desire to mount her horse and ride to Kearney's side. *He'd get himself killed trying to protect you,* a voice in her mind told her. *You serve him best by remaining here.* Realizing this did nothing to reassure her or lessen her frustration, but it did keep her from doing anything foolish.

Look at him, the voice said, as her gaze returned to Kearney. *Do you honestly believe that he needs your protection?*

Confusion and violence swirled all around the king. Everywhere Keziah looked she saw men dying. Battle-axes and pikes and swords glinted in the sunlight, steel and flesh alike bore the stain of blood, and a thin haze of dust hung low over the plain. A thousand voices seemed to be screaming out at once, cries of fear and pain, battle lust and death mingling into an incomprehensible din.

Which is why, when Keziah first heard the name called out—"Lenvyd"—she knew she must be imagining it. How could she possibly pick out a single voice in the midst of this clamor? Unless it was the name. For she knew a man named Lenvyd. He was a healer who they had left back in Audun's Castle, an older man whom the master healer had deemed too aged to make the journey northward. More than that, it seemed that the name had been shouted by another of the healers, a man who would also have known the old Qirsi. Looking at him now, she saw a second Qirsi beyond him, tall and thin, his back bent with age. And seeing this second man's face as he turned for just an instant, a name—the full name—immediately leaped to mind. Lenvyd jal Qosten.

"He shouldn't be here," she murmured, her eyes following him.

Yet there he was, and hadn't he been with them since they marched from the City of Kings? She had taken little notice of the healers during their journey. Certainly it was possible that the master healer had changed his mind about Lenvyd. Minqar would have known that there would be no shortage of wounded men; he might have decided that the addition to their company of even one skilled healer might well turn the tide in this war. Keziah had never seen Lenvyd minister to a patient, so she had no idea how fine a healer he was, but there could be no denying his courage. Even now, he was venturing closer to the battle line, braving the carnage to reach yet another fallen soldier. Indeed, it seemed this was why the other healer had called to him in the first place.

Only when Keziah had convinced herself that the old healer had been with them from the outset and had turned her attention back to Kearney, did she notice how close Lenvyd was to the king. It occurred to her then that every time the man had hurried to the side of another soldier he had also closed the distance between Kearney and himself.

This too, she was ready to dismiss as mere coincidence. But then Lenvyd stood. His back was to her, but she knew that he was staring at the king.

Terror seized her heart. She opened her mouth to scream a warning, fearing that already she was too late. But before she could make a sound, she sensed someone behind her, far too close.

"Archminister," a voice said.

She spun, found herself face-to-face with Abeni ja Krenta.

"Archminister!" she said in return.

Unable to help herself, she glanced back over her shoulder in time to see Kearney's mount rear. He clung to the beast, but almost immediately it reared again.

"You look like you've seen a wraith," the woman said, forcing Keziah to look at her before she could see whether Kearney was able to withstand Lenvyd's second attempt to unseat him.

"What? No. I . . . I'm just watching the . . . the battle." She laughed, short and abrupt. She sounded mad to her own ears. "I'm afraid I'm not very well suited to war."

Abeni raised an eyebrow. "No? What are you suited to?"

A cheer went up behind her, and whirling around once more, Keziah searched frantically for any sign of Kearney. After a moment she spotted his mount, but the saddle was empty.

"It seems the king has fallen," Abeni said. "Surely you had hoped for that."

Keziah faced her again, feeling dizzy and weak. Just because Kearney had been thrown from his mount didn't mean that he was dead. He was a fearsome warrior, and there were as many of Eibithar's men around him as there were soldiers of the empire. She needed to concentrate. The woman standing before her was dangerous; not only was she a chancellor in the Weaver's movement, she was also a shaper. And just now, when she spoke, there had been something strange in her tone.

"What do you mean by that?" Keziah demanded, winning herself just a bit more time to clear her mind.

Kearney!

The archminister smiled, a predatory look in her yellow eyes. "I must ask you again, as I did earlier today, what is it the Weaver has asked you to do?"

"As I told you, I don't think—"

"Yes, I know: the Weaver wouldn't want you to say. That strikes me as being a very convenient excuse."

She could barely stand for the trembling of her legs. "I don't understand."

"I don't believe you." Abeni eyed her briefly, her eyes narrowing, as if she were looking for a flaw in a newly forged blade. "Do you know that the gleaner has a sister?"

Keziah opened her mouth and closed it again. The sky above her seemed to be spinning, the world falling away beneath her feet.

Abeni stepped closer to her so that when next she spoke Keziah could feel the woman's breath against her cheek, warm and soft as the whisperings of a lover.

"I'm a shaper," she said, so softly that Keziah had to strain to hear her. "If you call for help or cry out, I'll break your neck."

"But I—"

Pain lanced through her hand, making her gasp.

Abeni held a finger to her lips. "Shhhh," she said, smiling again. "That was just the bone in your little finger. I can do far worse, but I'm hoping I won't have to."

"What do you want?" Keziah asked, sobbing, her eyes closed.

"Walk with me."

"No. You'll kill me as soon as you have the chance."

This time she heard the bone break—same hand, the ring finger. She clutched the mangled hand to her breast, tears streaming down her face. Had there been food in her stomach she would have been ill.

"I won't kill you unless you make me. You're more valuable to us alive, Keziah. Surely you see that. Grinsa jal Arriet's sister. The Weaver will be so pleased." The smile vanished from her face. "Now walk, or you'll die. And any you call to your aid will perish as well."

Her hand throbbing, her sight clouded with agony and de-

spair, Keziah made herself walk. It wasn't surrender, she told
herself. Hope remained so long as she still drew breath. She
had only to find some way to escape the chancellor.

But she was addled with grief. Walking through the camp,
past soldiers still recovering from yesterday's wounds and
the cold, blackened remains of the previous night's fires, she
could think only of Kearney and her brother, and how she
had failed them both.

Chapter

Eighteen

G rinsa had heard it said that a warrior who marched
to war without passion—be it hatred of the enemy,
or fear of death, or love of country—was doomed
to walk among wraiths before the battles were
ended. Clearly it was an Eandi saying, for his people, he still
believed, were never meant to be warriors, and on this day he
was proving that by relying on magic a man could survive a
battle for which he had no enthusiasm at all.

The Weaver was close. Grinsa could feel the man's approach the way a ship's captain might sense a coming storm.
This battle, born of stubbornness and pride and too many
centuries of hatred, was weakening them just when they most
needed to be strong. Kearney knew this. Despite his refusal
to listen to reason at their parley earlier this very day, the
Braedony captain who led the empire's army might well have
known it too. That they fought anyway reaffirmed for him
once more Dusaan's cunning; he knew the Eandis' vulnera-
bilities all too well.

Grinsa had no desire to kill the men before him. He neither
hated the empire nor so feared its warriors that he fought with
the battle lust he saw all around him. He raised his blade only

to keep from being killed himself and to keep the warriors around him from doing too much damage to each other and themselves. It was, he had quickly come to realize, a poor way to fight. His reactions were too slow. Each time he looked for some way to bring down one of the enemy without killing him, he left himself open to another attack. Several times already he had been forced to draw upon his shaping magic in order to shatter blades that would otherwise have bit into his flesh. And twice he had been left with no choice but to break the bones of men who persisted in attacking him even after he rendered their weapons useless.

Naturally, his efforts to save lives had no effect on those around him, who continued to slaughter and be slaughtered with terrible persistence. He should have given up and simply fought as he had been trained so long ago, but he couldn't. That the battle was clearly going Eibithar's way was of little consolation. Tavis was still alive, as was Xaver MarCullet, who fought beside him. But like the soldiers around them, they fought as men possessed, and though Grinsa was grateful for anything that kept the two boys alive, he couldn't help but disapprove. Tavis, at least, knew what was at stake.

Grinsa's fighting also wasn't helped by all that Keziah had told him of the traitors among Sanbira's Qirsi. He should have been prepared—the ministers on this battlefield were among the most powerful and influential in all the Forelands, just the sort sought out by Dusaan jal Kania for his movement. But for so many of them to have turned . . . Grinsa had seen the arrival of Sanbira's queen as a source of hope, as a sign that the leaders of the Eandi courts were capable of reaching past old rivalries and antiquated practices in order to combat this new enemy. And while all of this might be true, it now seemed that the Weaver had been just as eager to have Olesya and her company reach the Moorlands. Grinsa didn't care to dwell on what this might mean for their prospects in the coming war, nor did he have time to do so.

With so many dangerous Qirsi about, he had to be alert to the possibility of attack, readying himself to fend off enemy magic even as he parried Eandi assaults with his steel. As a

Weaver he could sense not only what powers a Qirsi possessed, but also when they were used. At any moment he expected his sword to shatter, or, worse, one of his limbs or his neck. He had chosen to fight on the ground this day, rather than mounted, fearing that the horse would only offer his enemies another target.

So it was that he perceived the attack, knowing immediately that it hadn't been intended for him. For a long time, he had sensed only healing magic—a good deal of it. When the other power intruded on his thoughts, as jarring in his mind as a sour note might be to an accomplished musician, he jumped away from his Eandi attacker, spinning around swiftly, locating the source of the magic almost immediately. Language of beasts. From the old healer standing near Kearney, just to the east of where Grinsa was fighting.

He reached for the man, trying to take hold of his magic before he could make the animal rear, or bolt, or whatever he had in mind. But the Eandi soldier was on Grinsa again, and the gleaner had to fight him off, parrying two blows before finally breaking the man's blade. When the soldier came at him once more, this time brandishing a dagger, Grinsa shattered the bone in his leg, cursing the warrior's stupidity. He whirled to look for the healer, turning just in time to see the king topple from his horse. Several Braedony soldiers shouted in triumph, surging toward the spot where Kearney had fallen. They were met, however, by an equal number of Eibithar's men.

Torn between his concern for the king and his need to stop the healer from doing more damage, the gleaner hesitated, though only for an instant. The soldiers could protect their sovereign. He might well be the only person who knew that the healer was responsible. He strode toward the old man, who was still standing, staring at the king's horse and the tumult around the beast, as if unable to fathom what he had just done. Reaching him, Grinsa spun the man around and grabbed him by his arms, forcing the healer to look him in the eye. He had a thin, angular face, with an overlarge nose and small, wide-set eyes. Grinsa didn't recognize him.

"Who are you?" he demanded.

"I'm . . . I'm just a healer!"

"Liar! You used language of beasts on the king's mount!
Now tell me who you are!"

"How can you know that?"

"I'm a Weaver, you fool! Haven't you heard your fellow
traitors speaking of me? I'd imagine it's all they can talk
about."

"I don't know what—"

Grinsa slapped him hard across the face, leaving a bright
red mark high on his cheek.

"Lie to me again and you'll get far worse!"

The man started to say something, then stopped himself.
For several moments he merely glared at Grinsa. Then he
grinned maliciously, all pretense forsaken.

"What is it you think you can do to me? I'm a dead man no
matter what I say, so the threat of killing me won't help you."

"There are other ways."

The healer actually laughed. "You mean torture? I'm an
old man. I'll die before you learn anything of value."

"Perhaps you didn't hear me a moment ago, healer. I'm a
Weaver. I have mind-bending magic."

The man's face fell.

"You'll tell me everything I want to know, simply because
I ask it of you. One way or another, you'll talk. The question
is, how much do you want to suffer for each answer you give.
I'm told that mind-bending power can hurt when used too
roughly. Of course, I don't know for certain. The last man I
used it on died before I could ask him." This time it was
Grinsa's turn to grin. "So I'll give you one last chance. Who
are you?"

The healer didn't answer at first. He clamped his mouth
shut, his eyes still fixed on Grinsa's face, as if he were preparing himself to resist the gleaner's mind-bending power. After
some time, though, he looked away, and gave a small shake
of his head.

"My name is Lenvyd jal Qosten," he said at last.

The name seemed familiar somehow, though Grinsa
couldn't quite place it. "You came here as a healer?"

"Yes."

"From where? I don't recognize you. Are you one of the queen's Qirsi, or do you come from one of Eibithar's houses?"

He smiled thinly. "No. I came from the City of Kings. Just because you didn't notice me doesn't mean that I wasn't there."

The gleaner nearly struck him again. "You think that justifies it, don't you? You aren't noticed enough, you want to be praised, and instead you're ignored, and that's reason enough to betray your king and your realm."

"I wouldn't expect you to understand. Your eyes may be yellow, but your blood runs Eandi."

Grinsa had once been married to an Eandi woman; he'd had the barb directed at him too many times for it to bother him anymore. "What else have you done for the conspiracy?"

"You'll have to take that from me, gleaner. Use your mind-bending magic if you must. I'll tell you no more willingly."

He narrowed his eyes. "Gleaner?" he said.

The healer smiled again. "Oh, yes. I know who you are. I didn't know that you were a Weaver, but I know you. You were a Revel performer once—that strikes me as even more pathetic now that I know how powerful you truly are. And then you were Tavis of Curgh's toady. I take it you're his squire now."

"What else have you done for them?" Grinsa demanded, struggling to keep control of his temper.

"Actually, there is one thing that will interest you," he said. "The woman in Audun's Castle, the one who betrayed our movement—I killed her."

It hit Grinsa like a fist to his stomach, knocking the air out of him. He knew she wasn't dead—he'd entered her dreams too recently; the healer couldn't possibly have killed her since then and still made it to the Moorlands so quickly. But he should have known the name as soon as he heard it. Lenvyd jal Qosten. He could hear Cresenne speaking of him, telling Grinsa of the poisoning that nearly took her life.

Abruptly the gleaner's sword was in his hand, though Grinsa didn't remember pulling it free. The man's eyes widened at the sight of his steel, but Grinsa didn't even give him a chance to speak. He grabbed Lenvyd by the shoulder with one hand, and drove the point of his blade into the healer's heart with the other. Lenvyd opened his mouth, as if to scream, but he could only manage a wet gasping sound, as his eyes slid briefly toward Grinsa's face, then rolled back in his head.

"You didn't kill her," the gleaner said, pushing the man off his blade. "You failed. You're lucky I got to you first. Your Weaver would have been far more cruel in meting out his punishment."

Perhaps he should have been ashamed. Against him, Lenvyd had been defenseless, an old healer, with barely enough magic to be a threat to anyone. As Grinsa himself had said, the man had only succeeded in making Cresenne ill. He was but a foot soldier in the Weaver's army.

Yet in that one moment, he had been the embodiment of all that had been done to Cresenne in the Weaver's name. There was no real vengeance to be found in the killing; only an outlet for rage and frustration and grief. Had Tavis done something similar, Grinsa would have railed at him. But in this case the gleaner couldn't bring himself to care. It was a murder, nothing more, and certainly nothing less. Given the opportunity to do it again, he would have, without hesitation.

He stooped to wipe the man's blood from his sword, glancing briefly at the healer's body. Then he turned and strode toward the soldiers who were fighting for Kearney's life.

They had chosen to fight near the king because they didn't dare remain too close to their fathers, who were fighting at the head of the Curgh army, west of Kearney's force. Had Hagan seen Xaver with a sword in his hand, blood trickling from a small cut above his eye, he would have flown into another rage. And since Tavis had fought and marched with both the king's army and that of his father in recent days, none would think it strange to see the young lord and his liege man fighting under Kearney's banner.

They remained on the fringe of the battle, both of them putting to use all that Xaver's father had taught them in the

wards of Curgh Castle as they tested their skills against the
brawny swordsmen of the empire. Tavis had done his share
of fighting in recent days and felt confident enough to wade
farther into the melee. He sensed, however, that while Xaver
was glad to be fighting, he remained unsure of himself. Tavis
made no effort to take them closer to the center of the battle,
and his friend gave no indication that this troubled him.

At least not until Kearney fell.

They were resting when the king's horse first reared. Tavis
had just succeeded in wounding his foe and had turned his
blade on the young soldier Xaver was fighting. Faced with
two adversaries, this man retreated, a gash on his thigh and
another high on his sword arm. Xaver had done well.

"Thanks," the liege man said, lifting a hand to the cut on
his brow and wincing slightly. "I was getting tired."

"I couldn't tell."

Xaver smirked. "Right."

"No, I'm serious. You fought well."

His friend regarded him for several moments, as if surprised by the compliment. "Thank you," he finally said. "I'd
say the same about you, but I was too scared to look away
from the man I was fighting."

Tavis laughed, but before he could say anything more, he
saw Xaver's eyes go wide and his face blanch. Following the
line of his gaze, the young lord looked just in time to see the
king tumble from his mount into a sea of warriors.

Xaver didn't falter for even an instant. Tavis was still trying to decide what he ought to do when he saw his friend running to the king's aid, his sword raised, a cry on his lips.
There was nothing for the young lord to do but follow.

The two boys quickly found themselves surrounded by
scores of Eibithar's men, all of them pushing forward, trying
to reach the king. And for once, their slight builds helped
them. Squeezing past several of the other men, all the while
keeping the king's horse in view, as if the beast's regal head
were a beacon, they soon found the king. He was on his back
still, kicking out with both feet, parrying chopping blows
from the empire's men with his sword. Several soldiers of
Eibithar were with him already, some fighting off the enemy,

others trying to help Kearney to his feet. But the press of Braedon's men was relentless. The king and his guards had little room in which to maneuver.

Xaver leaped forward, joining those who were opposing the empire's men. Tavis, with another of the realm's soldiers, bent over the king, took Kearney by the arm, and hoisted him to his feet.

"My thanks to both of you," the king said, looking a bit shaken.

They didn't have time for more. Braedon's warriors were everywhere. It seemed that when they saw Kearney fall, they concentrated their assault on the very center of Eibithar's army. Within moments Tavis realized that he, Kearney, Xaver, and a small number of the king's guards were surrounded, cut off from the rest of Eibithar's army.

None of them spoke. They didn't have to; all of them knew it. Wordlessly they formed a tight circle, their backs to one another, their weapons held ready, glinting in the sunlight. Two of the larger soldiers stood on either side of Kearney, as was appropriate. Tavis and Xaver stood together on the opposite side of their small ring. There was a soldier on Tavis's other side, no doubt one of the many among the king's men who still thought him a butcher who had murdered Brienne and earned every one of the scars given to him by Aindreas of Kentigern. Tavis wondered briefly if the man would see this as an opportunity to get the young lord killed.

"Don't break formation," the king said, his voice low and taut. "If the man next to you falls—no matter who he is—don't stoop to help him. Close the gap as quickly as possible and keep fighting."

Xaver and Tavis exchanged a brief, silent look. An instant later, they were battling to stay alive, outnumbered by the empire's men and unable to give ground without endangering the lives of the others in the circle. Braedon's warriors weren't fools. Seeing the two boys standing shoulder to shoulder, thinking them the weakest swordsmen in the ring, they concentrated their attack on the young lord and his liege man.

Tavis found himself fending off several enemy soldiers at once, their blades hacking at him from all angles. Had he not been wearing a coat of mail, he would have died in those first few moments. As it was, he soon had gashes on his neck, face, and both hands, and welts covering much of the rest of his body. Yet he also realized early on that again his was the quickest sword—the men facing him were larger and stronger, but they fought sluggishly, without imagination. Once more, as he had so many times in this past year, he found himself silently thanking Xaver's father for all the years of training. He might have cursed Hagan a thousand times for his exacting sword drills and the extravagant punishments he devised for laziness and lapses in technique, but the swordmaster had taught them well. After a time, Tavis found that his foes were tiring, their sword strokes becoming less precise and forceful, their defenses slackening. He was able to parry more and more of their blows, and on several occasions he even had opportunity to lash out with his own attacks, surprising the Braedony soldiers with his speed. He wasn't able to kill any of them, or even drive them to the ground, but he did keep them at bay.

Even as his confidence grew, he didn't dare look away for the merest instant. He sensed rather than saw that Xaver was still beside him, on his feet, his blade dancing. The soldier on his other side was also still standing, his shoulder nearly touching Tavis's. Whatever the man thought of Tavis, he seemed to understand that if one of them fell, they all might die. In fact, as far as the young lord could tell, all in their circle were still alive, including the king and his guards. When at last Tavis's father and Hagan MarCullet reached them, fighting through the horde of enemy soldiers and forcing into retreat those they left alive, every man in the ring greeted the Curgh warriors with a hoarse cry.

As the fighting around them subsided, Hagan and Javan approached the two boys, Hagan looking none too pleased, and the expression on the duke's face making it clear to the young lord that he should expect no help from his father.

"I'll take the blame," Tavis whispered to his friend. "Just keep quiet and leave this to me."

Xaver said nothing.

Tavis turned to look at him, and saw that the boy's eyes were fixed elsewhere. Before he had the chance to ask Xaver what he was looking at, or even to turn and look himself, his friend bolted forward, shouting a warning.

Without thinking, Tavis ran after him, and so saw too late what his friend had spotted. One of the Braedony soldiers, a man whose right shoulder was a bloody mess, had crept back within striking distance of the king, his sword held low, but a dagger flashing in his good hand. Tavis heard Hagan behind him, calling to his son, but Xaver didn't hesitate for even a moment.

Kearney seemed at last to have sensed his peril, but before he could raise his sword to defend himself, Xaver crashed into the Bradeony soldier, knocking the man to the ground and falling on top of him. They grappled for a moment, the soldier, despite his wound, quickly overpowering Xaver and raising his dirk to strike. By then, however, the king and several of his men had come to Xaver's aid. They pulled the empire's man off of him, the soldiers beating the invader with their fists until he crumpled to the ground.

The king offered a hand to Xaver, who stared up at him for a moment before taking it and allowing Kearney to pull him to his feet.

"I'm in your debt, Master MarCullet."

"N-not at all, Your Majesty."

The king smiled, glancing at Tavis and then Hagan, both of whom had stopped a short distance off.

"He's quite a warrior, swordmaster. You should be very proud."

Hagan bowed his head, his color rising. "You honor us, Your Majesty."

"I thought you were fighting with your father's army today, Lord Curgh."

It was Tavis's turn to feel his face redden. "Yes, Your Majesty. Xaver and I . . . we . . ."

"I asked them to convey a message to you, my liege," Tavis's father broke in. "The fighting must have started before they could return to the Curgh lines."

"Indeed," the king said, raising an eyebrow. "And what message was that?"

Javan allowed himself a small smile. "I'm afraid that in the excitement of the battle, I've forgotten."

Kearney nodded. "I see. Well, it's fortunate for me that they were here, no matter how that came to pass."

"Fortunate for all of us, my liege."

"Thank you, Javan. How goes the rest of the battle?"

The duke's expression sobered instantly. "The enemy has been driven back, my liege. They lost a good many men. To be honest, I don't see how they can continue this war."

"And what of our losses?"

"Not nearly as bad as the empire's, my liege, but still more than I would have hoped."

"Damn."

Before either man could say more, Grinsa joined them, looking grim.

"Your Majesty," the gleaner said, dropping briefly to one knee. "I'm glad to see you're unhurt. I feared the worst."

"Thank you, gleaner." Kearney narrowed his eyes, as if the full import of the gleaner's presence there on the battlefield had finally reached him. "Was it magic that made my horse rear?"

"Yes, it was. I tried to stop him, but couldn't act quickly enough."

"Who was responsible?"

"One of your healers, Your Majesty. A man named Lenvyd jal Qosten."

The king frowned, seeming to search his memory. "The name is vaguely familiar. An older man, isn't he?"

"Yes. He was left behind when you marched from the City of Kings. He followed you here, later, though only after making an attempt on Cresenne's life."

"It seems the gods were with me today."

"Yes, Your Majesty."

"Where is this man now? I want to speak with him."

Grinsa looked away. "He's dead."

"Dead? You killed him?"

The gleaner's mouth twitched, and he didn't meet the king's gaze. "Yes, I did."

Kearney started to say something, then he glanced at the others standing with them and appeared to think better of it. In the end, he merely said, "We'll speak of this again, gleaner."

Grinsa inclined his head slightly. "As you wish, Your Majesty."

Kearney began to lead his men and the other nobles back toward the camp. Hagan put an arm around Xaver's shoulder and steered him after the king, his anger seemingly overmastered by his relief, at least for the moment.

"You and I will speak a bit later, as well," Javan told Tavis, sounding cross, and fixing him with an icy glare.

"Yes, Father."

The duke turned and walked away, leaving Tavis alone with Grinsa.

"Sounds like we're both in a bit of trouble," the young lord said.

"I suppose."

"Why did you kill that man, Grinsa?"

"I don't want to talk about it." He started away, but Tavis grabbed his arm, forcing him to stop and face him.

"That's too bad. I want an answer."

Grinsa shrugged off his hand, just as Tavis would have had their roles been reversed. "You want . . ." the gleaner repeated, shaking his head. "What business is this of yours?"

"I'm your friend, Grinsa. It's as much my business as everything else that's happened in the past year. And if that's not enough, it's my business because I'm depending on you to defeat the Weaver. So is everyone else on this plain. I need to know if you're able to do that, or if your feelings for Cresenne are going to get in the way."

"How dare you!" The gleaner spun away again.

"You killed him for vengeance, didn't you?" Tavis called after him. "You once accused me of pursuing Cadel just to get revenge, but you just did the same thing. Isn't that so?"

The gleaner halted, his hands balled into fists. After a moment, he turned, and stalked back to where Tavis still stood, looking so angry that for a moment the boy thought Grinsa was going to hit him.

"This wasn't the same," he said. "The man was Qirsi. He had language of beasts. He was still a threat to the king and everyone else with a mount."

"Cadel was still an assassin. Wasn't he a threat?"

"The Weaver could have contacted this man. He could have learned a great deal from him."

"How much more does the Weaver need to know, Grinsa? He knows where we are, how many men we have."

Grinsa looked off to the side, his lips pressed thin. It was, Tavis realized, the first time he had ever seen the gleaner truly ashamed of something he had done.

"I don't blame you for doing it," the young lord said, as gently as he could. "I would have done the same thing."

Grinsa's eyes flicked in his direction for just a second.

"Of course, that might only make you feel worse."

The gleaner smiled, shaking his head again. After a moment he began to laugh quietly. "Well, it doesn't make me feel any better."

Tavis laughed in turn.

"The truth is, I'm not sure why I killed him," Grinsa admitted, turning serious once more. "I did it without thinking. He told me that he had poisoned her, and I killed him. It wasn't out of vengeance. It was just rage."

The young lord nodded. "I understand. But it's one thing to act on your rage with a healer. It's quite another to do it with the Weaver."

"I don't need you telling me that. Truly, Tavis, I don't."

Tavis shrugged. "Then I won't speak of it again."

They returned to the camp, where they found the king speaking with Sanbira's queen and the rest of the nobles. A few of the Qirsi were there as well, but not many.

"Gleaner," Kearney called as they approached. "Have you seen the archminister?"

Grinsa faltered in midstride. "Demons and fire! Keziah!"

"What is it?" Tavis asked.

"I've no time to explain. We have to find them!"

"Them?"

"The archministers."

Her hand still throbbed, but Keziah's tears had stopped. She refused to grieve any more. Either Kearney had died, or he hadn't. Either Grinsa would find a way to overcome the betrayals of the Qirsi around her, or he wouldn't. She couldn't help her beloved king, nor could she fight her brother's battles for him. All she could do was fight for herself, and she had every intention of doing that.

Abeni was still with her, as was the first minister of Macharzo, whose name, it seemed, was Craeffe. A third traitor, a man who served as first minister of Norinde, was nearby, apparently watching for any sign that others were headed this way, though Keziah couldn't see him. They were in a tight circle of hulking boulders, sheltered from the wind and the failing sunlight, and hidden from view.

"They're going to be missing her," Craeffe was saying now, her thin face looking grey in the shadows. "We should kill her and be done with it."

Abeni looked bored. "We gain nothing by killing her. If she turns up dead, suspicion will fall on us and we'll have gained nothing. Alive, she's a valuable tool, and a way of controlling Grinsa."

"She betrayed the Weaver. Don't you think he'd want her dead?"

"Actually, I expect he'd want to kill her himself." She looked at Keziah. "Don't you agree, Archminister?"

"Craeffe is right," Keziah said, through clenched teeth. "You should kill me and be done with it. I'll never help you, and—"

The rest of the thought was lost in a paroxysm of agony as yet another bone in her hand shattered. That made four now. Only her thumb remained whole. And, of course, the other hand. Better just to die than endure this.

"Don't be so certain that you won't help us," Abeni said. "Torture does strange things to people."

"We can't keep her hidden forever."

"We don't have to, Craeffe. It will be nightfall soon, and the Weaver should be near. Once it's dark, we'll strike out westward until we're clear of the camps. Then we'll turn toward the north and find the Weaver's army."

"They'll be looking for us, for her. We'll be killed before we ever get near the Weaver."

"What was it the Weaver told you to do?" Abeni asked her again, bringing her face close to Keziah's.

She closed her eyes and looked away, bracing herself for what she knew would come. Even so, when the bone in her thumb broke, she collapsed to the ground, crying out in pain and cradling her hand.

"It's a simple question, Keziah," the archminister said, standing over her. "Surely it can't be worth all this. Besides, I think I know. He wanted you to kill the king, didn't he? That was why that other man was doing it, and you were watching, looking so horrified it was almost amusing." Abeni kicked Keziah's hand. The bones within her discolored flesh felt as if they were aflame. "Am I right?"

Keziah merely whimpered, unable to say more.

"This isn't getting us anywhere. Just kill her already. We can claim that she was a traitor to her realm, that we saw her flee after the king fell."

"Her brother won't believe that. Besides, we really have no choice but to keep her alive. If I'm not mistaken, she's already told Grinsa that we're with the movement. Haven't you, Keziah?"

At that, Keziah opened her eyes, glaring up at the woman. "Yes, I did. He knows about all three of you, and he'll never give you the opportunity to get away. You're going to die on this plain, Abeni. You might as well kill me, too. That's the best you can hope for."

Abeni's brow creased, and she crouched down beside her. "Why are you so anxious for me to kill you? Is it fear of the Weaver? Is it that you know what he'll do to you when next you sleep?"

She looked away again.

"Yes," Abeni said, standing once more. "I thought so. You're right to be afraid. The pain in your hand will be nothing next to his punishment." She turned back to Craeffe. "The gleaner knows that we're with the movement. Keziah here is our only hope of getting away alive. If we kill her, Grinsa won't hesitate to kill us. But so long as she lives, he'll try to find some way to save her. Won't he, Keziah?"

Before she could think of a response, the other Qirsi stepped into their small shelter.

"What is it, Filtem?"

"Someone's coming. A Qirsi. I couldn't make out his face."

"Did he see you?"

"I don't think so."

"Good. Be silent, both of you." An instant later Abeni was beside her again, hurriedly binding her hands and tying a gag over her mouth. "Not a sound," she whispered, her mouth almost touching Keziah's ear. She pulled her dagger free and held the hilt of it just over Keziah's hand, as if ready to strike her. "You'll suffer mightily for any noise you make, and whoever he is will die if he comes near us."

Keziah eyed the woman, wishing she could kill her, cursing Qirsar for giving her magics that could not avail her in such times. But in the end she just nodded, drawing a dark smile from the archminister.

She strained to hear, desperate for any sign that someone had come to rescue her, but she heard nothing, save the breathing of the three traitors. At one point, she thought she heard a light footfall just beyond the stones that surrounded them, and she knew a moment of hope that almost made her forget her anguish. But no one entered the circle, and after hearing nothing more, she felt her despair return, and with it the brutal pulsing in her hand.

Abeni made a small motion, catching Filtem's eye. She pointed at him, then gestured toward the narrow entrance to the circle and pulled her dagger free.

Filtem appeared to understand. Drawing his own blade, he crept to the entrance and slipped out, as silent and graceful as a cat.

This time she definitely heard something, or someone. It sounded like a brief struggle, just beyond the stones, and then a quick, sharp intake of breath. A moment later, a thick mist began to seep into the circle. It built quickly, until Keziah could see nothing of her captors or the boulders surrounding them. She heard footsteps within the circle, though they seemed unsteady. One of the women shouted something and there was a dry cracking sound followed by the thud of a body falling to the ground.

A sudden wind swept through the stones, clearing away the mist. And there, in the center of the circle, lay Filtem, a dagger jutting from his chest, his eyes open but sightless, his legs bent at improbable angles.

"Filtem!" Craeffe shrieked, flying to his side and cradling his head in her lap.

"Damn," Abeni muttered.

Craeffe glowered at the archminister, her face streaked with tears. "You fool! Look what you've gotten us into!"

"Shut up and let me think."

"What's there to think about? The gleaner's out there! We're dead!"

"Don't be an idiot. If it was Grinsa, he wouldn't be playing these games. He'd simply take hold of our magic and destroy us." Abeni shook her head. "No, it's someone else." After a moment's consideration she roughly pulled Keziah to her feet and held her dagger to the woman's throat.

"Show yourself," she called out, "or the archminister dies!"

There was no response.

With her free hand, Abeni pulled off Keziah's gag. "Tell him," she commanded.

"She's a shaper!" Keziah shouted immediately. "And she has mists—" Agony. A terrible pain in her ear and hot blood running down the side of her head and neck.

Abeni pressed the bloodied blade against her throat again. "Damn you! I should kill you now!"

"You can't, and you know it."

White-hot pain exploded in her other hand.

"Get up, Craeffe. I need your help."

The other woman gazed down at Filtem for another moment, crying still.

"He's dead, Craeffe. There's nothing more you can do for him. But we can still save ourselves."

"How?"

"We've still got the advantage. That's but one man out there. If there were two they'd have attacked by now."

Craeffe climbed to her feet, wiping the tears from her face. "What do you suggest?"

"We need to remain together. I should never have sent Filtem out there alone—that was my mistake. But as long as we stay together and keep the archminister with us, there's nothing he can do. We're both shapers, after all."

As Abeni spoke, she relaxed her grip on Keziah slightly. Not much—the woman probably didn't even notice that she had done so. But Keziah did, and now she did the only thing she could. Moving as quickly as she ever had, she stamped her foot on Abeni's and at the same time threw back her elbow, catching the woman full in the breast.

Abeni gasped, then cursed, but Keziah had already flung herself away from the woman, falling to the ground and rolling until she reached the edge of the ring.

The pain in her hands was nearly more than she could bear, but she managed to shout out, "I'm free!"

Immediately, mist began to fill the circle again, driven by a strong wind. There were footsteps, the sudden rustling of cloth, and then that awful, familiar sound of snapping bone. A moment later a second body fell to the earth.

Keziah felt as though she had been kicked in the stomach.

Yet another wind whipped through the circle, and when the mist had cleared, Keziah nearly cried out with joy.

Craeffe was lying on the grass, utterly motionless. And standing over her was Fotir jal Salene, his brilliant yellow eyes fixed on Abeni.

"It seems you and I wield the same powers, Archminister," he said to her. He glanced at Keziah for just an instant. "Are you all right?"

"Well enough."

He nodded, facing the traitor again.

"Take even a single step toward me, and I'll break her neck," Abeni said. "If you're a shaper, you know that I can."

"And you know that I can do the same to you."

"Then it seems neither of us has the advantage."

How many times had Keziah found herself in such a circumstance: helpless to defend herself, depending on another—Grinsa, or Kearney, or Gershon Trasker, or Fotir—to guard her life? She was tired of feeling helpless, of living in fear of the Weaver and his servants, of accepting the suspicions of others as the price of her decision to join the conspiracy. She ached to strike out at any one of her many enemies. And here was Abeni.

Fotir and Sanbira's archminister were too intent on each other to take notice of her, or to see what she did as she looked up at the two of them.

High over the ring of stones, black as night against the deepening blue of the twilight sky, a lone falcon was gliding in slow circles. It was a long way, and Keziah was weary with grief and pain. But still she cast her thoughts upward, reaching for the bird's mind, and touching it with her magic. Language of beasts. Many times she had used this power to calm an anxious horse, and once, years before, she had escaped uninjured from an encounter with a wild dog in the Glyndwr Highlands. But never before had she attempted to communicate anything to a wild bird, much less one as fierce as this hawk.

At first she feared that the creature would refuse to heed her request. But she maintained her hold on the falcon's mind, conveying to it all that Abeni had done to her, and after several moments she sensed the bird's acquiescence. She saw it pull in its wings and begin a steep dive toward the circle of stones.

Glancing at Fotir and Abeni again, Keziah saw that they were still staring at one another. Fotir was saying something, but Keziah could not hear him, so absorbed was she in the strange thoughts of the falcon—dizzying images of hunting on the wing, of tearing into the warm, bloody flesh of a ptarmigan, of the bird's sickening descent toward the Qirsi woman standing over her. Keziah shook her head, trying to break free of the creature's mind.

In the next instant, she heard Abeni scream in shock and

pain as the bird raked the back of her head with its out-stretched talons. The falcon called out as well, a sharp, repet-itive cry that echoed among the boulders as the bird climbed into the sky again.

Releasing her hold on the falcon, Keziah found her sight momentarily clouded, her thoughts muddled. By the time she could see and think clearly again, Abeni lay prone on the grasses beside Craeffe, their heads jutting from their bodies at similar angles.

"You killed her," Keziah said, knowing that she sounded simple.

"You didn't want me to?"

"No, I did. I just . . ." Abruptly she was sobbing, her body shaking so violently that she wondered if she would ever be able to stand. "Thank you," she managed.

Fotir crossed to where she lay and reached to untie her hands. When she gasped at his first touch, he stopped, winc-ing as if he too were in pain.

"I'm sorry. Should I leave the bonds?"

She shook her head, taking a long breath. "Please, untie them. I'll bear it as best I can."

Keziah had to grit her teeth and bite back more than one cry as he struggled with Abeni's knot, but in a few moments her maimed hands were free.

"Thank you," she whispered again.

"Of course. Let's get you to a healer."

"Take me to my brother."

Fotir frowned. "Your brother?"

With all the secrets she had kept and revealed in recent turns, not only to this man, but to so many others, she found it hard to remember what remained hidden and what didn't.

"Grinsa," she said. "Grinsa is my brother."

He stared at her a moment, shaking his head. "Your brother," he whispered. "Yes, of course. I'll take you to him."

He lifted her into his arms as if she were but a child and carried her out of the ring of boulders.

"Is Kearney all right?" she asked suddenly, remembering all that happened before Abeni began to hurt her.

"I don't know," Fotir said. "The gleaner asked me to keep watch on you. I left the battle before it ended."

"He asked you to watch me?"

Fotir smiled, his eyes so golden they appeared almost orange in the evening light. "Does that surprise you?"

Chapter

Nineteen

ed by Grinsa, Kearney, and the queen of Sanbira, Qirsi and Eandi alike had begun a frantic search of the camp for Keziah and Olesya's archminister. Tavis heard several of the king's soldiers speaking of it as a hunt for traitors, but he didn't bother to correct them, not knowing himself whether Grinsa and Keziah wanted it to seem just that. In fact, Tavis didn't fully understand why Grinsa was so eager to find the archministers until Fotir walked into camp amid the commotion of the search carrying Keziah in his arms, her mangled hands livid and swollen in the twilight.

Grinsa was at the minister's side almost immediately, taking Keziah from him and laying her gently beside a fire.

"What happened?" he asked, his brow deeply creased as he examined his sister's hands.

Fotir and Keziah exchanged a look, as if unsure as to which of them should speak. Other nobles and ministers began to gather around them, as did many soldiers from the various houses of Eibithar and Sanbira.

"Three of them had taken her captive," Fotir finally answered. "Sanbira's archminister and two of her first ministers—Macharzo and Norinde, I believe."

The queen gaped at him, her face white as bone. "Demons and fire! Three of them, you say?"

"I'm sorry, Your Highness."

"Where are they now?" Grinsa demanded, murder in his eyes.

"They're dead, in that cluster of boulders back there."

The gleaner blinked. "You killed all three of them? By yourself?"

At that, Fotir smiled, sharing another look with the arch-minister. "Not entirely, no."

Grinsa faced his sister again. "Keziah?"

Before she could say anything, Tavis heard a voice shouting, "Where is she? Is she alive?"

A moment later, Kearney reached Keziah's side, relief plain on his face. "Gods be praised. Are you hurt?" His eyes fell to her hands and he grimaced. "Damn!"

"I was just about to begin healing her, Your Majesty."

"Who did this to her?" the king asked.

"I'm afraid it was my archminister, Your Majesty," Olesya said. "And two more ministers from houses in my realm. It seems the conspiracy struck hard at Sanbira, and I brought its servants into your midst."

"These renegades have plagued all of us, Your Highness. A healer from my own castle nearly killed me today. None of us has been immune." He looked at Grinsa again. "I take it the traitors have been dealt with."

"They have, Your Majesty, thanks to Curgh's first minister."

Kearney turned to Fotir and placed a hand on the Qirsi's shoulder. "Then I'm indebted to you, Minister."

"You honor me, Your Majesty."

"Were these ministers acting on the Weaver's orders?"

"Forgive me for saying so, Your Majesty," Grinsa said. "But such questions can wait for a bit. I'd like to heal the archminister's injuries."

"Yes, of course, gleaner. Forgive me." This last Kearney said to Keziah. He gazed at her a moment, then caressed her cheek with the back of his hand, seemingly heedless of all who were around them. "I don't know what I would have done had I lost you."

Keziah blushed. "You're too kind, Your Majesty."

The king cleared his throat, standing once more and facing Grinsa. "If you need anything for her, anything at all . . ."

"Yes, Your Majesty."

Kearney cast one last look at his archminister, then motioned to the others standing around her. "Come. Let's leave the gleaner to his work."

Tavis and the others followed the king as he walked a short distance from Keziah and Grinsa.

"Tell me what happened, First Minister," Kearney said, looking at Fotir.

"Grinsa asked me to keep watch on her, Your Majesty. He expected something like this might happen. I saw them taking her south from the camp and followed at a distance, afraid of alerting them to my presence." He shrugged, then shook his head. "As it turns out, had I acted more quickly, I might have kept them from hurting her."

"You saved her life, Minister. I'm certain of it." Kearney glanced at Javan and Tavis. "Indeed, this is a fine day for the House of Curgh. First Master MarCullet saved my life, and now the first minister has saved my archminister. The people of Glyndwr will remember your deeds for centuries to come."

Javan bowed. "You honor my people and my house, Your Majesty."

Xaver, who was standing nearby beside his father, turned bright red, a small smile playing at the corners of his mouth. Tavis was pleased for his friend, though he also felt himself grappling with an unexpected surge of jealousy.

"I'm sorry to have to ask you this, Your Highness," Kearney said to Sanbira's queen, "but do you have any reason to believe that the other Qirsi in your company are disloyal?"

Olesya shook her head, but she looked uncertain. "I don't, Your Majesty. But rest assured, I intend to speak with all of them before this night is through."

"I think all of us would be well served to do the same. I'd like my nobles to speak with their ministers immediately. Gershon," he said to his swordmaster, "I'd like you to speak with the healers."

"How can we be certain that they won't simply lie to us,

Your Majesty?" Marston of Shanstead's eyes flicked nervously from face to face. "After today, how can we be certain of anything?"

"Surely after today you no longer suspect Keziah of being a traitor, or Grinsa, or Fotir."

Marston lowered his gaze. "Of course not, Your Majesty."

"Even under these circumstances, Lord Shanstead, we must find it within ourselves to trust and be trusted. Without Grinsa and the other Qirsi we have no chance against the Weaver and his army. Speak with your Qirsi, discern what you can from your conversations, and trust in yourselves to find the truth. That's all any of us can do."

"Yes, Your Majesty."

"We'll speak again later," the king said, dismissing them. "Feed yourselves, see to the wounded among your men."

They began to disperse, and Tavis thought to return to Grinsa's side, in case he needed any assistance.

"Wait a moment, Tavis," his father said, before he had even taken a step. "I'd like a word with you."

Tavis cringed, then turned. Javan was standing with Hagan and Xaver. The swordmaster and duke were regarding him with the same severe expressions, while his friend simply looked chagrined.

"Walk with us," Javan commanded, starting southward, away from the other soldiers and nobles.

Tavis had little choice but to join them, falling in step beside his father and walking through the matted grasses in the gathering gloom. None of them spoke, until finally Javan halted, forcing the others to do the same.

"Would one of you care to explain to me what happened today?" he asked looking from his son to Xaver, then back to Tavis.

"Xaver saved the king's life," Tavis said, careful to keep both his voice and mien neutral.

Out of the corner of his eye, he saw Hagan suppress a grin. But clearly the duke was not amused.

"That's not what I meant, and you know it! I did not give Xaver permission to fight, nor did I give you leave to take him into battle with you under the king's banner! In fact, I don't remember giving you leave to fight with the King's Guard yourself! This is the second time in as many battles that something of this sort has happened, and I grow tired—"

"Oh Father, please stop it."

Javan gaped at him, opening his mouth to say something, and then simply closing it again.

"Xaver and I are a full year past our Fatings, and while I would never question your authority to command the Curgh army, I do believe that over the past year I've earned the right to make such decisions for myself."

"When you ride with my army, you submit yourself to my command!"

"Yes, I do. But by law I remain under the king's authority, or, more precisely, under the authority of his son, the duke of Glyndwr."

"Kearney the Younger?"

Tavis shook his head. "That's not the point. I'm not merely your son anymore. I've spent the last year fending for myself, and doing a passable job of it."

"You're still a noble in the House of Curgh."

"Yes, I suppose I am. But I'm also more than that now. And perhaps less, as well. Whatever I am, I made a decision to fight, as I saw fit, and I don't apologize for that. I also made a decision to take my liege man with me, and in that I erred." He turned to the swordmaster. "I owe you an apology, Hagan. I put your son's life at risk, and I shouldn't have, not without speaking first with you. I'm sorry."

"It's not his fault, Father," Xaver said quickly. He hesitated, then bowed to Javan. "Forgive me, my lord. I made Tavis take me with him."

"I doubt that, Master MarCullet. It seems that no one is capable of making my son do anything."

Glancing at Tavis, Xaver smiled. "Actually, I am."

In spite of all that had happened that day, the duke smiled, though only for an instant. "Someday you'll have to explain to me how you do it."

"I begged him to let me fight," Xaver said, looking once more at his own father. "I knew you'd keep me out of battles forever if I didn't prove to you that I could defend myself.

And I didn't come all this way just to watch the rest of you defeat the empire's army."

Hagan made a sour face. "You're both fools," he said, eyeing the two boys. "Wanting to fight." He shook his head. "Didn't I teach you anything?"

"Apparently you did, Hagan. Your boy saved the king."

Xaver looked at the duke. "Tavis would have done the same thing, my lord."

"No," Tavis said. "That was all you, Stinger. I didn't even see the soldier until he was almost on Kearney."

"Well," the duke said, "from this day on, you both fight under Curgh's banner unless you have leave from me to do otherwise. Is that understood?"

Both of them nodded.

"Hagan, would you please see to the wounded? I'll be along shortly. I'd just like another word with my son, in private."

"Of course, my lord."

The swordmaster nodded toward Tavis, then placed an arm around Xaver's shoulders and led him back toward the camp.

Tavis expected his father to berate him once more, but this time the duke surprised him.

"What did you mean before when you said that you might be less than a noble in our house?"

Tavis shrugged, abruptly feeling uncomfortable. He had always been far more at ease with his father's wrath than with his concern. "I don't know. I . . . I'm not entirely convinced that the people of Curgh will ever accept me as their duke. Certainly I don't believe that your soldiers will ever willingly take orders from me."

"They might surprise you. You should have heard them speaking of how you fought today beside the king. Not only Curgh's men, mind you, but Kearney's as well."

"It's more than that. We nearly lost this war because Galdasten wouldn't fight with us. Nor would Eardley or Rennach, or most of the other minor houses. The realm might still fall because they're not here. And that's all because of me."

"After all this time, you don't really still believe that, do you?" Javan smiled again, a kinder smile than the duke had offered Tavis in many years. "It wasn't you, Tavis. Your mother and I both know that, and so does anyone with even a bit of sense. It was the conspiracy all along. A man doesn't succeed as a noble because of what others think of him. He succeeds with courage and wisdom, strength and compassion. You're young still, you've much to learn. But I believe that someday you'll make a fine duke."

Tavis nodded and smiled. "Thank you, Father," he said, and meant it. It was as close as Javan had ever come to expressing pride in him. A part of Tavis wondered, though, if he still even wanted to be duke.

Fotir wandered about the camp as long as he could bear, giving aid to healers who were tending to the wounded from the most recent battle. He didn't possess healing magic himself, but he knew something of herbs and tonics, poultices and splints. And he welcomed any opportunity to keep his thoughts from wandering to all that had happened this day.

At that moment, most ministers in the camp were speaking with their nobles, so that the Eandi might determine if there were any other traitors among their Qirsi. Fotir had long been above such suspicions, for which he was grateful, and all that he had done in the past few hours had only served to enhance his reputation. Everywhere he went, soldiers cheered him, clapping him on the back and inviting him to sit and share their meager food. Always he declined, with a smile and a polite wave. Still, there could be no denying that he was a hero, his valor established beyond doubt by the three bodies he had left among the boulders and grasses.

He had killed before—during the siege of Kentigern, when he fought alongside his duke to repel the invasion from Mertesse, he killed more soldiers than he could remember. In the course of that fight, he had used his magic several times to shatter the blades of his opponents, so that he might dispatch them more quickly with his sword. In all his years of service to the House of Curgh, however, he had never actually used his power to take a life. On this day he had done it twice.

He wasn't fool enough to believe that he'd had any choice in the matter. Had he not killed the two women with his shaping magic, they would have killed him, and surely they would have killed the archminister. And that brought him to the core of the matter. For even as he struggled to justify the killings, he understood that he would kill again without hesitation if it was the only way to save her.

Fotir had devoted his life to serving his duke and his house, and though he had sacrificed much for that service, he had never once regretted his choice. True, he had effectively ended his relationship with both of his parents, who saw service to an Eandi noble as a betrayal of the Qirsi people, and who probably would have joined the Weaver's cause had they lived long enough to see this day. It was also true that he had never married or started a family. Still, serving the duke offered its own rewards—travel to the great cities of Eibithar, the opportunity to shape the future of the realm by offering counsel to a powerful duke and his fellow nobles, and an ever-deepening friendship with Javan, whom Fotir believed to be a truly great man, despite his faults.

Perhaps because he was the most powerful minister in all the dukedom of Curgh, there had been no shortage of women, Qirsi and Eandi both, offering to warm his bed. Nor had Fotir been shy about encouraging their advances. None of these women, however, had ever managed to capture his heart the way Keziah had.

It was not just that she was beautiful, and brilliant, and kind, though she was all of these things. She was also the bravest soul he had ever met. Anyone who was willing to risk the power and wrath of the Weaver so that she might destroy his movement deserved to be counted among the true heroes of the Forelands. It made laughable the celebrity he was enjoying this night. It humbled him. In all his life, no one had affected him so—certainly not a woman with eyes the color of sand on a quiet seashore, and hair as fine and lustrous as spun gold.

For years he had heard rumors of a forbidden love affair between Kearney of Glyndwr and his exquisite first minister, but always he had chosen not to give credence to what he heard, believing such talk unseemly. But since Kearney's ascension to the throne he had spent a good deal of time in the company of the king and archminister, and it seemed clear to him that there was more to their rapport than met the eye. Only today, though, seeing how the king looked at her, did he know for certain that the rumors had been true. Kearney had been horrified by her wounds, and so relieved to find her still alive that he could barely speak. And Fotir had also seen how she looked at the king, her breath catching at the mere sight of him, her skin seemingly aflame with his caress.

How could a mere minister compete with a king, particularly one as noble and strong as Kearney? Why would he even try?

So Fotir wandered the camp, helping as he could, avoiding Grinsa and the archminister. Until at last his need to see her again overwhelmed his good sense.

The king was there when he reached them, and Fotir tried to turn away without being noticed. Kearney saw him before he could flee.

"First Minister!" the king called. "Please join us for a moment."

How had he come to this? He hardly recognized himself. Fotir was renowned throughout the land for his formidable intellect and powerful magic. And here he was wishing he could run and hide, like some lovelorn schoolboy. It would have been laughable if . . . Actually, it was laughable.

"Yes, Your Majesty?" he said as he drew near the others.

Grinsa was still intent on Keziah's injured hand, but the king was grinning at him, still grateful no doubt, for Keziah's rescue. For her part, the archminister favored him with a smile, but said nothing.

"We were just discussing something, and it seems from what I've been told that you're one of the few others in all the Forelands who can offer an informed opinion on the matter."

Now that he was closer to the man, Fotir realized that the king's smile a moment before had been forced. Kearney didn't look at all pleased, and Grinsa seemed to be concentrating on Keziah's hand so that he wouldn't have to meet the king's gaze.

"How can I help, Your Majesty?" Fotir asked, all other considerations forgotten for the moment.

To his surprise, it was Keziah who answered. "I believe, First Minister, that both my king and my brother would like you to convince me that I'm a fool."

"That's not fair," Grinsa said, his eyes snapping up to meet hers.

Once again, Fotir found that he had been wrong. It seemed that Grinsa wasn't angry with the king, but rather with Keziah.

"The gleaner's right, Archminister. Neither of us thinks you a fool, nor do any of us question your courage. But what you propose is lunacy."

"So now you think me mad?" She laughed, though it sounded forced and, Fotir had to admit, just a bit crazed. "That's hardly more flattering, Your Majesty."

"Keziah, if you'd just listen for a moment—"

"No. The king asked Fotir to join us so that he might render an opinion. We should let him."

"I'm not certain that I want to get in the middle of this."

Grinsa glanced at him, shaking his head. "I'm certain that you don't."

"Come now, First Minister. You were brave enough to rescue me once. Surely you won't hesitate to do so again."

Fotir felt his face redden. It was far too close to what he himself had been thinking not long ago. "I don't wish to put myself between you and the king, Archminister," he said, and immediately regretted his choice of words.

Keziah regarded him for a moment, then turned to her brother.

"That feels much better, Grinsa. I'm grateful."

The gleaner nodded, still looking grim.

"Let me tell you what it is I want to do," she said, facing the first minister again. "And if you truly feel that I'm foolish—" She cast a quick look at Kearney. "Or mad—then I'll relent."

"All right."

"You know that I've joined the Weaver's movement, or at least feigned doing so in order to win his trust. You also know what he did to Cresenne when she betrayed him, and so you have some idea of what he'll do to me when he learns that I've been deceiving him all this time."

Fotir nodded, shuddering at the memory of Cresenne's scars.

"Now that the other, true traitors among us are dead, I'm apparently the only one of his servants remaining on this plain. He'll be suspicious of this, of me, especially since he ordered me to kill the king, and the king still lives."

"You expect him to enter your dreams tonight?"

"We expect him and his army to reach us tomorrow. I'd be very surprised if he didn't come to me before morning."

"Which is why you shouldn't sleep at all tonight," Grinsa said. "By this time tomorrow, all of this will be over, for good or bad. Why risk dreaming of him at all?"

Fotir had to admit that the gleaner made a good point.

"You agree with him," Keziah said, eyeing the minister, a pained expression on her face.

"I don't know yet what you propose, Archminister. I'll make no judgments until I do."

She looked relieved. "Thank you. I think we should let him enter my dreams, and I think Grinsa should be there as well."

"Is that possible?" Fotir asked, looking from Keziah to the gleaner.

"She wants me to use her mind to strike at him, to make her dreams into a battlefield."

"He asked if it was possible, Grinsa, and you know that it is. We both do."

Fotir sensed that there was far more at work here than there appeared, but he didn't presume to ask questions. What Keziah suggested struck him as extraordinarily dangerous, but also cunning. If Grinsa managed to hurt the Weaver in this way, or—dare he think it?—kill the man, it might save thousands of lives.

"Can you fight him as she says?" Fotir asked.

Grinsa nodded reluctantly. "I believe it's possible, but only at terrible risk to her."

Fotir could tell from the look in the gleaner's eyes and the tone of his voice that there was more at work here than just concern for his sister. Grinsa feared the Weaver. He didn't believe fully in his ability to defeat the man, be it in Keziah's mind or on the battle plain.

"If it seems the battle isn't going your way, can you wake her in time?"

"You would actually consider this, First Minister?"

Fotir faced the king. "I share your concern, Your Majesty." *I love her, too.* "But I see much promise in Keziah's idea. If the Weaver can be defeated in this way—"

"We don't know that he can!"

Keziah placed her healed hand on the gleaner's arm. "Let him finish, Grinsa."

"If he can be," Fotir went on, "and this war can be prevented, it might be worth the risk."

"And what if I fail? What if I'm not strong enough to defeat him or even to protect her?"

"If you can't defeat him," Keziah said, drawing Grinsa's gaze once more, "he's going to kill me anyway. Maybe not tonight, but soon." Grinsa looked at her with such tenderness that the archminister actually smiled. "You can't protect me forever, Grinsa." She glanced at Kearney, the expression in her eyes almost seeming to ask the king's permission. "None of you can."

"So you mean to go through with it."

Before any of them could speak, a voice called to the king.

"What now?" Kearney muttered.

A moment later the thane of Shanstead joined them in the firelight, the young duchess of Curlinte beside him. "Pardon me for interrupting, Your Majesty."

"This really isn't a good time, Lord Shanstead. Can it wait until later?"

"Actually, Your Majesty, I wished to see how the archminister is faring, and to have a word with her."

The king bristled. "To what end?"

"It's all right, Your Majesty," Keziah said. Looking past him, she went on, "I'm feeling much better, Lord Shanstead. You're kind to ask."

"Not at all, Archminister." He hesitated. "I wanted . . . well, I felt that I owed you an apology. And you, too, gleaner. It seems I misjudged you both."

Kearney glanced at his archminister, and she at him. "That can't have been easy for you to say, Lord Shanstead."

"No, Your Majesty."

"It takes an honorable man to admit his errors. Your father would be very proud."

"Thank you, Your Majesty."

"How fares your queen, Lady Curlinte?"

"Abeni's betrayal was a blow, Your Majesty, as was her death. But Her Highness is known as the Lioness of the Hills for good reason. She'll be ready to do battle come morning."

"I've no doubt."

There was a brief, awkward silence. Then Marston bowed, forcing a smile. "Well, I'll let you return to your conversation. Forgive the interruption."

"Not at all, Lord Shanstead," the king said. "We'll speak again later."

The thane nodded, and he and the duchess walked away.

Kearney stared after them. "It seems you've won them over."

Keziah smiled grimly. "And all it took was two broken hands and quite nearly my death."

"Eandi suspicions won't vanish overnight, Archminister."

"No, Your Majesty. Indeed, I expect they'll outlive us all, even should we defeat the renegades."

"We can deal with that later," Grinsa said. "Right now, all that matters is the Weaver."

Keziah could still see Shanstead and the duchess making their way through the camp. "I will say this: they make a fine couple."

"A couple?" Kearney said, frowning. "Are you certain?"

Keziah turned to Fotir. "Don't you think so?"

The minister shrugged. "I can't say that I noticed."

She rolled her eyes. "How can men who see so much on

the battlefield be so blind when it comes to matters of the heart?" She cast a look at her brother. "I suppose you didn't notice either."

"I don't think I want to answer."

Kearney and Fotir laughed. Keziah merely arched an eyebrow.

"When would you do this?" the king asked at length, growing somber once more. "When would you confront the Weaver? Tonight, obviously. But when?"

"It will be a few hours still before he tries to reach for me," Keziah said. "Perhaps when Panya rises."

Grinsa shook his head. "I've lost track of the days. I don't even know how deep into the waning we are or when the moons will be rising."

"We've five days left until Pitch Night," Fotir told him.

"Then, yes. We should wait for Panya's rise."

"Very well," Kearney said heavily.

"We have your permission, Your Majesty?" Keziah asked.

"Would it matter if you didn't?"

"Of course it would. You're my king. If you command me not to do this, I won't."

"As your friend, I'd gladly give such a command. But as your king, I know that I can't." He paused, still looking at her, but then turned to Grinsa and said quietly, "Guard her well, gleaner."

"You know I will, Your Majesty."

Kearney nodded to Fotir, then strode away, as if suddenly eager to be as far as possible from the three Qirsi.

"He's frightened for you," Grinsa said.

Keziah shrugged. "He's an Eandi king who's being forced to rely on magic that he doesn't fully understand. That's what frightens him."

"It's more than that, and you know it."

Keziah eyed Fotir briefly, appearing uncomfortable. "I suppose," was all she said.

"I should leave you," Grinsa said. "Rest. Just don't sleep."

She grinned. "I won't. Thank you for healing me, Grinsa."

He started away. "Of course."

"Wait, gleaner," Fotir called, stopping him. "I'll walk

with you. Will you be all right alone?" he asked the arch-minister.

"It hardly seems that I have a choice." Fotir wasn't certain how to respond, and clearly Keziah sensed this. "I meant it as a joke, First Minister. I'll be fine."

He nodded and smiled. Then he joined the gleaner and they made their way through the camp toward Javan and the Curgh army.

"You fear what you're about to do," Fotir said, eyeing Grinsa as they walked.

"Very much."

"I had the sense a moment ago that you're unsure of whether you can defeat the Weaver."

Grinsa looked at him sharply, then faced forward again. "You saw that?"

"A minister learns to judge much from a person's expression and tone of voice."

"Well, you're right. What Keziah wants to do is terribly dangerous. Yes, we may be able to strike at the Weaver, but he'll have an opportunity to strike at us as well. We'll be on equal footing. I'll have to protect Keziah and myself." He shook his head. "I think it's a grave mistake."

"I understand your reluctance, truly I do. But I also believe that the archminister's idea has much to recommend it. It seems that the Weaver is always a step ahead of us, but I can't imagine he'll be expecting this."

Grinsa nodded once, as if conceding the point. "Probably not, no. I suppose that's worth something." He eyed Fotir briefly, a small smile on his face. "You're quite taken with her, aren't you?"

Fotir faltered in midstride. "What makes you say that?"

"I may be slow to fathom matters of the heart as my sister says, but not when it comes to her."

For several moments, the first minister offered no reply. "Please don't say anything to her," he said at last. "It would only make matters worse. Besides, her heart belongs to an-other."

"It did once. I don't know that it still does."

Fotir shook his head. "Nevertheless, I'd rather she didn't know."

"Your secret is safe, First Minister."

"I'm in your debt. I should return to my duke. No doubt he's wondering where I am. But if you need my help, you know where to find me. I may wish to keep my feelings for Keziah hidden, but I'd do anything to keep her alive, and you as well."

"You've already done much today, First Minister. But I'll keep that in mind."

Fotir gripped his arm briefly, then went to join his duke. He was embarrassed by the ease with which the gleaner had divined his thoughts, but he was certain that Grinsa would keep what he knew to himself. Who kept a secret better than a Weaver?

Grinsa found Tavis on the fringe of the Curgh camp, sitting alone, of course, eating a small meal of roast fowl and bread. The young lord looked up at the sound of Grinsa's approach, regarding the gleaner with a slight smile, his brow creased.

"Why are you looking so pleased?" he asked.

Grinsa did nothing to conceal his surprise. "Am I?"

"More than I've seen you in some time."

"Well, I've just come from Keziah, and . . ." He paused. He had been thinking about his sister and Fotir. For too long she had mourned the end of her love affair with the king. Perhaps, with time, Fotir could help her heart to heal. Still, the first minister served in the court of Tavis's father, and Grinsa had given his word that he would say nothing of this to anyone. "And I'm pleased by how well she's healed from her injuries," he said, for that also was true.

"I'm glad to hear it. You must be tired." Tavis gestured at his plate. "Do you want some of this?"

"Aren't you going to eat it?"

"I've had plenty."

Grinsa sat and took the offered food. "Thank you." He bit into the fowl. "It's good. Where did you get it?"

"Actually some of my father's men gave it to me." He grinned. "So I suppose there's a chance it's poisoned."

"I doubt that. Hungry soldiers wouldn't waste good fowl to poison a noble. Careful with the wine, though."

Tavis grinned. "It seems I've won back a bit of their respect."

"You fought bravely today. Kearney told me so himself."

"Xaver was the brave one."

"Is that why you're here alone?"

The boy scowled. "No!" A moment later his expression softened. "Maybe. I'm happy for Xaver, really I am. What he did today showed great courage. I've no doubt that he saved Kearney's life. And he's my best friend." He glanced at the gleaner. "Or at least one of them. I'm glad that he's getting so much attention."

"But?"

He smiled for just an instant. "But just once I'd like it if someone thought of me as a hero."

"That might not be your fate, Tavis."

"Are you saying that as a gleaner or a friend?"

"Both. That doesn't mean it's true—as I've told you before, our fates are constantly shifting, changing. But I'm afraid your future will always be dogged by shadows from your past."

He nodded, gazing across the camp, the bright fires and torchlight sparkling in his eyes. "I think you may be right."

"That doesn't mean you can't be happy, nor does it mean that you won't reclaim your place among Eibithar's nobility."

"I understand."

Grinsa started to say more, then stopped himself, sensing that the young lord really did grasp the import of what he was saying.

"There's something I need to tell you," he said instead. "Something Keziah and I are going to try later tonight. It doesn't involve you, but I wanted you to know." He explained briefly what his sister and he had in mind to attempt.

"That sounds like it could be dangerous for both of you."

"For her more than for me."

"Knowing the two of you as I do, I'm not certain that you can separate one from the other."

Grinsa hadn't thought of it in those terms. "Perhaps not."

"Is there anything I can do to help?"

"I'm afraid there isn't. But if I fail, and . . . and I'm lost, I want you to ride south from here tonight—"

"What?"

"Please, just listen." Grinsa paused, finding that there were suddenly tears in his eyes. "If I die, no one will survive the Weaver's assault—he'll kill all of you. One sword more or less won't make any difference at all. I want you to ride to the City of Kings as quickly as you can. Take Cresenne and Bryntelle away from here. I don't know where. I'll leave that to you and Cresenne to decide."

"Grinsa—"

"Let me finish. I know that you can't protect them with magic. But you can watch over them, guard them with your blade, make certain that Cresenne isn't attacked in her sleep."

"You'd trust me with this?"

At that the gleaner smiled, though tears still rolled down his cheeks. "Whom else would I turn to, Tavis? Aside from Cresenne and Keziah, there's no one in this world who knows me better than you do, or who I know to be a more faithful friend."

Tavis stared at Grinsa, seemingly struck dumb by the gleaner's words. But at last, he gave a small nod. "I swear to you that I'll keep them safe," he said. "So long as I draw breath."

Chapter
Twenty

Qirsi camp, north of the battle plain, the Moorlands, Eibithar

He had only to wait one last night. Dusaan had led his army to within just a league of where the Eandi forces had been doing battle, weakening themselves, spilling one another's blood as if at his behest. Tomorrow, he and his warriors would sweep across the Moorlands, their white hair flying like battle flags, their pale eyes shining in the light of a new day. And drawing upon the vast power of those around him, Dusaan would destroy his enemies, his shaping magic cutting through their ranks like a scythe, his conjured fires eradicating them from the face of Elined's earth.

All his life, he had waited for this moment, anticipating his victory and all that would come after it. One might have expected that this night he would be crazed with anticipation, unable to sit still, his mind tormented with worries about the soundness of his plans.

Nothing could have been further from the truth. Never had he felt so confident. The Eandi were nothing. Cresenne ja Terba, whose betrayal had plagued him for too long, would soon be dead, if she wasn't already. Even Grinsa jal Arriet could not stop him from extending his rule over all the Forelands. Though the gleaner didn't know it, he was surrounded by servants of the movement, and he faced a force that would easily overwhelm the few who remained loyal to the courts.

On this night, on the eve of war, Dusaan was more at peace than he could ever remember being—an irony that he would savor for the balance of the night.

This was not to say that he had nothing left to do. Jastanne and Uestem would continue well into the night to work with the Qirsi commanders, and before dawn, Dusaan would join them, so that he might make certain that his warriors were ready. And before then, there were conversations he needed to have with his other chancellors.

He reached for Abeni first, knowing that she was near, and that she would expect to speak with him this night. Twice he combed the Moorlands, seeking her mind, growing more agitated by the moment. When at last he was forced to conclude that she was dead or had left the battle plain for some reason—impossible!—he reached for the other Sanbiran woman. She wasn't there either, nor was her lover, Norinde's first minister. Then he tasted fear, acrid, like bile. How long had it been since he had truly been afraid, since he had doubted that he would win this war? He searched for the healer, but even he had vanished. He gritted his teeth, his apprehension now mingled with rage. Grinsa. It had to have been the gleaner.

Among his servants on the Moorlands, the only one he sensed was Keziah ja Dafydd, Eibithar's archminister. Dusaan started to reach for her, then stopped. He still had doubts about this one. She had pledged herself to his cause, but what had she done on his behalf? He had ordered her to kill Cresenne, but she had failed, claiming that the opportunity never presented itself. He had commanded that she kill her king, the man who had spurned her, the man she now professed to hate. Yet as of their last encounter, Kearney still lived. And now, all those who served him and awaited his arrival on the Moorlands were dead, save this woman.

Had she betrayed him? Dusaan remembered now that she had not been surprised the first time he entered her dreams. Her father, she told him at the time, had been a Weaver and she had often communicated with him in that way. And the Weaver had believed her; he had been eager to do so. Fool! Had she joined his movement as an agent of the courts? Had she been deceiving him all this time?

Fear was gone now. He still had an army of more than two hundred. No one could stand against him, certainly not

Grinsa and his paltry collection of faithless Qirsi. The Weaver had no cause for concern. But fury. Yes, he had ample justification for that.

He thrust himself into Keziah's mind, intending to exact a measure of vengeance before he slaughtered her.

For a single disorienting moment, Dusaan thought that he had opened his eyes to daylight, that he had fallen asleep and dreamed it all—Abeni's death, Keziah's betrayal. But then he realized that there were two suns shining on the plain, his brilliant white one, and a second—golden, dazzling, oddly familiar.

All of these thoughts crossed through his mind in the time it took him to step into the woman's mind—less than the span of a single heartbeat. Abruptly he felt someone grappling with him for control of his magic. His defenses failed him for just an instant, and suddenly he was on the ground, his head aching, blood flowing from a wound on his temple.

It's the gleaner. Fighting Grinsa's assault, staving off panic as best he could, Dusaan gathered his magic to him, wresting his powers from the gleaner's control, grappling first for those that could be used against him. Fire, shaping, delusion—

He shrieked in pain, feeling the bone in his arm splinter, not as it would from an attack by shaping magic, but more insidiously, as if the bone were breaking apart from the inside. Healing.

"That's how you attacked Cresenne, isn't it?"

His first mistake, and the one that probably saved Dusaan's life. In the time it took Grinsa to speak the words, the Weaver was able to wrest the last of his powers from the man. His arm was screaming, his head throbbed. But he was safe. In just a few moments he was able to heal his arm and the gash on his head.

He climbed to his feet, sensing Keziah. She was afraid. She knew how angry he was, how much he wanted to hurt her. But there could be no doubt as to where her loyalty lay. Probably there never had been.

"I'll enjoy killing you, Archminister. When the time comes."

Grinsa tried to take hold of his magic again, but Dusaan was ready this time, despite the agony in his arm.

"No, gleaner. You won't catch me unawares again. You had your chance—I'll give you that. Had you acted quickly enough, had you been a bit more precise with your magic, you might have killed me. But not now."

And with that, Dusaan launched an assault of his own. For if Grinsa could control his magic, couldn't he use the gleaner's in turn? Grinsa was ready, though. He repelled the attack with ease, a feral grin on his face. The Weaver sensed no fear in him at all.

"Twice you've bested me, Dusaan, but not this night."

"That remains to be seen, gleaner." He turned to Keziah. "I'm disappointed, Archminister. I'd hoped that you would survive this war, so that I might make a noble of you, allow you to see what it is to rule, rather than just truckle to those with power. Speaking of which, I assume that your king still lives?"

She said nothing. She barely seemed willing to hold his gaze.

"You won't be making nobles of anyone," Grinsa said, sounding too confident, "nor will you be leading your army of traitors into battle."

The Weaver raised an eyebrow. "You intend to kill me?" he asked with a laugh. "Don't deceive yourself, Grinsa. You're not powerful enough to destroy me here, not without killing the archminister as well."

"The one has nothing to do with the other."

"Not necessarily, no. I'm not saying it can't be done. I may well kill you before this encounter is ended. But you haven't the power or knowledge to do it. Unless you've been honing your abilities since the last time we spoke."

This time the gleaner's attack was entirely predictable. Dusaan was never in any danger at all.

"Tell me what you did to Abeni and the others," the Weaver said, as if nothing had happened.

"They're dead."

"I guessed as much. But how is it you knew enough to kill them?"

For the first time, he sensed hesitation on both their parts. Here was their weakness, whatever it might be.

"They learned that I was a Weaver and moved against me."

Dusaan shook his head. "I don't believe you." He stared at the woman, probing her mind with his own. "It was you they were after, wasn't it? They learned that you were deceiving me."

Grinsa tried once more to take possession of his magic. Healing, shaping, fire. But the Weaver had little trouble fighting him off.

"I told you," the gleaner said. "They moved against me. Keziah refused to join them, and they turned on her."

"Your hands have been healed recently. Both of them. I can feel it. There's a residue of pain there. Did they torture you?"

Grinsa attacked again, even going so far this time as to step in front of Dusaan and strike him with his fist. The blow did nothing, however. It was as if the gleaner's hand passed right through him.

"Why would they hurt you in this way?" Dusaan asked, looking past Grinsa to the archminister. To her credit, the woman held his gaze, but she said nothing, her face nearly as white as her hair. "If they had merely learned that you betrayed me, or that you were a threat to the movement, they would have simply killed you. But they didn't, did they?"

Grinsa looked back at her.

This isn't working. Wake up, Kezi!

At first Dusaan thought that Grinsa had said this aloud.

No! We have to keep trying!

It's too dangerous!

It took him several moments to understand that they were sharing these thoughts, the words reaching him as the whisper of a gentle wind. And he used this opportunity to try again for Grinsa's power. With his thoughts directed elsewhere, the gleaner was ill prepared for the assault. Still he held tight to his powers, the deeper ones in particular. But fire . . .

Grinsa's sleeve suddenly burst into flame, and he cried out, batting at the flames with his other hand—the instinctive reaction. It took him but an instant to reclaim control of his magic and extinguish the flame in that way. But that was all the time Dusaan needed. With Grinsa's attention diverted, he struck at Keziah.

Had she possessed healing magic, or shaping, he could have killed her instantly. But she didn't, and that made hurting her much more difficult. Instead, he stopped her breathing, using his own delusion power to convince her that she couldn't draw breath. Her eyes widened, and she clutched at her throat.

Breathe, Kezi. Just as you always do. He can't do this to you if you don't let him.

Dusaan felt her struggling with her terror, fighting to overcome the belief that he could actually strangle her. A moment later, with a shuddering gasp, she inhaled.

Grinsa attacked again, but Dusaan brushed the assault away as if it were a fly.

"You call her Kezi. You've known each other for a long time."

He nearly laughed at what he saw on the gleaner's face. "Yes, you fool, I can hear your thoughts. I'm as much in her mind as you are." Dusaan looked at her again. "Kezi." He nodded. "It suits you. Were you lovers once? Is that it? Was that tale about you and the king merely another deception?"

But even as he asked the question, he knew that this couldn't be. He'd felt the power of her love for her king, as well as her heartache at losing him. Such things could not easily be feigned. Nor was there any memory of passion between these two.

"No," he said, before either of them had time to lie. "You weren't lovers. But then what?" Then it came to him, and he smiled broadly. "Of course! You lied to me that first night," he said to the woman. "You told me your father had been a Weaver, and that was why you weren't surprised by my presence in your mind. But it wasn't your father, was it? It was your brother."

The Weaver eyed them both, grinning at the dismay he saw in their eyes. He would never have said that they looked alike, but searching now for the resemblance, he saw it. The

similarities were subtle—the high cheekbones, the shape of
their eyes, even the way their jaws clenched in anger or
fear—but knowing to look for them, he realized that they
were unmistakable.

"The archminister of Eibithar is sister to a Weaver. How
splendid!"

The onslaught came so swiftly, with such fury, that Dusaan
was unable to ward himself. Grinsa didn't make the mistake
of throwing a punch this time. He remained perfectly still as
he seized Dusaan's magic with his mind. Not shaping, for
that was the most dangerous, and thus the one the Weaver
guarded first. Healing again.

Dusaan felt the skin on his face opening, wide gashes from
which blood poured like rain-fed streams from the Crying
Hills. He fought to regain control of his power once more,
only to find that he had it without having struggled at all.
Grinsa had relinquished the healing magic and had taken
hold of the Weaver's shaping power, lashing out with what
would have been the killing blow. Dusaan actually felt pressure building on the bone in his neck.

Never in his life had he known such terror. It almost
seemed that Bian was at his shoulder, waiting to carry him to
the Underrealm. Had he faltered even in the least, he would
have died then. But drawing upon all his strength, managing
in that moment of abject fear to keep his mind clear, the
Weaver fought, mastering first his fright and then the gleaner.
It was over in but a moment, though it seemed an eternity.

His magic was his again. The gleaner stood before him, his
chest rising and falling, his face flushed, as if he had just
come through some great bloody battle.

Dusaan healed the wounds on his face with a thought,
though he could do nothing about the blood that stained his
surcoat. "As I told you," he said, his voice raw, "you'll not kill
me tonight."

"Then I'll have to wait until tomorrow."

The Weaver grinned. "Brave words, but empty ones. You
know that. You may be strong, Grinsa, and more cunning
than I had credited. But you can't defeat my army. You think

that Abeni's death will save you. You're wrong. She was one chancellor among many. You killed four of my servants today. But I still command hundreds. How many are in your army, Grinsa? Ten? Twelve?" He shook his head. "I should have seen this attack coming. I understand that now. It was your only chance to defeat me. You've failed, and tomorrow I'll destroy you." He eyed the archminister, then made one last desperate attempt to turn his power against her, but Grinsa was ready. Dusaan grinned. "No matter," he said, still looking at Keziah. "Come tomorrow, your life is forfeit. I'll enjoy killing you almost as much as I will your brother. I wouldn't sleep for the rest of the night, Keziah. It might not be safe."

With that, he opened his eyes to the fire burning low before him. The world seemed to heave and spin, as if he were on some storm-tossed ship in the Scabbard, and he squeezed his eyes shut once more, fighting through a wave of nausea.

"Damn them," he muttered, his teeth clenched.

Again he opened his eyes. The dizziness was subsiding. Neither his face nor his arm pained him anymore; he seemed to have healed fully, notwithstanding the dark bloodstains on his clothes.

He would enjoy killing them both.

It troubled him that Kearney lived still, but in past conversations with the archminister he had sensed her reluctance to carry out his orders. On some level he had expected this. Come the morrow, it wouldn't matter.

"Weaver?"

He knew the voice immediately. Nitara. Better that she didn't see him like this, bloodied and shaken.

"What is it?" he asked, not looking at her.

"We heard you cry out. We were . . . I wanted to make certain that you were all right."

Dusaan had no idea that he had made any sound at all beyond Keziah's mind. He turned just a bit, enough so that she would see his face. "I'm fine," he told her. "Go to sleep. Tomorrow is going to be a great day."

Her eyes widened. "There's blood on your face!"

The Weaver touched his cheek, felt the blood there, still sticky. He turned his back to her once more. "It's nothing. I told you I was fine. Now leave me."

"But you're hur—"

"Go!"

Dusaan sensed her hesitation, then heard her withdraw. He lightly traced a finger over the places where Grinsa had cut him, feeling blood everywhere. He must look a mess. He ran a hand through his hair, knowing that he shouldn't have yelled at Nitara. It was Grinsa who did this to him, who filled him with rage and clouded his mind.

He would have to clean himself and change his clothes. He would have to find some way to still his trembling hands. And then he would make himself sleep as well. What he said to Nitara was doubly true for himself. Tomorrow did promise to be a great day, the culmination of years of planning and a lifetime of dreams.

Tonight the gleaner had won, but his was a hollow victory. Dawn would bring the end of Eandi rule in the Forelands, and the ascension of a new Qirsi Supremacy.

"He wants his shapers and those with mists and winds on the flanks," Jastanne said, her eyes flicking from Uestem to the three commanders sitting with him. "They're our best defense against the Eandi archers. As long as we can guard ourselves from their arrows, we've nothing to fear."

"So fire and language of beasts will take the center?" one of Uestem's commanders asked. It took Jastanne a moment to remember her name: Rov.

"Yes. Neither magic offers much in the way of defense, and language of beasts, at least, is better suited to close fighting."

"He was wise to divide us so," Yedeg said, as if glimpsing the Weaver's purpose for the first time.

"Did you have any doubt as to his wisdom, Commander?"

Yedeg's face colored. "No, Chancellor, of course not. I just . . . It took me some time to grasp the intricacies of his plan."

"He's as brilliant as he is powerful, Commander. That's why we're destined to prevail."

"Yes, Chancellor."

"You're not to use your magic on your own," she went on, speaking to all of them again, "unless it's the only way to save your life or that of one of your fellow warriors. You must make certain that those under your command understand this. The Weaver will be wielding power from over two hundred of us, and if all of us are using magic on our own, particularly if we're using powers other than those to which we've been assigned, it will only make matters more difficult for him. Discipline and precision will win this war. The one exception is those with language of beasts. They may have to use their power individually. It's simply the nature of the magic and I've explained as much to Nitara."

As if responding to the mention of her name, Nitara came into view, striding back toward the fire. The chancellors and commanders had heard the Weaver call out a short time before, and the minister had gone to see whether he had been summoning one of them. As the woman drew nearer, Jastanne saw that her cheeks were ashen, her eyes wide with fright. This in itself was not cause for concern—the minister was young, and, of course, she remained quite taken with the Weaver, though as far as Jastanne could see, he had done nothing to encourage her in this regard. Still something in the woman's manner troubled her.

"Commander? Is everything all right?"

Nitara met her gaze for a moment, then glanced nervously at the others. "I'm not certain."

Jastanne cast a quick look at Uestem, who nodded to her.

"Why don't you and I speak in private," she said, standing and taking Nitara gently by the arm. They walked a short distance, until they were beyond the hearing of anyone in the Qirsi camp. "Now," the chancellor said, "why don't you tell me what happened."

"I think the Weaver was hurt."

"Hurt?" Jastanne frowned at the very notion. "By whom?"

"I don't know."

"What makes you think—?"

"There was blood on his face, and I think on his clothes also, but I couldn't see very well. He refused to look at me."

Jastanne just stared at her. Surely the woman had to be mistaken. "Blood? Are you certain?"

"Yes, at least about the blood on his face."

"There must be some explanation." *Blood! On the Weaver!*

"I tried to help him, but he sent me away."

Of course he would. "As I say, there must be a reason for all this, and he probably didn't want to alarm the rest of us." She paused a moment, wondering what to do. "Whatever the truth of this, Nitara, we can't risk allowing word of it to spread through the camp. Don't mention what you saw to the others, not even your closest friends. I won't say a word either. Agreed?"

The woman nodded. "What are you going to do?"

"I'll speak to him," she said, making herself smile. "As I say, I'm sure there's an explanation."

Usually, Nitara would have bristled at the notion of Jastanne speaking with the Weaver in private. She had been slow to overcome her jealousy of the chancellor. But now she merely nodded.

They returned to where Uestem and the other commanders were sitting. Uestem looked up expectantly as they approached, but Jastanne shook her head, as if to say that there was nothing of substance to Nitara's concerns. She and the merchant had told the commanders all they needed to know for the next day's battle, so they dismissed them and watched them walk off.

Only then did Uestem ask about Nitara. "What was troubling the woman?"

"It was nothing."

"I'm not sure I believe you."

Jastanne smiled thinly. "Very well. I don't know what to make of it, but I intend to handle it on my own."

He opened his hands and shrugged. "That's all you had to say."

She laughed. She still wasn't certain that she trusted the

merchant, but she had begun to like him. "Good night, Uestem."

He nodded and walked away.

Jastanne took a breath, then walked toward the south edge of the camp, where the Weaver usually ate his meals and slept in solitude. Chances were he would send her away, just as he had the commander. But if he really was wounded and their cause was threatened, someone needed to know. Best it be her.

When she reached his small fire, however, he was nowhere to be seen. For the first time, Jastanne found herself growing truly apprehensive.

"Weaver?" she called, pitching her voice to carry, but keeping it low enough that she wouldn't draw the attention of the other Qirsi.

"Who is that?" he answered from the shadows.

"Your chancellor, Jastanne."

He stepped into the firelight, and Jastanne's breath caught at the sight of him. He was shirtless, his broad chest and shoulders gleaming like polished marble. His face appeared clean and unmarked, his golden eyes shining.

"Forgive me, Weaver. I didn't mean to disturb you. I was . . . I'll leave you."

"You came because of Nitara, because of what she saw."

"She told me there was blood."

He inhaled, straightening. "There was. But I'm fine. You've no cause for concern."

She heard no anger in his tone, yet she felt compelled to apologize once more for her presence there, the doubts that it implied.

"I'm sorry." She thought to say more, then decided against it, turning to go.

"Wait," he said.

Jastanne faced him once more, gazing at his body, his hair, his eyes, wanting to touch him, wanting to feel him touching her.

"I won't speak of this with anyone, Weaver. Neither will Nitara—I've sworn her to silence."

"Good. But that's not why I stopped you."

She felt her pulse quicken.

"We ride to war with the dawn. Tomorrow we'll remake the world. I don't know yet who I'll choose to be my queen, but I do know that of all who serve me, none has done more for this cause than you."

Her skin seemed to burn with the anticipation of his caress. Her throat ached with desire of him. But she managed to say, "You honor me, Weaver."

"This is not a night for either of us to be alone."

He held out a hand to her then, and when she took it, he pulled her to him, taking her in his arms and lifting her off the ground to kiss her, long and deep.

After that, Jastanne lost all sense of time, surrendering utterly to his touch and the cadence of their movements in the cool grasses and the soft glow of the fire. His hunger seemed a match for hers, their passion bringing them together again and again, until at last they lay together beneath the star-filled sky, sated and exhausted.

Jastanne felt herself drifting toward slumber, happier than she had been in many years. She felt him beside her, restless and alert, and knew that he wasn't ready for sleep. But she couldn't help herself.

Just as she was about to give in to her weariness, he sat up.

Jastanne forced her eyes open. "Forgive me, Weaver," she said. "But I'm so tired."

He shook his head, his face somber in the dim light. "It's all right," he said. "You should sleep." He smiled, though it seemed to take some effort. "Thank you for this night. My . . . my need was great."

"As was mine."

"I have one thing more to ask of you."

"Of course, Weaver. Anything."

"Tomorrow, when the fighting begins, I'll be matched against another Weaver. You've heard me speak of him before, though others haven't."

She nodded. "Grinsa jal Arriet."

"Yes. Defeating him will take much of my attention. But there's another who has to die, and I want you to kill her for me. She deceived me and she seeks to destroy all for which we've toiled these last several years."

"Who is she?"

"Her name is Keziah ja Dafydd. She's the archminister of Eibithar. Her powers are considerable, and they include language of beasts, but she possesses neither shaping nor fire. You shouldn't have trouble killing her."

Jastanne nodded. "She won't survive the day, Weaver. You have my word."

Again he smiled, easily this time. "You serve me well," he said, brushing her cheek with his fingers. He stood, naked, glorious, and began to dress. And Jastanne closed her eyes, allowing sleep to take her, hoping that she would dream of him and of what they had shared this night.

She sat alone by the small fire, staring into the darkness, waiting for Jastanne to return. Silence settled over the camp like a warm blanket—all around her, Qirsi slept, horses stomped and snorted, a gentle wind rustled the grasses and hummed as it moved among the boulders. And still Jastanne didn't come back from her conversation with the Weaver.

Finally, Nitara realized that the chancellor wouldn't return, at least not until dawn, and she feared that her heart would simply stop beating. She had expected this since the first time she saw Jastanne, with her exquisite face and lithe form, and her golden eyes, so like Dusaan's that it seemed Qirsar had marked them for each other.

It would have been easier had she still hated the woman as she did that first day. But Nitara had come to respect her, even to like her. And how could she blame Jastanne for desiring the Weaver, when she herself had imagined a thousand times what it would be like to lie with him?

"The movement is everything," he had said to her once, before they took the palace from Harel, as he was explaining why he couldn't love her. "Devote yourself to our cause, and you devote yourself to me; give it your passion, and you give that passion to me."

"But that's not enough," she said at the time.

And he replied plainly, though not without sympathy, "It will have to be."

As far as she knew, he hadn't loved any woman since then. That is, until tonight.

Wasn't it possible then, that with victory within reach, with the Forelands about to be his, he was ready to take a wife? Or perhaps several. Just after joining the Weaver's army Jastanne sensed Nitara's jealousy and spoke to her of the possibility that Dusaan would have as many women as had Braedon's emperor. "Do you really think that a man like that—a Qirsi king—will take but one wife?" Jastanne had asked her that day. Maybe, she suggested, he would choose to love both of them. In which case, didn't the fact that he was with Jastanne tonight suggest that some time soon he might call Nitara to his bed?

It wasn't exactly what she would have chosen—if she could claim Dusaan as her own, she would. But Jastanne was right. A man like the Weaver could never belong to but one love. Better she should be one lover among many than never know what it was to give herself to him. That would be too great a loss to contemplate.

So at last, reluctant to give up her vigil, but knowing that she needed to rest before the morrow's battle, Nitara lay down on her sleeping roll and closed her eyes. She quickly fell asleep, and almost immediately found herself in a dream.

The minister was on a plain and a Qirsi man stood before her, wind whipping his hair around his face. She had heard some of the other Qirsi—the chancellors and a minister from Galdasten—speaking of dreams in which the Weaver came to them, walking in their sleep to give them instructions, and for one disorienting moment, she wondered if this was what was happening to her.

Then she recognized the man, and knew this wasn't so. His eyes were brighter than Dusaan's, his face leaner, more youthful. He was neither as tall nor as broad as the Weaver, though he did have a muscular build. She still remembered the smooth, solid feel of his back and chest from the nights they had spent in each other's arms.

"I'm dreaming," she said aloud, as if hoping to wake herself.

"Yes," Kayiv jal Yivanne answered, walking toward her. As he drew near, she saw bloodstains on his ministerial robes and the dagger jutting from his chest. Her dagger.

"What do you want of me?"

He stopped just in front of her, so close that the hilt of the killing blade nearly touched her breasts. "You ride to war. There's to be a great battle tomorrow."

"What of it?"

"You expect to win. You think that your victory will justify what you did to me, what your Weaver has done to the Eandi in Curtell and Ayvencalde and Galdasten, what all of you will do to the armies of Eibithar and Braedon."

"It does justify it. We're going to change the world. You never understood that."

"I understood. I just chose not to be a part of it." He smiled, a dark, terrible smile. "And for that, I died by your hand."

"I won't listen to this."

"Then send me away, if you can."

She tried to wake herself, or she thought she did. It was so hard to know what she was dreaming and what was real.

"Do you remember what I said to you?"

"When?" she asked. But she knew. Gods, she knew. His last words, whispered on a dying breath.

The smile faded, chased away by a single tear, which was far worse. "I loved you so."

Nitara closed her eyes. Or did she? Wasn't she already asleep?

"That's what I said. 'I loved you so.' "

"I remember," she said, shuddering.

"And now your Weaver loves another."

"No!"

"Maybe you shouldn't have killed me after all."

"I had to!"

"For him," Kayiv said.

"Yes, for him."

"Then I have to do this for all the others, all who would die if I didn't."

He pulled the dagger free from his chest, the blade emerging as clean and brilliant as the day she bought it. And raising it high, so that it gleamed in the morning sun, he plunged it into her neck.

Nitara screamed. Yet somehow she still heard him say, his voice so sad that it made her want to weep, "I loved you so."

She opened her eyes to starlight and the dim glow of the moons. Her heart was pounding so hard that her chest hurt, and her clothes were soaked with sweat. She raised herself up on one elbow and looked around the camp. No one else appeared to be awake. Jastanne was nowhere to be seen.

"Damn," she whispered, running a hand through her hair.

After a few moments she lay back down, staring up at the stars, knowing she should sleep, but afraid to close her eyes again.

"We're going to change the world," she said to the darkness, as if Kayiv might hear her. "That's why I had to do it."

Chapter
Twenty-one

The Moorlands, Eibithar

eziah awoke as soon as the Weaver left her dream, opening her eyes to find Grinsa still sitting beside her, concern etched on his face.

"Are you all right?" he asked.

She nodded. As encounters with the Weaver went, this one had been relatively easy for her. "Are you?"

He shrugged, glowering at the fire that burned a short distance away. "I had him. Twice, really. And both times he managed to fight me off."

"You hurt him, Grinsa. And maybe more important than that, you frightened him. He won't be so confident tomorrow, and that has to be to our advantage."

"Maybe. I fear he was right though. Any victory I might have won just now will be meaningless in the end. In order to defeat him I needed to kill him, and I couldn't." He swung his gaze back to her. "You'll have to be especially watchful tomorrow, Kezi. He's vengeful—we know that—and now he has ample reason to want to punish you."

She sat up, her head spinning, though not as it had after previous dreams of the Weaver. Could it be that she was getting used to this?

"I'll be careful," she said, "although I imagine he'll be most intent on killing you. Every time he thinks he's added a woman to his movement, you seem to take her away. I can't imagine that he likes that."

Her brother grinned. "No, probably not."

"We should tell Kearney what's happened. He'll want to know."

Grinsa nodded, standing and helping Keziah to her feet. They crossed the camp and found the king sitting outside his tent with Gershon Trasker.

Keziah and Gershon had hardly spoken since the swordmaster's arrival on the battle plain. Once they had been fierce rivals for the king's ear and had disliked and distrusted each other. Later, when Keziah began trying to join the conspiracy, she was forced to rely on Gershon as a confidant, and they came to an understanding of sorts. More than once during the march north from the City of Kings, Keziah had been surprised to find that she missed his company. She thought about seeking him out upon his arrival, but at the time she was still posing as a traitor, and she couldn't risk being seen with him.

Both Gershon and the king stood as Keziah and Grinsa approached.

"Are you all right?" Kearney asked, looking the archminister up and down as if he expected to see wounds on her.

"I'm fine. Both of us are."

"Did it work?"

"No, Your Majesty," Grinsa said. "I'm sorry."

"Damn. What happened?"

"Grinsa tried!" Keziah said.

Kearney cast a dark look her way. "I don't doubt that he did, Archminister. I'm merely asking that he tell me what happened."

Grinsa laid a hand on her shoulder, as he briefly described for Kearney their encounter with the Weaver.

"I'm certain that you did all you could, gleaner," the king said when he had finished. "I'm grateful to you for making the effort. And I'm grateful to you, Archminister. I have some idea of how much you risked."

"You honor me, Your Majesty," she said, her gaze lowered.

Gershon looked at Kearney and then at Grinsa. "So what do we do now?"

"We ready ourselves for war. Isn't that so, gleaner?"

"Yes, Your Majesty, I suppose it is."

"You'll lead the Qirsi, of course."

"The few I have left."

"How do you suggest we array the armies?"

Grinsa rubbed a hand over his face. "To be honest, I'm not very knowledgeable when it comes to military tactics. The swordmaster probably knows better than I."

"I doubt that," Gershon said. "I've never fought a Qirsi army."

"I'm not interested in hearing which of you knows less about fighting this kind of war! I simply want your recommendations."

"Let me ask you this, gleaner," Gershon said. "If you were leading an army of Qirsi against us, what could I do that would confound you the most?"

Grinsa appeared to consider this for several moments. "It all comes down to the archers," he said at last. "Swordsmen will never get close enough to do any damage, but the archers may be able to reach them."

"How?"

"Spread them. Have arrows flying at the Qirsi from as

many different positions as possible. Force them to summon winds from several directions at once. Either the Weaver will have to relinquish his hold on some of those who have mists and winds, which will make the gales they raise less effective, or he'll have to keep his full attention on sustaining all the winds. One way or another it helps us."

"Good," Kearney said. "What else?"

Grinsa fell silent once more, staring at the fire, slowly shaking his head. "The queen's army should remain on foot," he said after some time. "All of us should."

"But won't the Qirsi be mounted?"

"Yes. But the Weaver will have many warriors with language of beasts."

Neither Kearney nor Gershon appeared convinced.

"You can't think of them as you would an Eandi enemy, Your Majesty," the gleaner went on. "As simple fighters, they won't be the equal of your soldiers. It's their magic that makes them dangerous, and so we must do everything we can to eliminate that advantage. They will be mounted, which means that I can use magic against their horses. We'll be better off if they can't do the same."

The king nodded, though he still looked unhappy. "Very well, gleaner. Anything else?"

"Not that I can think of, Your Majesty. But if more comes to me, I'll let you know."

"Of course. You're probably weary. Get some sleep, gleaner. And again, you have my thanks for all you've done."

Grinsa bowed. Then he turned to Keziah. "You'll be all right?"

"Yes."

"If you find that you're having trouble remaining awake, find me, and wake me. I'll watch over you."

"That's kind of you, but it's more important that you get some rest."

Gershon frowned. "Why can't she sleep?"

"The Weaver threatened me at the end of our encounter tonight," she answered. "I'm not certain that he'd really make an attempt on my life on the eve of battle, but it's probably best that I don't give him the opportunity."

"Until the morning then," Grinsa said, kissing her cheek. He nodded to Gershon, then walked toward the Curgh camp.

For several moments the three of them stood silent watching her brother walk away.

Finally, Gershon cleared his throat, and said, "Well, I should probably sleep, too." He remained where he was, however, eyeing Keziah. "It seems you survived your deception of the Weaver. Whatever happens tomorrow, you don't have to pretend anymore."

"No, I don't. Thank you, swordmaster."

He glanced at the king, his cheeks shading to crimson. "For what?"

"For keeping my secret. For protecting me."

"I didn't do much, Archminister."

She smiled. "You did more than you know. And like it or not, you gained a Qirsi friend." She stepped forward, raised herself onto her tiptoes, and kissed him.

Gershon scowled at her. "What was that for?"

"It seemed the best way to aggravate you. I've missed doing that."

Kearney laughed.

"You always did excel at it," the swordmaster said, sounding cross, though it seemed to take an effort. After a moment, he offered a smile of his own. "You've done us all a great service, Archminister. And I promise you that every man under my command will know of it. I'm aware of how they've treated you these past several turns and I intend to put a stop to it."

"That's not necessary."

"I believe it is."

She had no desire to argue with the man. "All right then. Again, you have my thanks."

"You're welcome." Gershon bowed to the king. "Your Majesty."

"Good night, Gershon."

In recent days, Keziah had tried to avoid being alone with the king, but that was where she now found herself. Kearney stared into the fire, but occasionally his eyes would flick toward her.

"Twice today I've feared that I might lose you," he said, breaking a lengthy silence. "I can't tell you how the thought of that frightened me."

"I'm grateful to you, Your Majesty."

He looked up, his eyes meeting hers. "I didn't say that as your king."

Keziah shivered. How long had she waited to hear him say such a thing to her? And yet now that he had at last spoken the words, she wondered if she still wanted him. Her ambivalence surprised her. It even frightened her a bit. She could hardly remember a time when she hadn't loved this man.

"Forgive me, Your Majesty. But you *are* my king, and all that you say to me, you say as a king to his archminister."

"We've been so much more than that to each other, Kez. Can't we be again? I've missed you. With everything that's happened today I've realized again how much I still need you."

She smiled, despite the tears in her eyes. "I'll always love you, and not only as my king. But it's been so long . . ." She faltered. "Maybe too long. I don't know if I can go back."

"So we can never be together again? Not even tonight, on the eve of a war that could end all that we've known and fought together to preserve?" He smiled playfully. "You have to stay awake anyway."

Keziah laughed, though her heart was aching. He had always been able to find humor in even the most difficult of circumstances. It was one of the reasons she had fallen in love with him.

She walked to where he stood and put her arms around him, resting her head against his chest. "Not even tonight," she whispered. "I'm sorry."

They stood that way for a long time, until at last she turned her face up to his and kissed him one last time. Then she pulled back and left him, wiping the tears from her cheeks.

A year ago, on the night he agreed to assume the throne, on the plain just beyond the walls of Kentigern Castle, she had refused him in much the same way, though it had nearly killed her to do so. Tonight was different. She was different. And as she walked away from the man she had once loved more than she ever thought possible, Keziah ja Dafydd surprised herself again, this time with the direction in which her steps carried her.

He watched from a distance, waiting until the king was alone before approaching him. He was surprised to see Kearney and the archminister embrace, even more so when they kissed. Like others, he had heard rumors of Kearney's affair with the woman, but he hadn't known whether or not to believe them. Not long ago, Aindreas would have thought to use what he had seen as a weapon against the king, another way, perhaps, to challenge the legitimacy of his rule. But not anymore.

"You're doing the right thing, Father."

The duke turned at the sound of Brienne's voice. She was beside him, her golden hair stirring in the light wind, her grey eyes luminous with the light of torches and stars. He didn't say the obvious, that he was doing the only thing he could, and coming to it late, very nearly too late. Instead, he merely smiled at her, wishing that he could cup her cheek in his hand, or kiss her smooth brow, knowing that she existed only in his mind and was beyond his reach.

"It's not going to get any easier, Father."

Right. Facing Kearney again, he stepped forward into the light of the king's fire, his hands trembling, beads of sweat running down his temples.

"My pardon, Your Majesty. May I have a word?"

The king spun around at the sound of Aindreas's voice, his hand straying to the hilt of his sword. Seeing the duke, Kearney frowned but he didn't relax his stance.

"This isn't a good time, Lord Kentigern. Can it wait until tomorrow?"

"No, I'm afraid it can't. Tomorrow might be too late."

Kearney narrowed his eyes. "What is it you want?"

Aindreas stared at him, noting that his hand was still on his weapon. "You think I've come to kill you."

"Have you?"

"Of course not!"

"You say that as if I should know it without asking. But considering the matter from my point of view, do you really think the notion that far-fetched?"

This was why he hated the man, why he hated Javan as well. The arrogance, the self-righteousness. He should have known better than to approach this imperious king.

"You've thought the worst of me from the day you took the throne," Aindreas said, sneering at him. "You've sided with Javan from the beginning, allowing him to poison your mind against me! You give no thought at all to how we've suffered this past year!"

"This isn't my fault, Aindreas! You've defied me at every turn, fomented rebellion throughout the land, and weakened our realm when it's most vulnerable! I've given you ample opportunity to put your house in good standing once more, and you've refused."

"I'm here. I marched with your swordmaster and joined him in defeating the Solkarans. I've fought against the empire. What more do you want?"

"Allowing you to fight with us was Gershon's decision, and I won't question his judgment. But neither am I ready to forgive all simply because you've finally upheld your duty to the throne and the realm."

"You have no right to judge me or my house!"

"I have every right! I'm your king! And it's about time you treated me as such!"

Aindreas nearly left then. How could he be expected to make peace with such a man? How could he possibly confess to Kearney all that he had done when the king already regarded him as a traitor? He actually turned to go, but Brienne was there, standing in his path, a hard look in her eyes.

The duke halted, closing his eyes briefly and taking a long breath. "You're right," he said. He turned back to Kearney. "Your Majesty."

The king regarded him doubtfully. "Suddenly, I'm right?"

"Not suddenly. You've been right for some time now, about many things."

"What about all that you just said to me, about how Javan had poisoned my mind, and I had never given any consideration to your house?"

Aindreas rubbed his eyes with his thumb and forefinger. "I'm a fool, Your Majesty. Surely you've reasoned that out for yourself by now."

A wry smile touched the king's lips. "I've had some inkling, yes. But I never thought I'd hear you admit it."

"Yes, well, there's a good deal I need to admit."

"I don't understand."

Abruptly the duke's eyes were stinging, and for a moment he feared that he might begin to weep. How had he allowed matters to progress so far? Yes, the Qirsi had deceived him, preying on his grief and his desperate need to avenge Brienne's murder. But he had once thought of himself as a strong man, a deeply intelligent man. It seemed an eternity since he had behaved as either. He gazed past the king and saw Brienne staring back at him. She didn't look angry anymore, or even ashamed. She just looked sad.

"Aindreas?"

"I've betrayed the realm," he said. "And I've shamed my house." Just saying the words, the duke felt something loosen in his chest, though he also began to sob.

Kearney regarded him with pity, a pained expression on his face. "It's not too late for you to reclaim Kentigern's place among Eibithar's great houses."

"No. You don't know what I've done."

"Perhaps you should tell me then."

Aindreas opened his mouth, but the words wouldn't come. He had to bite back the bile rising in his throat.

"Does this have something to do with the men I sent to the tor some time ago?"

The captain Kearney had sent to Kentigern, the one the Qirsi woman attacked. Aindreas could still see the man lying on the floor of his presence chamber, blood pouring from the gaping wound at his throat. Jastanne had wielded the dagger, but Aindreas knew that he had killed the man, just as surely as if he had dragged the blade across the captain's neck himself.

"No, and yes."

"You're speaking in riddles, Aindreas. I haven't time for this."

"I've allied myself with the Qirsi."

Kearney gaped at him. "What?"

"I even signed a document pledging my support to their movement."

One might have thought that Aindreas had confessed to killing his own daughter, such was the expression on the king's face. "Why would you do such a thing?"

"I was grieving. I was certain that Tavis was guilty and that you and Javan had contrived together to destroy my house."

"But to join with the traitors . . ."

"It seemed the only way to strike at you. Alone, I was weak. And even with the other houses supporting me, I could do no more than defy you and wait for you to crush me."

"When?" Kearney asked, as if in a stupor. "When did you do this?"

"Long ago. During the snows."

"What have you done on their behalf?"

"You know most of it. I've defied you, I've sought to turn the other houses against you, and at first I allowed the Solkarans to march past Kentigern on their way here. I also stood by and did nothing as one of them killed your captain in my castle."

"And what have they done for you in return?"

"Nothing yet. Our agreement was that I would help them defeat the Eandi courts and when the time came, they would spare Kentigern. I don't know if they intended to honor their end of our bargain, but I was interested only in seeing you destroyed."

"You hated me that much."

Aindreas nodded. "I hated everything that much. You and Javan most of all."

Kearney exhaled through his teeth, shaking his head slowly, his eyes fixed on the ground. "Well, you've certainly made a mess of things, Aindreas. I'll grant you that." He glanced at the duke, looking disgusted. "I can't believe you actually pledged yourself to their movement in writing."

"It was the only way to get them to agree," he said, as if that excused it.

If the king was thinking the same thing, he had the grace to keep it to himself. "What made you change your mind?" he asked instead.

"I don't want Ennis to inherit a disgraced house."

"It may be too late for that."

"I know. When the Qirsi see me fighting beside you tomorrow, they'll know that I betrayed them and they'll reveal to all what I've done."

"You could leave tonight. We'd need for your men to remain, of course, but they can fight under the banner of another house. It would raise some questions, but it might save you the humiliation of being exposed as a traitor."

"You'd let me go?"

"I've no desire to see your son disgraced, Aindreas. You seem to forget at times that I'm a father, too."

"I appreciate that, Your Majesty," the duke said, and meant it. But he knew that he couldn't leave. That path led to a different sort of shame. "But I don't wish to leave. I came north with Gershon so that I could fight for the realm, as the duke of a great house should. I won't run away now."

"I'm not certain that I can help you then."

"I don't expect you to, Your Majesty. I wanted to confess this to you because it was the right thing to do. It's been a long time since I did anything for that reason alone."

The king appeared to consider this, nodding at last. "I believe I understand. I also think that the judgments of history are based on all that we do, rather than one large thing, be it good or evil. If we prevail tomorrow, and you play a role in that victory, your deeds will reflect on your house and your son."

It was a greater kindness than Aindreas had any right to expect, and proof once more of how greatly he had erred in opposing this king. "Again, Your Majesty, I'm grateful to you."

Kearney offered a thin smile by way of response, but said nothing. Aindreas sensed that the king wanted him to go.

"I'll leave you, Your Majesty. I hope you know that my

sword and my men are yours to use as you will. Perhaps together we can defeat this enemy."

"Perhaps. Good night, Aindreas."

The duke turned and made his way back to where his soldiers were sleeping. Glancing to the side, he saw that Brienne was with him, looking more at peace than he had seen her look in so long.

"I'm proud of you, Father," she said. "Farewell." And with that, she vanished.

He had just fallen asleep, or so it seemed. One moment he was closing his eyes, allowing himself at last to give in to his weariness, and the next he was dimly aware of someone standing over him, then kneeling beside him. Fotir forced himself awake, and found himself gazing up into the eyes of the archminister.

His first thought was that he had been wrong all this time. Since the day he met Keziah, he had thought her eyes the color of sand, but seeing them now in the torchlight, he realized that they were more like flames, bright and entrancing. His second thought was that he must have looked a mess.

He sat up quickly, running a hand through his hair. "Is there something you need, Archminister?"

"No, I—"

"Have you already had your encounter with the Weaver?" he asked, abruptly remembering all that had happened earlier that night. "Are you all right?"

"Yes, thank you. I'm fine. But Grinsa wasn't able to defeat him."

"But he came through it unhurt?"

Keziah nodded.

"Well, good. I'm sorry that he wasn't able to do more, but the important thing is that both of you are safe."

"Yes," she said, grinning mischievously. "I could see how concerned you were for us. You almost managed to stay awake."

"No, it's not . . . I was . . ."

She was laughing at him, her eyes dancing. "It's all right, First Minister. You should have been resting. I would have, had I been in your position."

"You mean prone?"

Her mouth fell open. "Was that a joke? I don't think I've ever heard you say something humorous."

Fotir looked away. "That's not fair. I'm not as serious as all that."

"Aren't you? You remind me of Grinsa sometimes. You seem to carry the weight of the world on your shoulders."

"These are dark times. Is it any wonder?"

"Even in the darkest of days, we have to be able to laugh. If we can't, we've lost already."

"Perhaps you're right," he said. "Is this why you woke me? To coax more humor from me?"

She shrugged, smiling. "I can't sleep."

"After the day you've had, I'm not surprised."

"No," she said, with a small laugh. "I mean that I can't risk trying to sleep. The Weaver threatened to kill me if I dared sleep again tonight. I was hoping you might be willing to keep me company while I await the dawn."

He was as flattered as he was surprised. Mostly, though, he was at a loss as to what he should say. "I'm honored that you'd ask me," he said at last, inwardly cringing at how formal he sounded. "Of course I will."

For several moments neither of them spoke. The archminister was staring at her hands.

At last she faced him once more. "I want to tell you how much I appreciate your words of support earlier tonight. If you hadn't said what you did, the king might not have given us permission to make the attempt."

"You're welcome. Though it seems that it didn't do much good."

She frowned. "Do you think now that it was a mistake?"

"Not at all. I thought it quite a fine idea. I just . . ." He shook his head, wishing that he had kept his mouth shut. "Never mind."

They lapsed into another silence. Fotir had to keep himself

from staring at her as he cast about for something—anything—to say.

"Are you certain I'm not disturbing you?" she finally asked. "Perhaps I shouldn't have woken you."

"You're not disturbing me. I'm just not very good at this."

Her eyebrows went up. "Good at what?"

Fotir felt the blood rush to his cheeks. Why was it that he always found himself so flustered when he was with this woman? "Making conversation," he said.

"You're first minister to a major house. Surely you're accustomed to speaking with nobles and ministers."

"Somehow this is different." *You're different.*

She gave a kind smile. "Would you like to walk?"

Even if he had wanted to refuse her, he hadn't the power to do so. "Of course," he said, standing.

She offered him a hand and he pulled her gently to her feet, their eyes meeting for just an instant.

"Is something the matter?"

His cheeks still burning, Fotir looked away and shook his head. "Not at all."

They started away from the camp, southward, picking their way among the grasses and boulders. Panya, the white moon, shone low in the eastern sky, thin and curved, her edges as sharp as an Uulranni blade. As they walked, Keziah took Fotir's hand, her skin cool and soft.

"What about the king?" he asked, the first words that came to mind.

As quickly as she had claimed his hand, she let it drop.

"What do you mean?"

He squeezed his eyes shut for just a moment, cursing his stupidity. "Forgive me, Archminister. It's really none of my concern."

For some time Keziah said nothing, and though they continued to walk, Fotir suddenly sensed a great distance between them.

"It's not really something I can discuss," she told him at length, her voice so low he had to lean closer just to hear her.

"You don't have to. I shouldn't have—"

"No, you had every right. I just thought . . ." She stared straight ahead, looking as if she might cry. "I should have known better." They walked a bit more, and then she stopped, facing him with a smile that was clearly forced. "Perhaps we should return," she said.

"I didn't mean to offend you."

"You didn't. You asked a question that I'm not ready to answer. And I shouldn't have come to you until I am."

She started away, but Fotir merely stood there. After a moment Keziah stopped, facing him again.

"I don't want to go back," he said.

She looked so sad, so beautiful. "Neither do I. But I think it's best that we do."

Keziah started walking once more, and Fotir could do nothing but follow, railing at himself for speaking so carelessly. She led him toward the king's camp, but stopped a good distance from Kearney's tent, the same difficult smile on her lips.

"Thank you," she said.

Fotir frowned. "For what?"

She started to answer, then faltered and shook her head. "It's hard to explain. But I'm grateful to you." And stepping forward, she kissed him lightly on the lips. Then she left him, hurrying away without a backward glance.

Grinsa spread out his sleeping roll near where Tavis slept, trying his best to make no noise. He was more weary than he could ever remember being. The day's battle, the search for Kezi, his confrontation with Dusaan—it had all left him utterly spent, as if he had just done a hundred gleanings at one sitting. He needed desperately to sleep, yet he knew that even a full night's rest wouldn't do him much good. Far more than merely being exhausted, he found that he was without hope. As much as he had feared for his sister, he had also known with the certainty of a man facing his own death that tonight's attempt on the Weaver's life was their last best hope of defeating Dusaan and winning this war. Their failure struck at his heart like a blade.

He wasn't certain any longer that the Weaver was more powerful than he was. He had thought so for many turns, but after this night he felt a bit more confident in his own abilities. Not that it mattered. He could have been far stronger than Dusaan, and still his own power would not make up for the sheer number of Qirsi under the Weaver's command. Dusaan commanded an army of over two hundred. Grinsa had a force—if it could be called that—of thirteen. Perhaps a few more of the healers would join them in the end, but while they might number twenty before all was said and done, that still was not enough. Not nearly.

Yes, they had the Eandi warriors, and Grinsa spoke of them to the others as if they might actually balance the coming battle. But he knew they could not. He was a Weaver and so he knew what a wind summoned by so many sorcerers could do to the arrows of even the finest archers. He had healed wounds and burns and mangled limbs, and so he knew what Qirsi fire and shaping power could do to mortal flesh and bone. This war—and again, he wondered if the word was appropriate in this instance—would be quick and brutal. It would be a slaughter.

He should have told Kearney and Sanbira's queen and their soldiers to flee while they still could. Better to make Dusaan hunt them down. Perhaps a series of wars, scattered across the Forelands, would offer them some hope. Perhaps over time, they could whittle away some of the Weaver's army. Then there might be a chance.

But Eandi warriors didn't think this way. They heard Grinsa speak of an army of two hundred Qirsi, and they tried their best to understand what that meant, how much power such a force might wield. But in their hearts, they scoffed at his warnings. They envisioned a puny army being overwhelmed by steel and muscle and courage, failing to realize that they would never get close enough to Dusaan and his servants to pull their blades free, much less fight. Keziah and Fotir and the other Qirsi understood, but though they might have spoken in support of retreat had Grinsa suggested it, their nobles would not have listened. Not now, after all that the Weaver's movement had wrought.

No, the war would be fought on the morrow. And by night-fall every person in these camps would probably be dead.

Grinsa lay down, but he didn't even try to sleep, staring up at the stars and the moons instead.

"You're alive," Tavis said sleepily.

"I didn't mean to wake you."

"It's all right. How's the archminister?"

"She wasn't hurt. The Weaver's still alive."

"I assumed that. You would have woken me had you managed to kill him."

"Probably, yes."

"What's troubling you?"

Everything. We're all going to be killed. "I'm just tired."

"It's more than that." The young lord sat up. "Was he too powerful for you again?"

"No," Grinsa said, his voice flat. "Actually, I got the better of him this time. I couldn't kill him, but I did hurt him."

"Then what's the matter?"

The gleaner shook his head. "Please, Tavis. Let it be."

He closed his eyes, hoping that the boy would lie down and go back to sleep, knowing that he wouldn't.

"You're thinking about tomorrow, aren't you? About the battle?"

The gleaner sighed. "If you must know, yes, I am."

"I've been thinking about it, too."

Something in the way he said this made Grinsa sit up as well, and eye the boy with interest. A year ago he wouldn't have given much consideration to anything Tavis had to say on such a matter. But he had come to appreciate the young lord's insights on all things, even Qirsi magic.

"What have you been thinking?" he asked.

"That it all comes down to numbers. The Weaver isn't any smarter than you are, and despite your doubts, I've never thought that he was any more powerful. But he has far more Qirsi with him."

"Obviously."

"And that led me to a question. It might be foolish, but if it's not, it could be of some help to you."

"What is it?"

Tavis told him, and long after he had spoken the words, Grinsa merely continued to sit there, staring at the boy as if he had suddenly conjured golden flames or made his dark scars disappear.

"Grinsa?" the young lord finally said.

"It's far from a foolish question, Tavis. It's brilliant." He stood. "We have to find the others."

"The others?"

"Kearney, the queen, the other Qirsi. We have to tell them." He smiled, daring to hope for the first time in so long. "You may have just saved us all," he said.

Tavis beamed.

Chapter

Twenty-two

Southeast of the battle plain, the Moorlands, Eibithar

n all probability she had maimed herself for life. There hadn't been time to allow her shoulder and leg to mend themselves properly, and though the bones hadn't broken again as she rode northward, neither had they healed as they should. Evanthya couldn't walk without limping, nor could she move her mangled arm as freely as before. Fetnalla's treachery, which had scored her heart in ways none could see, had also left its mark upon her body.

Still, she had managed to continue her pursuit, following as the woman she loved rode headlong toward her Weaver and his war. Nothing else mattered to her. She knew better than to think that she could turn Fetnalla from the path she was on. Whatever hope she once had of being able to reason with her love, of convincing her that she had erred in casting her lot with the Weaver, had died with the shattering of her shoulder and the snapping of the bone in her leg. She now meant only to stop Fetnalla, even if that meant killing her.

Once they had struck at the conspiracy together, paying the assassin to kill Shurik jal Marcine. Since then, Evanthya had hungered for another opportunity to fight the renegades. Emboldened by their one success, she had imagined herself a warrior of consequence, someone who might tip the balance in the coming war. Not anymore. The fate of the Forelands would be decided by the powerful. Evanthya cared only that Fetnalla not join the Weaver's horde. It wasn't that she thought her love's presence on the battlefield would matter much one way or another, or even that she sought to deny the Weaver as many of his servants as possible. Rather, she knew that history would remember those who had betrayed their realms to fight for the Weaver's dark cause, and she didn't want Fetnalla's name listed among them. In a sense, she wished to save Fetnalla from herself. Already her love was infamous—the traitor who killed Brall, duke of Orvinti, as he marched to break Solkara's siege of Dantrielle. That was bad enough. Evanthya couldn't allow Fetnalla to do more.

She owed Fetnalla that much. Whatever had become of their love, once it had filled her world with light and laughter and passion. That was how she intended to remember Fetnalla.

She rode through heat and hunger and thirst. She rode through pain. Every step of her mount jarred her tender bones, until at times, thundering northward across Eibithar's Moorlands, she felt lost in a haze of agony and was forced to rely on her horse to keep them headed in the right direction. Occasionally she thought she caught a glimpse of Fetnalla in the distance. Often at night, she spied a fire burning ahead of her, a tiny spark of light on the horizon. Sometimes in the morning, as she resumed her pursuit, she found the charred remains of the blaze or a patch of crushed grass where her love had bedded down for the night. These discoveries kept her moving, spurring her on when her body screamed for her to stop.

Fetnalla had to know that she followed still; no one knew

her as well as did her love. Yet Fetnalla made no more effort
to stop Evanthya, nor did she quicken her pace. This, as much
as anything, gave Evanthya some small cause for hope. She
could almost imagine Fetnalla watching for her fires, fearing
their next encounter, yet drawing comfort from her proximity.

And Evanthya had to admit that she preferred it this way as
well. Even had she been able to close the distance between
them, she wasn't sure that she would. Fetnalla had hurt her
badly the last time they faced each other. Who knew what she
would do next time, or what she would force Evanthya to do?
Who could say how it would end? There was more than a little consolation to be found in this uncertainty. At least for a
short while, they both lived knowing that the other was safe
and nearby.

All that had changed late this day, when Evanthya first saw
the thin lines of smoke rising into the sky. It seemed a vast
host was encamped ahead of her. The battle plain. What else
could it be? Surely Fetnalla had seen the fires as well, and
had turned so that she might skirt the edge of the plain and
ride on to join the Weaver. But would she turn west or east?
After considering the matter for only a few moments, Evanthya turned east. Fetnalla would not risk the western course,
where she might be seen by the Eibitharian warriors, a dark
form against the fiery western sky.

Evanthya rode on, even after the sun had set, her eyes fixed
on the north, searching for some sign of her love. When the
small fire jumped to life some distance ahead, she smiled
grimly, steering her horse toward the light as if it were a beacon at sea, and she a lost ship.

It was completely dark by the time she drew near to Fetnalla's blaze. Stars glowed brightly in the night sky, but this
late in the waning the moons were not yet up, and Evanthya
could barely see the ground in front of her. She could see Fetnalla, though, sitting beside her fire, poking at the coals with
a long stick, her face bathed in the warm light. Evanthya dismounted a short distance from the fire and covered the last
bit on foot. A few strides from the fire, she reached for her
sword, only to remember that Fetnalla had shattered it during

their last encounter. She pulled her dagger free instead, continuing forward warily and silently. Or so she thought.

"I've been waiting for you," her love called before Evanthya had reached the circle of light created by the flames.

Evanthya hesitated, unsure of what to say or do.

"Come on, Evanthya. Let me see you." Fetnalla had stood and was peering into the darkness, trying to catch sight of her.

"How do I know you won't try to kill me again?"

"If I'd wanted to kill you, you'd be dead. I healed you, remember? If either of us has murder in her mind, it's most likely you. I'd wager you already have your weapon drawn."

"I don't have shaping magic. I need to protect myself somehow."

"A dagger will do you no good, and you know it. I can break that blade as easily as I did your sword."

"As easily as you did my shoulder and my leg?"

"You gave me no choice, Evanthya! I warned you time and again!"

"Yes, you warned me. And I chose to believe that you wouldn't be able to hurt me, that you loved me too much. It seems I was wrong."

"That's not—" Fetnalla shook her head. "This is ridiculous! Come here where I can see you. I feel like I'm speaking with a wraith."

Evanthya took a long, steadying breath and sheathed her dagger. Then she limped into the firelight, her eyes fixed on her love's face.

Seeing her, Fetnalla let out a small cry, her face contorting with grief and pity. "Look at you!" she whispered. "Look at what you've done to yourself!"

"Done to myself?"

Fetnalla hurried to where Evanthya stood and guided her to a spot beside the fire. "I told you to rest. I warned you that the bones needed time to mend."

Evanthya sat, and Fetnalla knelt before her, placing her hands first on Evanthya's leg, and then on her shoulder, her eyes closed, her brow furrowed in concentration.

"The bones have knitted poorly." She opened her eyes

again, shaking her head. "But they're set now. I don't think there's anything I can do for you."

"I wouldn't want you to, even if you could."

Fetnalla sat back on her heels, her expression hardening, her lips pressed thin so that her mouth was a dark gash on her face. After a moment she stood and walked to the other side of the fire. "You're a stubborn fool."

"Better that than—"

"Don't say it!" Fetnalla said, whirling on her and leveling a rigid finger at her heart.

"Don't say what? That you're a traitor? A murderer?"

"Stop it!"

Evanthya almost said more. But she stopped herself, realizing that no good could come of it. Fetnalla had called her stubborn just a moment before, but the truth was that she, and not Evanthya, had always been the stubborn one. Even under the best of circumstances her love found it next to impossible to admit when she was wrong; she would never do so now.

"You look like you haven't been sleeping," Evanthya said at last, gazing at her across the fire.

Fetnalla shrugged, her arms crossed over her chest. "I sleep well enough."

"I don't. I dream of you every night, and each time, when I wake up alone, I can't get back to sleep."

Her love looked away, though a small smile tugged at the corners of her mouth. "You're lying, but thank you."

"I am not lying."

"Of course you are. In all the time we were together you never dreamed of me. Why would you start now?"

It was true. She never used to dream of Fetnalla, though her love claimed to dream of her often. Fetnalla had teased her about it for years. But it was equally true that Evanthya had dreamed of her several times since last they spoke, dark visions in which her love shattered her bones one by one, while a shadowy figure—the Weaver, no doubt—stood nearby, laughing.

"I'm afraid for you." *I'm afraid of you.*

Fetnalla's smile vanished. "And I'm afraid for you. You should leave here, Evanthya. Tonight. If the Weaver finds you, he'll kill you. He knows that you'll never join his movement, and so he sees you as a threat, not only to me, but to him as well, and to everything for which we've worked."

"I can't just run away. You know me better than that. I hate him and all that he's done to this land. I have to fight him."

"Then you have to fight me."

Her shoulder began to throb at the mere thought of it.

Fetnalla walked to her mount, reached into the leather bag hanging from her saddle, and pulled out a small pouch.

"You must be hungry," she said. "I don't have much—some hard bread and cheese—but you're welcome to it."

"What about you?"

"I've eaten already." She smiled sadly. "And before long, I'll either be able to get all the food I need, or it won't matter what I have left."

Evanthya was famished, and after a moment she stood, stepped around the fire, and took the food. Sitting, she began to eat, shoving bread and cheese into her mouth as quickly as she could, barely chewing one mouthful before taking another.

"You're going to make yourself sick eating that way."

She forced herself to stop, closing her eyes and slowly chewing what she had taken.

"Have some of this," Fetnalla said, handing her a skin of water.

"Thank you."

"When was the last time you ate?"

"I don't know. It's been a day or two."

"Evanthya!"

"You didn't stop. How could I?"

"You're mad!"

"I thought I was a 'stubborn fool.'"

"You're all of that, and more. You should have just let me go."

"Is that what you would have done had it been me?"

Fetnalla straightened. "Yes."

"I don't believe you," Evanthya said, grinning.

"I wouldn't have starved myself, and I certainly wouldn't have . . ." She looked Evanthya up and down, her gaze lingering on Evanthya's crippled shoulder. "You've sacrificed too much."

"I've suffered less than others."

Fetnalla opened her mouth as if to argue, then stopped herself and just shook her head.

Evanthya took another bite or two of bread and a few sips of water. Then she handed the food and skin back to Fetnalla. Hungry as she had been, she filled up quickly.

"Don't you want more?"

"Not now. I'm grateful to you, though."

Fetnalla returned the pouch and skin to her bag before facing Evanthya once again.

"What are we going to do?" she asked, firelight shining in her pale eyes. "I don't want to fight you, and I know better than to think that I can turn you to the Weaver's cause."

"You could come away with me."

Her beloved frowned. "This is no joke, Evanthya."

"I know that. Leave here with me tonight."

"Impossible. I'm a murderer, remember? I'm a traitorous minister who killed her duke. That's what the Eandi will say. I can't ever go back to Aneira."

"Then we'll go somewhere else. Wethyrn or Caerisse or Sanbira. We can join the prelates on Aylsa for all I care. As long as we're away from the Weaver and his war." She swallowed, trying not to cry. "As long as we're together."

"You're serious, aren't you?"

"I am."

"A moment ago you said that you had to fight the Weaver. That you hated him too much to run away from this war."

"My love for you is stronger by far than my hatred of the Weaver."

"You'd leave Tebeo? You'd give up your service to Dantrielle?"

She nodded. "If it meant being with you."

Fetnalla smiled at her, the tender, loving smile Evanthya recalled from so long ago, before they had ever heard of the Weaver and his conspiracy. Tears glistened on Fetnalla's cheeks and she wiped them away. "I'd like that very much."

"Then come with me."

"It's not that easy."

"It can be."

"No, it can't. The Weaver—"

"Forget about the Weaver!"

She shook her head, tears flying from her face. "You don't understand! He'll think that I betrayed him. He walks in my dreams, Evanthya. He can find me anywhere and kill me in my sleep."

A comment leaped to mind, another barb about the Weaver's cruelty and Fetnalla's willingness to follow him in spite of it. But Evanthya kept this to herself.

Instead she asked, her voice as gentle as possible, "Are you certain that he would? Are you that important to him? Or is it possible that after this final war, should he survive, he won't care enough to come after you?"

She feared that Fetnalla might take offense, but her love merely stared at her. "I don't know," she said. "I suppose it's possible."

"What choice do we have, Fetnalla? If we remain here, either you'll have to kill me or I'll have to kill you. Failing that, one of us is likely to die. Is that what you want? For one of us to be alone for the rest of her days? Wouldn't it be better to take this chance? At least we'd be together, with a chance at a new life. If the Weaver finds us, so be it, but at least we'd have some hope."

"You make it sound so simple."

"I'm not as foolish as you think I am. I'm not saying that escape will be easy. Merely the choice." She grinned. "That is, if you don't mind living out your days with a cripple."

She meant it to be humorous, but abruptly Fetnalla was bawling, tears coursing down her face.

"I'm so sorry," she managed to say, her body quaking with her sobs. "Hurting you that way . . . That was the worst thing I've ever done."

Evanthya should have gone to her. She should have taken Fetnalla in her arms and told her that she was forgiven, that all she cared about was being with her, that none of the rest mattered. She wanted to, yet she couldn't bring herself to move her feet. For the first time, it dawned on her that she might not be able to love this woman anymore. She was still in love with the Fetnalla she knew a year ago, before any of this began, but could she ever really trust her again? She was in love with an idea, a memory. For as long as she lived, she would be. But for the rest of her life, she would also remember the sound of her bones shattering, the pain tearing through her shoulder like a battle-ax. How could she ever love someone who had assaulted her? Yes, Fetnalla had healed her bones, but for all her talents with such magic, her love couldn't mend the wound on Evanthya's heart.

"You were angry," Evanthya offered, feeling that she had to say something.

"That doesn't justify it."

"No, it doesn't."

Fetnalla's sobbing began to subside. "Can you forgive me?"

Evanthya stared down at the fire. "I don't know," she admitted. "I want to try."

"But you speak of going away with me. How can we do that if you can't forgive what I've done?"

"I'm sure I can with time."

"But—"

"Can't we just go? It's harder with the Weaver so close and war in the air all around us. We'll leave here together, go someplace safe. Everything will be better then."

But Evanthya could feel her hope slipping away. For just an instant she had believed that this might work, that Fetnalla would go with her, that they could escape the darkness that was blanketing all the Forelands. Not anymore. The moment had passed, and once more she found herself face-to-face with an enemy she loved, a lover she could never trust again.

It seemed that Fetnalla sensed this as well. "It sounds nice," she said quietly.

For some time neither of them spoke. A soft wind blew across the grasses, and an owl called from far off, sounding ghostlike and lonely.

"Do you remember the first night we . . . we lay together?" Fetnalla asked, breaking the silence.

"Of course I do."

"You told me that you'd gone to Dantrielle hoping to join the Festival, that you'd never intended to serve in an Eandi court."

"It was true. I never did intend it. But I feel fortunate to have found my way to Tebeo's castle."

"I know you do. But I never felt that way about my life in Orvinti."

"I don't believe you. You always told me that serving Brall—"

"I know what I told you. And I'm telling you now that it wasn't true. I wanted it to be. I always hoped that someday I'd be as content serving my duke as you were serving yours. But it never happened, and then he started growing suspicious of me."

She stared at Fetnalla, fighting back tears she couldn't explain. "Why are you telling me this?"

"Because I want you to understand." She held up a hand, silencing Evanthya before she could speak. "I know it doesn't excuse what I've done. But even before I joined the Weaver's movement, I was unhappy in my life as a minister. I thought you should know that."

Evanthya shook her head. "I don't know what you want me to say."

"I don't want you to say anything. I'm just . . ." She trailed off, a puzzled look on her face. She was looking past Evanthya, her eyes narrowed, as if she were straining to see something in the darkness beyond the firelight. "You . . ." she whispered.

Before Evanthya could turn and look for herself, she heard a footfall just behind her, light and sure, and far too close.

He hadn't expected the Weaver to walk in his dreams again. They had spoken only a few days before, and the Weaver had told him then all that he needed to know. War was at hand. In another few days they would meet on the battle plain and the Weaver would reach for his magic—mists and winds as well as shaping. He would have to be prepared for this. He would have to open his mind to the Weaver's power. This was no time for any Qirsi in his army to be hesitant, or to resist the Weaver in any way.

All this and more the Weaver had explained to Pronjed the last time they spoke. The archminister understood perfectly. He might have made some mistakes during his service to the movement—he still shuddered to think of how close the Weaver had come to killing him after he decided on his own to murder the king of Aneira, whom he had served—but Pronjed was determined not to fail on the battle plain. By good fortune and the Weaver's mercy, he remained a chancellor in the movement, which meant that he would likely be one of the Weaver's nobles once the Eandi were defeated and Qirsi ruled the Forelands. He had no intention of squandering his claim to nobility. He had pushed himself to the limits of his endurance and now he was within a day's ride of where the Eandi armies had gathered, and only two days' journey from joining the Weaver's company.

Which was why he had been so surprised to find himself walking the familiar plain again soon after falling asleep only two nights after the previous dream. This time the Weaver didn't force him to climb that torturous incline, or even to wait for his appearance. Pronjed opened his mind's eye to the dream, and there was the Weaver, framed by the familiar radiant light.

"Weaver—"

"We've spoken before of the woman from Orvinti, the first minister."

"Yes, Weaver. I remember."

"She follows you still. She's but a day's ride behind you. I want you to find her."

"Of course, Weaver. Is she in danger?"

"Not as you mean, but yes. There was a task I wished her to complete, and she's failed, to the peril of us all."

"Are you certain?" he asked, without thinking. He knew of this task. She was to kill Evanthya ja Yispar, Dantrielle's first minister, who had also been her lover. The last time Pronjed saw Fetnalla, she had been waiting for Evanthya on the Moors of Durril, intent on doing the Weaver's bidding though clearly the very notion of it pained her deeply. Still,

Pronjed should have known better than to question the Weaver's word. As soon as he spoke, he regretted it, wincing in anticipation of punishment.

It never came. Fortunately, the Weaver appeared to understand his response. "I believe she wanted to succeed, but her love for the woman overmastered her judgment. She rode north from Aneira without having killed the minister, and she allowed herself to be followed."

Again, Pronjed wanted to ask how the Weaver could be certain of this, not because he doubted that it was true, but rather because he longed to understand better the power this man wielded. He kept silent, however, knowing how dangerous it would be to question the Weaver a second time.

"When I reached for the one to enter her dreams," the Weaver said, apparently reading his thoughts, "I sensed the presence of the other."

"They're together?"

"No, though the distance between them is little enough for the minister to know that the other pursues her."

Pronjed couldn't help thinking that Fetnalla's love for the woman had to be powerful indeed to make her defy the Weaver in this way. "Is it possible that Dantrielle's minister might still be turned to our cause? If they love each other that much . . ."

"Were that possible, they'd be together. No, the woman from Dantrielle is determined to stop her, perhaps even to oppose the movement. She must be killed."

"I understand, Weaver."

"You may have to fight both of them. Fetnalla couldn't kill her. She may be relieved to have this task fall to you. But it's also possible that she'll try to stop you. Like you, she's a shaper. Her other powers are of no consequence. The other woman has language of beasts and mists, but nothing that can harm you."

"Very well. Where do you want me to do this?"

"Fetnalla should come within sight of the Eandi encampment tomorrow, and when Dantrielle's first minister sees how close she is to the battle plain, she'll make every effort to catch up to her. You shouldn't have to journey far to find them."

"I'll see to this, Weaver. I give you my word that Dantrielle's first minister will never live to see your victory."

"Good," the Weaver said.

Pronjed expected the dream to end then. But the Weaver seemed to hesitate.

"I don't want you to use magic, if you don't have to," the man said at last.

"Weaver?"

"I want any who find the minister's body to think this the work of Eandi soldiers. There will be enough killing of Qirsi by Qirsi on the battle plain. Fetnalla will know the truth, of course, but the rest need not know that we had to kill this woman. Do you understand?"

"Yes, Weaver."

"Ride north when she's dead, with Fetnalla if at all possible."

An instant later, Pronjed awoke.

That was the previous night. As the Weaver predicted, Fetnalla appeared on the southern horizon this very day, just as the sun began its descent into the west. Pronjed marked her progress northward, but made certain to keep out of sight. He watched her stop for the evening and make camp, and, soon after darkness fell, he heard a second rider approaching, drawn to her fire as if a moth.

He watched the two women together and could see how powerfully they were drawn to one another. He strained to hear their conversation and was able to make out most of it. At first, he believed that they might leave the plain together and he struggled with himself, unsure of what he would do. Surely these two, if they fled, intending to make a new life for themselves elsewhere in the Forelands, were no threat to the Weaver and his movement. But would the Weaver view them that way, or would he see such a choice on Pronjed's part as yet another failure, and reason to deny him a place of honor in the new world he was shaping?

To the archminister's profound relief, it was not a decision he was forced to make. Within moments the women abandoned their plans, perhaps sensing, as he did, that the Weaver would find them no matter where they went. Or maybe they realized that all that divided them from each other had grown too powerful to be overcome.

Whatever the reason, he took this latest turn in their conversation as an indication that the time had come to act. He started forward as stealthily as possible, circling their fire until he was directly behind Evanthya. He pulled his sword free as he crept toward them, sliding the blade free of its sheath slowly and silently. Neither of the women appeared to take any notice of him at all, and within moments he was close enough to hear the settling of the embers in their fire and to see the tears on Fetnalla's face.

He was close enough to have killed Evanthya with his magic, but the Weaver had made his wishes quite clear, and so Pronjed crept closer. At last Fetnalla did see him, faltering in what she had been saying and straining to recognize the shadowy form lurking behind her love, but by then he was close enough.

"You," the minister said, catching a glimpse of his face, and alerting Evanthya to his presence.

He saw her begin to turn, but he didn't give her the chance to ward herself. His heart suddenly pounding in his chest— was it fear, or the exhilaration of the kill?—he drew back his weapon, and plunged it into her back.

Fetnalla saw Pronjed pull his arm back, saw as well his sword glinting in the firelight. Then he struck at her love. Evanthya's back arched violently, her mouth opening in a sharp, abbreviated cry, and the blade burst from her chest, gleaming still, stained crimson.

They remained in that pose for what seemed a lifetime, Evanthya's eyes wide and raised to Morna's darkened sky, Pronjed lurking at her shoulder like some demon sent by Bian himself, his teeth bared, his free hand gripping her neck. Fetnalla wanted to scream. She wanted to run to Evanthya's side and free her from the archminister's grasp. But she couldn't move, she couldn't even make a sound. All around them was silence and blackness, as if all the world were holding its breath.

Then it seemed that the world exhaled. Pronjed pulled his sword free, allowing Evanthya to topple to the ground. Somehow Fetnalla shook off her stupor and rushed to her love's side.

"Why did you do that?" she screamed at Pronjed, her vision clouded with tears and grief and rage.

"The Weaver commanded it of me. I'm sorry."

It made sense, of course. Surely the Weaver knew that she had failed to kill Evanthya on the Moors of Durril. No doubt he knew that she would never be able to fulfill her oath to him.

"Fetnalla?"

Her love's voice sounded so weak. A growing circle of blood stained the center of her riding cloak. Her eyes were glazed, as if she were half asleep.

"Yes, I'm here," Fetnalla whispered.

"Who was it? Who killed me?"

Fetnalla looked up at Pronjed briefly, then placed a finger lightly on Evanthya's lips.

"Shhh. I can heal you," she said, not at all certain that she really could.

Pronjed stepped farther into the firelight. "Please don't, First Minister. If you do, I'll have no choice but to kill you as well."

"I don't care."

She placed her hand over Evanthya's bloody wound, but her love put her own hand over Fetnalla's, shaking her head with an effort that seemed to steal her breath.

"Don't, Fetnalla. It's too late."

She choked back a sob. "No, it's not! It can't be!"

"First Minister, please," Pronjed said. "Don't make me do this."

"You want me to just let her die?"

"How else was this going to end? Did you really think that the two of you could find some way to end this war? Or did you intend to go your separate ways, thinking that the Weaver would accept that? Evanthya had to die, and since you couldn't kill her, I did."

"No," she said, shaking her head. She looked down at Evanthya again. There still might be time. Her love's breathing had slowed so much it was difficult even to see the rise and fall of her breast. Yet she was alive, and so might be saved. But wasn't it easier this way? She would never have found the strength to kill Evanthya herself. That Pronjed had done it for her was a blessing of sorts, a gift, to both of them really. And so, despite her tears, despite the voice within her mind that screamed for her to do something—anything—to save the woman she loved, despite the grief that struck at her own heart, as if Pronjed's sword had pierced her flesh as well, she didn't draw upon her healing magic. She merely knelt beside Evanthya, sobbing until her throat ached, watching her love's life bleed away.

"Fetnalla," Evanthya said again, barely able to make herself heard.

Fetnalla leaned close to her, tears falling from her face and darkening Evanthya's cloak like rain. "I'm right beside you."

"Don't let him win. The Weaver. Don't let him."

"You shouldn't worry about him. You shouldn't worry about any of it. We'll go away. Just you and me, just like we talked about."

"Look what he's done to me, Fetnalla. He can't win. He'll do this to everything."

She bent and kissed her love's lips, which were as cold as mountain water. "Hush," she said. "Save your strength."

"No. My strength. Is for you. Fight him."

Somehow, Evanthya managed to take Fetnalla's hand in her own. The pressure of her fingers was so light that Fetnalla hardly felt it at all. Yet she sensed that Evanthya was squeezing with all her might.

"My strength to you," she murmured.

"My love," Fetnalla whispered, kissing Evanthya's brow.

She made no reply.

"Evanthya?"

Fetnalla stared down at her. Evanthya's eyes were still open, but her breast rose no more, and her hand had gone limp. Fetnalla kissed that hand, crying still, gazing at her love's face. It remained just as she remembered from the day they met, her skin as smooth as a child's, the small lines around her mouth making it seem that she was ready to break into a smile at any moment. After some time, Fetnalla let the hand fall, and closed her love's eyes. She wiped her tears, but they wouldn't stop.

At last, she looked up at Pronjed. He stood a short distance from her, still holding his sword, eyeing her warily.

"I'm sorry," he said. "Truly I am. But the Weaver . . ."

"Yes," she said. "The Weaver."

"I was prepared to let the two of you go, if it had come to that."

"The Weaver wouldn't have been so generous. He'd have found us, and he probably would have punished you, as well."

"I'd like to sheath my sword."

"I'm a shaper, Pronjed. If I wanted to avenge her, your sword wouldn't stop me."

"I'm a shaper, too. You should know that."

Fetnalla climbed to her feet, shaking her head. "We're not going to fight," she said, and meant it.

Pronjed might have struck the killing blow, but Evanthya's blood wasn't on his hands any more than it was on hers. Or any less. Hadn't she chosen not to save her? Didn't that make her as responsible as Pronjed for Evanthya's murder? In the end, neither of them had much choice. The Weaver had made it clear some time ago that he wanted Evanthya dead. Both she and Pronjed were merely following his commands. *Don't let him win.*

She crossed her arms over her chest, shivering in the night air. "As you said, how else was this going to end?"

"Thank you for understanding," he said, returning his blade to its sheath. "I was hoping that you and I would ride north together."

Fetnalla found that she was staring at Evanthya again. She hadn't meant to. In fact, she tried to look at anything other than her beloved's body, but she couldn't help herself. "North," she repeated absently.

"Yes. To join with the Weaver's army. He's expecting us.

We ride to war tomorrow, First Minister. Surely you knew that."

She nodded. Tomorrow. Yes, she had assumed that it would be soon. It might as well be tomorrow.

"I think we should leave here," Pronjed said.

She was still doing it. Staring at Evanthya. Shouldn't they have built her a pyre? Didn't her love deserve that much?

"First Minister? Fetnalla."

It was her name that reached through the haze in her mind. She tore her eyes from Evanthya's face and looked at the archminister. He was watching her, concern written on his bony features.

"You should saddle your horse," he told her, "and gather whatever you need to take with you. I'll . . . I'll see to the rest."

Somewhere, deep in her mind, a small voice cried out in protest. Who was this man to give her orders? Who was he to offer his sympathy and his friendship? But she hadn't the will to resist. She stepped to where her saddle lay, put it on her steed, and began to fasten the straps. Once it was secured, she turned, glancing about her camp, feeling that surely she was forgetting something. All she saw, however, was Evanthya, blood staining her cloak, firelight warming her cheek.

After several moments, Pronjed returned, frowning as he glanced back into the darkness.

"Do you have language of beasts?" he asked.

"No. Evanthya did."

"I can't get her horse to leave or come with me. It just stands there. Could you—?"

"No. As long as she's here, he'll stay just where he is."

"Someone may see it."

Fetnalla glanced at Evanthya, then quickly made herself look away. "It can't be helped."

"No, I suppose it can't." He hesitated. Then, "Are you ready?"

She nodded and swung herself onto her horse, refusing now to gaze at her love.

"We're part of a great cause, First Minister," Pronjed said gently, as if he might comfort her with such words. "We're going to change the world. Some, I'm afraid, simply weren't ready for the future the Weaver has envisioned."

Hadn't she told herself much the same thing several times since leaving Aneira? Since murdering Brall? Evanthya could never understand all that the Weaver had given to Fetnalla and others devoted to his cause. She could never embrace the true meaning of the Weaver's movement. Her view of the world was too narrow, too strongly tied to old notions of loyalty and service. Each time Fetnalla considered what it might mean to kill her love, that was how she justified it.

My strength to you, Evanthya had said, as the life bled from her body. Then why did Fetnalla feel so terribly weak?

Chapter

Twenty-three

City of Kings, Eibithar

resenne held Bryntelle in her arms, watching the morning dawn from the ramparts atop Audun's Castle. A light wind sweeping down off the Caerissan Steppe rustled the pennons above them. The eastern sky glowed pink and orange, like the flames conjured this past night by the sorcerers who came to the castle.

The Revel was in the City of Kings, chased south from the coastal cities by invasion and war. Usually the festival would be in Thorald now, having arrived there from Galdasten. But with the Braedony invasion, the performers had fled across the Moorlands to the safety of the City of Kings. Here they had remained for the better part of a turn, awaiting word that the invaders had been repelled so that they might resume their journeys across Eibithar.

It seemed the people of the city had grown weary of the performances, for last night the fire sorcerers and tumblers had come to the castle, where they performed for the queen and those soldiers who had remained behind when Kearney marched to war. For Cresenne, who remained a prisoner in the castle, and who had spent countless nights in solitude, walking the corridors of the fortress or the empty paths of the castle gardens, the performers provided a welcome diversion. For Bryntelle, they were a spectacle.

The babe squealed with delight at every somersault turned by the tumblers. She stared with rapt attention at the hands of the Qirsi, watching as flames of gold and red, blue and purple, orange and green crept over their skin. She grinned, wide-eyed and enthralled, at the songs of bards and pipers. Most nights, the child napped at least once, usually twice. She hadn't slept at all this night. Long after the performers left the castle, she continued to laugh and coo.

For Cresenne the night was spoiled only by the appearance of a face from her past. While holding Bryntelle so that the baby could see one of the bards, she spied a bald, fat Qirsi standing near the other musicians. She recognized the man immediately. Altrin jal Casson, one of the gleaners with whom she had worked in Curgh just over a year ago, when she first met Grinsa and began plotting the murder of Kentigern's Lady Brienne. Seeing him, she quickly turned away, so as to hide her face. Bryntelle, of course, began to cry, because she could no longer see the singer, and thus drew more attention to her. When Cresenne faced the musician again, Trin had vanished. She didn't see him again for the rest of the night. But she suspected that he had noticed her and remembered, and she dreaded having to speak with him. He had been kind to her during their brief friendship, but the Revel was a small community, and she had little doubt that he had heard of her betrayal.

With the sky brightening and the castle beginning to wake, Cresenne knew that she should return to her quarters and sleep. As long as the Weaver still lived she needed to take her rest during the day. But like Bryntelle, she was wide awake, her mind alive with visions from the previous night. So she remained where she was, watching the sun rise, feeling the air grow warmer.

It had been several days since she last spoke with Grinsa. No doubt he was occupied with other matters—for all she knew he and the Weaver had already met in battle. She shuddered at the thought. Her magic ran no deeper than that of most other Qirsi, but she felt that if Grinsa had died, she'd have sensed it somehow. This was what she chose to believe, what she would continue to believe until she heard tidings to the contrary.

She thought it likely that he knew how difficult it was for her to have him in her mind, to feel his caresses and kisses in that way. He was brilliant and he knew her better than did any other man she had ever known. He couldn't have helped but notice how, in the aftermath of the Weaver's last assault, she shied from his touch. Cresenne was desperate to believe that all this would change when they were truly together and he could hold her in his powerful arms. The Weaver had violated her mind far more than her body. Perhaps when Grinsa could touch her without having to enter her dreams she would rediscover her passion for him. But until then, until she knew for certain that the Weaver was dead, she preferred that Grinsa didn't disturb her sleep, though this meant having no word from him at all.

At last, as the sun began to grow hot against her face, and the night guards, weary and bored, were replaced by rested men, Cresenne carried Bryntelle to the nearest of the tower stairways and descended to the lower corridor, intending to eat a small breakfast and then return to their quarters.

Before she reached the kitchen, however, she saw a familiar form walking toward her, a warm smile on his round face.

"Cresenne ja Terba," Trin said, opening his arms in greeting. "I thought it was you last night, though I thought I'd inquire of the soldiers before I approached you."

She smiled in spite of herself and allowed him to embrace her.

"And who is this lovely young lady?"

"Her name is Bryntelle."

Trin regarded her for a moment, his yellow eyes dancing. "Bryntelle ja . . . ?"

Cresenne had to laugh. How could anyone be so transparent? "Bryntelle ja Grinsa," she said.

The fat man grinned. "Ah! I thought so. I always knew that the two of you were destined for one another. I believe I told you so at the time."

"Yes, you did, much to Grinsa's embarrassment."

"The boy needed a push, that's all." He looked at the baby again. "She's quite beautiful. Not that I'm surprised, mind you."

"Thank you."

"Where were you off to?" he asked. "I'll walk with you."

"Actually, we were on our way to the kitchen."

"Better still!" he said brightly. "I've already eaten, but I've never been one to refuse a meal." He patted his ample belly. "Particularly a free one."

Again she laughed. Trin was just as she remembered, and though she had dreaded this encounter, she already found herself grateful for his companionship.

They walked to the kitchen and then sat eating a small breakfast. All the while, Trin regaled her with tales of the Revel, describing for her the public humiliations and private indiscretions of seemingly every Qirsi and Eandi in the festival. Some of the names she recognized from her days as a gleaner, others she didn't, but she had to admit that she found all of it quite entertaining. Bryntelle appeared to as well, laughing every time Cresenne did, and smiling at this strange bald man who told such clever stories. It occurred to Cresenne that the child had never heard her mother laugh so often or so loudly. That, as much as anything, may have been what the babe found so amusing.

At last, Trin ran out of tales, or at least chose to make it seem so. He stared at her, his smile slowly fading, a kindly look in his eyes.

"So tell me, cousin, how is it you've come to live in Audun's Castle?"

It was a polite question, but likely an unnecessary one. A

man with Trin's penchant for gathering information about others could hardly have spent so much time in the City of Kings without hearing talk of the Qirsi traitor living under Kearney's protection.

"I think you know."

He tipped his head, conceding the point. "Word travels the streets. But what's Grinsa's connection with all of this? The last I saw of him, he was searching for you. He accused me of aiding the conspiracy, and even struck me."

Her eyes widened. "He didn't! When was this?"

"Long ago, at Kearney's investiture. I forgave him, of course. Had I been so in love with you, and so desperate to find you, I might have done the same. Still, for a man such as myself, who makes a point of knowing as much as possible about the affairs of others, it was rather confusing."

"I can imagine." She looked at Bryntelle, smoothing the wisps of white hair that covered her head. "There's so much to explain, Trin, much of it too painful or too humiliating to tell. It's enough to say that our love affair began as a seduction and deception."

"You were acting on the conspiracy's behalf."

"Yes."

"And that's why you fled."

She nodded.

"Where did Grinsa find you?"

Cresenne smiled. "I found him, just before Bryntelle was born."

"I see. And how is it that our friend, the Revel gleaner, has become guardian to a disgraced lord and an advisor to kings?"

Once more, she shifted her gaze to the child. "He's a wise man, Trin. And he's somewhat more than he first appears."

"That tells me nothing."

"Still, it's all I can say. I'm sorry."

He laid a meaty hand over hers. "No need for apologies, my dear. I offer none for my prying—you should give none for telling me that it's none of my concern." He grinned, for just a moment, then grew serious again. "Tell me, though, what does the future hold for you?"

Cresenne shrugged, her stomach balling itself into a fist. "Who can say? If the W—" She looked up to find Trin eyeing her intently. "If the conspiracy wins this war, I'm probably a corpse. If it can be defeated . . ." She made a small gesture with her hands, unsure of what to say. "I suppose this is my future."

"Do they treat you well, these Eandi who call you traitor behind your back?"

"How do you—?"

"I told you: word travels. Do they?"

"Well enough."

"Do you trust them to keep you safe?"

"I trust . . ." She had intended to say that she trusted Grinsa to keep her safe, but that would have raised more questions than it answered. "I trust myself."

Trin smiled. "Well, good for you. I wish I had your strength, cousin." He leaned closer to her. "Just the same, take a word of caution from an old, fat Qirsi who trusts no one, himself least of all. Be watchful. I know that there have been attempts on your life, though some of what I've heard I don't quite understand. And I expect, from what I've been told, that there may be others. Kearney's guards have grown somewhat lax with the Revel in their city. I walked in here today with little trouble—the soldiers at the gate hardly gave me a second look." A mischievous grin lit his face for just an instant. "Though I gave them several. I do love a man in armor." Just as quickly as it had appeared, his smile vanished, leaving the old gleaner grim and earnest. "My point is this: if I can come and go as I please, so can other Qirsi with darker intentions. Be careful, cousin. Now that we've renewed our friendship, I'm loath to see it end prematurely."

She just stared back at him. Notwithstanding her brave words a moment before, she felt frightened and terribly small. She wanted to rail at the guards for their laziness, but she knew that would do her no good. And already another thought had entered her mind. Some time ago she had spoken with the queen—a chance encounter in the gardens. Leilia told her that if she needed anything, she had only to ask for it.

Cresenne had been reluctant to request anything of the woman, assuming that the queen had long since forgotten their conversation. But perhaps in this case she could best serve herself and her child by being a bit brash.

"I'll see to it," she said at last. "Thank you, Trin."

He raised an eyebrow. "You'll see to it? Now I am impressed. I wonder if Grinsa knows just what he's gotten himself into."

Funny that this strange man should find it so easy to make her laugh, even when it seemed that she was threatened from all sides.

"Right now, I'm sure that I'm the least of his worries," she said.

"I don't claim to know the man very well, cousin," Trin told her, patting her hand. "But I expect you're wrong about that."

It was long past time for Bryntelle to sleep, so Cresenne walked Trin to the castle gate, bade him farewell, and asked, in all sincerity, that he come to see her again when he could find the time.

"Finding the time is a simple matter, my dear. The other gleaners know me too well to expect me to do much work, and I seldom disappoint them."

Still smiling from this last quip, still intending to approach the queen later, after they had slept, Cresenne made her way back to her chamber, singing softly to Bryntelle, who was nearly asleep by the time they turned into their corridor.

So it was that Cresenne didn't notice the Qirsi woman lurking by her door until she was almost upon her.

The stranger's clothes were worn and travel-stained. She wore her white hair short, so that it framed her round, pretty face. From the lines around her mouth and eyes and her bent back and rounded shoulders, Cresenne guessed that she was in her late thirties, old for a Qirsi. She had her arms crossed over her chest, and her expression was solemn and wary. But it was the woman's eyes that drew Cresenne's attention. They were deep gold, like a merchant's coins, and they reminded her strongly of the Weaver's.

"Cresenne ja Terba?" the woman asked.

Cresenne halted, sensing that she was in danger. "Who are you?"

The woman opened her mouth to reply, but then lunged at her, brandishing a dagger that she had held hidden within her sleeve. Cresenne tried to jump away, but the stranger moved with speed and grace that belied her aged appearance. She tried to ward herself, but she would have had to drop Bryntelle to do so. In the end, she was helpless to do more than watch as her attacker hammered the blade into her heart. Pain blinded her, stole her breath, her strength. Somehow she was on her back, struggling to remain conscious. She heard Bryntelle crying, realized that she no longer held the baby in her arms. But she could do nothing. She felt the life gushing from her body, staining her clothes and the stone floor. Gods it was cold. Bryntelle. Grinsa. How could she have failed them both this way? How could she have let the Weaver win?

She had journeyed eastward in secret, resting by day, moving in stealth through the nights.

"No one will know you," the Weaver had told her one night more than a turn before. "No one will think to stop you. You'll be able to go anywhere you choose, anywhere I tell you. You will be a walking wraith."

And so she was. Once she had been first minister of Mertesse, one of Aneira's proud houses. Now she was a pale shadow, invisible to the world around her. Bereft of her mount, her beloved Pon, she had been forced to travel the entire distance—more than sixty leagues—on foot. More than once, she had nearly given in to her fatigue, knowing that she was too old and too weak. She had to steal what food she could find, or forage for it off the land like some wild creature. But she persevered, drawing on resources she hadn't known she possessed, driven in equal measure by her grief for Shurik, which lingered still even after so many turns, and by the Weaver's promise, offered to her in the shadow of Kentigern Tor. When those nearly failed her as well, and her strength withered in the face of hunger and the mere fact of her physical limitations, she found, much to her surprise, one last source of strength: pride.

She might not have been the most valued of the Weaver's servants, nor the most powerful, even when the magic still flowed freely through her body. But he had trusted her, Yaella ja Banvel, to see this matter to its end, and she refused to fail.

"I have a task for you," he said that night in her dream, as the siege of Kentigern wore on and she recovered from her injuries. "A dangerous task. I can't say for certain that you'll survive, even if you succeed. But you will be doing a great service to the cause we share, and I believe that you'll find peace before you die."

She had been frightened of course. How could she not be, speaking to the Weaver of her own mortality? But she was exhilarated as well, eager to fulfill this destiny he had seen for her.

"There is a woman, a traitor to our cause," he said, and then spoke the name. "Cresenne ja Terba. She is as dear to Grinsa jal Arriet as Shurik was to you, perhaps even more so, for she bore him a child. I want you to kill her."

Yaella had never thought of herself as vengeful, but she was drawn to the notion that she might strike back at this other Weaver who had taken Shurik from her. In the end, with her magic a mere shadow of what it once had been, and her body little more, she had reached the City of Kings because the Weaver managed to give purpose to her life once more. Grief had consumed her; this quest for revenge had restored her, at least long enough.

She had expected all along that gaining entry to Audun's Castle would be the greatest challenge of all, a formidable test of her cunning. When at last she saw the City of Kings from her hiding place along the slope of the Caerissan Steppe, its massive walls gleaming in the late-day sun, the great towers of the fortress rising into a sky of brilliant blue, Yaella quailed, wondering how she could ever hope to get past such massive battlements and the soldiers guarding them. Still she went on, covering the remaining distance during the night and passing through the city gates when they opened in the morning. Only then, as she entered the city and saw the grand tents of Eibithar's famous Revel, did she begin to believe that the gods might be with her in this endeavor, watching over her and the Weaver's cause.

When night fell, she slipped into the castle with ease, following a small group of Qirsi performers and stepping past the guards with a confident smile and a nodded greeting, as if there were no question but that she belonged there.

The Weaver had told her where she could find the woman's bedchamber. How he knew this, she couldn't say, but she followed his instructions and waited by her door, knowing from all the Weaver had told her that the traitor would return to the chamber with first light.

"The woman sleeps during the day, so great is her fear of me," he said. "You will show her that she can't escape her fate so easily."

Yaella remained in the shadows by the woman's chamber for some time, struggling to slow her racing heart, fearing that she would be discovered by a guard or one of the queen's ladies. The night ended and morning broke over the royal city, and still she waited, until she began to fear that somehow she had reached the chamber too late, and that the woman was already within, asleep behind a locked door. When she tried the door handle, however, her hand trembling, she found that the chamber was unlocked. Peering inside, she saw no one. Had the Weaver been wrong about the location of the woman's chamber? Had Yaella taken too long to reach the City of Kings? Had the woman left Audun's Castle? She was nearly ready to leave the corridor, although she wasn't certain where she would go next, when at last she heard someone approaching, light footsteps echoing softly in the nearby stairway.

A moment later the woman came into view.

The Weaver had told Yaella of Cresenne's beauty, even confessing to her during her extraordinary dream that he had once thought to make this woman his queen. So she was prepared for that. Yaella wasn't prepared, however, for just how young the woman appeared. Seeing Cresenne approach, Yaella's resolve wavered, albeit for only a moment. Still, when she allowed herself to be seen and spoke the woman's name, Yaella was shaking in every limb. The Weaver had wanted her to announce to Cresenne that he was responsible for her murder, as if the woman could have doubted such a thing.

"This is what becomes of those who betray the Weaver and his cause," she was supposed to say, before striking the killing blow. But it had been all she could do just to say the woman's name aloud; she couldn't bring herself to say more. Instead she just leaped at her, moving faster and more nimbly than she had imagined she could.

For a moment, after Cresenne fell, Yaella could only stand there, staring down at her, watching the blood flow from her heart, like a dark river in flood. Then the sound of the child's crying reached her and with it yet another memory from her last encounter with the Weaver.

"I don't want the child harmed," he said. A small grace, for she was certain that she could never have killed a babe, no matter who its father might be. "Take her with you if you can. Otherwise leave her there."

The corridor was empty, and the Weaver had told her of a sally port through which she could leave the castle undetected. She bent quickly, gathering the babe in her arms, and with one last backward glance at Cresenne, she started toward the west end of the fortress.

She hadn't even turned the nearest corner, however, when a man appeared before her. He was Qirsi—the fattest man of her race Yaella had ever seen—and he smiled a greeting when he first saw her. But then his eyes strayed to the child and he slowed his gait. Looking past her, he saw Cresenne, his pale eyes widening.

"Demons and fire!" he said, halting and blocking her way. "What have you done to her?"

She pulled her dagger free again and held it before her. The man appeared to falter at the sight of it, but only for the briefest moment.

"Give me the child!" he said. "Now!"

Yaella laid the blade on the babe's throat. "I'll kill her."

Again he hesitated, glancing at Cresenne once more and licking his lips nervously, as if he saw his own future in her fate. He was sweating like an overworked horse and Yaella thought she could see his hands quaking. At last, though, he shook his head. "I don't believe you will. Your masters sent you here for the babe. They'll be angry if she dies."

I don't want the child harmed. This was probably no more than conjecture on the part of the fat man, but it was unnervingly accurate. Her eyes flicked to the child, who was screaming. A dark lump had swelled on the babe's forehead, no doubt where she had struck the floor when her mother dropped her.

"They want me to join them. They don't care about the child."

"You're lying."

"Not about my willingness to kill her. If you let me go, I promise she'll be safe. You're right: I was sent to kill the mother and bring back the child. The Weaver will see that she's cared for."

The man stared at her. "A Weaver?"

She hadn't time for this. It was only a matter of time before they were discovered by soldiers of the king.

"Yes, a Weaver. And he doesn't deal kindly with those who meddle in his affairs. Now out of my way."

"A Weaver," he said again, as if he hadn't heard. "Of course."

Yaella could delay no more. She pressed herself against the stone wall and began to edge past the man, still holding the dagger at the babe's neck.

"Let me pass," she said.

"Never." He moved to block her way, just as she knew he would.

With a sudden thrust, she drove the blade into his flesh. She missed his heart, catching him closer to the shoulder, but still the man grunted in pain and slumped against the wall, the dagger jutting from his round body. Yaella hurried to get away from him.

As she reached the corner, however, flames abruptly flared before her, bright and angry, their heat making her flinch.

"Another step and you die!" came a voice from behind her.

Yaella turned at the sound, clutching the child so close to her breast that it began to cry anew. Her dagger was in the fat man. Fire was at her back. And staring at the apparition that faced her now, she felt Bian the Deceiver hovering at her shoulder, waiting to take her to the Underrealm.

No.

There was comfort to be found in death. Peace at a time when all the land was descending into war. Shelter from all that the Weaver had done to her. Release from a life that had strayed so far from what she had foreseen as a girl.

But no.

It was Bryntelle who reached her. The sound of her crying. Or, more precisely, the retreat of that sound. At first Cresenne thought that she was just fading, the last of her life's blood draining from the gaping hole in her chest, cold closing in on her, like the snows advancing on Wethyrn's Crown after a long harvest. But Bryntelle's cries only retreated for a moment. Then they were joined by voices, a man and a woman. The woman. The one who had done this to her, whose blade had killed her.

But no. Not yet.

The woman was taking her child, or attempting to.

She forced her eyes open, stared up at the stone ceiling. She tried to raise her head so that she might look at the wound, but she hadn't the strength even for this.

Wouldn't it just have been easier to surrender, to embrace peace and shelter and release?

She lifted her hand, heavy as a smith's anvil, and laid it on the wound. Warm blood still flowed, but so weakly. A trickle compared with what it should have been. She probed the wound with cold, leaden fingers. Straight as the blade that pierced her flesh, long enough to kill, but easy enough to heal. She reached for her healing magic. Also a trickle, spent like her blood, but not done quite yet. The effort brought tears to her eyes, made her stomach heave. But after a moment the power welled up within her. And the wound began to close.

Magic seeped into her, warm against the deadly cold, and the thaw brought with it pain that death's chill had masked. She gritted her teeth, squeezed her eyes closed once more.

But she did not relent. Bryntelle's cries still echoed in the corridor, as did the voices.

Soon the wound had closed. She could feel her heart beating within her bruised, aching chest. With more time and more magic, she might have eased the pain somewhat, but she didn't dare.

Instead, she fought to turn over, gasping with every least movement. She pushed herself onto her hands and knees, then clawed her way up the wall beside her until she was standing, her legs nearly buckling, her sight swimming. She saw two figures a short distance away. The woman and Trin.

An instant later something glinted in the dim light and Trin fell back against the stone.

The woman began to stride away. Bryntelle was in her arms.

Cresenne didn't even think, but merely cast the flame, reaching for the wall once more to keep from collapsing to the stone.

"Another step and you die!"

The woman turned slowly to face her, her cheeks ashen, Bryntelle held before her as if a warrior's shield. "You should be dead," she murmured.

"Give me my baby."

The woman glanced about, as if looking for some path to freedom. "I'll kill her if I have to."

Cresenne was wearier than she had ever been, but she kept the flames burning at the corridor's end, determined not to let the woman escape.

"The Weaver doesn't want her dead. We both know that."

"You're a traitor. How would you know what he wants?"

"You didn't kill her when you had the chance. You took her instead, just as he instructed. He's wanted this child for himself since before she was born."

"Is that why you turned on him?"

She wasn't certain how much longer she could maintain the conjured fire, or even remain on her feet. "Give her to me."

Cresenne saw the woman waver, her eyes flicking toward the dagger in Trin's chest, as if she were gauging the distance she would have to cover to retrieve it.

"Please," Cresenne said, her voice breaking, tears stinging her eyes. "I just want my baby back. Put her down and I'll let you go."

"No, you won't. You'll kill me."

"I hope she does," Trin muttered, glaring up at the woman and pulling the blade free. "You deserve no less." He flung the dagger toward Cresenne so that it clattered across the stone floor, stopping at her feet. "There you go, cousin. End this."

Cresenne stooped to pick it up, then decided against it, straightening again. "No. Put down my child, and you're free to go."

Before the woman could respond, Cresenne heard shouts coming from beyond the flames. It had to be Kearney's guards. She let the fires die away, hoping that she was right about the soldiers, knowing that she would never find the strength to raise the flames again if she were wrong.

Two soldiers stepped into the corridor, swords drawn. Cresenne knew one of them; he had guarded her chamber during her time in the prison tower.

"What's all this?" he demanded, eyeing the three Qirsi with manifest distrust.

"This woman tried to kill me," Cresenne said, leaning against the wall. "She attacked my friend as well, and she's trying to take my child."

The woman raised Bryntelle over her head, as if intending to dash the child against the floor.

"Not another step," she said, facing the guards.

Cresenne cried out, taking an unsteady step forward. But she needn't have worried.

No sooner had the woman lifted Bryntelle than she lowered her again, tears on her face. "What am I doing?" she whispered. She held out the child to the guards, shaking her head. "I'm sorry."

One of the guards took Bryntelle and the other grabbed the woman, turning her so that she had to face Cresenne.

Cresenne staggered forward until she reached the man who held her child. Taking Bryntelle from him, she began to sob, fussing over the babe, kissing the bruise on her head.

"Are ye all right, m'lady?" the guard asked. Maybe it was the sight of her, bloodied and unsteady on her feet, or the piteous cries coming from Bryntelle. Perhaps the soldier finally realized that there were Qirsi in the Forelands who were worse by far than she. Whatever the reason, this was as much courtesy as any Eandi warrior had ever shown her.

"I need a healer," she said. Then she nodded toward Trin. "So does my friend there. And my child."

The man nodded and left them at a run.

"Wha' should we do with 'er?" the other guard asked, still holding the woman, one hand pinning her arm to her body, the other gripping her hair.

Cresenne looked at him and then at the woman. After a moment she started walking to where her attacker stood. She nearly fell, but then managed to steady herself against the wall and make it the rest of the way.

"Who are you?" Cresenne asked, stopping just in front of her.

The woman just stared at her for several moments, looking like a waif beside the guard.

At last she dropped her gaze. "I was once first minister of Mertesse."

"Mertesse?" the guard repeated, glowering at her, hatred in his eyes. An Aneiran as well as a Qirsi traitor. It was a wonder the man didn't kill her where she stood.

"What's your name?"

"Yaella. Yaella ja Banvel."

The other guard returned, and with him came Nurle jal Danteffe, the healer who had saved Cresenne's life after she was poisoned by yet another servant of the Weaver.

"Are you all right?" Nurle asked, frowning with concern.

"I'm well enough," she said. "Help Trin."

He nodded once and went to the gleaner.

"She deserves t' die," said the soldier who held Cresenne's attacker. "With wha' she's done t' ye and th' child. Say th' word an' we'll take care o' her. No one need be th' wiser."

"Let them do it, Cresenne," Trin called to her. "He's right: she's earned this death."

Nurle cast a look her way, but said nothing.

Cresenne shook her head. "There were those who would have done the same with me when I first came here," she said. "And it may be that the queen will put her to death before long. But I don't want any more blood on my hands."

The woman laughed. "You think yourself noble, compassionate. Let them kill me. That would be an act of mercy."

"Certainly it would be an easy end for you."

"Easy? You don't know what you're saying. I'm old. Nothing is easy anymore. A year or two ago, this brute holding me would be afire already, this corridor filled with a concealing mist as I made my escape. But I've nothing left. No magic, no strength. Nothing."

"You had a dagger, and that was nearly enough," Cresenne said, and started to turn away.

"Aren't you going to ask me why I tried to kill you?"

"I don't have to ask. You're here because the Weaver wanted me dead."

"So did I. Your Grinsa jal Arriet was responsible for the death of the man I loved. I came here to avenge him."

"What man? What was his name?"

"Shurik jal Marcine."

Cresenne nodded. "I know that name. Kentigern's first minister."

"Another traitor," the guard muttered.

The woman scowled at him. "Betrayal wears many faces, Eandi. He devoted himself to a great cause, just as I have." She faced Cresenne again. "He's the reason I came. I failed him today even more than I did the Weaver."

Cresenne regarded her a moment, then laughed, short and sharp. "You're a fool. You belong to the Weaver's movement; nothing else matters. He wanted you to kill me and so you made the attempt. You're deceiving yourself if you believe anything different. He controls those who serve him as a master controls a slave. It's been half a year since I renounced him and still he governs my life, forcing me to live like some wretched creature of the night." She gestured at the bloodstains on her clothes and the scars on her face. "Look at me. I've never truly met him, and yet he's left scars all over my body." She shook her head. "No, your thirst for vengeance had nothing to do with what happened today. All of this was the Weaver's doing."

The woman glared at her, her color high. "He hates you, you know. He'll never stop trying to kill you. You might have survived today, but you'll be dead soon enough."

"That remains to be seen," Cresenne said. "I've made it this far. And he hasn't won yet."

With that, she turned her back on the woman, listening as the guards led her away. There were tears on her face again, but she brushed them off with her sleeve and smiled down at Bryntelle, who had finally stopped crying.

"You need healing," Nurle said.

Cresenne nodded. "Yes. And then we need to sleep. Already the day's nearly half gone."

Chapter
Twenty-four

The Moorlands, Eibithar

he morning dawned bright and clear, the eastern sky aglow with fiery shades of red and gold, the western sky gradually lightening from black, to indigo, and finally to azure. The air was utterly still and the moons still hung overhead, white and red, bone and blood, as if awaiting the coming battle.

Nitara was awake at first light, as were the Weaver's other warriors. Jastanne returned to her side of the camp soon after the minister awoke, but she would not meet Nitara's gaze. It was all the confirmation Nitara needed that the chancellor had spent the previous night in the Weaver's arms.

She had expected to be enraged and aggrieved, to feel jealousy gnawing like wood ants at her mind. But on this day no such emotions could reach her. Today, she rode to war, a soldier in the Weaver's army, a servant of his movement, an apostle of his vision. Tomorrow, perhaps, she would lament that he had chosen to love Jastanne rather than her. Or maybe their victory today would purge her of envy and resentment.

The vision of Kayiv that had darkened her sleep remained fresh in her mind, but even this memory could not distract Nitara from her purpose. Jastanne had chosen to make her a commander in the Weaver's force, a decision to which Dusaan himself had assented. She intended to justify the faith they had shown in her. The Weaver's army might yet be defeated—although she could not imagine how or by what force—but it would not be through any failure on her part.

In many respects hers was the most dangerous command of all. The other powers—fire, shaping, mists and winds—could all be wielded to good effect from afar. Language of beasts worked best at close distance. The other magics lent themselves naturally to the Weaver's power; the greater the number being woven into a single force, the more devastating the magic. But language of beasts had to be wielded with precision and usually was most effective when used individually, one Qirsi whispering to one animal. That was why Nitara and the Qirsi under her command would be positioned close to the center, as far as possible from the Eandi archers. Bowmen would not be on horseback, and Nitara and her soldiers could do little to block the enemy's arrows. They would be at the heart of this battle, facing down Eandi riders, doing all they could to evade the steel of Eibithar and Sanbira's warriors.

It was a role she relished and as she called her soldiers to her, she saw the same eagerness on many of their faces. She saw fear as well, but this was to be expected.

"You know what the Weaver expects of us," she said. Several of them nodded, but most of them merely stared at her, waiting.

"Ours is a unique mission in this war. We cannot depend upon the Weaver's magic to bolster our own, nor can we watch this battle unfold from a safe distance. We may not wield the deepest magic in the Weaver's army, but we will stand at the core of his force and keep the riders of the Eandi at bay."

A murmur of agreement and more nods. A few of them smiled, the fierce, courageous smiles of warriors.

"It will be dangerous work," she said, feeling more and more like a commander with every word she spoke. "Some of us may not live to see the end. No doubt that frightens many of you. I'd be scared as well, were it not for one simple truth: I'd rather die in the service of our Weaver, wielding my powers on his behalf, than live out the rest of my days in a world ruled by the Eandi."

She expected more nods and mumbled assent. Instead, these last words were greeted by a deafening cheer that startled Nitara and made her horse whinny and rear.

The minister glanced about and saw that the other commanders were watching her. So was Jastanne, an amused grin on her pretty face.

"That's all," Nitara said, abruptly feeling self-conscious. "Go ready your mounts. We ride at my signal."

The others turned away, their expressions grim but determined. Whatever fear she had seen in them before seemed to have vanished.

"What in Qirsar's name did you say to them?"

Nitara turned. Jastanne was approaching, still grinning.

She shrugged. "I'm not really sure. I just told them that I'd rather die for the Weaver than grow old in a land ruled by the Eandi."

The chancellor nodded. "I like that. Do you mind if I use it, too?"

"Not at all."

Jastanne stopped in front of her, but then stared down at her feet, seemingly unsure of what she wanted to say. For the first time since the day they met, Nitara felt that she had the woman at a disadvantage, and though she had already resolved not to give in to her jealousy, she couldn't help but be pleased. "Was there something you wanted, Chancellor?"

Jastanne nodded, meeting her gaze for a moment before

looking off to the south. "Yes. I'll be leading our half of the army into war, just as we planned, but once we reach the battle plain, I may have to leave you and the others for a time."

"What?"

"The Weaver has asked me to see to a matter of some importance, and it may require that I relinquish command. Just for a short while. I want you to be ready to assume command in my place."

Nitara gaped at her. "I'm . . . I'm not sure I can. Leading a part of this army is one thing, but leading all the Qirsi under your command is another entirely."

"No, it's not. There's really very little difference."

"Can't the other chancellor—?"

"He has his own force to command, Nitara. Besides, as powerful as he is, he doesn't possess both mists and language of beasts, as you do." She smiled, though only for an instant. "For that matter, neither do I. No, you're the logical choice."

Nitara nodded, taking a breath. "All right."

"Just follow the Weaver, as always. And allow your instincts to guide you."

Another cheer went up from the far side of the camp. Both women turned toward the sound, and Nitara saw that several Qirsi were already on their mounts.

"You'll be fine," Jastanne said, facing her again.

"What is it the Weaver's asked you to do?"

The chancellor hesitated. "He wants me to kill a woman who betrayed the movement. It shouldn't take me long."

"Very well," Nitara said. "Qirsar guard you, Chancellor."

"And you, Nitara."

Jastanne started away.

"Did you and he—?" She stopped, ashamed of herself for blurting out anything at all.

The chancellor turned slowly, her brow knitted. "Nitara—"

"Forget that I said anything. Please. I'm happy for you. For both of you."

"It was one night, Nitara. That's all. Who knows what today is going to bring?" She turned again and walked away, leaving Nitara feeling alone and terribly young.

After a moment, the minister glanced about to see if any of

the others were watching her, or had heard their exchange. No one appeared to be paying her any attention at all.

She strapped on her sword, saddled her mount, and swung herself onto the stallion's back. Surveying the camp again, she saw the Weaver on his horse, sitting motionless, his hair gleaming in the early morning light, his eyes fixed on the southern sky. He said nothing, but all of them seemed to sense that he wanted them to gather around him. Within just a few moments a tight cluster of Qirsi had surrounded him, their gazes fixed on his regal face. Nitara wished that she could be next to him, but she made no effort to press forward. She merely waited for him to speak.

"This is the day we've been planning for," he said at last, his voice even, but loud enough to be heard by all. "This is the day we fulfill our destiny. Nine centuries ago our people came to the Forelands as would-be conquerors. Like you, they were willing to die for their cause. Like you, they lent their power to a Weaver. They were the greatest army ever to ride on these moors, and they scattered Eandi armies before them in their march toward dominion. They nearly succeeded; they would have had it not been for the betrayal of one man." He regarded them all. "Carthach," he said, echoing the name that resounded in Nitara's mind, no doubt in the minds of all who had assembled around him.

"I speak his name not to open old wounds, but to remind you of how close we once came to victory, and of how long we have waited for redemption. For nine hundred years we have suffered for his treachery. For nine hundred years we have waited to fulfill the promise of that first Qirsi army. Today our long wait finally ends. Today we cleanse our history, we wipe away the stain of Carthach's treason. Today, we begin anew. From this day forward we will rule the Forelands, just as we should have so long ago. Together, you and I will remake the world." He raised himself out of his saddle, standing in his stirrups. "We fight for the glory of Qirsar!" he shouted, drawing a mighty roar from his warriors.

"Our magic is yours, Weaver," Jastanne said, after the din had subsided. "Weave us well."

Dusaan nodded once. "Into your units," he said. "It's time to ride."

The Qirsi quickly returned to their brigades, and were soon thundering southward across the Moorlands. Nitara and Yedeg, Jastanne's other commander, rode just behind the chancellor; Rov and Gorlan followed Uestem. Two more Qirsi had joined them during the night. One, a tall, thin man with an angular face, Nitara understood to be the archminister of Aneira. The other was a lanky woman with a haunted look in her pale eyes. Both of them were shapers; they took positions in Gorlan's force.

At the head of the army rode the Weaver, his white hair flowing in the wind like the great mane of a god. From all that Nitara had ever heard about war and armies, she knew that the morn of a battle was the most difficult time for a warrior. This was when thoughts of death entered a soldier's mind, when fear took hold of the heart. But none of the men or women around her seemed frightened. With the Weaver leading them, they appeared confident, at ease. It was as if he was already using his magic to impart to them his courage. Nitara doubted that the Eandi soldiers awaiting them on the plain felt so certain of their fates.

After only a brief ride the Qirsi encountered a small force of Eandi soldiers, all of them wearing the white, gold, and red of Braedon. One of the men, a captain no doubt, rode forward from the others, most of whom were on foot. He had his hand raised in greeting, as if calling for a parley.

"The remnants of the emperor's army!" the Weaver called, a grin on his face. "Shapers!" he said, turning toward Uestem's force. The captain reined in his horse, a puzzled look on his face.

"High Chancellor?" he called to Dusaan.

The Weaver offered no reply, and an instant later, the Eandi fell, his body appearing to break like a child's toy. The Qirsi rode on, bearing down on the other soldiers who now tried to flee. Many of them died without drawing their weapons. The Weaver and his warriors didn't even bother to slow their charge.

A short time later, the Qirsi army topped a small rise, and Nitara saw before them the armies of the enemy. Confident as she was, the minister couldn't help but be daunted by the size of the Eandi force. There were thousands of them, their helms and armor glittering in the sunlight. They were spread wide across the plain, in a vast crescent, so that they appeared ready to block a Qirsi advance in any direction. Already, the Weaver and his warriors had defeated armies far bigger than their own, but never had they faced anything like this.

After a moment, Dusaan raised a hand and his riders halted. He turned in his saddle, glancing back at Jastanne and Uestem, and beckoned them forward.

"Commanders," Jastanne said quietly, as she spurred her mount forward.

Nitara and the others followed, stopping just behind Dusaan.

"What do you see, Chancellor?" the Weaver asked.

Jastanne eyed the Eandi armies for a moment before responding. "None of them are on horseback."

"Meaning?"

"We'll have to fold those with language of beasts into the other units."

"Yes, those with other powers of use to us. Very good. What else?"

"They've spread the archers along the breadth of their lines," Uestem said.

"Yes, they have. Why?"

"To keep us from using a single wind against them."

"I expect so. Jastanne, we'll have to keep the winds turning, give them no time to adjust."

"Yes, Weaver."

Dusaan looked back at Nitara. "Commander, I understand that you may find yourself leading the chancellor's army for a time."

"But my unit—"

"Your unit may be blended into the others, but that doesn't change the fact that you're a commander, and that you possess mists and winds, as well as language of beasts. You should be prepared to lead the others. Do you understand?"

She nodded, her throat suddenly dry. "Yes, Weaver."

For a few frenzied moments Nitara and Jastanne divided those Qirsi who had been in the minister's unit among the other brigades. A few, those who didn't have mists, or shaping, or fire, were told to remain behind, but the others quickly took their places behind the other commanders. Nitara remained with Yedeg and Jastanne.

"The enemy has been clever," the Weaver said, when they were ready. "No doubt the Qirsi among them—all of them traitors to our people—aided the Eandi with their preparations. But none of what they've done changes anything. Mounted or on foot, spread wide or clustered like a herd of drel, the Eandi can't defeat us. These are the last desperate measures of a foe we've already defeated." He pulled his sword free and raised it over his head. "We ride to war!"

With a full-throated cry, the other Qirsi kicked at their mounts and rode forward, following Dusaan and pulling their weapons free as well. Nitara had time to remark to herself how curious a gesture this was, considering that the only weapon the Qirsi hoped to use was their magic.

And then everything began to go horribly wrong.

They were quickly closing the distance between themselves and the Eandi lines. Nitara was eyeing the bowmen to her right—the closest of the Eandi archers—waiting for them to launch their first volley of arrows, when she felt a sudden pulse of heat. She looked to her left in time to see several of Rov's riders fall to the ground flailing at flames that had engulfed their hair and clothing. In front of her, Dusaan halted, incredulous and enraged.

"What in Qirsar's name is happening?" he demanded.

"We're under attack!" came the reply, although Nitara never saw who it was who spoke.

An instant later, she heard a rapid succession of muffled cracks and then howls of pain. On the far side of the Weaver's army, where Gorlan sat at the head of his brigade, at least a dozen more warriors fell, many of them writhing in pain, a few completely motionless.

It did seem that they were under attack. She was about to say so when her horse reared and at last she understood the nature of this assault, though she didn't know how the enemy managed it. For as she toppled off her mount, landing hard on the ground and just barely missing a hulking boulder, Nitara realized that she had unhorsed herself. Or, to be more precise, someone had used her magic to make the beast throw her.

Someone other than her Weaver.

That it was such a simple question did nothing to diminish its brilliance. It had never even crossed Grinsa's mind, though he had been thinking of nothing but the coming war for longer than he could say. But Tavis had a nimble mind and a unique way of looking at the world. And in this instance, he had given them cause for hope, slim though it was.

"Is it possible," he had asked Grinsa the night before, "for a Weaver to use the magic of another Qirsi even if he doesn't want you to?"

The answer, of course, was yes.

It wasn't easy. A Qirsi who knew that the Weaver was about to try such a thing could close his or her mind and resist the intrusion. But a Weaver could usually overcome the defenses of a less powerful sorcerer, and on those occasions when the sorcerer wasn't prepared there was little he or she could do to ward off a Weaver's assault.

He and the young lord had gone to Kearney immediately, and Grinsa and the king had spent much of the night devising their strategy for this day's fight. It was simple really—there remained little for them to do against so formidable an enemy. But with the archers spread as Grinsa had recommended earlier in the evening, it was possible that he could create enough confusion among the Weaver's army to allow the bowmen to have some effect.

"You say this was Tavis's idea?" the king asked him after they had spoken for some time.

"Yes, Your Majesty, it was."

"He's come far in the past year."

"I think the promise was always there, but yes, he's grown considerably since your offer of asylum."

Kearney had smiled at that. "You put it most generously,

gleaner, but you and I both know that I had nothing to do with his transformation. He's spent this past year in your company and to the degree that anyone other than Tavis himself deserves such credit, it should go to you."

"I suppose. In the end, I think I've learned as much from Tavis as he has from me."

"Well, he's given us an opportunity at least. Let's make certain that we put it to good use."

In the light of morning, watching how the Weaver's advance slowed and then stalled, his lines crumbling in a tumult of flame and anguished screams, Grinsa found himself believing that they were on the verge of doing just that. Already he had killed or wounded nearly three dozen of the Weaver's servants, and now he waved an Eibitharian banner over his head, signaling to Kearney that the king should begin his attack.

Immediately, the king shouted orders to his lead bowmen, one of whom unfurled a banner of his own. A moment later, a swarm of arrows leaped into the sky, soaring toward the Qirsi army from several directions at once.

Grinsa felt a wind begin to rise from the north, but he knew it wouldn't gain strength fast enough to block the assault. And just to make certain of this, he now reached out with his power, sensing where the Weaver had positioned those among his horde who possessed mists and winds. Seizing the power of as many of them as he could tear away from the Weaver—about twenty in all—he robbed their gale of much of its strength.

Seconds later, the arrows struck, bringing new cries of pain from the Qirsi and panicked whinnying from their mounts. Many fell—Grinsa and the loyal Qirsi were still vastly outnumbered, but the Weaver's advantage was shrinking by the moment.

Dusaan himself remained seated on his mount, which he steered from side to side, making the beast dance as he shouted commands to his foundering warriors. Another volley flew from the bows of the Eandi archers, but already the Weaver had coaxed a wind from his sorcerers, one that built rapidly and began to swirl, weakening the flight of the arrows. Grinsa tried once more to use his power on Dusaan's Qirsi, but they were ready for him now. Not only did the sorcerers resist him, but he could feel Dusaan tightening his hold on their magic. Gazing across the battle plain, he saw that the Weaver was staring back at him. Their eyes met, and Dusaan shook his head, a feral grin springing to his lips.

Grinsa knew that he wouldn't catch the Weaver unaware again.

Most of the second wave of arrows fell short of Dusaan's army, and those that did reach the Qirsi did little damage. Kearney's archers sent up another barrage, but the Weaver defeated this one with ease.

Grinsa reached again for Dusaan's shapers and managed to wound several more of them. But he could hear the Weaver shouting at his warriors once more, and when the gleaner tried to use the enemies' fire magic against them, he encountered too much resistance.

"Damn!" he muttered.

Tavis looked at him sharply. "What is it?"

"Dusaan has warned them against me. It's going to be far harder now to turn their magic back on them."

"You can still try."

He faced the young lord, shaking his head. "It's not worth the effort, and if I don't start weaving the others now Dusaan will use the same tactic against us."

Tavis frowned, staring across the plain once more.

Grinsa knew what he was thinking. In the first few moments of the battle they had managed to destroy nearly a third of the Weaver's army, but it wasn't enough. Not nearly.

"We made a good start, Tavis, in large part thanks to you."

"Yes, but now what?"

Before Grinsa could think of a response, Dusaan offered one of his own. The gleaner sensed the magic as it surged toward them, feeling it on his skin as one might a close lightning strike, tasting it as one might blood, and he reached desperately for the shapers along the Eandi lines—Fotir and Xivled, Evetta ja Rudek, who was Tremain's first minister, and Dyre jal Frinval, who served in Kearney's court with Keziah. With an effort that stole his breath and brought beads of sweat to his brow, he sent forth his own burst of power that he hoped would meet the Weaver's. But Dusaan's magic and that of his servants overwhelmed the meager power that Grinsa could muster. Had the gleaner done nothing nearly half of the Eandi soldiers might have been killed. As it was, he was able to save a good number of them.

Still, Dusaan's onslaught crashed into the soldiers as an ocean wave would a wall of sand. Hundreds were lost, many of them screaming in agony, others silenced before they even knew what had happened to them.

"Gleaner!" he heard Kearney shout, but Grinsa had no time to answer.

Dusaan and his army were advancing on them once more, and already the gleaner could see the next attack building. A glimmering flame that rose from the land like a wraith and began to speed toward them. Drawing on the power of his fellow Qirsi—Evetta again, as well as Labruinn's first minister, the old minister from Brugaosa, whose power had diminished to almost nothing, and a number of the healers who also possessed fire magic—Grinsa countered with a blaze of his own. He'd had more warning this time, and his fire met Dusaan's a good distance from the Eandi lines. Still, he could only hope to diminish the potency of the Weaver's assault. When Dusaan's fire crashed into the Eandi army it killed scores, and wounded many more. But it didn't obliterate Kearney's force, and Grinsa could ask for little more.

"At this rate it won't be long before our entire army is gone."

Grinsa cast a withering glare at Tavis, but said nothing. The boy was right.

He couldn't allow the Weaver to continue his offensive against the Eandi soldiers, and there seemed to be only one way to stop him. Reaching for his shapers once more, the gleaner directed an attack against Dusaan himself. The Weaver would be expecting this—Grinsa had little hope that he could actually hurt the man. But at least Dusaan would have to defend himself, making it impossible for him to launch attacks of his own.

As he expected, the Weaver turned his magic away with

ease. Grinsa thought he actually heard the Weaver laughing, but he didn't falter even for an instant. He reached for the fire magic again, sending a ball of flame at the man. Again Dusaan blocked the attack, but already Grinsa was drawing on Keziah's magic, language of beasts. This, it seemed, Dusaan had not expected, for his mount suddenly reared, neighing loudly. For just a moment, Grinsa thought that he might succeed in unseating the Weaver. But Dusaan quickly calmed the beast. Again the gleaner drew upon his shaping magic.

By this time though, he was beginning to tire. Here was the flaw in this tactic. It was born of desperation and it demanded a great deal of effort on Grinsa's part with little opportunity for rest. In time he would grow too weary to fight at all, and then all would be lost. In truth, he had known all along that he would have to resort to these attacks eventually. He just hadn't known that his plight and that of his allies would grow so dire so quickly.

"What can I do?" Tavis asked.

Grinsa shook his head, having no answer at first. His teeth were clenched, his mind fully occupied by the weaving of magic and his mounting exhaustion. "Wave the flag," he said at last, tossing the Eibitharian banner to the boy. "Maybe the archers can do some good."

"There aren't many of them left. Most died by the Weaver's magic."

"Those who are left then. Quickly, Tavis!"

The young lord raised the flag over his head and moments later arrows soared into the morning air. There were pitifully few of them, and the Weaver's Qirsi managed to defend themselves with winds and shaping even though Dusaan couldn't weave their powers together.

"Again!" the gleaner called.

He saw Tavis wave the flag, but he never knew for certain whether the archers fired. At that same moment Dusaan retaliated with an attack of his own. Shaping at first, then fire, then back to shaping once more. Grinsa held tightly to his magic, easily resisting the Weaver's assault. Unlike Dusaan, the gleaner wasn't on horseback, meaning that there were fewer powers for the Weaver to try to control. Except that in the next instant, Dusaan had taken hold of Grinsa's power of mists and winds—Grinsa hadn't even thought to guard that magic.

A gale started to rise, and the gleaner struggled to regain control of his magic.

"Grinsa?" Tavis's voice seemed to come to him from a great distance. He didn't reply.

In the span of a single heartbeat, Dusaan released the one power, trying once more for shaping and then fire. Grinsa fought to ward himself, attempting to anticipate the Weaver's attacks. But he was weary, and with each moment that passed it grew harder for him to keep the Weaver from taking hold of his shaping power, the one Dusaan seemed to want most of all.

How had the Weaver turned the tide of their battle so quickly? Just a few moments before Grinsa had Dusaan reeling, clinging desperately to his mount and laboring to maintain control of his magics. Now Grinsa was the one scrambling simply to stay alive.

He heard Tavis say something else, but he couldn't make out what it was. Abruptly though, his battle with the Weaver ceased. He stared at the boy, astonished.

"What happened?"

"The archers finally managed to aim a salvo at the Weaver," the boy said. "He had to raise a wind to protect himself."

Grinsa nodded. His respite wouldn't last long, but he was grateful for any rest at all.

"How are we doing?" he asked.

"Our archers aren't having much effect on them," Tavis said, "and they won't come close to our swordsmen. But as long as you keep the Weaver occupied, they don't seem capable of doing much damage to our lines."

Right.

"I'll keep after him as long as I can," he said. "But you have to understand, Tavis: I'm merely delaying the inevitable. I can't keep this up forever."

"Neither can he. Just make certain that his strength fails first."

"You don't understand. With so many Qirsi on his side, the damage he's done thus far demanded far less of him than what I've had to do. I'm already weary—wearier than he. I can't win a battle on these terms."

Tavis merely stared back at him, the look in his eyes asking the obvious question. What choice did they have?

Grinsa looked across the battle plain once more. Dusaan called to his warriors, then glanced back at the gleaner. No time to waste.

He reached for the Weaver's magic again. Language of beasts, fire, shaping. Dusaan brushed him away as if he were no more than an irksome child. Before Grinsa could try a second time, the Weaver began to draw upon the vast power of his army. Shaping. Grinsa could see the magic shimmering before him, making the grasses and boulders of the moor waver, as if from the heat of a planting sun. He reached for the others again, wondering how much longer they could contend with the might of so many Qirsi.

But his allies were there—Fotir, Xivled, and the rest—and the stream of magic they sent back at the Weaver seemed stronger than any he had woven that day. It almost seemed that Fotir and the others, sensing his fatigue, had given more of themselves, offering their strength where his was failing. By the time the Weaver's magic reached the Eandi lines, it had dwindled to nearly nothing. A few soldiers were wounded, crumpling to the ground, but not nearly as many as Grinsa had feared.

"We were fortunate that time," he said.

Tavis eyed him, seeming at last to understand just how bleak was their situation. He didn't say anything. He didn't have to.

After a moment, Grinsa faced Dusaan again and tried once more to take control of the Weaver's power. He had little hope of succeeding. But he didn't know what else to do.

She felt useless, as she always did during these battles. A part of her had hoped that this day might be different, that despite the lingering pain in her hands she might prove herself as a warrior. Her brother was leading them to war. At last she had her chance to strike back against the Weaver, to repay the man for all he had done to her, and to Cresenne, and to everyone else who had suffered at the hands of his conspiracy. Finally, she could avenge the murder of Paegar jal Berget, who had once been her friend, despite his ties to the Weaver's movement.

But Keziah found that she could be of no help at all, even in a war of magic, a war between Weavers. Grinsa did draw upon her magic once, when he used language of beasts against Dusaan's horse, but little came of that effort, and almost immediately both Weavers turned back to the more menacing powers: shaping and fire. Ironically, had she truly been a part of the Weaver's army, she would have been called upon to raise a wind, but as of yet, Grinsa hadn't tried to raise an opposing gale.

She could only watch and wait, and hope that eventually, before all was lost, she would have her opportunity to strike at the enemy.

As Dusaan's warriors drew nearer to the Eandi lines, Keziah began to push her way forward, past astonished Eandi soldiers. She wasn't fool enough to fancy herself a skilled swordswoman, but possessing language of beasts, she thought that she ought to be where her magic would do Kearney's army the most good. She might not be able to strike a killing blow either with steel or Qirsi power, but she could make a horse rear at an opportune time, or coax a falcon out of the sky as she had done when Fotir saved her. No matter what she managed to do, it would be better than standing behind Kearney's men wondering how she might make herself useful.

Before she reached the front lines, however, she spied something that made her stop. It was a Qirsi woman riding in a wide arc around the eastern flank of the Eandi lines. Had there been more than this lone rider Keziah would have raised the alarm immediately. But it was just the one woman, and something in her manner gave the archminister pause. Keziah was watching her from some distance, but the rider appeared to be scanning the Eandi armies, as if searching for something, or someone. She was beautiful and so young in appearance, with golden eyes so much like those of the Weaver, that Keziah wondered for just a moment if she might be Dusaan's daughter. She knew it was impossible, but she was equally sure that the woman was powerful in her own right, no matter the nature of her ties to the Weaver. She moved confidently, as if she had complete faith in her abilities and her magic.

"Probably a shaper," Keziah muttered to herself, marking the woman's progress. Her hands throbbed at the mere suggestion. For as she stood watching the rider, Keziah sensed that the woman was searching for her. The Weaver had vowed to punish her and somehow she knew that he had chosen this woman to mete out whatever retribution he had chosen.

Her first thought was to flee. Perhaps she had time to find her horse and ride away from the plain. Abeni had hurt her so badly; she would rather die instantly by a warrior's blade than face such agony again. As quickly as the notion came to her, however, she dismissed it. If the Weaver wanted her dead, he would find a way to kill her. Better to face her doom now. Besides, she sensed that this woman would cut a swath through the ranks of Kearney's men to reach her if forced to do so. If Keziah was to die this day, she didn't want to face Bian the Deceiver with any more deaths on her head.

She made her way back through the soldiers to the rear of the lines and then walked a short distance from the battle plain, all the while watching the rider. The woman continued to scan the Eandi lines until at last her eyes fell on Keziah. As soon as the rider spotted the archminister, she kicked her mount to a gallop and rode directly toward her, white hair dancing in the wind.

The archminister kept her eyes locked on her attacker, readying herself to use language of beasts on the woman's mount. It seemed, though, that the Weaver had warned this woman against her. Long before she was close enough for Keziah's magic to have much effect on the creature, the woman halted and dismounted, continuing her approach on foot. Two soldiers charged her, but both collapsed to the ground before they were within ten fourspans of her. Keziah thought she heard the muffled snapping of bone as they fell.

This time fear got the better of her. Keziah turned, intending to run, but before she could take even a step, her leg gave way. She fell to the grass, pain clouding her vision. Her stomach heaved and she clenched her teeth to keep from being ill.

"Not so fast, Archminister," the woman called to her, killing another soldier without so much as a glance. "The Weaver wanted me to convey a message to you."

Keziah braced herself, knowing what was coming. *Why does it always have to be shapers?* she had time to wonder. Then torment. Not the hands this time, nor even a limb. She heard the cracking of bone, and felt as though a fire were burning within her body. She gasped, her agony only worsening. One rib. Then another. This time she couldn't keep herself from vomiting, though that too brought new anguish.

Several more Eandi soldiers converged on the woman, swords drawn, but before they reached her they were hammered to the ground, their bodies collapsing in grotesque positions as if they had been mauled by some terrible demon of the Underrealm. For just an instant the archminister thought that her attacker had done this herself, but when the woman looked back over her shoulder Keziah knew that it had been the Weaver, that he was watching them, waiting to see her die.

"He wanted you to suffer," the woman said, facing her once more, smiling faintly. "But I'm afraid there's no time for that now."

At least it would be quick.

"Hold, Jastanne!" came a voice from beside Keziah. "You'll not be killing anyone today."

Keziah looked up and, to her amazement, saw Aindreas, the duke of Kentigern, towering over her, his sword held loosely in one hand, a shield in the other.

Her first impulse was to warn him away, to tell him that the woman was a shaper and that no Eandi warrior, no matter his size, could contend with her. Then the full import of what he had said finally reached her. *Jastanne.* He had called the woman by her name.

The Qirsi laughed.

"Yes, Archminister. He knows me. You find that odd, don't you?"

A few others had gathered around them, though most on the battle plain remained oblivious of this second, lesser conflict. The handful of men who had followed the duke were soldiers wearing the colors of Eibithar: Kearney's men, who had treated Keziah with suspicion and contempt for so many turns, who had been told of Kentigern's defiance of the Crown, who had come to this plain to do battle with the empire's soldiers only to find themselves at war with a Weaver and his army. Most of them probably didn't know what to make of the scene unfolding before them. Keziah wasn't even certain that she did.

"How do you know this woman?" she asked, through gritted teeth.

The woman was smiling still. "Yes, my Lord Duke, can you explain that?"

Aindreas tightened his hold on the sword, his knuckles whitening. "It doesn't matter," he said, his gaze flicking from Jastanne's face to the faces of the soldiers. "This woman is a shaper," he said loudly. "She's more dangerous than any of you know. She can't be allowed to live."

Again Jastanne laughed. "And she can't be killed by the likes of you."

There was a chiming sound, and the duke's blade splintered like bone. An instant later Keziah heard the rending of wood, and Aindreas's shield broke in two. Three soldiers raised their blades as if to charge her. There were three muffled cracks, and the men toppled to the grass, two of them howling and writhing in pain. One of them didn't move at all. A sheen of sweat had appeared on Jastanne's face, and she was breathing heavily, as if she had run a great distance, but she seemed to have her strength still.

"I've wanted to kill you for some time now, Kentigern," she said, "but you've been too valuable to us. The Weaver wouldn't allow it. Now, though . . ." She shrugged and grinned. "The duke is a traitor," she said, pitching her voice to carry. "He pledged himself to the Qirsi cause, believing that your king was somehow responsible for the death of his daughter."

"That's a lie!" one of the men shouted back at her.

But Aindreas didn't deny it. He just glowered at her, gripping the useless hilt of his weapon.

"Is it?" she said. "Notice the duke's silence. Don't you think he would protest if he could?"

The soldier blanched, looking from the woman to Aindreas. The other men stared at the duke as well.

Jastanne, however, eyed Keziah once more. She said nothing. She didn't have to. Keziah knew that she was about to die.

Perhaps Aindreas sensed this as well. With a roar that would have made the bravest warrior quail, he charged the woman, his dagger drawn, his eyes wide and wild. And Jastanne didn't even flinch. She made a small grunting sound, as if pushing hard with her magic, but otherwise she didn't move. At least not at first.

Aindreas staggered before he reached her, his enraged bellow rising, changing to something more desperate, more awful. Keziah could hear the bones in his body breaking in rapid succession. The dagger fell from his hands. But he didn't fall, nor did he stop. Perhaps it was just the force of his initial steps, or maybe the force of his will. He continued toward the woman, flailing now, his face red, his steps unsteady.

Jastanne took a step back, pulling her sword free, and as the duke stumbled into her she thrust the blade into his chest. Still he tumbled forward, but now the woman simply stepped to the side, allowing him to stagger past her before he fell to the ground, driving the blade deeper. The other soldiers vaulted toward her, thinking that at last they had her defeated. But their swords broke in quick succession, and their necks after that.

Keziah was alone.

Except that when she looked at Jastanne again, she saw that another had come, one the woman hadn't noticed.

"How did you turn him?" Keziah asked, keeping the woman's gaze on herself, needing just a bit more time.

Jastanne's face had grown pale, and her hair, damp with sweat, clung to her brow. Keziah had no doubt, though, that she had strength enough to finish this.

"It was easy, if you must know. He came to us."

"I don't believe you," the archminister said, only half listening.

"I don't particularly care. It's the truth. He hated your king that much."

Keziah didn't answer. Her thoughts were fixed entirely on Jastanne's horse, which had wandered close, perhaps following the sound of the woman's voice. In these few seconds, the archminister had managed to bring him even closer. Hearing his steps, seeing the direction of Keziah's gaze, Jastanne spun. And at that very moment Keziah summoned an image of fire, thrusting it into the creature's mind as if it were a blade. The beast reared, kicking out with its front hooves. One smote the woman on the head, and she collapsed, sprawling on the ground beside Keziah. She let out a low groan and stirred, but the archminister grabbed a nearby rock and silenced her with a second blow.

Keziah closed her eyes briefly, taking a long, deep breath. Then, in a haze of pain, she forced herself into motion and crawled to the duke.

Aindreas lay on his side, his chest a bloodstained mess, his breath coming in great wet gasps, flecks of blood at the corners of his mouth. His eyes were open, but he seemed not to see her, even when her face was just in front of his.

"My lord?" Keziah said.

"Is it over?" he rasped.

"Not yet, my lord."

"Jastanne?"

"She's wounded, but she lives still."

"Kill her now, while you can. She's . . ." His voice gave way, and his enormous frame was racked by terrible coughs.

"I'll call for a healer, my lord."

"I'm dead already."

"No, my lor—"

"Yes." For the first time, his grey eyes seemed to focus on her face. "Tell the king . . . tell him that I died well."

"My lord—"

"It was a mistake. I know that now. The shame of it will stain my house for centuries. But perhaps dying this way . . . I'm sorry."

She heard footsteps behind her, the jangling of swords and armor. Turning with an effort, Keziah saw soldiers running toward her.

"Archminister!" one of them called.

"Get healers! Quickly!"

One of the men started back toward the camp, but the others hurried to her side.

"Is he dead?" one of the men asked, his gaze fixed on the duke.

Keziah didn't answer. Aindreas coughed again, weakly this time. His breathing had slowed, his skin was the color of high clouds on a warm harvest morning.

"Brienne," he whispered. "Forgive . . . me."

His mouth opened slightly, as if he intended to take another breath. But his chest was still, and what little life had remained in his eyes faded to nothing.

Keziah reached out and closed his eyes for him, wincing as she did. She couldn't bring herself to shed tears for the man, not after all that he had done. But she grieved for his family and his house.

"Thank you," she said softly, "for saving my life."

"Archminister?"

"He died a hero," she said. "He saved me from certain death." She glanced up at the man. "Make certain that your comrades know that."

"I will, Archminister." He hesitated. "Are you hurt badly?"

"My leg is broken, and my ribs. But I'll be all right once the healers arrive."

He nodded, then looked at the other soldiers, some of whom yet lived. At last his gaze came to rest on Jastanne, whose chest rose and fell, despite the darkening bruises on her head.

"What about her?" the man asked.

"Bind her hands and feet," Keziah said, ignoring Aindreas's words and the warning that echoed in her own mind. "Use silk if you can find it. Otherwise cord will have to do. And have her watched by at least four men."

"Four?"

"She's a shaper. I only hope that four will be enough."

Chapter

Twenty-five

It was a disconcerting way to fight a war. Fotir had no idea from one moment to the next whether he should be advising his duke and the king or lending his magic to Grinsa. Several times already this day, the gleaner had entered his mind without warning, taking hold of his shaping magic to counter one of the Weaver's attacks. It was disorienting enough having the man in his mind wielding his power. But to have this happen seemingly at random, with no time to prepare himself, left the minister dazed, his thoughts addled as if from a sharp blow. He could hardly follow the course of the battle unfolding on the plain before him. He knew only that it was going poorly.

Grinsa's attempts to use the magic of the enemy to his own advantage—apparently a tactic suggested by Tavis—had worked at first, disrupting the Weaver's initial attacks and costing the man a good number of his warriors. But the enemy had recovered quickly, reforming his lines and using the awesome power he wielded to devastating effect. The Eandi archers had inflicted some damage on the Qirsi army, but their ranks had been decimated by the Weaver's shaping and fire power; fewer than a hundred remained alive and uninjured. Thus far Grinsa had managed to keep the enemy from doing the same to the Eandi swordsmen, but Fotir sensed that the gleaner's strength was failing. Each new Qirsi assault exacted a greater toll than the previous one, and every time Grinsa reached for the minister's power to defend the Eandi lines the effort seemed more desperate.

Grinsa stood quite close to where Fotir and his duke were watching the battle progress, but it might as well have been forty leagues. Having rid themselves of most of the archers, the Weaver and his servants had closed the distance between themselves and the Eandi lines. The Qirsi remained far enough away so that any advance by Kearney's swordsmen would leave the Eandi soldiers exposed to the Weaver's lethal power, but they were close enough to give the gleaner precious little time to respond to each new attack that Dusaan unleashed. All of Grinsa's attention was directed forward, his gaze never straying from the Weaver.

"Damn them!" Hagan MarCullet growled, standing near Javan and Fotir. "Why won't they just fight us and be done with it?" He cupped a hand to his mouth. "Fight, ye cowards!" he shouted.

Fotir glanced at the duke, who was already eyeing him, his expression bleak.

"Perhaps it is time we took the battle to them," Javan said. "This doesn't seem to be working."

Hagan nodded. "Couldn't the gleaner and the rest of you raise a mist? With the proper cover, we might be able to attack."

The minister started to respond, but before he could say a word, Grinsa was in his mind again, drawing on his shaping power. Fotir could see nothing of the Weaver's magic, of course, nor could he sense it, as Grinsa apparently could. But there could be no mistaking the panic in the gleaner's thoughts.

"Get behind your shields!" Fotir called to all who could hear. "This is going to be bad."

It was.

Even with Grinsa wielding the magic of so many, Fotir felt the collision of the gleaner's power with that of the Weaver as if it were a body blow. He staggered, reaching out to steady himself on whatever was nearest, which turned out to be his duke's shoulder. Grinsa touched his mind a second time, sending out another pulse of power. Nevertheless, when the Weaver's magic hit the Eandi lines, it was like a storm tide rushing over castles of sand. The Qirsi attack shattered the bodies of hundreds of warriors, crashing through the King's Guard, the soldiers of Sanbira, and the forces of Kentigern, Thorald, Heneagh, Labruinn, Tremain, and even Curgh. No army was spared.

Those who were able to raise their shields in time found themselves holding mangled pieces of wood and steel. But at least they were alive.

"The gleaner's weakening, isn't he?" the duke said.

"There are just too many of them," Fotir answered, feeling that he needed to defend his friend.

"I'm not finding fault, First Minister, I'm merely making an observation."

Reluctantly, Fotir nodded. "I can feel his weariness."

"We should attack them," Hagan said, echoing the duke's words from a moment before. "Standing here waiting to die is not my idea of waging war."

Javan cast a hard look at the Qirsi army. "We should at least suggest as much to the gleaner and the king, while there's still time."

Fotir nodded his agreement, and they hurried to where Grinsa and Kearney stood.

Grinsa's face was as white as Panya's glow, and sweat ran like tears down his cheeks.

"Please pardon the intrusion, Your Majesty," the duke said, "but we've been wondering if it might not be time to alter our tactics."

Kearney wore a pained expression, as if hope had long since abandoned him. "To what end, Javan?"

"We should take the fight to them. Have the gleaner raise a mist to conceal an assault on the Qirsi lines."

"Any mist I raise the Weaver will defeat with a wind. I haven't enough Qirsi to sustain both a mist and an opposing gale. It would be a slaughter."

"It's becoming that already," the duke said.

Fotir thought the gleaner would argue, but he merely shrugged.

Kearney looked at Grinsa. "Can you keep the Weaver occupied for a time? Give us an opportunity to advance on him unseen?"

"Not without—" He faltered, his eyes widening slightly, though they never left the Weaver. "Actually there may be a way to give you that opportunity and perhaps win one for me, as well. Fotir, gather the Qirsi as quickly as you can. Bring them all to me. We haven't much time before the Weaver attacks again."

The minister glanced at his duke, who nodded immediately.

He sprinted off, running first to the west and then back to the east before returning to the gleaner. At one point he had to stop so that Grinsa could draw upon his power again and ward off another attack. Somehow, the gleaner was able to project more magic this time, and the Weaver's assault had little effect. It seemed that whatever hope Grinsa had glimpsed had strengthened him, at least for the moment.

By the time he returned, there were a dozen Qirsi gathered around the king and gleaner.

Still, Grinsa frowned when he saw the minister had returned.

"Where's Keziah?"

Fotir felt the blood drain from his face. "I don't know. I didn't see her."

"What do you mean you didn't see her?" Kearney demanded. "Where could she have gone?"

"It doesn't matter right now!" the gleaner said, though there could be no mistaking the concern in his pale eyes. "I need all of you who have mists and winds to raise a mist together. Summon the mist from the center of the battle plain and when the Weaver raises a wind to counter it—"

"Wait," Evetta said. "Aren't you going to be weaving us?"

Somehow Grinsa managed a grin. "No, I'm not. The Weaver will think I am, and when he pits his magic against yours, I'll strike at him." He turned to the king. "Your warriors won't have much time, Your Majesty. They must attack swiftly."

"Should we use the horses?"

"I still think that would be a mistake. Especially in a mist. With the Qirsi on horseback, your warriors will have no doubt as to who the enemy is. And with your men on foot, the Weaver will have one less magic at his disposal."

"Very well."

"We should begin immediately."

Kearney nodded. "We await the mist."

Grinsa eyed his fellow Qirsi once more. "When the Weaver raises his wind, you'll have to work together to fight against it. If this is to work, I can't help you."

"We'll do our part," Fotir said.

The gleaner smiled faintly. "I'm sure you will. Begin."

Fotir faced the battle plain and began to draw upon his power of mists and winds. Without the gleaner in his mind, bolstering his magic, blending it with his own and that of the others, he felt weak and small. But among the Qirsi standing with him, several wielded this magic, and in just a short time a heavy fog had settled over the moor.

"Your Majesty?" Grinsa said.

Kearney drew his sword, as did Javan, Tavis, Hagan Mar-Cullet and his son, and Gershon Trasker.

"Our lives are in your hands, gleaner," the king said. "May the gods be kind to us all."

"I'll do all I can to protect you, Your Majesty. If by my death, I can insure your survival, and that of the others, then so be it."

"I hope it doesn't come to that." Kearney faced his sword-master. "Gershon, signal the attack."

The swordmaster began barking commands, which were echoed along the Eandi lines in both directions. Within moments, soldiers were surging forward, their swords raised, war cries on their lips. It seemed that they had been waiting for this, impatient for the opportunity to fight back against this maddening, deadly foe.

The king and duke started forward as well, although not before Tavis turned to face the gleaner.

"When this is over," Tavis said, "I want a new Fating."

"What?"

The young lord was smiling, the scars he carried from Kentigern appearing to vanish for just a moment. Grinsa's brow was furrowed as if he were frowning, but there was a smile on his lips as well.

"I've never had a real one, you know, and I think I've earned it."

Grinsa laughed. "Fine. A Fating it is. Now go."

Tavis gazed at the gleaner a moment longer, then turned and ran to join the rest.

Fotir and the other Qirsi continued to weave their mists and soon the Eandi warriors had vanished in the grey cloud they had created, though their shouts could still be heard.

"Why isn't the Weaver doing anything?" Xivled jal Viste asked. "Why hasn't he raised a wind yet?"

Grinsa was frowning, his eyes on the mist. "Where in Qirsar's name is Kezi?" he muttered. Then, as if finally realizing that Xiv's question had been directed at him, he shook his head, as if rousing himself. "I'm sorry. What did you say?"

"I was wondering why the Weaver hadn't raised a wind yet."

"A good question. I think he may be confused. He's probably wondering if this is a feint of some sort, or an act of desperation."

"Little does he know that it's both."

Grinsa smirked. "Indeed."

"Can he sense that you're not weaving us?" Fotir asked.

"Probably, but even so, his lines are about to be attacked by more than two thousand men. He has to do something. The question is, will he strike out blindly, or try first to defeat the mist."

For the first time since leaving Braedon's Imperial Palace in the Weaver's company, Nitara felt herself growing truly afraid. The mist itself was nothing to fear. The Weaver would have little trouble sweeping it away with a wind; he had far more sorcerers at his disposal than did the Eandi.

But it soon became apparent to her that he was making no effort to do so. Did he want the mist to remain in place? If so, what was it he expected of the rest of them? And if not, why had he allowed it to remain? Was he engaged in some other struggle? Or worse, had he been hurt or killed? Nitara tried to tell herself that this was impossible, but the night before she had seen blood on his face and robe, and this very morning another Weaver—another Weaver!—had taken hold of her magic and made her tumble from her mount. She had tried to convince herself otherwise, but this was the only explanation for what had happened to her, and for what had been done to others in the Weaver's ranks. Where once, not more than a day ago, a mist like this one would have been of no concern at all, it now chilled her to her heart, as if Bian himself had summoned the vapor from his dark realm.

She could hear soldiers approaching. Hundreds of soldiers, perhaps more.

Abruptly she found herself helpless. She was on horseback, and she carried a blade, but she was no fighter. And without the Weaver, she had no magic with which to defend herself. She could raise a wind to blow away the mist, but what if the Weaver didn't want that? Her other magics— gleaning and language of beasts—were of little use to her. She'd heard it said long ago that her people weren't meant to be warriors, that their magics were not those of a conquering race. Indeed, these were words ascribed to Carthach himself, the traitor whose treason ended the first Qirsi War nine centuries before. But until this moment, she had never understood what he meant.

There were other Qirsi near her, barely visible through the dense mist, but none of them had said a word to her, and again, she wasn't certain what the Weaver expected of them.

She actually had started to consider retreat, when at last a wind rose, gathering speed swiftly and stirring the fog so that it began to dissipate. Still the mist surrounded them, and other winds blew, clearly intended to counter the one raised by the Weaver. In the next instant, though, the Weaver's gale died away, just as abruptly as it had appeared. Nitara began to hear voices calling out along the Qirsi front, the words impossible to make out at first. But it seemed this was a message that traveled the lines.

"Summon your own winds!" she heard. "Defeat this mist!"

She repeated the words, shouting them as well, listened as the command traveled past her and was lost in the wind and fog.

Before she could reach for her magic, the Eandi soldiers reached her. Nitara kicked at her mount, driving the beast directly at the men, hacking at them with her sword. There was no grace in her attack, no method. She was impelled by fear, and the certainty that if she didn't kill the men they would kill her. From all around her came the cries of warriors and the clash of steel. Winds rose and fell, stirring the mist into a frenzy so that it seemed wraiths were dancing all around the battle, but failing to clear the air.

She could hear the chime of shattering metal and the muted snapping of bone, and she knew that there were shapers nearby. She nearly gagged on the smell of charred flesh, saw dark grey smoke mingling with the sorcerous fog. There were other Qirsi nearby who were better suited than she to fighting these men. She lashed out with her blade, doing little damage to the enemy, but keeping them at bay at least for the moment. As she fought, she turned her mount once more and kicked the beast to a gallop, retreating from the combat.

"Where are you going?" a man's voice called to her. She stared into the swirling mist, unable to see more than a vague form, mounted and crowned with white hair.

"My magic won't avail me in battle," she answered. "From further back I can summon a wind."

She heard no reply, but thought she saw the rider nod before he vanished.

As soon as Nitara felt that she was safe from Eandi steel she halted and added her own wind to the muddled gale that raged over the battle plain. Still the mist lingered, giving an unearthly quality to the sounds of battle—the screams and moans, the clang of steel, and the dull pounding of horses' hooves. She tried to shift the direction of the wind she had summoned, but amid the magic of so many Qirsi, nothing she did seemed to have much effect.

The thought came to her with the brutal swiftness of a blow, stealing her breath and making her totter in her saddle.

What had happened to the Weaver? She and her fellow Qirsi were fighting this mist and their soldiers on their own, without his magic to bolster their power, without his vision to direct their efforts.

Was he dead? Was he locked in a battle of his own?

A second blow, even more potent than the first. The second Weaver. Who else could hope to engage him in combat for any length of time?

Before she knew what she was doing, Nitara was riding along the Qirsi lines searching for the Weaver, straining to see through the mist, desperate to catch sight of his chiseled face and regal mane. *Gods, let him be alive!*

She wasn't certain how she could help him—of what use could she be in a battle between Weavers? She knew only that she needed to be with him. Nothing else mattered. Without Dusaan, this war was lost. And even if Nitara and her fellow Qirsi managed to prevail without him, what would be left of their movement? Who would rule the Forelands if not her Weaver? He was their strength, their cunning. He was their future. So Nitara rode, standing in her stirrups, gazing intently into the maddening white mist, her eyes tearing with the effort. She sensed that he was close, and also that he was in danger. More, it seemed that no one else understood this. It all fell to her. She could save him and so save the movement. Or she could fail and bring all to ruin.

As soon as he sensed the wind rising, Grinsa attacked. Shaping, fire, language of beasts, delusion, shaping again, healing, fire, language of beasts. Each time Dusaan warded one magic, Grinsa reached for another. He was weary and fear had crept deep into his heart. But he refused to despair, and he fought the Weaver with all the fury he had held within himself over the past year. Was Dusaan stronger than he?

Perhaps. Grinsa didn't care anymore. He struck at the man as a battle-crazed warrior hammers at the shield of his foe. He abandoned all to cruelty and vengeance, hatred and bloodlust. Shaping, healing, delusion, fire, language of beasts. Pity was weakness. Mercy might prove fatal. For this one moment, this final battle, he knew only malice and savagery.

For good or ill, this was his last onslaught. He would spend all destroying this man and crushing his movement. For Cresenne and Bryntelle, for Keziah and Tavis, for this land and its people, so imperfect and yet so deserving of his protection despite their flawed humanity. He drew upon his love of all, of life itself, and through a dark and perverse alchemy transformed it into power more fell and terrifying than any he had wielded before.

Fire, healing, language of beasts, delusion, shaping.

Magic coursed through his body, hot and terrible, searing his limbs, his lungs, his veins. He was ablaze with it, incandescent, as if Morna's sun burned within him. Never before had he wielded power such as this; he had never even tried.

And within mere moments he knew that it wouldn't be enough. Not nearly.

No matter how quickly he shifted from one magic to the next, Dusaan responded, altering his defenses to match every assault. Grinsa gave the Weaver no chance to fight back and kept him from weaving the magic of the sorcerers in the Qirsi army, but other than that, his attacks had no effect. Still he fought on, looking for an opening, hoping that just once he would reach for a magic that Dusaan had left unguarded. He didn't.

Not even a Weaver could maintain such an attack forever. Already Grinsa sensed that he was nearing the limits of his endurance, and he knew that when his strength failed him, Dusaan would be ready. A voice within his mind—was it Cresenne's?—called for him to break off his offensive, to save some of his strength for whatever would come after this gambit failed. Yet, he didn't dare. He had sent Kearney, Tavis, and the rest of the Eandi forward under the cover of mist to bring war to the Qirsi army. As soon as he stopped trying to take control of Dusaan's power, there would be nothing to stop the Weaver from slaughtering them.

Instead, he continued to pound at Dusaan's mind with his own. Fire, shaping, delusion, fire, language of beasts, shaping. He could feel himself growing weaker. For a time, Dusaan had struggled to hold him off, like a swordsman parrying the attacks of a crazed foe. Now the Weaver seemed to be toying with him, as the same swordsman might play with a child, turning away his assaults with ease and unnerving confidence.

Still, when Dusaan's reprisal came, Grinsa was utterly unprepared. One moment he was attempting to seize the Weaver's healing magic, and the next he was on his back, the bones in both of his legs splintered like dry wood. Awash in a sea of pain, he never had the chance to scream. Suddenly he couldn't draw breath. It seemed that some great demon from the Underrealm was kneeling on his chest.

Cresenne! he thought, silent tears on his face. *I've failed! Forgive me!*

He heard laughter in his mind, and then a voice.

"No, gleaner. You'll not have such an easy death. You'll see it all before the end. My victory, the destruction of your Eandi friends, the broken body of your sister. All of it. You'll know torment and despair and humiliation before the sweet release you seek." Dusaan laughed again. And then, out of spite, or simply because he could, the Weaver smashed the bone in Grinsa's shoulder, the same one broken by the merchant Grinsa battled on the Wethy Crown. "That's for Tihod," he said, before leaving the gleaner with his agony and his sorrow.

Yes, there had been harrowing moments. Years from now when he looked back on this day, relishing once more his victory over the gleaner and the armies of the Eandi courts, he would admit that much to himself. Grinsa's attack, while not unexpected, had been far more furious than he thought it would be. In its first few moments, Dusaan truly feared for his life. It didn't take him long, however, to realize that the gleaner couldn't hurt him. Perhaps if this had been Grinsa's first attack it might have worked. But the gleaner was weary, his power diminished by all that had come before. The Weaver knew that he needed only to ward himself and wait. Eventually Grinsa's strength would fail, and then the war would be Dusaan's.

He would remember for the rest of his days how it felt to take hold of Grinsa's power and turn it against the gleaner. No vengeance had ever tasted so sweet. It almost seemed that he could hear the bones shattering, that he could feel Grinsa's hope wither and die. Was there risk in allowing the man to live? Of course, but not much. He was spent, broken, beaten. And he would die soon enough.

The Weaver could see nothing while the mist hung over the battle plain. It seemed that his warriors had managed to withstand the Eandi charge, but he couldn't be certain of this so long as he battled the gleaner. After defeating Grinsa, however, Dusaan summoned a gale that swept away the fog, revealing a pitched battle between his Qirsi riders and the soldiers of Eibithar and Sanbira. The dead and wounded lay everywhere. Most were Eandi, their bodies broken or charred or bloodied by a sword stroke. But there were Qirsi dead as well, stark crimson stains on their pale skin and white hair.

As soon as the mist vanished, warriors on both sides faltered, as if uncertain as to what to do next.

Dusaan wasted no time. "Shapers!" he cried.

There would be no magic to oppose him this time, no pulse of power to match his own. He could destroy the Eandi at will. Grinsa was trying to take hold of his magic again. Dusaan sensed the attack coming and started to ward himself, but the gleaner's attempt amounted to nothing. Grinsa had no strength left. His assault was so pitiful that Dusaan nearly laughed aloud. There was no one left to oppose him, at least no one who mattered.

The Weaver had thought to have the king of Eibithar murdered before this battle began, and his first thought now was to kill Kearney and thus deny the Eandi their leader. An instant later he reconsidered. By killing the king, he gave the man's soldiers reason to fight and others reason to resist his advance across the land in subsequent days. Better to destroy the army and force Kearney's surrender. He would ride at the head of Dusaan's army a prisoner, stripped of his sword, his head bent, his hands bound. Let any others who might think to stand against the Qirsi see that.

He glanced at his warriors, gathering their power so as to strike at the enemy. The Qirsi were watching him. Fatigued, but expectant. They, too, knew that victory was near. He saw pride in their pale eyes, a desire to finish this, to realize the vision of which he had spoken so often.

The Eandi eyed him as well, terror and loathing on their faces. How long had he waited for this moment? It was all that he had imagined it would be, and more. He was as strong as a god, as indomitable as Qirsar himself. Power filled him—his own, and that of his servants. He had only to choose where to strike. He surveyed the battle plain for just an instant. Yes, there. A smile touched his lips, and he let the magic fly.

It was like fighting in a dream. He knew that others were nearby—the king, his father, Xaver—but he couldn't see them and he hadn't time to search for them in the mist. Qirsi horsemen appeared before him, and Tavis fought. Twice his clothes had been set ablaze. The first time, he had dropped to the ground, rolled back and forth until he extinguished the flames, and stood once more to fight on. The second time he didn't bother with the fire on his shirt until after he had pulled the Qirsi from his saddle and killed him. He had burns on his neck and arm, but he didn't care. He had been lucky to face Qirsi with fire magic. Shapers would have killed him.

The soldiers who saw what he had done cheered him, and after that they fought alongside him, guarding him from attacks, treating him as one of their own. At long last he had earned the trust of Kearney's men-at-arms, perhaps even their respect. It was a shame that none of them would live out the day.

Even before the mist drifted away, borne on the sorcerer's wind, Tavis sensed that the battle wasn't going Grinsa's way. It was intuition, nothing more—a cold, sour feeling in his stomach—but he took it as prophecy. He had often heard Grinsa speak with frustration of his gleaning power, of how uncertain it could be at times, and it occurred to him to wonder if this was what it was like: elusive, insubstantial glimpses of the future. When the air cleared, he wasn't at all surprised.

The battle slowed, then ceased altogether, warriors on both sides staring up at the Weaver atop his mount, some of them with blades poised to strike. They remained that way for what seemed an eternity, though it was probably only a few moments. The young lord glanced to his left, saw Xaver standing motionless, his sword held loosely in his right hand, his eyes already fixed on Tavis. He opened his mouth and took a breath, as if intending to say something. And in that moment the Weaver struck.

Had Tavis been standing with his friend, he would have died as well, his entire body shattered as if some unseen fist had battered him to the earth. As it was, the Weaver's magic reached only so far, stopping just a few fourspans from where Tavis was watching, helpless and aggrieved.

Heedless of all else, he bounded to his friend's side, but it was already too late. Xaver lay lifeless on the grass, his body mangled, though there didn't appear to be a mark on him. His eyes were closed, his face so utterly composed that one might well have thought him asleep and lost in a dream, had it not been for the small trickle of blood that seeped from his nose.

Tavis cradled the boy's head in his lap, tears pouring down his cheeks and falling like rain on Xaver's brow.

After a moment, he looked up, glaring at the Weaver. "You bastard!" he shouted. "You cowardly bastard!"

The Qirsi gazed back at him serenely, saying nothing. Then he turned toward Kearney.

"Surrender now, Your Majesty, and I'll spare the rest of your men."

Standing just a short distance from where Tavis knelt in

the grass, Kearney gripped his sword and stood straight-backed, a gentle wind stirring his silver hair. "I'll not surrender to you."

The Weaver raised an eyebrow and gave a slight shrug. A moment later a sudden torrent of fire crashed into the other side of the Eandi army, searing flesh, hair, and clothing, scattering bodies as a gust of wind scatters seeds from a harvest flower.

The Weaver started to say something else, but Tavis heard none of it. At that moment Hagan MarCullet arrived, dropping to his knees beside his son's shattered form, sobs racking his body, his voice breaking as he said the boy's name again and again. Tavis laid the boy's head in Hagan's lap, drawing the swordmaster's gaze.

"I'm so sorry, Hagan," he managed to say. "If I hadn't convinced you to let him fight—"

"Hush, boy. It wasn't you or me. I know that; you should, too."

Tavis nodded, wanting only to kill the Weaver, even if he died doing so. He heard more screams, reaching him as if from far off. Perhaps the Weaver had struck at them again.

The young lord hardly cared. He couldn't take his eyes off Xaver, nor could he seem to stop crying.

"Lord Curgh," a voice said from just behind him.

Tavis didn't answer. This was the end. They'd die here on the Moorlands, or they'd be made slaves to the Qirsi. Either way, they had lost.

"Lord Curgh." More insistent this time. Still Tavis refused to turn. Why couldn't they just leave him alone?

"Tavis."

It was his name that reached him. Turning, he saw Marston of Shanstead standing over him, a look of deepest concern on his youthful face.

"What do you want?"

"It's your father. I think you'd better come quickly."

Tavis glanced quickly at Hagan, his blood turning cold. "Stay here," he said.

He stood and hurried after Marston, his apprehension mounting with every step, his legs trembling so badly he expected to stumble at any moment. The thane led him past living soldiers and then past dead ones. No one spoke, or if they did, Tavis didn't hear them. He just walked, following the man to where his father lay.

The duke lived still, but only barely. Like Xaver, he was unmarked. Shaping. How did one fight such an enemy?

"Your son, my lord," said a soldier who knelt by Javan.

The duke's eyes fluttered open. "Tavis?" he said, the word coming out as a sigh.

Tavis's tears were flowing once more. Had they even stopped?

"Yes, Father," he said, kneeling as well and taking his father's hand. The duke's skin was as cold as stone. "I'm here."

"Tell your mother . . . Tell her I'm sorry I didn't make it home to her."

"Father—"

"No. Listen. You lead our house now. No matter what. Curgh is yours. Even in defeat, you remain who you are. Never surrender."

Tavis didn't know what to say, and he couldn't have spoken if he had.

"This last year, you've made me proud."

"You should have been king."

Javan shook his head, closing his eyes. "No. The gods know. This was . . . my fate."

The duke's mouth opened, as if he was going to speak again. But he moved no more.

He should have taken his sword and rushed at the Weaver. He would have died, of course, but perhaps he would have inspired others to do the same. Maybe he could have turned the tide of this battle. But Tavis could do nothing more than kneel beside his father, the duke of Curgh, and surrender all to grief.

"Lay down your sword!" he heard the Weaver say, steel in his voice. "Save the lives of those few who remain under your command!"

"We don't fear death," Kearney answered, his voice equally strong. "Indeed, if surrender means submitting to the rule of a tyrant, we would rather die than yield."

There was a brief silence. Then, "So be it. You bring this doom on yourself, Eandi."

Wrenching himself out of his mourning, Tavis made himself watch. If this was to be the end of Eibithar, the end of the House of Curgh, he owed it to his father and Xaver to bear witness.

"Shapers," the Weaver said, his eyes never leaving Kearney's face.

She fought without purpose, without thought, without love or hate or fear. The Weaver drew upon her power as if it were ink in a well, using what he needed when he needed it. She offered neither resistance nor passion. Even when the mist surrounded her, and the Weaver no longer touched her mind, she didn't grow afraid. Soldiers appeared before her, brandishing their blades, eyeing her with contempt, and she struck at them, using her magic to break their swords. But she didn't kill. That she left to the other Qirsi. This was no attempt to embrace virtue. She knew that the Weaver used her magic to destroy Eandi warriors and that if Bian chose to judge her harshly when at last she died, he'd have ample reason for doing so. She simply didn't care enough about any of this to take the lives of those she rendered unarmed.

Watching her do battle, one might have thought her resigned to the inevitability of her death, but that wasn't right either. She didn't want to die. Or more precisely, she didn't want to face her dead in Bian's Underrealm. Not like this.

Yet even that didn't explain it.

It almost seemed that she was dead already. Nothing could be taken from her that she hadn't already lost. Nothing could touch her. Not grief, though she would have welcomed tears; not rage, though anger might have brought with it courage and resolve; not even the cold calculation of ambition, though she knew that others around her fought for the glory promised them by the Weaver.

She was aware only of what she saw before her, of what the Weaver expected of her, of what she had to do to survive.

That, and of the voice repeating itself in her mind, nudging her toward action.

Why did she resist? Was she afraid after all? Yes, it seemed she was. Not of death, but of failure which would bring pain and humiliation. Better to do nothing than to face those, for she would fail. She knew that as well.

Still, the voice remained with her, both gentle and insistent.

Don't let him win.

She didn't feel the Weaver's touch for some time, and she began to think that perhaps he had been defeated, that none of this would fall to her. But then a wind whipped past her, driving off the mist, leaving her squinting in the bright sunlight. A moment later the Weaver touched her mind once more, dipping into the well, using her power to kill hundreds.

He'll do this to everything. Fight him.

What could she do against such power? It would be a futile gesture, a sacrifice without meaning.

Again he took hold of her magic, crushing Eandi soldiers as if they were ants.

Don't let him.

She had let Evanthya die. Her cowardice had cost her the one love she had ever known. Now it held her again, robbing her of her strength, her will.

My strength to you.

"Lay down your sword!"

Eibithar's king stood defiant and regal, looking much as a king should. But Fetnalla knew that she didn't do this for him, or for any of the Eandi. She harbored no love for them. Even here, at the end, she still found herself unable to forgive Brall for his suspicions, his betrayal of their friendship. No, whatever she did would be for Evanthya.

"So be it! You bring this doom on yourself, Eandi."

The Weaver was already reaching for her power when he said, "Shapers."

It made this easier in a way, for he strengthened her himself. He augmented her magic, blending it with his own and that of the others. She needed only to direct it, to turn it back on him.

It was not until she tried to do just this, however, that she realized how great a mistake she had made.

The Weaver hesitated, and then his eyes snapped toward her, blazing like ward fires.

"What are you doing?"

She struggled to fight him, to strike at him with her shaping power. But her magic was part of a far greater force now, an alloy forged from the power of so many. It was enormous, a weapon far beyond her abilities. She could no more wield it than a child could a soldier's broadsword.

He glared at her, his eyes narrowing. Abruptly, she couldn't breathe. "Why?" he demanded. "What could make you do this?"

Before she could answer a second mind touched her own, and she sensed that there was magic here as well. It was no match for the Weaver's but still it was considerable, and it took hold of that great weapon, the one she hadn't the power to master herself.

"No!" she heard the Weaver roar.

This second presence held fast, struggling to break the Weaver's grip on her. She felt it growing more potent, as if feeding on the magic of the other Qirsi, until it equaled the Weaver's might. And then it struck.

Dusaan struggled to wrest control of the magic from this other force—Fetnalla understood that she had become a battlefield, that somehow the fate of the Forelands would be determined by this fight for her power. And after a moment's uncertainty, she chose.

Don't let him win.

There was, of course, an explanation for all that was happening around her, one that made sense within the natural laws that governed Qirsi magic. She didn't care. As far as Fetnalla was concerned, it was Evanthya fighting the Weaver, grappling with him for control of her magic, giving her the power to resist. *My strength to you,* her love had said.

Yes.

✦

How many times had he surrendered to despair, thinking that he had lost this war, only to find that hope yet remained? But on this day, at last, Grinsa knew that he had lost, that with his body broken and his power exhausted, there was nothing more he could do to combat the Weaver and his army.

Yet when he heard those words—"What are you doing?"—he lifted his gaze to the Weaver's face. And seeing doubt in the man's eyes he dared hope that there might still be one last chance to save all that he held dear.

He reached forth with his mind and immediately found the woman. There were still many Qirsi in Dusaan's army, but this one stood out like a gem among river stones. Bright, defiant, grieving, proud. He hadn't time to wonder who she was, or why she did this. He reached for her magic, took hold of it with all the strength he had left.

Doing so he found himself in possession of all Dusaan's servants, at least all those with shaping magic. For they were one, joined into a single force by the Weaver himself, ready to strike. He had only to seize them from the man, and they were his.

But he was weak, wounded, forlorn, and he would have failed had it not been for the woman. Her magic filled him, renewed him, restored his power and his spirit. Still, he hadn't enough to overmaster the Weaver. Not without help.

And who else should come to his aid in that one last moment, than Tavis of Curgh, who despite all that he once had been, was now a man of courage and keenest insight. Grinsa heard the young lord's voice cry out, saw him raise his sword and charge toward the Qirsi lines. His was a futile attack, an invitation to death, but it was also the last thing that Dusaan expected. The Weaver's attention wavered. It was only for an instant, but it was enough. Taking hold of the magic, of this great, shining weapon the woman had offered him, Grinsa ripped it away from the Weaver, and smote him, drawing upon all the strength he had left, knowing that he would have only this one opportunity.

Dusaan flew off of his mount as if swatted by the hand of a god.

A shrill cry of disbelief and anguish and fury was ripped from the man's throat as he tumbled through the air and landed in a heap just in front of his army. He stirred, reached one last time for his magic, shouting his rage. And Grinsa hammered at him again, crushing him, silencing him, ridding the Forelands of his malice and his terrifying magic.

For the span of a heartbeat, every man and woman on the battle plain was still. Qirsi, Eandi. None so much as took a breath. Grinsa heard no sound save the rustling of the grasses in the soft wind.

Then all was tumult.

She heard the king shout out for his men to attack, and she saw several of her fellow warriors turn their mounts and flee rather than face Eandi steel without the guiding power of the Weaver.

But Nitara paid no heed to any of them. Dusaan was dead. Her heart had been rent in two. She couldn't bring herself to fight, nor did she care enough about her own survival to retreat. Vengeance was all that was left to her, and she took it.

The woman who had turned on them sat motionless, staring at the Weaver's crumpled body, oblivious of all that was happening around her. There may even have been a tear on her face.

Nitara cared not. Raising her sword, she kicked at the flanks of her mount and charged the woman.

"For my people!" she shouted, and swung her weapon.

The woman looked up in time to see Nitara riding toward her, but she made no effort to defend herself. The blade sliced into her side and she fell to the ground, making no sound at all.

Nitara reined her horse to a halt, threw herself off of the beast, and strode to the woman's side. Blood poured from the wound, darkening the grasses and soil, but Nitara hardly noticed. She laid the tip of her blade at the base of the woman's neck, staring down at her, hating her more than she had ever hated anything or anyone.

"Why?" she shouted, tears suddenly coursing down her face. "Why did you betray him?"

The woman just gazed up at the sky, a slight smile on her lips. "My love," she whispered, and was still.

"Tell me!" Nitara cried, though she knew that the woman was beyond hearing. "Damn you!"

Aware once more of the battle raging around her, she looked up. Three Eandi soldiers were advancing on her, swords held ready. No doubt she should have retreated to fight another day, but as far as she was concerned there were no more days. The living world had become for her a wasteland. Grinning darkly, she raised her sword and awaited their assault.

Chapter

Twenty-six

Pronjed could hardly believe how quickly their fortunes had turned. Moments before the Weaver and his army had been on the verge of a great victory. Now the Weaver was dead, his army scattering over the battle plain, some fighting, others in flight. In the days leading up to this war, Pronjed had considered many possible outcomes, most of them turning on the simple fact that Dusaan jal Kania hadn't liked him very much and might well have killed him once the war was over. But the archminister didn't believe that he would see the Weaver defeated. He never imagined that he would watch the man die.

He had little interest in continuing this fight. Whatever his feelings toward the Eandi, he knew better than to think that he could stand against an army of them. His powers were considerable—having both delusion and shaping power, he could talk or fight his way past a good number of warriors.

And if those didn't work, he also had mists and winds. Nevertheless, he preferred to slip away, unnoticed and preferably alone.

But where to go? There was no future for him in Aneira, where by now he had been branded a traitor and sentenced to death. Nor could he remain in Eibithar, where his accent marked him as an enemy. He had no desire to live in Braedon or Wethyrn. The nobles of the empire would never again trust a Qirsi, and Wethyrn, for all its charm, was simply too small and weak to hold his interest. Which left him with Caerisse or Sanbira, and both lay to the south and west.

He made this choice in a matter of seconds and promptly turned his mount westward, intending to ride off at a full gallop.

"Hold, Qirsi."

A woman's voice, young but not without some mettle. A noble of some sort, probably a duchess. From Sanbira judging from the accent.

Pronjed turned slowly to face her. She looked even younger than she sounded and was every bit as beautiful as one would expect a noble of the southern realm to be. Her hair and eyes were black; with her long limbs and lanky frame she looked more like a festival dancer than a warrior. But she held a blade ready, and Pronjed felt certain that she knew how to use it. Four men stood with her, all of them holding bows.

Looking at the soldiers, the minister had the sense that they were swordsmen rather than archers; none looked comfortable with his bow. But all had arrows nocked and the bowstrings drawn. Whatever their skill, one of them would probably manage to aim true. Pronjed thought that he could snap all four bows before one of the men managed to loose his arrow, but he wasn't certain.

"My lady," he said, needing time, needing to take the measure of this bold duchess.

"Throw down your weapons and dismount."

He laughed. She might have been brave, but she was too young and foolish to represent any true danger. "My weapon?" He pulled his sword free and tossed it on the ground at her feet. "There. Do you truly believe that you've nothing to fear from me now?"

"Of course not, Minister. But my father always taught me that in disarming a foe, one should begin with the most obvious dangers."

Pronjed eyed her curiously. *Minister.* "Have we met, my lady?"

"I don't believe so. But you knew me for a duchess, and I know you for a minister. Is that so strange?"

Perhaps there was more to this woman than he had thought. "Who are you?"

"Off your horse, Qirsi. We'll have ample time later for such questions."

"Tell me," he said, and this time he touched her mind lightly with his delusion magic.

"My name is Diani. I'm the duchess of Curlinte."

Of course. He'd heard of this one, and of the attempt on her life. "Well, Lady Curlinte, I think I'd be better off remaining on my horse. I don't imagine your queen or Eibithar's king will be dealing lightly with men like me. Don't you agree?"

"Yes, I suppose I do."

The soldiers were glancing at one another, frowns on their faces. "My lady," one of them said.

The duchess shook her head, then looked up at Pronjed with a mix of horror and indignation. "What did you do to me?"

"As you see, my lady. That sword was the least of my weapons."

Before she could order the soldiers to kill him, Pronjed struck at them with his shaping magic, splintering the four bows. As an afterthought, he broke her sword as well, leaving the duchess and her warriors looking bewildered and afraid.

"I think I'll be leaving now," the minister said. He grinned. "Unless you intend to pull me from my mount with your bare hands."

But the duchess wasn't ready to surrender. Pulling her dagger free, she stepped in front of him. "Get off that horse." After a moment's hesitation, the four soldiers joined her.

"Don't be a fool. I'll ride you down. That is, if I don't snap your neck first."

"Then do it. But I won't just stand by as you ride to freedom."

Normally, this woman and her soldiers wouldn't have been of any concern to him. But it had already been a long morning, and he had used a good deal of power on the Weaver's behalf. He could kill the five of them, but how much magic would he have left if others confronted him before he escaped?

"Move!" he said, pushing again with his delusion magic.

The duchess took a step to the side, then stumbled, as if resisting his power. She lifted her hands to her head, grimacing in pain.

"Don't let him get away!" she said, her teeth clenched.

The soldiers, who by now also had their daggers drawn, stood shoulder to shoulder in front of him. He read doubt in their faces, but he saw nothing to indicate that they were about to flee. Reluctantly, Pronjed reached for his shaping magic.

At the first touch on his mind, the minister thought that the Weaver had joined his fight, that he wasn't dead after all. But rather than feeling his power bolstered by this new presence in his mind, he felt it bound. The other Weaver. Somehow the man had sensed his power and taken hold of it. Abruptly, shaping was lost to him. He reached for delusion, but he could no more use that magic than the other. Mists and winds. Nothing.

"No!" he cried, without thinking.

The sound of his voice seemed to propel the duchess and soldiers into motion. Powerful hands grabbed hold of his leg and arm, and yanked him off of his horse. He landed hard on the ground, but still Pronjed fought to break free, even as he continued to battle the intruder in his mind. In all ways, however, he was helpless. A moment later, he felt the point of a dagger at his throat and he stiffened, ceasing his struggles.

The duchess seized a handful of his hair, forcing him to meet her gaze. "If you so much as blink, I'll kill you."

How he longed to shatter that blade, or better yet, to force the woman to turn it on herself, as he had done to Carden so long ago. But the other Weaver held him fast.

"Get rope," the duchess said. "Irons are no good against a shaper."

"Yes, my lady."

"Or better yet . . ."

He knew what was coming before she pulled the dagger away. He would have done the same had he been in her position.

"Damn," he had time to mutter.

Then he felt an explosion of pain at the back of his skull, and the minister knew no more.

The healers did what they could for her, mending the shattered bones in her leg and body, and easing her pain somewhat. Keziah had been through this before, however, and far too recently. She knew that it would be days before she could move without discomfort.

She also knew that she was fortunate to be alive at all, that had it not been for Aindreas of Kentigern, she too would have been counted among the victims of the Weaver and his war.

"Where can we take you, Archminister?" one of the healers asked, when they had finished ministering to her leg.

Keziah could hear soldiers cheering to the north. It seemed that the Weaver had been defeated. Somehow, incredibly, Grinsa had prevailed. Keziah felt that she was living some marvelous dream; for just an instant she feared waking to find that none of it was true, that the war had yet to be fought, that her survival and Grinsa's remained uncertain.

"I want to see my—" She felt her face color. "The gleaner. I want to see Grinsa." She tried to stand. "But I can go to him myself."

The healer laid a gentle but firm hand on her shoulder. "No," he said. "You can't. You'll be walking on your own soon enough. Tomorrow perhaps, or the day after. But for now, I'll carry you."

She started to object, then stopped herself. It hurt just to breathe, much less move. "Very well."

He lifted her effortlessly, and began walking toward the center of the Eandi lines. Resting in the healer's arms, Keziah suddenly found herself thinking of Fotir and Kearney and even Tavis of Curgh, wondering if they were alive, hoping desperately that they had survived the battle.

So it was that she was already looking for Curgh's first minister when he spotted her and called out her name. Fotir ran to her, grinning like a young boy on Bohdan's Night.

"You're alive!" he said. "Earlier, when we couldn't find you, Grinsa and I feared the worst." He looked at the healer. "Thank you. I can take her."

The healer glanced at Keziah, grinning slightly, an eyebrow raised.

She smiled in turn. "It's all right. He'll see to it that I don't walk."

The healer laughed. "Very well."

Fotir took her from the man.

"Thank you," Keziah said, as the healer began to turn away.

"Of course, Archminister. Stay off that leg."

"I will."

"What happened?" Fotir asked her, when they were alone.

She met his gaze briefly, then looked away, abruptly remembering the awkwardness of the night before. "The Weaver sent a shaper to kill me."

"What is it with you and shapers?"

"Careful, First Minister. As I remember it, you're a shaper."

This time it was Fotir who looked away. "True. Well, in any case, I'm glad you managed to defeat him."

"Actually, it was a woman, and I was saved by the duke of Kentigern."

Fotir stared at her, his bright yellow eyes wide. "Kentigern?"

"Yes. He died rescuing me." She almost said more, but thought better of it. "He wanted nothing more than to redeem his house."

"Perhaps by saving you he did."

She feared that redemption wouldn't come so easily for the people of Kentigern, but she merely nodded and said, "Yes, perhaps." A moment later, their eyes met again. "Where's Grinsa?"

"I'll take you to him." Fotir began to walk, carrying her past clusters of soldiers, some wounded, others simply smiling, sharing tales of the recent battle. "He was hurt," the first minister said. "The Weaver broke both of his legs and his shoulder."

Fear seized her heart. "But he's alive."

Fotir smiled reassuringly. "Yes. And he'll be very happy to see you."

They reached her brother a few moments later and Fotir lowered her to the ground beside him. Three healers knelt beside him, their hands on his legs and shoulder. Grinsa's eyes were closed and his face was damp with sweat.

"Grinsa," she said, shocked to see him looking so.

His eyes flew open. "Kezi!" He gripped her hand so tightly that it hurt. "I thought I'd lost you. Are you all right?"

"Not too bad. Better than you, it would seem."

He gave a small frown. "I'm fine. I was just helping the healers."

"Please talk to him, Archminister," said one of the healers, an older woman. "He's supposed to be resting."

"The sooner they're done with me, the sooner they can help someone else."

The healer continued to look at her, pleading with her pale eyes.

"I think it's best that I stay out of this." She glanced up at Fotir. "Don't you agree?"

But the minister was staring northward, his expression grim. "Excuse me," he said after a moment, and walked off without waiting for her reply.

Keziah looked at her brother, who merely shrugged.

"Tell me what happened," she said after a brief silence.

Grinsa began to describe for her his battle with the Weaver, and for a long time she forgot about Fotir and Aindreas and the woman who had nearly killed her, so rapt was she held by Grinsa's tale.

"Do you know who she is?" she asked when at last he had finished. "This woman who saved us?"

He shook his head. "No. But the Weaver spoke to her, so others may know what she did. I fear for her."

Keziah nodded.

"What about you?"

She told her story in turn, once again saying nothing about all that had passed between Aindreas and the Qirsi woman. Grinsa, however, seemed to sense that she had left something out.

"How fortunate for you that the duke happened upon you when he did."

Her gaze flicked toward the healers. "Yes."

Grinsa was watching her, and he nodded, seeming to understand her reticence.

"Do you know what happened to Tavis?" Keziah asked.

His brow furrowed. "No. I saw him charge the Qirsi lines, but I lost track of him in all that happened after."

"I'm sure he's all right," Keziah said, knowing how empty the words would sound, but feeling that she should say something. "It seems you were right about him. He did have a role to play in all this."

Before Grinsa could answer, the healers sat back on their heels, all of them looking worn.

"That's all we can do for you now, gleaner," the woman told him. "The rest will take some time. The bones in your leg have knitted well—you should be able to walk normally in just a few days." She hesitated. "Your shoulder . . . It had been broken before . . ."

Grinsa sat up slowly and smiled, though Keziah could see that it was forced. Her chest ached for him.

"It's not your fault," he said. "How bad is it?"

"You'll be able to move the arm, but not as you once did. And it will never look quite right."

He nodded, smiled again. "It could have been much worse. Thank you—all of you—for what you did."

They bowed to him, then moved off.

"I'm so sorry, Grinsa."

"It's nothing," he said. He looked at her, his eyes meeting

hers. "Truly, Kezi. With all that could have happened, this is a trifle."

"Of course," she said. But there were tears on her face.

"We should find someone who can help us up, and then search out the king and Tavis."

"Yes, all right."

Grinsa laughed. "We're quite a pair, aren't we. Unable to walk, barely able to sit up. It's a wonder we survived at all."

But Keziah knew better; surely her brother did as well. She was alive because Aindreas had given his life to protect her. Grinsa had prevailed because one woman in the Qirsi army had dared to oppose the Weaver, though she might well have died for the choice she made. There was nothing miraculous about their survival. It had been purchased with far too much blood.

Tavis stood alone in the middle of the battle plain, his sword held ready. He turned a slow circle, looking for someone to kill, or for someone who might kill him. He didn't care which just then. He wanted only to lash out with his steel, to feel his blade bite into flesh or armor or the edge of another sword. Already, he had killed two Qirsi in the time since the Weaver died. But it wasn't enough, not nearly.

"Come on!" he shouted, watching Eandi soldiers chase down the few renegades who remained on the plain, searching for just one white-hair of his own. "Cowards!"

"Tavis!"

He ignored the voice, though for just a moment it sounded like his father's.

"Tavis, lower your sword!"

Maybe it was Xaver calling to him. Perhaps he was surrounded by wraiths, the shades of all his dead.

"Tavis," came the voice again, softer this time, and much closer.

He spun, prepared to strike at the white-hair he saw standing before him.

"I can break your blade if I have to."

Tavis blinked, realized it was Fotir.

"Please, my lord."

He lowered his sword, abruptly finding that he was too weary to hold it high anymore. "First Minister," he muttered.

"I'm so sorry, my lord. To have lost one of them would have been bad enough. But to lose both . . ." He shook his head, looking like he might weep. "There's been no darker day in the long history of our house."

Tavis should have known what to say, but his battle rage had sluiced away, leaving him utterly spent. Even had he wanted to cry, he couldn't have. He could only nod dully, his eyes fixed on the ground at his feet.

"Let me take you back to the camp, my lord. Grinsa is eager to see you."

"He survived," Tavis said.

"Yes, my lord. He was injured, but the healers have treated him. He'll be fine."

"Good." He nodded again. "That's good."

Fotir put an arm around Tavis's shoulders and began to guide him back toward the Eandi lines. After only a few steps, however, Tavis stopped, turning his gaze to where his father had fallen.

"I should . . . He shouldn't just be left there."

"He's already been borne back to the Curgh camp, my lord. So has Master MarCullet."

They began to walk again. Tavis realized that he still held his blade in his hand, and he sheathed it.

"Should we send a messenger to my mother?" he asked.

"Truly, my lord, I don't know. It might be easier for her to hear these tidings from you."

Tavis looked up at that, meeting the minister's gaze. He nearly told the man to send a messenger, for he had no stomach for that conversation. But something stopped him.

For too long he had considered himself a coward, seeing in his failures as a warrior and the craven manner in which he had killed the assassin in Wethyrn, all the evidence of this that he needed. And though ashamed of his weakness, he had chosen to accept it as part of who he was. Today, he had acquitted himself well in combat, only to realize now how poor a measure of bravery was one's performance on a battlefield.

More to the point, on this day, he had become duke of Curgh. It was not a title he wanted, not so soon. But it was his nevertheless. The facile acceptance of his own limitations was a luxury he could no longer afford.

"You're right," he said. "I should be the one to tell her of Father's death." He straightened, even managed a small smile. "Thank you, Fotir. I know how much you cared for my father, and how much he valued your service to our house. I'm a poor substitute for him, but still I hope that you'll continue to serve as Curgh's first minister."

"If you wish it, my lord, I'd be honored."

"Thank you, Fotir."

"Lord Curgh!"

They halted and turned. Kearney strode toward them, followed by Gershon Trasker and the thane of Shanstead.

Tavis knelt, as did the minister. "Your Majesty."

"Please rise."

They both stood again.

"I'm pleased to see that you're all right, Tavis."

"Thank you, Your Majesty."

"I was deeply saddened to hear that your father was lost. He was as fine and noble a man as I've ever known. The Underrealm will shine like Morna's sky with his light. I can say the same of Master MarCullet. The House of Curgh has paid a dear price for the freedom of the Forelands. All in the land shall hear of the valor of her sons."

Tavis looked away, his eyes stinging. "Thank you, Your Majesty."

"I take it you were on your way to see the gleaner."

"Yes, Your Majesty."

"I'd like to join you if I may. He's earned our thanks and more."

"Of course, Your Majesty."

They began once more to walk, Tavis dabbing at his eyes, hoping Kearney wouldn't notice. A few moments before, he couldn't bring himself to shed even a single tear. Now he couldn't stop his tears from flowing.

They found Grinsa sitting on the grass beside his sister. His face was the color of ash and his clothes were soaked dark with sweat. But he smiled when he spotted Tavis and even raised a hand in greeting.

Kearney hurried forward to the archminister, hesitated briefly, then stooped and kissed her quickly on the cheek.

"I feared for you," he said, a bright smile on his lips.

Keziah's cheeks colored. "Thank you, Your Majesty."

"What happened?"

"The Weaver sent an assassin for me. I would have died had it not been for Lord Kentigern."

"Aindreas?" the king said, clearly surprised. "Where is he now?"

"He's dead, Your Majesty."

The king's smile vanished. "Damn. We lost too many today."

"Tavis?" Grinsa was eyeing him grimly, as if readying himself for dark tidings. "Tell me."

"My father," Tavis said, his voice breaking. "And Xaver."

The gleaner closed his eyes for a moment. "I'm so sorry, Tavis."

They were all watching him, pity in their eyes, and though he knew that they meant well, Tavis couldn't bear their stares or their sympathy. He turned abruptly and started away. "My pardon, Your Majesty," he called over his shoulder.

Tavis knew just where he was going, or rather, who he was looking for: the one man on the Moorlands who understood what he was feeling, who fully shared his grief.

It took him some time to find Hagan MarCullet, but he spotted the swordmaster at last, sitting on the grass some distance to the south of the Eandi camps. He had his back to the armies, and as Tavis approached he suddenly found himself hesitating, wondering if he should leave the man to his solitude and his anguish. At last he halted, intending to turn back.

But at that moment, Hagan turned to look at him. There were tears on the swordmaster's ruddy cheeks, and his eyes were swollen and red.

"I'm sorry, Hagan. I . . . I didn't mean to disturb you."

The man beckoned to him with an open hand. "It's all right, lad. Come on, then. He'd want us to be together. Both of them would."

Tavis nodded, walked to the swordmaster, and sat down beside him. Hagan held a sword across his lap. Xaver's sword.

"All that I taught him," Hagan said, his voice even despite the tears streaming down his face. "I thought that it would prepare him for any enemy, that it could save him from . . . from this." He shook his head, sobbing. "It was all for nothing."

"That's not so, Hagan," Tavis said, tearful once more. "There was nothing you could have done to prepare us for this war. But I wouldn't have traded those days in the castle wards for anything, and neither would Xaver. The lessons themselves were what mattered most. Don't you know how proud he was to be your son, to train with you, to hear the castle guards speak of you with such awe? Even as a boy, he loved being called Stinger, because it marked him as Hagan MarCullet's son. You taught him well, swordmaster, just as you did me."

Hagan nodded, though his sobbing continued. Tavis laid a hand on his broad shoulder and said nothing more. But the two of them sat there for some time, their backs to the armies, their faces warmed by the sun and brushed by a gentle wind, their tears somehow less bitter for being shed together.

"He's suffered too much for a boy so young," the king said, watching as Tavis hurried off.

Grinsa's heart ached for the young lord, but he thought it important that the others begin to see Tavis as he did, especially now, with the dukedom thrust upon him. "He's not as young as you think he is."

Kearney looked at him, frowning. "He's but a year past his Fating, gleaner. He may have matured, but he's still a boy."

"Yes, he is. But he's strong, and wise beyond his years. And he has more mettle than even he knows." Grinsa stared past the king, following Tavis's progress as the young noble made his way through the camp. "I wouldn't have said this when I met him, but I think he'll make a fine duke."

"I agree with you," Kearney said. "Still, I lament that he'll have to prove himself in the court at so tender an age."

Keziah touched Grinsa's arm, as if telling him to let the matter drop. She was right, of course.

For several moments, none of them spoke. Grinsa could hear warriors laughing and singing throughout the camp, which was as it should be. They had won a great victory today. But in this small circle, the king, his nobles, and their ministers were subdued. Too many soldiers had died, too many nobles had been lost. And though the Weaver was dead, the rift between Qirsi and Eandi remained, wider than it had been in centuries.

A man from the King's Guard approached them, his uniform of purple and gold torn and bloodstained.

"My pardon, Yer Majesty," he said, bowing to the king. "But th' archminister wanted me t' tell 'er when th' woman was awake."

"What woman?"

"The one who attacked me," Keziah said, drawing Kearney's gaze. "She's a shaper, which means that she's a danger to all of us."

"You can control her, can't you, gleaner?"

"Yes, Your Majesty, I can."

Keziah shook her head. "You've been hurt. It's too soon for this."

"It's all right, Kezi. As you said, she's a danger to everyone in this camp. We can hardly afford to wait."

Kearney eyed him. "You're certain?"

"Yes."

"Very well," the king said. "Bring her here. I want her escorted by four swordsmen and an equal number of archers."

"Aye, Yer Majesty," the man said. He bowed and hurried off.

"This is going to be a problem for some time to come," Marston of Shanstead said to no one in particular. "Plenty of renegades survived this day and we have no idea what powers they possess. Shaping, fire, maybe worse. It's going to take years to hunt down all of them."

Grinsa and Fotir shared a look, but neither of them offered any response.

"The gleaner knows," said Caius of Labruinn. "Don't you? A Weaver can just look at other Qirsi and know what powers they possess. Isn't that right?"

"Yes, it is."

Again, they lapsed into silence. Grinsa was troubled by what he had heard from Shanstead and Labruinn, but he kept his misgivings to himself, at least for the time being.

It wasn't long before the guard returned leading a cluster of soldiers, all of them looking nervous. At their center, looking like a mere child beside them, walked an attractive Qirsi woman with shoulder-length hair that she wore loose, and bright, golden eyes. She wore a slight smirk on her full lips, but her gaze was watchful, her lean frame tense, as if at any moment she might attempt to escape. There was a dark, ugly bruise on her brow, and another one, flecked with blood, on the side of her head. When she was close enough, Grinsa reached into her mind and took hold of her magic. Immediately, her gaze snapped to his face.

"So you're the other Weaver," the woman said, as she and the soldiers drew near. She looked him over as if he were a blade for sale in a city marketplace. "I expected more."

"Who are you?" Kearney demanded.

The woman glanced at him, then faced Grinsa once more. "Why would you choose these fools over your own people? Is the blood in your veins so weak that you truly consider yourself one of them?"

"I can make you answer the king's questions," Grinsa said placidly. "You know that."

She paled, but the smirk lingered. "They have you on a short leash, don't they?"

"Her name is Jastanne," Keziah said.

"Yes, it is," she said. "Why don't you tell them how you know that, Archminister."

Keziah glared at her, perhaps wishing that she had kept silent.

"No? Then I will. The duke of Kentigern knew it. He saved

her life, but only because he knew enough to look for me. You see, he was a traitor. He hated you so much, Your Majesty, that he forged an alliance with our movement in an attempt to save his house and destroy your kingdom. You think he died a hero, but in fact he was a traitor."

Caius pulled his sword free. "You lie, white-hair!" But there was doubt in his eyes and desperation in his voice. Marston of Shanstead looked appalled, as did the soldiers standing beside the woman. For his part, Grinsa believed her. Not only did he think Aindreas capable of such a thing—he had seen what the duke did to Tavis in the dungeons of Kentigern—but he sensed the truth in her words. The Weaver had succeeded all too well in dividing them.

"I can prove that I'm telling you the truth."

"You mean the paper he signed?" Kearney asked.

The woman stared at him, her smirk gone, disbelief in her eyes. "How do you know about that?"

"Do you really believe that the duke of a major house would cast his lot with your conspiracy?"

"He did!"

"Yes, with my blessing."

"That's . . . No! You're lying!"

Moving so quickly that his hand and steel were but a blur, Gershon Trasker pulled his sword free and laid its point at the base of her neck, just above her heart. "Tread lightly, white-hair," he growled. "That's the king of Eibithar you're talking to."

But she was right. Kearney was lying. Grinsa sensed that as well. For whatever reason, he had chosen to shield Aindreas and his house from this disgrace. It was an act of surpassing generosity, one of which few would ever know.

"He allied himself with our movement! He betrayed all of you!"

"No," the king said, and now he was the one smirking. "He deceived all of you. And today he proved both his loyalty and his valor. Now I'll ask you again: who are you?"

She opened her mouth. Closed it again, clenching her jaw.

"Gleaner?"

Grinsa touched her mind with his delusion magic. "Answer him."

"My name is Jastanne ja Triln. I'm a merchant and sea captain."

"What else?"

"I'm a chancellor in the Weaver's movement."

"What powers does she possess?" the king asked.

"In addition to shaping, she has mists and gleaning."

Before the king could ask anything else, a voice called to him from a distance. A woman's voice. A moment later, the duchess of Curlinte stepped into their circle, accompanied by several soldiers and a tall Qirsi man who was walking unsteadily and bleeding from a wound on the back of his head. This Qirsi also had shaping, as well as delusion magic, gleaning, and mists. No doubt he, too, was one of Dusaan's chancellors.

Grinsa took hold of his magic.

"You!" the man said in a whisper, staring at him wide-eyed. "You're the one who stopped me from killing them."

"Yes."

"He's a minister, Your Majesty," Diani said. "From Aneira, if his accent is any indication."

"Actually," Grinsa said, remembering descriptions of the man that he and Tavis had heard while journeying through the southern kingdom, "he's more than that. If I'm not mistaken, this is Aneira's archminister."

"Is this true?" Kearney asked. "You're Pronjed jal Drenthe?"

Grinsa expected the man to deny it, or at least to refuse to answer. But he merely nodded, hatred in his eyes as he looked sidelong at the gleaner.

Diani still had her dagger drawn. She hadn't taken her eyes off the man. "He has shaping power," she said. "And he used another magic on me, one that forced me to do things."

Grinsa took a breath. He could see where this was going. "It's called delusion. I've also heard it called mind-bending power."

Marston had moved to stand beside the duchess and he

was watching the minister warily. "Whatever it's called, he's clearly as dangerous as this woman, perhaps more so."

"I agree," the king said. "How do we guard Qirsi with such powers, gleaner? You can't watch them all the time, and our weapons are of little use against them."

The thane shook his head. "They shouldn't be imprisoned. They should be executed. They're traitors and murderers, and they deserve no less."

"I agree," Gershon said.

Keziah looked at him, but said nothing.

Caius was gripping his sword tightly, as if he would have liked to strike the killing blow himself. But he kept his distance from the two Qirsi. "How do you execute a shaper? Our weapons are useless against them."

Marston nodded toward Grinsa. "The gleaner can kill them. He can use their own power against them."

"I can," Grinsa said. "But I won't."

"What?"

"I fought for the courts, and was glad to do so. But I won't execute prisoners for you."

"Not even if His Majesty orders you to?"

Grinsa held the thane's gaze. "Not even then."

"You know what they've done, what they'll do again, if only we give them the chance. And still you refuse? All you white-hairs are the same!"

Xivled jal Viste stepped forward, glowering at Marston. "White-hairs?" he repeated. "You haven't learned a damn thing from all this, have you?"

The thane's eyes widened. "Xiv, I—"

"No, my lord. You need to hear this. We've just come through the most horrific war our land has known in centuries. I never thought I'd see so many killed in my lifetime, much less in a single day. And all of them died because our people—yours and mine—have paid more attention to the color of each other's eyes and hair, than to all that binds us to one another. It has to stop, my lord. Your suspicion, your prejudice—we can't afford them anymore. We need to find some way to trust one another, to put these ancient hatreds to rest finally and for good. If we can't, we're doomed to repeat this war."

"Of course, I know that. But this gleaner—"

"This gleaner saved us all, my lord. He's done enough. If you can't see that, then I'm not certain that I wish to continue serving in your court."

Before Marston could respond, his minister turned and walked away, leaving the thane looking perplexed.

For some time, none of them spoke.

"He's right, of course," Keziah said at last.

"Let it be, Kez," the king said in a low voice.

"No, Your Majesty, I won't! That's what we've done for too long. We've refused to talk about it, hoping the problem would simply disappear, and as a result it nearly destroyed us. We can't wait any longer."

"All that may be true, but this is a discussion we can have later."

"When? When the dead have been buried? When the rest of the renegades have been found? When the wounds of this war have healed? Or must we wait even longer than that? Shouldn't we do this now, before your dukes return to their castles?"

"You're wasting your breath, cousin," Jastanne said, an insolent smile on her lips. "The Eandi will never change. They hate us, and do you know why? It's because they fear us, they fear our magic." She shook her head. "No, you can't change them. Your only hope lay with the Weaver and his movement, and now you've destroyed that."

Kearney stared at the woman, as if seeing her for the first time. At last he faced Keziah again. "We won't wait long. Discussing this matter before we bid farewell to the dukes strikes me as a fine idea. I give you my word. For now though, we should deal with these two, and any other renegades we can find."

"Your Majesty—"

"Have done, Marston. Please. I have no intention of ordering the gleaner to do anything that he does not choose to do voluntarily."

Grinsa tipped his head. "Thank you, Your Majesty."

"Nevertheless, Grinsa, I do agree that this man and woman should be put to death, and I need to know if you intend to intervene on their behalf."

Grinsa felt the others watching him, waiting. Gershon still held his weapon, as did the duchess, Caius, and several of the soldiers. He was quite certain that they were prepared to fight him if they thought it necessary.

"No, Your Majesty, I have no such intentions. If you think it best to execute them, you should do so."

Kearney nodded.

Keziah glanced Grinsa's way, then said, "You should blindfold them, Your Majesty. Keep their hands bound, and bind their ankles as well. You should also have several archers watching them at all times."

"Thank you, Archminister." The king turned to his soldiers. "You heard what she said. See to it right away, and have preparations made for their executions. I want them dead before nightfall." He looked at Grinsa again, nodded once. "Gleaner."

The king strode away, followed closely by Shanstead, Labruinn, and the others.

"I'm sorry," Keziah said when they were gone.

"For what?"

"For telling Kearney how he should guard them. The truth is, I want them dead. I never thought I'd say it, but in spite of everything else, I agree with Marston: they deserve to die."

"Actually, I agree with him, too."

Her eyebrows went up.

"It's true," he said, feeling terribly weary. "I just didn't want a hand in their deaths. Is that so difficult to fathom?"

His sister looked pained. "No, not at all. I should have understood."

He shrugged. "It's been a long day. For all of us."

She summoned one of the soldiers with a gesture. "I'm going to get some food. Why don't you join me? You must be famished."

Grinsa made himself smile. "I'll eat soon. First I want to speak with Cresenne."

"Of course."

The soldier helped Keziah to her feet and led her away, leaving Grinsa alone on the cool grass. He could have slept for hours, and he wasn't certain how long he could keep himself in Cresenne's dreams. But it was growing late; she would be waking soon to another lonely night, and he didn't want to wait even one more day to tell her that Dusaan was dead.

Closing his eyes, he sent his mind southward to Audun's Castle. He found her quickly and entered her mind. Immediately he felt the dull pain in her chest. Had she been attacked yet again?

"Cresenne!" he said as soon as he saw her.

She gazed toward him, then took a tentative step forward. It occurred to him that in her dream he would be sitting, just as he was in the waking world.

"It's all right," he said. "It's me."

"Grinsa?"

"Yes. I was hurt, but I'm fine now."

She ran to him, dropped to her knees beside him. Despite the scars that he still saw on her face, he thought that she had never looked more beautiful. She kissed him lightly on the lips, then sat back meeting his gaze, fear and hope mingled in her eyes.

He reached out a hand and cupped her cheek. "He's dead. It's over."

For a moment she merely stared back at him. Then tears flooded her eyes and she began to sob. "Are you certain?"

"Yes. He can't hurt you anymore." He found that he was crying as well, though he was also smiling.

"A woman attacked me today. I nearly died again, and she nearly took Bryntelle. I went to sleep thinking that this would never end, that I'd be fighting off his servants and living in fear of his dreams until he finally managed to kill me."

"I don't know how many more of his servants are out there," Grinsa told her. "But Dusaan will never walk in your dreams again."

She put her arms around him, still weeping, and for a long time they held each other.

"How bad was it?" she finally asked. She pulled back quickly. "Is Keziah all right?"

"She's fine."

"And Tavis?"

"He's . . . it's complicated. He survived the fighting, but his father was killed and his closest friend."

"I'm sorry for him. Truly."

"You said that Bryntelle was nearly taken from you. Is she—"

"She's right here beside me. Trin saved her. He saved us both."

Grinsa gaped at her. "Trin?"

She nodded.

"Trin," he said again. After a moment he laughed. "What a day."

"Tell me what happened."

"Not now," he said, shaking his head. "I need to rest. But soon. I'll tell you everything, I promise."

"All right." She kissed him again, deeply this time. Then she smiled, the dazzling smile he remembered from so long ago. He hadn't seen her smile like that in more turns than he could count. "I love you."

Grinsa brushed a strand of hair from her face. "And I love you."

He opened his eyes to the late-day sun, blinking against the brightness. He sat there a moment, then forced himself to his feet, wincing at the pain in his shoulder. His legs felt well enough, though—the healers had worked their craft well—and he turned gingerly to face the battle plain.

Dusaan's body still lay amid the grasses. Other bodies, Eandi and Qirsi alike, had been moved. But no one had bothered with the Weaver. Or maybe none had dared go near him.

Grinsa reached out with his magic and tried to touch the Weaver's mind, much as a soldier might prod a fallen enemy with the toe of his boot. Nothing. Dusaan was dead; his war was done. Over the next several turns, perhaps stretching to years, all the realms of the Forelands would continue to pay a price for what the man and his movement had done. Even now, Grinsa could hear Gershon Trasker in the distance, barking commands to the archers who would soon execute Jastanne and Pronjed. In the days to come, parents would weep for children lost in battle, sons and daughters would learn their first painful lessons about war and death, lovers would grieve at the realization of their worst fears.

But too, the land would begin to heal itself. At least Grinsa could hope as much. Throughout the Forelands, suspicions ran deep and in all directions, like fissures in dried earth. It would take time, he knew, for trust to take root again. Already though, he saw signs that the process was under way. Kearney had lied to preserve Kentigern's honor. Soldiers in the king's army were treating both Keziah and Tavis with the courtesy and respect that were their due.

These were trifles, to be sure. But they were a start. And on this day, when so much blood had been spilled and the Weaver had come so very close to defeating them all, Grinsa could hardly ask for more.

Chapter
Twenty-seven

Curgh, Eibithar, Morna's Moon waxing

They remained on the Moorlands for several days, collecting the dead, building pyres from the scant brush found among the grasses, and sending dark black clouds of smoke into the clear planting sky. At the insistence of Kearney and Sanbira's queen, even the renegades were given the honor of a single vast pyre that for hours poured foul smoke into the air. Only the Weaver's body was left to rot under the sun, its putrid remains picked at for days by crows and vultures.

Tavis's father and Xaver MarCullet were given over to flame and vapor the first night after the battle, as stars burned brightly over the moor and slivers of moonlight shone weakly in the east. Tavis stood with Hagan MarCullet, his hand resting on the swordmaster's stooped shoulder, his vision blurred with tears. He hadn't cried so much in a single day since he was a child, and his throat and chest ached. Later that night, Aindreas of Kentigern was laid out on his own pyre, and Tavis watched that one burn as well, his emotions as roiled as a river in flood.

The following morning, the last of Adriel's turn, he penned a message to his mother, informing her that he would be returning to Curgh early in the new turn, accompanied by the king and a number of nobles. He had planned to tell her of the duke's death upon reaching the castle, but she needed to know that Kearney was coming, and she would not have wanted to have the king there when she learned that her husband was dead. As it was, he needed only write of their plans to tell her all she needed to know. Had Javan been alive, he, and not Tavis, would have sent such a message.

At first, Tavis had been reluctant to have the king accompany him back to Curgh. He liked Kearney a great deal, but even without accepting the king's offer of asylum and a home in Glyndwr, he had lived under the protection of the Crown for too long. Kearney had argued, though, that now more than ever, Tavis needed his help.

"You lead your house now, Lord Curgh. We must make it clear, to friend and foe alike, that I trust completely in your innocence and your ability to govern a major house."

His innocence. Tavis knew that some in the realm would die of old age still believing that he had killed Brienne, and he no longer cared to try to convince them otherwise. But he was wise enough to recognize the generosity of Kearney's offer, and to know that he would have been a fool to refuse him.

And had he not, Fotir, ever the first minister, would have prevailed upon him to accept anyway.

"He puts himself at risk for you, my lord," the Qirsi told him quietly. "There are many, including ministers in his own court, who would tell him that you're not worth the cost of such a gesture."

"I know. I have no intention of refusing him. I just wish for a bit of peace."

Fotir had smiled at that. "I don't doubt it, my lord. You'll have it soon enough."

When at last they set out for Curgh, Tavis was accompanied by a host of soldiers, nobles, and ministers. Not only did Kearney ride with him, but so did Lathrop of Tremain, Caius of Labruinn, Marston of Shanstead, and their companies. Naturally, Grinsa rode with him, too, although not without some reluctance, for he was eager to return to the City of Kings and see Cresenne and his daughter. Tavis noticed as well that the duchess of Curlinte rode with Marston rather than setting out for Sanbira with her queen.

Well before they reached Curgh, Tavis began to feel that he was home at last. He hadn't seen the castle of his forebears in more than a year, since he set out with Xaver and his father for Kentigern. In the time since, he had sailed the waters of Kreanna to Wethyrn and had battled the assassin Cadel on the rocky shores of the Wethy Crown. Yet only now, still leagues south of the castle, but sensing the first hint of brine in the wind, did he find himself thinking of the high cliffs of Curgh and the frothing waters of Amon's Ocean below.

They came to the great walls of Curgh City late on the fourth day of their journey from the battle plain. The King's Guard and the armies of Thorald and Tremain stopped at the gates and made camp in the shadow of the city. Kearney and the other nobles followed Tavis through the gates and into the streets of Curgh, where they were greeted by cheers from the city folk. For Tavis, it was a bittersweet homecoming. He had assumed since Kentigern that he would never hear his name shouted with such reverence by Curgh's people. But he sensed as well the shock of those lining the streets at not seeing their duke in the king's company. Upon entering the castle, he leaped from his horse and rushed to his mother's outstretched arms. For several moments they held each other, heedless of the king and the protocol of royal visits, and they wept, grief for Javan mingling with joy at Tavis's redemption.

"If I could have saved him, I would have."

"I know that."

At last, Shonah released him, wiping the tears from her face and curtsying to the king.

"Forgive me, Your Majesty," she said.

"There's nothing to forgive, my lady. I hope that you'll accept my condolences on the loss of your husband. He was a wise leader, a courageous warrior, and a good friend. The land grieves for him."

"You honor us, Your Majesty."

"You do us the honor, my lady, by making us guests in your home at such a time."

The duchess curtsied again, then turned to Hagan, who had yet to dismount. She favored him with a smile, then faltered searching the ranks of Curgh's army. After a moment, she spun toward Tavis.

"Xaver?" she whispered.

Tavis swallowed and shook his head.

"Oh, Hagan." She walked to the swordmaster and took his hand, her face streaked with tears once more. "I'm so terribly sorry."

The swordmaster nodded but said nothing. He remained on his horse, looking straight ahead, his jaw quivering, as if it was all he could do to keep from bawling like a child. Shonah brushed the swordmaster's hand with her lips, then faced Kearney and the other nobles once more.

"Please make yourselves welcome. Quarters have been arranged for you and your ministers and there will be a feast tonight to celebrate your victory over the enemies of our realm."

The king and his company dismounted and followed Shonah into the castle. Tavis hesitated, eyeing Hagan, wondering if he should remain with him.

"Leave him," the gleaner said softly. "He'll join us when he's ready."

Tavis knew he was right. He cast one more look at the swordmaster before leaving the ward with Grinsa.

The next few days seemed a blur of feasts and ceremony. Tavis's investiture was a modest affair, as ducal ordinations tended to be. It had been several centuries since dukes of

Curgh wore any sort of crown, and never had they held scepters or other tokens of their title. But Tavis did take his father's sword as his own, and after a brief ceremony in the castle's lower ward at which he swore fealty to the Crown, he hosted yet another banquet, this one open to the people of Curgh City.

The following morning, a rider arrived from Heneagh bearing a message of sympathy to Shonah and congratulations to the new duke. Later in the day, similar missives arrived from Domnall and Sussyn, two houses that had supported Aindreas of Kentigern in his feud with the king.

"Perhaps this will bring the other houses back to the fold, Your Majesty," Tavis said, showing the messages to Kearney in his father's old presence chamber.

"We can hope so," the king said, sounding skeptical. "I expect it will take some time for Galdasten and Kentigern to sort through all that's happened in the past year. Aindreas's boy is still several years shy of his Fating, and Renald's sons were killed by the Qirsi. Both houses have a good deal to sort through. I don't imagine they'll be ready to reconcile with your house or the throne any time soon." He smiled thinly. "And Elam has always been a stubborn fool, so if I were you, I wouldn't be sitting atop my ramparts waiting for messengers from Eardley."

Tavis grinned. "Yes, Your Majesty."

"How is Hagan?" the king asked, his smile fading.

The young duke shrugged, then shook his head. "Not well. The Hagan of old would be scouring the countryside for probationers to replace the men we lost on the moor, and he'd be working those soldiers who remain day and night. Instead he walks the castle corridors or locks himself away in his chamber. He won't even speak with my mother."

"It's bound to take some time."

"I suppose. At least when he lost Daria, he still had Xaver to care for. But now . . . He speaks of returning to MarCullet and the home of his youth. He's still an earl, you know."

Kearney raised an eyebrow. "I had no idea."

"I never thought of him as the kind of man who could live

a noble's life, but maybe that's what he needs, at least for a while. Mother thinks so."

"Your mother may well be right. Perhaps Hagan can find peace in the home of his forebears."

"I hope so, Your Majesty."

One final matter remained before Kearney and the other dukes left Curgh for their homes, one about which Tavis knew little until Grinsa explained it to him the following morning. It seemed that Kearney had agreed to a conclave of sorts between the nobles and their Qirsi, an opportunity for men and women of both races to speak of recent events and all that lay behind them.

"He agreed to it just after the battle with Dusaan," Grinsa told him, as they walked through the castle ward. "It was Keziah's idea, but I think that one of the renegades goaded the king into agreeing to it. I can't believe he's eager to hear what Keziah and the others have to say."

"I don't imagine. I'm not sure that I am, either."

The nobles and their Qirsi met in the castle's great hall, where Tavis's father had welcomed so many dukes and thanes, honoring them with feasts. Fotir was there, of course, having made all the arrangements for the discussion with the approval of Tavis's mother. Sitting with him were Keziah, Xivled jal Viste, and the ministers of the dukes of Labruinn and Tremain. They sat on one side of the great table, across from Marston, Caius, Lathrop, Diani of Curlinte, and Gershon Trasker. Tavis and Grinsa entered the hall in silence, taking their places on either side of the table. On this day, Tavis gave up pride of place to the king, allowing him to preside, as was proper. Servants had put out cheeses, breads, fruits, and flasks of wine, but no one ate or so much as filled a goblet. None of them even spoke.

"I'm afraid I'm at a loss as to where to begin," Kearney finally said, looking around the table.

"Perhaps the archminister would like to tell us why we're here," Marston said.

Xivled bristled, and it occurred to Tavis that he hadn't seen the thane and his minister together since they arrived in Curgh.

"All I meant was that we're here at her request," Marston went on, casting a quick look at his minister. "I'd like to know what she hopes to accomplish with this discussion for which she was so eager."

"That's a fair question, my lord," Keziah said.

Xivled shook his head, glaring at the thane. "I think you're too generous, Archminister. It should be obvious to all why this meeting was necessary."

"What's obvious to the Qirsi at this table might still be a mystery to the rest of us," Kearney said. "Please, Minister, tell us why you think we're here."

"To put an end to the mistrust," Xivled said, as if the rest of them were simple. "To begin to repair the damage that's been done by this war and the conspiracy."

"You can't think to do that in one day, lad," Lathrop said, his tone gentle. "These conflicts are as old as the kingdom itself."

"I know that, my lord. But we have to begin somewhere."

"And where would that be?" Caius demanded, sounding far more belligerent than had the duke of Tremain. "What is it you're asking of us?"

"You might begin, my lord, by not treating every Qirsi you meet with such disdain."

"I don't believe I do, Minister."

Xivled started to respond, but Keziah silenced him with a sharp glance.

"I believe what the minister means, my lord, is that while we treat our lords with deference, we in turn are often treated with somewhat less respect."

"Demons and fire, woman! We're nobles! Do you expect us to bow to you?"

"We don't have to bow to them to show them courtesy, Lord Labruinn," Tavis said. "But in the past, nobles in the Eibitharian courts have spoken of collecting Qirsi ministers as one might horses or fine swords." He glanced at the duchess of Curlinte. "Nor was that practice unique to our realm. It's time we began to see the Qirsi as something more than chattel."

"That seems a small step," Lathrop said. "From what I understand, the Weaver was speaking of creating a new nobility of Qirsi lords and dukes. If that's what the Qirsi in Eibithar truly want, we're doomed."

"That's not what we want," Xivled said.

Marston eyed him briefly, then looked down at his hands. "Perhaps you don't, but some might."

"There!" the minister said, pointing at his thane. "That's what I object to. The suspicion. You assume the worst about us, though you have no cause."

"No cause? Xiv, consider what's just happened throughout the Forelands! How can you say that I have no cause?"

Tavis cast a quick look at Grinsa, only to find that the gleaner was already watching him. After a moment, Tavis gave a small shake of his head. This was going poorly.

"Ambition and treachery can be found in any heart, my lord," Xivled said. "Eandi or Qirsi."

Marston looked like he wanted to say more, but he wisely chose to remain silent.

"You're awfully quiet, gleaner," Gershon Trasker said after a time. "You had much to say in the days before the war. What say you now?"

Grinsa shrugged, the deformity of his shoulder making the movement appear awkward and strange. "There's little I can say, swordmaster. You're all speaking of trusting one another, of taking the first tentative steps down a long, difficult path. I'm a Weaver. There's no place for me in your society, at least not for now. In a sense, this discussion has nothing to do with me."

Fotir turned to face him, his brow furrowed. "Surely you can offer us some counsel. How are we to overcome these divisions?"

"Truly, I don't know. The only advice I can give you is to be patient. As Lord Tremain has said, this question is old as the seven realms. It won't be answered in a day, or a year, or even ten years. And in the meantime, you must guard against falling back into old conflicts, into fear and mistrust. Patience, and tolerance—they will see you through."

"It seems you had counsel for us after all, gleaner," the king said, smiling. "You have our thanks, once again, as well as my promise that we'll heed your words." He reached for a flask of pale wine and filled his goblet. "Come friends. Let us eat, and enjoy one last day of Lord Curgh's hospitality. It's important that we speak of these matters, but there comes a time when we must simply live and do the best we can."

Slowly, the others filled their cups. When they had, Kearney raised his goblet. "To Eibithar," he said. "Long may she know peace."

"To Eibithar," the others answered.

Their small feast lasted much of the morning. Soon after the ringing of the midday bells, the nobles and their ministers began to say their farewells and leave the hall. Most, it seemed, intended to leave Curgh the following morning. Marston and Lady Curlinte were among the last to leave, and though Tavis hadn't known what Xivled would do, in the end the minister followed his lord from the great chamber. Soon, all had left the hall save for Tavis, Grinsa, and Kearney. They sat together in silence for some time, until at last the king cleared his throat. "I think it's time I was returning to the City of Kings," he said. "I'm grateful to you for your courtesy, Tavis, but I have a family as well, and I'm eager to see them."

"Yes, of course, Your Majesty."

"If you'd like, I can leave a small contingent of soldiers, at least until you've had some time to rebuild your army."

"Thank you, Your Majesty, but I don't think that's necessary. Curgh has protected her own walls for centuries, and she can do so now."

The king nodded. "Very well. Then I'll be riding in the morning."

Grinsa, who had been staring at his wine, looked up at the king. "If I may, Your Majesty, I'd like permission to ride with you."

"You're leaving, too?" Tavis said, though of course, he shouldn't have been surprised.

"It's been too long since I saw my daughter, Tavis. You didn't really think I'd remain here forever, did you?"

"No, but . . ." He shook his head. "No."

"You're welcome to ride with me, gleaner. But what will you do once you reach the City of Kings?"

"That depends in large part on you, Your Majesty. Cresenne remains a prisoner in Audun's Castle. And it's now common knowledge that I'm a Weaver."

Tavis had wanted to say something during their discussion, but the time hadn't been right. Now, though, he didn't hesitate. "After all that Grinsa's done, it shouldn't matter that he's a Weaver!"

"But you know it does, Tavis," the king said. "Even before we left the Moorlands, nobles were speaking to me of having him imprisoned or even put to death. Throughout Eibithar, people are more frightened of Weavers than they've been in centuries. I can't simply ignore the laws of the realm."

"Even if those laws are unjust?"

"We'll try to change the laws, and perhaps over time we will. But as Grinsa himself has said, we're just starting a long and difficult process. The people aren't ready to have Weavers living among them, not so soon after this war." Kearney looked at Grinsa. "As I've told you before, I have no desire to see you executed, nor do I wish Cresenne ill. But I'm at a loss as to what to do."

"I have an idea," Grinsa said. "But it will demand some pliancy on your part, Your Majesty."

Kearney regarded him a moment, then nodded. "I'm listening."

Since arriving in Curgh, Keziah had managed to avoid them both. She walked in the city marketplace or wandered the castle wards and gardens. She attended the feasts, of course, as well as Tavis's investiture and this day's discussion. But she always kept to herself and she excused herself from the celebrations and feasts as quickly as she could. Anything to avoid being alone with Kearney or Fotir. Soon she would be leaving for Audun's Castle, and none of this would matter anymore, but until then, she had no desire to speak with either of them.

Or so she wanted to believe.

Her wounds had healed. The bones in her ribs and leg no longer ached as she walked, and her hands, shattered by Sanbira's archminister, hadn't hurt for several days now. She had slept better over the past several nights than she had in more than a year. What a joy it was to lay down at night without dreading her dreams. A part of her, she realized now, had never truly believed that the Weaver could be defeated, or that she would ever be free of him. Their victory on the Moorlands had come at a great price, but it seemed to her miraculous nevertheless.

So why did she remain so unhappy?

Late on this day, the ninth of the waxing, she found herself in the gardens once more, strolling past brilliant, fragrant blooms of rose and sweet violet. The sun angled sharply across the courtyard, casting long, dark shadows that cooled the air. Her thoughts had turned again to Fotir, as they often did these days. They had hardly spoken to one another since reaching Curgh. The first minister was occupied with Curgh's young duke and its grieving duchess. They needed him far more than did Keziah, and it was only right that he should be more concerned with them than with anything, or anyone, else. She couldn't help but remember, however, how their conversation ended the night before the war with Dusaan. She could still feel the warmth of his hand holding hers. And she could still hear his question, so deserving of an answer, so difficult to address.

What about the king?

Indeed.

She heard footsteps on the stone path behind her and she turned, half expecting to see the minister. Instead it was Gershon Trasker.

"Am I disturbing you?"

"Not at all, swordmaster. Is there something you need?"

"I just thought you should know: the king has decided that we're to leave tomorrow morning."

Why did that make her so afraid? "All right. Thank you."

She thought he would go, but he didn't. He glanced about, looking at the flowers as he might a collection of daggers or battle shields. Keziah couldn't remember ever seeing Gershon in the gardens of Audun's Castle, or Glyndwr for that matter.

"Have your injuries healed?" he finally asked.

"Yes, thank you."

"Good. And my men are treating you better?"

Keziah had to smile. "Yes, they are. Thank you for that, as well."

"It's the least you deserve, given all that you've done for us."

"I did it for myself, swordmaster. You speak as though I did the Eandi a favor. That wasn't it at all. I was trying to protect my king, my realm, and my people. I was trying to save myself." She looked away. "Besides," she went on, trying to soften what she had said, "I'm not certain that what I did mattered in the end."

"Of course it did."

"The Weaver very nearly defeated us, despite my efforts. And I had little to do with our victory. That was Grinsa, and a woman in the Weaver's army who turned against him at the end. We don't even know her name."

"You showed courage and loyalty. You helped us kill the three traitors from Sanbira. They might well have tipped the balance in the Weaver's favor before the end."

There was no point in arguing the matter. Gershon was showing her as much kindness as he ever had. Best just to accept his praise and be grateful.

"Again, swordmaster, thank you. Had it not been for you, I never would have made it through these past several turns."

He shrugged, looking embarrassed, as he always did when she paid him compliments. "Well, maybe you'll show your gratitude by not making yourself such a nuisance all the time."

Keziah laughed, though abruptly her chest was aching. She stepped quickly to where he stood, kissed his cheek, and ran from the gardens, knowing at last what she had to do.

By the time she reached the king's chamber, her heart was pounding, her courage failing her. Resisting an urge to flee, she knocked on his door.

"Enter!" came the reply.

She pushed the door open and walked in. To her relief, he was alone, save for a young servant.

Kearney was sitting at a small writing table, but seeing her, he quickly stood. "Ke—" He glanced at the boy. "Archminister."

"Forgive me for disturbing you, Your Majesty." She realized that she was wringing her hands, and she allowed them to fall to her sides.

"Not at all. Is something troubling you?"

She hesitated, her eyes welling.

"Please leave us," he said to the servant.

The boy let himself out of the chamber.

He crossed to where she was standing and took her hands. "Now, what's happened?"

She opened her mouth to speak, but began to cry instead.

"What is it, Kez?"

She was trembling, her legs shaking so badly that she had to tighten her grip on his hands just to keep from collapsing to the floor.

"Kez?" he said, sounding truly afraid.

"I can't go back with you," she blurted out.

He blinked. "What?"

"I can't do this anymore."

He released her hands and took a step back. "Do what?" he asked.

But he already knew. She read it in those grey eyes. Strangely, seeing such hurt in them now emboldened her, convincing her that she was doing the right thing. Finally. She wiped her tears away.

"There was a time when I loved you more than anything in the world," she told him. "In a way, I always will love you. But we can never be together again, and so long as I remain in your court, I'll never be able to love another."

"All the more reason to keep you as my archminister." He smiled halfheartedly, then looked away, shaking his head. "That was meant as a joke. I suppose it wasn't very funny."

"I'd ask you to release me from your service, Your Majesty. I think it's best for both of us."

"Do you love another, Kez?"

"I'm not certain."

He frowned. "You're not certain?"

"It's possible that I do, yes. But that's not the reason I want to leave your court, at least not entirely. I see the way you look at me. It's only a matter of time before others notice as well."

"I look at you that way because I love you."

"I know. And that's why I have to leave you."

"Where will you go?"

"Actually, I was going to ask Lord Curgh if I might serve in his court."

Comprehension lit his face, and for a moment she feared that he would grow angry. But he merely smiled. "I hope you'll be very happy here. If Tavis is as wise as I think he is, he'll soon find himself being served by the two finest ministers in Eibithar."

"Thank you, Your Majesty."

He stepped forward and put his arms around her, kissing her brow. "I'll miss you, Kez," he whispered.

"And I you."

He held her a moment longer, then stepped back. "I hereby release you from service in the court of Audun's Castle. May you find happiness on whatever path you choose."

She smiled, tears on her cheeks once more. "Thank you, Your Majesty," she said softly, and left him.

She hurried through the castle corridors, nearly breaking into a run. Coming at last to Tavis's presence chamber, she knocked and let herself in at the duke's summons.

Fotir was with him. Of course.

"Archminister," Tavis said. "What can I do for you?"

"Actually, my lord, I no longer go by that title."

The two men shared a glance.

"What do you mean?" the young duke asked.

"I've left the king's court. I asked him to release me from his service, and he kindly granted my request."

Fotir shook his head. "Why would you do such a thing?"

"I was wondering, my lord," she went on, ignoring him for the moment, "if you might have use for another minister in your court."

Tavis's eyes widened. "My court?"

"Yes."

"I . . . I have first and second ministers already. Curgh's wealth is substantial, but I can hardly afford—"

"You wouldn't have to pay me much."

Fotir was smiling now, regarding her with astonishment. "Why are you doing this?"

Their eyes met, and Keziah realized she was grinning stupidly. "Why do you think?"

Tavis looked from Fotir to Keziah and then back again, amusement and puzzlement on his scarred face. "What do you think of all this, First Minister?" he asked. "After what I said today about not collecting ministers as if they were Sanbiri swords, can I really add another to my court?"

The minister didn't take his eyes off of her, but he began to laugh. "I'm not certain that I can offer an objective opinion on this, my lord."

"Then don't."

At that, Fotir turned to the young duke, gratitude written on his features. He really was quite handsome. "Yes, my lord, I think you can."

"Very well." Tavis faced Keziah once more. "Welcome to the Curgh court, Minister."

"Thank you, my lord."

"I suppose this means that you won't be riding south with your brother."

"My brother?" she said.

"Yes. He's leaving with the king tomorrow."

It made sense. No doubt Grinsa was eager to return to Cresenne and Bryntelle. But there was something in the duke's tone . . .

"You haven't spoken to him," Tavis said.

"No, my lord."

"I think you should. He's in his chamber, I believe, preparing for his journey."

Keziah started to leave the chamber, then faltered, meeting Fotir's gaze.

"It's all right," he said. "We'll talk later."

She nodded and went in search of her brother. There was a

knot in her stomach, though she wasn't sure why. Reaching his chamber, she found the door ajar. She knocked once before stepping inside.

Grinsa was bent over his travel sack, but he straightened at the sight of her. His face was pale, his expression grim. Keziah shuddered and crossed her arms over her chest.

"You're leaving," she said.

"Yes. I'm riding south with you and the king."

"I'm not going south."

He frowned. "You're not?"

"I'm no longer archminister."

"What?"

"It was my choice. I can't serve Kearney anymore. It's just too difficult."

"Where will you go?"

A small smile touched her lips. "I'm staying here in Curgh."

"Oh, Kezi," he said, taking her in his arms. "That's the best thing I've heard all day." He looked down at her. "Fotir's a good man."

"Who said anything about Fotir?"

He raised an eyebrow.

"It's not fair," she said. "How is it that I can never surprise you?"

"You have surprised me, again and again. You surprised me when you risked your life to deceive the Weaver, and again when you suggested that we strike at him through your dreams the night before the battle. And you surprised me just now. A year ago you wouldn't have been able to make such a choice."

"I think you're right."

He took her hand and kissed it. "I'm going to miss you."

"Just because I'm no longer archminister doesn't mean that I can't visit Audun's Castle."

"I won't be staying in Audun's Castle."

Keziah shivered again. "Tell me," she said, not wanting to hear.

"It's nothing you don't already know. Cresenne is a prisoner of the realm, and I'm a Weaver. We have no future here—certainly Bryntelle doesn't."

"But the war is over. Surely you have nothing more to prove to Kearney and the rest. And Cresenne has suffered enough for what she did."

"There are many who would disagree with you. I love her, but if I didn't, I'm not sure that I'd want to see her go free. As for me, the law is quite clear on what's to be done with Weavers."

"Kearney can change the law! I'll talk to him!" She was shaking once more. She had finally found the strength to live without Kearney. But how could she ever live without Grinsa?

He touched her cheek, looking at her with so much love. "I don't want you to talk to him."

"Then what are you going to do?"

"Something I've always dreamed of doing. We're going to the Southlands."

"The Southlands?" she said, her voice hardly more than a whisper. "How?"

"I don't know yet. I expect we can find a merchant ship to take us. There are still a few Qirsi ships that sail beyond Sanbira on the Sea of Stars. Or maybe we'll cross the Border Range. We've still several turns before the snows."

"Does Cresenne know?"

"Not yet. But aside from Bryntelle and me, there's nothing holding her here."

"The Southlands," she said again. Keziah had never thought that anyplace could sound so far away. She pressed her face against his chest, muffling her sobs. "I'll never see you again."

"You don't know that. And besides, I'm a Weaver. I can always find my way into your dreams."

"It's not the same."

"I know."

"What will I do without you?"

"You'll live a long, happy life. You'll serve a young duke who may yet prove himself one of the great leaders this land has ever known. You'll love a fine minister who will be devoted to you. And you'll find that you're stronger and more capable than you know."

She smiled at him through her tears. "You gleaned all that?"

"I didn't have to glean it. I know it in my heart."

He kissed her forehead again, and Keziah held on to him as if she never intended to let go.

Chapter
Twenty-eight

City of Kings, Eibithar, Morna's Moon waning

T he journey southward from Curgh to Audun's Castle took nearly half a turn. Grinsa understood that most of the king's men were on foot, but still he found their pace maddeningly slow. Every day he found himself wishing that he could simply kick his mount to a gallop and cover the distance as swiftly as the beast could manage. But he remained a free man solely because Kearney had chosen to ignore Eibithar's laws regarding Weavers, and it would have been inappropriate for him to ride ahead of the king.

As it was, all that made the long ride bearable was Tavis's presence by his side. He had urged the young duke not to accompany him to the City of Kings.

"You've only just become duke," he had said the morning they left, when Tavis appeared in the castle's lower ward, dressed in rider's garb. "You should remain here with your mother and your people."

To which the boy had calmly replied, "I don't want to. And anyway," he added, "You made a promise."

Grinsa still believed that Tavis should have stayed behind, but he was glad to have the young noble with him. They rode together each day, saying little, merely enjoying each other's company.

One morning, as they passed near the banks of the Sussyn, Tavis suddenly asked, "Can a Weaver enter the dreams of anyone, or only a Qirsi?"

"I believe only a Qirsi. When I enter someone's dreams, I touch their magic, just the way I would if I was weaving their power with my own. I don't know how I could do that with an Eandi." He glanced at the boy, sensing that this was not the answer he had wanted. "Still, I've never tried to enter an Eandi's dreams. I suppose it may be possible."

Tavis nodded, but said nothing more.

It was the only time they even came close to speaking of Grinsa's impending departure.

When at last the host came within sight of the royal city, just before dusk on the twelfth day of their journey, the gleaner's impatience got the better of him.

"Your Majesty, may we have your permission to ride ahead? I'm . . . I'm quite eager to reach the castle."

Kearney smiled and nodded. "Of course. I'll ride with you." He looked back at Gershon Trasker. "Swordmaster, I'd like you to remain with the men for the rest of their march. We three are going to ride on to the city."

"Yes, Your Majesty."

It was late in the waning, and though they pushed their mounts, the three riders still hadn't reached the city walls when night fell. Grinsa raised a bright yellow flame to light their way, and some time before they came to the walls, they were joined by a large contingent of soldiers who had ridden forth at the sight of his fire. Recognizing their king, several of the men returned to the castle, shouting news of the king's return. By the time Kearney, Tavis, and Grinsa rode through the south gate, bells were tolling throughout the city and thousands of people had lined the streets to cheer their sovereign. They regarded Tavis and Grinsa warily, but if they still thought the young noble a butcher, they kept it to themselves.

Grinsa, Tavis, and Kearney entered the castle, only to find

that most of the soldiers who had remained behind when the king rode to war had gathered in the main courtyard to greet them. It promised to be a lengthy welcome.

"Your Majesty . . ."

Kearney grinned. "Go, gleaner. Tavis and I will find you later."

He was off his horse almost before the king had finished speaking. "Thank you, Your Majesty," he said with a quick bow.

A moment later he was running toward the chamber in which Cresenne had stayed before being moved to the prison tower. He could only assume that she had been returned to the same room after Kearney and the nobles left Audun's Castle.

He needn't have even wondered. She was waiting for him at the entrance to the corridor, Bryntelle in her arms, torch-light glittering in her pale eyes, starlight shimmering in her hair. He strode to her, wrapping her in his arms and kissing her long and deep.

"I can't believe you're really here," she murmured, her breath warm on his cheek.

They kissed again, only to be interrupted by a loud squeal from Bryntelle.

"I think someone else would like a hug."

Grinsa laughed. Had he ever been this happy? "Look at you!" he said to his daughter. "She's so big!"

"She can sit up by herself now. And she's making all kinds of sounds."

The child was every bit as beautiful as Cresenne. Her mouth and nose were just like her mother's. Her eyes were more like his in shape, and their color was a perfect blending of Grinsa's and Cresenne's.

"She's exquisite."

"Isn't she?"

He glanced at Cresenne, kissed her again.

"Do you want to hold her?"

Grinsa nodded. Cresenne put Bryntelle in his arms, and, of course, the child immediately began to cry.

"She's not used to you."

"It's all right," he said, rocking Bryntelle gently. "She has plenty of time."

He smiled down at the girl, gently stroking her cheek with a finger and whispering to her. Eventually her crying subsided and she grabbed hold of his finger with a tiny hand.

"I've spoken to the queen a few times recently," Cresenne said at length.

"The queen? Really?" he said, his attention still fixed on Bryntelle.

"She's been kind to me. She says that she can give us a bigger chamber, if Kearney will agree."

He looked up. "That's kind of her. But I have something else in mind, if you're willing to leave the City of Kings."

Cresenne regarded him skeptically. "Leave? I didn't think Kearney would ever allow it."

"He'll let us go if we agree to leave Eibithar."

"And you'd be willing to do that?"

He smiled. "I'll go anywhere, as long as I'm with the two of you."

Her face brightened. "All right. Where?"

"The Southlands."

Grinsa hadn't been certain how she would respond to this. He feared that she might be reluctant to go so far.

But there was wonder in her eyes as she said, "It's perfect."

They had surprisingly little to do in preparation for their journey. Cresenne had few belongings and all that Grinsa had brought with him from Curgh was already packed and ready. Cresenne still had a bit of gold, as did Grinsa, and Tavis had given the gleaner a good deal more, insisting that it was the least he could do to repay Grinsa for all he had done.

"I have an entire treasury at my disposal now," Tavis had said, insisting that the gleaner accept his gift. "Let me do this for you."

"I've been living off your gold for too long," Grinsa told him.

"Fine then, after this I won't give you any more."

At last, Grinsa relented. "Very well. Thank you, Tavis. I'm in your debt."

"Just keep your promise, and I'll consider us even."

Only two days after Grinsa's arrival in the City of Kings, he and Cresenne were ready to leave. They had agreed that they would seek passage on a ship and brave the highlands of the Border Range only as a last resort. Grinsa couldn't remember ever being this excited.

They had an audience with the king in the morning at which Kearney formally gave them permission to leave the castle and the realm.

"Go in peace," the king said. "Both of you. I hope you find happiness in the Southlands."

Grinsa bowed to him. "Thank you, Your Majesty. I've called Eibithar my home all my life. Leaving it could never be easy. But I'm comforted knowing that I leave it under the authority of such a noble and fair-minded man."

"I'll do everything in my power to make certain that your roles in our victory are never forgotten. Perhaps with time, my people will be ready to embrace a Weaver as both ally and neighbor."

"Yes, Your Majesty." But Grinsa doubted that he would see such a change in his lifetime.

Grinsa, Cresenne, and Bryntelle left the king, made their way out of the castle, and walked toward the city marketplace, where they were to meet Tavis.

"I can't believe he's making you do this," Cresenne said, smiling slightly.

Grinsa grinned and shrugged. "I did promise. And really, it's the least I can do for him."

"You're fortunate that the Revel's still here. Normally you'd have to go all the way to Eardley this time of year."

They made their way to the gleaning tent, where they found Tavis standing by the entrance with Trin. The old gleaner hadn't changed much since Grinsa last saw him: he was still fat and bald, with round, pink cheeks and a sly smile.

"It's good to see you, cousin," he said, taking Grinsa's

hand in both of his. "I'm glad to know that all my efforts to get you and this lovely woman together weren't for naught. It seems I know something about love after all."

Cresenne laughed, but Grinsa remained serious.

"Cresenne tells me that you saved her life, and kept Bryntelle from being taken away. She also says that you did all this at no small cost to yourself."

"Mere foolishness on my part," Trin said. "I've spent a lifetime cultivating a reputation as a coward. I'd be most grateful if you didn't speak of this again."

Grinsa had to smile. "Very well. But you have my gratitude just the same."

"And you mine."

"What for?"

"I've heard a bit about your exploits since last we saw each other. I think all of us owe you a word of thanks. Don't you?"

Grinsa gripped his shoulder. "You're a good man, Trin."

"Yes, well, I don't want that getting around either." He gestured toward Tavis. "I've been explaining to our young friend here that we don't usually allow anyone—Eandi or Qirsi, noble or common—a second Fating. But he seems to feel that his previous encounter with the Qiran was not all it was supposed to be, and he told me that you would say much the same thing."

"He's right. I think he's earned this second Fating. I'd be most grateful if you'd allow us a moment with the stone."

"Very well." Trin pushed the tent flap aside and motioned them inside. "The stone awaits." He glanced at the duke. "May it prove kind."

Grinsa cast a quick look at Cresenne. "This shouldn't take long."

"We'll be fine," she said.

Trin took her gently by the arm and began to lead her toward the marketplace. "I'll take good care of them both," he said over his shoulder.

Grinsa entered the tent, with Tavis following close behind. Inside, it was just as Grinsa remembered: overly warm and sparsely furnished. The Qiran, jagged and glowing, sat on a small table, the polished face of the stone turned toward a chair on the far side of the table where Tavis was to sit. Grinsa crossed to a second chair, nearer to the tent entrance.

It was strange being in the tent again. He felt like he had left this life behind centuries ago, yet the heat and the glow of the stone were all so very familiar.

"Are you certain you want to do this?" he asked.

Tavis had already taken his seat by the Qiran.

"Why wouldn't I be?"

"I just want you to be sure. Most people fear their Fatings. And your first one was rather unpleasant."

"I'm not the same person I was then. And even if I was, how could this one possibly be worse?"

Grinsa tipped his head, conceding the point. But for several moments he merely sat, staring at the stone.

"Grinsa?"

"You're right, Tavis. You're not the same person. Since the day I met you, I've seen your promise, I've seen glimpses of the man you would become. There were times when that man seemed impossibly far away, but I never fully lost sight of him. Still, even sensing your potential, I never imagined that you could come so far in so short a time."

"I suppose that's testimony to how miserable a creature I was when first we met."

"No, it's not. I was—"

"I'm kidding, Grinsa. Thank you. If I've become the man you and Xaver and my father wanted me to be it's only because the three of you never lost faith in that promise of which you speak. If it weren't for you, I'd still be the brat whose future you gleaned the last time we were in this tent."

"I'm not so sure of that."

"I am. And I'm grateful to you."

Grinsa smiled. "Whenever you're ready, my lord."

Tavis took a breath. "On this, the day of my Fating, I beseech you, Qirsar, lay your hands upon this stone. Let my life unfold before my eyes. Let the mysteries of time be revealed in the light of the Qiran. Show me my fate."

Even as Grinsa began to blend his magic with the power of the stone, he watched Tavis's face, the shifting light of the Qiran making his scars darken, then fade, then darken again.

He didn't have to look within the stone to know what the young duke was seeing, for he had dreamed Tavis's fate the previous night. It appeared to be, for all that had come before, a rather ordinary life: a long reign as Curgh's duke, marriage to an attractive dark-haired woman the gleaner didn't recognize, several children, including two sons. He saw nothing to make him believe that Tavis would ever be king, but he sensed that Tavis had abandoned that dream long ago.

When it was over, and the bright glimmering of the stone had given way to a softer, plainer glow, Tavis sat back in his chair, looking profoundly relieved.

"You saw?"

Grinsa nodded. "Yes."

"There was nothing bad, at least not that I could see."

"I've told you before, Tavis, the stone shows us our fate at any particular moment. Just because you saw no tragedy today doesn't mean that your life won't be marked with some loss."

"I know."

"That said, I think you've earned a bit of happiness, don't you?"

"I'm not sure it works that way. Look at Hagan."

Grinsa shrugged, then nodded. "You may be right. But I still think you're due for good fortune."

"Perhaps I am."

They stood and stepped out of the tent. A cool breeze touched Grinsa's face and stirred the boy's hair. Trin and Cresenne were nowhere to be seen, and Grinsa suggested that they walk through the marketplace and try to find them.

"You should go ahead," Tavis said. "It's time I was on my way back to Curgh."

Grinsa nodded, surprised to feel his throat tightening.

"Tavis, I—"

Before he could finish, Tavis had rushed forward and wrapped the gleaner in a hard embrace.

"I love you, Grinsa," he whispered. Then he pulled away quickly and started striding back toward Audun's Castle. After a few steps he broke into a run, disappearing amid the crowds of people enjoying the Revel.

"And I love you," the gleaner said softly.

Wiping a tear from his cheek, Grinsa walked into the marketplace. He soon found Cresenne and Bryntelle, but Trin wasn't with them anymore.

"He's haggling with a merchant over a Caerissan ring," Cresenne explained. "He said to tell you that you should take good care of us and stay out of trouble."

The gleaner grinned and kissed her. "Sound advice."

"Where's Tavis?"

"He's gone back to the castle. I think he's eager to be returning home."

"So are we ready to go?"

Grinsa looked around the market and then gazed up at the castle walls looming in the distance. "I am if you are." He took her hand and pressed it to his lips.

They led the mounts given to them by the king to the city's east gate, intending to make their way to the port of Rennach. Bryntelle was chattering excitedly as Grinsa handed her up to Cresenne, her eyes wide, a toothless smile on her lovely face. He climbed onto his horse and they started riding to the east along the base of the Caerissan Steppe, toward Raven Falls.

"I think she's even happier to be out of the castle than I am," Cresenne said, gazing at their daughter, a bright smile on her lips.

"It seems so."

"Are you all right?"

Grinsa smiled, as well. "Yes, fine."

"Did Tavis's Fating go well?"

"You know that I can't answer that."

She arched an eyebrow. "Not this again."

Grinsa began to laugh.

"You're not going to tell me, are you?"

He leaned toward her and kissed her lightly on the lips. "No, I'm not."

"Fine," she said airily. "I did my share of gleanings, you know. I just won't tell you about them. I'll only speak of them to Bryntelle."

Grinsa suppressed a smile. "That's fair."

They rode in silence for a few moments.

"What possible difference would it make if you were to tell me?"

The gleaner laughed again. "It was a good Fating," he said at last. "Tavis is going to be just fine." He looked at her. "Truly."

Cresenne nodded, looking relieved as she faced forward again. "I'm glad," she murmured.

He reached out a hand and she took it briefly, giving his fingers a gentle squeeze.

Grinsa knew that he had spoken true. Tavis would be fine, and so would Kezi. Even without him. For so long he had carried the world's cares in his heart, its burdens on his shoulders. Relinquishing them had proven harder than he had expected. But riding eastward toward the sea and an unknown future, he at last felt that great weight lifting, floating free, leaving him feeling that he might rise off his mount and fly with the swifts and swallows darting overhead.

"Grinsa, what is it?"

He glanced at her, smiling, and shook his head. "It's nothing. I just . . ." She was so lovely, as was the girl she held in her arms. His family. How long had he wished for this, fearing even to believe in the possibility? "I'm ready to go home."

Cresenne frowned. "Home? What do you mean?"

"I'm not certain yet. But we'll know it when we find it." And this he also knew to be true, for he was a Weaver.

And now a sneak peek
at the first book in

BLOOD OF THE SOUTHLANDS

David B. Coe's
exciting new series

The Sorcerers' Plague

Available now from Tor Books

TOR® A TOR HARDCOVER

ISBN-13: 978-0-7653-1638-7   ISBN-10: 0-7653-1638-2

"Is it the pestilence, Papa?" asked Blayne, the younger of her two brothers.

"I don't know!" Papa snapped. He shook his head. "Maybe. Qirsar save us all if it is."

Mama staggered back to the doorway, stood there briefly, then whirled away and was sick again.

Papa looked at Delon. "Go get the healer."

Delon nodded once and ran out the door.

For some time Jynna, Blayne, and their father just stood there, the only sound in the house coming from Jynna's mother and the fire.

"You two should eat," Papa said at last.

Jynna and her brother exchanged a look. She was too scared to take even a bite, and judging from the expression on Blayne's face, she guessed that he felt the same way.

"Well?" Papa said, his voice rising again.

"I'm not hungry, Papa."

Blayne shook his head. "Neither am I."

Jynna thought Papa would make them eat anyway, but in the end he just shook his head, and muttered, "I don't blame you. I don't much feel like eating either."

As he said it, Jynna realized that he appeared flushed as well, though she couldn't tell if he was just worried about Mama or if he was starting to get sick also.

Mama appeared in the doorway again. She didn't look flushed anymore. Instead she was deathly pale, her face nearly as white as her hair, and her bright golden eyes sunken and dull. Only the dark purple lines under her eyes gave her face any color at all. She looked like a wraith.

"I need to lie down," she said, the words coming out as a whisper.

Papa hurried to her side, lifted her as if she were a child, and carried her to their bedroom.

He came out again a few moments later, his expression grim, his cheeks nearly as red as Mama's had been a short time before.

"She's already asleep," he said. "And to be honest, I'm starting to feel it, too."

"So it is the pestilence," Blayne said.

At that moment Delon returned.

"The healer says she'll be along when she can," he told them all, looking scared. "But there's lots of people sick."

"Damn," Papa said, sighing the word. He glanced at Blayne. "Well, there's your answer. It's probably too late, but I want the three of you outside. You're not sick yet. Maybe you'll make it through."

"But Papa—"

"I know what you're going to say, Delon. But there's nothing to be done now. Either your mother and I will live or we won't. But you haven't any way to save us, so it's best you save yourselves."

"I have healing magic," her brother said. "Blayne's come into his power, and he has it, too. We *can* save you, if you'll just let us."

Papa glared at him, the muscles in his jaw bunching. For just an instant, Jynna thought he might strike Delon for what he had said. "Never utter such words in this house again. Do you hear me?"

Delon lowered his gaze. "Yes, Papa."

"You're past your fourth four. You're a man now. If your mother and I . . . if the healer can't help us, then it'll fall to you to take care of your brother and sister. You're old enough that you should know better than to speak against the god like that." He started to say more, but then stopped and ran out the door, grabbing at his gut just as Mama had done.

None of them said anything, but Jynna found herself wishing that her brothers would use their magic, just as Delon had suggested. Surely the god would understand this one time.

"So what do we do?" Blayne asked, looking at Delon. Jynna couldn't be sure, but she thought he was probably thinking the same thing.

"We go outside," Delon said. "And we wait for the healer, just as Papa told us to."

The boys held each other's gazes for several moments, but they said nothing, and at last they ushered Jynna out into the darkness. Papa was still on the porch, leaning heavily on the railing. They didn't speak, though all three of them stared back at him as they descended the stairs. Eventually he went back into the house, leaving them alone in the cool night air. The sky was clear and the moons shone overhead, both of them still well short of full.

"What if they die?" Jynna asked, starting to cry.

Blayne shook his head. "They're not going to die." But he wouldn't look at her as he said it, and she knew he was lying.

"They might," Delon said. "Don't lie to her. Not about this." He took her in his arms and kissed the top of her head. She couldn't remember him ever doing such a thing before. His shirt smelled faintly of hay and sweat, as Papa's often did, and she pressed her cheek against it. "The healer's going to come, and maybe he can save them. But if he can't, we'll take care of you. We'll all take care of each other, all right?"

Jynna nodded, but she couldn't stop crying.

They sat down on the grass to wait, and after some time Jynna lay down, her tears still flowing, her stomach hurting, though because she was hungry or sick, she couldn't say. Eventually she woke up again. The boys were standing a short distance away, both of them doubled over.

"Hasn't the healer come yet?" she called to them.

She saw Delon shake his head. "Not yet," he answered, his voice hoarse.

"And now you're both sick." She flung it at them, an accusation. *Who's going to take care of me if you die too?* she wanted to ask, but she couldn't even choke out the words. *I'll be all alone!* Better she should die than face the world without her parents and brothers.

Neither of them said anything, and in the next moment, matters grew far worse. The sky over the village suddenly flared bright yellow, and an arc of fire streaked across the night, as if Eilidh herself had declared war on the people of Tivston. Again the fire flew and a third time.

"What's happening?" Jynna cried. Somehow she was on her feet. She started toward her brothers, but stopped herself after only a step. Who would protect her? "Is it a war?" she asked. She knew how foolish the question sounded, but she couldn't help herself.

She heard a long moan from within the house—the sound she imagined a ghost might make—and an instant later a bolt of flame crashed through the roof of the house. Burning slats of wood spun into the air and fell to earth, smoking, charred at the edges. Again the moan. It was her mother's voice. She had fire magic, Jynna knew, though of course she never used it. Until tonight. Flame burst through the roof again and Jynna heard a scream. Only when the scream kept going, long after this second flame had died away, did she realize that she was the one screaming.

She forced herself to stop, and doing so she realized that others were screaming as well, in the village, in the houses around them. The sky was aglow, orange like a smith's forge. She could hear the rending of wood and the panicked howling of dogs, the neighing of horses and strange, otherworldly cries coming from the cattle and sheep. Flames and smoke began to rise from her house. The boys hurried toward the door, but both of them seemed unsteady on their feet. Before they could reach the top of the stairs, though, the front wall of the house exploded outward, throwing the boys onto their backs, knocking Jynna to the ground, and showering them all with embers and smoking scraps of wood.

When Jynna looked up again, there were her mother and father, leaning on each other, struggling to get free of the wreckage that had once been their home. They managed to descend the stairs to the ground; then both of them collapsed, their chests heaving with every breath. Mama lay on her back, and abruptly she thrust both hands skyward. Flame shot from her palms as if she were a goddess, or a demon from Bian's realm.

Delon gaped at her. "What's happening to you?"

"I can't control it!" Mama said. "I'm trying, but I can't stop!"

Papa rolled himself onto his knees and let out a piercing cry. And then the skin on both his forearms peeled open, like the rind of some pale, evil fruit, and blood began to run over his hands and soak into his clothes.

It took her a moment to understand what was happening to him. Healing magic. Papa had it, too. Except that he could no longer control it, just like Mama couldn't stop using her fire magic. Was this what would happen to Delon and Blayne? Would it happen to her as well?

She crawled backward, away from them all, tears coursing down her face. "No!" she cried. "No. No. No."

"Jynna!" her father gasped, staring at her, the blood on his arms gleaming in the moonlight. "Go! Get away from here! Get help!"

She shook her head so hard that the tears flew from her face. "Where? Where can I go?"

"Anywhere! Away from here!" He stared at the ground for a moment before meeting her gaze again.

Another pulse of fire flew from her mother's hands, but it seemed dimmer this time, weaker.

"Go north!" her father said. "You know which way is north?"

She nodded.

"Go to the lake. Then follow the shore to Lowna. They're Fal'Borna there, not Y'Qatt. They can help you. They can help us."

"You mean with magic?" she asked, her eyes wide.

He hesitated, nodded once. "With magic. Now go! Quickly!"

She stared at him a moment longer. More screams rose from the village. More streaks of flame lit the sky. Not a war, she knew now. A pestilence. A plague. An Y'Qatt plague.

"Go, Jynna!" her father whispered, collapsing onto his side, his blood staining the grass.

She stood and ran.

About the Author

DAVID B. COE, the author of nine epic fantasy novels, won the Crawford Award for Best First Fantasy for *Children of Amarid* and *The Outlanders*, the first two books in his LonTobyn trilogy. *Weavers of War* is the final novel of the Winds of the Forelands, which includes *Rules of Ascension*, *Seeds of Betrayal*, *Bonds of Vengeance*, and *Shapers of Darkness*. His most recent novel is *The Sorcerers' Plague*, the first in a new trilogy, Blood of the Southlands. He lives with his family on the Cumberland Plateau in Tennessee.

Go back to the beginning...

READ

David B. Coe

Winds of the Forelands

SERIES

**TITLES AVAILABLE
IN PAPERBACK**

Winds of the Forelands

SERIES

Rules of Ascension

BOOK ONE

978-0-8125-8984-9
0-8125-8984-X

"War and politics, love and magic, all drawn in detail against a vividly imagined feudal background. A complex and excellent book."

—David Drake

Seeds of Betrayal

BOOK TWO

978-0-8125-8998-6
0-8125-8998-X

"Both action and the cast loom large; the members of the latter are well drawn; and Forelands politics are as complex as any tracked by the daily media."

—Booklist

Bonds of Vengeance

BOOK THREE

978-0-8125-9018-0
0-8125-9018-X

"David Coe writes fantasy that is intelligent, gripping, and real. Action and intrigue pull you into the story, and his sharply drawn characters keep you there."

—Kate Elliott

Shapers of Darkness

BOOK FOUR

978-0-8125-9021-0
0-8125-9021-X

"Those familiar with previous events will welcome the increasingly complex plot. Fans of Terry Goodkind's brand of fantasy intrigue will be pleased."

—Publishers Weekly